About the author

R. F. Delderfield was born in South London in 1912. On leaving school he joined the *Exmouth Chronicle* newspaper as a junior reporter, where he went on to become Editor. From there he began to write stage plays and then became a highly successful novelist, renowned for brilliantly portraying slices of English life.

With the publication of his first saga, *A Horseman Riding By*, he became one of Britain's most popular authors and his novels have been bestsellers ever since. He died in 1972.

Praise for R. F. Delderfield

'He built an imposing artistic social history that promises to join those of his great forebears in the long, noble line of the English novel. His narratives belong in a tradition that goes back to John Galsworthy and Arnold Bennett'

Life Magazine

R. F. DELDERFIELD

The Avenue Goes To War

HODDER

First published in Great Britain in 1964 by Hodder & Stoughton Ltd
An Hachette Livre Company

This paperback edition published in 2008

4

Copyright © 1958,1964 R. F. Delderfield

A CIP catalogue record for this title
is available from the British Library

ISBN 978 0 340 96378 4

Typeset in Hewer Text UK Ltd, Edinburgh

Printed and bound in Great Britain by Clays Ltd, Elcograf S.p.A.

Hodder & Stoughton policy is to use papers that are natural, renewable
and recyclable products and made from wood grown in sustainable
forests. The logging and manufacturing processes are expected to
conform to the environmental regulations of the country of origin.

Hodder & Stoughton Ltd
338 Euston Road
London NW1 3BH

www.hodder.co.uk

For my Brother Bill
in acknowledgement of
thirty years' encouragement
R.F.D.

Contents

CHAPTER I
An Avenue At War

THE Avenue stretched in a wide curve from Shirley Rise, just off the Lower Road, to the gates of the Rec', at the junction of the Avenue, and Delhi Road. Its pre-war trimness had disappeared with the summer. People had been too busy, and too distraught, to use shears on the privet hedges, and long shoots were already straggling over and through the lengths of looped chains, that had formerly swung clear of the hedges connecting the dwarf pillars that separated the houses. Over at Number One Hundred and Twelve, for instance, the lilac now covered the entire front garden, and almost opposite, at Number Ninety-Seven, a 'To Let' notice was lashed to the trunk of the familiar laburnum.

There were other 'To Let' and 'For Sale' notices along the Avenue, nearly a score of them, and some of the boards had been there for the better part of a year. There was, as yet, no grass in the street, but there would be before very long, and weeds too, from seeds blown south from the old Nursery, behind the even numbers, or north from the meadow, that separated the backs of the odd numbers from the Manor Wood, where the old white mansion, empty and desolate these thirty years, was crumbling to final decay.

Very few children were seen in the avenue these days. Almost all of them had left more than a year ago, before the first siren wailed out from the A.R.P. Centre, in Shirley Rise, or the smug Baskervilles, of Number Eighty-Four, had scuttled into their bomb-proof shelter, excavated by Mr. Baskerville during the Munich crisis.

Most of the children had crept back in the New Year, their parents fearing no retaliation to the R.A.F. leaflet raids over Berlin, but by the late summer of 1940, they had all hurried away again, some of them as far away as Canada, and the United States, but the majority not quite so far, to Somerset, like Archie Carver's family, of Number Two, or to a thatched cottage, on the Totnes Road, like Eunice Godbeer, of Number Twenty-Two.

The adults left in the Avenue missed the noise of the children playing in the street after tea, and on Saturday mornings. When dusk fell there was nobody to knock at their doors and run away, as the elder Carver twins, 'The Unlikes', had done so long ago, when people in the Avenue were making crystal-sets, and Avenue daughters, in cloche hats, and knee-length frocks, were known as 'flappers', not 'judies', and young men who took their wooing seriously were invariably known as 'Sheiks'.

Apart from the evacuation of school children most of the young folk of the Avenue had dispersed, and some would never again turn into the Avenue from Shirley Rise, to pass along the crescent to their front-gates. Casualties, so far, had not been heavy. There was silent grief at Number Six, where Mrs. Hopper had lost her only son on the *Royal Oak*, and in lesser degree at Number Seventy-Eight, where Grandpa Barnmeade had managed, despite his advanced years, to die for democracy.

Grandpa Barnmeade had surprised everybody along the Avenue, in September, 1939. Up to that date nobody had paid much attention to his secondhand stories of the Battle of Ishandhlwana, or the camel charge at Omdurman, but when the call went out for air-raid wardens, the old man had somehow contrived to get himself appointed. Throughout that first winter, when everyone was unfamiliar with the art of blacking-out, his neighbours had been obliged to take him very seriously indeed. Night after night he had pounded the pavements, his service respirator at 'the ready', his mace-like torch directing a powerful beam on odd and even numbers alike, and he himself poised for a panther spring at every chink of light that winked along the crescent.

Whenever he saw such a gleam he charged, uttering high-

pitched howls of rage, and promising to fill fleets of Black
Marias with Avenue folk who, judged by their behaviour, had
arrived at a covert agreement with Goering, and his Luftwaffe squadrons.

In late September Grandpa Barnmeade died at his post,
just like the Roman sentry at Pompeii, just like 'Boy' Corn-
well, at Jutland.

Scrambling on to the porch of Number Four, at 2 a.m.,
with the intention of smashing the windows of Becky Clegg's
bedroom, and extinguishing the glow that leaked from behind
her lath and paper black-out screen, he had slipped, and
fallen headlong on to the flagged path, ten feet below.

Edith Clegg, hearing the impact, and the warden's final
yell of indignation, had run out, and found him lying there.
He was unconscious, and she had hurried along to fetch Jim
Carver, of Number Twenty; there was little Jim could do but
telephone for the ambulance from the Post, and sweep away
the fragments of Grandpa Barnmeade's huge torch. The old
veteran had broken his neck.

They gave him a spectacular Avenue funeral, and Edith
Clegg wept when the hearse passed the house, for she recalled, with a wave of self-reproach, that Becky's light had
caused the tragedy and that she had once called the old hero
'Little Hitler'. He was buried in Shirley Churchyard, and Jim
was one of his bearers. That night everyone along the Avenue was very careful about their black-outs, reasoning, perhaps that from his new vantage point, the old warden could
see chinks that were invisible to his easy-going successor.

* * * *

The residential rump at the Shirley, or golf links, end of
the Avenue, had remained much as it was throughout the
'twenties' and 'thirties'.

Little Miss Baker, the semi-paralysed spinster of Number
One, still peeped from her downstairs window at the even
numbers opposite, and could still tell you what was what, and
who was who. She had been sitting there a long time now—
since the middle of the First World War—and had resisted
all endeavours, on the part of good-intentioned relatives, to
evacuate her to the country. She reasoned that she had little

enough to lose, for she had to be carried to and from her room on the rare occasions she left it. For the greater part of her adult life this end of the Avenue had been her window on the world. She was a patient and reserved little body, friendly with all, but intimate with none, except, possibly, Edith Clegg, who sometimes crossed the road, and took tea with her, at the three-legged table in the window.

Miss Baker remembered most of the neighbours moving into their houses, and she was quite determined to sit this second war out. Her range of vision reached as far as Number Twenty-Four, and she could have told you, at any particular time, where any of the people in the twelve houses opposite were, and usually, what they were doing at a particular time of day.

Across the road, at the corner shop that had once been Toni Piretta's, but was now A. Carver Ltd., Archie Carver appeared from time to time, opening and closing the double doors, that he had caused to be cut in the garden wall of Number Two.

Archie was forty now, and acquiring a paunch, but he was an extremely active man, and set out on his rounds before most of the Avenue families had finished breakfast, or emerged from their front gates, to hurry down to Woodside Station, for the 8.45 to town.

Archie was obliged to start early. He now had nearly twenty businesses to attend to, and trade was very brisk indeed, for Archie was one of the few along the Avenue who had profited by the respite offered by Mr. Chamberlain's umbrella. From September '38, onwards, Archie had bought wisely and very extensively. Three rented houses in the area were stacked with tinned goods, that were becoming scarcer every day, and in his store behind Number Two, were dozens of racks, each supporting a crate of sugar, tea, coffee, or some other rationed commodity. The racks represented more than a thousand pounds of Archie's ploughed-back capital.

Nor did the crates constitute the sole treasure in Archie's storehouse. Under the floor, in a specially hollowed-out cavity, that dated back to Archie's private declaration of war— his war against the Inland Revenue—were Archie's oil-drums, holding his Floating Reserve.

Once upon a time these drums had contained mere half-crowns, and florins, the gleanings from Archie's tills, after the blinds were down, and new and fictitious till-rolls were made out, but now with trade booming, Archie could ignore half-crowns, and was collecting paper gleanings, to put into fire-proof tin boxes, which he buried in the oil-drums, and covered over with sawdust.

He took up his floorboards once a week, and only one other person knew of the existence of the vault. That person was not Maria, the Italian-born daughter of old Toni, who had persuaded Archie to marry her, and come into partnership with him in the mid-twenties. The other person who knew all about the oil-drums was Archie's elder son, Anthony, now in his final term at public school, in Somerset. Anthony had been told because he was the Crown Prince to the Empire of Twenty Pop-Ins.

Archie Carver had spent the greater part of his life forging his chain of pop-ins—small, undistinguished little grocery shops, scattered about the new housing estates, along the Kent-Surrey border. In the beginning the pop-ins had been a means to an end, that end being a bank balance just large enough to enable Archie to live the sort of life he had planned to live, since he was a grocer's errand boy, during the First World War. Today, however, the shops, and their turnover, were ends in themselves, for he had forgotten almost everything else, and his wife and family hardly ever saw him, not even when one or other of them returned to the Avenue from the comfortable Georgian house he had found for them in Somerset.

So, in the very early hours of each successive Sunday morning, when the Avenue was very still, and the double gates giving access to his yard had been bolted and padlocked from the inside, Archie selected a yale key from the huge bunch he carried everywhere he went, and let himself into the store behind the house. It was the store where his mahogany-faced father-in-law had once played so many games of bears with the children, when they were tiny. Here Archie began at once to drag crates of expensive camouflage from a furthermost corner, and lay bare the cunningly-fitted floorboards that led down to his Floating Reserve. Edith

Clegg, at Number Four, beyond the wall, sometimes heard the muffled thumps of the crates he moved, but she was a very uncomplicated person, and did not connect them with buried treasure. Instead, she reflected: "That poor Mr. Carver does work hard! He never seems to go to bed at all, poor, dear man!"

. . . .

Yet Archie sometimes did go to bed, went, in fact, the moment he had relocked his store. Had Edith been a prying woman she might have considered it very odd that Archie did not spend Saturday nights in his own home but went, instead, out into Shirley Rise, and through a gap in the hawthorn hedge, that led to the meadow immediately behind the odd numbers.

Once here, he slipped along the path in the shadow of the boundary fences, crossed the open track that was the sole break in the even sweep of the crescent, and let himself in at the back gate of Number Forty-Five, the home of Elaine Fraser, whose husband, Esme, was away serving with the R.A.F., in the Midlands.

Archie's regular Saturday night call at Number Forty-Five was the nearest he ever came to taking a holiday. He seldom stayed more than a few hours, preferring to leave again before it was light. He had many customers in the Avenue, and his presence at Number Forty-Five, during the hours of darkness, might be commented upon, and ultimately affect his business. There had been a time when Archie had made a habit of combining business with pleasure, but that was long ago, before one of his assistants had robbed him of nearly a hundred pounds, and laughed in his face when he had discovered the theft. Nowadays Archie took his fun more soberly, and paid for it on the nail, or rather on Elaine Fraser's bow-fronted dressing-table, where he left his keys, loose change, and gold cigarette-lighter, after he had undressed.

Their relationship was a very business-like one, and both of them preferred to keep it so. This was easy enough to achieve now that Esme Fraser had joined up, and was considerate enough to 'phone his wife whenever he managed to wangle a forty-eight hour pass, and hitch-hike home from the Midlands.

Prior to that it had meant they had to meet far afield, and rent a room, which wasn't easy these days, with London so full of homeless foreigners, and uniformed wayfarers.

Archie had grown fond of Elaine. In addition to possessing striking good looks, and a sturdy, but pleasing figure, she had the enormous advantage of being without a conscience. She solaced him and took his money, without commenting upon their association. She was as brisk and as business-like as was he himself, when handing groceries over the counter. She was always there waiting for him when he arrived, and she never committed the error of trying to elevate their association to an emotional plane, as so many of Archie's women had tried to do in the past. She was not out to snare him, enslave him, or compromise him, merely to accommodate him, at the agreed price. Between his visits, if he thought of her at all, it was with mild gratitude. It was a great pity, he reflected, that there were not many more women like Elaine, and an even greater pity that he had not made her acquaintance years ago, when she was growing up, and cloistered with her family, at Number Seventeen, just across the road.

* * * *

Apart from Archie's occasional visits Elaine led a solitary life. There was no contact these days between her and her mother, or her brother Sydney, who still occupied Number Seventeen, a few doors away. It was now more than seven years since she had walked out of the house, and followed her father, Edgar, to Wales, where he was now living over a little antique shop with Frances, the 'other woman', and Frances' daughter Pippa.

Edgar had found Elaine a nice, steady job as a hotel receptionist, but she had not stayed there very long, for during her early adolescence Elaine Frith had dreamed a dream, and the dream had shaped her life for many years now, driving her out to tour the country in the company of a second-rate illusionist, and after that to cross to the Continent, as the mistress of a middle-aged variety agent.

Neither of these haphazard partnerships had breathed reality into her dream, for it was a lavish and extravagant dream, involving a terrace, with a swinging hammock, a flock of male courtiers, wardrobes full of expensive clothes, a yacht that dropped anchor in Monte Carlo, and Majorca, and, above all, a Great Provider.

Her brief and painful liaison with Tom Tappertitt, the proprietor of the circus that she had joined after leaving Benny Boy, the agent, had been equally unprofitable. That ridiculous episode had ended face down on a bed, in a small, private hotel, with an irate Mrs. Tappertitt, who happened to be a professional strongwoman, enthusiastically tanning her bare bottom, while husband Tom moaned from the confines of the shallow cupboard, into which his energetic wife had thrust him while she administered justice on Elaine.

After that Elaine had renounced hit-and-miss tactics, and had married young Esme Fraser, the boy who had been mooning after her since the late 'twenties. There were two reasons for this decision. First the necessity of acquiring a base from which she could sally out to search for the Great Provider, and secondly because of Esme's modest fortune, which turned out to be more modest than she had been led to believe.

Up to the moment of the outbreak of war Elaine had been ready to write off her marriage as yet another false start, but now she was not so sure. Their child, born on the actual day of the declaration of war, had been taken off her hands, and now Esme too had disappeared from the scene, and only appeared in the Avenue at irregular, and widely-spaced intervals. In view of all this there was still something to be said for a husband with a small unearned income.

Meantime, there had been Stevie, the big Polish airman, since posted overseas, and later Archie, who, carefully handled, might yet provide the terrace hammock, and yacht, not withstanding his Italian wife, and young family down in Somerset.

Had she been less experienced Elaine might have settled for Archie there and then, but she hesitated because her dream was not a static dream, but a dream that was constantly expanding. If the war went on long enough who could tell what possibilities lay ahead, providing she kept her eyes open, and saved her steadily increasing capital?

On Sunday mornings, after Archie had dressed, and slipped out by the way he had entered, Elaine would sometimes lie relaxed, and watch the light flicker through the black-out curtain. Her mind would range, not over the remote, or recent past, but far into the golden future, across the Atlantic even, where some said that real money was waiting. Archie's five pound notes were all very well to go on with, of course, and he was very useful in other ways, with his gin, groceries, and nylons, but after all, Archie, notwithstanding his chain of suburban pop-ins, was still very much of the Avenue, and Elaine had never been reconciled to the Avenue, or to any suburban feature of it.

Somewhere, sometime, bigger, better, and more stream-lined game awaited her. She was only twenty-nine; there was time in hand.

* * * *

Like her daughter, at Number Forty-Five, Esther Frith led a solitary life, more solitary these days than that of anyone in the Avenue. She had never made any friends there, and after her divorce, and Elaine's flight, she had shared the house with Sydney, her only son. Now that Sydney was gone she worried about him unceasingly for he was all she had left in her life to worry about. She had once been devoted to her Methodist Chapel, in Croydon, but since Sydney had joined the Air Force she had stopped attending public worship, feeling that she needed a more personal approach to God, if He was to find time to maintain a duration-of-war watch over Sydney.

She spent nearly an hour on her knees before she climbed into bed each night, and her prayers had a single, repetitive theme:— *'Keep Sydney safe! Keep Sydney away from the bombs! Anything can happen to anyone only keep Sydney intact! Keep him away from the bombs!'*

She might have spared herself a nightly vigil on the cold linoleum, for God was already keeping Sydney as safely as anyone could be kept in the Britain of 1940.

Sydney had joined the Volunteer Reserve of the R.A.F. nearly a year before the war, and he was now a Pilot Officer,

in the Accounts Branch. By day he worked under the heavi-
ly-reinforced roof of Station Headquarters, and whenever the
siren wailed he was authorised to dive into a deep shelter,
carrying with him his loose-leafed ledgers, some long sheets
of blotting paper, and a ready reckoner.

Esther Frith might have been excused for devoting her
prayers to her own safekeeping, for all that stood between
her and the Luftwaffe, was a thin screen of slates, but it had
never occurred to her that she might be hit by a bomb. She
was a very sound sleeper, and slept through most of the
alarms, while her neighbours were crowding into their An-
dersons, and Morrisons, or fussing about their houses with
flasks of tea, cushions, and trailing blankets. Sometimes, just
before she went to sleep, she thought of Edgar, her former
husband, and whenever she did so she experienced anew the
cold wave of shock that his original confession had once
brought her . . . Edgar, the mild, the drab, the hopelessly
ineffectual, but an Edgar madly and recklessly in love with a
woman at the shop, a woman who, so she had been given to
understand, had already given birth to a love-child by a
soldier of the last war!

The sheer staggering improbability of these facts buffeted
Esther particularly when she recalled her husbands' feeble
reaction to her decree that they should sleep apart, after the
birth of their second child, Sydney. She remembered how he
had received this ultimatum, how he had been content to
mumble something into his straggly moustache, and drift
away to tend potted hyacinths in his greenhouse. It was
curious how, during all the years when the children were
growing up, Edgar must have continued to think about *That
Thing*, the *Thing* that had come between them during the
first hours of their Bournemouth honeymoon, when she had
at length been brought face to face with the appalling demands men could make upon the women they married! Even
a man like poor, wispy, skimpy, little Edgar!

* * *

Just across the road, at Number Twenty-Two, lived another wartime recluse, white-faced, earnest and amiable Harold

Godbeer, solicitor's clerk, of Stillman and Vickers, St. Paul's Churchyard.

Before the war Number Twenty-Two had been among the most contented homes in the Avenue. Eunice Godbeer, formerly Eunice Fraser, had married her Harold in the mid-twenties, after a courtship lasting several years. Courting had begun on Harold's part, after Eunice's appeal for professional advice, following the death of her Scots mother-in-law.

Eunice was a soft, small-boned, flaxen-haired, little woman. In those days she had reminded the bachelor Harold of helpless Mrs. Copperfield, adrift in a world of widow's problems, the solving of which would be a privilege to any susceptible bachelor. For years, however, his courtship did not prosper. Esme, Eunice's only child by her first marriage, had interposed between Harold and his heart's desire, for young Esme was a romantic, and had made a hero out of his dead soldier father. Because of this he did not take kindly to a stepfather who made his living in an office, drafting conveyances, and scratching about in the deed-boxes of the dead.

Then, unexpectedly, the fog had lifted, and the way to the altar was clear. Esme, and his friend little Judy Carver, next door, had become embroiled in a ridiculous dispute about a bag of confetti, sold to them by a huckster, at the Shirley Easter fair, and Harold, a bespectacled knight-errant, had come galloping to the rescue. As a direct result of this encounter Esme's entire attitude towards clerkly stepfathers had changed overnight, and Harold had won his fair lady in a canter.

Then Esme had grown up, and married Elaine Frith, the dark, exciting, rather mysterious girl who lived directly opposite to Number Twenty-Two, and the young couple had delighted everybody by making their new home further down the Avenue.

In less than a year, little Barbara had been born, giving all of them such short-lived delight, for Barbara was now the cause of her grandparents' separation, and in his lonelier moments Harold could not help asking himself why it should be he, a mere step-grandfather, who was denied the comfort and solace of his wife for the duration, when the child's mother, Elaine, could have evacuated herself at will, taken charge of the child, and sent Eunice home to the blitz and Harold.

In the days before the war Harold had sometimes yearned for solitude. He was the kind of man who liked to come home from the office, eat a cold supper, put on his slippers, and lose himself in a careful scrutiny of *The Times*.

After that he liked to listen to brass bands on the radio, or potter about the house, embellishing it, and increasing its capital value, by applying little touches of primrose paint, or installing extra cupboard-space.

He soon discovered, however, that Eunice much preferred light conversation, but in more than ten years of married life he had still not acquired the habit of seeming to listen without listening, or of making a tame husband's monosyllabic replies to his wife's endless small-talk.

After Esme had married, Harold had lost a valuable ally, and was left to swim against the tide of small-talk alone. The result was that he sat down to read an article on far Eastern policy, and then, unaccountably, found himself running an eye up and down the stock market column, or studying the obituaries. He also lost patience with Eunice sometimes because of her irritating habit of performing several trivial tasks at once, particularly late at night, when he was tired and anxious to sleep.

He would lie in bed, with the sheets up to his chin, glumly watching her, as she pottered to and fro in a pretty pink nightdress, or sat brushing her long, soft hair, rubbing her cheeks with cream, or hanging and re-hanging frocks in the mahogany wardrobe. Contemplating her at times like this he would marvel that any woman alive could take so long to achieve so little.

On these occasions his mind sometimes slunk back to his cosy bachelor lodgings, in Outram Crescent, beyond the Nursery garden, but he was always able to dismiss these regrets when, at long length, Eunice turned out the light, and snuggled down beside him, warm, soft, and delicately perfumed.

She would then take his hand, tuck it possessively under her breast, and murmur "Goodnight dear, it's been such a nice day, hasn't it?" And he had to agree that, taken all round, it certainly had.

The days were not anything like so nice now, or the nights either, what with crowded trains to and from the city, cheerless news about shipping losses, the terrifying isolation of dear Old England, and the constant, stomach-churning wail of the siren from the A.R.P. post, in Shirley Rise. It was a miserable business to get up and dress after a broken night's sleep, and come downstairs to make one's own toast on the gas-stove, in a fireless kitchen. It was just as depressing to come home, tired and low-spirited to an empty hearth, at the end of the day, to thresh about the big double bed, night after night, to reach out one's arm, and find nothing but emptiness, to yearn and yearn for the warmth of a silly, pretty, chattering little woman who, never once, in all the years they had been married, had been anything but submissive and generous to him, once she really had turned out the light, and could think of no new topic to discuss with him.

One way and another Harold was having a tiresome war, and if it had not been for his new-found friendship with Jim Carver, the big, solemn Socialist, next door, he might have thrown up the sponge long since, resigned his head clerkship, and hurried down to Devonshire to dodge bombs, and keep Eunice and little Barbara company.

By way of contrast Jim Carver of Number Twenty was by no means as depressed by the war. Jim had been a widower many years, and his elder daughter, Louise, had cared for him, and for the rest of his family, with great skill and thoughtful economy, ever since his wife had died in the 'flu epidemic shortly before he came home from France, in 1919.

Since Dunkirk Jim Carver had been more at peace with himself than he had been since the days of the General Strike, for at last his crusading zeal had been released into an officially authorised assault on the triple citadel of graft, cruelty, and social injustice.

Ever since Armistice Day, 1918, Jim Carver had been crusading. On that momentous day he had seen a vision that seared his soul, even as the soul of St. Paul had been seared, on the road to Damascus. On that day he had seen a dead boy on a bank, just outside Mons, a boy he believed to have been sacrificed not to freedom, or democracy, but to the

stupidity and vanity of a potbellied base major, who had
ordered a last-minute suicidal attack on a German machine-
gun post.

Over the corpse of the boy whom he believed to have been
the final casualty of the First World War, Jim Carver had
sworn an oath. He had sworn to devote the remainder of his
life to the abolition of war, and the system that made wars
inevitable.

So far as he was able he had kept that oath. For years
now he had stumped about the suburb, preaching the gospel
of the Brotherhood of Man, and the League of Nations, but
so far his only reward for these endeavours had been a
flagrant succession of betrayals. He had been collectively
betrayed by the governments of the world, and by his own
government in particular. He had seen the workers betrayed
by white-collar volunteers in 1926, and again, by their own,
worthless leaders, in 1931. He had seen Abyssinia betrayed
by the City of London, in 1935, Spain betrayed by the
League itself in 1936, and Czechoslovakia betrayed by all
and sundry in 1938. The final betrayal, the most shattering of
all, had come from the Left, in August 1939, and when, not
long afterwards, Russia had swept into Poland, and then
turned its guns on Finland, Jim came very near to despair,
which seethed within him right through the period of the
phoney war, until it erupted over the beaches of Dunkirk.

Then, at one minute, fifty-nine seconds to doomstroke,
Winston Churchill had spoken up—Churchill—a man who,
until that historic moment, Jim Carver had always disliked,
and distrusted, the politician whom he had labelled a
turncoat, and a typical autocrat of the ruling caste, but a
man who, at that hour, said the things that Jim would have
liked to have said, and did things that he would have liked to
have done, and in the way that Jim would have said and
done them!

For a day or two, before Churchill took office, Jim hovered over the abyss of utter hopelessness, and then, under the
impetus of Churchill's fight-on-the-beaches broadcast, he
moved cautiously into the Valley of Hope. Here, Jim told
himself, was a Man, and a man worth following! Here was
someone who, for all his shifts, and cynicisms in the past,

knew England, and Englishmen, and knew what he was
fighting for, a man, moreover, who was not prepared to fool
himself or anyone else about the bloodiness and immensity of
the tasks ahead.

Already a full-time A.R.P. worker, Jim at once joined the
Home Guard. One glorious morning, when crippled Junkers
came fluttering over the suburb, he actually took a pot shot
at Fascism with a real rifle, and saw the aircraft explode in
flames, on a patch of gorse just over the hill. He cheered and
danced as though his shot had brought the aircraft to earth.

From the summer of 1940 Jim dedicated himself to war
with all the single-mindedness that he had dedicated himself
to peace. There was no effort that he would not make to
further the cause of democracy. In between long spells of
duties at the A.R.P. Centre, he somehow found time to
instruct middle-aged neighbours in the art of grenade-
throwing, and when this was done, he hurried home to help
Jack Strawbridge, Louise's ponderous husband, to dig for
victory, in the old Nursery, behind the house. He encouraged
Harold, his next-door neighbour, to start a local Savings
Group, and when this was underway he moved from house
to house along the Avenue, soliciting aluminium cooking
utensils for Beaverbrook's Spitfire drive.

He was exalted, and inspired, as he had not been since 1914,
when he had walked into a Hammersmith recruiting office, and
volunteered to fight Kaiser Bill.

The war had scattered Jim's family. His foureen-year-old
quarrel with Archie, over the boy's betrayal of the workers'
cause by enrolling as a Special during the General Strike, had
been set aside for Louise's wedding before the war, but it had
never really healed, and when father and son passed one
another in Shirley Rise they did no more than exchange a
casual greeting. Nowadays, however, Archie's approach to life
ceased to worry Jim, who was too busy to ponder what the
boy was doing at that corner shop of his, or what part he was
playing, if any, in the overthrow of tyranny. Archie was a bad
egg, and best forgotten. Fortunately this was easily done, for
Jim had two younger sons of whom to be proud.

Bernard and Boxer, the Unlike Twins, whom he had dismissed in pre-war days as empty-headed, speed-crazy young

idiots, had turned up trumps after all. They had been out with the B.E.F., in '39, and had fought their way home across the entire breadth of France, to turn up unscathed, weeks after the wreck of the army had trickled back from Dunkirk. In their own way they had been heroes, slightly comical heroes, perhaps, but deserving an Avenue triumph, for all the might of Hitler's panzers had not vanquished them, and now they had volunteered to train as Commandos, and were gleefully scaling cliffs, and blowing up buildings, in a Highland stamping ground.

They turned up in the Avenue from time to time, having thumbed or fiddled their way across England, using the same methods, one assumed, as they had employed in France. They were taut, bronzed, and spoiling for a fight, and Jim looked at them with quiet pride, as they sat wolfing his bread and tinned beans, in the kitchen of Number Twenty. The thought of what they would do to the next Nazi they encountered uplifted him, and increased his confidence in ultimate victory.

Jim had one other member of the family serving in the Forces—Judy, his younger daughter, and the favourite among his children.

Judy had joined the W.A.A.F. a week after she received news that her husband, the young infantry officer whom Jim had met but once, at the wedding, had been drowned in a torpedoed troopship. Poor Judy, he reflected, had only been married about a month, and his heart bled for her, but she seemed to have rallied very quickly, and found some kind of anodyne for her grief on the plotting tables of a fighter-station, during the Battle of Britain.

When she came on leave, in September, Jim gained the impression that she was over the worst of it, and might even marry again given time, perhaps to one of those slim, clear-eyed youngsters, who had put up such a wonderful show over South-Eastern England during the summer.

As it happened Jim was wrong about Judy, but he was a man who saw life in broad outline and was by nature prevented from estimating, even approximately, the extent of the damage that the death of Tim Ascham had done to the heart of his favourite child. He had no means of knowing, nor indeed had anyone else, that when Judy's daily spell of duty was done, when she had undressed and climbed into her little iron cot, alongside girls gaily discussing forthcoming dates, she sometimes had to drag her mind away from Tim Ascham's infectious chuckle, and his plain, freckled face, lest she should suddenly break down and sob like a child, or scream at her room-mates—"For God's sake stop talking about men as if they were trophies! They're going to die! Almost all of them are going to die, just as mine died!"

Of course she never did lose control, and her billet-mates thought of her as a shy, rather mousey little thing, a shade too conscientious about her work, and too fastidious to profit from the unit's access to an almost unlimited number of young men.

Jim's youngest children, the girl twins, known along the Avenue as Fetch and Carry, or simply as 'The Likes', had not joined the Forces. The outbreak of war found them serving as waitresses in a West End café, where the tips were good, and the customers moderately gallant. Both had inherited Jim's big, muscular frame, and long, loose limbs. They were approaching their twenty-second birthday now, and a generation earlier they might have been described as 'fine women'. They were certainly robust, and could whisk across a room carrying a tray loaded with heavy china, or kick open a service door with large, square, feet. They sang and whistled as they worked, and when they laughed in the kitchen all the customers heard them in the shop. Like their twin brothers, Bernard and Boxer, they were seldom seen apart, and always operated as a team, but in their case nobody could have said which of them took the lead. They seemed to arrive at conclusions simultaneously, and when they spoke they usually said the same thing, the one a split second after the other, so that hearing them was rather like listening to an echo.

They still lived at home, travelling up on the 9.5, so as to be on duty in time to serve morning coffee, and returning on the 6.35, after the dinner team had relieved them. In the train they read *True Love Stories,* buying only one copy, and holding it between them all the way home.

They were never any trouble to Jim, to their sister Louise, or to anyone else. They minded their own, and each other's business. Everyone in the Avenue liked them, but somehow they did not impress people as did the older twins, Berni and Boxer.

* * * *

Over at Number Forty-Three, where Ted Hartnell the jazz orchestra leader had lived with his wife Margy since the early 'thirties', the house was often empty and silent for weeks at a time. Ted was away at sea, a steward on a tanker, and Margy, who had been queen of the Hartnell Eight before the war, and had succeeded, in that capacity, in converting her shambling sunny-natured, tune-tapping husband into a professional musician of some standing, had assembled a new orchestra and taken it away on an E.N.S.A. tour to the camps.

There had been heartache and disappointment at Number Forty-Three since Dunkirk. Ted was almost forty years of age when war broke out, and had never had an unsyncopated idea in his head until he engaged a Bavarian refugee to play in his band. The Bavarian was a Jew, known as Nikki, who had escaped from the Nazis by the skin of his teeth, in 1937. His father and brothers had disappeared into a concentration camp, and he himself had been badly shaken by his own experiences when he had met Ted, and given him a first-hand account of what it was like to be a Jew in Hitler's Germany.

From the moment of his meeting with Nikki, Ted changed. Like everyone else in Britain he had read newspaper reports about concentration camps, and uniformed bullies, who called on their victims by night, but somehow it had not registered with him until he actually heard it described first-hand by Nikki. Once the facts were absorbed by him they drove jazz music out of his head, and made him long to become an active crusader, like Jim Carver, across the road.

Margy, his wife, was very irritated by the change in him. Throughout the long, dull months of the phoney war she had argued interminably with him, pointing out that no matter how terrible things might be in Berlin, or in Munich, they had nothing whatever to do with the engagement book of the Hartnell Eight, an orchestra sponsored by a man well over military age.

But Ted couldn't see it this way at all. He said that he was still young enough to do *something* to dismay Heinrich Himmler, and Margy was obliged to resort to desperate measures to prevent him from enlisting in the Pioneer Corps, the day after the Invasion of Poland.

Up to that moment they had both been too busy and too mobile, to start a family, but when Margy saw that nothing else was likely to dissuade him from making a fool of himself, and sacrificing their goodwill and broadcast dates on the altar of Democracy, she at once set about starting one, and her announcement did succeed in compelling him to postpone enlistment for a spell.

For a very short spell, however, for the Dunkirk epic started it all up again, and the threat of invasion turned Ted into a patriot of the 1914 vintage. Without saying another word to her he went off and enlisted in the Ordnance Corps, and was called up shortly before Margy's baby was due to arrive.

The child was stillborn, and no wonder, moaned Margy, for Ted was invalided out of the Ordnance Corps almost at once, but instead of coming home with the good news the fool dropped in at a shipping office and put down his name for sea service in the cook's galley!

The Merchant Service it seemed, was not nearly so fussy about physical fitness as the Ordnance Corps, and before Margy was out of the nursing home Ted was away on the high seas, en route for Venezuela!

She had one letter from him, posted in the Madeiras, but after that no further word for months and months. Half mad with anxiety, and bored stiff with waiting about the house for the postman, she marched out of Number Forty-Five one morning, swept together the wrecks of three disbanded orchestras, and set out on a tour of the camps. At one of their two-night stands she ran into Nikki, the refugee, but although by no means a vindictive woman, she could not bring herself to discuss Ted with him. If it hadn't been for Nikki, she reflected, she and Ted might have made a good thing out of the war, and ultimately fought clear of suburban engagements, and modest summer tours. Nor was that all! By some tortuous process of reasoning she persuaded herself that

Nikki, blast him and his concentration camps, was responsible for the stillbirth of her child!

. . . .

Few households in the Avenue had changed as little as that of Number Four, where Edith Clegg, and her sister Becky, had now lived quietly for nearly thirty years.

The Clegg sisters had lived in the Avenue longer than any other family, and people who moved in during the First World War remembered that Becky had once been regarded as rather less than half-witted. She had, they were told, some sort of mental ailment, that drove her to appear at her garden fence, from time to time, clad only in a night-dress, in order to summon her cat, Lickapaw, who had lived wild for long spells, in the abandoned nursery behind the even numbers.

Lickapaw was dead now, and lay buried in the garden of Number Four, under a headboard marked with his name and age, but although Becky had long ceased to appear at the fence in night attire, her reputation for feeble-mindedness lingered among the older residents, and they were not unduly surprised when they heard, via Mrs. Hooper, of Number Six, that 'the fair-haired one was having her spells again'!

Becky's spells as they were called, had been a great trial to her plump and sweet-tempered sister, Edith. They had begun early in the century, after Becky, then a handsome girl of twenty-two, had been rescued by her sister from a tenement in Lambeth, after a disastrous runaway marriage to a wandering artist whom the sisters had met in their Devon village, where their father had once been priest-in-charge.

Edith had found her, several months after the elopement, badly bruised in mind and body, and poor Becky had never quite recovered her wits. At certain times she would retreat wholly into the past, and imagine that they were still the rector's daughters, in a village on the shores of Bideford Bay, or that she was still living with her husband, Saul, and expecting his child, or simply preparing supper against his return.

In the early 'twenties', soon after Edith had taken in Ted Hartnell as a lodger, and the three of them began living such pleasant, musical lives at Number Four, Becky's spells had become far less frequent, although she was still liable to confuse tradesmen who called at the back door with boys who had been killed on the Somme, years and years ago. Under the impetus of war, however, her wits began to fail again, and about the time of Dunkirk she had returned from a shopping visit on the Lower Road one evening, and set about frying supper for Saul, whom she declared she had encountered outside the Odeon.

For a time Edith was half-convinced that she really had seen the man with whom she eloped all those years ago, but then Becky had begun to knit for her baby, and Edith, sick at heart, soon realised that the shock and excitement of the war had caused the spells to begin all over again. She called in the doctor, and was relieved when he assured her that there was no immediate danger of 'putting Becky away', but that she would need 'keeping an eye on'. This injunction did not worry Edith unduly. She had been keeping an eye on Becky for nearly forty years, and was on very friendly terms with dear, strong Mr. Carver only a few houses away, who would always come to her aid if she needed him. It would mean, however, that Becky could not be left alone for long, and this looked like curtailing Edith's visits to the cinema, which was a great shame seeing that she had only just recaptured her earlier enthusiasm for films, after seeing the epic 'Gone With the Wind', in glorious technicolour.

Edith had once worked in the Odeon as pianist, but that was in the old silent-picture days, when it was called the Granada, and poor, dear Rudi was alive, and no one had heard of Al Jolson. After Mr. Billington, the Granada proprietor, had installed the talkie apparatus, in 1929, Edith had lost her job, and she had been years getting accustomed to stars who used their lips instead of their eyes, and a heaving bosom, to convey a simple statement such as *'I love you, I'll always love you!'*

It was the depressing aspect of the Avenue under the strain of total war that had driven Edith back to the cinema, and she had been immensely cheered to discover that it still retained its magic for her, and only needed 'a little getting used to'. Perhaps their girl lodger, Jean McInroy, would take charge of Becky once a week, and enable her to sit through at least one feature film a week, providing she attended matinées. After all, she reflected, everything worth while was being spoiled or dislocated, by that awful man Hitler. Surely the occasional solace of the cinema would not be denied her?

. . . .

Like her neighbour Jim Carver, Jean McInroy, Edith's lodger since the week after Ted Hartnell had married, was finding some consoling factors in total war.

Jean was a commercial artist, and up to September, 1939, she had earned a reasonable living illustrating magazine stories, and press advertisement copy.

She was a very pretty girl, and almost every man who passed her in the street, or sat opposite her in the 'bus, kept her in view for as long as was practicable. For all that she was now twenty-six and still unclaimed.

Young men seemed to go to extraordinary lengths to get acquainted with her, but these friendships never developed into courtship, the reason being that poor Jean had a large cavity in the roof of her mouth, that made coherent conversation with her almost impossible. She could make a variety of gobbling, nasal sounds, and people who were used to her, like Edith for instance, had little difficulty in understanding her, but the affliction proved a hopeless handicap in the early stages of courting, and Jean had long since abandoned any idea of forming a permanent association with one of the young men attracted by her pretty face and figure.

Instead of grieving over what couldn't be helped she did a sensible thing, the kind of thing that one might expect from a girl with sensible Scots blood in her veins. She created her own man, a dream man, and called him The Ideal British Male. She went one better. She made him provide for her, by putting him into almost every sketch she sold to the advertisement agencies, for whom she worked on commission.

Almost everyone in the Avenue was familiar with Jean's Ideal Man although, to all but Edith, he was simply a sketch inside the frame of an advertisement or story illustration. They all knew him, however, without connecting him with his creator, Jean. He was six feet in height, had broad shoulders, nice, but not effeminate wavy hair, a long, lean, leave-it-to-me-little-woman jaw, a slightly sunburned complexion, radiant good health, and blue, Empire building eyes. He also possessed the distinct advantage of being able to supply his wife and family with anything on the market, from a sleek white sports car, like the one Archie Carver drove, to a surprise box of chocolates for stay-at-home-wifie, or a tin of high-grade sardines for the children's tea. He was incapable of letting anyone down and he was the perfect lover, always saying the right things in the right way and at the right time, and always tender, manly, true, and courageous things, like: *"This isn't the end, Jean darling. Some day I'll return to you, and when I do your heart will tell you how I regarded you through the empty years between. . . ."*

Fetch and Carry, the twins of Number Twenty, were very familiar with Philip, the Ideal British Male, whom they encountered each day in their magazines, and even the sour Esther Frith, of Number Seventeen, was dimly aware of him, for he appeared in advertisements for washing powders in all the daily papers. Only Jean, his creator, however, knew that he actually existed in the flesh, and that on Mondays, Wednesdays, and Fridays, her duty nights with the Auxiliary Fire Service, at the Fire Station in Cawnpore Road, she had the heavenly privilege of handing him a cup of tea in an enamel mug, and watching him demonstrate the use of the stirrup-pump to beginners.

After years and years of scrutiny in trains, 'buses, and crowded city and suburban streets, Jean had at last come face to face with the Ideal British Male in the person of Chief Officer Hargreaves, head of the suburb's fire service. She had lost no time in joining the A.F.S., in order to be near him, and watch over him, and see that he got his tea hot, fresh and strong, whenever he needed it. He was almost unaware of her, of course, and had hardly addressed a word to her in all the time she had known him, but he smiled his warm, kind smile when she put his mug of tea down in front of him, and said: "Thank you, Miss McInroy," in the soft but deep-throated voice she always knew that Philip would use when she found him.

One day, perhaps, something would happen that would bring them together.

He was unmarried, and appeared to be without attachment of any kind, besides which, God would hardly have brought them together so miraculously had He not had some positive development in mind.

So Jean slipped gaily into her blue slacks on Mondays, Wednesdays and Fridays, and tripped blithely down Shirley Rise to the fire station, while overhead the enemy bomber fleets began to multiply with the shortening of the days, and the people of the Avenue waited to see what Armageddon had in store for them, both individually, and as a community.

CHAPTER II

Incident

ON the night of November 5th, 1940, Jim Carver went on duty at eight o'clock, moving along the Avenue, head down, shoulders hunched against thin, driving rain.

As he was turning into Shirley Rise, to make his way up the hill to the Aid Post, the siren began to warble, and he quickened his step, his rubber boots clumping over the wet flags, his khaki haversack, packed with Louise's sandwiches, bumping against his hip and reminding him, almost without him being aware of it, of blundering ration-party trips up the Line, under very similar weather conditions, more than twenty years before.

He walked surely in almost complete darkness, his hands stretched out to break the force of a collision with a lamp-post, or telegraph pole; as he edged round the wide bend, towards the junction of Upper Road, he saw a faint glow in the sky over to the north-east. They were making another night of it apparently. Before midnight the suburbs would have bonfires enough, and on a scale undreamed of in pre-war Guy Fawkes' celebrations.

His mind travelled back a decade and he remembered the bonfires he had made for his children in the 'twenties' and early 'thirties'. He recalled how Boxer, who always delighted in these occasions, had thrown a twopenny cannon into the garden of Harold Godbeer, next-door, and received a smart box on the ear in consequence. He remembered another year, the year a spark from the bonfire had landed in the cardboard box containing the family's pooled fireworks, and the whole evening's fun being concentrated into one mad, explosive minute, with crackers leaping in every direction, and Judy screaming with fear, while that young devil Boxer capered about in the midst of the constellation, shouting with laughter, and looking like a demon from the pit.

The glow in the sky broadened and his mind returned to the present. How were people taking this non-stop assault? How long would it be before they cracked under the strain of terror, and sleeplessness? It was only November now and before them stretched months of long, winter nights, most of which looked like being spent on makeshift beds, in minute-by-minute expectation of sudden death. It was well enough for men like himself, men who had endured, and survived, years of concentrated bombardment, under far worse conditions. An experience like that helped to put the thing in a proper perspective. Out there the German gunners had usually had the line taped to an inch, and had sometimes strafed it for hours on end, without killing or even wounding, more than a tenth of the trench garrison. The chance of being hit and killed by a bomb dropped at random, on a city the size of London, was negligible. There was more chance, they said, of being run over in the blackout, and casualty returns had so far proved as much. But how did you convince people of things like this? How could you persuade dear old souls like Edith Clegg, of Number Four, or poor old Harold Godbeer, next-door, that it was more than a thousand to one against their being killed by blast, or crushed under falling masonry?

So far everyone had behaved extraordinarily well, as good or better, than the new drafts of youngsters pushed into the line after the 1918 break-through had behaved, but would it last? Could untrained civilians stand up to this kind of punishment?

Jim was familiar with the art of public pulse-taking. For years now he had been assessing public opinion, on one or other of the great political issues of the day. His guess now was that it would take at least a year's pounding to beat London to its knees and batter its population into a frame of mind where they ran into the street, howling for peace at any price. The rest of the winter, and possibly one more summer, like last summer. After that anything might happen.

That, then, had been Hitler's mistake, his worst mistake so far, if one discounted his failure to follow up Dunkirk with invasion. The price he demanded was too high, higher than death itself. It was like a pair of purses, held out to two heavyweight boxers in the ring. Victory for one meant more conquest, and loot. Defeat for the other meant slavery under impossible conditions, the exile and sterilisation of adult males, the splitting up of families, the wholesale slaughter of women and children, racial persecution on a scale unprecedented in barbaric wars of the past. What was death by bombs compared with such an accumulation of horrors? No wonder London was 'taking it'.

He turned into the sandbagged entrance of the post, and hung his haversack on a nail, lifting his hand in greeting to a group of men hunched round the coke fire, and glancing at the map of the suburb, with its box of flags ready to mark incidents.

* * *

Back in the Avenue, the residential rump had already completed its air-raid drill, performed, in most cases with a phlegm that implied years, rather than weeks of practice.

Edith Clegg had coaxed Becky into the Morrison, and had then climbed out again, in order to turn off the gas at the main, and collect the metal box containing their insurance policies, keepsakes, and deeds.

Esther Frith had finished praying, and had climbed into her glacial bed, where she lay rubbing one foot on the other, and listening, during the few moments it took her to get to sleep, for the intermittent buzz overhead that meant the passage of German bombers over the suburb.

Harold Godbeer, whom the siren had caught slumped over his little fire, reading an inspired account of Wavell's attack in Libya, got up and went out into the scullery, where he mixed himself his nightly dose of bicarbonate. Having swallowed it he wriggled under the kitchen table, and wedged himself against the projecting buttress of the unlit stove. Harold had not yet got an indoor shelter and had discussed, with Jim, the safest and most blast-proof corner of Number Twenty-Two. Jim had toured the downstairs rooms, made certain adjustments to the position of furniture, and pointed to the heavy table.

"Under there is as good as anywhere, old chap," he told Harold, kindly, "but you know what we used to say in the trenches—if your name's on one it'll find you."

Harold envied him his quiet courage, the kind of courage that enabled him to walk upright in the open, during a raid. As he settled himself among cushions, and adjusted the plaid rug that they had so often used for picnics in Manor Wood, his hand groped along the skirting until it touched the framed photograph of Eunice, that he kept in his dug-out. He drew it out, and studied it, in the dim light of the 15-watt bulb, noting the tendril of flaxen hair that had escaped from the right 'earphone' (Eunice had never had her hair bobbed or shingled, she was far too proud of her tresses) and he brought the picture up to his pale lips, pressing them gently on the glass.

Down the road Archie Carver, who shared his father's contempt for shelters, got up from his supper as soon as he heard the siren and carried a spare fire-extinguisher out of the back door, standing it against the door of the store, in the yard. He was not afraid of being killed by blast, or buried alive in wreckage, but he was not going to stand by helplessly while an incendiary sent his stock and Floating Reserve up in smoke.

Almost opposite, little Miss Baker switched on her bedside light, and picked up her Rupert Brooke, a book she already knew by heart, but one that she liked to hold when the house began to vibrate with the passage of enemy aircraft overhead. At the first double throb she began to read:

> 'Blow out you bugles,
>   Over the rich dead . . .'

She mouthed the words lovingly, and half audibly, savouring each of them like a sweetmeat, and as she read her memory conjured up a portrait she had once seen of the poet as a schoolboy. She remembered how eager, sensitive and noble he had looked—'washed by English rivers, warmed by English suns!'

* * * *

The bomb fell about a hundred and fifty yards from the golf-links end of the Avenue, obliterating the first three odd numbers of Delhi Road, that bordered the northern side of the Old Nursery and scattering rubble far over the potato rows of Jack Strawbridge's dig-for-victory patch behind the first houses on the Avenue's even side.

The explosion rocked every house in the crescent and splintered almost every window that faced the open space. Everyone in the Avenue flinched and hissed at the terrifying nearness of the blast. Harold Godbeer's low-powered bulb winked out and the glass in Eunice's photograph frame cracked under his thumb, causing him to drop it like a hot brick.

Immediately the blast wave had passed, and the roar of tumbling bricks and plaster had died away in a long, echoing rumble, the broken throb of aero-engines was heard overhead with dreadful clarity. Everybody in the Avenue waited for the second, and inevitably louder explosion, that would probably mean the end for all of them.

When it came it was from further off, out somewhere beyond the Lower Road, and they breathed again, smiling to themselves, and cocking their ears like terriers for subsequent bangs.

Up at the post in Shirley Rise there was a brief moment of confusion, as the telephone shrilled, and the heavy rescue squad surged round the hooks and lockers that contained their equipment. Jim roared an order and somebody started up the crash tender, a light lorry fitted with a powerful engine. Outside a fire-engine rushed past and the Post telephonist catching Jim by the sleeve, shouted: *"Delhi Road—this end!"*

Jim made his dispositions, the plotter marked the map, and the tender shot through the double doors, wrenching itself into a right-angled turn as Jim scrambled down beside the driver and the other men clung to the heavy equipment, clamped in the back.

When they got there Chief Officer Hargreaves was already in position, and his men and girls were running out hose to turn on a blazing house, adjoining the smoking rubble that now filled the gap where, only fifteen minutes before, three terraced houses had stood.

Jim had a quick word with Hargreaves, who turned aside from his work as soon as he recognised him.

"Direct hit ... there may be people under there ... we've already got one out, a passer-by, poor devil!"

Jim saw the casualty being carried into the ambulance, and at once began to deploy his men over the half-acre of bricks, splintered beams, and laths.

In the glare of the fire he saw an arm protruding from beneath a pile of guttering. He began to pull at the debris, piece by piece, until he had exposed the head and shoulders of an elderly woman. There was blood on her grey hair and Jim saw at once that she was dead. He gave orders for her removal, and then moved forward into the blast area, to search for the living.

A faint hail came from the most solid patch of rubble, and Jim stumbled towards it, clawing his way over the loose bricks, and an abattis of shattered furniture.

"How many of you?" he shouted, and then, over his shoulder, "Turn on the light! Give me some light, damn you!"

The stairway of one of the houses was still standing but it led to nothing. The front door of the house had been ripped from its hinges, and flung slantwise against the little cave formed by the stairs. It had saved the occupants of the broom cupboard of Number Two, for the fragments of the upper storey had cascaded down over this improvised glacis, sealing it off, and making its occupants a casual gift of their lives.

Jim tore at the bricks and shouldered the door aside, shining his bullseye into the hole, and directing the beam on its three occupants, a thin woman, and two girls, aged about seven and ten. The woman seemed very calm and the children more excited than terrified.

"Bring Junkie ... don't forget Junkie!" piped the younger

child, as Jim gathered her up, and passed her to Hopner, who stood at his elbow.

"How many are you?" he repeated, reaching back for the second child.

"Only three of us," said the woman irritably, "Junkie's her blasted monkey . . . here you are Rita, take it from the gentleman, do!" She sounded like a harassed housewife, disturbed in the process of preparing a meal in a hot kitchen, and Jim, noting this, repressed a chuckle. She gave Jim a large, woolly monkey, covered in powdered plaster, and Jim passed it across to the child, who clutched it joyfully as Hopner lifted her and bore her away.

"By God, that's one up for the 'under-the-stairs' theory," said Jim, as he helped the woman over the shifting bricks.

"Gran didn't get to us," said the woman, "I told her to stop messing about with the blackout, and come on in, but she wouldn't, she *would* potter! Is she all right?"

Jim thought of the old woman under the guttering, but decided to let someone else break the news. There were probably other survivors, and this one, who did not appear to be suffering from shock, might be able to help account for the families.

"Who lives on each side of you, ma'am? Both houses have copped it."

"Mrs. Purvis and her lodger, Miss Gilbraith, live in Number Two, but they usually go to the shelter. I only hope they did this time! A Mrs. Brooking, and her family, are in Number Six. They've already been bombed out once, in Catford. There's five of 'em, counting the old man. Are they all right?"

"We'll soon see," Jim told her, "you and your girls go on up to the Rest Centre, and get plenty of hot sweet tea inside you!"

The woman took a single, swift look at the ruins of her home.

"We been here since we was married," she said, bitterly. "We've only just finished paying for it! It's a bit much, isn't it?" She shrugged, and a smile flashed through the mask of plaster and grime on her narrow face. "You wait 'till my old man hears about it, he won't half be mad, I can tell you!"

"Where is he?" asked Jim, with an answering grin.

"God knows," said the woman, "last time I heard he was
in Africa, pasting the Eyeties!"

Jim picked his way over the rubble to the wreck of
Number Six. Where the kitchen had been Hopner met him,
and Jim noticed that the fellow seemed badly shaken. His
voice quivered as he said:

"They're dead, all five of them! Christ, it's a bloody shambles in there! I hope to God we'll be dishing it out, soon
enough. No more bloody leaflets, eh?"

"No," said Jim, "no more leaflets!" And then: "Can I get
through to them?"

"In that gap by the sink," said Hopner, and stood aside,
awaiting Jim's lead.

Jim crawled through the rubble beside the sink, holding his
bullseye at arms length. Most of the kitchen ceiling was
down, but near the door, where it led into the hall, he found
all five bodies, an old man, a plump, middle-aged woman,
and three boys, the eldest about thirteen. They were dead but
not mutilated, having been killed instantaneously by blast as
they scampered in a group from kitchen to hall, making for
the stair cupboard, no doubt. The woman and two of the
children had been stripped by blast, and their naked bodies,
sprawled one upon the other, looked pitiful and obscene.

Jim climbed in, calling to Hopner over his shoulder.

"Stand by to take them out, Fred. They've all copped it!"

He heard Hopner retching, as he picked up the boy nearest
to him, and he kicked savagely with his boots to enlarge the
aperture.

The child's body was no weight, and as he crossed the
beam of the bullseye, wedged in the splintered window
frame, he looked down at the face. Pity shook him, then
rage.

"God help me, I must get out of this," he thought, "I must
get into something where I can hit back, and kill, kill with
the bayonet, the Sten, and the grenade! Kill the bastards with
anything, anything at all!"

He passed the body to Hopner, and turned back for the
others.

· · · ·

The Delhi Road incident always remained fixed in the memory of Jean McInroy, because it was the occasion when Chief Officer Hargreaves had isolated her from the others and first addressed her as someone who was part of his team, not merely as a brewer of tea at the fire station.

There were many calls that night, and the local Service was ordered to send men and equipment over to Clockhouse, where a shower of incendiaries had started a big fire.

The Delhi Road fire was soon out, but Hargreaves always left someone on duty, in case it started up again. On this occasion he chose Jean, addressing her as she was rolling in hose.

"You live quite near here, don't you Miss McInroy?"

Jean nodded, breathlessly, delighted to discover that he already knew her name and the district in which she lived.

"Okay, then you stand by, and keep an eye on this place. I'll leave you a spare stirrup-pump, but if it looks serious don't waste time tackling it yourself, get through to the post, and I'll send someone at once."

She nodded again, and he looked at her curiously. He knew nothing about her cleft palate, but just that this girl seemed keen and was not given to gossiping, or skylarking, like some of the other volunteers.

"You don't mind being left here on your own?"

Jean smiled, murmured something, and shook her head, vigorously. He patted her shoulder. "You're a good kid," he said, and then, "I'm relying on you!"

He turned aside, and shouted to the driver to clamp up, and get ready to move off.

The men climbed aboard, and the engine and tender clanked off towards the Lower Road.

Jean remained on the brick-strewn pavement, her heart thumping painfully, but her soul buoyant with ecstasy. He had touched her, patted her, praised her! He had actually noticed her, and in the midst of all this responsibility, and horror! She was a 'good kid', and he 'was relying on her'!

She stooped, and lifted the stirrup-pump as though it was a wedding bouquet. Just let it break out again, just *let* it! She would soon show the Ideal British Male the kind of wife she would make him in God's and his own good time!

When Jim came off duty the moist sky was shredding to grey over Manor Woods, south-east of the Avenue. He clumped along to the gate of Number Twenty, and was fumbling for his key, when somebody called to him from the porch room window, of Number Twenty-Two. He looked up, and saw Harold's tousled head, and a face bearded with lather.

"I say, Carver old man, you look as if you'd had a bad night of it! I've just made tea! Would you care for a cup?"

Tea, Jim thought, always tea! No matter what happened, what time of the day or night it was, how many people had been mauled, or blown to pieces, the entire suburb dived head foremost into a row of teapots! He himself must have swallowed quarts of it since going on duty a few hours ago.

"I'll come in and yarn Godbeer! I daresay Louise can do with an extra half-hour in bed. Is everyone along here all right?"

"Fine," said Harold, withdrawing his head, "I'll come down and let you in, old man!"

They went into the kitchen, and sat at the table, sipping. Jim briefly described the Delhi Road incident, but it was soon clear that Harold was not listening. He looked strained and jittery. His long, white, clerical fingers kept tapping at the cracked frame of his wife's photograph, that lay face uppermost on the table.

Presently he said: "Do you mind if I ... I talk quite frankly, old man?"

"No," said Jim. "But you needn't apologise for being a bit edgy. Another split second on that Jerry's bomb-release and it would have been curtains for this end of the Avenue!"

Harold began to talk, rushing his sentences, but holding his glance down on Eunice's picture.

"I thought it was superstition at first Carver ... you know ... at times like this we're all inclined to get little whims and fancies! I was frightened all right, but I felt I could cope with it, until this ... this picture cracked in my hand. Then it seemed to me that it was a ... well, a kind of omen. I thought 'I'll never see my Eunice again . . . I'll be dead before Christmas! Or she will, or we both will!' No, no, let me finish old man ..."—as Jim lifted his hand,—"then I decided that it wasn't really an omen at all, but that I was telling myself it was, and using it as an excuse to run, to get to hell out of it, by the next train!"

"Well," said Jim, "and why not? What's to stop you joining her down there? I daresay you could get a job in Torquay easily enough, couldn't you?"

"Oh yes," said Harold, "I could even open a branch office down there. As a matter of fact our Mr. Vickars is all in favour of it, with things like they are in the City, but . . . well . . . the fact is I couldn't live with myself if I did that, it would be too much like running away."

"That's absolutely cockeyed," said Jim, shortly, "there's damn all to keep you here is there?"

"There's nothing to keep you, or Miss Clegg, or that girl lodger of Miss Clegg's," countered Harold, defensively.

"Dammit, I'm a full-time A.R.P. worker, and that girl you mention is in the A.F.S.," argued Jim. He was genuinely puzzled by the man's manner and line of reasoning.

"I can't do anything like you're doing," said Harold, "I'd like to, but I know that if I did I'd only crack up, and get in the way! The Savings Group you put me on to . . . it's not much but, well . . . it is better than nothing. Apart from that, I want to stick it as long as people like you stay. You see . . . I believe in this war, and I don't want other people to fight it for me! If there's nothing else I can do, at least I can hang on, and not let them chase me out of my home."

Jim looked at him with affection. This was the kind of thing he had been thinking about on his way up to the post last night. Here was the staying power of the British, revealed in the person of a pigeon-chested little city clerk, hanging on to his terraced home in the suburb, while all hell broke loose round him, hanging on and staying put, simply because he was vaguely aware that, by so doing, he was identifying himself with the clear-cut issues of right and wrong, and with the one basic principle of democracy that everybody understood—the right to let people and nations muddle along in their own way, without any pressure from outside.

"Does that seem well . . . does it seem pompous to you, Carver?" asked Harold, after a pause.

"No," said Jim slowly, "it's what we're all fighting for, after all."

"But I *can't* stick it any longer alone," said Harold suddenly, "It isn't fear of being killed, or smashed up, it's ... it's the loneliness, it's not being able to talk to anyone, when things start to happen."

He looked Jim full in the eyes, for the first time since they had sat down. "Would you think it infernal impudence on my part if I ... if I asked you to ... to take up quarters in here?"

He went on, before Jim could exclaim: "We'd muck along together ... you could have the back bedroom, where Esme used to sleep, and I could do things for you ... make tea, etc., and clean up and ... well, all sorts of things, that you haven't time to do. After all, your daughter must have her hands full. She's a husband, and the twins to look after, as well as doing for young Judy, and the two boys, when they come on leave."

And why not, thought Jim, still struggling to conceal his surprise. There was more room in here, and obviously the poor chap was near the end of his tether. He thought back to the summer, to the night the twins got home from France, when he had almost despaired, and this little man, sucking his pipe at the front gate, had pumped new courage into him, simply by voicing his confidence in the country's ability to stand up to Hitler, and defy an invasion. Well, Godbeer had been right on that occasion, and now that the Germans were trying to blast the country into submission, Godbeer himself stood in need of a little encouragement, encouragement that would spring from living cheek by jowl with someone physically engaged in the struggle.

He smiled, and held out his hand.

"Why not, Godbeer? I'll move in with you! It's a deal!"

Harold gulped, beamed, and then wrung his neighbour's hand.

"I'll start getting the room ready now," he babbled. "My word, but this'll make all the difference, all the difference in the world! I'll leave the key with you when I go to work today, and I'll ... I'll 'phone Eunice, the minute I get to the

office! She'll be tickled to death, Carver, and so will Esme
... I'll drop Esme a line tonight!"

He darted about the kitchen like an excited child, and Jim
leaned back in his chair, and stretched. As he brought his big
hands forward again he noticed that they were grey with
dirt, and that there was dried blood on his forearm, where
the head of one of the children had rested as he handed the
body out to poor old Hopner.

"I think I'll start by having a wash-and-brush in your
bathroom, Godbeer," he said.

"Yes, yes, by all means," said Harold, "soap ... towel ...
you'll find everything there, but here, let me pull off those
boots ... you must be all in!"

Before Jim could protest he had knelt and lifted Jim's right
foot, tugging at the boot, and covering his hands with mud
and damp plaster.

"No, no," protested Jim, "dammit, you're the landlord, not
the bootboy!"

But Harold would not be denied and drew off both boots.
Then Jim laughed outright, and Harold laughed too, and
nothing for either of them seemed so sad, or so hopeless, as
the first light of dawn crept through the shattered kitchen
window, and the whiff of charred homes drifted over from the
smouldering rubble in Delhi Road.

CHAPTER III

Exercise 'Make-A-Way'

BERNI and Boxer, the Carver twins, were enjoying life in the Commandos, more than they had enjoyed their schooldays, or their Speedway days, or even their provincial tour as The Suicide Twins, with the Wall of Death outfit.

Stimulating as these experiences had proved, their capacity to enjoy them had been limited by rules and regulations, devised for the comfort of ordinary citizens. No matter how exciting, or how provocative the opportunities that presented themselves in schoolroom, team-race, or fairground, star-turns were still expected to behave more or less like normal people; even their overseas campaign, with the B.E.F., had been soured by workaday obligations, like equipment cleaning and road safety precautions.

Being a Commando was different, so different that even now they experienced some difficulty in adjusting themselves to the role of outlaws who were encouraged by the newspapers, and even by their own officers, to cut clean through rules and regulations and concentrate solely on the business of learning to kill Germans.

They were proving ideal material for a Commando unit. All their lives they had craved speed, noise, excitement, and modest acclaim. All their lives, in one way or another, they had been waging jolly, uninhibited warfare on the long-suffering British public, knocking at doors and running away, smashing windows with catapults, practising the string-and-parcel game on unsuspecting pedestrians, clambering about on schoolhouse roofs, thinking up new and explosive jokes to

38

test the disciplinary powers of their schoolmasters, or devising new thrills to test the nerves of fans.

Later, when they had left school and became Speedway aces at Crystal Palace, they were often in trouble with the Police during off-duty periods, never for anything amounting to a felony, but simply because of their unspeakable contempt for the rules laid down for ordinary road-users. Later still they had made quite a name for themselves as riders on the Wall of Death, until Boxer, the more slow-witted of the two, had lost them their jobs, by getting drunk, and involving himself with Jackie Gulliver, madcap daughter of the industrialist, whose machines they rode.

They operated, as always, in a team—just the two of them, with Boxer as the more forward in action, and Bernard, the smaller, fair-haired one, as brain and seconder. They had always operated in this way, ever since, at the age of eight, Boxer had fallen through the ice of the frozen pond in the Lane, near the Avenue, and had been saved, miraculously, by Bernard. From that day forward they were not to be parted and Bernard had accepted responsibility for everything his brother said or did.

Whenever there was a decision to be made it was Bernard who made it; Boxer never made up his mind on any issue, without first appealing for Bernard's sanction.

"Whadysay Berni, whadysay?" he would ask, his bullet head cocked, like that of an eager mastiff. Bernard would suck his lips, and pretend to ponder a moment, while Boxer hovered, awaiting his brother's curt nod, or shake of the head, that signified approval or otherwise. When Bernard had pronounced Boxer never questioned his decisions. They were infallible as far as Boxer was concerned.

In action they were superb. Boxer had slow, ponderous strength, his brother an ape-like agility, and the speed of a striking cobra. They were popular with the unit, but they were seldom seen in their comrades' company off duty. Just as, in their schooldays, they had found all the comradeship they needed in each other, so, as men, they preferred to seek their relaxation unhindered by a third, or fourth party. It was probably their preference for one another's company that had kept them unmarried throughout their early manhood, for women found them attractive and either could have married a dozen times during their motor-cycling heyday.

They were much admired by their officers, who considered that their genial aggressiveness, and reliance one upon the other, exemplified the Commando team-spirit. They were always the first to arrive at the cliff top, or aboard the moored pontoon. They were always first in and first out of a position, marked down to be stormed, or demolished. They loved knocking things down and blowing things up. They won the unarmed combat contests outright and amused the adjudicating officer by flatly refusing to fight one another.

They were wonderfully skilful providers during the unit's outdoor bivouac spells, helping themselves to game and farmhouse food, with the stealth of country-bred poachers and the skill of trained housebreakers, and when the unit was briefed on 'Exercise Make-a-Way' they made no attempt to conceal their elation, for this, they felt, promised to prove the supreme lark of the course.

Under 'Exercise Make-a-Way' the men were ordered to leave the base near Killiecrankie and make their way to the unit's London depot. They had to accomplish the journey in twenty-four hours, without spending a penny on food, drink or transport. The police, and local Home Guard units were to be alerted, and had promised to do their utmost to arrest any man wearing the distinctive flash in his beret.

The pairs set off a few minutes before dawn, carrying their weapons and a ground-sheet. Most of the men made for the main road, hoping to thumb lifts as far as Edinburgh, or Glasgow, and thus accomplish the first leg of the journey as the daylight traffic began to flow south.

Bernard, however, had a much better idea. He was hungry, and was not disposed to begin a four-hundred-mile hitch-hike on an empty stomach.

Boxer hoisted him through a skylight in the shop-door of a local bakery and here they stuffed themselves with pies, and pastries, taking care to carry away a surplus for the journey south. Boxer wanted to stay and make tea, in the scullery adjoining, but Bernard forbade this on the grounds that they might have to manhandle the baker, whose pasties had been tasty and satisfying. So they broke into another shop, lower down the street, and there helped themselves to a few bottles of mineral waters and fifty cigarettes apiece. After all, Bernard argued, the police had been alerted and two robberies would probably detain half the local constabulary in the area all morning, giving the unit time to clear the area.

A mile or two along the road to Perth they stopped a motorist, who was travelling in the opposite direction. Bernard would have preferred to have obtained a lift on a south-bound car, but the commercial traveller they encountered was the first motorist they met and so they made the best of him. He was abandoned by the roadside, speechless with indignation, while they reversed his Austin and drove off at high speed towards Perth.

They did not enter the city for Bernard remembered that there had been a 'phone box near the point where they hijacked the car and he reasoned that the motorist would be certain to make for it and report the number and description of the car. Accordingly, they ditched the Austin in a builder's yard and borrowed the builder's lorry, which had been immobilised in accordance with national instructions, but not sufficiently so to defeat a pair of trained mechanics like Boxer and Bernard.

They drove over the Ochil Hills to within a few miles of Stirling, where they ran out of petrol, and parked the lorry at a crossroads. They left it on the crown of the road, confident that its presence there would soon be the means of providing them with fresh transport.

They were not disappointed. In less than five minutes a roving section of the local Home Guard came bowling along, in a jeep. Perched on the vehicle were three Home Guardsmen, heavy, middle-aged Scots, who at once recognised the flashes of the two Commandos and leaped from the jeep with Gaelic whoops of triumph.

In ninety-four seconds two of them were lying trussed in the back of the lorry, and the third, whom Boxer had been obliged to rabbit-punch, was on hands and knees, being sick in the ditch. The twins took the jeep, drove it round the parked lorry and set off, munching pasties, in the general direction of Glasgow.

By mid-day they had crossed the Border at Carlisle, leaving behind them a trail of abandoned vehicles, pilfered shops, groggy Home Guardsmen, and two footsore policemen, whose bicycles they had borrowed whilst the owners were signing on duty.

Telephone wires began to buzz and the adjutant in the orderly room of the Killiecrankie base was kept busy all morning, dealing with a spate of testy enquiries. Meanwhile, the twins pursued their way blithely across the fells in an ironmonger's van, singing their twenty-year-old signature tune, *'Everybody's Doing It'*, at the top of untuneful voices.

At Skipton they ran into a road-block, and had to jump for it. Their pursuers harried them out of the town, and up on to the open moor, towards Earby, but they shook them off easily enough and lay up in the gorse near the main road, munching the last of their stolen provisions and taking their ease, until a likely-looking car presented itself.

They let several cars pass and then Bernard walked into the road and flagged a plump police inspector, who drove up in a new Morris. He was alone, and incredibly naïve.

The Inspector, one of their Skipton pursuers, stepped from the car with a broad smile.

"That's the spirit, sonny! You've had a good run for your money, haven't you?" and he jerked his thumb genially towards the rear seat of the car.

Bernard got in without a word and the Inspector climbed in after him, pressing the self-starter, and letting in the clutch.

The engine started but the car did not move, so the policeman revved up and strained forward, throwing a puzzled glance over his shoulder at the solemn-faced young man who was sitting meekly behind him.

When Bernard looked meek his expression was not far off that of an idiot's, so that even then the policeman did not suspect a trap.

"That's very odd," he grunted, slipping into neutral again and opening the door.

It was not in the least odd, as Bernard could have told him, for while they had been setting themselves in the car Boxer had emerged from the bushes a few yards down the hill and slipped a large, squarish block of limestone against the forward tread of the offside rear tyre. By the time the Inspector had climbed out and opened the bonnet, Boxer was in the driver's seat. He reversed a yard, swerved left, struck the Inspector in the chest with the offside front wing and roared off down the road. Bernard blew a kiss to him out of the rear window.

It had all happened so quickly, and so expertly that the Inspector had not even time to note Boxer's features and had seen him only as a blurr of khaki, before falling on his back in the gorse.

"Silly old sod," said Boxer, "didn't he remember there were two of us?"

That was the point, both then and later. People never remembered that there were two of them. As long as Bernard stood before them, looking solemn, and slightly pained, they were wide open for attack from behind by the lumbering Boxer, and in this way the twins idled south, in vans, in cars and, on the final stage of the journey, in a single-decker 'bus, from which six bewildered passengers had been ejected.

They drove the 'bus right up to the depot gates, and the sergeant of the guard, who had been warned of their almost certain arrival, regarded them with awe, as he marched them into the duty officer, and clocked up their time-of-arrival in the guardroom.

It was not long after dusk and they had accomplished the exercise in a shade over half the allotted time, arriving four hours ahead of the next pair, and in much better condition.

Over a drink in the ante-room the following night the section-commander discussed the exercise with the C.O.

"Off the record, would you call it a success, sir?"

The Colonel thought of all the new files that had been opened since lunch, files already bulging with complaints, scattered throughout a dozen counties.

"Well, yes," he said, "I suppose we could, but off the record the sooner we get boys like those Carvers into action the better chance we have of getting the civilian population acclimatised to the waging of total war! Do you follow me?"

"Yes, sir," said the lieutenant, dutifully, "I think I do, sir!"

CHAPTER IV

For Them That Trespass

NOBODY in the Avenue recalled a Christmas as drab and cheerless, as this one of 1940.

The four Christmases of the First World War had been shorn of many of the customary festivities and towards the end, after the shattering casualty lists of 1917, few civilians had felt like celebrating. They had, however, made some kind of effort in those half-forgotten days. There had still been trees in the windows and plenty of children in the suburb to sing carols. They had still had Christmas displays in the big shops of Croydon and Fairyland basements for children to visit in order to meet Santa Claus.

This year, however, the second Christmas of World War II, nobody seemed to remember that it was Christmas. There were so many more immediate matters to occupy their minds, for the Avenue was now undergoing a siege and hardly a night went by when the siren was not heard at dusk, or the 'All Clear' sounded before it was time to wash, shave, prepare a makeshift breakfast, and hurry into Shirley Rise for a train that, as likely as not, was over an hour late, on account of incidents higher up the line.

It was cold too, no sort of weather for hanging about the draughty station platforms at Addiscombe and Woodside and the news was as depressing as ever, not as terrifying as it had been earlier in the year, but still without a gleam of hope anywhere, and reminiscent, the older folk felt, of the stalemate period of 1916 and 1917, when the old war had looked as if it was going on forever.

44

As yet the Avenue was untouched, though Jim Carver had already dug families out of shattered houses in Delhi Road, Cawnpore Road, Lucknow Crescent, Outram Crescent, and at several points on the Lower Road. Perhaps the open spaces, at each end of the Avenue, or the presence of the Manor Woods, just across the meadow, had saved the crescent, or perhaps it was just a matter of luck. Blitzed or not, the families who remained in the Avenue had to endure the same rigours as their neighbours sleeping crowded together in inadequate shelters, wedged under their staircases, waking from fitful dozes, with dry and bitter tastes in their mouths, feeling jumpy, irritable, and uncomfortably clammy in siren suits and thick, woollen sweaters.

Apart from the bombs there were other gross inconveniences. Everyone along the Avenue was already sick and tired of exchanging little bits of paper for rations, and waiting for news of the lucky ones in the Forces, who were surely unable to realise what it was like to go for weeks at a stretch without a real night's rest?

Edith Clegg, at Number Four, was one of the few who made an effort to celebrate Christmas. Each December since she and her sister Becky had lived in the Avenue Edith had bought a Christmas tree at the seedsman's, in the Lower Road and had planted it in a huge, green fern-pot, in the front window, decking it out in fairy lights, and crowning it with a four-inch fairy doll, waving a tinsel wand.

She had always had an electrician call on her specially to fix the lights and she never hesitated to fetch him back again if something went wrong with them and they winked out before Christmas Eve. She was also in the habit of buying a few shillingsworth of holly each year, and sticking sprigs behind all the pictures in the house. Sometimes in addition, Becky sat in the kitchen, with a bowl of home-made paste in front of her and made long, paper chains that were then suspended from the centre lights of the hall and sitting-room.

This year Edith was disappointed when she called at the seedsman's, on December 21st.

" 'Olly, *and* a Christmas Tree, m'm? I'm afraid you've had that, this year," said the man, massaging his bald patch, and looking at her with astonishment.

Edith was not at all familiar with the new Air Force slang and not unnaturally misunderstood him.

"Indeed I haven't had it," she protested, rather testily for her, for her temper had been subjected to the same stresses and strains as everybody else's in the Avenue. "How could I have had it? I only remembered it this morning and came out straight away to buy it."

The man grinned.

"I mean you *can't* have it, because there *isn't* any," he explained, making a mental note of the conversation with the intention of passing it on to his son Roddy, who was serving in the R.A.F. "It's just that we haven't any trees at all this year and as for 'olly, well, I reckon there's plenty about, but no one's got round to picking it and bringing it in for sale!"

"But that's very extraordinary, isn't it?" argued Edith, "after all, it is Christmas week."

"There's a war on, m'm," said the seedsman, and grinned so offensively that Edith had to resist an impulse to strike him smartly on his bald patch with her shopping bag, as she had once struck Mrs. Rolfe, of Number Eight, when the horrid woman had been so rude about poor dear young Edward and his nice Mrs. Simpson, in 1936.

Edith returned to the Avenue in very low spirits, reflecting how, in the past, she had taken Christmas trees and Christmas holly very much for granted, just as she had taken for granted so many aspects of life in the Avenue. Now, it would seem, festive decorations had gone the way of almost everything else that was pleasant and familiar in life, swallowed up in the welter of shortages, restrictions, and prohibitions of total war, like the amount of butter one might spread on one's bread, or the number of sugar-lumps one could put in one's tea.

A little spurt of rage followed these reflections, and it was rage directed against that dreadful little man with the toothbrush moustache, who was responsible for all this upset. Why didn't one of his own countrymen assassinate him and restore things to normal? Why didn't God, who must surely regard him as the Arch-fiend personified, strike him dead with that cancer in the throat that the newspapers said he was already afflicted with? How long Edith asked herself, was he going to be *allowed* to make their lives so drab and wretched? Nobody had had a moment's peace since he began to rant and roar into microphones and march his savage-looking hordes into other people's countries!

Two years ago Edith would have been horrified to catch herself hoping that even Adolf Hitler would die of cancer of the throat and even now, as her natural kindness flooded back, she felt a little ashamed of such dreadful thoughts. After all, it *was* Christmas, and even the Germans celebrated Christmas, didn't they? *'Silent Night'* was a German tune surely, and didn't Christmas trees originate from Germany, or from somewhere near Germany?

She paused at the gate of Number Four, as a new thought struck her. Why not go out and *find* a Christmas tree? Why not take the secateurs from the kitchen tool-box and go out and *steal* holly from the nearest wood?

The prospect excited her and gave her spirits a distinct lift. The Manor Woods were just across the meadow and there was bound to be at least one little Christmas tree somewhere among that tangle of briars and close-set timber. Holly too! She remembered seeing holly bushes there, when she had walked in the woods before the war. Surely no one would miss a few sprigs of holly, particularly as no one seemed to own the Old Manor nowadays.

She made up her mind on the spot. Going into the house she walked through to the kitchen, found the secateurs, a ball of string, and her gardening gloves, and went briskly out again, crossing the meadow by the cart-track and taking the winding path that led towards the lake in front of the Manor.

She kept a sharp lookout for holly as she pushed her way along the overgrown bridle path. The long briars caught at her thick, woollen stockings and at the hem of her skirt. There were beech trees, oak trees, larch trees and elm trees by the score, but no fir trees and no holly bushes.

She pushed on until she came to the boundary wall of the old kitchen garden, flanking the paved forecourt. The weeds here were waist high and the broken paving was very rough underfoot. She climbed the broken wall of the terrace, and passed along the face of the mansion, where coping stone had crashed down from the first storey and half buried the broad flight of steps leading up from the lake.

The gazebo beside the water had fallen in, and the lake itself was covered with vivid green weed. There was plenty of ivy here but still no holly. Ivy would do, she supposed, but somehow it was not as Christmassy as holly, despite the words of the old carol.

Over on the islet Edith could see fir trees, but there was no means of crossing to them. The punt, that had been moored near the gazebo, had long since rotted through and now lay in two feet of water on the margin of the lake. It had been there since the mid-twenties, when Esme Fraser, and his shield-bearer, little Judy Carver, had been shipwrecked in it, whilst enacting 'The Passing of Arthur'.

Then, when she had almost made up her mind to abandon the crazy idea and return home empty-handed Edith saw a tiny sapling, growing at the extreme edge of the wood, on the far side of the house. It was a little Scots fir that must have seeded itself and to reach it Edith had to wade through a patch of reed higher than her shoulders.

The embankment here had crumbled away, and lake water had seeped through on to what had once been a croquet lawn. The water was higher than her ankles, but she plunged on, beating her way through the reeds, and wrenching one foot after the other, until at last she climbed the slope to the beech wood and reached the tree.

The little trunk was too thick for her secateurs and she saw that she would have to tear it up by the roots. Small as it was it was deeply rooted and resisted her for some time, but she persevered and finally got it free by scratching away at the loose earth and bringing the secateurs to bear on the slack fibres underneath.

When it came out she grunted with triumph. Her legs, hands and face were plastered with mud, she was sweating freely and her hairpins had fallen out during the struggle, so that long wisps of grey hair now hung down on each side of her face. She laid the tree on the ground and sat down on a fallen beech to recover her breath.

Then she saw the holly bush, about fifty yards off. It was a huge, straggling bush, spreading out between a beech and an elm. Even at this distance she could see there were plenty of berries on the sprigs and getting up she almost ran across the wood, forgetting her gloves that she had peeled off and thrown down whilst she was digging at the tree root.

She penetrated the bush and for ten minutes hacked away at the lower branches, cutting some twenty pieces of holly and pricking her fingers and thumbs in a dozen places. Reaching up for a long, heavily-berried sprig, some five feet from the ground, she felt the elastic supporting her bloomers snap but even this fresh disaster failed to check her enthusiasm and she cut the long sprig and tossed it after the others into the clearing.

Then, holding the secateurs in one hand, and supporting her sagging bloomers with the other, she ploughed her way out of the bush and set about bunching the sprigs. When the bundle was firmly tied it was almost as much as she could drag. She wound the loose end of string round her wrist and hitching at her drooping bloomers with her free hand, she stumbled back to where she had left the tree.

Here she was obliged to consider her position. It was going to be very difficult to return the way she had come, across the marsh, and over the wall, dragging the holly, carrying the tree, and supporting a pair of heavy bloomers, wrinkling about her knees.

She decided that something must be done about the bloomers and after a hasty glance around she cut a length from the string, hitched up her skirts and knotted the cord round her middle.

It crossed her mind then to wonder what her father, the rector, would have said, if somebody had told him that his elder daughter, fifty-eight years old, had tied up her bloomers with string, whilst in the act of trespassing, uprooting trees, and stealing holly from somebody else's woods. It was, she thought with a surprised giggle, the most improbable situation in which she had ever found herself, so improbable, in fact, that it demanded audible extenuation.

"I'm sorry," she said aloud, "but how was I to know that such a silly thing would happen, while I was picking a bit of holly for Christmas?"

She took the long way home, round the edge of the wood,

across the brook and behind the mansion, to the point where she guessed a foothpath would join the wider ride that opened on to the meadow.

She had never walked along this path before, and it did not appear that anyone had trodden it in years, for it was scarcely more than a rabbit run. The going was terribly hard, so hard indeed, that once or twice she almost abandoned the trailing bunch of holly because it would catch on roots and briars, making every yard of her progress a back-breaking struggle.

The brook, when she reached it was the worst obstacle of all. It was not deep, but its banks had been undercut by the rains of fifty winters and the bridge between them looked so frail and worm eaten that Edith dare not test her weight on it and was obliged to wade across.

Halfway over she lost a shoe and with her hands so full was quite unable to recover it. She staggered up the far bank, gasping, and almost in tears. In her struggles to save the shoe the waistband of her bloomers had worked free of the string girdle and the wretched garment was once again about her knees, making upright movement impossible.

She put down the tree and the holly and retied the string, this time boring a hole in the waistband with the secateurs, and threading the string through the hole, in order to guard against a third descent. Then she faced up to the prospect of pushing through brambles without a right shoe, and after a moment's thought she took off her woollen scarf and wrapped it round and round her right foot, knotting it securely across the shin.

Gathering up the holly and the tree she set off on the final stage of her journey, emerging some fifteen minutes later into the meadow and crossing it in a series of spurts, spaced by two-minute breathers.

By the time she reached the boundary wall of Number Seventeen she had ceased to care what she looked like. Esther Frith, standing on a chair in the back bedroom and making some adjustment to the blackout curtains, saw the strange, mud-daubed figure walk crabwise into the Avenue. For a moment Esther failed to recognise the occupier of Number Four. The Thing—it could hardly, thought Esther, be a human being—wore one mud-caked shoe and stocking on its left leg, and a plaid scarf wrapped round its right leg. Its hat—Esther supposed it was a hat—was tipped rakishly over its left eye and its iron-grey hair hung in festoons about hunched shoulders. Its garments, such as they were, were ripped in half a dozen places, it clutched an uprooted fir-tree to its muddied bosom and dragged behind it a huge bunch of holly, tied on the end of a length of string!

Esther stared and stared, but still did not know what to make of it, and as she watched the figure passed out of her line of vision and staggered right-handed towards the golf-links end of the Avenue.

The only other person who saw Edith cross from the track to the gate of Number Four was the postman, who was making his mid-day deliveries. He knew Edith well but even he, face to face with her as she came out of the front gate of Number Six, had some difficulty in reconciling the battered, mud-caked figure that limped past him, with the placid little body who gave him half a crown every Boxing Morning, although she rarely received anything more exciting than a circular during the postal year.

"I say, Miss Clegg," he called out, "you had an accident, m'm?"

Edith paused and faced him. She was breathless, battered, scratched, bruised, and ready to faint with exhaustion. Her clothes were in tatters and her wretched bloomers were on the point of slipping to her knees again. Her scarf-bound foot throbbed and ached after contact with hundreds of brambles, nettles, and sharp stones. Her hair, damp with sweat, obscured her vision, so that she seemed to regard the postman through a shredded mat, but she minded none of these hurts and indignities. Her heart glowed with triumph. Now that she was clear of the woods she felt as though she, personally, had inflicted a crushing defeat on the Forces of Evil, represented by the Wehrmacht, the Luftwaffe and the U-Boat packs. She pushed aside a hank of hair with a scratched and bleeding forearm.

"No, postman," she said slowly and deliberately. "I've *not* had an accident, I've been getting my decorations for Christmas!" And when the man's jaw dropped, and he made no immediate reply; she added: "After all, I don't see why we've *all* got to forget it's Christmas, just because That Little Beast doesn't believe in it, do you?"

"Well ... nnno ..." stuttered the postman, "no, I suppose not, Miss Clegg," and he stood watching her fumble with her elbow at the latch of her gate, far too astonished and overcome to leap forward and assist her.

CHAPTER V

Music At Sea

ONE other member of the Avenue's pre-war community thought of Christmas decorations on that particular day, December 21st, but he had no opportunity to gather any. The memory of Edith's Christmas tree, as it had appeared in the window of Number Four every year before the war, invaded his waking dreams, as he lay drifting in an open boat, some three thousand miles from the wood in which Edith was trespassing.

The Christmas tree had come into his mind because he had got his dates mixed, and was convinced that it was already Christmas Eve. It was difficult to make an accurate reckoning of the time they had spent in the boat, since the tanker had exploded after two direct hits by a U-boat. Sometimes, it seemed to Ted Hartnell, one-time stonemason, subsequently jazz-drummer, that he had been lying here, his head on the gunwale, his face upturned to a brassy sky, for the better part of a lifetime. At other times he did not seem to be at sea at all, but back on the ragtime circuit, with Al Swinger's Rhythmateers, beating it up in some airless, suburban institute, or dance-hall, rattling away at 'Yes Sir, that's my Baby', or one of the wonderful hit-tunes of the early days, a tune like 'Valencia', or the record-breaking 'Goodnight, Sweetheart'.

The waltzes returned to him more frequently than the quicksteps, or fox-trots, for the slow slap-slap of the sea against the thwarts was a waltz measure.

They had been adrift now for eleven days, the tanker having gone to the bottom on the night of the tenth, when

53

the ship was less than a week out of Montevideo. Since then they must have drifted hundreds of miles west.

Gunter, the second mate, who was in nominal charge of the lifeboat, told them that prevailing winds and currents would carry them due west and that soon, at any time now, they would see the coastline of South America.

They had all believed him at first, until Lofty, the big stoker, had gone raving mad waiting for the coast to show up and had leapt overboard and disappeared, before they could throw him a line, or tell him that what he thought was land was only a bank of low cloud. The cloudbank faded out soon after Lofty, abandoning the boat to a limitless space of flat water and empty sky, in which the sun glowed and glowed from first light until merciful dusk.

There were only nine of them left in the boat now, for Chips, and the Negro greaser, had been badly scalded in the second explosion, and had both died on the third day adrift. They had stopped rowing after that, husbanding their strength, such as it was, for a concerted signalling effort if they saw a smudge of smoke on the horizon.

The only breaks in the monotony of the long days were Gunter's night and morning issue of rations, two malted milk tablets and about a wine glass full of water apiece, just sufficient to make them start sweating again and clamour for their turn under the awning of shirts and swabs that had been rigged in the narrow bows. There was only sufficient space under the awning for two at a time, so they took turn and turn about, lurching forward when Gunter, who sat rigidly in the stern, issued the command.

Now that Lofty was gone they seemed to have exhausted all topics of conversation. Lofty had kept them amused for more than seventy-two hours, describing the women that he had consorted with in the shanty-towns of ports all over the world, dilating on the various merits of Creoles, and Papuans, and the horizontal accomplishments of West Indian mammies and Boston dolls. Now Lofty had gone, 'to look for a mermaid' as Gunter had put it, rather unfeelingly thought Ted, who had been fond of the big, jolly stoker.

In the intervals of dreaming about Edith's pre-war Christmas trees, arguing with the Second-Mate about the date, and humming dance tunes of the 'twenties', and 'thirties', Ted Hartnell put in some repair work on his Mexican harmonica, the one piece of personal property that he had saved when he slid down the davits, and fell into the starboard boat a few minutes after the first impact.

He had purchased the harmonica at their first port of call, never having seen an instrument like it in a London musical store. In his jazz-band days he had not been much attracted to harmonica playing. For him it lacked the beat of the banjo, ukelele, banjolele, or even the mandolin, all of which he played expertly. Neither did it possess the blare and summons of conventional wind instruments, like the sax', or the trumpet, and it was without the compelling 'itchiness' of drums and clappers, or the nostalgic wail of the accordion and concertina.

It had, however, the one merit of being portable. That was why he had had it with him when the ship went down. He had been practising on it in the galley between the skipper's strident demands for tea and snacks, just before the first explosion had hurled him against the bulkhead. The harmonica was then in his hip pocket, and had thus taken the greater part of the impact on its stout, nickel-plated sheathing.

When he remembered it, and fished it out, he was distressed to find that it had a long, shallow dent along its centre. He could extract music from either end but not from the middle. No matter how hard he sucked, the only sound that emerged from the centre notes was a thin, despairing wail, like the protest of a maltreated cat. Lofty had listened to him trying it out, hopefully at first, but impatiently later on, for finally he said:

"Pack it in Ted, for Chrissake! It sounds like a camel's fart, straight it do!"

Now that Lofty had gone overboard to look for his mermaid, and all the other survivors were sunk in silent despondency, Ted tried again. He thought that if he could unscrew the outer casing and prise from the inside, he could soon straighten the dent and restore the damaged notes to something approximating to their original key.

He borrowed the surly donkeyman's penknife and worked away at the tiny brass screws, hour after hour, ultimately getting them out and placing them carefully in his trouser pocket. Then he used a bent nail to bring gentle pressure to bear from the inside of the frame and when the dent was as smooth as he could get it, he screwed the fastenings back again, using the edge of his identity disc as a screwdriver.

Gunter, who had been watching him for the last hour said:

"Okay! Give it a go, Steward! We could do with a tune, I reckon."

Ted played a few bars of his favourite melody, *'Charmaine'*, and the Second Mate's lips cracked in a grin.

"Say, that's swell! I remember that tune! Play it right through, Steward!"

Ted played it through, softly and melodiously. The repairs had been adequate and the key was as near perfect as mattered. As he played, it was easy to forget heat, sunblisters, boredom, and raging thirst. The dip of the stern, where Gunter sat, became the dip and sway of his customers, in the 'twenties'. He saw, without conscious effort, the tide of bobbed heads and the steady circular sweeps of a hundred closely interlocked couples, the girl's eager faces looking up at him as they passed the dais, the men dancing with confidence, for it was always easy to waltz to *'Charmaine'*.

A middle-aged seaman amidships shifted his position, and smiled across at Ted.

"Play some more, Bud! I kinda like that! Play us a carol."

Ted played *'While Shepherds Watched'*, and the remaining men began to lose some of their apathy and regain something of the chirpiness they had shown before Chips had died and Lofty had dived overboard.

"Aw, to hell with that," said The Kid, a freckled boy, barely eighteen, whose face was now burned the colour of a fresh lobster. "There's no bleedin' shepherds watching us, is there? Play something more up to date, play *'Scatterbrain'*."

Ted played *'Scatterbrain'*, and the tune seemed suited to the harmonica. Halfway through The Kid began to croak the lyric.

'... pretty as a picture
As refreshing as the rain

Isn't it a pity that you're
Such a Scatterbrain...'

When the song finished he got a hoarse bravo from the
other seven. Ted tapped the harmonica, and moistened his
lips with sea-water.

"What now?" he asked, as Gunter nodded encouragingly
across the men sprawled between them.

There was a clamour from them all. It was strange, Ted
thought, how each generation clung to its own numbers,
'Dad' Mckintyre the cook, wanted *'Dolly Grey'*, and *'Won't
You Come Home, Bill Bailey'*, tunes he had learned at the
music-halls in his mashing days. The men in their early
forties wanted World War One tunes, *'Tipperary'*, *'Hold
Your Hand Out, Naughty Boy'*, and *'Long, Long Trail'*. The
storeman, who was about Ted's age, preferred the hits of the
'twenties', silly, sentimental numbers, like *'Babette'*, and *'Carolina Moon'*.

"I've always liked *'Babette'*," he told everybody, "I met
my missus when they were playing *'Babette'*, on the old pier,
at Eastbourne. I always called her 'Babs' after that! Kind o'
joke between us."

Ted played *'Babette'* and *'Carolina Moon'* and all the
other moons, over all the other States, until the heat went
out of the sun and the flat sea around them turned mouse-
grey, and Gunter shouted: "Tea up!"

Then they forgot Ted and his harmonica for a few moments, watching with unwavering eyes, whilst Gunter measured the few thimbles of water into the enamel cup, and saw
it was passed from hand to hand with the reverence of
communicants.

When Gunter had recorked the bottle, and they were
sucking their malted milk tablets, Ted began again, playing
until the gross, copper moon rose over the water and the sea
danced with phosphorescent light, as one by one the men
dozed off, lulled into a fitful oblivion by the steady slop-slop
of the water against the gunwale.

Ted slept too, dreaming of Margy, his wife, and seeing her,
big with child, plugging a number at the song-counter at
Woolworth's, in the Old Orchard Road. He woke up with a

start, remembering the dream, or enough of it to reflect on its absurdity, for their child had been still-born but a few months ago, and Margy had not been a song-plugger at Woolworth's since the early 'thirties', when they met.

. . . .

Day succeeded day. The cook died, but the remaining eight hung on, even Gunter losing count of time, as the boat idled between sea and sky and the empty water bottles rolled to and fro, to and fro, in the triangle formed by The Kid's legs.

Sometimes an hour would go by without any one of them moving, or speaking. They had abandoned their routine of taking turns under the awning. The two who were there, Hoskins, and Paddy O'Sullivan, lay half in and half out, their bare feet thrust across Ted's legs.

Each time a silence seemed unusually long Ted would lift his harmonica. At first he played a few odd chords for his own amusement, but as time dragged by his tunes became the main factor in their survival. Ted did not understand how this came about, but on the third day following his repair of the instrument he realised that it was so, for Gunter, who was still rigid at the tiller, within reach of the last remaining water bottle, and the tin of malted milk tablets, began to make signs at him whenever he stopped playing. They were not clear, unmistakable signs, like a smile, or a nod, but long, steady glances, or a sudden twitch of his lips, that Ted interpreted as a plea to begin playing again.

It was not easy now to coax music from the harmonica. The instrument was in good enough shape, but Ted's lips were not, they were raw and puffed, and every suck of breath required an effort. He kept at it, however, laving his mouth with sea-water between spells of playing and some-times gargling a little, or trying to gargle.

When there were no longer any request numbers he racked his brain for one or other of the hardier tunes, out of the past. He played 'Red, Red Robin', the refrain that had once cost him his job as a stonemason, when the rhythm had magnetised the end of his chisel, and caused him to multiply the inverted commas on the headstone of one, Thomas Hitchcock.

He played all the hit tunes of the vo-deo-do era, '*Crazy Words, Crazy Tunes*', that had been so popular in the Charleston days, '*Bye, Bye, Blackbird*', '*Sonny Boy,*' the hit of the first feature talkie, and many, many others. Then, when he began finding the breaks, or what The Kid called 'the twiddly-bits', too difficult and painful, he played slower measures, '*Blue Danube*', '*Tales from Vienna Woods*', and sleepy-time tunes of the Deep South.

He was playing '*Poor Old Joe*' when Gunter suddenly let out a hoarse squawk and tried to inch himself upright in the stern. Ted stopped playing and followed the direction of the Second Officer's half-raised hand. Gunter was pointing into the south-west, where the sun hung low in the sky, a huge sizzling disc, poised on the very edge of the horizon.

Ted put the harmonica aside, and dashed salt water into his eyes, rubbing away the brine that had gummed up his sore lids. He could hardly believe what he saw, for steaming slowly across the face of the sun, was a ship, a big ship, and not far away, for he could see the dark cloud of smoke mushrooming from its single, squat funnel.

The men lying between Ted and Gunter began to stir. Ted tried to shout, but no sound emerged from his lips. Gunter also was trying to say something, and was finding speech equally difficult. He kept making stiff, jerky movements with his right arm, and Ted knew what he wanted—someone must open the small box, amidships and fire the Verey pistol.

Nobody seemed to be taking any notice of Gunter, they were all looking in the direction of the ship, heaving and slithering, opening and closing their mouths, like a catch of newly-landed fish. At last Ted pushed himself free of the thwart, and fell forward on his knees, knocking open the box with the butt of his hand and groping for the heavy pistol. He found it, and tried to crawl astern to Gunter, but the Second Officer shook his head, and mouthed the words: "Fire it . . . fire it!"

Ted held the pistol in both hands, the butt hard against his breastbone, and pressed the trigger. It moved at last, and the flash of the cartridge almost blinded him. He dropped the pistol as the signal hissed up in a wide arc and burst over their port bow.

After that everything was muddled and confused. It was as if he had dozed off in a railway station buffet, and heard sounds and voices on every side, without being conscious of them as distinct noises, each with an independent origin.

This state of confusion seemed to last a long time, but at length his brain cleared, and he saw that they were swarming up and down ropes and cradles. He heard The Kid croak: "It's Christmas Day! God Almighty, it's Christmas Day!"

Then many hands lifted him from the bottom of the boat and, as they did so, his own hand reached out and up for the harmonica, which he remembered having dropped in the thwarts the moment he saw the ship.

A sailor, who seemed to speak in a strong level voice, said: "Lumme! We mustn't forget that, must we chum?"

Then Ted's senses slipped away from him once more, and he remembered nothing until he awoke in a white cot and saw Gunter grinning at him from a range of a few inches.

"Feel like a tune, Steward?" said Gunter, and held up the harmonica.

He must have noted Ted's bewilderment, for he added: "It was a British ship, the *Hyacinth*, on the way to the States. They left it a bit late, didn't they? One more day and we'd have been done to a turn! Go to sleep again, I'll look after this! By God, it was a damned good job for us you had it with you, chum!"

Ted went back to sleep, alternately dozing, and dreaming, until they dropped anchor in Charleston, the vessel's first port of call.

It was here that Second Officer Gunter made out his first report and handed it to the British Consul. The final paragraph of the report read:

"In my opinion most of the men in the boat owe their lives to Steward Edward Hartnell, and his harmonica. Although himself in the last stages of exhaustion, the Steward continued to cheer his comrades with a variation of tunes, sometimes playing for hours at a stretch. I consider his example worthy of recognition, showing, as it did, remarkable qualities of courage and devotion to others."

The paragraph ultimately crossed the Atlantic, where it earned Ted Hartnell, ex-stonemason, ex-jazz orchestra leader, and war-time sea steward, the George Medal.

It was the first decoration to be won in the Avenue.

CHAPTER VI

Archie In The Doldrums

ELAINE FRASER, née Frith, formerly of Number Seventeen,
now of Number Forty-Three, won no medals during the war,
but some would have said she earned one, if only for achieving the distinction of being the one person in the Avenue,
who never once allowed the exigencies of war to limit her
dreams.

Elaine had come to terms with life long, long ago, when
she had first dreamed her dream, in the limited privacy of the
little porch-room she had occupied, in her mother's household.

Today, at twenty-nine, she saw no reason why the crazy
antics of an Austrian house-painter should induce her to
vary her plans in the smallest particular. She remained aloof
from the war, and when the waging of the war by the people
all about her caused an occasional obstacle to be raised in
her path, she went over, or under it, with the adroitness of
a professional athlete.

Good food was scarce, but she got all she needed from
Archie. Smart clothes were in short supply, but she had
plenty of money put by and more flowing in all the time,
so that she came to a certain arrangement with the manager
of the fashion house that she had patronised before the war,
and was now the best dressed woman in the Avenue. The
blitz did not worry her, for she was a fatalist, without even
being aware of it, and having converted the dining-room at
the back into a bedroom, and called in a carpenter to strength-
en the walls and the ceiling with some beams salvaged from

a less fortunate local householder, she slept soundly through all but the noisiest raids. Even the blackout did not worry her. She was the kind of person who could see all she cared to see, with or without a light.

Sometimes, when she was curled up on her settee, reading a novel, sipping a gin and tonic, and dipping steadily into one of Archie's boxes of chocolates at her elbow, she looked rather like a large, comfortable Persian cat taking its ease on the hearthrug. The war news never caused her a moment's concern, for she neither listened to it, nor read about it. She used the chic, portable radio that Esme had given her for programmes of light orchestral music, and although she bought all the glossy magazines that she could lay hands on, she found nothing to interest her in the newspapers, and had long since ordered her newsagent to stop delivering them.

In a way she too performed war work and had done from the outset. From time to time she had made a number of fighting men very happy indeed and what more could a woman do, when happiness was so hard to come by nowadays?

There had been Stefan, the Polish airman, whose corpse was now washing about in the Channel somewhere. She had made Stefan happy for weeks, for since his flight from Warsaw he had found Englishwomen excessively cold and unresponsive, until he ran into Elaine at an Allied Relief Fund Dance. After Stefan there had been the Dutchman, who also left the house sweating and beaming, and whenever her husband Esme came home on leave, she made him happy too, giving him no opportunity to voice the doubts and dreads he had experienced during the night watches in the Midland orderly room that he inhabited.

In addition to all these endeavours she made Archie Carver happy every Saturday night, sirens notwithstanding, and Archie was a much-harassed man these days, greatly in need of a little relaxation. The blitz was becoming an obsession with him, not because he feared that it might cut short his life, but because the Luftwaffe crews had taken to using incendiaries and oil-bombs and at any moment one might fall on his store at the back of the corner shop, destroying goods that could not be replaced, not even by a man as enterprising as Archie.

Elaine knew nothing whatever about Archie's private strongroom and its oil-drums, now almost full, but she knew that a stock of rationed goods was more valuable than money and that the careful deployment of Archie's stocks (the product of inspired buying during the busy year spent under Mr. Chamberlain's umbrella) was no guarantee at all against the greater part of these goods going up in smoke. Bombs were falling everywhere nowadays and it was quite within the bounds of possibility that a heavy raid in South London would account for half a dozen of his rented store-houses, scattered though they were over a wide area, between Catford and Wickham.

She noticed how jittery he was getting when he made his weekly call on her one night early in the New Year. She was already in bed, reading, when she heard him dump the heavy cardboard box containing her rations on the scullery table, just inside the back door.

She called, cheerily: "Hullo there? I'm not asleep," and he slouched in, looking drawn and haggard, not at all like the old, purposeful Archie, who had knocked her down with his sports car at the bottom of Shirley Rise on that awful day that the doctor told her she could expect Esme's child in August.

His movements were heavy and resigned, as he sat on the foot of the bed and dragged off his brogues. His broad face seemed a little thinner and he blinked and blinked in the soft light, as though his eyes pricked, and smarted.

"You look all in, dearest," she said, sympathetically. She called all her men friends, 'dearest'. 'Darling' had ceased to mean anything, and she disliked the American terms 'cutie', 'sugar', and 'honey'. Neither was the word even used by her hypocritically, for the man who happened to be sitting on the end of the bed, at any particular time, really was her dearest, and remained so until he had gone, and another had taken his place.

"It's these bloody incendiaries," he told her, glumly, "I don't mind H.E., you could salvage most of the stuff after an H.E., but once the place is alight, what chance has anybody

got? You'd simply have to stand by and watch a fortune
blaze up under the blasted hoses! It's not just that either!
Sometimes I wonder what the hell it's all in aid of!"

"You mean the war?"

"War? War, no—everything—*life!*"

Most women, most wives indeed, would have tried to
reason with him, to point out that he was overtired, and out
of sorts, that London was a big place, that there were
millions of square yards to receive a limited number of
incendiary bombs, and that the chances of one of his stores
being demolished was therefore remote, if one weighed the
risks objectively. He would then have begun to argue about
it, getting more and more irritable in the process, and clinging more and more obstinately to his own gloomy points of
view, so that in the end they would have bickered and
sulked, and the entire evening would have been spoiled.

Elaine knew men much better than this. She knew that in
order to soothe him she would have to switch his mind right
away from incendiaries and food stocks. Fortunately the
means to achieve the diversion were at hand. She slipped out
of bed, poured him a whisky and soda, let fall her pink
nightdress, and offered the drink with a little curtsy.

"Your refreshment, O Master!"

He took the glass with a tired smile and began to sip it,
but without taking his eyes from her.

"I don't know how the hell I'd cope without you, Elaine,"
he admitted, "I look forward to coming here all the week."

She made a pert and familiar movement with her lips, and
crossed to the stool, in front of the dressing-table. His eyes
absorbed every part of her, as she intended they should. He
noted her long, straight back, her big breasts, and pale,
pear-shaped behind. She was sturdier and heavier, than most
of the women who had attracted him in the past, particularly
since he had outlived his twenties. Sometimes she reminded
him a little of Rita Ramage, the wounded officer's wife, in
Outram Crescent, who had been his first mistress and had
been so difficult to ditch. The similarity was purely physical,
however. Elaine could be relied upon not to make a hysterical scene in public, supposing he suddenly stopped coming
here; neither would she hold it against him if he took it into

his head to seek relaxation elsewhere. She was like he once had been, a person able to live for the day, fearing no one,

He finished his whisky, got up, and slipped his arm round her, brushing the top of her head with his thick lips.

"I'm tired," he said, "I'll stay here all day tomorrow, if that's okay with you."

"That's okay, Archie."

Suddenly he caught her in his arms and began kissing her hair, cheeks, and shoulders. He had never kissed her like this before and it frightened him a little to realise how important she had become to him, how eagerly he was beginning to look forward to his Saturday nights with her, and how dull, and lonely, it would be in the Avenue without her.

The 'All Clear' howled over the Avenue, but if they heard it they made no comment. Elaine turned out the light, and for an hour or more they lay still, listening to the new, small-hours sounds that the loom of war was weaving into the pattern of the suburb; Jim Carver, clumping off-duty in his heavy gumboots, the wail of sirens in distant suburbs, the clank of a fire-tender, climbing Shirley Rise on its way to the A.R.P. Centre, on the Upper Road. Then they slept, Archie's head on her breast and Elaine's plump arm thrown protectively across his broad shoulders.

She brought him tea about midday. It was part of her service on the odd occasions that he stayed over. As he sat up to sip it she broached the subject that had been in her mind before she slept.

"You ought to take a few days off, Archie. If you don't, you'll crack up."

His fears had gone with the darkness.

"That's crazy," he told her, "I couldn't leave here, and besides, where the hell could we go? Where *does* anybody take a holiday these days?"

She noticed that he said 'we', and it pleased her. When she thought about it she realised that she too could do with a few days' change.

"Oh, there's places," she said, "and of course you can go! If anything did happen, being here wouldn't make the slightest difference would it? You can get one of your branch managers to sleep over the road. Why don't we go up to Blackpool, for a week?"

He considered the proposal. Blackpool, so he had heard, was one of the few places in Britain where fun and games could still be had, albeit in limited doses. The R.A.F., and hordes of civil servants, were said to be billeted up there of course, but a commercial traveller had told him, only last week, that there was still plenty of entertainment available and that a few good hotels were still open to the public.

The more he considered the idea the more it appealed to him. He had been to Blackpool on several occasions in the 'thirties', and had always enjoyed himself, as he knew how to enjoy himself when he did get away from his shops, and the vast amounts of paper work they entailed nowadays, unless, of course, one was prepared to hand over most of one's profits to the Inland Revenue.

Elaine saw that he had made up his mind.

"We'll go next week-end " she said, "can you manage the petrol?"

He chuckled. "I've got a reserve pool for the vans," he told her, "so you don't want to worry about petrol. How about Esme?"

"You don't have to worry about him, either," said Elaine, "poor Esme's on a course, and he won't get leave until it's over."

Archie stretched himself and rolled out of bed. He felt relaxed and excessively good-humoured, so much so that he could spare Elaine's long-suffering husband a sympathetic thought. This was rare, for ordinarily they never mentioned Esme to one another.

"Why the blazes don't you divorce that poor blighter?" he asked suddenly.

Elaine called, from the kitchen.

"Why should I? I've got nothing against Esme!"

He laughed outright, whilst in the act of donning his trousers.

"You're a pretty hard case, Elaine! Damn it, he must have rumbled you by now!"

"He's in love with me," said Elaine, coming in with a

breakfast tray containing toast and fresh tea, "but you wouldn't understand that, would you dearest?"

"No," said Archie, soberly, "I'm jiggered if I would, but I'd sooner be with you than any woman I know, and that's a step towards it isn't it?"

"It satisfies me," said Elaine shortly. "Do you want marmalade?"

* * * *

Elaine had oversimplified Archie's worries that evening. It was true that Archie feared for his stocks, and his hoard of notes, but these were occupational risks, and when he was not overtired he faced them boldly enough. At the moment his principal worry had nothing whatever to do with his businesses, it was a purely personal problem, and concerned his elder son, Anthony.

The difference between Elaine and Archie was that Elaine was an uncomplicated soul and Archie Carver was not. Most people, Elaine included, would have judged him so, and written him down as a person to whom the piling up of money, in one form or another, was the only thing that mattered.

There had been a time when this estimate would have been an accurate one. This was in what Archie now called his 'middle period', that is, the years immediately following his alliance with old Toni Piretta, and the forging of the first few links in his chain of pop-ins about the suburbs. It was before Anthony, his elder boy, had begun to occupy his thoughts. Up to the time that the Munich evacuation had separated him from the family. Archie had hardly noticed the boy and even now he was barely aware of his younger son, James, or the girl, Juanita. Since his last visit to Tony's school, however, he had found himself thinking a great deal about his elder boy and had begun to relate his own efforts in the sphere of business to the boy's future, as his partner, and successor.

Ever since he had been his own boss Archie had been a supreme individualist. The money he made, and such power as he acquired, was for him, and him alone. His family had never entered into his calculations. They were simply a tiresome by-product of his bargain with Old Toni, whose terms had been, in effect 'Marry my Maria, give me some grand-children, and we go fifty-fifty on everything!'

Both men had fulfilled their sides of the bargain, and from both their standpoints it had been a fruitful and satisfactory arrangement. Neither Toni, as a father, nor Archie, as a husband, however, had ever viewed it from Maria's point of view, and as the years went by, and the children, growing up, had occupied more and more of her time and kept her out of the shop, she had drifted outside the orbit of Archie's activi-ties. There had never been an open quarrel, not even after Toni had died, but sometimes almost a week would pass without the exchange of more than a few monosyllables ... 'Yes', 'No', 'Sure', 'Can't', 'Might'.

She knew as much as she wanted to know about his casual infidelities. She knew also, and this interested her far more, that he had cash stacked away somewhere and not in his banking accounts. She did not know where this money was hidden but simply that it was there, within yards, perhaps, of their parent shop, at Number Two, The Avenue.

He did not keep Maria short of money, for meanness had never been one of his characteristics, but his indifference to her and to her children, had soured her during the first years of marriage, so that now she had come to regard Archie as the representation of all men, in all places, and all countries, and her antipathy to men as a sex extended to her own male children. She reserved all her natural warmth and tenderness, for Juanita, the twelve-year-old girl, who lived with her in Somerset.

From time to time Archie went down to visit them for a few hours, and on these occasions he usually drove the few miles further west, to Hearthover, where young Tony was at school.

Archie, who had left a Council school when he was thir-teen, in order to begin work as an errand boy at a multiple grocer's, was fascinated by Hearthover. To him it was the epitome of all the schools that he had once read about in boys' magazines, schools with elm-fringed quadrangles, tuck-shops with fat boys and lithe, young adolescents who looked you straight in the eye, and had pretty mothers, who some-times attended speech days wearing big, floppy hats.

Hearthover and everything Hearthover stood for, was, so to speak, the chink in Archie's cash-box, and money could run through that chink as fast as it liked. Such romantic inclinations as he had once possessed had been ironed out of Archie during his errand-boy days in World War One, and in the course of his struggles to acquire wealth and power in a chosen sphere of business, but somehow his romantic notions about the public schools of twopenny magazines had survived, and because of this he approached Hearthover with the reverence of a pilgrim entering a hallowed shrine.

To Archie, Hearthover was Harrow, the Glorious Fourth, Greyfriars, and Billy Bunter. It was more, for Archie, who scorned patriotism, unconsciously identified Hearthover with Britain's Glorious Past and if he envied anyone at all it was Tony, his own boy, who had the immense privilege of being a cog in Hearthover and an important cog too, for the boy had done very well there, both academically and on the games field. He was now in the Sixth, a prefect, and in the running for the post of Captain of the School, providing he stayed on for a term following his eighteenth birthday.

Tony Carver's progress at Hearthover and at the Eastbourne preparatory school that had preceded his entry there, was a triumph of the alchemy of environment over that of ancestry.

Tony had been born in a room over a suburban shop. His father had begun life as a grocer's errand boy, and his grandfather on an even lower social plane—barefoot, in the slums of Naples. His mother, Maria, had once served fish and chips in the Lower Road, and had had her bottom nipped night after night by high-spirited customers but no one would have suspected these ancestral backgrounds had they witnessed young Tony Carver winning the mile at the interschools sports meeting, or regaling his fellow prefects with a detailed account of a fumbled pass as he sat, ministered to by adoring fags, at his study tea-table in Chiver's cock-house at Hearthover.

He looked and behaved, exactly like the typical public schoolboy of the school classics. He would have earned an approving nod from Doctor Arnold, and any of H. A. Vachell's heroes would have courted his friendship. He said the right things in the right accent. His opinions and his outlook, were as orthodox and uncomplicated as those of a mid-Victorian foreign secretary. He believed in God and in democracy, a carefully-graded democracy, of privilege, patronage, and class-comradeship, that belonged to the age of Liberal supremacy in the first decade of the century. His body was well washed and so were his thoughts. He was feared by the louts and the frowsters, particularly those who made a habit of dodging the games practices, and was worshipped by the juniors, who fell over one another in their eagerness to oil his cricket-bats, or scrape mud from the studs of his football boots. He was attentive, but not particularly studious in class, maintaining a judicious position between the head and the tail of his cadre, but winning an occasional prize. He was sometimes chosen to recite the Latin ode on Speech Days. He was clean, fearless, honest, truthful, loyal and terribly, terribly dull.

In view of all this it is not surprising that Archie was worried by the letter he had recently received from Tony's headmaster, a letter in which he expressed his desire to discuss Tony's future with his father.

It was obvious, from the tone of the letter, that the boy had been more frank with his headmaster than he had been with his parent, for Archie had on several occasions tried to bring their hesitant conversations round to the subject of Tony's career, but the boy had failed to respond, and had given Archie no opportunity to say that Tony was, in due course, expected to come into the business, as Crown Prince of the Pop-In Empire.

There was, of course, the hurdle of the call-up to be negotiated. Tony would be eighteen in June, and would be obliged, therefore, to join one or other of the Services. But Archie had anticipated this and had worked out a scheme involving indefinite postponements, occasioned by an extension of Tony's technical education. This extension was ostensibly directed towards making Tony a more useful officer when, at length, he was moved to join the colours.

Archie had given a good deal of thought to Tony's enlistment and no one was better aware than he of the existence of several loopholes, available to the knowing, and the prudent. There was the Catering Corps, for instance, the officers of which required a long course at the depot. There were several technical units that required even longer spells at a University. There were the government laboratories, where one might, if fortunate, avoid a uniform altogether. All these possibilities had been studied by Archie, and he only awaited the boy's preference, before making up his mind which of them to pursue.

He drove down to Hearthover a few days before beginning his holiday with Elaine and turned his long, white sports car into the West Avenue, steering between the long lines of beeches, that led up the hill, to the huge mass of grey stone that was the school.

As he dropped down into second gear and passed the playing fields on his right, Archie felt the old magic of Greyfriars and St. Jim's steal over him. A Rugby match was in progress on Lower Side, and Archie could hear the wild cries of the touchline spectators . . . "Pass, idiot, *pass!*", "Get it back, oh, *get it back!*" Then, after a brief silence during a line-out, the long, dolorous, organised cheer of shivering juniors, chivvied by stump-wielding seniors and house-colours: "*Come alonnnnnng Schoooool!*"

He grinned, parked his car and went through the wicket-gate into the field. The visitors had just scored a try and he arrived at a distressing moment for the home supporters. Almost the first boy he saw was Tony, his face clouded with worry and disappointment, as he strode up and down the touchline, looking like a young general witnessing the crisis of a battle on which hung the fate of his country and the chastity of his wife and daughters. He frowned when he saw Archie.

"Hullo, Gov . . . heard you were coming . . . excuse me a minute, this second-fifteen game is dicey . . . Heslopp has just muffed a punt and they rushed him and touched down between the posts . . . Ohhhh, *hell* . . ." as the try was neatly converted, "That's eight down! Pull yourselves together school, for heaven's sake! Pull yourselves together . . . !"

Archie had never played rugby football and did not understand a word of his son's complaints but he looked at Tony with quiet pride and noticed how all the smaller boys made way for him, and looked after him, as he bustled down the field towards the further goalposts.

The game was less than halfway through, so Archie thought that he might as well have his chat with the Headmaster and see Tony later. He strolled back to the school and was shown into the chilly visitors' room, and from thence, in due course, into the great man's study, that looked out over tennis-courts and miles of rainswept moor.

"Ah, Mr. Carver, make yourself comfortable ... glad you could come ... bit of a break for you, I imagine. News isn't too good is it? I hear they've been hammering non-stop up in town. Have you been blitzed yet?"

No, Archie told him, not yet, but that was a chance that every Londoner had to take. The man's faint air of patronage irritated him and he realised that his awe of Hearthover did not extend to its staff and headmaster. He had always found schoolmasters fussy and irritating. They were inclined, he thought, to treat all parents as if they were new boys, just settling in. He decided to speed up the interview.

"You wrote to me about my boy," he said, flatly.

"Yes I did ... and a fine boy too, Mr. Carver ... a credit to you, and a credit to us! He's done well here, as well as any lad I ever recall having."

"I'm glad," said Archie, "then what is it you wanted to see me about? Should he stay on here a term or two?"

The Headmaster slewed round in his swivel chair and as they came face to face it crossed Archie's mind that the headmaster of a school like Hearthover should take more pains with his clothes. The Head's dark grey suit sagged and bulged over his paunch. He wore no suspenders and a few inches of hairy shin were revealed as he threw one short leg over the other.

"It seems that you have got something lined up for the old 'Butcher'," said the Head, with a warm smile that was meant to put this rather testy parent at his ease. Then, noting Archie's puzzled frown, "I'm sorry—we all call Carver 'The Butcher' here ... 'Carver'—'Butcher,' d'you see? They nearly all have some sort of nickname like that, at least, all the successful ones do. Sometimes it's dubbed on them the first week. I'm not supposed to use it, of course, at least not until they get into the Sixth! After that it's optional."

"He never told me he had a nickname," said Archie a little sulkily, and proceeded to dismiss the subject, which he considered childish. "Yes, I've got something 'lined up' as you say . . . I want him to come into my business ultimately, but I realise that he'll have to go into something else while the war lasts. Is he any good at chemistry?"

"Chemistry?" The Head seemed genuinely puzzled. "Why chemistry, Mr. Carver?"

"Because I don't want him killed if I can help it," said Archie bluntly. "I didn't work all these years to see my eldest son's life thrown away by some clot of a general, and if I can keep him out of harm's way I intend to do it."

The Head coughed. He was unused to frankness of this sort, for among the visitors who had occupied the leather armchair, now filled by Archie's capacious behind, had been a number of generals, clots and otherwise, and even a stray admiral or two. He spoke seriously, weighing his words.

"I don't think you're going to be able to do anything like that Mr. Carver, not with old 'Butcher'. You see, he's a very spirited lad and he seems to have his future pretty well worked out. As a matter of fact, I had a chat with him on Monday, after callover, and that was why I wrote to you."

"How do you mean, he's got things 'worked out'?" asked Archie. "How can a kid like that work anything while he's tucked away down here?"

"It seems that he wants to make a career of the Army," said the Head, watching his visitor carefully.

Archie was so surprised that he forgot himself. He had never forgotten himself on previous visits to the school. When he visited Hearthover he always made a great effort, for Tony's sake.

"Christ!" he said, and his face flushed.

"Are you so very much against it?" pursued the Headmaster, politely ignoring the exclamation.

"Why of course I'm against it," roared Archie, "and so should you be! What sense is there in it, at a time like this?

Even supposing he survived the war, what sort of future is there in the Army, these days?"

"I imagine we'll always have to have an army," said the schoolmaster, stiffly, and wondered how it was possible that this coarse, irritable tradesman and 'dear old Butcher' came to be father and son.

For a moment Archie was disposed to argue with the man, then he realised that he would find it far too difficult to keep his temper while he did so and that he might say something he would regret.

"I think I'd better see Tony before we pursue this subject," he said, levering himself out of the deep chair.

"By all means," said the Head very much relieved at Archie's decision, "I'll send a runner for him now. He's probably on Lower Side, watching the match."

He touched a bell, and the duty monitor came in, a fourteen-year-old, with freckles and stiff red hair.

"Give Carver my compliments, and ask him to meet his father in his study now," said the Head, shortly.

"Yes, sir," said the boy, and after a single swift glance at the Great Carver's governor, he skipped out of the room.

"I daresay your boy will entertain you to tea," said the Head. "In the meantime, if you'll excuse me, I'll find somebody to take you along to the studies. Perhaps we can meet again after callover, when you've had a talk with him."

Father and son had their talk, and it was a sterile one from Archie's point of view.

There were no recriminations, and neither raised their voices, but Archie left Hearthover without resuming his discussion with the Head.

He drove away with sullen anger in his heart, for Tony had been unexpectedly obstinate, and had flatly declined to consider any alteration in plans that he had already made for himself, made, Archie reflected bitterly, without consulting either of his parents.

"I couldn't wriggle out of it like that, Gov," he had told Archie, when the various avenues of evasion were outlined to him. "Hang it, the Hun has already wiped out fifteen Hearthovereans! What sort of example would I be setting the kids here, if I spent the rest of the war frowsting in a bugs lab? I can get into a good regiment, if I decide to make a career of it. Take Frobisher-Clarke, he left only last term, and he's already at Sandhurst! Take Levison II! He's going into the Guards, of course, and I don't imagine I could swing that, but it ought to be easy enough to wangle the Tank Corps, and if I muff that I shall try for a fighter-pilot."

Archie felt no disposition whatever to take Frobisher-Clarke or, for that matter, Levison II. He felt baffled and defeated in this atmosphere of aggressive patriotism. He argued and reasoned for ten minutes more, before giving up. He had sold too many pounds of groceries, to too many housewives, not to recognise a stonewall sales-resistance when he encountered it. He said his final piece about the businesses, but Tony barely paid him the compliment of listening. As soon as a bell clanged, from somewhere down the corridor, the boy got up and opened his study door.

"I'll have to go now, Gov, I'm taking callover. Will you be staying in the locality overnight, with Mummy?"

It was curious, thought Archie, as he was escorted past scuffling groups of boys in the draughty quad, it was curious that someone on the point of enlisting in the Tank Corps, should still use the word 'Mummy'. Perhaps it was a fad— these places were full of fads. One term it was 'folks', and 'mater', the next 'people', and 'Mummy'. The whole set-up was beyond him, as remote from his counters and his coupons, as the present age was removed from feudalism.

He shook hands, climbed into his car and made up his mind to put Tony and Hearthover out of mind for a few days. He was very glad now that Elaine had talked him into taking that little holiday.

During the drive home he tried hard to forget Tony but he did not wholly succeed. There was little traffic on the road and under hooded headlights the journey seemed unusually long and cheerless. Somehow his visit to the school, his talk with the Head, and the hour or so he spent in Tony's study, had combined to put his past and future into a much sharper focus than he preferred. All these years he had been absorbed in making money, but now, he asked himself, what did it all amount to? Tony wanted neither the money nor the businesses. Measured alongside his childish eagerness to come to grips with scuttle-helmeted Germans, Archie's chain of pop-ins, and all they represented in terms of toil and hard cash, were too trivial to merit a single thought on his part, for the boy hadn't even bothered to listen to him, so obsessed was he with dreams of active service. Those other young idiots he had referred to, Frobisher Something-or-other, and Levison II, meant far more to him than Archie, his money and his pop-ins put together! What was the point of building up a business and a fortune if, when one began to fatten and tire, no one was interested in nursing it, or preventing it from disintegrating? What could he do with all that money in the tins, except throw it away on women like Elaine in return for a tumble or two on a bed, or a few hours' company?

He wondered, for the first time, whether he had made a mistake in sending the boy to a place like Hearthover. Wouldn't it have been wiser to have put him to work in the shop, at fourteen, and teach him that the only protection against the buffets life had in store for you was a credit balance at the bank and a secret cash reserve? If he had done this, would Tony still have wanted to go out in search of a military funeral?

He realised that he could only guess the answers to these questions. Tony's patriotic urges, a sentiment obviously shared by all his schoolfellows, and actively encouraged by that slovenly idiot of a Headmaster, were so alien to Archie that he could not even begin to understand them. Such friends and acquaintances as he possessed, were of his own kind, men who, at best, paid lipservice to the struggle going on around them and men who, if truth were known, had welcomed the war, with all its personal risks and inconveniences, as the one sure route to quick and easy profits. Like Archie they were aware of the sacrifices others were making—some of them even had sons and brothers serving in the Forces— but the popular issues did not touch them, never would, and never could touch them. It was as though, Archie reflected, the contestants were not really divided into Fascists, and Democrats, Germans and British, but simply into two races of individuals, those who believed anything and everything they heard on the radio, or saw in print, and the others, who had learned long ago that each man's duty was to himself and that all else was claptrap.

His mind went back to his first meeting with Rita Ramage, the officer's wife he met and lived with when he was only seventeen. Because he was well grown she had imagined him to be of military age and had asked him, during their first meeting, why he was not in uniform. He had immediately recognised her for one of his own kind, and had replied: "Because I don't believe in it!" She had laughed outright, and replied: "Neither do I, and what's more I never have, not even poor Little Belgium!"

Well, that was more than twenty years ago, and now, instead of Poor Little Belgium, it was the poor little Jew, or the poor little Pole. Yet youngsters fell for it just as they had in 1914, and some of them couldn't wait to get within range of the guns. And all the time fools like that Headmaster stood by waving flags! That was what one paid nearly three hundred a year for—the privilege of having a boy taught to take everything that he read in a penny newspaper at its face value!

He drove into the Avenue and through his double-gates just after midnight. A patrolling warden, caught in the headlights, stood aside and touched his cap, respectfully.

"Quiet tonight, sir!"

Too damned quiet, thought Archie, who, for once, would have preferred to have seen the sky criss-crossed with searchlights and have heard the bombs thud and the siren screech. He felt lonelier and more depressed, than he had felt for years and the prospect of getting himself a cold supper, and going to bed in the empty house, was too bleak to be contemplated. He yearned to talk to someone sufficiently adult to class the war, and the principles it involved, with toy soldiers and nursery rhymes, but there was no one like that in the Avenue except Elaine and it was Wednesday, not Saturday.

Oh, to hell with it, thought Archie, I'll pop over and tell her we'll go to Blackpool tomorrow, instead of Friday! Who cares if the blasted incendiaries set the place alight while I'm away? What point is there anyway, in working oneself to death simply to hoard money in tins, under the floor?

He crossed the road, too impatient, and too irritated, to

take the usual precaution of making a circuitous approach, via Shirley Rise. Fifty yards down the crescent he slipped into the alley, between Number Forty-Three, and Number Forty-One.

The warden, who saw him go, cocked an eyebrow, and murmured 'Ha-Haaa!', as he hunched his shoulders, and continued his solitary beat along the Avenue.

CHAPTER VII

Eunice Watches Boats

EUNICE GODBEER, wife of Harold Godbeer, of Number Twenty-Two, and formerly Mrs. Fraser, widow of Lieutenant Fraser, killed on the Marne, was enjoying her exile from the Avenue. She enjoyed living beside the sea, and she enjoyed even more her responsibilities as nurse and guardian of little Barbara, Esme's baby, now seventeen months old.

It had never taken very much to make Eunice happy. At forty-nine she had the mind, as well as the features, of a placid girl of fourteen. No wisp of grey hair showed in her carefully-coiled, honey-coloured 'earphones', themselves a relic of her youth in the early 'twenties'. No frown had worn a furrow across her smooth, white forehead, or puckered the corners of her small, ripe, sweet-tempered little mouth.

After upwards of twenty years of life with Eunice, Harold had at last concluded that his wife's girlish appearance was the direct result of mental vacuity. Although he was very proud of what he sometimes called her 'Dresden shepherdess prettiness', it sometimes annoyed him to reflect that her freshness and charm were legacies of a lifelong habit of letting other people do her worrying.

He could not recall a single instance of her worrying about anything more serious than the delay of bread deliveries, or a bank of cloud that threatened to spoil a projected picnic. When he had first met her he imagined that she must have worried when her soldier husband was killed and she was left to bring up Esme alone, but he had since learned that this was not so. A scrutiny of her personal papers, soon after they were married, had told him that all the worrying on that occasion had been done by her Scots mother-in-law and after the old lady had died he himself had taken over Eunice's life, first as her solicitor, subsequently as her husband.

It was the same apparently, with her evacuation into the country, for this did not seem to worry her either. Since she had taken little Barbara to Torquay, on September 4th, 1939, they had met once a month, but she always greeted him as though he had just returned to the Avenue, on the 5.25, after a normal day at the office. It was not, he told himself, that she lacked affection. She could be very affectionate indeed whenever he wanted her to be and he had never had the slightest doubt but that she loved him dearly and would miss him very much if he was killed by a bomb. In the same way, of course, she would grieve over Esme, or little Barbara, should anything unpleasant happen to either of them, but nonetheless he had an unworthy suspicion that, should circumstances widow her a second time, she would not remain unsolaced for very long. Someone, some big, patient male, would soon become aware of her inability to memorise the times of buses, or the day of the week, and would melt under a helpless glance of those china blue eyes and hurry forward, with an eager offer of assistance. This, thought Harold gloomily, would inevitably lead to the altar and then the same thing would begin to happen all over again.

In a sense (although Harold did not know it) it was already happening. Eunice and little Barbara occupied a pretty thatched cottage, on the outskirts of Torquay, and down the road was a large shop, temporarily housing an R.A.F equipment depot. Dozens of officers were attached to this depot, and by no means all of them were of the type solicited by poster artists, in their fly-with-the-R.A.F. recruiting efforts. One particularly, Wing Commander Glynne, the Commanding Officer of the Depot, had already made the acquaintance of the pretty little evacuee and her baby, and regularly performed a number of small services for her, such as fitting blackout curtains in the cottage, detailing men to clean the cottage windows, or running both her and the baby, in and out of the town for their daily shopping.

Wing Commander Glynne was a very courteous officer, and expected little or nothing in return for these little services. He was satisfied with a sweet smile from Eunice, and a fond gurgle from the baby, or sometimes, when he was really in luck, a grateful pat on the back of the hand, as he helped Eunice in or out of his Vauxhall and promised to 'keep an eye open for her', if he saw her standing at the bus stop on his way home.

Eunice spent the greater part of her day in the shopping centre. All her life she had been able to occupy herself for hours at a stretch by drifting along pavements and gazing rapturously into large, plate-glass windows. It was by no means necessary to her enjoyment actually to enter a shop and make a purchase. In some ways she preferred not to, for this always put a period to the expedition, and she was obliged to spend the remainder of the afternoon at the counters. When this happened she was usually spotted and claimed by Wing Commander Glynne, with a little parcel swinging from each finger and thumb, and nothing but coppers in her handbag.

Once inside a shop Eunice was a wonderful customer, open to every suggestion made by the assistants who served her. She was the kind of woman whose mere presence in a shop improved the relationship between manager and staff. The dullest and most impatient shop assistant could sell her anything, from a packet of pins to a beach outfit, from a small bottle of perfume to an electrical gadget for removing a roll of flesh under the chin that had yet to reveal itself.

When she wasn't in a shop, or had wandered away from the windows, she chattered gaily to little Barbara, the baby. Barbara looked adorable, with dark ringlets peering from poke bonnet and huge brown eyes, that reminded Eunice so poignantly of Esme before he took to playing rough games, but in addition to looking so bewitching the baby was an excellent listener. Her vocabulary was still limited to an odd word or two, and she therefore made no demands on her grandmother's inventiveness and Eunice did not have to cast about for fresh topics of conversation, an exercise that exhausted her.

Sometimes Eunice would wedge the pram against a seat on

the Marine Parade, and the two of them would spend a pleasant, placid hour, looking down on the boats moored in the harbour. Eunice would describe what they saw, in simple, uncomplicated terms: "There's a blue one, with a man in a jersey! What's he doing? Tying a rope I think! I wonder what for? To catch fish? I shouldn't think so, Baba, he'd have to go out to sea to do that wouldn't he?"

They made an enchanting picture sitting by the quay and no one ever identified them for what they were, grandmother and granddaughter. Elderly people would hover as they passed and smile down at them, and occasionally someone would ask after the baby's father and whether he was abroad, fighting. Eunice was always flattered by these implications and never enlightened people as to the true relationship. It was very pleasant, she felt, to be thought young enough to be a soldier's bride in a second World War after having actually been one in the first! Sometimes she almost thought of herself as Barbara's mother, for it seemed to her, as she watched young men in uniforms go swinging by, that time had stood still, and that she was back in Kensington Gardens, in the spring of 1915, with Esme instead of Baba in the pram, and squads of young men marching and counter-marching about the park, as she sat throwing crusts to the ducks in the Serpentine.

She liked best her long, peaceful evenings, after Baba had been put to bed, and she could settle by the fire, with *East Lynne*, or an Ethel M. Dell. She read the books of Mrs. Henry Wood, and Miss Dell, over and over again. She had a dreadful memory and they always seemed fresh to her. She wrote to Harold twice a week, and to Esme once a week, but she had to make herself perform these duties, for writing letters did not come easily to her. She never knew what to say and sometimes she sucked the pen for ten minutes, after writing 'My Own Darling', an introduction that served for each of them.

It never occurred to her to wonder how long the war would last, or whether she would ever return to the Avenue, where she had spent so many happy years between the two wars. That was something that dear Harold would see to when the time came. In the meantime, there were the shops, and Baba's spinach to buy, and *East Lynne* to re-read, and the boats to look at.

Day followed day, with scarcely any variation, except a little chat with the laundryman (such a nice, cheerful, flattering laundryman) or perhaps a ride to Totnes and back, with that sweet old R.A.F. officer. She was in no hurry to go back to the Avenue (though she would go, of course, the moment Harold sent for her) for down here the war and the bombs, seemed very remote, and the air was so good for Baba, who would now say 'fisherman', and 'anchor', clearly enough for even passers-by to understand.

* * * *

One sunny morning in March, about the time that Archie and Elaine were exploring the wartime delights of Blackpool, Eunice decided to avail herself of the Wing Commander's car once more and convey herself, Baba and Baba's large pram, down to the shops. She had all sorts of things to buy, and it was nice to be able to dump all the heavier purchases in the pram-well, under Barbara's feet, leaving the carrier basket free for any personal purchases that she might have to make.

The Wing Commander put her down near the Pavilion, and she set out intending to push the pram along the harbour edge to the Clock Tower, where there was a shop that changed its window every day.

The harbour seemed particularly busy that morning. All the usual fishing boats were there, but so was a row of squat-looking launches that she had never seen before. Somebody told her they were Air-Sea Rescue launches, used for saving airmen from the sea, and because Esme was in the Air Force, and might, at some time, be called upon to sit in just such a boat, Eunice thought it right that Barbara should be properly introduced to them. She lifted the baby out of her pram, and held her up, so that she could look over the wall, and 'see the big boats that Daddy used'.

Eunice was holding her like this, and steadying herself against a buttress, when she was conscious of a vague stir in the immediate area. She saw a group of men run up the steps in a body and heard people shout from the other side of the road.

At the same moment an insistent blaring smote her ears, as though a hundred car hooters were being pressed from only a few feet away. Then, above the immediate racket, she heard the roar and splutter of aero-engines, and glancing up she saw three aircraft, at hardly more than rooftop level, skimming in from the sea, zooming right above her head, and making the most unearthly din in flight.

She did not recognise these aircraft as German hit-and-run-raiders. If she saw the markings on them she did not identify them with the frantic scurrying of the people beside her. It all happened so very quickly; one second she was holding Baba against the wall, and the next she was instinctively thrusting her back into the pram, bending over her and adjusting the little wool blanket, the one with yellow chickens embroidered on the corner.

Then somebody hurrying by punched her in the back, and she wondered how people could be so rude and so careless towards a woman attending to a baby. At the moment of impact little Barbara, terrified by the noise no doubt, set up a long thin wail, and after that the seawall seemed to disintegrate and the waves rushed in and Eunice thought how horrid and noisy and disappointing everybody was being, on what had promised to be such a nice, sunny morning at the shops.

She felt no pain and hardly any physical shock, just a small and final spurt of irritation.

In less than a minute the aircraft had racketted away beyond the Tor and people came running, telling one another in high-pitched voices how amazing it was that the Luftwaffe had at last noticed Torquay and how lucky everybody had been to escape, and what terrible gunners Goering's airmen must be! Then somebody noticed Eunice, slumped over the pram and heard the baby's voice raised in a protesting wail, and the man nearest the pram said: "Hullo? Somebody's copped it!", and they all looked to see blood staining the pretty cot blanket.

Gently they lifted Eunice clear of the pram and laid her down on a mackintosh, spread under the wall. Other people succeeded in quietening the baby, lifting her out while someone ran for a policeman. The policeman arrived almost at once and began sorting through Eunice's capacious handbag and copying her address into his notebook.

Then the ambulance drew up and people with wildly beating hearts crowded round, to see the poor woman driven away to the mortuary and the woman who was cooing over the baby being asked by the policeman to accompany him to the station, for he was a bachelor, and did not feel confident of handling the situation alone.

Ambulance and police car sped away in different directions, but because the people who were there knew nothing of Eunice, or her suburb, nobody thought it strange that a woman who had never had a sour thought about anyone, should be the first person in the Avenue to die under the bullets of German machine-guns.

* * * *

They got through on the 'phone to Harold about 2 p.m., when he had just finished eating his sandwich lunch, and was looking up a precedent for a party wall dispute, in Stone's *Justices Manual*.

The line was bad, and they had some difficulty in making him understand. He kept saying: "I beg your pardon . . . please speak up . . . I can't hear . . . my wife . . . what about my wife . . . ?"

Eventually they did make him understand and he cried out, dropping the receiver on the desk, where it continued to squawk and crackle, until Miss Redvers, his secretary, gently replaced it and summoned help from the outer office.

Miss Redvers was well trained and resourceful. She managed to get the name of Esme's camp from the gibbering Harold, and after a tiresome delay getting the confidential number from Whitehall, put through a call to the Commanding Officer. The C.O. was very sympathetic, and promised to interview Esme immediately. He also promised to fix him up with a week's compassionate leave, but he warned them that it was unlikely the man would be able to get home until very late that night, or early the next morning.

In the meantime, Blane, the articled junior, had brewed Harold some black coffee, and forced him to swallow it, and Miss Redvers had dissolved three Aspros into the cup without

Harold noticing. By dusk he was sufficiently recovered to be escorted to the station and put on his train, but Miss Redvers insisted on accompanying him to his home in the Avenue, where she was relieved to find Jim Carver, eating his high tea in the kitchen, preparatory to going on duty at the Post.

Jim took charge of Harold at once and she was able to make her way home. She had acted throughout from motives of disinterested kindness, but as she paced about Woodside Station, awaiting her train back to Streatham, she could not help wondering if Harold would want to marry again, once the poor dear recovered from the terrible shock. It was an interesting possibility and occupied her mind throughout most of the journey to Streatham.

Esme, pale and haggard, arrived soon after midnight, and went into Number Twenty before calling at his home, just across the road.

Jim let him in and told him that he had been able to switch duties with a colleague at the Post and had remained to look after Harold, now sound asleep and 'doped to the eyebrows'.

"Are they quite sure Barbara's okay?" Esme asked him, fearfully.

Jim told him they were sure, for he himself had spoken to the Superintendent of Police on the 'phone an hour or so earlier. The baby was now being cared for by the resident nurse at an Evacuee Centre and could be fetched home any time that he or Harold found convenient. The Superintendent had also asked if they wanted him to take any steps about the funeral.

It was the mention of the word 'funeral' that brought the fact of his mother's death home to Esme. All the way south, in the stuffy, crawling train, his mind had resisted the information passed to him by the C.O., at the camp. It seemed incredible that poor Eunice had been machine-gunned to death, on the Torquay sea-front, when all the people here in the Avenue were still alive after months of bombardment. His senses shied away from the monstrous idiocy of the facts, of a harmless, fluffy, chirrupy little thing like Eunice Godbeer, becoming a target for young Teutons, who came zooming over the Channel from Le Mans, or Chartres. What could anybody hope to gain by such indiscriminate killing? How could the snuffing-out of a million Eunices affect the course of the war one way or the other?

Jim Carver tried to make some sort of sense of it.

"I suppose they've got a screwy idea that if they kill off a sufficient number of civilians we'll all start screaming for peace," he said, quietly. "By God, but they must want their heads examined over there! Even the Hohenzollerns weren't that dim . . . there was some sort of crazy logic in sinking the *Lusitania* and shooting Nurse Cavell!"

"I'd better go across to Elaine," said Esme, after refusing cocoa and sandwiches. The thought of food revolted him. He had been unable to take more than a bite out of a pork pie they had given him when he left the camp.

Jim looked uncomfortable. "I . . . er. I'm afraid she's not there," he said, "Harold went over about seven, and I tried again just before you got in."

Esme looked puzzled. "If she was going away she must have told Harold," he argued.

"There was this," said Jim, and gave Esme a used envelope, with a drawing pin stuck through the flap. "I found it fastened to the back door," he explained.

Esme glanced at the envelope. On it, in Elaine's large, legible scrawl, was the message: *'No milk until Tuesday'*.

"Where the hell could she have gone?" he demanded. "Could it be up to her father's, in Llandudno?"

"That seems the most likely bet," said Jim. "Are they on the 'phone up there?"

"Yes, I'll slip over to my place and get through at once. Will you be staying with Harold for a bit?"

"I live here," Jim told him, "Harold invited me, some time ago."

"Oh yes, I was forgetting," said Esme, vaguely, and left.

Number Forty-Three was cold and silent when he let himself in. He went into the downstairs bedroom and looked first at the dressing-table. If Elaine was spending a night away from home she would never have left without the array of pots and bottles that stood in a long row against the mirror. The space was empty and he double-checked by searching the cupboard for her soft, leather grip, and then glancing behind the bathroom door, to see if her dressing gown was there. Bag and dressing gown were missing, and so he went into the front room, lit the gas-fire, and put through a call to Edgar Frith, her father.

He was a long time getting through and during the delay his indignation mounted. What sort of woman was she, to go off like this, without even leaving a message with Harold, just across the road, or with Margy Hartnell, next door? Why wasn't she with the baby anyway, instead of gadding about on her own, and letting his mother take all the chances? Then he had a chastening thought. Perhaps she had taken it into her head to slip down to Torquay and spend a few days with the child? Perhaps, at this very moment, she was knocking at the door of the cottage, on the Totnes Road, and getting no answer, or being told the news by a policeman?

The thought made him jiggle the hook, and shout: "Hullo, hullo!" into the receiver. Eventually Edgar's tired voice was heard at the other end, and Esme, after apologising for waking him at 2 a.m., at once asked if Elaine was there. Edgar seemed surprised at being asked such a question.

"Elaine? Why, no, my boy ... no, no, of course she isn't! Why should she be?"

Esme briefly explained what had happened in Torquay, and he heard Edgar expel his breath.

"I say ... I'm terribly sorry, old chap, ... I'll come down ... I'll come right away ..."

No, no, Esme told him, he and Harold were leaving for Torquay in the morning, and Elaine would turn up sooner or later. She had probably got fed up with the bombing, and had gone into the country for a few days. She was like that Esme explained, as if Edgar, her father, didn't know, she was always doing things on impulse, and was always surprised if people expected her to behave differently.

He said goodnight to Edgar, took a final look round the bedroom, where Elaine's perfume still hovered, and then re-crossed the road to Number Twenty.

"She's not there," he told Jim, shortly, "I can't imagine where she is."

Jim could imagine, but he said nothing. After all, Elaine's wartime reputation was only an Avenue rumour, originating,

as far as he could discover, from that fatuous ass Grubb, the
A.R.P. warden, who had succeeded the punctilious Grandpa
Barnmeade.

"You get some sleep," said Jim, "try, anyway! You've got
a rotten time ahead of you. Would you care to stay here?"
Esme declined, returning thoughtfully to Number Forty-
Three.

He and Harold travelled down to Torquay and collected
Barbara the following afternoon. The child beamed with
pleasure on seeing Esme, who fondled her thick, dark curls,
so like her mother's in softness and texture, and hugged her
close, under the weepy glances of the volunteer nurse.

"I'm so terribly sorry about your wife," she murmured.

"She wasn't my wife, she was my mother," he explained,
with a tired smile, and reflected how Eunice would have
trilled with delighted laughter at the woman's mistake.

"Oh I . . . I'm terribly sorry," stuttered the nurse, and
then, more soberly, "the Warden told me to ask if you
wanted to see . . . your mother."

"No," said Esme quickly, and then, despite the wretched
triteness of the remark, "I'd sooner remember her alive."

Harold preferred otherwise. Despite Esme's protests he
insisted on going over to the mortuary. He came out tottering rather than walking, and Esme, encumbered as he was
with Barbara, had difficulty in getting him up to the cottage
and was glad of assistance from an unexpected quarter, the
R.A.F. Equipment Depot at the top of the town. The C.O., it
seemed, had known Eunice, and pulled up alongside them, as
they waited at the 'bus stop.

"I recognised the baby," he told Harold quickly introducing himself. "I say, my deepest sympathies old chap, she
really was a charming little woman, and quite wonderful with
that youngster. I often gave them a lift into town; you
know!" He turned to the blank-faced Esme. "You must be
feeling pretty dicky, my boy. Would you and your father like
to pop into my place for a snifter, on the way home?"

Harold thanked him, but declined. He had never been
much of a drinker, and he felt sure that spirits were not
going to help him much now.

They spent a wretched night at the cottage and Esme

persuaded Harold to order a local funeral. What was the point, he argued, of taking poor Eunice all the way back to Shirley Churchyard? They had no family grave there, and she had been happy down here. Blast the bloody Germans, she had been happy everywhere, he reflected, savagely.

"We spent our honeymoon here," Harold reminded him.

"I know," said Esme, attempting the weakest of jokes, "I was there too, remember?"

They travelled home the morning after the funeral, and Esme, occupied with Barbara, did not notice how ill Harold looked, until he began coughing while they waited in the taxi queue at Paddington. Then he realised that his step-father was on the point of collapse and paid the driver two pounds to drive them the twelve miles to the Avenue, instead of taking them over to Charing Cross.

When they reached Number Twenty-Two, good old Jim Carver was there, with Edith Clegg, from Number Four, and Harold did collapse and Jim had to carry him up the narrow stairs and put him to bed, where he remained for more than a fortnight, nursed, alternately, by Jim and Edith. By that time, Esme had disappeared from the Avenue as abruptly as his wife, taking the baby with him, and, like her, leaving no message for any of them.

CHAPTER VIII

Gaslight In Reverse

BLACKPOOL did not disappoint Elaine and the celebrated breezes soon swept Archie from the doldrums, once he had enjoyed a good night's sleep following the tiring drive north.

The town seethed with airmen, billeted by the thousand in the terrace houses of the drab roads, leading off the Marine Parade.

Many of the pre-war centres of amusements that Archie remembered were open and thriving. There was even a small amusement park with its usual assortment of booths and freak shows.

Elaine, who had once worked in a fairground, during her travels in search of The Great Provider, felt very much at home in this atmosphere and amused Archie by winning two prizes at a shooting booth.

"I used to load rifles on one of these," she told him. "The secret with tufted darts is to aim low, at least an inch below the bull. They fly up, don't you see?"

She carried away a large celluloid doll and a hideous brown ashtray. Archie, who examined the prizes closely, made a rapid calculation of the promoter's margin of profit, and decided that if the prizes were purchased by the gross the promoter could afford to present a prize to every third marksman and still make a profit.

He told Elaine this and she laughed, affectionately squeezing his arm.

"Oh, forget profit and loss for a bit, Archie! We're here to enjoy ourselves, aren't we?"

Enjoy themselves they certainly did! They ate oysters at a bar, drank a good deal of gin, idled in the cafés during the afternoons, watched the recruits drilling on the front in the mornings, danced every night in the Tower Ballroom, sat through several cinema shows and even visited the theatre, sitting in a box, and listening to a popular radio star croon, 'Over the Rainbow', and 'The White Cliffs of Dover'.

They went to bed in the small hours and had their breakfast served on trays at 10 a.m. Archie complained a little at the quality of the food and made a mental note to bring his rations with him when they came here again, but he had no reason to complain of Elaine's share in the entertainment, finding her relaxed, and as generous as ever. She even gave him the impression that he could, if so disposed, come to mean something more to her than a weekender, with plenty of money to burn.

In a strictly limited sense he was right. Elaine liked his breezy masculinity and the fact that he made no demands at all upon her emotions. Even the casual men, in her vaudeville days, had sometimes tried to pretend that they were in love with her as a person, and not simply as a congenial bedfellow. Eugene, the Illusionist, had grossly deceived himself in this respect, and Benny Boy, the agent, had been tiresomely jealous if she flirted with a man at the next table. As for poor Esme, he had made impossible demands on her during the first months of marriage, swearing eternal fidelity to her (as if that was possible, at his age!) and refusing to be satisfied with the purely physical manifestations of her affection.

Another of Archie's characteristics that attracted Elaine was his normality. She had the strongly-sexed woman's contempt for mattress frivolities, the kind that were often paraded as freedom from inhibitions, and she knew enough about the male's sexual habits to recognise these tricks for the exact reverse of what they pretended to be. She preferred her lovers to observe certain fixed rules of conduct and to refrain from making a drama of the relationship. Archie never attempted to make an issue of it, he simply got down to business, in a sane, healthy manner, and once the act was accomplished, he never referred to it again until next time. She found this approach restful yet refreshing, for it left her mind free to explore other fields. Some of the men she had made free with had half-persuaded her that no other fields existed.

Up here, with so many airmen about, all marching to and fro in their ridiculous little caps and turning this way and that under the hoarse commands of jerky little N.C.O's, Elaine found herself remembering Esme now and again. She wondered how he had reacted to these idiotic manoeuvres, when he had been a recruit in Blackpool, the previous summer. Very sulkily, she imagined, like that man with horn-rimmed glasses, who kept getting it all wrong, and attracting the invective of the one with the stripes tied to his arm!

Watching the training of recruits was one of Blackpool's free shows in 1941, and the numerous civilians about the town took full advantage of it. Their presence was sometimes resented by the hard-pressed N.C.O's. One morning, when Elaine and Archie were leaning casually on a bandstand rail, watching a squad perform an energetic exercise known as 'feet-astride-jumping-arms-upward-raising', the corporal in charge, a hardbitten regular, barked the order:—"Stead-eee!", and then looked directly at his audience. In the silence that accompanied this scrutiny he suddenly exclaimed: "Oi! You there in the gran'-stand! Come back after break, and you c'n all throw bleedin' nuts at us!"

Archie was stung by this remark, but Elaine only laughed, as the crowd of sheepish bystanders melted away.

"Well, we did rather ask for it, didn't we?" she remarked to the glowering Archie.

Her attitude was, perhaps an indication of the subtle difference in their respective outlooks on war. Elaine was that rare person able to cruise along quite untroubled by conscience. Never once had it occurred to her that the men in uniform were anything more than a troop of clowns, performing these antics for a fixed rate of pay.

Archie, on the other hand, found the presence of so many men in uniform slightly irritating. Their enthusiasm, and their plight, also, reminded him of his son Tony, who would soon be one of them. Deep, deep in the heart, securely anchored by the profit-urge and the fear of insecurity that had fed his go-it-alone philosophy all these years, was the instinct of a fighting animal, the instinct that had prompted him to go out and win independence in the first instance. It is probable that, under different circumstances, he might have developed into a first-class resistance fighter, and had there been no such thing as military discipline, or the necessity of submitting to it, Archie might even have been in uniform himself. He had more physical courage than most men and, in addition, a certain pride in his physical fitness. At forty he was still a lusty, agile man, and he told himself that, had he cared to enlist, his worth would have been instantly recognised by his superiors. He had, however, a whole battery of arguments to convince him of the folly of enlisting, and against these arguments his aggressive instinct was powerless, or almost so. His outlook was based, in the main, on his powers of observation, and whenever he needed to extinguish the faint spark of patriotism that glowed in him, he had only had to remind himself of his father's desperate hunt for work, when he returned from World War I, or of the parties of ex-servicemen, legless and armless some of them, whom he had seen drifting along the pavements of the suburb, begging to the tune of '*Keep The Home Fires Burning*'.

. . . .

They returned to the Avenue on Thursday evening. Archie left her at the junction of Lower Road, and Shirley Rise, in order to give her time to walk up the hill and let herself into Number Forty-Three, before he drove into his yard and garaged the car.

It was dusk when she turned into the crescent and a glance told her that no disaster had overtaken her end of it during the interval. Strips of paper were still pasted over the windows and the dwarf walls, shorn of their swinging chains and iron supports in the scrap-iron drive of previous months, were otherwise intact.

She let herself in and pulled at the front-door blackout curtain, before switching on the light. The house felt damp, and she shivered, hurrying into the bedroom with the intention of lighting the fire and pouring herself a drink. Then she stood still, seeing that the bed had been disturbed, and noting, in the same glance, the presence of Barbara's blue bonnet on the dressing-table stool.

For a moment she stood with her hand on the light-switch, her mind sorting the various possibilities suggested by the turned-back coverlet and the presence of the bonnet. The bonnet told her that somebody had brought the baby home from Torquay and Elaine's first reaction was irritation. Then she felt momentarily confused, for her eye, surveying the room, took in the blue-grey haversack, and service respirator both hanging on the chair-back near the window. She called, softly:

"Esme? Are you there Esme?"

She heard him then, moving about in the porch room upstairs and expected the eager rush of feet on the landing. When he seemed in no hurry to descend she went into the hall, and called again:

"Esme darling ... it's me ... Elaine ... I've been away, dear!"

He came downstairs very slowly and she saw at once that something had happened to change him since their last meeting. His small, delicate features were frozen in an expression that was half sullen and half pained. She had seen the expression before, during some of their lopsided quarrels, quarrels in which she had steadfastly refused to engage and had thus ensured putting him in the wrong, whatever the cause of the tiff. She realised that he was annoyed at coming home unexpectedly and finding the house empty, and her mind instantly began to grapple with the means to deal with the situation.

She smiled up at him, a warm, welcoming smile.

"All right Esme, you needn't look so tragic! How was I to know that you'd be home? You said you wouldn't get any leave until the course finished, in April."

He reached the foot of the stairs, but he did not advance and throw his arms about her, showering kisses on her hair, and cheeks, and mouth, as she expected him to do. He stood stockstill, on the bottom stair, with his left hand clasping the smooth wooden ball that terminated the bannister.

"Mother's been killed," he said slowly. "I've brought Barbara home!"

She started, violently, catching her breath. She was fond of Eunice, in some ways an ideal mother-in-law, but because Elaine was fundamentally a generous person, her own sense of loss was at once swamped in a rush of sympathy for Esme and for poor old Harold, across the road.

"Oh, God," she exclaimed . . . "*God!* Poor Eunice . . . ! *How* . . . When . . . ?"

"Last Thursday," he said, "in a hit-and-run raid, on Torquay. She was buried on Monday. Where have you been, Elaine?"

Half her mind absorbed the tragic fact of his news, while the other half fumbled wildly for a plausible explanation of her week's absence. Thursday, he said . . . that meant he must have come home on Thursday night or at latest, early on Friday morning, only a few hours after she and Archie had begun their journey up to Blackpool. He must have been awaiting her the better part of a week!

She tried to stall for time by asking questions.

"Where have you been . . . ? Did you go down . . . ? Did Harold go down with you? Was Barbara with her, when it . . . when it happened?"

"We both went down," he said, and she was disconcerted by the steadiness of his eyes. "Barbara was with her when Jerry came over, but she's okay. The point is, where the hell have *you* been?"

"To Blackpool," she said, flatly, and then, before he could exclaim, "I . . . I got fed up with the bombing, and they said Blackpool was the only place to go for a break."

"Who said so?"

This was unlike Esme. He was not in the habit of asking unpleasantly pointed questions like that, so she fell back on impatience, her panic getting the better of her shock.

"What does it matter who said so . . . somebody did —anyway, I went! After all, how was I to know you'd come? You said you wouldn't have any leave."

"But you didn't tell anyone you were going! You didn't even tell Harold! Nobody knew where you were, I even rang your father, to see if you were there."

"I'm terribly sorry I wasn't here Esme. I just went off on

impulse. I was sick and tired of that siren, and of all the muddle, and fuss . . . I . . . I hadn't been sleeping too well."

She saw that she was making some sort of progress, for his features relaxed a little, and he began to look worried and harassed, rather than tragic, and accusing.

Then the telephone bell in the front-room rang, and she made the tactical error of leaping sideways to answer it. Ordinarily she would never have made such a mistake, but her mind was a turmoil of conflicting emotions, grief, anxiety, irritation, and bewilderment, all struggling to assert themselves. He at once noted her eagerness, and she saw that he had noticed it.

"I'll get it," she said, moving quickly towards the open door, but he was a split second ahead of her.

"No, *I* will, Elaine!"

He strode across the threshold, and snatched the receiver.

As he did so Elaine knew that she was adrift again, that this odd but convenient marriage would dissolve at the breezy crackle of Archie's voice, and even as she heard Archie begin to speak it occurred to her that a girl never stopped learning in this business and that, if any ringing was to be done, it would have been so much wiser if she had arranged to ring Archie. In the dim light of the shaded hall lamp she studied Esme's face, as Archie said: "Hello there? I've just got in! What's new? Did any complications pile up while we were away?"

She felt a slight but distinct impulse to giggle. Any complications! Eunice dead, the baby home, Esme here, holding the telephone, after demanding to know where she had been all the week! Any complications?

"Who *is* that?" asked Esme, and his voice seemed to her to be shrill, like a small boy's, angry, but pleading.

"Who . . . ?"

Just that one word, then a metallic click, as Archie swiftly replaced the 'phone. He wasn't very bright either, she reflected. They had both handled the situation like hopeless amateurs.

"Don't you know who that was?" she asked, suddenly tired of melodrama.

"No, how should I? Only that it was the person you've been with, all the week."

She found this the most incredible aspect of the farce. Esme didn't even recognize the voice, or connect her absence with Archie Carver, the grocer, across the road. He did not even link the voice with that huge casket of fruit that had arrived at the nursing home, when Barbara was born, or with the steady supply of rationed goods that had trickled into Number Forty-Three since rationing first began. Quite obviously it had never crossed his mind that there might be an arrangement behind such prodigality, that some kind of payment might be expected for all the butter and cheese that he had eaten during his leave periods and crafty week-ends.

"It was Archie," she said, "Archie Carver, from across the road."

"You've been away with him? With Carver?"

She nodded, and then, recognising the futility of further discussion, she left him standing just inside the front-room, and went into the bedroom that had once been their dining room.

He followed her and watched her reach into the cupboard, and yank out the gin bottle and a half-bottle of lime cordial.

"I need a drink," said Elaine calmly, "and I expect you need one too!"

She found two glasses and began to pour, but when she looked up he was gone from the doorway. She heard him clump upstairs, in his ugly Service boots, and walk across the floor of the back bedroom, immediately overhead.

She wondered, as she sipped her gin, what he would do now, whether he would walk out of the house, or stay up there by himself, trying to come to terms with the situation and plot a new course if he could find one. She heard him opening and shutting drawers, and decided that he was going to decamp, here and now, that he would probably go straight across to Harold, pour out his tale and set about writing her one of his long, drivelling letters.

Her moment of sympathy for him had passed. Their association had already lasted too long, much longer than she had meant it to when they had married in the autumn of 1938. She was no good to him anyway, with his quaint romantic notions of Arthurian chivalry, and his pitiful attempts to mould her into his kind of bride, an enchained, unsullied bride, for ever menaced by dragons.

Swiftly, as she poured her second gin, she went back over their relationship from the very beginning, from the moment of their first encounter at the Stafford-Ffoulkes Junior Imperial Ball, when he was sixteen, and she a year older.

He had been out of date even then and he was just as out of date now. She had taught him the Charleston and had been trying to teach him something more profitable ever since—how to impress a woman, how to dominate a woman, how to see life as it was and not as it might have looked to a high-minded knight, riding under a balcony in Camelot!

It had been useless, all of it, and she had known that within a week of their Paris honeymoon. People like Esme never learned the kind of things she could teach because they did not want to learn them. They were afraid of reality, afraid to name their fears. They persuaded themselves that reality was ugly and that the colours of romance had faded once women took to riding bicycles and going out to work. Some people could get away with this lifelong pretence at living, but not many. Those who did were usually women, like poor Eunice, from whom, no doubt, he had inherited all this tiresome flapdoodle. Well, even Eunice hadn't got away with it in the end. The machine-age had at last caught up with her and killed her, and probaby the same thing would happen to Esme, unless he woke up.

She heard him coming downstairs again, treading carefully, as though heavily laden. She put down her glass and moved into the hall. She was on the point of saying something to deter him from carrying melodrama to the point of absurdity and walking out into the night like a wronged husband in a bad film. She had been going to say; "Oh be your age, Esme! There's a war on, and people are fed up! They *need* fun . . . !" or something like that. Then she noticed that he was carrying Barbara, who was still asleep, and wrapped in an eiderdown and a cot blanket.

"Where on earth are you going with her at this time of night?" she demanded.

He made no reply, but half-turned to twist the knob of the

front door, raising his knee to support the bundle he carried. She had another impulse to giggle, for here, it seemed, was the Victorian novelette in reverse, a man leaving the house with a whimpering bundle, while the woman of the story remained behind in the warm, sipping gin and lime.

Then he got the door open and went out, hooking it closed with a back-kick, and leaving her standing there, looking across the empty hall.

"Well, if that's how you feel . . .", she shouted, and then, recoiling from the prospect of Harold calling on her to cajole, reason, and condemn, she shot the bolt of the door and went back into the bedroom, slamming the door after her.

She kicked off her high-heeled shoes and wiggled her toes in the luxury of freedom. She turned on the radio and wondered for a moment if she should ring Archie and tell him what had happened. Then she decided to postpone this irksome necessity until the morning, for she was by no means sure of Archie's reactions and needed time to think.

The Small Provider had gone and The Great Provider had yet to be found.

CHAPTER IX

Baby In Camp

ELAINE was wrong in her guess that Esme marched out of Number Forty-Three and crossed the road to Harold, at Number Twenty, in search of sympathy. She was unaware that Harold was at that time running a high temperature, but even had his stepfather been in his normal health it is doubtful whether Esme would have hurried to confide in him at that particular moment.

Esme was facing a personal problem that could not be solved by advice or symapthy from anyone. Years ago, when Elaine had told him of her intention to leave the suburb, and to follow her dream along paths that he was not invited to tread in her company, he had carried his troubles to Harold and had received good advice, but Esme had not followed it, for Elaine remained in his thoughts throughout his entire adolescence and they had married after all, soon after she had returned to the Avenue, in 1938.

No amount of self-deception on Esme's part could persuade him that the marriage had been a success, and since he had left home to join the R.A.F., he had become increasingly aware that their relationship was deteriorating. He knew this, but he had been unable to come to terms with the fact. Over the years he had had ample opportunity to study Elaine's attitude to men in general and to himself in particular. Harold had once said that she was incapable of entertaining deep feelings about anyone, or anything, and Harold had been quite right. Yet Harold himself had been beguiled by Elaine during the weeks preceding her marriage to Esme and had been more than half-convinced that he had misjudged her, and that her tawdry experiences in vaudeville had taught her the hidden values of domesticity in the suburb. Esme, who had wanted so badly to be hoodwinked, had been an even easier victim.

At last, however, there was no advantage in continuing to hoodwink himself and in a way he welcomed the crisis. Ever since he had joined up he had been aware that his wife was deceiving him, but each time he had returned to the Avenue he had been able to persuade himself that she indulged in nothing more serious than an occasional wartime flirtation, the kind of light-hearted association that any lonely woman might encourage—up to a certain point. He did not believe that she had been unfaithful to him, for he was more naïve than most men and found it hard to fuse her outwardly affectionate approach to him with adultery. Duplicity, of that kind, he reasoned, was alien to the people of the Avenue. It belonged in higher places, in mews flats and country houses. It had never flourished in rows of terraced houses, where nobody earned more than a few pounds a week.

This reasoning was not as naïve as it would appear to be. Esme was a child of the suburbs. He had grown up believing in the solid virtues of the poor and the undistinguished. He believed in the majesty of the law, an incorruptible police force, in trains that ran to time, and husbands who spent eight hours a day in offices, two hours a day in suburban trains, and mowed their lawns regularly on Saturday afternoons! He believed in correct change, prompt payment of rates, and good faith. A person like Archie, or Elaine, would have said that he still believed in Santa Claus.

His unhappy months of doubt did not help him to absorb the shock of Elaine's frank admission regarding her association with Archie Carver. Esme had always been aware of the man as big, florid and cocky, so unlike his sober father, Jim, his hard-working elder sister, Louise, or even his unpredictable brothers, Bernard and Boxer.

The identity of Elaine's lover exacerbated his hurt. To him it was a betrayal among neighbours, an Avenue let-down, and it magnified his wife's disloyalty. He asked himself how she could bring herself to go away with a man like that,

when her husband was in uniform, and her child was being
cared for by someone else, two hundred miles away? What
did she think when she was being pawed by him, in some
second-class hotel bedroom, or worse, in an Avenue house,
which her cuckolded husband owned?

As he threw together his belongings the enormity of her
powers of deception made him choke with humiliation. As an
orderly room clerk he had become familiar, of late, with this
kind of situation. He had sorted through the green confidential files made out in respect of various men of the unit who
were having 'domestic troubles', and had actually filled in
forms applying for legal aid on their behalf. He had read
some of the letters they brought back with them as evidence,
sordid little exchanges for the most part, full of sloppy
endearments, and repetitious words like 'ducks' and 'lovey'.

There had been one in particular that had quite disgusted
him—an aircraft factory hand's detailed description of the
steps he intending taking in order to console a serviceman's
wife, as soon as the husband was safely on board the troopship.

Now, he reflected, he would have a green, confidential file
to himself and the facts concerning his own wife, and her
liaison with a middle-aged grocer over the road, would be
bandied about between Flight Lieutenant Dyson, the camp
mouthpiece, and lawyers representing Elaine and Archie.

In the meantime, what was he to do with the baby? In the
grip of a cold, helpless rage, he had bundled the child in a
blanket and eiderdown, and carried her out of the house, but
it was a gesture that had little sense, for his compassionate
leave had already expired and he was due back at the camp
at 0800 hours next day. It was after dark now, and the siren
might sound at any moment.

The final thought sobered him and he paused at the end of
the Avenue, outside Number One. Obviously the sane course
would be to take Barbara over to Number Twenty, and there
discuss the situation, if not with poor Harold, then at least
with Jim Carver, the father of the man who had so generous-
ly supplied Number Forty-Three with extra rations.

Esme almost made up his mind to adopt this course,
before he recalled the nature of the man who had lived next

door to them for so many years. Esme had grown up regarding Jim Carver with a mixture of awe and faint distrust. True, he and Harold seemed to be boon companions these days, a fact that Esme still found difficult to understand, for he remembered Harold assessing his neighbour as 'a Bolshie'. Jim Carver had, it was rumoured, actually taken part in the burning of a 'bus, during the General Strike and the memory of this fifteen-year-old story was sufficient to make Esme think twice of acquainting this man with his eldest son's part in wrecking a serviceman's marriage. Jim was the kind of man, he felt, who would roar with rage the moment he heard the facts and then stride off down the Avenue to Number Two, to have it out with his son and thus feed the episode to the Avenue gossips. Such action could hardly mend matters—they were past mending anyway—and Esme was far too sensitive to want his shame advertised in the Avenue windows.

Then if not Harold, or Jim Carver, who else? There was no other person in the Avenue with whom Esme was on intimate terms. After all, one needed to know a person reasonably well, to turn up on the doorstep at nine o'clock at night, and enlist his help as custodian for a seventeen-month-old baby, recently snatched from a faithless wife. There seemed no alternative to taking the baby back to camp and dropping the whole problem into the lap of the R.A.F. They would have to grant him additional leave, in order to find accommodation for the child, at least until Harold recovered, and then, perhaps, he would be able to make more permanent arrangements, possibly with Elaine's father or mother.

Well, and why not? Esme asked himself, standing indecisively at the junction of Shirley Rise, and the Avenue. He had put his own life aside, in order to serve in the R.A.F., and now the Service could start doing something for him. He had, in fact, little doubt but that it would try, for he had witnessed, at close quarters, the genuine concern of the authorities for men enmeshed in 'domestic problems', and he had been struck by the size and scope of the machinery set up to deal with this by-product of war. His own Commanding Officer, a Squadron Leader, was a bluff, middle-aged, ex-seaman, who, after years in aircraft carriers, had strayed

into the R.A.F. as a regular, in time to catch the floodtide of
wartime promotion. Esme had watched him deal with a
variety of delicate, personal problems and had been greatly
impressed by his common sense and gruff kindness. He was
typical, Esme learned, of all regular officers, a type that he
had been prepared to dislike and distrust, for he had once
shared the civilian's prevailing contempt for enlisted men,
and thought of them as misfits who signed on because nobody
could be found to employ them.

After only a few weeks in uniform Esme realised that this
was nonsense. He found that the regulars were, for the most
part, decent, kindly, and by no means unintelligent, far more
likeable indeed, and far better officers, than some of the
bumptious youngsters of the Reserve, week-end fliers, without
real experience of handling men or machines. The pick of
these volunteers, he discovered, swiftly graduated to the
operational units, leaving the least admirable, men like Sydney Frith, Elaine's odious brother, to officer the rapidly-
expanding Training Command, in which Esme had the mis-
fortune to serve.

At the memory of 'Collie', his C.O. at Queen's Norton,
Esme made up his mind. Fortunately the night air was mild,
with a soft, south wind blowing in from Manor Woods and a
sky bright with stars. Barbara did not seem to have been
disturbed by her outing and was still asleep in the folds of the
blanket, but Esme realised that it would be folly to attempt
the hundred-mile journey back to the camp by rail, when it
could be accomplished, in much shorter time, and in considerably more comfort, by hire-car. So he went down Shirley
Rise to the Lower Road, and looked in at Skelton's, the
all-night garage, where he had once hired a car after over-
staying his leave.

The prohibitive cost of the journey did not worry him. His
salary was made up by the Scottish newspaper that he had
represented before joining the Service, and, in addition, he
drew a regular five pounds a week from his own investments.
He was one of the few rankers at Queen's Norton who
seldom thought about the fortnightly pay parade until it
came round.

He secured car and driver almost at once and was dropped

off outside the guardroom, just before midnight. The baby had continued to sleep soundly throughout the journey, only waking when Esme had to shift her position, in order to extract his wallet and pay the fare.

Then Barbara began to wriggle and whimper and the corporal of the guard, who had lounged out from his hut on hearing a car drive up, came through the wicket gate and regarded him curiously. He was a big Westcountry man, with the camp reputation of a humorist, and he at once recognised Esme as the L.A.C. who had obliged him by getting his leave pass signed a fortnight ago. Because of this his approach was cordial

"Eh, eh, eh ... What you been up to, Fraser? Are you 'aving us on?"

Esme, tired, depressed and much harassed, was in no mood for jokes.

"I'm just back off leave, and I've got to see the C.O. or the Adj. right away! Are either of them about?"

When the corporal had first approached Esme he had been convinced that his leg was about to be pulled, but by this time Barbara was wide awake, and not at all sure of herself in the glare of the corporal's torch. She set up a loud and protesting bellow and the corporal jumped back as though he had been stung.

"Christ!" he stuttered, "you really 'ave got a tacker there! What's the idea? Where'd you find it?"

"I didn't find it, you clot," snapped Esme, "it's my kid and you'll have to run us down to H.Q. in the guard wagon."

The corporal pulled himself together.

"Streuth!" he gasped. "You been bombed out, chum?"

"Yes," said Esme, anxious to cut the interview short.

The corporal was instantly sympathetic.

"Hard luck, mate—here—half a sec' ... hi *you*"—to the helmeted sentry, who was gaping at them from his box—"tell one of the others to take over and run this L.A.C. and his kid down to H.Q. Jump to it, or someone'll be mistaking it for the ruddy siren!"

The sentry doubled into the guard hut and the corporal turned his torch downward, drawing aside the folds of the blanket and beaming down at Barbara's puckered face.

"Arrr, but she's a right pretty li'l maid! How old?"

"Seventeen months," said Esme, and suddenly experienced a wave of relief that he was back among friends. "I had to bring her, there was nowhere I could take her, not at this time of night."

He rocked the baby gently and the wails slowly subsided, culminating at last in a series of small hiccoughs. He smiled, for the first time since they had told him of Eunice.

"All right, Babs, take it easy, we're going to make a W.A.A.F. out of you!"

The corporal chuckled. "Sure thing!" he said, and then: "*Bloody* sure thing! Here, hop in mate, and I'll hand her up to you."

Esme felt a powerful kinship with the man, so powerful indeed, that he instantly regretted his lie about the bombing. "I'll tell you what really happened at N.A.A.F.I. break, tomorrow," he promised, "and thanks for the lift, I've been in a terrible flap all evening!"

"It'll be okeydoke," said the corporal, "the Old Man was here less than half an hour ago, and he won't have finished his rounds yet. You'll probably catch him at H.Q., now."

The station-wagon drove into the camp, passing between the long lines of blacked-out huts. The sentry drove slowly and carefully, as though transporting a cargo of explosive, and he kept glancing sideways at Esme, as though he badly wanted to say something but was unsure how to begin.

When they got to Station Headquarters he jumped out and ran round, reaching up to help the encumbered Esme to the ground.

"Careful—mind the step—it's okay, the C.O.'s here, I can see a chink in his blackout!"

Esme carried Barbara down the narrow passage and straight into the orderly room. The duty clerk was sitting at the registry desk, sorting posting notices, and he looked up with a wide yawn.

"Hullo, Fraser? What's cooking?"

"I'm going in to see the Old Man," Esme told him. "Is anyone else in there?"

"No," said the clerk, "he's signing the stuff I've been working on. I say—what the hell have you got there?"

"My kid," said Esme, and then, seeing the man's jaw drop, "I've been bombed out!"

He tapped at the communicating door before the man could exclaim, and a deep voice at once boomed: "Come in."

'Collie' was sitting at his desk, scrawling signatures across a fanned-out sheaf of documents. He looked up with the impatient expression that Esme had once thought of as a sign of permanent irritability, but had now ceased to fear. The C.O. was a thickset, grizzled man, in his mid-fifties. He wore the observer's badge, the 'O', sprouting a single wing, that everybody in camp called a 'Flying Orifice'. His broad face was seamed and tanned, and there was a sadness in his eyes that Esme knew had been put there by the death of his younger son, shot down over Lille, during the Battle of France.

"Have you got a baby there, L.A.C.?" he grunted, but without, Esme thought, a note of surprise.

"Yes, sir, my daughter, sir," said Esme, half coming to attention, but relaxing as the Squadron Leader waved his hand.

"H'm! What happened? Blitzed?"

"No, sir," said Esme, "not exactly."

The Squadron Leader leaned back and jerked his head towards the only other chair in the room.

"Well? What's the score, L.A.C.?"

Esme sat down and told him, simply, and in briefest outline. "I don't know why I took the kid, sir ..." he concluded, "it was pretty silly I suppose, but anyway I did! If we could park somewhere for the night, I daresay I could 'phone someone, and make other arrangements."

"I don't blame you for taking her, L.A.C.," said Collie, slowly, and began rubbing his chin in long, sweeping movements. For a moment there was silence, except for the dry rasp of the Squadron Leader's horny palm on his stubble.

"Know anything about feeding kids?" he asked, suddenly.

"Well yes, sir, a bit I suppose, but I didn't bring any of the stuff with me. It didn't occur to me."

Two more rasping sweeps and then the C.O. picked up the 'phone. "Get me through to the Waffery," he grunted to the switchboard operator.

Esme heard a series of metallic clicks, as the operator

plugged in, and then Collie saying: "Who *is* that?" and a girl's voice, answering. "Well listen," Collie went on, "one of my clerks has just breezed in with a baby ... that's it ... *a baby!* Well, it'll have to stay the night in camp and maybe most of tomorrow! Have you got anyone over there who can cope, providing I fix the grub with the Catering Officer?"

The girl at the far end of the 'phone said something in reply, but Esme was only half listening; he suddenly realised how terribly exhausted he felt.

"Okay," he heard Collie say, "I'll bring 'em over right away!"

He replaced the receiver and turned back to Esme.

"The W.A.A.F. officer's in bed, and there's no point in getting her out. She wouldn't have a clue anyway, but they've got a new sergeant over there, I saw her yesterday, and she's buttoned up—a good type! I'll run you over, then you'd better get some sleep and we'll chew it all over in the morning, with Flight Lieutenant Dyson. He'll know all the angles, it's his job! Fair enough?"

"Fair enough, sir," said Esme, gratefully, "but I'm ... I'm not dead sure of the W.A.A.F. orderly room, I've only been over there once, sir."

"I said I'd run you over, didn't I?" grunted Collie, and got up, lifting hat and gloves from the 'In' tray. He paused in his stride for the door and peered over Esme's arm at the baby. Barbara was sound asleep again and at each exhalation a stray curl stirred on her cheek.

"Say, she's a honey!" said Collie, readjusting the blanket.

He hesitated a moment longer, blocking the door, and it seemed to Esme that he was making up his mind to say something else. Finally he turned, his hand on the door-knob, his eyes regarding Esme paternally.

"Will you take a tip from me, L.A.C., before the legal boys get to scratching around in your affairs? *Wipe it,* son!— *Just wipe it*! I've seen a lot of this sort of thing. I'm fifty-five now, and I've served with married men all over the world. The only thing to do in a case like this is to make up your mind to scrub it, and start fresh! Don't look back, and for Christ's sake don't drive yourself crazy sorting through the 'ifs', and 'might-have-beens'! You've been caught out in the

rain see? So you got wet, wet right through! Okay! Dry
yourself, and then lay out a fresh kit! You don't have to keep
reminding yourself how wet you got! That's what's important! You don't remember how wet you got, or how silly you
looked, with the rain running down your neck!"

He gave Esme a gentle push and their eyes met, each of
them smiling. Esme said nothing, he would have found
speech difficult, but followed Collie into the orderly room,
past the motionless clerk, down the passage and out into the
main lane. There was a glow in his heart, and as they climbed
into the C.O.'s car it seemed to spread down to his stomach
and loins.

They drove silently across the dispersal area; towards the
huddle of Nissen huts, where the W.A.A.F. flight was housed.
As they climbed out Collie said:

"It's through there, and it's all fixed, I'll join you in a few
minutes, I've got to contact the duty cook and fix the rations."

Esme mounted the steps, and went down the passage past
Signals, towards the W.A.A.F. orderly room. A girl, hearing
his steps, called: "Hullo there! Is that the baby?", and then
the door opened, flooding the narrow corridor with light.

The girl, a sergeant, had stripes tied to her rolled-up
shirtsleeve. She stood on the threshold and Esme stopped
too, a few feet away; for a long moment, they stared at one
another, each too surprised, and delighted to exclaim. Then
the sergeant gave a little gasp, and ran forward, exclaiming.

"*Esme!* Oh *Esme* . . . it *couldn't* be . . . ! It *couldn't* . . ."

Perhaps Esme had had a surfeit of shocks in the last few
days and was growing impervious to new ones, or perhaps,
subconsciously, he had half-recognised the girl's voice on the
C.O.'s 'phone. At all events he was the first to recover, as the
glow inside him spread.

"Hullo, Judy? So you're the new sergeant, the 'good type'
who's 'buttoned up'?"

. . . .

There was no reason why Judy Carver should have been so
overwhelmingly surprised to see Esme. She was aware that he
was on the strength at Queen's Norton, for one of her first

jobs, on being posted to the O.T.U. after her promotion, had been to check through a nominal roll of the permanent staff, sent for duplication to the typing pool.

She had been intrigued, but not particularly elated, to come across Esme's name in the Headquarters Section. Once upon a time such a discovery would have sent her into transports of joy and despatched her fancy along the familiar road that led away from the Avenue, up the Rise to Shirley Church, and from thence to a semi-detached villa, on one of the new housing estates. Here she would have dreamed of Esme's return on the 6.10, and pictured herself preparing his high tea, and talking to their baby, styled, in her dream, 'The Cherub'.

This was Judy's oldest dream and reached back to the long, dry summer of 1919, when she was seven years' old, and for more than a decade it had no serious rival. Most of the time between then and now she had lived next door to Esme, and when she wasn't following him about, rescuing him from dungeons, binding up his 'grievous wounds' for the barge journey to Avalon, concealing him in corn stooks from the probing bayonets of 'Butcher' Cumberland's troops, or standing beside him during a cannonade, in which he was killed and spared the gibbet at Execution Dock, she was writing about Esme in her diary. This diary, containing a day-to-day record of her dream, had been long since burned in the dustbin, of Number Twenty. It was destroyed on the day following Esme's purchase, in the shop where she had worked, of a powder-compact, his Christmas gift to Elaine Frith, of Number Seventeen.

After that they had drifted apart, for Esme was engaged in other, and slightly more adult games of make-believe, and by the time Elaine had left Number Seventeen, and joined her father in North Wales, Judy had replaced Esme with her new and absorbing interest, at the riding school, over towards Keston. Later still, when she had attained her B.H.A. certificate, and gone down to Devonshire to help her employer found a bigger riding school, the Esme-hurt had healed, leaving but a small scar, small enough, indeed, to forget to ache when she fell gently in love with Tim Ascham, drowned off the Lizard within a month of their marriage.

From time to time, during the bleak months that had followed Tim's death, Judy had returned to the Avenue and heard her sister, Louise talk about Esme, and his prodigal bride, Elaine. Louise said she often saw them going in and out of Number Forty-Three, opposite, and that Elaine now had a child, born on the day that Hitler had invaded Poland, and that the child was a pretty little girl, with dark curls, and was called Barbara.

Louise kept Judy well informed on these things, but no more accurately than she reported upon all the other families in the Avenue. Ted Hartnell, the jazz band man, had won a medal. Young Brooking, the ginger-haired boy of Number Seventy-Six, had been taken prisoner. Grandpa Barnmeade, the Air Raid Warden, had broken his neck, outside Miss Clegg's. There had been a bomb on the Shirley Rise end of Delhi Road, killing several people. Judy liked hearing the Avenue gossip from Louise, for although she had now been resident in Devonshire for several years, and her main interests were rural, rather than suburban, she was still very much attached to the Avenue and it would never cease to be home.

She was still fond of Esme, too, but in a painless way, in the way one is fond of summers long ago. She could never see foxglove spires in Devon woods, for instance, without remembering how excited Esme had been by the first foxgloves they had found growing in the wrecked kitchen garden of the Old Manor, where they had played so often.

She was fond of Esme, but she no longer linked him with Shirley Church, orange blossom, and confetti, or saw him marching up and down the lawn, pushing a mower among the new houses of the Wickham estate. Whenever she did remember him it was with warmth and gratitude, as a slight, intense little boy, who had sprinkled stardust up and down the Avenue and had lit and trimmed for her a small, magic lamp, that even now was capable of defying the blackouts of wartime winters.

When the C.O. had rung through, and broken the tedium of the night watch, by telling her about an airman who had arrived with a baby, she had been pleased, and excited. It did not seem to her a remarkable thing that a man should walk into camp, at 23.59 hours, with a baby in his arms. Happen-

ings like this were common enough nowadays, with whole
households going up in clouds of dust, and men being rushed
off on compassionate leave, to scratch among the ruins of
their homes for all that was left of their pre-war lives.

She made a bed in the duty W.A.A.F.'s bunk, and slipped
across to the billet for a hot-water bottle and a clean pillow-
slip. Then she heard the poor chap clumping along the passage, opened the door, and there stood Esme, holding the
baby she had heard Louise describe so often, but had never
yet seen!

As soon as their first greetings were over, they put Barbara
to bed and left a low-powered bulb burning, in case she woke
up, and was frightened by unfamiliar surroundings. Then the
duty cook came in, carrying a cardboard box containing the
various ingredients for Barbara's breakfast, the result of a
long and earnest 'phone discussion between the duty cook and
a sleep-bemused Catering Officer. Then the C.O. looked in
again—he never seemed to go to bed at all—and learned,
with mild interest, that his L.A.C. clerk and the new Sergeant
W.A.A.F., had been next-door neighbours in London, before
the war. He was not taken aback by this coincidence, for his
life at sea, before his transfer to the R.A.F., had been full of
strange encounters. He had once found himself afloat on a
hen-coop off Auckland, with a man who had stolen his watch
in Rosyth!

Finally he did get to bed, and left L.A.C. and Sergeant
gossiping over mugs of cocoa and plates of sausage and
mash. Esme told Judy what a smashing officer Collie was, and
how hopeless the volunteer reservists were, and Judy told Esme
about life on an operational squadron, during the Battle of
Britain, and how pretty Barbara was, every bit as pretty as
Louise had described.

At length Esme, who somehow did not feel tired any more,
told Judy how his mother had been killed in a hit-and-run
raid, and ultimately the truth about how Barbara came to be
with him. He remembered, just in time, that the coincidence
of their meeting like this was even stranger than it appeared,
for his wife's lover was Judy's eldest brother. He found
himself unable to tell her this as yet, so he described Archie
as a nameless 'civvy', whom Elaine had 'run across some-

where'. She would find out sooner or later, of course, but that could wait, and he much preferred her to find it out from someone else.

It was three o'clock before he left her and crossed the silent disperal area to his billet. He slept soundly until the Tannoy clicked and the men around him dragged themselves from their beds as the first news bulletin of the day began to crackle from the amplifier, and a cheerful riser began to bellow—

"There'll be blue birds overrrr ...
The White Cliffs of Dover ...
Tomorrow, just you wait and seeee ..."

To the other men in the hut it was just another day. To Esme, lying still, and recalling the events of yesterday, it seemed more like rebirth.

His day proved a very crowded one. First there was a succession of 'phone calls and discussions, then a longish session with Flight Lieutenant Dyson, the unit 'mouthpiece', and afterwards a quick peep at Barbara who, far from being upset by her succession of moves during the last week, was already queening it in the midst of a circle of cooing W.A.A.F.s, over whom Sergeant Ascham presided, like the senior nanny at a royal christening.

When Esme looked in and they all made way for him, and Barbara called: "Dada!", reaching out her arms, Esme blushed under the chorus of "Oooos" and "Ahhhs", but Barbara soon forgot him in the assortment of playthings that were produced, as if by magic, from kitbags and lockers.

Thus he was able to compose a long, explanatory letter to Harold, and enclose with it another for Jim Carver, from Judy. Bewildered reading it made for the Avenue recipients, as Harold, his temperature at last down to normal, sat up in bed, spooning Edith Clegg's mutton broth into his mouth, while Jim sat beside him, still wearing his lime-dusted gumboots and read the letters loud, rapidly at first, then carefully, with numerous asides.

In a way the news was good for Harold. It gave him something to think about, and helped him to forget his loss.

Jim, noting this, discussed the situation in detail and persuaded him that Esme's decision to convey the baby to Elaine's father, in Wales, was a sensible, if temporary solution to a complicated situation.

Harold, to Jim's astonishment, was not much surprised by Elaine's behaviour.

"I've had my suspicions for some time, old man," he croaked, "but it wasn't for me to say anything, that is, not without some sort of proof. I knew she was gadding about, but then, isn't everyone gadding about these days? People are coming and going, here, there and everywhere, and all hell's let loose every night. Just fancy my poor Eunice . . . I mean to say, how's a man to know what to do for the best? We send her into the country, and we stay on here, getting blitzed round the clock, yet it's she who gets it, and we don't! Sometimes it makes a man feel like packing everything in, and just letting go!"

Jim was not much worried by this pessimistic speech, for by this time he knew Harold well enough to wait for his essential level-headedness to return. People like Harold, who had worked thirty years in one job, and carried their modest salaries back to the Avenue every Friday, were not likely to be bowled over by a single, personal tragedy, no matter how poignant their loss, or how desperate their grief during the days following the first shock. People like Harold, he reflected, invariably survived personal losses, just as they survived the bombardments, the boredom and muddle of war. Jim had no doubts whatever about their staying power, having fought alongside them in the slush of the Somme, and the thin rain of Ypres. Harold would survive, and so would all the other people of the Avenue, and crescents of the suburb, no matter how battered, and scattered were their homes and possessions, when madness had run its course across the Channel. He wished he felt as sure of the stamina of younger chaps, boys like Esme Fraser, but they, poor devils, had had a lot to put up with lately, too much perhaps, as events over the road were proving.

Pondering these things Jim folded the letters, and placed them on Harold's bedside table, wondering, as he did so, what kind of a man this nameless civvy could be, who would set his cap at the wife of a man serving in the Forces and fighting a war for survival.

* * * *

Jim need not have worried about Esme. In some ways he was a good deal happier and less worried than he had been for years.

The period of doubting and compromise was over. He had, in fact, already taken his C.O.'s advice. He had 'scrubbed it', and was making a real effort to discard the past, once and for all.

After the machinery for divorce had been started by the unit lawyer, who worked from facts told him by Esme at their first interview, he began to experience a sense of relief. From now on, he told himself, Elaine could go her own way, and he would go his, and when Elaine wrote saying that she would not defend a divorce, he found that at last he could study their relationship objectively, and see it for what it was, instead of what he had striven to make it. He was surprised to discover that he felt little or no bitterness towards her, acknowledging the fact that their failure, as man and wife, in no way differed from their adolescent courtship. It had always been slavish adoration and endless extenuation on his part, mild affection and thinly disguised impatience on hers.

He could see that, on the whole, she had been more honest with him, than he with her. Many times she had told him frankly that she was not in love with him, and never would be, but his pride had never been able to absorb this, and he had gone on, month after month, telling himself that sooner or later she would 'discover' him and value his love accordingly. He knew now that this was wishful thinking on his part, but it was not merely the end of doubting that brought comfort to him that spring but something that he derived from the active sympathy of the people around him.

Esme had volunteered for the R.A.F. because he had come to believe that defeat by Germany would be worse than extinction. Like Jim Carver, and like Harold, he had weighed the alternatives, and persuaded himself that the British were fighting for survival, not merely as members of an independent sovereign state, but as a people, and a people who believed that life without human dignity was not worth having.

In the year that he had served, since Dunkirk, his views' had not changed, but the ideals that he believed himself to be fighting for had struggled free of newspaper clichés.

Like all the other young men who had grown to maturity in the hesitant 'thirties', Esme had engaged in hundreds of casual discussions about war in the abstract. Looking back on these arguments in pubs, in offices, and trains, he could now recognise their fatuity. All the talking-points of that period— sanctions, the League, pacifism, democracy, world federalisation, were of no importance. What was important, what gave real purpose to this war, was the fundamental decency of the ordinary people who were engaged in it, men like old Collie, the C.O., and the man in his billet, who made up his bed the night he returned and had stolen a cheese sandwich from the cookhouse, laying it on his pillow in case Esme had travelled back to camp on an empty stomach.

Ever since he had packed up his civilian clothes at the Receiving Depot, Esme had been touched by the kindness and thoughtfulness of the majority of the men around him, touched also by the easy, unselfconscious way in which they shared things. He had acquired that sense of *belonging* that the uniform seemed to give all who wore it. It was as though every man who dipped his 'irons' in the trough of hot-water that stood outside the cookhouses, performed, by so doing, some mystic ceremony that made him a permanent member of one huge, sprawling, joke-cracking, grousing family.

This was something he had been unable to find in civilian life, though he had looked for it at school, at his work, and on his travels about the country. He had always been a solitary person, and the sense of belonging brought him relief, and an end to the loneliness that his marriage had intensified, rather than banished.

His natural shyness, inherited from his Scots ancestors, had made him seem aloof, and slightly pompous, particularly with women, but the easy comradeship of the forces encouraged him to develop two aspects of his character, the ability to spin yarns, and a strong sense of humour. These characteristics made him popular among the men, and when the story of his domestic trouble leaked out, as it was bound to do in the circumstances, he discovered that he was more popular than he had imagined. The strong sympathy of the men about him was not demonstrative, but it was undeniably there, and he could sense it in the billet, and orderly room. It was a kind of closing of the ranks against the outsiders, the scroungers, the civvies, and in a curiously final way it helped to heal his pride.

Barbara remained in the camp two days, while Esme was engaged in trying to contact Edgar Frith, his father-in-law, in Llandudno. Edgar and his wife, Frances, were away from home, and it was not until the evening of the second day that Esme spoke to him, and was invited to bring the baby at once.

He went into the C.O. for his pass, and was surprised to find Judy in the office.

"The Sergeant has applied for escort duty," said Collie, with a grin. "Does that appeal to you?"

"I should be very glad of her company, sir," said Esme, adding, with an answering smile, "I did feel the most awful clot, walking in here carrying the kid the night before last, sir!"

"You looked one, too," said Collie, handing over the passes. "Here are two forty-eights, and you can pick up early chits from the W.O. If I were you I'd thumb the station wagon, I daresay we've got something to fetch from the station!"

"Thank you, sir," said Esme, saluting.

They went out, and stood for a moment in the winter sunshine, alongside G.H.Q. flagpole.

"I suppose it was cheek of me to ask the C.O., without consulting you Esme," said Judy, "but it's a long way to Llandudno, and I didn't like the idea of you coping on your own. Besides. . . ." She smiled, wrinkling her nose, "I could do with a crafty forty-eight myself, and I've never seen North Wales!"

He thought how trim and taut she looked in her best blue. The colour suited her, and so did the cap that made so many of the girls look like clippies. Judy's was set at the slightest angle, and a long roll of chestnut curls escaped from the back, defying regulations and touching her shoulders. He had never thought of her as a pretty girl, and indeed she was not, for her nose was short and slightly snub, and her mouth was too small, but her brown eyes were alight with friendliness, and as he looked more closely at her he remembered, so clearly, the first day they had smiled at him, the day she had followed him on his solitary exploration into Manor Wood. He remembered too how they had climbed the broken wall to the lakeside, and played Sleeping Beauty in the old sum-mer-house, and as the scene returned the curious rhythm of life struck him, a chance encounter between two children, more than twenty years ago, and now here were these two facing one another on an airfield, waiting to share the job of conveying a child across the country.

"We did some curious things together in the old days, Judy," he said, smiling, "but I imagine this tops them all! I'll find the W.O., and get the early chits. Is our W.O. authorised to sign one for W.A.A.F.s?"

"Why naturally, the C.O. fixed it, didn't he? I say, Esme, he's a regular sweetie isn't he? I'll wait for you here, and if the station wagon comes by I'll hold it. We can pick up Barbara on the way out. She's all ready, the girls are seeing to her!"

When he returned she had a lorry waiting. They drove across the dispersal area towards the Waffery and two L.A.C.W.s emerged, one carrying a spruced up Barbara, and the other Barbara's freshly ironed blanket. Behind them came an overalled A.C.W., with a small armful of toys, and behind her yet another girl, carrying Judy's attaché case.

"Good God," laughed Esme, "it's a ruddy ceremonial!"

"Call again any time," said the L.A.C.W. with the blanket, "linen laundered, children welcome, single airmen entertained after lights out!"

"And the next time see that she goes on ration strength," said the girl in the overall, "she's been eating like a horse all the time we've had her!"

The guard came out to the wire gate to watch them pass through into the road, and as the lorry driver slipped into neutral, he winked down at the corporal, and jerked his head to the nearside of the cabin, where Judy sat, with Barbara on her knees.

The corporal took the hint.

"Preseennnnnnt *hi!*" he shouted, and the men about him, quickly catching on, shuffled into line, and smartly presented arms.

"You see?" said Judy, to the smiling but embarrassed Esme, "she's practically a V.I.P. around camp!"

CHAPTER X

First Gap

SPRING, 1941, and the Avenue still intact!

Behind it, at the corner of Delhi Road, and in several places along the Cawnpore Road, and Lucknow Road, the scars of the winter siege showed in uniform façades. Immediately west of the Avenue there were several large craters in the downsweep of the links, and a huge pyramid of freshly-turned soil where the Ninth green had been sited, against the dwarf oaks of The Lane.

Eastward, the 'Rec' itself was showing scars. The bowls pavilion was in splinters, hit by a land mine, that had showered wreckage as far away as the back gardens of Outram Crescent. Where the bandstand had once stood, and Ted Hartnell had played for a season of open-air dancing, were now piles of wrecked and twisted seats, scattered here and there in the uncut grass, with buttercups already thrusting up among the rusting frames.

There had been one or two minor incidents on the night of the Great Fire, when the sky beyond the nursery turned bright orange and people in the back rooms of the even numbers had read newspapers in the glare of burning office blocks. A stray incendiary had whipped through the roof of Number Eighteen, next door to the Carvers, but Jack Strawbridge, fire-watching in the back lane, had been on the spot within ten seconds and had dealt with it in twenty more.

Over at Number Ninety-Seven, the Baskerville Family, snug in their de luxe shelter (now fitted with spring bunks, a radio, and electric light) had had their anxious moment, when anti-aircraft shrapnel smashed down on their green-house only a few yards away, but no one was hurt, and Mr. Baskerville had poked his head out and reported, chirpily: "Just the glass! Just the glass! What goes up has got to come down, kids!"

Under the impetus of the blitz, Mr. Baskerville, always the Avenue's jolly-man, was developing into a tireless raconteur. He now had an endless fund of blitz stories, acquired during his regular journeys to and from the City each day. It was unfortunate that he could never remember which of his neighbours he had travelled up or down with on the previous day, so that some of the more long-suffering Avenue husbands were obliged to hear the same stories twice or thrice, and were unable to head them off, because Mr. Baskerville seldom listened to anybody, but did most of the talking himself.

Poor Harold Godbeer, now almost himself again, was obliged to copy the tactics of a fugitive resistance fighter when he saw Mr. Baskerville hurry along the pavement for the 8.40 each morning. He had to gauge whether or not he was out of earshot of Mr. Baskerville's hail and then act accordingly, either scrambling out of the gate, and increasing the distance between them by breaking into a trot, or flattening himself behind the privet hedge that bordered his front-garden and remaining there until Mr. Baskerville had passed on and buttonholed somebody else. Of these two methods of Baskerville-dodging Harold much preferred the former, in spite of the fact that a brisk trot down Shirley Rise brought on his asthma. If he concealed himself, and let Baskerville pass, he had to dawdle all the way to Woodside and chance missing his train.

Over at Number One, little Miss Baker had successfully weathered the blitz and could now write triumphant letters to her brother and his wife, safe in the Lake District. They were gay, brave, letters and might have proved interesting, had Miss Baker's relatives been familiar with all the Avenue families. As it was Gregory Baker found them slightly irritating. He was a stranger to the suburb, and had moved north to avoid being bombed. He found it embarrassing to receive a stream of wish-you-were-here messages, from a woman who was semi-paralysed, yet preferred, for some inexplicable reason, to hang on in her dreary little house, risking violent death night by night.

As it happened little Miss Baker was thoroughly enjoying the blitz. In pre-war days Miss Clegg had been her only regular caller, but nowadays all sorts of visitors rapped on her windows, or came round by the alley and let themselves in by the back door.

"You okay, Miss Baker? Can I get you anything, Miss Baker? What price Nicolson Terrace, Miss Baker—four houses down, and only one ruddy canary dead!"

It was all very matey and stimulating and if it wasn't for the poor people who sometimes got themselves killed she wouldn't have minded it continuing indefinitely. Air Raid Wardens popped in for cups of tea, at all hours of the day and night, using her gas-stove, and bringing a chipped mug to her bedside. Fire-watchers, like jolly Jack Strawbridge across the road, whistled and waved, as they paced past her window, and on one memorable occasion the chairman of the local Council called on her, and she had her picture taken by a newspaper photographer, and published under a caption: *"Move out! Me! Not Pygmalion Likely!"*

There was a charm and a friendliness about the Avenue, that it had lacked in pre-war days. It had never housed a cheek-by-jowl community. In spite of its terraced rows, separated here and there by narrow alleys, the families had never developed a community spirit, like those in the streets nearer the Thames. People had always been civil to one another, and some of the families intermingled, but even these seldom used each other's Christian names, and hardly anybody along the road would have 'popped in next door', to borrow a cupful of sugar, or rice.

Only one member of the Avenue rump continued to live in isolation. Esther Frith, at Number Seventeen, had resisted all efforts on the part of her neighbours to loosen up, to mingle on the pavement, or to gossip over the back fence.

Number Seventeen had always been a very silent house, but now it was more silent than ever, for most of the time Esther lived there alone, without even a cat, or a budgerigar, and the only time the people opposite, or the Crispins, on her immediate right, saw any movement in and out of her front gate, was when Esther went shopping, or when Esther's son, Sydney, came home on leave, from the R.A.F.

Neither was Sydney given to mingling very freely. The only time he had ever been seen to speak to anyone in the Avenue was when he reprimanded young Albert Dodge, of Number Ninety-One, for passing him without giving a salute due to an officer.

Albert was a paratrooper, home from Egypt after an adventurous spell in Crete, and it is doubtful whether Albert would have saluted an R.A.F. officer had he been wearing wings, which Sydney was not.

Sydney, at this stage of the war, was the only commissioned officer in the Avenue, but he was the kind of man who valued salutes, and was very punctilious about returning them. He returned this one before he got it, which was very embarrassing, particularly as Albert Dodge chortled aloud when it happened.

Sydney almost ran after him, piping "I say ... I *say* there!" and Albert, a genial soul, obligingly stopped, and turned round, with an expression of polite interest on his broad, sweating face.

"You called me?" he asked, as Sydney drew level.

"Don't you salute an officer when you see one?" demanded Sydney, breathlessly.

"Not officers like you, I don't," replied Albert truthfully.

Sydney gasped. He had had several previous encounters of this sort, but none of the rankers he had reprimanded had been openly insolent towards him.

"I'd think I'd better have your name and number," he said, "I daresay you'll hear more of this."

"I doubt it," said Albert, who had volunteered for a second spell of overseas service before coming on leave. He gave his name and number, however, for he was an obliging young man, and he thought it might be amusing to bait Sydney.

Sydney left him, and turned, glowering, into Number Seventeen. He said nothing of the incident to Esther when she set his lunch before him.

The role of mother and son had been reversed in the last few years. Throughout his boyhood Sydney had crept about the house in terror of Esther, who kept a lithe, twopenny cane behind the picture entitled 'A Tempting Bait'. She had hardly ever used the cane on Sydney, who was her favourite, and upon whom she relied for a steady flow of information about his sister, Elaine, but Sydney occasionally saw it descend on his sister, and until he had passed his seventeenth birthday he had gone out of his way to propitiate his mother.

Since Edgar had run away, and Elaine had followed him, Sydney had usurped the throne at Number Seventeen. He now treated his mother like an old, and exasperating housekeeper. He accepted her slavish ministrations as his right, and when he brought home his fiancée, Cora, he hardly bothered to introduce her to Esther, but said, with a lordly wave of his hand: "This is Miss Gilpin, from the camp. She'll be staying until Sunday night, mother!"

Cora Gilpin was a civilian typist, attached to Sydney's accounts section, at Beacon Down Technical Training Depot. She was tall, pale, slightly round-shouldered, and extremely talkative. Sydney had cultivated her after he had failed to make headway with the few W.A.A.F. officers stationed at the camp. There were plenty of other W.A.A.F.s available, but a regulation (of which Sydney wholeheartedly approved) forbade an officer to walk out with a W.A.A.F., so that he was obliged, at length, to fall back on Cora, a civilian seconded from Works and Bricks Section.

Cora dressed well. She could afford to, for she earned three times the amount the W.A.A.F. clerks earned for doing precisely the same work. She had the additional advantage of being free to leave Camp at 5 p.m. without first looking at Daily Routine Orders, to discover whether her name was down for fire picket, or duty clerk.

She was an ideal mate for Sydney, for she shared the same horror of being thought 'common'. That was why she had hurried into Works and Bricks, and put herself down as a civilian clerk. She had no wish to be put into a common uniform, and share a common billet, with common girls, fishergirls some of them, straight from the herring-sheds of Grimsby, girls who swore freely, and used common expressions, like 'Wrap up', and 'Get knotted'. Cora used but one expletive, that did for almost anything. It was 'Jeepers-Creepers', and no one had ever told her it was a genteel cousin of Jesus Christ, so she went on using it, sandwiching it between long and detailed descriptions of how a typing ribbon had become frayed, and jammed the carriage, or what a masterful way Flight Lieutenant Frith had with airmen, at flag-hoisting parades, that she watched each morning from her office window.

A guest of honour, at Number Seventeen, Cora talked and talked and talked, mostly about Sydney, how highly Sydney was regarded by his Commanding Officer, how briskly Sydney presided over pay parades, and how strict Sydney was about the accounts section's gas-drill.

Esther said little or nothing in reply, but she fed them adequately, using up her own rations, and building a generous coal fire in the front room, where they could be alone, and get on with their courting.

They were here, on the last night of April, when, at about ten o'clock, the Shirley Rise siren sounded, and the Avenue folk, who had slept undisturbed for four nights in a row, began to go through their shelter-drill with the precision of veterans.

Unfortunately neither Sydney nor his fiancée were familiar with air-raids in this district, while Esther, who had now been in bed for more than an hour, had not even told them whether or not she had a shelter, or what she did, or where she went when there was a raid.

Sydney jumped up from the sofa, and drew aside the blackout curtain, in order to look out, and see if he could get a cue from a neighbour, but a warden must have been very close at hand, for a strident voice bawled: "Put that light out, damn you!" with a promptitude that would have warmed the heart of the late Grandpa Barnmeade.

Sydney hopped back in alarm, and Cora, who had become rather tousled in the process of resisting Sydney's cautious advances, stood up, smoothed down her frock, adjusted the shoulder-strap of her slip, and exclaimed: "Jeepers-Creepers! Where do we go from here?"

Sydney did not know where they should go, and freely admitted as much. He ran into the hall, and up the stairs, tapping on Esther's door, and calling:

"I say, mother . . . ! I say there . . . ! Where's your shelter?"

Esther had heard the siren but, as usual, had ignored it, reposing her trust in God, and in the slated roof above her head.

When she heard Sydney call, however, she climbed out of bed, threw a mackintosh over her shoulders, and pattered to the door. She was surprised by the urgency in his voice. After all, he was a soldier, and he surely must be accustomed to air raids by now.

"What did you say, dear?" she asked, opening the door an inch or two.

"I said 'Where's your shelter'?" said Sydney testily, "what do you do, when there's an air-raid?"

Esther blinked once or twice. "There isn't any shelter in the house, dear, and I've never done anything. I believe there is a public shelter in the 'Rec', but it's rather damp, I think. The woman from over the road was telling Mr. Carver only yesterday that. . . ."

Sydney was not interested in the views of the woman from over the road, and grunted his impatience. Back in the camp they had very good shelters, well below ground, lined with concrete, and heavily bunkered above. They were said to be proof against anything but a direct hit, and on the few occasions they had had a raid on the camp all the administrative staff, with the exception of those on duty, had filed into the shelter and waited for the all-clear.

He had imagined, until now, that similar accommodation was available to civilians, and if he had thought about it at all, which he had not, he would have supposed that immediately the siren sounded, Esther would slip into some clothes, and hurry along to the public shelter with everybody else in the neighbourhood. It amazed him that she could be so offhand and casual about air-raids, when bombs had already destroyed whole blocks of houses as close as Delhi Road, beyond the nursery garden.

"Get your things on, and hurry," he said, cocking an ear for the double throb of enemy aircraft.

But Esther still seemed bemused. "Hurry *where,* dear?" she asked, mildly.

"To the shelter, where else?" demanded Sydney, with the edge to his voice that he reserved for recruits.

"But I never go there," protested Esther, "I've just told you, Sydney, it's so damp and. . . ."

Cora called urgently, from the foot of the stairs. She had donned her coat and scarf, and was clutching her handbag.

"Come *on*, Sydney," she shouted, "come on—do!"

A few hundred yards away, at the A.R.P. Post, in Shirley Rise, Jim Carver looked up at the sky, and yawned. Another nuisance raid, he imagined, and wondered what had caused this sudden scaling down of the raids. There had been no big attacks now for more than a month, yet small units of the Luftwaffe continued to roam haphazardly about the sky, blitzing here and blitzing there, giving London a small ration, every now and again and behaving, he thought, like a dazed heavyweight boxer in Round Twelve, still hitting out, but soggily, unscientifically.

Then he heard the familiar *burp-burp* approaching from the south-east, and his ear, trained to an accurate pitch throughout the winter assault, told him that heavy aircraft were moving diagonally across the suburb, heading north-west. Perhaps it was Ealing, or Chiswick, but whoever got it would not have to endure much of a raid. There was no real 'weight' in the sky.

Sydney heard the throb of aircraft clearly, yet he remained fidgeting about the landing, barking at Esther through her half-open bedroom door.

"For goodness *sake*, Mother . . . make up your mind . . . ! We can't just stand here! Where do you *go*? What sort of *drill* do you follow?"

And then, from Cora, at the foot of the stairs, a short burst of direct questions:

"Are we going, or aren't we? Is there time? Is it wise? Is it far?"

And from Esther, stumbling about in the bedroom:

"I should have to get dressed, Sydney! Often nothing happens, dear, but you go, if you want to, by all means go if you wish to, Sydney . . . !"

Sydney, standing on the polished linoleum of the landing, felt himself sucked into this maelstrom of indecision. If Esther had panicked he would have known exactly what to do, or if Cora had stopped calling up the stairs he could have made up his mind, but with a havering woman on each floor he felt bewildered, and quite helpless. His instinct was to abandon them both, to tear out of the house, and bolt down the Avenue towards the 'Rec', to get underground, to get something thick and solid, between himself and the bombs. But Sydney had pride, and he knew that he could not abandon mother and fiancée in such a shameless fashion. He knew that, as an officer, he should set an example, be casual and jocular, even while devising a masterful plan that he could impose upon them by a single word of command.

Then the whistle of a descending bomb drove every other thought fom his mind, and he was conscious only of an agonised contraction of his stomach, a shrinking that forced the breath from his body, and the stability from his legs.

The bomb's descent sounded like a tragedian's sigh, half moan and half wail, and it ended in a shattering roar, that seemed to split his eardrums, and sent him crashing against the flimsy door of the airing-cupboard.

It fell, the first of a stick of six, on the Lower Road, about two hundred yards in direct flight from where he stood, but before he had regained his balance, and steadied himself by grabbing the stairhead rail, a second bomb landed in Delhi Road, and then the third, in the Nursery, directly opposite.

He heard Cora's scream from the hall, and the harsh jingle of splintering glass, as the blast emptied the lead frames of the front door. The house seemed to rock, like a vessel struck broadside on by a tidal wave, and he pitched forward across the landing, his head almost touching Esther's bedroom door, that appeared to fly away from him as he shot towards it. He had a glimpse of Esther, standing by the bed, fawn mackintosh draped over her long, linen nightdress, her dark hair clamped under gleaming clips, and in the moment of impact he thought it odd that she had not been thrown down, as he had been, but had managed to remain bolt upright, looking across at him, with an expression of surprise.

Then the fourth bomb fell, but no one in Number Seventeen heard its approach. It whistled down just like the others, but their ears were still singing with the previous explosions, beside which the descending whistle was like the chirrup of a sparrow.

It burst squarely on the small concrete slab, immediately outside the kitchen window, and the sole witness of the explosion, a War Reserve constable sheltering under the bank in Shirley Rise, saw Numbers Seventeen, Fifteen, and Thirteen bulge out, hover, and then rocket away almost brick by brick, into the meadow behind the Avenue.

He remained crouched until the other two bombs had exploded, over towards Addington, and then he remembered his duty, and ran, whistle shrilling, into the reeking Avenue.

As he pounded along, he heard the ambulance bell clanging in Shirley Rise, and before he had recovered from the spasm of coughing, brought on by the clouds of brickdust, both ambulance and heavy rescue tender, had swung into the Avenue, and the scene was alive with running figures, shouting to one another across a pile of debris masking a large crater in what had been the gardens of Numbers Seventeen, Fifteen, Thirteen, and Eleven and Nine.

Long before the all-clear had sounded neighbours had begun to drift out of the houses opposite, and gape at the havoc a five-hundred pound bomb had made of the odd numbers across the road.

Searchlights were turned on the rubble, but the rescue work was half-hearted, for it seemed clear to the most optimistic that nobody in the group of houses nearest the corner could have survived.

They were wrong, however, for they soon discovered that somebody was alive in Number Thirteen. They could hear screaming, and Jim's second-in-command, old Hopner, the man who had been so upset by the shambles in Delhi Road, but had since learned how not to be sick during rescue operations, was detailed to dig his way into the ruin through the front-room windows. Here, pinned by the foot under a heavy dining-room table, he found old Mrs. Coombes, very much alive, swearing like a bargee, and obstinately refusing to yield up the tin box that contained her jewellery and insurance policies.

Everyone else in the stricken houses was dead. Mrs. Coombes' lodgers, Mrs. Crispin, and her two nephews, whose father was far away in Palestine, and the morose Mrs. Frith, who had lived at Number Seventeen for as long as anyone could remember, and whose husband, they now recalled, had run away with someone else before the war, and now lived in Wales. Outside Number Seventeen, in front of the ragged oblong where the front path had been, they found the body of an unknown young woman.

Jim knew Mrs. Coombes' lodgers, and the Crispin family, and was also able to identify Mrs. Frith, but there was doubt about the identity of the young woman, who was thought to be a passerby until Albert Dodge, of Ninety-One, joined the rescue team as a volunteer. Albert told them that this young woman must be Sydney Frith's girl-friend, who had been staying in the house, and this set them digging for Sydney, whom they did not find until noon, the following day.

They found him eventually, or all that remained of him, for Sydney had been caught by the blast soughing between the thick wall of the stairs, and the thinner, interior walls of the main bedrooms. The wave had sucked him clear of the wreckage, and out across the gardens, flinging him over the little greenhouse, where his father had once consoled himself with potted hyacinths, and tossing him into the brick-strewn meadow, fifty yards or more from the house.

No one had thought of looking for him here, until one of the rescue squad found part of an R.A.F. tunic draped on the fence of Number Five, nearer the corner. It was Albert Dodge who found him, and helped to cover the body with a tarpaulin. As he did so he remembered Sydney's rebuke, of the previous day, and found himself wishing that he had given the poor little beggar an old 'one-two' after all, for what did it matter now? What would it have cost him, to do a silly, little thing like that?

Soon the casualties were tabbed, and driven away, two from Number Thirteen, three from Number Fifteen, three more in Number Seventeen, four from the remaining houses, a total of twelve human sacrifices to a madman's dream of world conquest.

The rubble was levelled, relatives were notified, and the people in the houses opposite found that they could now look right across the meadow to the woods.

There was one other casualty in the avenue that night, 'Strike', Jim Carver's retriever, whose heart burst at the

impact of the third bomb, the one that fell in the Nursery.
Jim found the dog dead in his basket when he returned to
Number Twenty for a short break during the morning. Everybody had been too busy to notice him until then, for he
had grown very lazy lately, and spent most of his time
asleep, beside the kitchen fire.

Jim called to him as he stirred his tea, and was surprised
when Strike failed to poke his yellow head over the rim of
the basket, and roll his eyes at his master, the way he had
done every morning when Jim came in from next door. Jim
called again:

"Strike! Strike, old boy! Did they give you a bit of a
shake-up last night, boy?"

When there was no answering creak from the basket, and
the tail did not stir, Jim got up, and knelt down beside the
hearth. He saw then that Strike was dead, and his teeth bit
sharply into his lip, for he was very fond of his pet. Strike
was at least fifteen, a great age for a golden-haired retriever,
and although Jim had long since been resigned to Strike's
death, from old age, it hurt him to realise that the old dog's
heart had succumbed to the roar of high explosive, and that
no one had even noticed his passing.

He called to Louise, who was upstairs, making beds.

"Come down, Lou! Old Strike's dead ... the bastards have
killed old Strike!"

Louise came running, tears in her eyes, and they turned the
dog in his basket, confirming their fears.

Jim straightened, and tugged at his moustache, his teeth
still pressed to his lower lip.

"He was a damned good dog, Lou, a damned good dog!
No one ever had a better dog!"

He sat down, and swallowed a mouthful of tea, regarding
the basket sadly, and thinking of the circumstances in which
he had acquired Strike, back in the week of the General
Strike, in 1926.

"He must be about fifteen and a half," he mused. "He was
only a pup, when I fished him out of that 'bus, at the
Elephant and Castle. I often wondered how he came to be
there in the first place. He saved me a month or so in clink,
I reckon, for if I hadn't picked him up, and pushed a way

out of the mob, the bobbies would have run us all in for industrial sabotage!"

"He had a good life, Dad," said Louise.

"That's so," he replied, "better than most people, and I don't suppose he felt anything. I'll bury him in the garden later on. I've got to get back over the road right now."

He came in again at dusk, and carried Strike, wrapped in his own shredded blanket, down to the Nursery fence, where he dug a hole in the soft soil, where the loganberries grew.

As he laid the dog in the hole an odd thought crossed his mind. He thought of all the cats and dogs in German homes, and how some of them must have been driven mad by the retaliative bombing of the R.A.F. The day's work had saddened him.

"What's the point of it all?" he asked himself. "Where the hell is it getting any of us, any one of us? That's what the politicians never tell anyone!"

Some of Jim's complacency disappeared after this incident, and he no longer wondered why the Luftwaffe had slackened its attack. Houses on each side of the gap took stock of their own scars. Miss Baker of Number One, asked Jack Strawbridge to fit a new frame and glass to her dining-room window, and Elaine Fraser, who had been out when the bomb fell, asked Archie to find her a man to renew the rear windows of Number Forty-Three, and cover them over with adhesive paper.

Glaziers, carpenters, and bricklayers were busy all down the odd side of the Avenue that week, but almost at once the incident was obscured by a fresh sensation. An early morning news bulletin was issued about Rudolf Hess, Hitler's deputy, who had puzzled everybody, including his Fuehrer it seemed, by stealing a fighter aircraft and parachuting into Scotland, supposedly to pay a social call on a duke.

This was news indeed, for surely it meant that Germany was putting out a peace feeler! Otherwise why should Nazi Number Two do such an extraordinary thing in the middle of a war?

One ex-member of the Avenue rump did not find it so easy to forget the bomb. This was Edgar Frith, antique dealer, the divorced husband of Esther, and father of Flight Lieutenant Frith.

Edgar hurried down from Llandudno to attend the double funeral, and later in the day he called on his daughter, Elaine, at Number Forty-Three, with the intention of scolding her for failing to attend at the graveside of her mother and brother.

Edgar had not seen Elaine since her wedding, in 1938, and he was a little shocked at the change in her appearance, and general demeanour. She was disposed to be friendly, however, and seated him in the front room, brewing him tea, after he had refused what she called a 'glass-of-buck-you-up-o'.

Edgar eyed his attractive daughter uneasily, as she sat poised on the piano stool, facing him, and sipped what seemed to him, a very generous measure of gin and vermouth. Her voice was huskier than he remembered, and she seemed to be much slimmer, as though she was no longer bothering to prepare proper meals for herself.

She was as frank, and as down-to-earth as ever, in her conversation, and he wondered, not for the first time, how a nervous little man like himself, and a frigid, circumspect woman, like poor Esther, had managed, between them, to beget a handsome extrovert like Elaine. In her presence he did not feel like a father at all, but more like a shy adolescent, trying to ingratiate himself with a pretty and sophisticated aunt.

"We're all alone now, Elaine," he said, as he addressed himself to a vigorous stirring of tea. "Perhaps we ought to try and see a bit more of each other in the future?"

"We've always been alone, Father," she told him, very condescendingly he thought, "for neither one of them were anything to us! Why do we have to pretend, just because they're dead?"

He was profoundly shocked, the more so because he had never quite rid himself of a feeling of guilt about his desertion of Esther. She had behaved intolerably towards him, of course, but that was certainly no excuse to speak of her with contempt.

"Now, now, Elaine, you shouldn't talk like that, really you shouldn't," he protested.

She laughed, finished her gin, and leaned back against the piano, shooting her long, elegant legs towards him, and looking, he thought, like a lithe, and freshly groomed cat, stretching itself in the sun.

"Why oughn't I? I'm all sorts of things, but I've never been a hypocrite! You aren't really, you couldn't be, or you'd never have run off with Frances, the way you did! But you're talking like a hypocrite right now, and beginning to act like one too, Daddy, and what's more you know it! What point is there in pretending to feel grieved over Mother and Sydney? I couldn't stand the sight of either one of them when they were alive and living a few doors up the road, and nothing has happened since to make me alter the way I felt about them. 'Ah, but they're dead,' you say! Well, and so what? It might have been us, mightn't it? It might still be us, any time, and would it do *us* any good if the people round here thought more of us simply because we'd been killed in an air-raid?"

He made a series of deprecating clicking noises with his tongue, but she ignored them. "Think back, to the time when we were all living together, in that awful house! Mother treated you like an elderly lodger, and me—she got a hell of a kick out of thrashing me every time I put a foot wrong. I don't say it was altogether her fault, I always thought there was something a bit queer about her, something that they put people away for, if it gets too bad! You were perfectly right to leave her, and go off with a nice normal woman, like Frances. And me? I was perfectly right to leave, too, the minute I was old enough to fend for myself. Why should we spend any more of our lives than we need with a person like that, someone who finds pleasure in being miserable? And how does her being killed in an air-raid make her a good mother, or a good wife? Then there's Sydney ... what was he, but a spiteful, sneaky, smarmy little devil, from the time he was old enough to spy on us? I can see him now, with his piggy little eyes, looking us over before he scampered off to Mother, to earn me a welt or two with the cane. Of the two of them I must say I preferred Mother, but I'm not shedding tears over either of them. I'm sorry they were killed, in the way a person is sorry about strangers killed in a rail accident, or something of that sort, but I don't feel sorry inside, and it's no use asking me to pretend that I do, for the benefit of the neighbours!"

He was silent for a moment, considering her explanation with the same deliberation he employed assessing the genuineness of a piece of china, or a set of Georgian spoons. Finally his honesty won through.

"I daresay you're right, Elaine," he said, with a sigh. "We all make an attempt to register conventional emotions at a time like this, but I suppose it's only because we're afraid people will think less of us if we don't." He changed the subject abruptly.

"Are you and Esme really breaking up?"

"It looks like it," she told him, again without a trace of concern in her voice, "we weren't really much good for each other. It was wrong of me to marry him, I suppose, but nobody could have convinced him of that at the time, could they?"

Edgar remembered an earnest young man, calling on him at Llandudno in the first year of his second marriage, and asking, pitifully he thought at the time, if he had received any news of Elaine. He remembered the same young man's shining eyes, when he had seen him and Elaine off as a honeymoon couple. Finally he recalled Esme's tired face not long ago, when he had brought the baby up to Llandudno, to be cared for by Frances, and her daughter, Pippa.

"No," he said, "it's no use pretending about that either, Elaine. I'm sorry about little Barbara, though. She's a lovely little kid, and no trouble at all. Frances and Pippa are spoiling her quite shamelessly, and she'll make us all suffer for it I daresay, but she's going to be very pretty, very pretty indeed! She reminds me of you, when you were her age."

"She won't be much like me," said Elaine, and for the first time he thought he detected a trace of wistfulness in her voice. "She's half Esme's, and she'll put on his rose-coloured spectacles the moment he offers them to her!"

"Are you going to . . . to marry this other chap, the grocer over the road?" asked Edgar, tentatively.

"God knows," said Elaine, "we'll cross that bridge when we come to it! He hasn't asked me yet, though I've got a feeling that he will before long. He's coming over directly, would you like to meet him?"

"No ... no. ... I ... er ... don't think that would be very wise," said Edgar, "not with a divorce pending ... I mean ... ! Besides, meeting me would embarrass him, wouldn't it?"

Elaine laughed. "It might embarrass you, but it wouldn't embarrass Archie! However, suit yourself, and thanks for looking in, Daddy, I'll keep in touch."

He got up, gladly enough, and she handed him his bowler hat, and dark, woollen gloves. He followed her into the hall, hesitating a moment as she opened the front door.

"Well ... good-bye Elaine ... if you want to talk you can always ring ... I'm in the shop now, most of the time," and he bobbed forward, kissing her lightly on her cheek and hurried out in the Avenue.

He turned right at the gate, averting his eyes as he passed the ragged gap where Number Seventeen had stood. What a mess they were making of everything! And what a mess most people made of their lives! Surely, at a time like this, the only sane thing to do was to snatch at every dandelion clock of happiness as it drifted by, to live by the hour, and let the rest of the world go hang!

He was grateful to be going back to Frances, Pippa, and the baby, and to be leaving the Avenue, with all its memories, behind him. They were not very pleasant memories and he would never come here again, not if he could avoid it.

CHAPTER XI

Harold Talks Sense

ONE Sunday morning in late June Harold brought a cup of tea into Jim's room and Jim, who had been on duty until the small hours, continued to sleep after Harold had rattled the cup. He reached out, and gently shook his friend by the shoulder.

Jim sat up instantly. He had never lost his trench habit of shaking off sleep in a matter of seconds, and he noticed that Harold was excited about something.

"He's gone into Russia," said Harold, sitting on the end of the bed, and beaming at Jim through his thick-lensed spectacles. "I heard the tail-end of the news, but it didn't seem to make sense, so I popped out and stopped somebody who had heard the beginning. He said it was quite right! He's gone into Russia!"

Jim was wide awake at once, for this was news indeed! The Germans had moved east, turning their backs on an unsubdued West, and this in spite of the Hitler-Stalin pact that had thrown the Left into such hopeless confusion two years ago, in spite of the cynical partition of Poland and the Fascist-like invasion of Finland, in 1940. The uneasy partnership of extreme Left and extreme Right had cracked, as he had always hoped and prayed that it would, and now Germany was facing Bismarck's old nightmare, the war on two fronts.

He forgot his tea and threw back the clothes, swinging his long legs to the floor.

"Are you sure? Are you certain, Harold?"

139

"Of course I'm sure," said Harold indignantly, "I wouldn't joke about a thing like that would I?"

"I'm not suggesting you're joking," said Jim, "but did you get it right? Are you *sure* you've got it right?"

Harold looked offended. "I say, old chap," he protested, "there's nothing wrong with my hearing is there? And anyway, that insurance chap from Number Sixty-Two heard the eight o'clock from the beginning. I daresay there'll be more of it by this time. You'd better drink your tea and come downstairs."

Jim gulped his tea and tore downstairs in his pyjamas. He fiddled with Harold's set and finally tuned in to a special bulletin. He sat there for the better part of an hour, constantly shushing Harold, who was rattling crockery in the kitchen as he prepared breakfast, and as the information was fed to him Jim's mind conjured with the vast possibilities the new development presented.

When finally he had turned off the set, and obeyed Harold's repeated requests to 'get something inside him old man,' he was as jubilant as a schoolboy on the last day of term. Harold had never seen him so cock-a-hoop, and he listened, smiling tolerantly, while Jim expounded theories involving the collapse of Fascism all over the world.

"I tell you it's the beginning of the end, Harold! The man's raving mad ... absolutely raving mad! The Germans will bleed to death in that vast country! Look what happened to Napoleon, and he was a professional soldier, not a piddling little house painter, with intuitions! They'll simply lead him on and on, the way they always do. His armour'll get bogged down in those forests for the winter, and then God help them! God help every one of them! They'll never get out, *never*! We can attack from this side, and crack 'em wide open, just like a nut! I tell you Harold, this is the beginning of the end!"

Harold was by no means so confident, but he did not say so, for he regarded Jim Carver as a superior strategist and a man who had actually fired weapons in anger and taken part in great battles. In addition he had an uncomfortable suspicion that any comment he might make on Russia generally would blunt the fine edge of his friendship with Jim, who had been recognized as the Avenue rabble-rouser ever since the days of the General Strike.

Harold had voted Conservative in more than a dozen consecutive elections. He had always been persuaded that Russia was every bit as undemocratic as Germany, and his suspicions, he felt, had been amply justified by Stalin's behaviour in 1939, and 1940. It would take him a long time to get used to Russia as an ally, and to Stalin and Molotov as champions of free speech and free elections. He had heard it said that Russia had concentration camps on a scale unheard of in Germany, that nearly half its population worked under the lash and the revolver, in Siberia. He had read that the M.K.V. was the parent of the Gestapo and that people who raised their voices against Communism disappeared even more abruptly than those who protested again Fascism. It was not easy to shed these convictions at the peep-peep of the time signal, prefacing the news. Winston Churchill, whom he revered above all men, might announce over the air that any enemy of Hitler was a friend of Britain's, but Harold's mind did not possess a politician's elasticity, and he had military as well as political misgivings. The papers had derided the efforts of the Red Army to overcome little Finland a few months ago, and if it took the Red Army months to reach Helsinki, Harold asked himself, how long would they spend on the road to Berlin?

He pondered these things as he ate his powdered egg, bacon, and fried bread, but he let Jim run on about the certainty of another retreat from Moscow, for Jim Carver's friendship, and his presence here in Number Twenty-Two, was far more important to Harold than ten thousand Red Armies, with or without guns mounted on sledges, and hordes of women snipers, who, so Jim told him, would now scatter into the birch forests and snipe the Germans unmercifully.

It might have been a very happy week for Jim, had it not been for a few lines of print in an issue of the *News of the World*, a day or so after this jubilant Sunday morning.

They had kept the identity of Elaine's co-respondent from him for as long as possible. Nobody wanted to be the first to tell him that his eldest son, besides being a war profiteer, had been instrumental in breaking up a Serviceman's home across the road. Harold had wanted to tell him on numerous occasions, and had even tried to persuade Esme to tell him, when he came home for a few days' leave at the end of his air-gunnery course, in the Isle of Man. Esme's moods, however, were puzzling Harold these days for the boy's whole attitude to the divorce seemed very casual, and when they had discussed the matter Esme did not appear to regard Jim Carver's knowledge of the facts as in any way important.

"Oh, scrub it, Harold," he told his stepfather, when the latter had taken advantage of Jim's absence on duty to raise the matter that was bothering him. "What the hell does it matter *who* made a monkey out of me? If I've put it out of my mind why can't everyone else? It's all over and done with! Barbara's okay in Llandudno, and I've managed to get clear of the ruddy orderly room at last, and do something a bit more useful than type a stencil of *'Officer's Behaviour in the Anteroom!'* "

So Harold did put the matter out of his mind, half hoping that Louise, or Jack Strawbridge, or even Jim's younger daughter, Judy, would break the news to Jim before the divorce found its way into the papers.

Perhaps, he reflected, it never would. There were so many divorces, and nothing very special about this one, so that perhaps after all Jim wouldn't hear about it until it was all too far in the past to matter.

Jim might not have heard about it, for he read only the war news as a rule, and when the divorce was made public, and Esme was granted a decree nisi, with the custody of Barbara, the bare facts were sandwiched into a quarter-column announcement embracing dozens of undefended cases; Esme's case occupied but two lines of small print, just names and addresses.

Then, to Harold's embarrassment, that old fool, Hopner, at the A.R.P. Post, had to blurt it out, just as Jim was going off duty one morning.

"I say Jim, is that your boy who's mixed up in that divorce?"

Jim made a natural mistake. "No, Charlie, it's the stepson of the chap I dig with. . . . Damned disgusting business. . . . The wife lives just over the road from me."

"Oh I know *her*," pursued the unwary Hopner, "she's practically a tart. She'll kip down with almost anyone, so they tell me, but I'm right sorry that she got your lad involved. It must be extra rations she was after, I suppose! Marvellous what some women'll do nowadays, for a pound of granulated and a tin of pineapple chunks, isn't it?"

Jim stared at him, bleakly. "What the hell are you drivelling about?" he asked. "What's my boy, Archie got to do with it?"

Hopner realised, too late, that he had put his foot in it, but he was fond of Jim and anyway it was impossible to back out now.

"I say, I'm sorry, old chap," he said, "I didn't realise you didn't know! It's in the paper . . . look," and he passed Jim a folded copy of the *News of the World*.

Jim read it carefully, and when he had absorbed the announcement he remained quite still for a few minutes. Hopner, watching him out of the corner of his eye, pretended to be busy repacking his respirator. At length Jim turned to him:

"Have you finished with this paper, Charlie?"

Hopner nodded. "You can take it, Jim."

Jim put it carefully into the pocket of his leather-faced jacket, and left without another word.

"Lumme!" murmured Hopner to his relief, "have I dropped a clanger!"

. . . .

Harold was brushing his clothes, preparatory to hurrying off for the 8.40., when Jim strode into the narrow hall, slamming the front-door behind him, and whipping the paper from his pocket. He flourished it angrily under Harold's nose.

"Did you know about this, Harold?"

Harold blinked, then nervously cleared his throat.

"Well yes . . . actually I did . . . I've known about it from the start."

"Why didn't you tell me? Why did you hint that the chap was a stranger?"

"I don't know—I suppose because I knew it would upset you!"

"You knew I was bound to find out sooner or later?"

"Not necessarily, and anyway, it wasn't really my business to tell you, Jim."

Jim recognised a note of pleading in Harold's voice.

"No, I don't suppose it was," he said grudgingly, "but all the same, I'd much rather have known. Does everybody else in the Avenue know?"

"Everybody who is interested," admitted Harold. Then, quickly: "But who *is* interested in that sort of thing nowadays?"

"*I* am," said Jim, quietly, suddenly peeling off his jacket, and unbuckling the broad leather belt that he always wore in addition to braces.

"What ... what are you going to do, Jim?" enquired Harold, forgetting that he had a bare ten minutes to get to Woodside in time to catch the 8.40.

"I'm going round to belt some decency into that bloody son of mine," said Jim shortly.

Harold acted instinctively. He reached out and grabbed the buckle of the belt, holding on to it tightly.

"You aren't going to do any such thing," he declared. "That won't help anybody, and it'll only get you into trouble! Besides, Archie's bigger than you, and a good deal younger, so you wouldn't be capable of doing it, anyway."

"I'll have a bloody good try," roared Jim, tugging hard at the belt, and jerking Harold halfway across the hall. "Let go of that buckle, damn you!"

"No," squeaked Harold, "I won't! I'm not going to let you make such a fool of yourself, Jim!"

"You've just said it was none of your business! Let go, blast you!"

"No, I won't, and it *is* my business. I think you're behaving stupidly, and I'm going to stop you if I can! You've been a good friend to me and. . . ."

He was unable to complete the sentence, for Jim's fist struck him on his long, thin nose, and he crashed back against the hallstand, losing his balance, and sliding to the floor.

The hall-stand ricochetted from the wall, and fell forward on his shoulders, bouncing off, striking the bannister, and finally coming to rest as a barrier between the two men. The belt remained swinging in Jim's hand.

For a few seconds neither of them moved. Then Jim peered over the hall-stand and regarded Harold with dismay. With his spectacles suspended from one ear Harold was groping for his handkerchief. Blood from his nose gushed over his white shirtfront, and dripped down his jacket on to the polished linoleum. The sight of the blood restored Jim's self-control.

"I say ... I'm sorry Harold ... I lost my temper ... ! I didn't mean to hit you like that! Here, take this handkerchief! You're bleeding all over the blasted hall!"

Without a word Harold reached up for the handkerchief, as Jim lifted the hall-stand, replacing it against the wall, and began gathering up an assortment of walking-sticks and umbrellas that had rattled from its racks.

Harold rose slowly to his feet, dabbing his nose, and breathing heavily through his mouth.

"I think I'd better go into the scullery," he said. "I've missed the 8.40 now and just look at me? Just *look* at my coat!"

Jim followed him into the scullery, and turned on the cold tap. For a few moments Harold dripped into the sink; then Jim said:

"You'd better lie on the floor and give it a chance to clot."

Harold obediently lay on the floor, and Jim bent over him, gently sponging chin and coat with a dish rag. When the bleeding had stopped Harold sat up and Jim, without another word, put on the kettle for tea.

As soon as it boiled they sat down facing one another. Harold smiled.

"Well, I stopped you, didn't I?"

Jim made no reply.

"You do see that you'd have made a fearful idiot of yourself, don't you, old man?"

"Yes," said Jim gruffly, "I see that, but it doesn't make me feel any better, I can tell you that!"

"Look here, old chap, I'd like to talk frankly if I may. May I?"

Jim grunted and Harold accepted the grunt as an affirmative.

"Well, it's like this, Jim! Here's a marriage that's gone on the rocks because of a war. At least, that's what we tell ourselves. We say it only happened because a husband went to the Forces, and a civilian moved in and took his place. But the fact of the matter is that it isn't the real reason at all! This was one of the marriages that would have gone on the rocks, anyway!"

"How can you assume that?" asked Jim.

"Because I know the girl, and I know the family! Hang it man, I acted for Elaine's father, years ago and she's a bad egg, Jim, bad right through! I've known that for some time, not from the beginning I grant you, because I don't mind admitting that at first she fooled me as much as she fooled Esme, but the fact remains that she's no good, and never will be. If it hadn't been your Archie, then it would have been someone else!"

"Is that supposed to make me proud of being Archie's father," growled Jim. "However, go on, since you seem determined to make light of it all."

"I am not," said Harold, in his best courtroom voice, "making light of it! I am simply attempting—and at considerable personal risk so far as I can see—to prevent you from washing a second lot of dirty linen in public before the first lot's dry! Go ahead! Make a newspaper story of this by assaulting your son! That way you'll expand the two lines in that paper to a front-page story for the whole country to read about!"

"Ah," said Jim, slowly, "you've got something there, Harold. I admit I hadn't looked at it like that. But by God, I'd like to tell Archie what I think of him, sitting there piling up money, and then shutting his shop and climbing into bed with your boy's wife!"

"Well," said Harold, beginning to feel more sure of himself, and pressing his advantage, "there's nothing whatever to prevent you from telling Archie what you think of him, but do it in private, with the edge of your tongue, and not in public with the buckle-end of what looks to me like a road-mender's belt!"

"I've always known Archie was a wrong 'un," said Jim gloomily, ignoring Harold's feeble joke, "he took a wrong turn somewhere, 'way back, when he was a boy, and he's left it too late to straighten himself out! I suppose that's the price a man pays for four years away in the trenches, when his kids are growing up, and he should be around keeping an eye on them! It'll be the same with half the kids today, you see if it isn't! The women too, they need the business end of a strap, some of 'em! It makes a man sick, when we're supposed to be fighting a war for national survival!"

"The war hasn't all that to do with it, Jim," said Harold. "I saw plenty of this sort of thing before the war. If people are born without a sense of responsibility they'll make a hash of marriage, war or no war. As for Esme, I can't help thinking that the boy is well rid of her, and I think he knows it. That's why he talked himself out of a safe job, and volunteered for air-gunner."

Jim set down his cup. "He's done that? Young Esme, put in for air-crew?"

"Didn't your girl, Judy tell you? She's still at the same camp isn't she?"

"No, she didn't tell me," said Jim, thoughtfully, "but I think I see what you mean about Esme. That's a direct result of his mother being killed, and then his wife letting him down?"

Harold shook his head. It was queer, he thought, how much better he was beginning to understand people, and people's notions lately. It was as though, through all these years, his blind devotion to Eunice had stood between him and everybody around him. Six months ago he too would have concluded that Esme's determination to volunteer for air-crew was a mere defiant gesture, something prompted by grief and bitterness, but now he knew that this was not so, that it was simply a part of Esme's growing up and was therefore inevitable.

"No, Jim, this is nothing to do with heroics," he said. "Esme tried for air-crew right at the beginning, but they turned him down on account of a slight defect in his vision. They're not so fussy now it seems. I remember thinking that he was relieved at the time, and settled gladly enough for an office job, but now he's beginning to see things as they really are, and that makes him want to play a more active part in this business. You see, Esme's a romantic, and until quite recently he's been content to see life as he wanted to see it, and as he'd always seen it, right from the time he was just a little chap. He always seemed to be shying away from life as it was, and creating a world for himself to live in. You remember how he was always dressing up, and pretending to be someone out of a book?"

Jim remembered. "My girl, Judy was a bit like that," he said. "It's a pity they didn't marry each other, and go right on living in a dream! God knows, there's enough of the so-called practical people about. We could all do with a bit more chivalry and make-believe. When I think of that son of mine. . . ."

Harold, anxious to keep the discussion in the abstract, hastily interrupted.

"You have to let people like Archie and Elaine go their own way for as long as they're able, Jim. They've got it coming to them, believe me! It's the decent people that are going to win out in the end and if I didn't believe that I'd cease to believe in everything!"

" 'As ye sow, so ye shall reap'. Do you really believe in that any more, Harold, do you *really* believe in payment deferred?"

"Yes, I do," said Harold, emphatically, "Because it's being proved all round us! Look at the way this country pulled up its socks when it had to, last year, and look at the way the people round here weathered the blitz, and held on until things began to look a bit brighter! They aren't Archies and Elaines, Jim, they're the majority, and that's what's important! If the majority has guts and decency what does it matter if a few here and there don't pull their weight? What does anyone gain by turning aside to knock sense and decency into them? If it isn't there to begin with it's a waste of time trying to put it there! Now do you see what I'm getting at, Jim?"

Jim Carver traced a pattern in a tea-stain on the American cloth table-covering before him. He was silent for a while, extinguishing the final flickers of anger against a son who had shamed and humiliated him. As the last embers of his resentment died he felt once more the surge of affection and admiration for the peaky-faced little clerk who reasoned with him so earnestly, and with such sincerity, and his mind returned to the previous occasion when this same man had revitalised him by falling back on the philosophy of the suburbs, a plain 'get-on-with-the-job-and-stop-whining' outlook, that epitomised every scrap of faith Jim had ever had in the common man.

"You're a good chap, Harold," he said, at length, "a real good chap, and you talk more common sense than anyone I know!"

His hand shot across the table and clasped Harold's. "I'm sorry I made such a bloody fool of myself, and I'm glad you stopped me making an even bloodier one!"

He stood up, suddenly: "To hell with Archie! To hell with all the Archies. I'll write young Esme a letter, and maybe send him some fags. I daresay he could do with 'em, I know I always could when I was in uniform!"

He kicked off his boots and went upstairs to his room. Harold looked at his watch and decided that he had time to wash up and catch the 9.24 from Woodside.

He felt pleased with himself, justifiably so.

CHAPTER XII

Night Ops For Archie

BY the end of October, 1941, the face of the Avenue had changed for the third time in three years.

In mid-summer, '39, it had curved between Links and Rec' with its sweep unbroken, save for the Manor meadow cart-track that ran out from between Number Seventeen and Nineteen. Its gardens, for the most part, were trim, and lovingly tended. Its dwarf walls were well pointed and their festoons of chains were intact.

By the time its small quota of sons had trickled home from Dunkirk, however, the long crescent had already begun to look like a road in a ghost-town, from which families had moved away, to build new homes elsewhere. The front gardens were no longer trim, but sadly weed-sown, and rapidly encroaching upon one another.

By the early spring of the following year there were more definite changes. The iron chains had gone, offered up for scrap, suburban ploughshares to be beaten into Churchill tanks. The long line of 'To Let' and 'For Sale' boards had been taken away. The big lilac, at Number One Hundred and Twelve, had now leaped a shoulder-high privet hedge into Number One Hundred and Fourteen, as though inspired by the wanderlust of Number Ninety-Seven's laburnum. This Avenue landmark, lacking its staked support, was leaning right across the path of Number Ninety-Five.

These changes, however, were superficial, and might not have been noticed by people who had not grown up in the Avenue. The big changes came later, after the bomb had torn a three house gap in the odd side. The blast wave of this explosion levelled a section of the dwarf wall, between Number Six and Eighteen, on the even side, and after that some of the houses were boarded up back and front, and all the occupied ones had their windows patterned with criss-crossed adhesive tape.

In the early summer the big gap was tidied but a good deal of the rubble remained. The smooth symmetry of the crescent had been destroyed and was never to be restored, for after this incident the Avenue put on its full battledress, and began to look like a neglected corner in a French battlefield. Then the grass really did grow in the street, pushing up between the cracked pavement slabs outside Number Fifteen, and surrounding the bronze chrysanthemums, that was all that remained of Nick Crispin's front garden. In less than a month ragwort, nettles and dock had secured a hold on the rubble behind Number Seventeen, and campion, willow-herb and viper's bugloss began to sprout in the oblong flower beds that Edgar Frith had tended so lovingly through all the years that he lived there.

Conversational topics had changed too, and so had the subject matter of Avenue jokes. Nobody spoke much of the blitz nowadays and as a station-platform topic it had gone the way of the *Graf Spee*, and Dunkirk. If people did refer to it they did so in the way that they had once spoken of the Somme, and of Passchendaele. Today the principal platform topic was Russia, and this meant that a whole list of new and almost unpronounceable names had to be memorised, names that did not roll easily to the tongue, dreadful names like 'Vitebsk', 'Mohilev', and 'Yekaterinoslav'.

Mr. Baskerville, he of the Avenue's first four-valve radio in 1923, and the Avenue's first 'bomb-proof' shelter, now found himself saddled with a new role, for besides that of fashion-leader of gadgets, he was now the Avenue Strategist, simply because he had acquired the knack of remembering the names of Russian towns, and Russian Commanders.

Several catchers of the 8.40 strove to compete with him in this new field, but they were never serious rivals. It was difficult to argue with Mr. Baskerville, because his information seemed to stem directly from the Kremlin. He was very open-handed with it and apparently did not take the careless-talk posters very seriously. He once told a covey of Avenue husbands, awaiting their train on Woodside Station, that Marshal Budenny now had a reserve army quartered in and around Kursk, and was only awaiting the arrival of the German spearheads before co-operating with Comrade Zukov in a two-prong pincer movement. This, he pointed out, would at once sever the Nazis' over-extended line, and isolate two army groups from base. Nobody contradicted him, after all, it might well be so, for all Mr. Baskerville's fellow-travellers were aware, as they had but British newspapers to feed upon, and Mr. Baskerville had long been referring to Joseph Stalin as 'Uncle Joe'.

Mr. Baskerville was militantly pro-Russian these days, and ready to cross attaché cases with anyone who doubted Russia's ability to withstand the weight of German armour. He sometimes hinted that a little Russian discipline might not come amiss at Woodside Station.

One day the 8.40 did not show up until past nine o'clock, and Mr. Baskerville, stamping his feet up and down the frosty platform, told them all how 'Uncle Joe' had recently shot the Moscow station-master for a similar delay in respect of the Tula express. When Mr. Mainwaring, a very kind-hearted man, pronounced this 'a bit much', Mr. Baskerville rounded on him angrily.

"Nonsense, Mainwaring! It was a clear case of exigency!" he retorted. "You couldn't have a clearer case of exigency!"

There were times, he added, when it became necessary for a State at war to be ruthless to the individual, in order to safeguard the majority. It was thus far, far better to shoot one station-master, than to keep ten thousand reservists away from the hard-pressed Mojaisk sector!

Mr. Baskerville was not the only Avenue train-catcher who conjured with topical words, like 'exigency'. Up and down the Avenue others were experimenting with unfamiliar words, and unfamiliar place names. Where one had once heard words like 'blitz' and 'panzer', one now heard terms like 'envelopment', and 'rapid deployment'. Nobody ever spoke of 'bulges', or 'bridgeheads', nowadays, but rather of 'perimeters', and the 'hedgehog strong-points'.

The jokes were different too, from those of the previous year. Mr. Baskerville had ceased to tell bomb stories, but had developed the even more disturbing habit of describing funny cartoons that he had seen in the evening papers. He never bothered to enquire whether his audience had seen the same cartoons but launched regardless into a detailed description of the drawing, and hooted with laughter when he quoted the caption.

"I say, Godbeer," he would gasp, running in pursuit of Harold, as they mounted the greasy steps to the 'up' platform, "I say old man, did you see: 'Wot a War', last night? There was a minesweeper, bearing down on a fishing boat, that was bobbing about near a mine, and the chap in the fishing boat was looking up at the minesweeper's captain with a grin, and saying: 'You don't 'ave to worry, skipper, I've knocked all the spikes off with me boathook!' Damned good, what? I don't know how they think of 'em, blessed if I do! Knocked 'em off with his boathook! Get me? Just imagine, swiping a floating mine with a boathook?"

Harold usually resigned himself to walking back to the Avenue in the trying company of Mr. Baskerville, and would endeavour to steer the conversation away from cartoons by mentioning one or other of the Avenue's more personal topics, like the posthumous V.C. awarded to Albert Dodge, for blowing up a viaduct near Bari, or the M.M. poor old Crispin had won in the Western Desert, on almost the very day that his family was wiped out on the last night of the winter blitz.

Little Miss Baker, at Number One, was missing the bombs, and begrudged Russia the almost exclusive patronage of the Luftwaffe. Like Harold Godbeer across the road it had taken rather more than Mr. Churchill's bland assurances to lay for her the ghosts of Lenin, and Trotsky. Try as she would she could never quite see Stalin as 'Uncle Joe', or rid herself of the suspicion that the bombs he was manufacturing by the million in the Urals ('Underground factories, mark you, and dug at least ten years ago, before anyone had heard of Hitler!') were not destined to be used against Nazis. She could never forget that these same men had once shot the poor dear Czar in a cellar, and that the man they murdered

had looked exactly like dear King George V, whose relation
he had been. It was also widely reported that this Stalin
everyone was making such a fuss about was once a bankrob-
ber. Notwithstanding the British Premier's adventurous past
Miss Baker did not find it easy to link dear Mr. Churchill
with the bomb-throwing bank robber. She confided these
unworthy doubts to Edith Clegg, when Edith came over for
tea one Thursday afternoon, and Edith promised to ask Mr.
Carver about it, and report back, but she forgot to do so
because troubles of her own were absorbing her attention just
then, to the total exclusion of the war.

Since the Avenue bombing Becky's 'little trouble' had
shown itself once again. Not only had her spells become
more frequent, but she had now taken to wandering away
from Number Four, on one occasion for two whole days, and
poor Edith was nearly frantic with worry and foreboding.
When she was found and reclaimed Becky always asserted
that she had met her husband, Saul, in the Lower Road, and
that he was making a home for her and the baby on the
proceeds of a lucrative commission for a landscape painting.

Edith knew of course, that this could not be so. Saul had
been in his early thirties when he had eloped with Becky,
and that was in the last years of Queen Victoria's reign. Saul
must now be approaching his dotage, even if he was still alive,
which must be extremely doubtful considering his mode of
life in days gone by. Becky's poor mind must have been
stirred up by the bombings, so much so that long buried
memories floated to the surface, causing her to identify
someone else with the man who had treated her so shamefully.

After a number of attempts to reason with Becky, Edith
consulted her neighbour, Jim, and together they had succeeded in tracking the ghost to a section of pavement, near the
Croydon Town Hall. It was here that poor Becky's fantasy
led her, day after day, to stand patiently beside a bedraggled
old man who sat cross-legged against the wall, sketching
flagstone portraits of Churchill, and lurid impressions of
aerial warfare, executed in coloured chalks.

Jim approached the elderly vagrant and talked to him

about Becky and the man readily admitted profiting by her regular patronage.

"She's alwuz 'ere, guvnor," he said, "but I carn't do nothin' to stop 'er, can I? It's a free country, or so they say, don't they, and she c'n stand here if she likes, I suppose, so long as she don't cause no obstruction. Bin real decent to me she 'as. Reg'lar two bob a day, and never nothing but kind words about me work neither! Wot's that, gov? *She thinks I'm somebody else?* Well, I carn't 'elp that neither, now can I? Orl right, gov, I'll keep an eye on 'er from now on. Tell you wot—just write 'er address on a bit o' paper, and I'll bring 'er back 'ome, pervidin' you'll stand the fares. Shirley an' Addiscombe ain't my way see, I got a room in Norbury."

After that things were a little easier for Edith. Whenever Becky did manage to slip out of the house she always turned up again by dusk, escorted home by the obliging pavement artist, to whom Edith paid a regular five shillings a week for his duties of chaperone.

It was all very trying, however, and sometimes Edith thought wistfully of the pleasant days between the wars, when Becky had seemed to recover most of her wits under the bob-bob-bobbing of dear Teddy, and they had all had such wonderful times singing '*Horsey, Keep Your Tail Up*' round the cottage piano in the front parlour.

* * * *

A close neighbour of Edith's was having his share of anxiety in the autumn of 1941.

Along at the corner shop Archie Carver was still coining money but he was not able to give his chain of pop-ins all the attention it demanded, for his mind was now obsessed by a whole string of problems, some of which had no bearing on profit and loss.

There was young Anthony, for instance, Officer Cadet Anthony now, and destined for the Guards Armoured Division. During their final interview, Anthony, who had developed into a very pompous young man, told his father exactly what he thought of men who obeyed the Government's injunction to 'stay put' too literally, and make money out of the present emergency.

Archie was not so much shocked, or shamed by this outspokenness as genuinely puzzled by the boy's abhorrence of commerce as a whole. What the hell was wrong with making money, anyway? Without it, he, Anthony, could never have lorded it in the prefects' common room, at Hearthover, and it was galling to be sneered at by a young man whose cricket boots had been bought with the profits of the businesses he so so arrogantly condemned. What did the boy expect his father to do about the war? Sell out at a loss, and enlist in the Pioneers? Or leave the pop-ins to take care of themselves, while he strutted up and down the Avenue in a tin-helmet, like all the other mugs? People had to eat didn't they? True, most of the stuff that went over and under the counter at the corner shop had first to be shipped across the Atlantic, at the risk of men's lives, but what else could happen to it once it was here but to be distributed from shops like Archie's pop-ins? The boy's attitude simply did not make sense. What was the difference between wartime grocery, and wartime stock-jobbing? How many of his friends' fathers were making a pile of money out of the war? Presumably all of them, if they paid the school fees out of income, and if they didn't, if they paid them out of capital, then it was almost certainly capital amassed and invested during the First World War!

Grudgingly Archie paid a hundred pounds into the boy's account at Coutt's, and told himself he was a damned fool for doing so, but he had heard that officers who overdrew their accounts were automatically cashiered, and Archie decided that a disaster of this sort would make nonsense of the entire Hearthover investment.

So he paid the money, and washed his hands of the matter, telling Maria, during the final family reunion before Anthony left for training, that it would damned well serve Anthony right if he was blown to pieces within twelve months.

The one bright spot in the episode as far as Archie was concerned was Anthony's quickness to take advantage of his school cadet training, and short-circuit the requisite three months, preliminary training in the ranks. It comforted Archie somewhat to reflect that his son was not quite a one-hundred-per-cent patriot, and was still sufficiently human to think up at least one little wangle.

During the period that he spent down in Somerset that summer Archie had a brief opportunity to study his two other children, James, the fourteen-year-old boy, and Juanita, his twelve-year-old daughter.

Maria told him that James was very backward at school, and spent most of his time ranging the hedgerows and woods, in search of birds and small animals. All the books that he owned dealt with wild life, and Archie found crude drawings of stoats and owls on the fly-leaves. Archie tested him at arithmetic, and found him very inadequate. Asked to choose between a pile of coppers and a shilling, James promptly chose the coppers, although there were only eleven of them. Archie reflected sadly that he would never have made a mistake like that, at the age of fourteen, and turned to Juanita for consolation.

He found none. The child was very pretty, and graceful, and lacked the coltishness of her age and sex. She moved, he thought, like a little ballet dancer, and Maria told him she was a good dancer and had recently been chosen to lead a company of much older children in a 'Savings Drive' dancing display, at Taunton. She had earned high praise in the local papers. He found her, however, extremely difficult to approach, for to all his praises and blandishments she showed no response but continued to regard him with polite, but unwavering hostility, as though he was a strange visitor, whose presence in the house interfered with her playtime. He was very puzzled by her attitude, and mentioned it to Maria: Maria said flatly:

"She doesn't like men! She never has!"

"But dammit, I'm her father," protested Archie. "I pay for her dancing lessons, don't I? Doesn't she realise that?"

"It isn't the sort of thing you can explain to a little girl of twelve," said Maria, stiffly.

She did not tell him that Juanita had been schooled to distrust and dislike men, or that in almost every conversation Maria had had with her daughter since the child could lisp one-syllabled words, her mother had let slip some remark calculated to develop in Juanita a suspicion for all men, except possibly her grandfather, Toni, who had died entertaining her in the meadow behind the Avenue.

This training was deliberate on Maria's part. It was her way of hitting back at Archie, for years of gross neglect and indifference and the fact that Archie was troubled by the girl's attitude towards him afforded her immense satisfaction. Maria had lost the sweet submissiveness she had possessed when her father had instructed her to marry Archie, and to bear children for his delight. The memory of her wasted life nagged at her unceasingly, so that she had engendered, at length, a sour hatred for this big, brisk, matter-of-fact man, who had never once kissed her affectionately. She warmed herself with the reflection that Juanita's indifference to him, and his disappointment in both the boys, was only the beginning of her revenge, and that one day she would strike him where it really hurt, straight in his cashbox. She was in no hurry, however, for her real revenge on him could wait; in the meantime, she could amuse herself by frustrating him in other little ways, in the matter of withholding a divorce if he asked for one.

Archie was depressed after leaving Somerset, and returning to the Avenue. He soon forgot Anthony's sneers, James' stupidity, and little Juanita's hostility, but there were other, and far more serious worries to take their place and these worries were looming against the background of teeming, harassing pre-occupations of a man trying to steer a fleet of grocery businesses through the sea of total war.

His pre-war stocks were being used up at an alarming rate, and were almost impossible to replace, despite shifts, bribes, and wangles on a scale unprecedented in 1939.

He bought wherever he could, and however he could, and did business with some very shady people in the process. Behind this struggle, hastening up like a reserve army of the enemy, was the constant pressure of his accountants in matters of purchase-tax, income tax, surtax, Schedule A, and God knew what other demands of his purse and ingenuity. It was sufficient, he sometimes told himself, to encourage a man to commit arson.

Occasionally, when he sat in his office behind the corner shop and worked late into the night, surrounded by cartons

of coupons, and columns of returns, he almost envied the
men on the high seas, like tha crazy jazz-drummer over the
road, or the men in the R.A.F., like that dreamy idiot,
Fraser, now cruising about the night sky in a four-engined
bomber. At least these people had but known enemies to
contend with, foes who declared themselves with torpedoes
and flak, whereas he, hedged about with batteries of forms
and ready reckoners, was liable at any time to be betrayed by
someone he had been compelled to trust solely because of the
fantastic difficulties he faced in keeping his shelves well-
stocked.

On these occasions, particularly when it was late at night
and he was tired, he would feel himself adrift on an ocean of
loneliness. There was absolutely no one to whom he could
turn for advice, not one single human being who cared
whether he sank or swam, or who could appreciate, even
partially, his cares and difficulties.

Elaine Fraser was still available across the road, but it was
impossible to discuss business affairs with Elaine. Sometimes
he almost made up his mind to ask her to marry him if he
could bribe Maria into giving him a divorce. Sometimes he
was half prepared to settle for a woman, who, as he was
aware, would never prove anything but an expensive luxury,
but one at least who shared his outlook and would prove
companionable. Once, indeed, he went as far as to sound her
on the subject and had been surprised, and slightly mortified,
by her seeming evasiveness.

"You and me ... ? Marry? Oh, I don't know, Archie, it
might work out, then again it might not! What's the hurry
anyway? You can come here whenever you feel like it, and
that's all you really want, isn't it?"

Was it? He was not sure any longer. Physically she more
than satisfied him and he was grateful to her for this, but in
the intervals between letting himself into Number Forty-
Three, and emptying his pockets of keys and coins on her
dressing table, while she sat hugging her knees and smiling
tolerantly from the bed, he sometimes felt that he needed
more than a soft, white, practised body, that he needed, if
not a wife and helpmeet, then at any rate a friend, someone

who could be relied upon to console him without a thought as to whether it was worth it or not.

. . . .

The two plainclothes men called on Archie about dusk one autumn evening, just as he had finished his cold supper, and was peeling off his jacket preparatory to a four-hour stint at his desk in the office above the store.

They were lean, casual, softly-spoken men, in raincoats and trilby hats, but he recognised them for policemen before they had produced their authority and had asked him, civilly enough, if he could 'spare them a few minutes to assist them in certain enquiries'.

He was obliged to spare them the better part of two hours, for one question seemed to lead easily to others, and Archie's iron nerve, and his astonishing memory for figures, was severely taxed during the interview.

Once he was obliged to excuse himself on the pretence of making some coffee, and take a quick look at his red pocket-book in the shadow of the step-ladder leading from store to kitchen.

At last they went away, presumably satisfied, and profuse in their thanks. But Archie was far from satisfied, and his head boiled with possibilities, particularly possibilities regarding the source of two cases of whisky and one case of gin, that a gentleman by the name of 'Swift' had acquired for him a month or so ago.

Archie had had his doubts about Mr. Swift at the time. He now recollected his mental appraisal of him, on the occasion of their first meeting. It was 'Swift by name and Swift by nature', but his doubts had not prevented him from making certain arrangements with the gentleman and at the time these arrangements had appeared to be wholly satisfactory ones, and had resulted in Archie being enabled to supply certain of his privileged customers with a limited supply of good cheer.

Now that the lean, raincoated gentlemen had called, however, and shown such a solicitous interest in his dealings with Mr. Swift, he was not at all sure that the acquaintanceship had been so satisfactory after all. He sat deep in thought for more than half an hour after the detectives had left, and then, after a couple of 'phone calls, he made his decision. If they called once they would call again and next time they might have a search warrant.

It cost Archie a very big effort to destroy, in cold blood, the equivalent of a hundred pounds' capital gain, and for a few moments he toyed with the idea of concealing Mr. Swift's cases of spirit on the premises and not of destroying them utterly.

The moment soon passed, however, and he made up his mind to cut his losses. He put on his heavy overcoat and gumboots and stumped downstairs into the store, where he foraged about among cartons and crates until he unearthed three half-empty cases. He loaded them into the back of his car, covered them with sacks and then stuffed some cardboard cartons on top of the sacking, until the whole space at the back of the car was filled. Then he unlocked his yard gates and drove out into the Avenue, turning right into Shirley Rise and making for the hills, beyond the Old Mill.

It was drizzling as he drove slowly and carefully towards the old Roman well, in the direction of Chislehurst, and he had turned into the road that bordered the pinewoods when a war reserve constable stepped into the beam of his headlights and signalled with his torch. Archie stopped and his mouth went dry, but he forced himself to sound tolerant and cheerful.

"Well, and what can I do for you tonight, officer?"

The reservist flashed his torch over Archie's head and into the back of the car.

"You're pretty well loaded, aren't you, sir?"

Archie twisted his thick neck. "Oh that? Yes, I'm still delivering. Can't get anyone to work overtime these days, so I have to turn to myself. I'm a grocer, and I'm all behind today. I've got fifty orders in there, and people have been screaming on the 'phone for them!"

"You're obscuring your rear window, sir. You couldn't see anything approaching from behind in your mirror!"

Archie relaxed. "That's right, officer, I couldn't, could I? Half a tick then, we'll see what we can do about it!" and he jumped out, and set about rummaging in the back, beating the

topmost cartons flat, until the window space was cleared, and
stuffing handfuls of bunched sacking down behind the crates
on the cushions: "How about that? Will that do?"

"That's all right, sir! Sorry I had to flag you but I've seen
some nasty accidents happen that way!"

"Damn decent of you to tell me," said Archie, breathing
freely again. "Miserable night for a beat. Have a fag?"

"Thank you, sir ... you don't mind if I don't smoke it
now, do you?"

"Not in the least," said Archie, checking an impulse to give
the man the packet. 'So long, then, and thanks once again!"

He got in and drove off, watching the pin-point of the
man's torch reflected in his mirror. The incident persuaded
him to go further afield than he had intended, and he back-
tracked along the far side of the woods, towards Westerham,
keeping a sharp look-out left and right for a likely dumping
place.

He found one at the bottom of a short, steep hill, where a
by-road led off into a hollow, and a slimy pond had formed
where the bank had subsided from a stubble field beyond it.

The road before and behind was empty. Having reconnoitred he turned into the lane, drove down it a distance of
about fifty yards, and stopped, switching off his lights.

It was not quite pitch dark, for the rain had now ceased
and faint starlight glimmered on the surface of the pond.
Archie opened the offside door of the rear compartment and
heaved out the top case, staggering with it to the edge of the
pond, and feeling his way with his feet into the margin of
slush.

When he was confident of keeping his balance he lifted the
crate above his head and hurled it towards the centre of the
pond. There was a noisy splash, but when he had found his
torch, and flashed it on the disturbed surface, there was no
sign of the case, just a jagged rent in the patch of weed.

Archie grunted with satisfaction, and returned for the
second case. Fearing the noise of another heavy splash he set
down this one in the mud, and threw the bottles into the
water one by one, finally returning to the car and repeating
this act of sabotage with the contents of the third and last
crate. He counted, bitterly, as he threw. Twenty-seven bottles

in all—worth, possibly, four to five pounds apiece at present black-market prices!

When he had finished he remembered the two empty cases at his feet. He shone his torch around and the beam showed him a roughly-made dyke wall, that held the pond water back from the road. The bricks were loose, and he was able to dislodge a dozen or so, which he loaded into the cases before wading out and launching them into deeper water.

The slush rose over the top of his gumboots and filled them, but this did not worry him, for bitterness had now left him and he was conscious of a feeling of achievement. Those nosey sods in raincoats could now come and go as they pleased, for with or without search warrants they would find nothing incriminating on his premises!

He plunged back to the road, sat down on the rear bumper of the car and began to empty his boots. He was thus engaged when he heard a soft squelching quite near at hand, and he looked up, quickly, his left boot in his hand.

A polite voice addressed him out of the patch of darkness towards the main road.

"Shall we resume our little chat now, Mr. Carver?"

Two torches flicked on, and Archie found himself held in their crossed beams, one waterlogged boot on, the other swinging from his hand. Two lean men in raincoats materialised out of the deep shadow, and stood quietly and inoffensively one on each side of him.

"Now then Mr. Carver, why not jump in beside me, and let me reverse you back to the main road," said one of them, as though conferring a favour on a stranded wayfarer.

Archie was too stunned to make a reply. He sat there, half supported by the bumper, one boot on, and one boot off, and suddenly both feet seemed to go numb, so quickly, and so completely, that he almost cried out in despair and discomfort.

CHAPTER XIII

Judy: Full Circle

AS soon as Esme had completed his operational training course in Gloucestershire he went on leave for fourteen days.

He spent the first week in North Wales, with Edgar, his wife Frances, and the baby but the weather was bad, thin, persistent rain misting the Snowdon range and making outdoor activities cheerless.

Little Barbara, who was now toddling about the flat over the shop, under the delighted tutelage of Pippa, Edgar's step-daughter, was not much interested in him but she talked incessantly. Esme was amused to note that she was queen of the little household, and by the mere wave of a pudgy hand could reduce not only Pippa, but Edgar and Frances, to the status of capering slaves.

Himself, she regarded gravely and he was moved when she clamoured for "Grannie Oooniss" as he tucked her up in her cot. It seemed to him strange that a child of thirty months should retain the memory of his mother, dead now for almost a year. He told her that "Grannie Oooniss had had to go away" and had sent Pippa to be a sister in her stead.

The child thought about this for a moment, then accepted it and called loudly for Pippa, who came running, leaving Esme standing helplessly by the rail of the cot.

He realised that, as Barbara grew up, she would have no memory at all of Elaine, her mother, and for some reason the chain of thought set up by this reflection led him to think of Judy, who was still stationed at Queen's Norton. He made a sudden resolve and kissing Barbara went downstairs and

164

'phoned a wire: *"Going back to Avenue tomorrow—stop—wangle week's leave join me."*

He excused his departure to Edgar and Frances by telling them that he felt he should spend part of his leave with Old Harold, but it was not really Harold who attracted him back to the suburb but a sudden nostalgia for Manor Wood, with its crumbling, blind-eyed mansion, and still, reed-fringed lake. It was here that he had spent the happiest hours of his life, through the long hazy summers of boyhood; it was here, in the company of the child who had been his constant companion of those years that he wished to go now, as he crossed the threshold of his first operational tour.

The excitement of actually flying, of being one of a team destined to set out, night after night, into the unknown, had ebbed during his active training period at the O.T.U. The act of flying, particularly by night, had brought moments of terror, and a kind of day-by-day drag of anxiety that was never completely swallowed up in the rough and tumble of air-crew camaraderie, but despite this he no longer regretted his decision to exchange the safety and boredom of the orderly-room for the cold and loneliness of a rear-gunner's turret.

Guns and gunnery appealed to him strongly, and his pass-out marks had been excellent. In addition, he had found in the compact world of a crew a sense of belonging that he had lacked all his life. The men of Bomber Command, he discovered, had very little in common with the traditional flier, the helmeted man of the posters, who had been so lionised during the Battle of Britain days, days that now seemed almost as remote as the 'Tipperary' era. The bomber crews displayed little of the strained flippancy and the raffish self-confidence of the young fighter pilots that he had met from time to time in camp and pub. Most of his comrades now were sober, dedicated men and their average age was several years more than that of their colleagues in Fighter Command. Esme's present skipper, Mike Ollerman, was typical of the heavy bomber pilot, a big, chunky, deliberate Midlander, with a wife and two children in a semi-detached home on a Nottingham housing estate and a junior partnership awaiting him in an estate-agency, if he survived to claim it. There was a cosmopolitan air about Esme's crew, embracing, as it did, three Englishmen, one Welshman, two Canadians, and a dark-skinned radio-operator, from Trinidad.

Of the six men Esme most admired Mike, the skipper, but he had made a special chum (if a special chum could be said to exist in such a close-knit group) of 'Snowball', the Trinidad boy.

Snowball was obsessed not so much with flying in general as with the mysteries of his apparatus. Esme, who shared a room with him, would sometimes watch him 'doing his homework' as Mike had put it, assembling, stripping, and then swiftly re-assembling a portable radio set that he carried from camp to camp and almost from pub to pub, as though the plastic case full of coils, valves, and wires, was a tiny, crippled child who could not be left unattended for more than a few moments.

Sprawled on his bed pretending to read, Esme would watch him and marvel at the deft movements of Snowball's brown fingers, as he prodded, threaded and sifted, his curly head bent over the table, his thick, pale lips pursed in a soft whistle, as he worked and worked at his endless task.

"Why do you do that, Snowball? What makes you want to keep fiddling with the bloody thing?" Esme had once asked him, for apart from guns Esme had the romantic's dislike for gadgets and all things mechanical.

Snowball had paused and looked up. "Ah dunno," he had replied, scratching his head, "Ah guess it kinda makes me *feel* somebody when all dese bits goes whar Ah say dey go!"

The reply set Esme pondering at the unlikeliness of it all, of all the strange journeys and enterprises over the past two hundred years, that led to this man being here at this particular time and place, crooning a plantation ditty composed by enslaved ancestors, as he tinkered and tinkered with a portable radio set because its assembly 'made him feel somebody'.

Musing to himself Esme pictured the Bristol slaver full of manacled Negroes, as it set out upon the infamous middle passage to the West Indies. He saw Snowball's greatgrandfather hoeing and singing as he worked along the rows of some rich man's plantation, and then Snowball's grandfather, and father, existing under hardly more favourable conditions, in some hovel near a white, tide-washed beach. It seemed to him as if Snowball's thread wandered back across the centuries, linking him with men who had lived out their lives in jungle clearings and had never heard the throb of aircraft, or dreamed that it was possible for anyone to pass over their forests in huge, complicated machines, like the one that Snowball climbed into each night.

He thought about Snowball again as the slow, crowded train carried him south-east to the Avenue, and he made a resolve to ask him home to Number Twenty-Two on their next leave, and show him the scenes of his own boyhood on the Kent-Surrey border. Judy would like Snowball and would be kind to him, without that slight touch of patronage that even the rest of the crew showed towards the Negro. Judy would be interested in his musings about Snowball, for always, he recalled, Judy had been interested in the same things as himself, right from the days when they had played King Arthur in the woods, and flung, oh, how many Excaliburs, into the Manor Lake?

. . . .

Judy wangled her pass and was back in Number Twenty late the same night.

She arrived after Esme and Harold had gone to bed and so she advertised her presence with a note, pushed through Harold's letter-box.

She awoke next morning with a feeling of exhilaration that had little to do with her being on leave. She had spent a number of leave periods in the Avenue during the past two years, and had usually been glad to return to the hurly-burly of the billet and N.A.A.F.I. queues. To her the Avenue now seemed sombre and almost lifeless. So many of the older people had departed and all the younger generation was away. Opposite her home was the melancholy, saw-toothed gap, where Numbers Thirteen, Fifteen and Seventeen had once stood, blocking her bedroom view of the woods.

She was sleeping now in the back room, overlooking the old Nursery, but even the Nursery had changed. It was no longer the briar-tangled wilderness that it had been but a two-acre plot of neat beds, laid out by Jack Strawbridge, her brother-in-law.

She climbed out of bed, pulled aside the curtains and looked across to the rubble heaps of Delhi Road and beyond them to where traffic could be seen passing up and down the Lower Road.

She was not used to this view, having slept throughout most of her girlhood in the front bedroom with Louise and the younger twins, Fetch and Carry. In those days Number Twenty had been a crowded household, particularly as regards sleeping space. There had been eight of them living there until Archie had married, and often seven of them up to the time that she left the Avenue and went down to Devonshire to join Maud Somerton.

She leaned out and twisted her head towards Number Twenty-Two, remembering that Esme's room was within almost a yard of her, and that he was sleeping there at this moment.

She pictured him, not as she knew him to be, with his dark hair receding slightly and his eyes deep-set and slightly brooding, but as the child she had known so well, restless, eager and imperious, his eyes flashing with enthusiasm as he seized her by the hand, and implored her to "go to the margin of the lake yet again, and bring me word of what e'er befalls!"

She smiled at the memory and with the smile came a rush of affection that flowed into the current of her exhilaration. Poor old Esme! He had set sail with such confidence, weighed down with a huge cargo of dreams and imaginings, and what had it all amounted to in the end? A series of bumps and buffetings ending in shipwreck and bewilderment? In the meantime, what of her own hopes and dreams, those dreams that, from earliest childhood, had been wrapped up in the boy sleeping next door? There had been that dear, familiar dream, of a white wedding in Shirley Church, the ecstatic honeymoon in Bournemouth, or Felixstowe, and the triumphant return to the semi-detached on the Wickham housing estate, with the baby in the pram on the lawn, the lawn that Esme would mow each Saturday afternoon, while she prepared his tea in the trim little kitchen.

Well, they had both had their honeymoons, and Esme had had his baby. She, at least, had a few weeks' of unforgettable happiness with poor old Tim to look back upon, but now even Tim was just a laughing, lovable memory; Esme too, she supposed, had enjoyed his brief ecstasy with Elaine. Then the world had gone mad and everything had begun to boil around them. People they had thought of as immortal had died, and the entire Avenue community had shifted and dissolved. Now there was not much time left for either of them. The war went on and on, and Esme was a fully-trained air-gunner, due at any moment to clamber into the belly of one of those squat, sinister monsters that she had seen on the airfields, probably never to emerge again, except as a mass of contorted limbs, flying through space towards red-winking chaos below.

Suddenly her exhilaration drained away and she found herself weeping, weeping for poor drowned Tim, for poor scared Esme, for the lost semi-detached on the Wickham Estate, and for every hard-pressed soul along the curve of the Avenue.

For a few moments she let the tears run. Then, feeling better for their release, she pulled herself together, slipped on a civilian blouse and a flared skirt that had been fashionable in 1938, and hurried into the bathroom to dab her eyes with Louise's flannel.

Louise called from the hall: "Breakfast, Judy!" Judith called back, tidied her hair, and ran downstairs, feeling, without knowing why, that those few moments spent looking out on the old Nursery marked the end of her youth.

* * * *

The sun was a dull, orange ball, hanging low over the wood, when they crossed the meadow and took the familiar path to the Manor.

They had no special destination but it was the kind of morning that suggested a walk in leafless woods. The grass of the meadow was crisp and white with frost and their breath hung on the air, so that Esme, in buoyant mood, quoted his favourite '*Morte d' Arthur*', beginning where Sir Bedivere, a role he had so often allocated to her, strode down to the mere to dispose of Excalibur.

> *'But the other swiftly strode from ridge to ridge,*
> *Clothed with his breath, and looking, as he walked,*
> *Larger than human on the frozen hills. . . .'*

As he spoke the lines she gave him a shy, sidelong glance, noting for the thousandth time how the wood succeeded in transforming him from the boy next door into the intense and mysterious being he had always been when they were alone on familiar ground. She noted too how surely the stresses of the last two years had matured him. His small, regular features were now sharper, his chin firmer and the skin of his cheeks more tightly stretched, making his cheekbones appear more prominent than she remembered. His eyes, however, were just the same, alight with a kind of quiet fanaticism, as though they had never quite ceased to look about the dream world he had inhabited when they trod these same paths as children, he in grey flannel shorts and open-necked grey shirt, she in the little red and white check frocks that Louise made for her from material bought for 'eleven-and-three-a-yard' at Bannock's, in the Lower Road. Dear, dear Esme, she thought, outside you've grown a little, but inside you haven't really changed a bit, not the tiniest bit!

She wanted to tell him this, for today she thought it would please him, but shyness prevented her; instead she made an indirect reference to their childhood Saturdays, by saying:

"This wood hasn't changed, Esme. Everywhere else has, almost all the roads, and allotments, the Rec', the links, and even The Lane, but not this wood! Do you think it ever will?"

They had come now to the crumbling wall that separated the trees from the ruins of the kitchen garden. It was this very spot, she recalled, where she had overtaken him that first summer morning, only a day or two after he and his mother had come to live in the Avenue, and she had tracked him along the tangled paths. He looked around, carefully.

"I hope not," he said, fervently, "I hope to God, not!

Whatever happens, if I get the chop, I'd like to go out remembering this place as it was, always."

"It's always meant so much to you, hasn't it? Why is that, Esme?"

He screwed up his eyes, a habit she had almost forgotten. "I suppose because the impressions of childhood are the only really permanent impressions," he said. "As time goes on, and you grow up, all kinds of things register—people, places, experiences, even new smells, and patterns of sound, but the first impressions of a place like Manor Wood are different. They're so vivid at the time that they become a kind of foundation for everything else. It's a sort of mental book-cover, that outlasts all the pages it holds together!"

His frown of concentration relaxed and he smiled at her.

"Do you remember that day soon after we met, when we came here and you thought I ought to be called 'David' because he was your favourite Biblical character? Remember how I played up to you because I wanted to show I was just as good as David with a sling?"

"It was the *first* day we met," she reminded him. "You made a sling out of your handkerchief and the stone went in the wrong direction, over your shoulder!"

"That's it, and I liked you for not commenting on it," he admitted, and as he remembered this fleeting thought, now nearly a quarter-century sped, he realised what it was about Judy that had made her such a pleasant companion in those days. It was the warm and generous understanding she showed of all he found romantic, and her subtle and stimulating appreciation of his ascendancy, as male and showman of the world of dreams.

For a moment, as he contemplated the long line of her jaw, and the curling lashes of her brown eyes, the years fell away, and he saw her again as she had stood before him as a child, so eager to serve and so dazzled by his majesty, the squire, the shieldbearer, the small but perfectly adequate audience for his essays in to the story-book world of plate-armour, and hell-raked galleons. He said, almost without hearing himself:

"How did we come to drift apart, Judy?"

She said nothing, turning quickly away to climb the wall,

for the tears had welled up again. They jumped, she first, into the wilderness of the kitchen garden and she pushed on ahead of him, taking advantage of the screen of the old boathouse to whip a handkerchief from her service-issue shoulder-bag, and dab her eyes.

"Dear God," she muttered to herself, "what the hell *is* the matter with me this morning? Why am I so damned weepy? It can't be Tim, for Tim never came here with me, and it can't be Esme, either, for I must be over Esme, after twelve years!"

He seemed aware of her embarrassment, for he dawdled over by the gazebo, the same octagonal structure in which they had played Sleeping Beauty on that first morning, and she had waited for him, terrified by the brooding stillness of the Manor, while he disappeared into the reeds in order to emerge as wonder-working Prince.

He had kissed her that morning, and had never kissed her again, not unless one counted kissing at Avenue parties, or hand-kissing when she was Guinevere and he was Lancelot about to set out on a quest.

That was very strange, she thought. Hundreds and hundreds of hours spent together, as they grew from childhood to adolescence, yet never a kiss, never a single step outside the world of make-believe and along the road that she once believed would lead to Shirley Church, and the semi-detached on the Wickham Estate.

She dabbed her eyes again and moved along under the sagging wall of the boathouse.

Presently he called:

"Here's the punt, Judy! It's still lying where it sank under us!"

She pulled herself together then and came slowly back across the shattered paving towards him. The air was crystal clear and the sun over the lake so bright that she had to shade her eyes to look across the flat expanse of water to the islet, the little islet that had been for them the unattainable Avalon.

"Did you ever get to that island, Esme," she asked, "I mean, did you ever get there without me, by yourself, or with Berni and Boxer?"

"No, I never did, Judy," he said quietly, and then shortly, "I could have gone there because, over on the other side, where the rhododendrons grow, the shore is much closer, and one year a big tree came down making a bridge. As a matter of fact it's quite easy to get there now."

The information surprised her. She knew, none better, how passionately he had once longed to reach that island, how he had talked of making a raft after the punt sank under them and how impatiently he had ranged the broken outhouses looking for wreckage that could be converted into a raft to carry them there. Now there was a tree bridge but he had never used it! She wondered why.

He told her, before she could ask him.

"It happened just before the war. I was mooching around one afternoon and I found the bridge. It probably came down in that bad gale we had, the one that brought down all those elms down on the edge of the links. I remember I was quite excited at the time and climbed up on the roots to cross over. Then I stopped." He broke off and looked away from her.

"Well?"

"I don't know, I suppose because it didn't seem right to go there without you, Judy. You see, this place, and the feeling I have for it, is still half yours, and I didn't want to share it with anyone else, not even Elaine, or your brothers!"

She had to wait a moment or two before she could trust herself to answer. He was still not looking at her and she was grateful for that. Finally she said:

"Let's go there now, Esme. I'd like to!"

He looked at her sharply and saw her tears.

"All right, come on!"

"*Come on!*"

He had said it as it had been said so many times. "*Come on! Follow me! Keep on my heels! Watch where you tread, lest the enemy pickets hear you! Lead the horses! Keep a sharp look-out for Sir Mordred's men! If they catch you give the curlew call, and I'll spur back.*" (How, she had always wondered, when she was leading his horse?)

They circled the lake to the west and crossed the soggy patch where Edith Clegg had come to grief in search of her

Christmas tree. On reaching firmer ground they moved through the rhododendrons until they were exactly opposite the Manor.

There they found the tree, a tall, leafless chestnut, its dead boughs curling up on each side of the trunk, its tip firmly embedded in the mossy bank that circled the islet on this side of the lake. It was easy to cross, for splintered boughs jutted like a handrail along the length of the tapering bole. He handed her up and then made his way to the bank.

When she had followed and had stepped down from the tree she noticed that he seemed to be very excited but this did not strike her as strange. Ever since she had known him he had wanted to cross to this islet, but for her today's achievement was his admission that he had preferred to wait until they could share the adventure.

The knowledge warmed her through. The dead dream that had lain like a withered stalk at her feet began to quicken and shoot up, flowering as it grew. Her heart beat so violently that she felt breathless; half-way up the bank she stopped and leaned against the trunk of a squat beech, the only beech tree on the island.

He had been clambering on to the ridge that crowned the islet, but when she stopped he paused, looking over his shoulder.

"What is it, Judy? Lost a shoe?"

She shook her head and smiled. For the second time that morning she could not trust herself to speak. He came back and reached down to her.

"Take hold and I'll pull you up! Look, we've never seen the old Manor from this angle! It looks so different! It looks as it must have looked when it was alive!"

She took his hand, finding it cool and firm. His touch steadied her and she struggled on to the summit, where a ring of spruce and fir crowned the knoll. Then she understood something that he must have guessed from boyhood.

Across the widest section of the lake the mansion squatted behind its forecourt, and for the first time she could appreciate its gracious symmetry. He was quite right. It no longer looked dead and blind-eyed. The edges of its crumbling walls were blurred by distance and the red sun, piercing the frosty air had turned its grey, peeling walls to a rose pink. It seemed whole and cared-for, almost as though it really was the palace of Sleeping Beauty, coming to life with the awakening of its Princess.

"It's a kind of miracle, Esme," she said softly.

He remained quite still, looking into the sun.

"I think I've been expecting a kind of miracle ever since I woke this morning, Judy," he said, and then, taking her by the arm, "Haven't you? *Haven't you, Judy?*"

She nodded, and suddenly the mansion was forgotten, becoming again the crumbling, blind-eyed ruin it had always been, but the miracle had touched them. He seized both her hands and they looked into each other's eyes for what seemed to her almost a minute. In that space of time they knew with certainty the purpose of the miracle and all that had led up to this moment across the years.

To Judy, the world about them seemed so still that it was as though everything in the scene had ceased to live. There was no ripple on the surface of the lake, no bird stirring in the rhododendron thicket beyond the chestnut-tree bridge, no movement, or sound, in the earth or sky under the fixed, red sun. Then the sun itself was shut out, as he threw his arms round her and covered her face with kisses, kissing on her eyes, cheeks, and mouth, and between kisses he was murmuring over and over again "It's *you*, Judy! It's *you*! It's always been you, Judy . . . darling Judy . . . it's *us* . . . it's always been *us*, Judy . . . !"

There was no need to confirm this by any means other than returning his kisses. There was no need to speak of the dream of long ago, of her moment of terror and fulfilment in the summerhouse, when he had broken the spell with his first kiss, and she had seen, for the first time, the vague outline of the future. She would tell him later, or perhaps she would not. Perhaps she would never speak of the long, bitter sweet process that had established in her mind the certainty of their standing together at the altar of Shirley Church, and sharing the semi-detached on the Wickham estate. It was not important now whether he knew or did not know of the dream that had seemed to die the morning she had learned of Elaine through the powder-compact he had bought at Boots, or of the dream that had seemed to replace it, conjured up by Tim Ascham on the edge of another wood, in Devon. Nothing mattered any more now that they had found each other, not the heart-aches of her girlhood, or the war, or Elaine, or even poor Tim. Nothing else in the world, past or present, was of the smallest importance; just Esme.

They remained there a long time, saying little, for there was little that needed to be said. The wonder of their discovery, and the relief it brought to each of them, precluded discussion of plans and the certainty of separation within days. For the moment they were obsessed by the magnitude of the discovery, and by its inevitability, so clear to each of them now. It was like an absurdly simple solution to a mystery that had baffled them all their lives.

Presently, Esme said:

"Let's stay here a while, Judy. Let's light a fire!"

Even his voice seemed to her to have softened. He was no longer issuing an order, as in the past—go here, do this, that's how I want it, that's how it should be done! His kisses had elevated her to equal rank and her shield-bearing days were over. Whatever they did now they would do side by side and it was clear that he too was aware of this readjustment in their relationship, for he awaited her nod and when she gave it he at once set about collecting twigs and cones, while she dived into her shoulder bag for old letters and scraps of paper.

They had the fire going in a few minutes and when it had burned up and the larger branches were beginning to splutter, he spread his great-coat at the base of a pine, and they sat on it, looking through the screen of wood smoke towards the Manor. Around them life stirred again. A moorhen trailed across the water and a pair of rooks sailed over the elms behind the mansion. The fire crackled pleasantly and Esme said:

"We ought to have potatoes to roast. We always used to roast potatoes in their jackets, remember?"

She remembered. Of course she remembered. There was nothing that she had forgotten. Sitting here, his head on her lap, she nursed her favourite memories like sleeping babies. She had not known that it was possible to be so happy and serene as this, for her dream had never carried her this far, never to the point of physical contact, of letting her hand slide along his temples and feeling the weight of his head on her thighs.

Her yearning for him swept over her in huge, measured waves, so that sometimes she felt she would drown under them. She cupped his face in her hands and kissed his mouth, gently and constantly and as her lips touched his she read gratitude in his eyes and knew that the majesty had gone from him and that from this point in their lives his need of her was the greater.

She told herself that this was her triumph but there was no room in her heart for triumph, only for fulfilment and harmony. Even the air-gunner's badge on his tunic communicated no fear. They would be parted soon but never in the sense that they had been separated in the past. She had loved Tim wholeheartedly but never with this certainty or serenity. There had always been something temporary about Tim, even when she had lain in his arms during their brief Cornish honeymoon, and perhaps this was the reason why Tim's death had ravaged her without surprising her.

With Esme it was so different. Today she was assured that no matter where he went or what he did he would return to her and she knew that she should convince him of this before they parted. She promised herself that she would do this tonight or tomorrow, but not now, not until the red ball of the sun had passed behind the elms, and the sweetness had gone from the day, for by then all the loose ends of their lives would have been tied and they would discuss practicalities like all other lovers. Then they could discuss Elaine, his child, Barbara, and their future generally, but in the meantime, for a little while longer, it could wait. It could wait until the fire died down, and they had recrossed the chestnut-tree bridge, and made their way back to the Avenue.

* * * *

Only little Miss Baker, of Number One saw their return and noticed that they walked hand in hand.

Their new intimacy warmed and excited her, for she had seen them grow up side by side and had never understood why her plan for them had gone awry. She reflected that perhaps war had something to be said for it after all. It did seem to jolt people out of their grooves, and here were two young people who had profited by it.

She thought, as they passed her window: "There'll be a wedding soon, and everyone along this end of the Avenue will be glad!" Then she smiled, reminding herself that when Edith Clegg came over with the news it would not be news at all but she would have to pretend that it was, for dear, loyal Edith always derived so much pleasure by imparting information of that sort.

Nobody at Number Twenty was suprised by the news that Esme and Judy were to marry very soon. Louise said: "There now! Just fancy! It's such a pity you can't go and do it tomorrow!"

Jim Carver said: "Well, I'm glad for you, I've always reckoned you were made for each other!"

Harold Godbeer, his brown eyes misting slightly behind his thick spectacles thought of Eunice and remembered how fond she had been of 'Esme's little friend', but he refrained from mentioning this to anyone, contenting himself with the half-jocular comment to Jim: "This makes me some sort of relation, old man, doesn't it?"

Esme's decree would not become absolute until February, so they decided to apply for leave towards the end of that month and marry by special licence in one of the airfield areas.

Esme did not relish the idea of using the registrar's office used by Elaine and himself, and as a divorcee there was no question of marrying in Shirley Church. Afterwards, he said, they could make a wartime base at Number Twenty, or Number Twenty-Two, whichever proved the most convenient. Number Forty-Three, across the road, he had already made over to Elaine, whom he had not seen since the night he took Barbara away but to whom he had written during the early stage of divorce proceedings.

He half-expected to meet Elaine during this leave, but he did not, and he was told that she had closed the house and gone away somewhere. Jim informed him that Archie was in some kind of new trouble, something to do with the black

market, but when Esme did not press for details, Jim went
on: "It's curious that Archie turned out like that. A chap at
the Depot was talking to me about the danger of adopting
war-babies the other day. He said one could never be sure
how they'd turn out. I told him he was talking a lot of cock,
and I ought to know it's cock, didn't I? How the hell do we
know how our kids will turn out? Take Archie! He's been a
wrong 'un from the word 'go', and I don't know where he
gets it! Neither my people, nor my wife's folks ever
amounted to much, but they weren't wrong 'uns, at least, not
so far as I know!"

The night before Esme was due to return from leave, they
all made up a party and went to the cinema to see *Forty-
Ninth Parallel*, the Leslie Howard picture that dealt with
fugitive Nazis in Canada.

Jim and Harold enjoyed it immensely for it expressed their
own sentiments exactly. Edith Clegg enjoyed it too, for Leslie
Howard was a great favourite of hers. Esme and Judy found
it difficult to concentrate on the film.

The screen flickered and then went dead, but before the
murmur of the audience had time to swell a slide bearing a
hastily-printed message was thrown on the screen, and suddenly everyone half-rose in their seats, exclaiming and turning
to one another with the excitement of a crowd that has just
witnessed a spectacular rescue, or a feat of skill.

The slide's message read:

> *'American naval bases at Pearl Harbour in
> Pacific attacked by Japanese aircraft early
> today'.*

Just that! Nothing about the success, or failure, of the
attack and nothing whatever about its repercussions on the
war as a whole. The stark fact, however, was more than
sufficient to make the continuance of the programme an
anti-climax and when the film returned to the screen hardly a
word of dialogue could be heard above the babel of speculation.

Within minutes the house lights went up and people began
to stream into the gangways and foyer. Stranger addressed

stranger beaming at one another, as though Japan had been an ally, and Pearl Harbour, wherever it was, was the capital of the German Reich!

Jim was almost incoherent with excitement and Harold hardly less excited. Poor Edith, who had been very anxious indeed to learn what happened to poor Leslie Howard in the end, and whether or not he was instrumental in getting that horrid U-boat commander behind barbed wire, was forced to admit that even Leslie Howard's fate was trivial compared with the fact that at last America was well and truly in the war. As Jim pointed out, this was the crowning blunder of the Axis, who now faced the united strength of the civilised world.

"Except for Sweden, Switzerland and Spain," protested Harold, whose long years in a solicitor's office had developed in him an insane passion for accuracy.

Jim turned on him with a snort.

"Now don't be ridiculous, old chap! Who the hell cares a damn about Sweden, Switzerland and Spain? Don't you see what this means? It means that Hitler has insisted on Japan attacking, in order to stop the Yanks from coming in with us, anyway! It means that the Yanks will now turn everything they've got on Japan, and come right out in the open with a flow of war material for us! By God, but this'll shake up the whole box of tricks, you see if it doesn't! The U-Boat blockade, the Second Front, the North African situation, and the Russian offensives! This means we *can't* lose, no matter what happens! It's just a question of time now before Jerry is sewn up like a cat in a bag! I tell you it's wonderful! It's the best news we've had since that dreary little maniac did a mad dog act in Russia!"

He went on talking in this strain all the way home, and all the time Judy was getting their supper, but he was not the only Avenue dweller who was cock-a-hoop that night, for up and down the crescent there were constant comings and goings, with people shouting at one another over back fences, and flagrant blackout offences being committed by the score as neighbours flung open their back doors and exchanged scraps of news heard over the radio.

Mr. Baskerville, of Number Ninety-Seven, who was

thought by some to be in the confidence of Joseph Stalin, was even more excited than Jim Carver. He ran up and down the Avenue knocking at doors and telling people all that he had heard of Moscow's bulletin, on his powerful set. He announced that Uncle Joe was overjoyed at the news and had said so, more or less personally.

Edith Clegg slipped across the road to discuss Pearl Harbour, and *The Forty-Ninth Parallel* with Miss Baker, and even Archie Carver, gloomily locking his yard gates, and reflecting that he had but five more days to complete his case and answer to bail in the matter of Mr. Swift's gin and whisky, paused to discuss the news with the Air Raid Warden, who had been attracted by the numerous gleams of light that were flickering over the Nursery, behind the even numbers. The warden himself was too excited to take blackout violations very seriously.

"I say, this is a bit of a picker-upper, isn't it, Mr. Carver?"

"It'll shorten the war! You can depend on that," growled Archie, but reflected, as he climbed the steps to his kitchen, that it would do nothing at all to shorten his sentence if they found him guilty of purchasing goods stolen from a N.A.A.F.I.

Judy was glad that the news had come when it did. It had given them all something to talk about, and helped to bridge over the last few hours to morning and a parting from Esme.

They left Harold and Jim still talking, and went into the kitchen of Number Twenty to say good night.

CHAPTER XIV

The Indestructible

CHRISTMAS came and went without incident in the Avenue. The third Christmas of the war and still no trees in the windows or paper chains suspended from centre-lights.

Even Edith was without a tree this year, for Miss Baker was ill with bronchitis and Edith had had no opportunity to repeat last year's expedition to the woods. She let Becky take her chance with Jean McInroy and the patient pavement artist, and spent most of her time across at Number One with the invalid.

At the corner shop Archie was equally busy. His case was down for January 1st, and long consultations with his lawyer left him no time to check his coupons, which were getting into a dreadful muddle.

Difficulties and irritations crowded in upon him with maddening multiplicity. One of his managers, at the Crowhurst branch, was injured in a blackout collision and another, spurred, no doubt, by lurid press accounts of Russian heroism suddenly threw up his job and enlisted in the Navy. What with one thing and another Archie hardly noticed Christmas, a shopping festival that had always been so important to him. Elaine was away and she had not even sent him a postcard, but he hardly thought of Elaine, he had so much on his mind just now.

The only two Avenue men who could be said to have enjoyed Christmas that year were Berni and Boxer, the Commando twins. The festival coincided exactly with their departure for Vaagso and the prospect of at last directing their tommy-guns upon live targets.

Their unit set out on Christmas Day but the weather was so heavy that their transport had to put into a Shetland Base for last-minute repairs. Here, in company with the few other men who had ridden the storm without loss of appetite, they sat down and consumed enormous helpings of tinned turkey and plum pudding, washed down by Danish lager, a case of which had been thoughtfully shipped home by a luckier unit.

By Boxing Day they were at sea again, huddled in the bucketing hold of the vessel, polishing their weapons, singing their lewd songs, putting last minute touches to their equipment and congratulating one another on the prospect of at last having unrestricted licence to blow things up and shoot things down.

They sat together, their backs to a bulkhead, roaring with laughter, and shouting, "Ooop she goes!" every time the vessel gave a particularly violent lurch.

All about them men were being sick and muttering, between obscenities, that they would make some bastard pay for their discomfort the moment they got ashore, but Berni and Boxer were neither sick nor sour. They had no especial hate for Germans and their stomachs had been subjected to a rigorous pre-war training during their employment as Wall of Death riders, so they sat polishing their grenades and tommy-guns, and shouting, "Ooop she goes!" as the vessel reared and slithered into the northern fogs.

Soon after dawn they were summoned on deck and leaned together on the rail, looking with keen interest at the spectacular snow-covered hills on the other side of the fiord. As the landing-craft were being slung out the guns of the naval escort opened up and the sound was like organ music to Berni and Boxer as they bobbed about waiting their turn to descend.

"Let's be first ashore! Let's be the first! Whadysay Berni, whadysay?" screamed Boxer, his face split in his habitual grin.

What Berni replied was inaudible, for all hell had broken loose before, behind, and on either side of them.

They were almost separated when an officer bellowed:

"No more in here!" after Boxer had jumped into the landing-craft and Berni was still negotiating the net, but the twins had not stayed side by side all these years, or travelled such a distance in order to be separated at the moment of action. Berni made a flying leap as the bows of the landing-craft turned away from the transport and landed squarely on Boxer's broad shoulders.

Boxer, somehow anticipating this, absorbed most of the shock as they sprawled face foremost across an ammunition box. Far from resenting the impact he shouted with laughter and when they had struggled upright and had freed themselves from the arms and legs of their comrades, their boat was running close inshore and a flight of Hampden bombers was roaring overhead, dropping a stick of smoke bombs.

They were not the first ashore but they were among the first half-dozen. They went racing through the smoke-screen into the broad main street of the town and whooping down on a house where Germans were lobbing percussion grenades from windows and doors.

Their orders had been the kind that always recommended themselves to the twins, namely, "Go in and keep pounding the bastards until they pack it in!"

They took these orders literally and the next hour proved the jolliest of their lives. First they blew up a small factory, from which a garrison was obstinately sniping the main street. Then they replenished their stock of grenades and used them on the office of a timber yard, where half a dozen Germans continued to maintain resistance after they had been surrounded on all sides. Then, when everyone inside the office was dead, and the yard itself a mass of flames, they answered a call for reinforcements at the far end of the town and attacked an isolated timber building reported to be Vaagso post office and telephone exchange.

Firing from the hip they joined a squad in rushing the main door and having won entrance went blithely from room to room shouting, singing and bundling their prisoners into the street, until a distant whistle sounded and the firing nearer the landing stage began to die away.

Berni said:

"I reckon they've about had it, Boxer! We'd better get back along."

Boxer, sensing the end of the adventure, was reluctant to go.

"We'd better blow the bloody place up, Bernie," he protested, and when Berni pointed out that they were now alone and had used up all their demolition charges, he conceded: "Okay then, but I gotter get Pop a souvenir! I just gotter get Pop a souvenir!"

They hunted around for a souvenir and came upon a dead German officer, his helmet still strapped under his chin. The helmet had a swastika badge and some other flashy insignia, so Boxer said that this was the very thing to take home to Pop in the Avenue.

He gave Bernard his gun and knelt down to unfasten the strap. Bernard watched him tolerantly, noting, with clinical interest, that the German officer lacked an eye and had gold fillings in his teeth.

At that moment there was a slight movement in the passage beyond them and Bernard looked up just in time to see a grenade roll into the room.

He screamed: "Watch out, Boxer!" and flung himself sideways, behind an up-ended table. There was a roar and a bright orange flash as the room disintegrated. Bernard was instantly half-buried under fragments of splintered planks and shattered furniture. The heavy pine table saved his life and in seconds he was on his feet again.

He turned his head to the right where Boxer had been kneeling but Boxer was gone; so was the dead German; so was the righthand wall.

Automatically he reached for his knife and at that moment a German soldier suddenly appeared in the ragged gap that had once been the door to the passage. He was a small, thin-faced man, and was holding both hands above his head.

Bernard blinked at him, his will-power consciously resisting the enormous weight of knowledge that Boxer was now dead, blown to pieces by this little snipe's grenade. He knew this to be so, but his mind fought and fought against it, for he was aware that, once it was fully acknowledged, his own life would be meaningless.

For perhaps three seconds the two men faced one another. Then, reading certain death in Bernard's eyes, the little German changed his mind and turned to flee.

He had moved but three strides when Bernard was upon him, leaping high on to his shoulders and bringing him down with a crash on the exposed joists of the passage floor. Here Bernard's knife rose and fell a dozen times and with each stab he made a queer, strangled sound, half grunt and half whimper.

The man was dead after the second stab but Bernard continued stabbing for almost half a minute. Then he jumped back and staggered into the space that had been the main room.

His eyes, bloodshot and smarting, narrowed to blue slits that peered here and there among the splintered planks and shreds of floor-covering. Down the street the whistle blew, shrilly and insistently this time, but Bernard did not hear it. He remained quite still beside the table top, his hands hanging down by his sides, the German's blood soaking his cuff, the knife still held in the stabbing grip.

He tried to call out but his throat was so dry and constricted that no sound emerged from his lips. Then, from close at hand he heard a whistle, not the recall signal but a human whistle, warbling a familiar stave.

He spun around and his eyes searched the disordered area immediately beyond the remains of the timber wall for it was from here, where the rubble was higher than himself, that the whistle seemed to come.

He cocked his ear like a terrier and suddenly he shouted with joy and agonising relief, for he recognised the stave as *their* tune 'Everybody's Doin' It', the tune they had whistled so often as they strolled down the Avenue in search of routine entertainment, a game of string-and-parcel, or knocking-down-ginger.

In two bounds he was beside the rubble heap and tearing away at the loose planks and plaster. First Boxer's boot emerged, then his knee, bare and bleeding, and finally, from under a window-frame, his wide mediaeval clown's grin, splitting his grimy face from ear to ear.

He said:

"Wotcher, Berni? Did you get that bastard?"

Tears were coursing through the dust and grime coating Bernârd's face but their flow relieved the remorseless thump of his heart. He licked his lips and tasted the salt.

"You . . . you okay, Boxer?" he managed to croak, at length, "you okay?"

"I dunno! I reckon so," said Boxer, and he prodded himself here and there as he struggled free and stood beside his brother, "I seem all right . . . bit of a cut on the knee but that's bugger all. How about you? You okay, Berni?"

Bernard nodded. "It's a bloody miracle," he said, "an absolute bloody miracle!"

Then, surveying the scene with a professional air, "I reckon it was the flimsiness of the place that did it. If it had been a brick house we'd have had it, the pair of us!"

"Ah, we oughter have looked," said Boxer, "we oughter have given the place a proper going-over, before we started mucking about looking for souvenirs. Just shows you Berni, just shows you! It's a pity about the helmet tho'! It was a corker that one, and old Pop would have liked it! Just a minute tho', what about the Jerry who lobbed at us? He'll have a helmet! Where is he, still inside?"

Bernard nodded but when Boxer made as though to move into the passage he suddenly reached out and grabbed his twin's arm.

"Oh, sod the souvenirs," he said, "leave that poor basket be, and find something down near the wharf. And *come on*, we got to get moving!"

Boxer did not argue for he never argued with Bernard, not once a decision had been made. All their lives it had been that way, Boxer making the proposals, and Bernard making the decisions. They found their weapons and clambered over the wreckage into the street.

The snow was a yellow slush beneath their feet, and the air was full of pungent woodsmoke and the reek of cordite. The firing had ceased altogether now and in the direction of the fiord they could see men moving along slowly in groups of three, each outer pair supporting a man in the middle.

Here and there, sprawled in the snow, lay still figures,

about three dozen of them and they stopped at each dead commando to collect paybook and identity disc.

They found their corporal awaiting them impatiently at the end of the town.

"Put a jerk in it, fer Christ's sake!" he said. "Is anyone else back there?"

"No," Bernard told him, "only the stiffs."

"They put up a pretty good show," said the corporal reluctantly, "but half our casualties were with that bloody smoke bomb we copped coming in! It fell smack into a landing-craft! Can you beat that? The R.A.F. dropping the ruddy smoke-screen *on* us, instead of in front of us?"

Bernard had noted the incident. He was a fair-minded young man.

"The poor sod was hit by ack-ack," he said, "and his kite was out of control!"

"Your brother looks as if he'd copped a basinful," said the corporal cheerfully. "Is he okay?"

"He's okay," said Bernard. "We were jammy!"

They formed up and moved off towards the jetty. Bernard was thinking: "That Jerry had his hands up but I fixed him simply because I thought he'd killed Boxer. I'm sorry now because he did have his hands up but what the hell? He threw the grenade first and surrendered after! You can't get away with a thing like that, not on this sort of lark! Besides, I thought he'd killed Boxer. I *still* can't understand how he didn't kill Boxer!"

The roar of the grenade still sang in his ears and he felt wretched and light-headed. His mind continued to revolve around the miracle he had witnessed and he thought: "Perhaps this means that nothing can kill Boxer, not while I'm around anyway! There was that icy pond! He was dead when I fished him up. Then there was that crash, the night of the Harringay match. He was as good as dead then in the pile up. Then there was just now—a ruddy grenade, exploding right beside him, and blowing him clean through a wall! I know what! He's bloody well indestructible!"

Suddenly his spirits soared, lifted on the conviction that Boxer was imortal, as long as he, Bernard, was still around.

He watched Boxer fall out and bend over a body in the slush.

"What you got now, Boxer?" he called.

"Cap badge! It'll do to go on with," Boxer shouted, adding regretfully, "I'd have liked that helmet for Pop! It was a real corker, that helmet was!"

Bernard yawned and stumbled. Suddenly he felt tired, terribly tired and listless. He cocked a bloodshot eye at his twin, who was running across the slush to rejoin the column, and he saw that Boxer was as buoyant and cheerful as he had been when they had first piled into the landing-craft. His thoughts became fanciful again!

Funny that Boxer should have whistled that tune, when he was buried under rubble! Funny thing that, and kind of ghostly, as though, even had Boxer been dead, he was still able to attract his twin's attention and be resurrected, as usual.

CHAPTER XV

Spring Roundabout

THE winters seemed to be getting harder and the springs more reluctant ever since the war had commenced, in 1939.

The Avenue people could now look back on three wartime winters, all of them colder, longer and more dismal than any winter of the 'twenties' or 'thirties'.

It was not just the blackout and the general shortages that made winter seem longer and darker than usual. There was snow for evidence, snow that hung about for weeks under the dwarf walls, and piled up on the rubble heap that had been Numbers Thirteen, Fifteen and Seventeen.

To the train-catchers it seemed as though they had now walked through slush for months as they made their way to Woodside and Addiscombe stations and when they returned to the Avenue, after dusk, the east wind whipped them when they turned in from Shirley Rise and seemed to pierce their clothing, whether they wore good quality garments, purchased before 1939, or the utility rubbish that outfitters were selling in all the shops nowadays.

Coal was poor quality too and very strictly rationed, so that it was not only Edith who made expeditions into Manor Wood in search of dead wood and kindling. Mr. Baskerville and his family went there regularly, pushing an old perambulator and returning loaded down with faggots. Jim and Harold spent odd afternoons in the thickets, cutting away at a fallen pine with Jim's cross-cut saw and the few children who remained in the crescent were always coming out of the wood with their sacks of twigs and fir cones.

Jim would have left the Avenue that spring had it not been for Harold. There was nothing much happening at the A.R.P. Centre. Air-raids over London seemed to have ceased altogether as the Luftwaffe pursued, what seemed to Jim, an idiotic policy of blitzing Cathedral towns in the provinces. 'Baedeker Raids' they called them and to his mind they were typical instances of Teuton stupidity, the shooting of Nurse Cavell, or the sinking of the *Lusitania*.

Jim toyed with the idea of getting a transfer into the Auxiliary Fire Service, and moving out to somewhere like Bristol, or Norwich but he held his hand, partly because he did not like to abandon Harold, and partly because, at any moment now, he expected to have to hurry off somewhere and give his daughter Judy away.

Judy was still stationed at Queen's Norton and Esme, halfway through a tour of operations, was stationed right up in Yorkhire, so that the two saw one another infrequently, and never seemed likely to remain together long enough to get themselves married.

To Jim the war seemed to have entered upon a kind of Western Front stalemate. Nothing very much seemed to be happening on the Allied side, apart from the monotonous bombing of rail yards at Hamm, or the even more monotonous 'elimination' of the German battleships *Scharnhorst* and *Gneisenau*, at Brest.

He had a bad moment when these oft-destroyed vessels escaped up the Channel, in February, and the R.A.F. and the Royal Navy were rumoured to have missed them on account of a stupid inter-service wrangle.

The Russian position worried him a little too, though not very seriously, for it was clear that his prophecy of the previous summer had been mainly fulfilled, and that the Wehrmacht was now bogged down in the Steppes.

He read the papers very carefully each day, looking for news of the Russian counter-attack that would sweep the Nazis back to the Pripet Marshes, but Joe Stalin did not appear to be in any particular hurry and Jim wondered if he too was awaiting the opening of the Second Front, the campaign that some of Jim's pre-war political colleagues were now demanding at mass meetings in Trafalgar Square.

He was not in the slightest bit worried about the ultimate outcome of the war, as he had been twelve months ago, before Russia was attacked and the British had met with one reverse after the other. All the same, it did seem to be developing into a leisurely war, and his own share in it bored him. He sat reading newspapers and drinking endless mugs of tea throughout his spells of duty at the A.R.P. post, wishing more than ever that he was twenty years younger and could join his twin boys in a Commando unit and have a real crack at the square-headed baskets!

The twins came home on leave after the St. Nazaire raid, in late March. Boxer brought with him a German gas-mask and a machine-pistol, to add to the cap-badge that he had brought home from Vaagso. Jim accepted these new gifts gravely but he was not really interested in souvenirs. He was much more actively interested in the information, passed on to him by Louise, that Bernard, the smaller twin, had now fallen in love.

It was curious, thought Jim, that Bernard should be able to fall in love without abandoning his chaperonage of Boxer, and even more strange that Boxer should accept the fact of Bernard having a girl without a display of jealousy or resentment. This, however, seemed to be the case, for Boxer now went off alone to the pub, while Bernard took long walks across Shirley Hills in the company of the sallow, solemn-eyed girl, whom Judy had brought home one day, explaining that she was the stepdaughter of Edgar Frith, Esme's former father-in-law, that her name was 'Pippa', and that she had come to London to make camouflage nets, at Beckenham.

Phillipa, or 'Pippa' as everyone called her, moved into Number Twenty as a lodger, in February, '42, and Louise took a fancy to her at once. This, thought Jim, was nothing much to go by, for Louise took a fancy to everyone. She even had a word or two to say in favour of Doctor Goebbels because, she said, the poor man had been born with a club foot!

Louise said that Bernard had fallen in love with Pippa and that Pippa returned his love. At first Jim found this difficult to believe, for Pippa seemed to him to be a mousey little thing, and not at all the kind of girl that he would have imagined Bernard might fall for. After he had watched them both for a day or two, he came to the conclusion that Louise was probably right, for Bernard, usually a phlegmatic young man, now seemed to be talking more than usual, and as he talked the girl listened, with her enormous brown eyes fixed upon him and her lips slightly parted, as though in breathless admiration. Jim did not pursue the subject very far. He had always found it very difficult to survey humanity individually.

In some ways the courtship of Bernard and Pippa was similar to that of Louise and Jack Strawbridge, in pre-war days. It was a very solemn, silent, take-it-for-granted affair, and had begun with a question on Pippa's part, continuing, from then on, a straight and uncomplicated course. As far as Jim could see it would lead, ultimately, to marriage, with Boxer as a kind of wedding gift to the bride.

Pippa had been living at Number Twenty for several weeks when the twins came home on leave but she had heard all about them from Judy. When they came trooping in from St. Nazaire she had an opportunity to watch them at close quarters and after a brief observation she suddenly button-holed Bernard in the back-garden and said, without preamble:

"Is it like having a baby who won't grow up?"

Bernard ought to have been shocked, or at least puzzled by such a question, but he was not, for somehow he recognised it as the remark of someone who had understood his lifework at a glance. It was the first time anyone ever had understood it, for until then everyone, including his family, had taken their relationship for granted. The mere fact that this girl had not done so at once recommended her to him as being an exceptionally intelligent person.

Until recently he had never felt the need to discuss his lifelong chaperonage of Boxer with anyone but after the incident of the grenade, at Vaagso, he did feel such a need. Indeed, it soon became urgent to him to confide in someone, and to get the relationship back into its proper perspective.

The thoughts he had been having just lately alarmed him, as though the roar and the flash of that grenade had loosened something in his head and encouraged the kind of speculation that belonged more properly inside the head of someone like Becky Clegg, the 'dippy sister', of Number Four!

Having decided that Boxer was indestructible Bernard now found himself wondering whether, in fact, he was really alive at all! It sometimes seemed to him that the real Boxer must have died at the bottom of the Lane pond all those years ago.

Bernard knew, of course, that this was simply a crazy fancy, that Boxer could be touched and seen, that he answered when addressed, and was in every way his old breezy, lolloping, harebrained self, but rationalisation of this kind did not help him to dismiss the thought that Boxer was really dead, or, at best, still a child, a kind of vivid materialisation of Bernard's picture of the man Boxer would have become had he been alive when fished from the bottom of the frozen pond.

It was because of these disconcerting fancies that the girl's question seemed to Bernard to be so logical. After all, he had been looking after a baby for twenty-odd years, and he found it very comforting that a complete stranger, such as this girl Pippa, should have recognised this after such a brief acquaintance.

He said, in reply: "That's it! That's what it's like and that's what it's always been like, right from the day he fell through the ice in the Lane!"

The girl nodded, sympathetically, though Bernard reasoned that she could not possibly know about the pond for they had never told anybody of the incident, not even Jim, or Louise, and they very rarely mentioned it to one another. It was something that had been sealed and packed away like a secret shame.

After this brief conversation Bernard wanted to see more of Pippa and the following Saturday he took her down the Lane, (still only half an Avenue, for all local building had ceased in September, 1939) to the spot where the pond had been.

Here he described the incident that had remained so vividly in his mind and the girl listened, without interrupting.

When he had finished all she said was:

"Perhaps he was meant to die then! Perhaps you interfered with something by bringing him back to life."

Bernard could hardly believe his ears. It was very uncanny and frightening that she should be able to read his mind as easily as that, but nevertheless he was drawn to her as he had never been drawn to any woman in the past. He felt certain that here, if anywhere, was someone who could help him and he was sure now that he needed help most desperately.

They went out into the Upper Road and on up the hill, past the Shirley Mill.

When they had reached the pebble slopes, where the old Bank Holiday fairs used to be held, he had made up his mind to confess.

"I think I'm going barmy," he told her, simply.

For answer she took his hand and led him along a path between the gorse thickets. At the top of the slope they stopped and sat down on a seat.

"Don't ever think that," she said, firmly, "and don't let anyone talk you into going to one of those psychiatrists they have in the army nowadays! There isn't anything wrong with you, Bernard. It's just that you've had to go through exactly twice as much as every other Commando! That's something you've got to understand, and make allowances for, right now!"

He discovered then that he did not want to leave go of her hand, for he felt that if he did his brain would burst, just like the grenade at Vaagso. He said shakily:

"All right then, you talk to me about it, Pippa, just go on talking to me about it!"

"It was all right in peace time," she explained. "Whatever you did for him then could be done without much strain, but it's so different now. Almost everybody's got as much to put up with as they can stand, without going mad! You've always been a very strong person, Bernard, but nobody's as strong as you're trying to be, and nobody could *do* the things you do, and then multiply it by two, every day!"

"I've never minded watching out for him," he said gruffly.

She had then to make a big decision. She had to decide whether she should try and explain that his endless, self-imposed guardianship of Boxer was simply the result of the pond incident and of the guilt he attached to it. That might help him but then again it might not, for it might even set him off into a labyrinth of half-baked speculation that would lead him straight to the medical people whom the soldiers called 'head-doctors'. Once there they would almost certainly treat him for the equivalent of what people once called 'shell-shock' and now called 'battle fatigue' and this would mean the end of his active service and an abrupt separation from his twin.

She did not think he could sustain the shock of such a separation, not, at all events, in his present condition, and she was determined not to confuse him with the little she knew of psychological treatment, being wise enough to know that her small stock of knowledge was hopelessly inadequate. What she wanted to do and what she yearned with all her heart to do, was to persuade him that his fancies were the result of months of physical strain, punctuated by short, murderous bursts of action, that he was not really sick but exhausted with the double burden he had been carrying for so long.

"It's like this, Bernard," she said, finally, "when you go back you've got to begin to relax, at least as far as Boxer's concerned! You've got to get used to letting him take his own chances, not only when you're fighting but at all other times, in camp and off duty. You've got to try and concentrate on looking after yourself for a bit and letting him learn to look after *himself*. If you don't you'll crack up and once that happens you'll be separated. Then he'll be on his own anyway. Do you see what I mean?"

"Aw, what does it matter, anyway," he argued but, without letting go of her hand, "I daresay we'll never get through, neither of us! We lose half our mob every time we go out!"

It would have astonished Boxer to have heard Bernard talking like this. Until then the war had always been such glorious fun and a show like Vaagso something to which they had looked forward. How was Boxer to understand that Bernard found it impossible to forget the shuddering shoulders of the little German who had tried to surrender after throwing the grenade.

Pippa said: "I think you'll come through Bernard because I think you've got the other half of your life to live. I think if you want that half enough you'll have it given to you but if you don't you won't. You see, you haven't really begun your own life yet but when you do you'll need someone to share it, because you've been so used to sharing that you wouldn't have any use for a life on your own. . . . When you remember that you'll come looking for me, and I'll be here, and we could be very happy together, because I love you and I'll always try and look after you the way you've looked after Boxer!"

She had made up her mind to say more. She was going to be quite ruthless and tell him that he would find no release until Boxer was dead, but suddenly his head was against her breast and he was sobbing, so that there was no point in saying more and she could only hold him there, soothing him, as though he was a child who had been desperately frightened and had run to her for help and comfort.

They remained still a long time but presently, when he was calmer, she inclined her head and softly kissed the short, fair hair on his neck.

He did not move when an elderly woman pedestrian walked past the seat and stared curiously at them. Pippa met her glance defiantly and the woman, suddenly embarrassed, looked away and quickened her step.

With hands coarsened by contact with miles of camouflage netting Pippa began to stroke his cheek. It was then that she saw, with wonder, that he was sound asleep.

* * * *

Archie had succeeded in talking his way out of the situation arising from his disposal of the gin and whisky, sold to him by the obliging Mr. Swift.

It is difficult to decide who was the more surprised by this, Archie, himself, or his lawyer, Mr. Roland Yelland-Parkes, of Parkes, Follett & Co. This was a firm to whom Archie had given much business in the past and who owed him, he felt, loyalty to the point of willingness to perform legal acrobatics.

Mr. Yelland-Parkes appropriated to himself most of the credit for the acquittal and Archie was too tired, and far too relieved, to begrudge him the credit. Probably honours were even, for while Mr. Yelland-Parkes took every conceivable advantage of the smallest fissures in the prosecution's case, it was Archie's brilliant performance in the witness-box that made the decisive impression on the jury, a jury that included two women, both housewives, and both over forty.

At the original hearing Archie took his solicitor's advice and elected to go to Quarter Sessions and be tried by jury and when it came up the case occupied the court the better part of two days. During the first day's hearing Archie had plenty of leisure to study the jury and determine the point of attack.

It was soon clear that the jurors had scant sympathy with Mr. Swift and his unlikely story of how he came by the goods featured in the indictment. His explanation was dismissed by them as an insulting fiction and Archie was not surprised, for Mr. Swift, heavy-jowled, lemon-eyed and pot-bellied, looked exactly like a current cartoonist's caricature of the black marketeer. He cut a pathetic figure in the witness-box and under cross-examination he lost his temper, said more than he had intended to, and ended in floundering. He was found guilty early in the second day's proceedings but because the cases were linked his sentence was postponed until Archie's had been heard.

The first part of Archie's defence was straightforward. He had been introduced to Mr. Swift by reputable wholesalers, whose names he obligingly supplied. He had purchased the cases of spirit in good faith and could produce a receipt (made out and back-dated an hour or so after the initial visit of the detectives) and the receipt was admitted as evidence, after a great deal of legal blather on the part of Mr. Yelland-Parkes and his learned opponent.

After that, however, the defence looked as if it had spent itself. As the prosecution was quick to stress, a man who has purchased two cases of spirits in good faith does not normally throw them into a pond on a dark night and do so, moreover, immediately after a conversation with detectives.

Archie met this challenge by facing it boldly and freely admitting that he had acted throughout like a hysterical fool. He was a much better actor than he knew and halfway through his testimony he began to gain ground. He dropped all his aitches and acted the part of a slow-witted, bewildered man, contrite and apologetic. He hung his head and several times hovered on the edge of a good, honest snivel.

"The fact is," he told the court, blinking his eyes to hold back tears of shame, "I was so overworked at the time that I 'ardly knew what I was doing! Fact is, I got into a muddle with my coupons and I'd been up, night after night, trying to make 'em come right! It's like this see, I try . . . well I try an' see everyone get their fair share and that's difficult when you . . . well . . . when you feel so sorry fer customers, especially the ladies, with big families. . . ."

He trailed off and glanced piteously at the nearest female juror, whom he had decided must surely be well acquainted with a grocer's difficulties in wartime.

Sensing his advantage he warmed to his work and stood up very well to his cross-examination, owning himself to be a fool, a hopelessly incompetent businessman, a soft touch, a stranger to simple addition, anything except a deliberate fraud. At one point his agony of self-abasement embarrassed the prosecution, for when he was asked, in crisp, pitiless tones, how he—as experienced grocer—could have been taken in by Mr. Swift's story of how he had acquired the spirits, Archie hung his head, and muttered: "I'm just a grocer, sir, not an educated man like you, sir! You see, I didn't get no schooling, not to speak of, on account of the last war! All me life, sir, I been getting diddled, sir!"

Mr. Yelland-Parkes, who had had the advantage of several long conversations with Archie, dropped his spectacles at this, but he recovered quickly, and nodded sympathetically when Archie returned to his errand-boy days and before being checked by the Judge managed to add a few, deft touches of colour to the outline of the narrative.

By the time the defence had been completed the jurymen, and certainly the jurywomen, were rather confused about Archie. He had been represented to them as being a slick, properous profiteer, a man who was gleefully battening on the country's agony and amassing a personal fortune by under-the-counter merchandising. He had been described, by implication, as a tradesman who, in his reckless pursuit of profit, was eager to consort with men like the wretched Mr. Swift and to buy rationed goods for resale at outrageous prices. The Archie they saw before them, however, bore no resemblance to this monster. He was an earnest, balding, browbeaten tradesman, tired to the point of a breakdown by the manifold difficulties of a wartime provisioning, and anxious only to make a clean breast of what appeared to be a childish act of folly on his part.

The jury was out for more than an hour and when they returned Archie was given the benefit of the doubt and Mr. Swift, who had a record, was sentenced to two years' imprisonment.

It might be imagined that Archie would be elated by his triumph, that it would restore to him his pre-war confidence in himself and send him out into the world taut and eager for fresh sallies into the haunts of other and more wary Mr. Swifts. Alternatively, it might be supposed that the margin by which he had missed accompanying his wholesaler to gaol would deter him from engaging in black-market activities, and he would now rest content on his legitimate and by no means inconsiderable profits.

In point of fact he followed neither of these courses, for as things turned out he was never given an opportunity to follow them. Mr. Yelland-Parkes, who was somewhat shaken by his client's virtuosity in the witness box, congratulated him rather hastily and departed, leaving behind him an impression that Archie would do well to find another firm of solicitors if he had need of one in the future.

So Archie drifted back to his corner shop and tried to pick up the threads of his businesses, lost during the anxious weeks preceding his initial hearing and his trial.

There was plenty to be done—staff to be sacked, new staff to be found, returns to be checked, coupons to be sorted, goods to be ordered, accounts to be examined, and heaven knew what else to claim his attention. For a month or two Archie tried hard to grapple with the complicated situation. He visited all his branches, sold off five of them, sat up over his ledgers until the small hours and generally made a strenuous effort to catch up with the clock. It was all in vain. Something had happened to him when those two lean men had loomed out of the dusk in the muddy lane down by the pond and he was now like a man trying to stem a torrent assailing a crumbling dyke. As soon as he had planted his feet and braced himself to hold out the water at one point it poured through at another, until at last he began to lose heart and seek relief in the bottle.

This (as he would have told you himself in the days before his nerve began to go) only made things progressively worse. He began to send wrong sets of papers to his accountant and make quick but ill-judged decisions on important issues. If Elaine had been at hand, and he could have relaxed now and again, he might have been able to pull himself together, but Elaine was far away in Cornwall, solacing a homesick Dutchman, and he found no relief in occasional expeditions to the West End, or in the arms of a shopgirl whom he succeeded in seducing. This last incident, indeed, ended humiliatingly for him, with the girl's brother committing assault upon him on the threshold of his Crowley Park branch.

As summer succeeded spring Archie began to grow desperate. In one last bid to sort himself out he suddenly disposed of all his remaining branches, except the Avenue shop, selling at a loss in order to be rid of responsibilities that threatened to drive him into an asylum.

For a month or so after this he wobbled along on a fairly even keel. Then the Inland Revenue representatives began to call on him and he was in no condition at all to take up their challenge but simply passed them on to his tame accountant, who settled for what seemed to Archie a fantastic sum of money rather than face court proceedings that might have been fatal to both of them.

Archie paid up but it cost him every penny he had in the bank. The night he wrote out the cheque he consumed a whole bottle of whisky and reeled off to bed still sober enough to remember, with gratitude, his iron rations in the oil-drums under the store.

He woke next morning with a throbbing head and a sour taste in his mouth, but he was accustomed to dealing with hangovers and set about vanquishing this one by holding his head under a running tap and swallowing pints of Alka-Seltzer and black coffee.

After a light meal he was much better, and felt more clearheaded than he had been for months.

He went up into the biggest bedroom overlooking Shirley Rise, the room in which his partner and father-in-law Toni had died watching the moon ride over the Lane elms, and began to review his position with something like his former detachment.

He was still, he told himself, several jumps ahead of most people, for he still had a sound, old-established business, and was done with the pestilential Inland Revenue for a spell. In addition, nobody of whom he was aware had got anything on him for under-the-counter wholesaling, whereas he still had capital, three large oil-drums full of capital! With this reserve, and the war still in full swing, he could always begin again, possibly in some other sphere, property perhaps, or government contracts of one kind or another. He would take a holiday first. God, how he needed a holiday! He would go down to Cornwall, and coax Elaine away from her Dutchman. That should be easy enough, with three oil-drums stuffed full of cash. They could go to Blackpool, where they had enjoyed themselves so much before this run of bad luck began, and after that he would set about making money again.

He got up, crushed out his cigarette, hitched his belt and almost ran down the wooden steps into his yard. In another moment he had the heavy doors of the store open and locked them behind him, and was moving the crates that concealed the trapdoor to the tiny vault.

The excavation was waist-deep and brick-lined. Archie had made it himself, acting upon the principles of those Elizabethan families who had constructed priests' holes on their domestic premises. The three oil-drums, two for the silver and one for the notes, stood in a row, buried under a litter of shavings and tissue paper that had once protected Jaffa oranges.

He jumped blithely into the pit but as he did so his foot glanced against the nearest drum. The hollow clang that resulted made him pause; he remembered that the drum containing the notes had stood furthest from the trap-door and there should therefore have been a *clonk* not a *clang*, from the drum he had kicked. Puzzled, he kicked it again and it rolled over, booming. He almost fell upon it, up-ending it, and shaking it in a frenzy of bewilderment.

It was empty and he flung it aside, reaching for the next drum but this too was empty! He flung it down, his brain recoiling from the implication, and braced himself against the sides of the opening for a moment, before projecting himself forward and falling on his knees beside the last and furthermost drum.

He tipped it towards him, twisted off the cap and squinted down into the hole, hoping against hope to see paper, wads and wads of paper. He saw only the yellow sheen of long-dried oil, for this drum too was empty!

Someone had been to the vault and eaten his iron rations!

For what seemed a long time he knelt there, telling himself over and over again that what was happening to him was only part of a nightmare, that, in a moment or two, he would wake up and find himself in bed, with the keys of his store on the bamboo table beside the bed.

Then his eye caught a dull gleam among the shavings near his right knee. His hand shot out and picked up an odd, shapeless lump of metal, about the size of a child's fist.

He looked at it in dismay and recognised it as a lump of half-crowns and florins, stuck together so firmly that they might have been welded. The exterior coins were a dull green and the gleam came from the milled edges of those in the centre.

He turned it over in his hands and the clammy feel of the metal restored him to reality. He knew now that this was not a dream, that he was actually here, in his own private vault, handling this ridiculous blob of coins that was all that remained of his reserve, the product of years and years of till-gleaning, dating right back to the day when he had opened his first sub-branch.

The enormity of the theft fogged his brain. There was no one, no one in the entire world save only his son, Anthony, who knew of the existence of this vault, and Anthony had landed in Egypt months before his father's last inspection of the drums. Apart from that, Anthony did not possess a key to the store, nor, indeed, did anyone but himself!

For a moment or two he considered the possibility of someone having spied upon him whilst he was visiting the vault but he soon dismissed this as an impossibility. Invariably, when coming here, he locked the doors behind him and there was no window or chink through which he could have been observed from the yard.

He did not see how the money could have been removed by human agency and although by no means a superstitious man the obvious alternative made him glance over his shoulder.

Finally he stood up and groped his way out of the hole and out of the store. His car was standing in the yard and he crossed to it and got in, leaving the store doors swinging open.

He sat for some minutes at the wheel, forcing himself to consider every possibility. Certainly not Anthony. Certainly not a casual thief. Then obviously someone who not only knew the whereabouts of the money but had access to the store and could enter without forcing an entry, traces of which must have remained.

He stared vacantly at the interior of the store in order to confirm this fact and it was then that he noticed a rusty hook, high up on the left-hand post of the door frame.

It was the place, he remembered, where old Toni Biretta had hung his store key during daylight hours. Toni had never taken precautions against thieves, for he had always lived on his premises and the risk of daylight robbery was therefore negligible. Every day, when he was passing in and out of the store, Toni had hung the key on that hook and every night, when he locked up, he had lifted it from the hook and carried it up to his bedroom.

In those days, therefore, there had been *two* store keys and one of the originals was now on Archie's key-ring. What then had happened to the other after Toni had died? Archie could not recall ever having seen it again!

As he thought this the entire situation began to clarify. Someone who knew about the money also knew about Toni's key, and that someone must have retained the key all these years, waiting and waiting for a chance to use it. . . . I

"*Maria!*"

He screamed the word as he flung himself out of the car. Maria had the key and Maria must have heard about the vault from Anthony, either by letter, or by word of mouth before the boy sailed for the Middle East! It was Maria who had robbed him, awaiting her opportunity, and probably watching him drive away from the house on one of his routine visits to the branches, or perhaps when she knew he was due in court and safely out of the way! Maria must have chosen this way to get even with him and it therefore followed that Maria must hate him with the vehemence that he reserved for the Inland Revenue, or the lean men who had caught him red-handed at the pond!

The more he thought about it the more certain he was of her guilt and of the pitiless treachery of the woman. The diabolical, Italianate cunning of her plot rose in his throat and almost choked him with fury. He ran into the yard, jumped into the car and reversed rapidly into the Avenue, almost colliding with Edith Clegg, who was walking along the pavement towards Number Four.

Without stopping to apologise, or to close either yard gates or store door, he roared into Shirley Rise, turned right at the junction and shot away towards Croydon and the Guildford Road.

He was heading for Somerset. He was going to get his money back if he had to beat Maria to a pulp to get it.

* * * * *

He never reached Somerset.

Once he had picked up the main coast road he felt a desperate need for a drink and stopped at a roadhouse, a few miles on his journey. He was well known at the pub and the barman, apologising for the house's lack of whisky, served him with two double gins.

Then Archie remembered that he had a half-bottle of brandy in the tool kit of the car. It was kept there for an emergency, just as his iron-rations had been put aside in the vault. He went out and found it and before starting up he gulped down the equivalent of half a dozen measures.

Then he set off again, leaving the built-up area at a steady fifty, his tyres screaming round the bends when he applied his footbrake, his body hunched over the wheel and his knuckles white with the intensity of his grip. About noon it began to rain but he did not slacken his speed. When the brandy bottle was empty he threw it over his shoulder into the space reserved for the folding hood.

He hardly saw the little cloud of cyclists, who emerged from a builder's yard at the entrance to the long, straggling village he swept through. He came tearing round a bend, his offside wheels a clear two feet over the white line and somebody on the pavement screamed. Archie, hearing the scream, automatically applied his brake, so that the big car skidded along the greasy surface, slewed round, and then went slithering forward at a barely reduced speed. It scattered the cyclists, spilling them in all directions, before shooting off at a fresh angle and crashing broadside on into a tall lamp-standard. Even this failed to stop it, for it glanced off the standard and finally came to rest in a shop doorway, missing two women shoppers by inches.

Archie himself was not seriously injured. The heavy car was coachbuilt and the chassis had absorbed the series of impacts. His head was cut open by the edge of the mirror and his knees by violent contact with the dashboard. They took him away in the first of the three ambulances. In the ambulance that followed were two of the injured, a cyclist and an A.T.S. girl, who had been struck by the falling standard. The A.T.S. girl died on her way to hospital.

Archie regained consciousness about an hour after they had stitched his wounds. The first thing he saw, when he opened his eyes, was a policeman sitting beside his bed, a pencil in his hand and an open notebook on his knee.

Archie stared at the policeman without speaking. He was fascinated by the hostility in the man's eyes.

CHAPTER XVI

End Of A Quest

THE day that Archie left hospital and limped down to attend the inquest on the victim of the crash, proved a notable one in the life of Jean McInroy, commercial artist, occupier of Edith Clegg's first-floor-front, and patient seeker of Britain's Ideal Male.

Many people along the Avenue, where Jean had now resided for nearly a decade, pitied Jean McInroy. They told each other that it was cruel that such an engaging and pretty girl should have her life blighted by a shocking impediment of speech, a defect that not only precluded marriage, but even prevented her from conversing with anyone who was unfamiliar with her disability and could not therefore be expected to understand her mumblings, and supplementary gestures.

It would have been much better, thought Harold Godbeer, and other kind souls like him, if Jean had been born deaf and dumb, for there was a certain dignity about a deaf mute that was altogether lacking in a pretty woman, with a deeply cleft palate. Most of the Avenue males were slightly embarrassed when they passed Jean coming out of Number Four, but they had all learned to smile at her, and raise their hats, and they were always rewarded by a shy smile acknowledging the gesture. No one except Edith however, went as far as to speak to her, but Edith had always had a way with the sick and disabled and after Jean had come to live with her, and Ted Hartnell had married and moved over to Forty Five, she was a mother to the girl, showering upon her the affection that had once been Ted's.

The Avenue's pity was largely wasted on Jean McInroy. She was not addicted to self-pity and the war that had brought misery and deprivation to so many people along the crescent brought Jean McInroy fulfilment in the person of Chief Officer Hargreaves, of the A.F.S., an organisation which Jean had joined in September, 1938, when she found herself unable to share Mr. Chamberlain's optimism.

In addition to possessing a very pretty face, a trim figure, plenty of Scottish common sense, and a sufficiency of talent with pens and Indian ink to earn a living illustrating advertisement copy and magazine stories, Jean possessed the rare privilege of being able to draw her dreams on paper.

For many years, prior to the outbreak of war, she had been steadily sketching her Ideal British Male, the solid, sunburned, pipe-smoking, home-making, rose-growing paragon of every domestic virtue in the glossies and the not-so-glossies, the man who looked equally attractive (but virile) in morning dress or bathing trunks, the man whose firm chin had been lathered by every brand of brushless shaving cream, the husband whose Empire-building eyes smiled at wife and kiddies from a kind of suburban Olympus, promising tenderness, fidelity and security to every woman who met his frank, manly, leave-it-to-hubby-darling gaze.

In the course of the last ten years Jean must have sketched thousands of Philips (she had always called him Philip and could never think of him by any other name) but it was not until war broke out, and she was attached as part-time driver to the local A.F.S., that she actually came face to face with him in the person of Chief Officer Hargreaves.

From that moment on her war-work became a pleasure. She drilled with fanaticism and once the blitz had begun, and she began to attend incidents in the company of Mr. Hargreaves, she soon distinguised herself by displaying a devotion to duty that earned her more than one citation in the official records.

She followed on the heels of Mr. Hargreaves like a faithful spaniel and when she became full-time, and Hargreaves needed a messenger, a driver, a tea-brewer, or a plotter, she was always the person selected, if only because she was at his elbow.

As time went on he began to notice her but in a vague and indeterminate way. When somebody told him about her cleft palate he went out of his way to be kind and considerate towards her, patting her shoulders and telling her she could leave early, or bringing her his cup to be washed and offering her a cigarette from his long, leather case.

She accepted these attentions shyly but never once pressed her advantage for she had discovered that he was unmarried and that his name was Philip, and she felt that these two coincidences had already marked him out for her. She was quite sure that if she bided her time then circumstances would surely arrive that would reveal her to him as his predestined mate. She was equally convinced that to do anything to hasten this revelation, would be unpardonable interference with the Divine Plan.

This childlike faith in Divine Justice came very easily to Jean. She was a tranquil, undemanding girl, reared on the Old Testament, and it did not seem unreasonable to her to believe that a God who could feed fugitives with manna, or cause water to gush from a rock, was also capable of steering her into the chaste embrace of the Ideal British Male, providing, of course, that she continued to play the game with God, and strove to be worthy of His interest.

She was nearly thirty now, however, and up to the time that she had joined the A.F.S. God did seem to be taking his time in the matter. It was not until she had sat through Chief Officer Hargreaves' first lecture on the use of a stirrup-pump that Jean's mind was set at rest and she knew that, sooner or later, something would happen to bring them together.

Sure enough something did happen and in the matter of Jean and her Ideal Male God ultimately behaved very well indeed, even going so far as to perform a small miracle in order to establish their relationship on a permanent basis.

Philip Hargreaves demanded even less of life than Jean. For years now he had shared a semi-detached house at Wickham with his elderly mother, and prior to entering the A.F.S. he had been manager of a small estate agency in Beckenham.

Such associations as he had formed with the girls that he met in his twenties and early thirties had not developed very far beyond the hat-raising stage, for long ago Philip had set himself a matrimonial target, and this target had never been reached.

Soon after getting his first job he had read somewhere that a man was foolish to marry on less than five hundred a year and because he was a very careful young man he had taken this advice to heart and had acted upon it.

Although his salary and commission had actually reached this figure in 1939 he was by then contributing two pounds ten shillings a week towards his mother's housekeeping purse, and he therefore considered he was still a hundred and fifty a year short of his target.

He was thirty-six now, still prudent, and much addicted to minute planning. He planned everything. If he intended using his Morris Minor on Sunday then he spent Saturday evening checking its tyres, water, oil, petrol and ignition. If he intended taking a holiday in August, then he booked his accommodation the previous October. Every detail of his life was planned in advance. The clothes he intended to wear on Monday were selected, and laid out in the spare room, before he undressed on Sunday night. He made long and detailed shopping lists for his mother and noted down the times when the shops were unlikely to be busy. He owned four pairs of shoes and chose a different pair every day, so that the soles of one pair were never more worn than any of the others. He was an excessively punctual man and had never been known to keep anybody waiting a single second. His preparations for everything that he did were made, as he was fond of telling people, in order to save time, but as his waggish brother Fred once remarked: "Phil never tells us what in hell he does with all the time he saves!"

Probably he used it to plan future economies of other people's time and efforts, and therefore his brother's supplementary opinion, that 'Phil was a bloody old maid' was unjust and abusive. Old maid or not he was a first-class fireman and his unit ran like clockwork.

The men and the girls at the depot put up with Philip's fussiness because they had seen him in action and had

learned to respect his coolness and personal courage. It might
have been argued that his coolness in action was merely the
result of minute planning, whereas his contempt for physical
danger was simply the evidence of a dull, unimaginative
mind. Young Simpson, his deputy, held this opinion, putting
forward the theory that Hargreaves was the kind of man who
collects a medal on the battlefield by walking straight up to
the enemy, demanding their surrender and getting it. Be that
as it may, Hargreaves was superb in action. He did not
flinch, or cower, or crawl because he was incapable of
imagining death or disablement. Other men got hurt, of
course, but usually through lack of planning. Nothing ever
happened to people who planned, and attended to detail.

. . . . .

It was Philip Hargreaves' addiction to long-term planning
that led to the temporary dispersal of his unit in the suburb.

Between the summer of 1941, and the spring of 1942,
there was little aerial activity in South London and having
brought his men and girls to a high pitch of efficiency during
the winter, Philip now found that their morale was being
adversely affected by enforced idleness.

He therefore sent a long memo to headquarters, suggesting
that part of his section should be converted into a mobile
reserve, ready to be rushed to any point in the country where
extra firemen were badly needed.

His memo coincided with the commencement of the heavier raids on the provinces and it was during the hammering of
Bristol that part of the local fire personnel, including Philip
and Jean, were sent down to the West for a tour of duty.

Here, in a terraced house in the battered suburb of
Bedminster, God performed his little miracle for Jean McInroy, of Number Four.

It began about eleven p.m., on the fourth successive night
that the area had been raided.

The unit was summoned to a short street off the Bath
Road, where a shower of incendiaries had started a serious
fire in a small biscuit factory, set in the heart of a thickly-
populated working-class district.

The blaze was promptly tackled and was soon under control, but before Philip judged it safe to move elsewhere, leaving a picket behind at the factory, a distraught man accosted him and told him that a child had been trapped in the basement of a half-demolished house a short distance down the street.

Philip directed him to the heavy rescue squad but the man was back almost immediately with news that the squad had its hands full two streets away; he begged Philip to send a couple of men to assist him in extricating the child.

The factory blaze was now well under control, so Philip called Jean and they hurried after the man, scrambling in single file over a tangle of hoses and debris and approaching the house by its short back garden. A hysterical woman met them in the alley and a man perched on the next-door fence called out:

"Watch out, guv! There's an unexploded bomb in there!"

Jean heard the warning but Philip, a few yards in advance of her apparently did not, for he scrambled over the rubble and at once entered the house through the kitchen window.

Almost immediately there was a long, dull roar and a blast wave that threw Jean flat on her back. The man close by tumbled off the fence but he reappeared almost at once shouting:

"Christ! I told him, didn't I? You 'eard me tell him, didn't you?"

For a few moments Jean was too dazed by the force of the explosion to understand what had happened. Men came running and a searchlight was turned on the back of the houses. As the dust settled horror overwhelmed her and she cried out, scrambling up and running towards the spot where the Ideal British Male had disappeared a moment before.

Other men appeared on the scene with more lights and somebody wearing a steel-helmet grasped Jean by the shoulder and shook her, demanding to know if anyone was inside the house when the explosion occurred.

"He was," she shouted, "*he* was! He was going in after a child . . . !" but he could not have understood her, for he kept repeating his question until she broke away and began to scrabble among the broken beams and bricks with her hands.

Others joined her and soon they were able to open up a hold that led into a small tunnel, formed by the ceilings and floor joists, supported by the stove and the big copper.

"Somebody can crawl in there, and look around," said the Warden, who had now taken charge. "Who's the skinniest round here?"

Before a volunteer could present himself Jean had dropped on her hands and knees and wormed her way into the triangular opening.

"You watch out, Miss," the warden called after her, "I can smell burning!"

Jean could smell burning too and saw that it came from some smouldering linoleum, half-screening the stove. The fumes made her cough and splutter as she crawled further into the house. In spite of a powerful beam, trained directly on the tunnel, she could see very little, for her body was blocking the small exit and the entire first floor seemed to have collapsed beyond the passage that led out of the kitchen.

She worked her hand down towards her thigh-pocket and dragged out her own torch, flicking it on and forcing her arm over her head so as to project the beam into the mass of obstacles ahead. Then she saw him, or rather his rubber thigh boots, projecting from beneath a joist so tightly wedged that it might have been cemented into the passage walls.

She tried to call, "Chiefie!", but the fumes of the smouldering linoleum caught her by the throat and she could only choke and writhe, her body full-length on the floor and her face touching the powdered plaster.

She lay still for a moment, unheeding the shouting behind her, seeing only the two upturned rubber soles less than a foot in front of her. When the spasm subsided she forced the beam of her torch to perform a half-circle and noted, about a yard to her right, a small space where she thought she might have room to rise to her knees and get her shoulders under the joist blocking the passage.

As she wriggled sideways she wondered whether his head was free beyond the obstruction or whether, like his knees and thighs, it was weighted down by rubble. The terrifying thought speeded her movements, and the rubble above her shifted slightly, squeaking and pattering as fresh trickles of plaster poured from above the joist, powdering her hair and half-filling her mouth with grit.

After that she moved more stealthily, drawing one leg after the other with infinite caution, until she reached the space and rose slowly on her knees, levering herself upward until her shoulders were straining against the edge of the timber.

The stench of the burning linoleum was now so pungent that she had the greatest difficulty in breathing and could only continue to do so by turning her head towards the exit. Forgetting that nobody would understand her she called:

"He's in here . . . I'm holding the roof . . . someone crawl in and take hold of his legs!"

The warden, who had been following her movements with his torch, called her gently: "Is there room? Can't *you* work him free?"

"No, no, I can't!" She was fighting hysteria. "Get that stinking lino out! Come in, quickly, quickly!"

Even had there been no impediment it is doubtful whether he could have heard and understood her, but he was an experienced and resourceful man and reached inside, dragging out the burning linoleum and then forcing his way into the narrow space beside her.

In the meantime, men outside were frantically enlarging the hole and when other men joined them they were able to pass back a hundredweight or so of bricks and mortar. Then, in the beam of their torches, she saw Philip's waist freed, then his chest, and finally his head.

When they eased him out into the open the rubble shifted again and the strain on her shoulders became intolerable. She dropped her torch, crying out and raising both hands to prevent the joist crushing her down to the floor.

The hole behind had now been further enlarged and the warden was able to crawl a little closer and take some of the strain. Together they managed to hold on until somebody passed through a billet, sliding it up between the warden's legs and wedging it under the joist at the instant of Jean's collapse.

The billet saved them both. They were seized and dragged

out feet foremost, to be laid on two stretchers that had been set down outside the hole.

When two men came to carry her away, however, she sat up, protesting.

"I'm all right . . . it's just my back. . . . What happened to Chiefie? What have you done with Chiefie?"

The man at her head grinned but said nothing beyond, "Relax, sister, relax!" as he lifted his end.

The man at her feet addressed his partner. "Lumme! I've heard o' perishing Sampson, but that there carry-on beats all, jigger me if it don't!" Then he smiled down at her as she sat up, steadying herself. "You ever tried all-in wrestling, Miss?"

She must have fainted then for she recalled nothing more until she found herself lying on a mattress, accepting a cup of Bovril from somebody.

She tried to sit up and ask after Philip again, but the effort made her sick and she was glad to lie still. Her shoulders felt as though they had been belaboured with an iron bar and her lungs seemed to be full of the fumes of that stinking linoleum and powdered plaster.

After they had washed her and given her another drink she slept, dreaming that she was looking out of the upstairs window of Number Four, watching Jim Carver's dog, 'Strike', run yapping under the wheels of a bicycle, ridden by Philip. Philip was wearing—heaven alone knew why—a *Wrinkless* support, like those she had been sketching to illustrate the advertisement copy of 'Trimfit'.

Jean was discharged from hospital in less than a week.

Her shoulders were raw and horribly bruised but there had been a large number of casualties in the last raid and the hospital was very short of beds. She was given a month's sick leave and a railway warrant back to London.

She did not use the warrant, preferring to remain in Bristol in order to see Philip on visiting days.

She found, when first admitted, that he too had had a very lucky escape. His right leg was broken, his collar-bone fractured and he had multiple minor injuries on chest and neck. They told her that he would be in hospital for at least a month and then asked her if she was a relative. She told them no but nodded when they asked her to write to his mother, whose address had been found on a label attached to Philip's identity disc. Jean did write to his mother and also to Edith, giving a brief account of what had happened and asking for a change of underclothes to be sent on to her hostel.

She spent most of her mornings sitting about in British restaurants, sipping tasteless coffee or drifting about the street, waiting and waiting for the visiting hour to strike.

On the first day that she was permitted to stay at his bedside for more than a few minutes, she showed him the gladioli and irises she had bought for him and watched the V.A.D. ease him into a sitting position, by manipulating the ugly pulley that supported his broken leg.

He seemed quite rational, except for the fact that he seemed to have forgotten about her inability to converse, for he began by asking her a number of questions about the technical side of the incident. How long had the section taken to get that factory blaze out? Was anyone else successful in extricating the child he had tried to rescue? Was their section likely to remain in Bristol, and if not would it go North or back to London?

She made no attempt to answer these questions, and had begun to blush even before the V.A.D., who had remained within call, started to wink at her in the strangest manner, and point meaningly to her ears.

Jean interpreted this as some kind of warning and looking at Philip she put a finger to her lips, indicating that he must not tire himself by talking too much. At this the nurse smiled approvingly and then jerked her head towards the other end of the ward.

Puzzled by this mime Jean left the bedside and walked down the ward towards the glazed swing doors, where the nurse was hovering.

"I forgot to tell you," she whispered, "he can't hear you, he's stone deaf!"

"*Deaf!*" murmured Jean. "*Deaf!*"

"Sister said it was blast," she added. "A bomb went off near him didn't it? He'll be all right apart from that, but he'll always be deaf. His ear-drums are perforated, both of them, poor chap!"

Jean looked back towards the bed and noticed that there was a certain vacancy in Phillip's expression. He was not looking at them but across at the patient immediately opposite. He seemed listless, so unlike the bustling, masterful Philip she remembered at the Fire Station, the man who never moved without a purpose, or turned his head to one side without knowing exactly what he was looking for at any particular moment.

The nurse lacked professional brusqueness and gave her time to absorb the shock of the news.

"We haven't told him yet," she said at length, "we were waiting until he's a bit better. He knows he's *temporarily* deaf, of course, so you'd better play along with us for a bit, there's a dear!"

She left her to answer a call from one of the other patients and Jean nerved herself to walk the short distance back to Philip's bedside. He smiled at her as she sat down, avoiding his eyes.

"They told me you saved my life," he said and she noticed that his voice was rather flat and toneless. "They told me all about it," he went on, "and I can't say that I'm that surprised. You're a good kid, Jean, one of the very best! I've written to H.Q. about it and I daresay it'll be in the papers sooner or later!"

She mumbled something in reply but still kept her eyes levelled on the floor. She heard him say:

"Of course I can't expect mother to trail right down here, so I wondered if you'd care to hang around and come here whenever you can?"

She was struck by the note of pleading in his voice, particularly when he went on: "You see, Jean, I don't know a soul in Bristol and it's very dull lying trussed up in this kind of contrivance all day!"

She looked up and nodded, her eyes full of tears. Then, without thinking at all about what she was doing, or what he would think, she caught up his hand and pressed it hard against her mouth.

He looked startled for a moment but then his pale features relaxed and he reached out with his other hand and gently stroked her hair.

"I say . . ." he faltered, "I say . . . *is* there anybody. . . ? I mean, well, when I get out of here, couldn't we. . . ? Supposing we. . . ?"

He was too overcome to be able to finish what he had meant to say. He had never addressed anybody in these terms before, this being the one occasion in his entire life when he had made a decision without a blueprint. As he watched her, however, even Philip was aware that no blueprint was need-ed, and that he had already said everything that needed saying. Presently she let fall his hand and bobbed forward, kissing him firmly on the mouth and ignoring the contemptu-ous snort of the old man in the next bed, and the amused glances of the row of patients on the other side of the ward, one of whom whistled in the way that she had sometimes heard young men whistle as she walked home to the Avenue on summer evenings.

. . . .

Jean and Philip were married three days after his dis-charge from Hospital and the section's departure for the Midlands.

By that time it was clear that Philip would never serve again in the A.F.S. In addition, his mother, who had gone to stay with her daughter, in Glasgow, wrote saying that she intended to remain in Scotland for the duration.

This unexpected news hastened the wedding and Jean, hearing that Margy Hartnell, of Number Forty-Five, was anxious to let her house before touring overseas with E.N.S.A., at once introduced her to Philip, who took the house and paid a quarter's rent in advance.

The details of the wedding were arranged by Edith Clegg, who had somehow managed to persuade Jim Carver to give away the bride.

"She's such a nice little thing, really," purred Edith, bub-bling with excitement at the prospect of yet another Avenue wedding, "and she hasn't a soul in the world, other than me!"

Jim protested that he hardly knew the girl but he let himself be talked into the job and turned up at Wickham Hill Congregational Chapel wearing his best navy-blue suit, the one he had purchased, ten years before, on the occasion of Louise's wedding to Jack Strawbridge.

The Avenue was well represented at the ceremony, for the *Advertiser* had recently published a quarter-column story of the happy couple's gallantry during the Bristol blitz. Harold Godbeer, in high collar and faultless grey cravat, represented Number Twenty-Two, and Jack and Louise Strawbridge joined Jim at the church.

Miss Baker, of Number One, was also present. Edith had seen to that by ordering an extra taxi 'with a driver accustomed to handling invalid ladies, please', and several families from lower down the crescent were there, including Mr. Westerman, the Avenue jester, Mr. Baskerville, the suburb's confidant of Joe Stalin, and all Mr. Baskerville's children, who brazenly defied the minister's ban on the use of confetti and danced with glee round the A.F.S. Guard of Honour, that lined the path when the couple emerged.

Mrs. Jarvis, of Number Six, was also there, and wrote an account of it to her son serving in Libya and so was Mrs. Hooper, of Number Six, and many others from houses nearer the Rec'.

Philip still limped rather badly and Jean was obliged to adjust her stride to his when they passed under the arch of firemen's axes, but this gave everybody time to remark how wonderfully pretty she looked, quite the prettiest bride, someone told Edith, that the Avenue had ever contributed to a local wedding.

Edith agreed, thinking that dear Jean looked just like a bride on the cover of one of those pre-war pieces of music that Ted Hartnell had left behind in the parlour of Number Four. Her eyes, she told Becky afterwards, shone like stars and her cheeks, under the Brussels veil that had been worn by Edith's grandmother nearly a century ago, looked like the petals of the cream roses that still grew in one or two of the Avenue's front gardens.

There was a modest reception at Number Four and Edith could not help remarking proudly to Jim that it was strange that she, an old maid, without a single niece or nephew, had now organised her third Avenue wedding in the space of ten years!

There were no speeches, apart from a brief expression of goodwill from Jim, and afterwards everyone trooped out on

to the pavement to watch Philip hand his radiant bride into
the taxi that was to take them to East Croydon, and thence,
by train, to Glasgow, where they were to pass a week-end
with Philip's relatives, before spending the honeymoon at
Oban.

Jean had once visited Oban as a child and had always
promised herself that she would honeymoon there.

As she leaned out of the taxi, to wave goodbye to the little
group round the gate of Number Four, Jim thought that he
had never seen anyone look so serenely happy and he commented on this to Harold who, because weddings always
reminded him of Eunice, seemed to be in low spirits as they
went into Number Twenty-Two to change.

"It's a curious thing," Jim remarked, "how unimportant
these disabilities are when it comes to the point. Take those
two! He's stone deaf and she can't get her tongue round a
two-syllable word without making everyone in earshot feel
sorry for her! Yet does it worry them? Either of them? Not a
jot, anyone can see that! Come to think of it, I've noticed this
before. I once knew a chap who had lost both his legs in a
factory accident. He started making pottery in his back-shed
and I never saw him when he wasn't on top of the world, and
making the rest of us feel damned ashamed of bellyaching
about trifles! It seems to me that you get a healthier perspective if you're deprived of something!"

Harold said nothing. He was remembering how enchanting
Eunice had looked in her little cloche hat at their wedding,
some twenty years before. Jim, however, had taken a drink
and was feeling very conversational.

"Take my eldest boy, Archie," he went on. "He's always
been a strapping great chap, with plenty of brains and never
a day's illness in his life, but what the hell has *he* done with
his life? Gets himself into one mess after another, and now
he's disappeared, put his shutters up and nobody knows
where he's got to. Take that girl that your boy, Esme, married! Good looks, good health and plenty of intelligence, but
what does *she* do with her life? Hawks her body from place
to place like a professional tart, and makes trouble, just like
my Archie, wherever she goes!"

Harold, however, was reluctant to be talked out of his

doldrums, so Jim left him and went off down the Avenue, ruminating on his neighbours as he passed their houses, and racking his brains for a theory that made sense out of their strivings and sorrows.

That afternoon the Avenue seemed to him to typify the bewildering muddle of life. Here was a lad like Albert Dodge, of Number Ninety-One, giving his life to blow up an Italian viaduct, and there a woman like Mrs. Crispin, of Number Fifteen, buried under the ruins of her home by a chance bomb that had been carried hundreds of miles through the sky by the German equivalent of young Albert Dodge! Here, thought Jim, were the people who were making the real sacrifices, the Dodges, the Crispins, the Hoopers, the Jarvises, and even the glum Friths, mother and son, who had been killed on their own doorstep.

Yet even here, in a little suburban Avenue, the sacrifices were monstrously unequal. A dozen houses in the crescent had been vacated on the first day of war and their owners were now far away, taking no active part in the struggle, but waiting for it to end before they returned and fell into step for the 8.40 again.

The same kind of thing, he supposed, must be happening in Russia, and even Germany. Some people were getting away with it and some were not. It was all a matter of luck, or the way the individual looked at things.

How would it end? What sort of future waited for a place like this Avenue when the final bomb had been dropped, and the last torpedo fired? Would the survivors inherit the new world that he had been promised in the trenches during the last war? Or would there be another decade or so of uneasy truce and industrial strife, before a third bunch of lunatics started it all up again, and deprived these people of their chance of finding a way through the difficulties that, come war, come peace, attended the seventy years or so they spent on earth?

He had to admit that he didn't know. There had been a time when he had thought that he did know, when he had believed that in Socialism he had an answer to humanity's woes, when he was convinced that all that was needed to build a Millennium, right here in Britain, was control of the

cartels and city speculators, and the public ownership of the
means of production.

In those days he believed in the integrity of everyone
earning less than three-fifty a year, in all the people who
caught the 8.40 and weeded their strips of garden at week-
ends.

He no longer had that kind of faith in Socialism, or any
other ism. Since the outbreak of war he had witnessed as
much greed and selfishness among the little people as he
expected of the profiteers. His own son, Archie, was typical
of those concentrating on grab, those who were seemingly
deaf, blind and indifferent to the responsibilities of Democracy. These people, the Archies, did not want freedom, certainly not the kind of freedom that Hitler and his associates were
trying to deny everybody; they preferred licence, licence to
enrich and indulge themselves, and it was nonsense to pretend that this preference was the prerogative of any one class
or income-bracket. It certainly began at the pinnacle, with
men who sat in comfortable city offices manipulating com-
panies and dividends, but afterwards it reached right down
into the Avenue, to people like Archie, who were not only
one's own class but often one's own flesh and blood!

Meanwhile, for those who did believe, for the mugs like
himself, and Harold Godbeer, for people like old Edith
Clegg, and that young starry-eyed couple who had just driven
off on their honeymoon, there was only one course to pursue—
to hang on and to hope, to stamp out militant Fascism on the
Continent, and then remain watchful for its revival in the
chaos that would surely attend the overthrow of the swastika.

Surely, Jim reasoned, that could not be so far off now?
Russia was roused, and America was fully committed; that
much at least was obvious from where he stood, in the
broad, winding path that led through the Rec' gates, for a
group of American GI's were playing baseball on what had
once been the football pitch, and they had attracted a group
of idlers, who stood watching a game that looked to Jim like
a hotted-up variant of rounders.

He joined the group and stood looking on for a moment,
noting that the ruins of the Rec' pavilion had been now

cleared and converted into some kind of American depot. Interested he moved nearer, recalling vaguely that he had heard his younger twins, Fetch and Carry, talk about the presence of Americans in the neighbourhood.

As he stood there somebody hailed him from the verandah of the new pavilion.

"Hiya, Pop!"

It was Carry, one of the twins, and he noticed, with slight irritation, that her jaws moved rhythmically up and down as she sprawled on the verandah seat, watching the game below.

Before he reached the pavilion Fetch, her sister, appeared, wearing a highly coloured apron, printed with the names of American states. Fetch's jaws moved too, in the same slow, circular movement, and the moment she saw him she called to somebody over her shoulder.

"Hi, Orrie! Mitch! It's Pop! Come an' say 'howdy!' It's my Pop! What-do-y-know 'bout that?"

Two G.I.s wearing khaki slacks lounged on the steps, one of them giving Fetch a resounding slap on her bottom as she passed. Jim regarded the quartette with dismay. His daughters seemed no longer to belong to him, or even to his country, but were now part and parcel of a transatlantic organisation that had been shipped in with jeeps, aircraft parts, and vast crates of chewing gum all draped in stars and stripes.

"What on earth are you two doing here?" he managed to say, as Carry introduced him to Orrie, the shorter, frizzy-haired soldier, and Fetch gave the taller, lantern-jawed man, ('Mitch' presumably) a return whack on the buttocks.

"We work here, Pop," Fetch explained, waving her hand towards the pavilion.

"Sure thing! Sure do!" corroborated Orrie; then, advancing, "Glad to know you, Pop! Kinda wonderin' when you'd show up, weren't we, Glam?"

"But I thought you worked over at Catford," protested Jim. "The last I heard you were waitresses, in the British Restaurant over there."

"That crummy joint?" exclaimed Carry turning to the others. "Get a load o' that, Fetch! Gee, Pop, we quit that flea pit a fortnight since! We met Orrie and Mitch at a U.S. hop, and soon as they knew we lived hereabouts they fixed us as waitresses in the canteen!"

"Orrie comes from Oregon, an' Mitch comes from Michigan," explained Fetch. "Kinda cute, don't you think?"

"Yes," said Jim, vaguely, "but why do we have to meet one another like this? Why not bring them home to supper tomorrow night? Louise would be delighted to meet them, I'm sure."

"You hear that, Mitch?" said Carry, laughing. "Pop wants to okay you! We go for that kind o' thing over here! Maybe he thinks you're kinda fresh, like I do!"

"Mighty nice o' you, mister," said Mitch, seriously, "but if we do come around I guess we'll hev to bring sumphn to help out."

"Bring something?" said Jim, "bring what?"

"Whatever's to hand, I guess," said the G.I. "It's like this, sir; our Top Brass is mighty perticular 'bout that! 'Don't none of you eat them pore bastards' rations!' he tells us, soon as we git here!"

"That's so, Pop," agreed Orrie, "we got it printed in a book, too! Take a looksee."

He extracted a small booklet from his hip-pocket and handed it to Jim. The brochure was entitled *'What to do and what not to do in Britain'*, and the sub-title read: *'A short guide for overseas enlisted men'*.

"That's extremely considerate of them," said Jim, smiling, "but you don't need to bring anything. We can run to a supper for allies, I guess."

"I guess!" Damn it, he thought, this clipped, outlandish jargon is catching! He grinned, shook hands and hastily excused himself, leaving the four of them to chew their way through the baseball game and discuss the impression that he had made upon the Americans.

"Nice guy," said Orrie, "but kind of educated! You never said your pop was a college man, Glam."

"I don't think he was, was he, Fetch?" said Carry.

Carry said no, she didn't think he was, but ever since she could remember Pop had spent most of his time addressing meetings, and reading piles of dull-looking books, so perhaps that accounted for the way he spoke.

Jim left the Rec' and returned to the Avenue. He was half-alarmed and half-amused at the chance encounter. He told himself that, as time went on, and he grew older and older, he began to understand less and less about the world he lived in.

* * * *

Orrie and Mitch came to Number Twenty for supper on the following evening.

Despite Jim's protest they brought with them a small sack of American canned goods and a large cardboard box, full of extravagant confections that they described, collectively, as 'candy'. This they presented to Louise, for whom the chief sacrifice of total war had been the strict rationing of sweets.

Jim, who came in with Harold about seven o'clock, had anticipated a dull evening and attended only because he considered it was his paternal duty to inspect the Americans at close quarters. His encounter in the Rec', had left him with an impression that the two Americans, the very first American soldiers he had met in this war, were a pair of boisterous extroverts, with whom he had little in common, beyond perhaps, a mutual antipathy for Nazis and Japanese warlords.

He was surprised, therefore and also somewhat nonplussed by Mitch's outspokeness on the conduct of the war up to the time of America's entry.

It seemed that Mitch, the unsmiling, lantern-jawed soldier, (who, so far as Jim could determine, favoured Fetch) had a poor opinion of British strategy as a whole and his views, which he went out of his way to declaim, immediately put Jim on the defensive.

Jim's view of American participation in the conflict was typical of the view taken by the Avenue as a whole. Everyone living in the Avenue resented America's claim to have won the first war, although Jim, as a front-line soldier, had never underestimated the part the Americans had played in the final offensive of 1918.

The few American soldiers he had run across in France he had rather liked and he was fully prepared to welcome those who had now appeared (very tardily to his way of thinking) to assist in vanquishing Hitler.

He was not, however, prepared to admit America into allied conferences as a senior partner—Russia perhaps, but not America, for Uncle Sam had failed democracy, and that almost fatally, by failing to join the Allies in 1939!

Harold shared these views but with a single reservation. What he did not share was Jim's enthusiasm for Cossacks, Joseph Stalin, girl-snipers and the partisans of the unending Steppes. Like Miss Baker, of Number One, he found it very difficult to shed the distrust of half a lifetime, and Red Russia was the one topic that he and Jim had learned to avoid, for fear it should provoke a serious quarrel.

Jim had resigned himself to Harold's distrust of Russia, writing it off as the result of years of ruthless propaganda by a capitalist press. Harold, on the other hand, easily persuaded himself that Jim's militant partisanship of Russia was merely a hangover from his friend's twenty-year championship of the underdog. It was thus sadly dated and belonged, properly, to the days of pogroms, smoking-bombs, and chain-gang migrations into Siberia. Both men were secretly sure that time would ultimately reveal the truth and convert each to the other's way of thinking.

When the unsmiling American began to inveigh against British military inefficiency, however, the neighbours promptly closed their ranks. Mitch, who had hardly given global politics a thought until the Japanese struck at Pearl Harbour, seemed to have made up for lost time by reading millions of words written by American war commentators. He had a capacious memory and sought to confound his hosts with strings of dates and figures, each dealing with the sorry progress of the war to date.

"You guys have been balling everything up by pulling your punches," he told them. "For crying out loud, mister, look at your North African campaign, in the fall of '40! You go for the Eyeties and scoop a cool hundred thousand of 'em into the bag! You get within spittin' distance of Tunis! Then what do you do? For Pete's sake, what do you *do*? You pull out and ship every man and every goddammed gun you got over to

Greece, and stand by while the poor guys get pitched into the Med by the Krauts!"

"That mightn't be very good strategy, I'll admit," said Harold, biting his lip, and checking Jim's retort by a prim, little wave of his hand, "but we British happen to be fighting this war for honourable reasons, and our government had given an undertaking to Greece that we would come to her assistance at once if she was attacked!"

"That's about it," added Jim, giving Harold a mental pat on the shoulders. "Over here we always try and honour our pledges, even if the maintenance of a pledge is temporarily inconvenient!"

" '*Temporarily inconvenient*'!" exclaimed Mitch, not at all impressed by Harold's line of defence. "Brother, it wasn't inconvenient, it was suicidal as far as you Limeys were concerned! Why, you lost your whole outfit didn't you, besides getting slung out of Crete and pushed back on the Gyppos! What sort of way is that to fight a war? You guys are still wearing kid mitts! You gotter learn to mix it, no holds barred! Take your bombing in Germany. . . !"

"What's wrong with the R.A.F.?" growled Jim. "Haven't they been knocking hell out of Germany's war potential?"

"Sure they have, sure mister, *by night*!" retorted Mitch. "What in hell's the use of plastering Krauts by night, when you can't see where you're hitting 'em? We're going over in daylight from now on and brother, are you going to see the dust fly!"

"Well, I'm very glad to hear it," said Harold, resignedly, "and as far as I'm concerned the oftener the better! But don't overlook the fact, old man, that until Russia came in we were tackling this job alone!"

Jim felt he could have embraced Harold on the spot and he cocked an eye to see how the American would accept the rebuke. Mitch certainly increased his rate of his chewing but apart from that shrugged it off quietly enough.

"Yeah, I guess that's so, feller, but you been getting a steady flow of war material from us ever since the startin' pistol!"

"Yes," said Harold gravely, "I suppose we have, but I don't think we *should* have done, if it hadn't been for

Roosevelt! Tell me now, are you a Republican or a Democrat?"

The American looked surprised. "Say, you're the first guy to ask me that over here!" he exclaimed. "I voted Republican ... I guess our family have always voted Republican."

"Ah," said Harold triumphantly, "then it looks to me as if we should have gone short of war material if your party had been in office!"

"Heck," said Mitch, "don't get me wrong, brother! We're *all* rootin' for you over there, and we have been, right from the start of it!"

"I don't doubt it," said Harold, "but cheering from the touchline wasn't very much use while the Nazis were swarming all over Europe!"

Mitch looked at Orrie for inspiration, but all Orrie said was: "This guy's sure got something," and then, enthusiastically, "Whatsay we quit chewing the fat an' put the radio on? You can get a swing programme round about now. It's pretty corny but I guess we could jive okay if we moved the furniture back!"

"Move anything you like! Make yourselves thoroughly at home," said Jim, grateful of the excuse to go next door and hold an inquest on the Americans, in the company of an Englishman whose quiet thrusts had seemed to him much more lethal than the bluster of public-house patriots.

The girls came in from the scullery, where they had been helping Louise to wash up, and to stack away the remains of the American bounty on half-empty larder shelves. It was a fine, clear evening and they opened up the French doors that led to the tiny verandah.

Orrie fiddled with the knobs of the radio until he found a wavelength that seemed to satisfy him. Then they pushed back the furniture and began to dance, "whooping it up", Fetch said, and seemed to be thoroughly familiar with steps that Jim had never seen anyone dance in the past.

Jack Strawbridge, smoking a Lucky Strike in the kitchen, watched them stolidly through the open window and Mrs. Hooper, from Number Six, heard the clatter and laughter seven doors away, and crept along the alley behind the gardens to see what was going on.

Safe in the kitchen of Number Twenty-Two Jim and Harold sat over a freshly-brewed pot of tea and discussed the American invasion.

"They've got a damn sight more bounce than I can stomach," said Jim, "and I'm glad you put that fellow in his place!"

To his surprise, however, Harold refused to enjoy his moral victory.

"We shouldn't argue with them, Jim! After all, they're over here to help us, and we ought to go out of our way to make them welcome!"

"My daughters seem to be taking care of that side of it," said Jim, grimly. "Just listen to 'em in there—'jiving' they call it! Like a bloody lot of savages celebrating a victory in the jungle if you ask me!"

Harold chuckled. "Ah, we're getting old, Jim," he said, "and I daresay we're getting left behind. I don't think they're bad chaps, in spite of their cockiness. After all, they can afford to be cocky. They've got all the money and we're absolutely dependent on them unless we want the war to drag on for the rest of our lives!"

"All I can say is, they might give us a bit more credit for sticking it out so far," grumbled Jim. "I'd like to know what sort of show America would have put up after Dunkirk, or during the blitz!"

"That isn't the way to look at it, Jim," said Harold, and as always Jim felt himself soothed, almost against his will, by this little man's homespun logic.

"Here's a family—Britain—up to its eyes in debt, and facing eviction! Along comes a rich uncle, Uncle Sam, and agrees to square up and give us a fresh start. Can we blame him for pontificating a bit, and letting us know that we're lucky to have him around? That's only human nature, Jim, and you can neither wonder at it nor grouse at it!"

"Damn it, don't talk as if they come in out of bigness of heart, man," argued Jim. "They wouldn't be here at all if the Japs hadn't kicked 'em into it at Pearl Harbour!"

"I don't care *why* they're here, Jim," pursued Harold, stirring his tea with the slow sweep of his hand that Jim had noticed during their innumerable sessions over this table. "I

only care that they *are* here, and that their being here means
that Hitler can't possibly win! That way we'll all get a second
chance and make better use of it than we did in 1918, I
hope!"

They went on to talk of other things, of the constantly
postponed wedding of Esme and Judy, who were still making
frantic endeavours to coincide a week's leave from their
respective airfields in Northamptonshire and Yorkshire; Boxer and Berni, now in training for the next show, that might
be the Second Front everyone was expecting; of Louise's
sallow, silent girl-lodger, Pippa, who was getting a stream of
letters from Bernard, a boy who had hardly put pen to paper
before his last leave, in April.

Next door the girls and their G.I. friends were still
'whooping it up'. They were dancing and singing to a chorus
beginning *'Praise the Lord, and pass the ammunition'*, and
their voices rang over the darkening Nursery, where Jack
Strawbridge had been digging for victory all spring and was
making a market-garden out of what had been a wilderness.

"Thank God I'm going on duty," said Jim, finally. "I don't
know how you can expect to get a wink of sleep with that
din going on! Shall I tell them to pipe down?"

"No," said Harold, "let 'em enjoy themselves while they
can. They're like young bears, Jim, with all their troubles
before them!"

"Don't you believe it, Harold," rejoined Jim, with a tired
grin, "Look at us, were into our sixties, at least, I am, and
you're not so far off, yet it looks to me as if there's just as
much trouble in front of us as there is behind!"

He stood up and lit his pipe, puffing at it meditatively and
looking up at the coral and purple sky beyond the saw-
toothed silhouette of Delhi Road.

"It's funny," he mused, "I remember the day I came home
here from Cologne. It was in the spring of 1919 and those
two youngest kids of mine were parked out somewhere
because the wife had died in the 'flu epidemic. I hadn't even
set eyes on 'em then. They were born on New Year's day,
and having 'em helped kill the missus, what with one thing
and another! I never thought that by the time they were
twenty-three we'd be halfway through another bloody war!"

"None of us did," said Harold, "but I'm glad we are all the same, because this war isn't like any other war, Jim. I never thought it was, and I still don't think it is! I don't believe this is a war to end war. That's a bit too much to hope, but at least it's a war that we couldn't avoid fighting if we were to have any hope in the future. I think people will come to realise that in the end and if they do, then it might have served its purpose in the end!"

He yawned and began to carry the tea-cups towards the sink.

"Here, leave those old chap," said Jim, "I'll do them before I go on duty. You get some sleep if you think that's possible."

Harold accepted his offer and smiled.

"All right. Good night, old man."

"Good night," said Jim.

Harold went slowly upstairs but Jim remained puffing his pipe for a moment and looking out over the nursery. The noise next door had subsided somewhat and from the other side of the fence came the soft strains of a vocal number, Vera Lynn singing about a nightingale she had seen in Berkeley Square. The melody seemed to have sobered the quartette, for presently Jim heard Carry say: "I like that number! I think it's a honey!"

"Sure is," Orrie agreed, "kinda gets you, like one o' Bing's. Where in hell is this place 'Berkeley Square'? Is it hereabouts?"

"Well, it's not far," Jim heard Fetch say. "We'll take you there when we go up West."

Jim smiled at the phrase 'up West.' It was so Cockney and so dated. His wife had always liked to go 'up West' on Saturday afternoons, and Edith Clegg still talked of 'going up West' whenever she intended to look at the shops in Piccadilly or Regent Street.

He pulled himself together, shook out his pipe and passed through the house into the Avenue, forgetting his promise to wash the cups.

The moon was riding high over the blurr of Manor Wood, a wood, so Orrie had told him, that would soon be the site of an American transport depot, with its headquarters in the old mansion.

A sense of peace and tranquility descended on Jim as he walked along the Avenue towards Shirley Rise.

The war, he reflected, was now almost three years' old and practically everybody in the world was drawn into it, just as they had been involved the last time. Harold was right, however, there was only one end to it, and ultimate victory for the Allies was now an absolute certainty.

Jim felt that he had acquired his second wind and could await the end with equanimity.

CHAPTER XVII

Edith Returns To Olympus

THE unexpected marriage of Jean McInroy precipitated another minor financial crisis at Number Four, where Edith Clegg had for some years depended on lodgers to supplement her slender income.

She was, however, well accustomed to these crises by now. She had weathered half a dozen since the day, soon after the end of the First World War, when her bank manager had pointed out to her that Parson Clegg's legacy was insufficient to maintain his two daughters in a world of steadily rising prices.

That had been the day she had decided to give music lessons, and to let her front bedroom, the day she had advertised for a boarder and attracted Ted Hartnell.

Later on, when Ted had been sacked from the stonemason's yard, and was out of work for a long time, she had found a new source of income as pianist at the Granada Cinema, in the Lower Road but she was ousted from the tiny orchestra pit by Al Jolson's Sonny-Boy. Then Ted had become well known as a jazz drummer, and had got married and gone to live over the road, which meant that his room had to be let to Jean McInroy, but now the room was vacant again and the budget of Number Four was down by thirty-five shillings a week.

Whenever she needed practical advice Edith sought out Jim Carver, a man for whom she had harboured an enormous regard dating from a winter's day, in 1920, when he had escorted her to the Abbey in order to pay her respects to the Unknown Warrior.

Edith now pointed out to him that the care of poor Becky was costing more than she could afford, and that the cost of running Number Four was eating into her limited reserves. Jim advised her to make another bedroom out of the parlour, and let both her main bedrooms to American officers, from the depot in Manor Wood. Accommodation in the suburb, he said, was very limited now, and he was sure that she would have no difficulty in finding a couple of regular boarders. American officers, he added, would eat in their mess and Edith would thus be under no obligation to stay home and cook for them. She might even get a part-time job, as there were plenty going nowadays.

Jim gave his daughter's friend, Orrie, a slip of paper advertising Edith's vacancies, and in due course two officers presented themselves, Major Leonidas Sparkewell and his middle-aged adjutant, Lieutenant Ericssohn. They moved in without any fuss, and in the months ahead they proved as satisfactory as Edith's previous lodgers, coming and going quietly about their business, and occasionally supplementing Edith's rations with gifts of tinned soups and candy.

Edith, liked the Lieutenant rather better than his younger superior, of whom she was a little afraid. He breathed hard through his nose, reminding her of Billy Bones, in *'Treasure Island'*, and whenever he stood aside to let her pass in the hall or on the stairs, she noticed that his breath smelled very strongly of liquor. Saul's breath had smelled like that when he had come courting Becky long ago, and perhaps it was because of Saul that Edith could not rid herself of a distrust of men who smelled of liquor, but she told herself that this was very unfair on Major Sparkewell, who always behaved towards her like a perfect gentleman, and even called her 'Mam' as though she was royalty.

The Major was a big, uncommunicative man, but in one of his rare confidences he told her that his adjutant, the lieutenant, was 'lousy with dough'. She discovered, after confiding in Jim, that this did not mean that he suffered from some obscure illness, but simply that he had plenty of money and was not dependent on his army pay.

The Lieutenant was a great contrast to the Major. He was slight, balding and at least ten years older than his superior. He wore rimless spectacles, and spoke with what Edith later discovered to be a rich, Southern accent.

Lieutenant Ericssohn was much more talkative than Major Sparkewell.

He came, he told her, from Carolina, where slaves had once worked on the plantations, and where they composed the songs that she, Becky and Teddy used to sing at their evening soirées round the cottage piano. This information interested her very much but she gathered that, prior to his enlistment after Pearl Harbour, Lieutenant Ericssohn had not been engaged in the planting of cotton but the more prosaic occupation of planting timber.

He was shy, courtly and inclined to blush, not at all like most of the Americans whom Edith saw crossing the meadow all that summer. Most of these soldiers looked untidy, yet happy-go-lucky, with their toadstool helmets, worn low on their sunburned faces, their unzipped windcheaters, and the everlasting rotation of their jaws.

Jim told her there were now hundreds of thousands of Americans in the country and that they had come here to prepare for an all-out attack across the Channel. She was a little intimidated by their raucous good humour and constant horseplay, but she went out of her way to smile at each one that she passed in the Avenue. They always smiled back and sometimes said: "Howdy, mor!", which she supposed to be some special form of transatlantic greeting.

The letting of her two rooms solved her financial problem and there was no need for her to go out and look for a part-time job, but it so happened that, in the August of that year, a job fell into her lap and set her once more upon the slopes of Olympus, where dwelt the heirs of poor dear Rudi and all the other gods and goddesses whose worshipper she had been when she had played '*Hearts and Flowers*', and Handel's '*Water Music*' in the orchestra pit of the Granada.

It had taken Edith a long, long time to adjust herself to talking-pictures. Her conversion had, indeed, been postponed right through the 'thirties,' until she witnessed, almost by accident, the epic *'Gone with the Wind'*, during the anxious summer of 1940.

The conversion was permanent for since then she had been a regular patron of the Odeon, that had now replaced the Granada under new and glossy management.

The young man who had stood in the gilded foyer of the cinema, wearing a smart dinner-jacket, had always a kind word for her when she went in and out of a matinée, but he had recently joined up and had been replaced by a jovial, corpulent manager, who bustled in and out of the cash desk and offices and seemed not to have time to chat with regular customers like Edith.

At least, so Edith thought throughout the early part of 1942, and she was therefore surprised and delighted when he hurried across to her, as she was leaving the cinema one afternoon, and greeted her by name. His booming voice reminded her of Mr. Billington, the original owner of the Granada, and the man who had first engaged her, nearly twenty years before.

"I say! You're *the* Miss Clegg, aren't you? You used to work here in the old days, didn't you? I wonder if you'd do me the honour of coming into the office for a cuppa, Miss Clegg? Nellie . . ." he snapped his fingers at a teen-age girl, who stood by in tight, grey trousers and a frogged jacket, "bring a pot of tea into my office! This lady and I are going to have a little business chat!"

Overwhelmed, Edith followed the manager into his plushy office and was bowed into a deep armchair. She was breathless and elated, for she had very happy memories of the Granada, and found it extremely pleasant to be shown so much courtesy by a stranger, whose office, did he but know it, was situated on the very spot where the fire emergency exit had been in her day.

Tea was brought in and they chatted about the film, an exciting war film, called *'One of Our Aircraft is Missing'*.

"You're a real regular of ours aren't you, Miss Clegg? I've always been meaning to introduce myself, ever since young Hedditch, my predecessor, pointed you out to me! I say, is it true that you used to work here in the flea-pit days?"

Edith remembered then that some people had always

referred to the Granada by this curious name, but she had never understood why, for in all the years that she had worked here she had never once encountered a flea and that despite Mr. Billington's reluctance to employ a regular charwoman.

"I was the pianist here for years," Edith told him, gravely. "It was a much smaller place then, of course. There was only Mr. Billington, his operator, and me. I ... I loved it here. You see, I felt I was actually taking *part* in the films while I was playing for them! I suppose that must sound rather silly to you but it was how I felt, as though poor dear Rudi and dear Buster Keaton, and all the others of those days, were ... well ... *friends* of mine, if you see what I mean?"

The manager, Mr. Bliss, did see what she meant. He recognised her at once as the kind of person he was looking for, someone who might prove invaluable to him in these days of acute shortage of staff and unpredictable decisions from head office.

"How would you like to work here again, Miss Clegg?" he asked, with an engaging smile.

Edith blinked at him. "*Work* here? *Me?* But you ... you don't have a pianist now? All the music and noises off come with the picture, don't they?"

Mr. Bliss chuckled. "Why yes, that's so, but I didn't mean as a pianist, I meant as a kind of ... well ... general factotum ... a relief in the cash-desk, a relief at the confectionery counter, and even a stand-in for me on my days off! A kind of under-manageress and usherette-supervisor you might say!"

Edith sucked in her breath and clenched her plump hands with excitement. *Under-manageress! Supervisor!* At a real cinema! With free access to every film that was shown! Then a doubt assailed her. There was poor Becky, who could not be left alone for more than brief periods, and there was the house to be looked after, and the Americans' rooms to be cleaned and tidied. Reluctantly she shook her head.

"I ... I'd *love* to come here and work but it's not possible ... you see, I've an invalid sister, and two lodgers. I don't cook for them it's true, and my sister isn't at all helpless, but. ..."

Mr. Bliss had been looking for someone like Edith for a long time and the fate of his weekly day off hung in the balance. Because of this he was disinclined to surrender Edith without a determined struggle. He pointed out that they could doubtless come to some special arrangement about hours of duty, and that she would find him far from unaccommodating in matters of time off, last minute readjustments of free periods and, above all, overtime rates.

She protested a little but in the end she promised to give the matter serious thought, and 'see what arrangements could be made about poor Becky'. She left him a less harassed man than she had found him, and as he later confided to his wife—"Here was an old duck who was really sold on corn, and likely to prove a godsend in the winter ahead!"

Mr. Bliss was a good judge of character. The necessary arrangements were made that very night. Mrs. Hooper, of Number Six, agreed to come in and 'do' for her neighbour for two hours daily, at half a crown an hour, and Louise Strawbridge, of Number Twenty-Two, agreed to give Becky a high tea each day, reluctantly agreeing to accept a fee of two shillings per meal.

"How much are they paying you?" Jim wanted to know, after Edith had explained the situation to him over a snack in Number Twenty-Two.

"That's funny," said Edith, her hand flying to her mouth, "I didn't ask him!" And when Jim roared with laughter, "Well, I hardly *liked* to! He was such a nice man, and so very polite to me!"

. . . .

They paid her five pounds ten shillings a week, for six hours a day, six days a week.

She went in at 3 p.m., when the matinée had commenced and left about 9 p.m., soon after the second-house had gone in and it was unlikely that fresh patrons would present themselves at the cash-desk.

Edith found the work easy and the atmosphere very congenial. When she had checked her cash, and transferred it to Mr. Bliss's office safe, she usually managed to slip into the auditorium in time to see the tail-end of the feature film before having her tea. She then picked up the beginning of the feature immediately after the news, about six-thirty in the evening, standing by the brass rail near the main exit until it was time for Elsie's break at the confectionery counter and returning, unless she was especially busy, when Elsie came back at seven o'clock and Maureen had totted up the first-house returns.

It was rather trying, at first, to follow the stories in this disjointed manner, but she soon grew accustomed to it and occupied her mind between times in spotting the villain or working out the dénouement.

She was surprised to discover how often her guesswork proved accurate and she soon came to bestow upon stars like Clark Gable, and David Niven, the same affection as she had once lavished upon Rudolph Valentino, and Ramon Navarro.

She liked best of all the war films, of which there were now a surprising number. She grew familiar with naval and air force slang, and could soon distinguish between destroyers and cruisers, Spitfires, and Heinkels. As in the far-off silent picture days, her personality began to reflower under the magic of the screen. She became more confident, more talkative, and as knowledgeable about screen personalities as she had been in the days when their private lives were recorded swimming-bath by swimming-bath, in film magazines.

She knew for instance, that David Niven, whose popularity increased with each picture he made, was actually a serving soldier in the Forces, and not just a make-believe soldier for the purposes of the film in which he was acting. She knew just how Veronica Lake kept her long, fair hair so sleek and exciting. She grew very fond of tough little Cagney, and elevated dear, gentle, mellow Mr. Tracy to a pinnacle within hailing distance of poor, dear, Rudi, whose wordless, eye-rolling proposals had yet to be matched in these days of outspoken desire.

She began to enjoy the musicals, particularly those starring that nice man, Bing Crosby, and she once shamelessly skimped her duties, in order to hear him sing '*I'm Dreaming of a White Christmas*' nineteen times, during a single week's showing of '*Holiday Inn*'.

She liked agile, whimsical Mr. Astaire, and his gay partner, Ginger Rogers, who could play dramatic roles, in addition to dancing so well. She liked them all, although the broad comedies seemed to have lost something by becoming audible, and she was always secretly hoping that Buster Keaton or Ben Turpin, would make a comeback in some of their extravagant two-reelers of the 'twenties'.

Dear Mr. Chaplin (who would not part, bless him, with his British nationality, in spite of making so much money in America) was still going the rounds, and she laughed until she cried at his portrayal of Hitler, in *'The Great Dictator'*, particularly his excruciatingly funny shaving of the fat German customer to the ever quickening rhythm of *'The Hungarian Rhapsody'*.

As time went on the war began to recede for Edith. Gradually she ceased to become aware of the actual fighting in Russia and Africa, or of the drone of R.A.F. bombers, winging their way towards the indestructible rail-yards at Hamm. She listened to, but without really hearing, endless speculation on the advance of the Japanese in the Far East, and the public clamour for a Second Front *now*, and every other topic that was being discussed up and down the Avenue. Sometimes she caught brief glimpses of current events in the newsreels, but the war news did not really interest her, and she much preferred to get through her work while it was being shown, in order to have a better opportunity to see what Mr. Cagney and Mr. Tracy, were up to that week.

Everyday worries receded from her once she had reported for duty, at 3 p.m., to begin yet another day in such splendid company, and sometimes it was difficult for her to disentangle the real war from the campaigns that she saw waged upon the screen. More than once she confused the battles of Errol Flynn, and Clark Gable, with the battles that were reported in the radio news bulletins.

Edith had, in fact, found her impregnable citadel against the assaults of rationing, shortages, blackouts and sirens. As autumn succeeded summer, and winter succeeded autumn, she lost touch with much that was going on in the Avenue' and had to remind herself, time and again, to ask after the Carver boys, and Mr. Godbeer's stepson, Esme.

That this was wrong and selfish of her she was well aware, but the heavy brass rail, opposite the main exit, was such a

comfortable place to lean nowadays and surely helping to run
a cinema, much patronised by the Forces, could be classified
as war work? That was what Mr. Carver told her anyway,
and Mr. Carver was usually right.

Everybody in the Avenue turned up at the cinema sooner
or later, even her own back-room lodger, little Lieutenant
Ericssohn, even that naughty wife who had been a Miss
Frith, of Number Seventeen, and later the guilty party in the
divorce of that nice, dreamy boy, Esme, whose poor, pretty
mother had been killed at Torquay.

Edith saw these two sitting very close together, in the back
row of the balcony one evening, and she thought it curious
that they should be together and quite obviously 'spooning'.

He had looked away, rather shamefacedly she thought,
when she accidentally flashed her torch on him whilst combing the row for a single one-and-ninepenny, so she had
hastily switched off her torch, and returned to the foyer,
deciding that it was no business at all of hers, as indeed it
was not, for Lieutenant Ericssohn did not have a framed
photograph of a Mrs. Ericssohn on the bamboo table beside
his bed, like the picture that Major Sparkewell had on his, so
he was obviously still a bachelor and entitled to all the
spooning he could get.

She dismissed the matter from her mind, hurried through
her returns, whisked the cash into the office safe and hurried
out again, just in time to see William Powell, rescued from
certain death by his wife, Myrna Loy, as she had felt certain
that he would be rescued when she had watched the first half
of the picture during the matinée.

CHAPTER XVIII

Elaine Falls Back On Base

ALTHOUGH Elaine followed her Dutch officer to various parts of the country throughout the spring and summer of 1942, she did not dispose of her Avenue base, Number Forty-Three; the house, together with its contents, had been made over to her by Esme immediately after the divorce, in February.

Esme's theatrical gesture, in thus parting with property worth some two thousand pounds at current prices, incurred Harold's displeasure but Esme was adamant. He had never returned to Number Forty-Three after the night he had taken Barbara to the airfield, and to put the house and furniture in the market, he argued, would involve a complicated clear-out, a humiliating division of goods, and probably an embarrassing auction sale. The property, he said, did not mean this much to him and he was certainly not in need of the money. His mother's legacy, and his increased rate of pay as aircrew, provided him with more than he needed, and now that he had made a final break with Elaine he shunned further dealings or even discussions with her or her solicitors.

Elaine accepted his gift of the house with considerable relief. Once before she had been homeless and she knew what it was like to lack a base. Indeed, it was this very lack that had provided her with the principal reason for returning home and marrying Esme shortly before the war.

In the interval between Esme's desertion, and her meeting with Captain Van Loon, of the Free Dutch Navy, she was not tempted to raise money by selling the property but preferred instead to draw upon her post office savings' account.

A base was very important to Elaine. It gave her a measure of independence and independence was something she treasured, having won it, in the first instance, against very heavy odds inside Number Seventeen.

She met her Dutchman, Van Loon, in a theatre bar, and had since accompanied him about the country as a kind of a *de luxe vivandière*.

She had been attracted to him, at the outset, by the knowledge that he was a diamond merchant in civilian life, and it had seemed not unreasonable to assume that a man who carried precious stones as large as peas in a wash-leather bag tied around his neck, might well prove to be the Great Provider for whom she had been searching since adolescence.

Van Loon had shown her the diamonds on the first night they had met and she now realised how very drunk he must have been, for she had never set eyes on them since! Had it not been for his gift of two insignificant stones she might have wondered if she had dreamed about the little wash-leather bag that dangled alongside his service identity disc.

Their relationship had not progressed since that first night. On closer acquaintance he turned out to be an unpredictable and mysterious man, who did not belong to wartime Britain, but between the covers of a paper-backed thriller featuring taciturn Continental agents, sudden departures to Buenos Aires, passwords, and radio transmitters disguised as suitcases.

Sometimes Elaine was a little afraid of him, particularly when he had been drinking. His favourite tipple was navy rum, of which he seemed able to procure vast quantities.

He was a tall, broad-chested man, in his late thirties, with immensely powerful arms covered with hair, and a chest that was even hairier, a thick, black mat, spreading from throat to navel. When he was drunk, and padding about in his pyjama trousers, he looked like a bewildered gorilla. His heavy features, cast in solemn mould, reminded Elaine of a face she had seen in a picture somewhere but the comparison eluded her until, one day, whilst turning the pages of an illustrated magazine, she came across the reproduction of a fifteenth-century portrait painting, and read that it was a portrait of Cardinal Albergati, by Van Eyck. She recalled then that she had seen this painting at an exhibition of Flemish work, to which the tiresome Esme had dragged her before they were married. She studied the painting carefully. It was, she thought, a pitiless face, and looked as if it might have been hacked out of granite and seamed with a chisel. It was a face that, diamonds notwithstanding, was not the kind a girl would accompany to bed from choice.

They had gone, within a few days of their first encounter, to a small Cornish resort, but they did not remain down there very long, for the Dutchman was engaged in some kind of mysterious war work concerned with anti-submarine measures and his activities took him to a large number of sea-coast towns where they usually remained for about a week, accommodated in the best available hotel.

This constant movement was all very well in spring, when, having established himself and 'wife' in a double room with bath, Van Loon at once went about his business, leaving her to her own devices until he returned to the hotel in time for dinner. Elaine had always been an expert idler and after eating breakfast in bed she cheerfully dawdled her way through the morning, bathing and dressing, and taking lunch downstairs. She spent the afternoons floating about town, having her hair set, reading light fiction, or, if the weather was dull, attending the matinée at the nearest cinema.

She liked this kind of life. It demanded nothing of her until bedtime, and even then Van Loon was a sound sleeper and a limited conversationalist. She often lay awake wondering about him after he had gone to sleep, and sometimes she asked herself whether he was what he pretended to be, a Dutch patriot who had sailed his vessel into Cardiff the moment he learned that the Germans had invaded his country, or whether his real purpose over here, and his constant journeyings to and fro about the country, had a more sinister purpose. She reasoned that, for all she knew, he might be a spy, a saboteur, or perhaps simply a shrewd businessman using a uniform to cloak illegal commercial activities.

Her speculations, however lurid, did not worry her. She had few convictions about the Allied cause and none whatever about laws aimed at suppressing black market activities. The war was something that was happening to other people, mostly stupid people, like Esme, his stepfather, those clodhopper Carver boys, and all the dreary girls whom she saw trooping here and trooping there in hideous hats, lisle stockings, and sexless uniforms.

Elaine had never wasted a single moment's thought on the progress of the war as an armed conflict but only on how its development and ultimate conclusion might affect her dream of financial security, the dream of terrace, courtiers, iced drinks, hammock, sports-car, yacht and Monte Carlo anchorage.

What did cause her concern, however, was Van Loon's parsimony and the conclusion that might be drawn from it. Perhaps she was exploring yet another blind alley in the search of a Great Provider. She was getting a little exasperated with blind alleys by this time and during her more pessimistic moods she sometimes went back over the years and tried to learn something from her long train of disappointments. Whenever she did this she was never able to discover exactly where she had lost her way, yet the' experiences of the past ten years did not, as she was obliged to admit, add up to any startling success on her part. She was over thirty now and had achieved but small and, for the most part, purely temporary gains. Viewed as a whole, her career as a professional adventuress was unremarkable.

There had been Eugene, the great Illusionist, great only by virtue of his billing and useful as a means of gaining an introduction to the stage. Beyond that he had been a dead loss, a tired, used-up man, with shrinking ambition and a tendency to let tomorrow take care of itself.

After Eugene there had been Benny Boy, Eugene's agent. He at least had provided a big car and a brief trip to the Continent, but in the end he too had failed her by going bankrupt, and turning her loose with nothing but a few trumpery gifts that she was obliged to convert into subsistence money until she had the ill-luck to run across little Tom Tappertitt, the circus-owning husband of a professional strong woman.

She did not like to dwell on the Tappertitt episode for it

had ended in shame and humiliation. Even at this distance Elaine's cheeks glowed in sympathy with her ill-used buttocks when she remembered lying helpless under the flail of Audrey the Amazon's large, right hand.

After Tappertitt came poor old Esme, and Elaine still thought of Esme with affection. He had been kind and generous to her right up to the very last moment and sometimes she half-wished she could have settled for him and his limited means. She might well have done so had she known that he was on the point of inheriting another income from his mother, when he had found out about Archie.

Archie she also thought of with affection, for something more than a physical relationship had existed between them and she had always been pleased to hear his key turn in the back door of Number Forty-Three.

Archie had been so easy-going and restful, despite his obsession with business, but business had won in the end and now, she understood, his greed had landed him in some kind of serious trouble with the police. She had seen Archie once or twice since his appearance in court but had recognised at once that recent experiences had shattered his nerve. She was accustomed to men who drank but not to the extent of carrying a bottle of brandy wherever they went. There was no future in Archie now, not her sort of future anyway, and besides, he was married to a Catholic who had refused to divorce him and it would be tiresome to go through life as a mistress who could be discarded the moment she began to lose her ground in the endless battle against waistline and wrinkles.

Finally there was this Dutchman, Captain Van Loon, who had appeared to be almost a certainty but had since turned out to be more disappointing than any of them, a man who had to be bullied into providing her with a pair of nylons and then grumbled like a volcano at the price he was asked to pay for them, a man who was so secretive with his briefcase, and his little wash-leather bag, that they must surely contain stones worth a fortune.

Elaine had discovered, in Van Loon's company, that she could forgive a man anything but meanness. Not one of the men in her past had been mean, not even poor old Eugene, who had never had two halfpence to rub together, whereas two of her lovers, Archie and Esme, had been extremely generous in their dealings with her. Remembering this Elaine sighed, and decided that, sooner or later, there would have to be some kind of showdown with 'Dutch'. He would have to make up his mind which he preferred to hang round his neck, her or his wash-leather bag. As it was she was wasting time, precious time, now that America had entered the war, for somewhere among the Americans there must be a man who would understand her yearning for terraces, sports cars, iced drinks, steam yachts and Mediterranean anchorages. If the cinema was to be taken seriously such men were commonplace in America, and what she had to offer in exchange was readily marketable among them judging by the whistles she heard when she happened to walk past a trainload of Americans on Crewe station the other afternoon.

The showdown with Dutch came sooner than she expected and without active encouragement on her part.

It was like all the other showdowns in Elaine's life, explosive, unexpected and by no means devoid of the elements of farce.

At their last stopping-place Dutch had made new arrangements regarding their accommodation. Instead of booking at a hotel he rented a small, detached bungalow, in a long row of similar bungalows, on the outskirts of the small Welsh port that they happened to be visiting.

Elaine disliked the arrangement from the start, for it meant that she would now be expected to do a certain amount of housework, making beds, cooking meals, and keeping the place tidy.

She grumbled about it the night they arrived but Dutch told her gruffly that there was no accommodation in either of the two local hotels and she would have to put up with the bungalow for a month, the period that he estimated they would remain in the district.

The town was one of the most depressing Elaine had ever visited, a jumble of wired-off wharfs, sagging sheds, and steep, seedy-looking streets, all leading down to a stagnant basin at the mouth of a muddy river. The air down here reeked of stale fish, tar, and diesel-oil from the shipping in the harbour and the same smell seemed to hang over the entire town.

Dutch seemed busier than usual and during the first week did not return home until dusk each evening. A minor heat wave was in progress but although the box-like rooms of the bungalow were stale and airless Elaine had little choice but to spend most of her time in them, for there was but one cinema and its programme ran from Monday to Saturday with no mid-week change of film.

Such cafés as existed were dismal, flyblown little establishments that used chipped cups, and offered a menu that, as Elaine declared after making a reconnaissance of the town, belonged in a community enduring a close siege rather than a war.

By the end of the second week she was bored and irritable and her irritability soon conveyed itself to Van Loon, who began to drink far more rum than was good for him. He began his drinking the moment he had finished his evening meal and had exhausted the limited possibilities of Elaine's magazines and the Forces' programme.

Under more comfortable circumstances Elaine might have derived a certain amount of gratuitous entertainment from watching him get drunk. His taciturn personality did not take kindly to the early stages of intoxication but it began to mellow after an hour or so when it assumed a kind of stilted drollery, fascinating to watch from a safe distance.

Later, if he continued drinking, his gaiety ebbed and was replaced by what Elaine learned to call 'The Poor-Rotterdam-Stage.' For an hour or more the Dutchman would beat his breast and commune with himself over persons and places he had lost in the initial air attack on that city. By this time, however, he would have reverted to his native tongue, so that she could only guess at at his meaning, gauging by tone and expression whether he was uttering maledictions against the Nazis or expressions of sorrow for their victims.

At last he would mix himself another stiff toddy and brace up, buttoning his lips and dashing the tears from his eyes. He would then attempt to make love to her but his movements were so heavy and clumsy that he usually abandoned the idea and reeled off to bed under her expert guidance.

She reflected, on these occasions, that had she been a different kind of woman she might have used these matchless opportunities to relieve him of one or two of the stones in his wash-leather bag. It was not fear of the possible consequences that prevented her but rather a kind of pride in her ability to handle a man, any sort of man, in any sort of condition. Apart from this she was shrewd and had long since decided that if her dream was to be fulfilled it would be fulfilled in a way that bolted the door against future disasters. In other words, once settled in the hammock on the terrace, nobody was going to tip her out of it or dispute legal possession of the terrace on which it was slung.

On this particular evening Dutch was a long time getting through his preliminary stages. He glared across at her and went on drinking steadily but without moving from the armchair in which he had seated himself. She pretended to be absorbed in a fashion magazine but she kept her eye on him and glanced across from time to time to see how his solemn jag was progressing.

At last he began to hum a tune and she knew that he was approching the mock-mellow stage. He got up, opened the french window and, still humming, peeled off his tunic and shirt and moved off into the little bathroom, where he commenced to shave with a cut-throat razor.

He was already drunk and she wondered whether he would cut himself but he did not and it occurred to her that perhaps he was not quite as drunk as he seemed. When he had finished shaving he began to run the bath water but before he actually climbed into the bath the lachrymose mood overtook him and he began to wail and gnash his teeth over the ruins of Rotterdam and the graves of his martyred shipmates.

He wandered, naked and lamenting, into the little lounge and passed through the open french windows into the garden. On the way he picked up his clarinet and began to play 'Shenandoah'. He was a spirited but indifferent performer on the clarinet and his repertoire was limited to two tunes, 'Shenandoah' and the Dutch National Anthem. The spectacle of him standing on the tiny lawn without a stitch of clothing, regaling the neighbours on each side of the hedge with an erratic rendering of the sea-shanty, diverted Elaine but she soon realised that the performance would have to be cut short before somebody summoned the police. So she went out and spoke gently to him, taking his arm and trying to lead him back to the house.

He took a good deal of persuading and in the interval both of them forgot that the bath taps were running. They were unpleasantly reminded of this fact by the appearance of a slow tide under the door.

She left him then and splashed into the flooded passage, but whilst she was struggling with the submerged taps he followed her into the bathroom and playfully upended her into the brimming bath.

At this point Elaine ceased to be amused and turned on him furiously, smashing a plastic bath brush over his head but in the end both of them went into the bath and for a moment Elaine thought she would be drowned under his immense bulk. They were facing different ways, and her violent struggles resulted in Dutch getting a heavy kick on the nose, which sent him yelping from the bathroom into the living-room, streaming blood and uttering a variety of obscure, Lowland oaths.

Elaine climbed out of the bath and locked the door before peeling off her clothes and wrapping herself in a bath robe. On the other side of the thin wall she could hear Dutch mumbling to himself and suddenly her irritation exploded into fury. She wrung out her clothes, flung open the door and marched into the living room, determined to be done with him then and there. She found herself looking into the levelled barrel of his .45 revolver.

Elaine was a courageous girl and accustomed to the antics of drunken men. Even so, it took her a few seconds to clear her brain sufficiently to grapple with the situation, for she was not at all sure whether or not the revolver was loaded. Usually it was not and she knew that he kept the ammunition in the little pouch, attached to the webbing belt that supported the holster.

She looked carefully on each side of him and was relieved to see the belt and its unbuttoned pouch lying on the bookcase, beside him. She decided then that he looked more absurd than frightening, hunched in the armchair, his nose dripping blood, his huge, swarthy body dripping water. She noticed too that his clarinet was on the mantelshelf, where he had placed it after she had coaxed him in from the garden.

She fell back on the sole armament at her disposal. Smiling archly, and letting fall the bathrobe, she unmasked her battery of charms at a range of less than six feet and in the gentlest of tones said:

"You don't have to persuade me with a gun, Dutch darling!"

As she said it he gave a bellow and dropped the gun, throwing himself forward, his head down and his arms spread to enfold her. She had, however, anticipated this and side stepping his rush she grabbed the clarinet, whirled it high, and brought it crashing down on the back of his neck.

He fell forward on his knees and as he pitched to the floor she raised the clarinet for a second blow.

It was not necessary. He lay full-length, wheezing like a punctured bellows, and she left him there after putting the revolver into its holster, and hiding the belt behind a long row of *Every Man His Own Lawyer*, that stood on the lower shelf of the bookcase.

He was sitting up when she had finished her packing. His nose had ceased to bleed and he looked very sick, but seemed more or less sober.

"I'm going now," she told him, "you'd better make yourself some coffee and then start clearing up this mess! I've emptied the bath and hidden your gun. You'll find it if you lay off the rum long enough. Good-bye now, Dutch!"

He said nothing but continued to stare at her. She went out into the kitchen to find something in which she could wrap her wet clothes, finally deciding to use the American cloth that was pinned to the table.

When she returned to the living-room for her suitcase he was still sitting there, ruefully examining his clarinet. She saw that it was cracked along its whole length and that some of its stops were twisted.

"Who did this?" he demanded, sullenly.

"I did! On you!" said Elaine lightly, and picking up her case she went out through the hall and into the road.

She caught the first available train to London, arriving at

Woodside about 6.30 a.m. There was no 'bus or taxi at that
hour, so she had to carry the case along to Shirley Rise and
up the hill to the Avenue.

It was a heavy case and she was panting when she turned
into the crescent and passed the gate of Number Four.

An American officer was emerging, a slim, middle-aged
man, with rimless spectacles. Elaine glanced at him, noted his
uniform, looked away quickly and then looked back, be-
seechingly.

He ran after her, calling out in the rich drawl of the Deep
South:

"Pardon me, ma'am ... let me help you with that baggage! Kinda heavy for a lady, isn't it? You live hereabouts,
ma'am?"

Elaine stopped and handed him the case. She smiled, and
thereby bestowed upon Lieutenant Ericssohn the fatal glance,
demure, yet vaguely promising, that she had once practised
before a wardrobe mirror not fifty yards from where they
now stood.

"You're so kind," she said, "but I'm not going far, only
across to Number Forty-Three ... *would* you ... it *has* been
a drag, all the way from the station. .. !"

They walked together across the Avenue and down the
odd side as far as the gate of Number Forty-Three.

"Thank you captain ... that was charming of you ... but
then, all Americans are gentlemen aren't they? Everybody
says so!"

He gazed at her rapturously as she fumbled for her key.

"Say ma'am—I'm billeted here, Number Four, party by
the name o' Miss Clegg. I'm from the dee-pot, over in the
wood, and ma name's 'Ericssohn', Lootenan' Ericssohn!"

"I'm delighted to know you, Lootenant," said Elaine offering her gloved hand.

CHAPTER XIX

Reconnaissance In Force

AN hour or so before Elaine dragged her heavy case up
Shirley Rise that August morning, two other members of the
Avenue rump were nearing the end of a more complicated
journey. They were heavily laden, but not with suitcases.
They carried, as well as their routine equipment, sections of a
Bangalore torpedo for the purpose of blasting a passage
through the wired gullies that led up towards the Hess bat-
tery, west of Dieppe.

Their troop was early in the field that morning, for the
main battle had yet to begin. The little convoy of landing
craft chugged across a calm sea, shrouded in the greyish
white mist of the hour known to Commandos as 'Nautical
Twilight' and the smaller Commando group, to which the
Carver twins were attached, headed direct for Vesterival. Its
members were armed, in the main, with mortars, and their
job was to engage the battery whilst a heavier column circled
it from Quiberville beach and then attacked from the rear.

The twins had passed close by Dieppe during their long
trek from the Belgian frontier two years before but their
familiarity with the landscape did not date from Dunkirk
days. They had since studied every yard of the Vesterival
beach and the village beyond from a scale model, built up by
their officers from hundreds of aerial photographs. They now
felt they knew the ground as well as they knew the Rec'
or the ploughland beyond Manor Woods, south-east of the
Avenue.

They stood, as usual, very close together in the bows of the landing craft and it was just light enough for Bernard to make out the outline of Boxer's bullet-head and powerful shoulders. They had not spoken since they had left the transport vessel. Boxer never spoke much on these occasions and this morning Bernard could not trust himself to speak.

He had never felt this way before, not even on the first occasion that they had gone into action, and certainly not at the outset of the bigger shows, like Vaagso, and St. Nazaire. On those occasions he had experienced successive waves of excitement that were almost pleasurable and his thoughts concerning the probable outcome of the raid had always been optimistic.

He did not feel this way today. Every few moments his stomach seemed to detach itself from his trunk and float away, as if attached to a long, tenuous cord which had to be gathered in before his stomach returned to its normal place. Then, when the stomach was back where it belonged, it was invaded by a large, malevolent crab, with ice-tipped pincers, that nipped and squeezed, causing Bernard to suck in huge mouthfuls of air and hiccough.

He wondered if any of the men standing close to him had noticed his hiccoughs. Boxer, who had his back to him, did not appear to have done so, for once or twice he half turned, and grinned his wide, clownish grin, jerking his head sideways, as if to express exuberance. When he did this Bernard almost hated him for his utter lack of nerves and his inexhaustible reserve of schoolboy *élan*.

As the boat pushed silently through the mist Bernard wondered if Pippa, the sallow, brown-eyed girl in the Avenue, was responsible for how he felt now. If so, then it was a pity that he had encouraged her by telling her about Boxer, and by writing her all those letters before their outgoing mail had been banned and they had been isolated behind wire in preparation for the big show.

He carried a bundle of her letters in his breast pocket, a dozen or more fat envelopes, making up a package the thickness of a small Bible, like the Bible that Lofty Burridge always carried into battle.

Bernard wondered if the reason why he had disobeyed regulations by carrying the letters across the Channel was in

any way related to the reason why Lofty Burridge carried his
Bible. Lofty was not a religious man but he had a superstitious belief in the power of a pocket Bible to isolate his heart
from a sniper's bullets. His father, so he told them, had met a
man in the trenches during the last war who had shown him
a New Testament with a small piece of shrapnel embedded in
its leaves. It was absurd to imagine that a packet of letters
would afford any protection against a bullet or a grenade
splinter. Nevertheless, Bernard had slipped the envelopes into
his left-hand breast pocket when he had been equipping
himself the previous night.

He gathered his stomach to himself once again and lifted
his hand to feel the letters. As he did so his mind's eye
conjured up a familiar image of their author, thin-faced,
earnest and immensely reassuring as she had seemed that day
on Shirley Hills, when he had made such a bloody fool of
himself by weeping on her breast and then, unaccountably,
dropping off into a heavy doze.

He remembered then what she had said to him about
looking after himself, about letting Boxer take his chance
when the fixed machine-guns began to chatter and the air
about them hissed with bursting mortar shells and exploding
grenades. The memory of her plea now seemed disloyal to
Boxer, and so he put it from his mind and reached out to
touch Boxer's hairy wrist.

"What is it, Berni-boy?"

Bernard swallowed and at last managed to speak. His
voice was midway between a croak and a hoarse whisper.

"Don't forget, Boxer, we stay together, no matter what!
You remember that, Boxer! Don't you go whooping off on
your own, like you did last time!"

Boxer chuckled, his shoulders shaking.

"Why sure, sure! That's what we fixed, didn't we?"

And then something of his twin's tension must have communicated itself to him, for he half-turned and peered more
closely at Bernard.

"You okay, son? You okay, Berni boy?"

The big crab began another deliberate exploration of Bernard's bowels but he managed to say:

"Sure I'm okay! Don't worry about *me*! Just you remem-

ber what I said, that's all. Just don't lose touch on the way
up!"

Bernard was not able to discover whether this repetitive
statement reassured Boxer, for at that moment a shower of
star-shells exploded about the winking beacon of the Pointe
d'Ailly lighthouse. Simultaneously an air-raid siren began to
wail from somewhere in the town, on their port quarter.

The man behind Bernard said: "Look! That must be the
Spits going in! It's any minute now!" but there was still no
unmistakable sign that the coast ahead had been alerted, no
crescendo of sound, as at Vaagso or St. Nazaire, that announced that they were recognised and being fired upon.

The blaze of light from the star-shells and the throb of
aircraft to starboard helped to calm Bernard, so that he
forced himself to assess the known factors from a military
rather than a personal standpoint.

"What's the chances of catching 'em napping, Ginger?" he
demanded, of the man on his right.

Ginger, a thickset man of Boxer's temperament, rolled
chewing gum on his tongue and cocked an eye towards the
lighthouse. The main stream of their assault group had already veered off to the west and were due at any moment to
ground on the shingle at Quiberville.

"I dunno," said Ginger, at length and then, carelessly: "A
bit less'n bugger all, I should say!"

Boxer heard the grim joke and chortled.

"Pipe down there," muttered an officer, from his position
in the bows, "we're almost in, chaps!"

Any minute now thought Bernard and his brain seethed
with alternatives. Let Boxer go and play safe himself, doing
exactly what he had been told to do, no more and no less.
Hold Boxer back, as he knew, no matter what kind of hell
they faced on the beach, he was capable of holding Boxer
back. The Commandos had had Boxer but two years but he
had made Boxer's decisions for twenty-two. Compromise
between these two alternatives, forge ahead with Boxer, as at
Vaagso, and thereafter rely on his own quickness of eye and
on Boxer's astonishing proficiency with firearms, to keep
them both alive until the recall, until Verey lights from
beyond the battery told them that the main column was

attacking and the mortar party was free to retire? Or one other course; let things slide, trust to luck and do what seemed the right thing to do at the climax of each successive moment?

His mind exploded like a box of ammunition, conflicting resolutions shooting this way and that, demolishing each other in flight, but beyond it all he could still see the solemn, narrow face of the girl, Pippa, and he began to curse her for the confusion she had created inside his head. On all previous occasions it had been so simple and uncomplicated, simply *'Look after Boxer! Watch out for Boxer! Keep Boxer alive! Stop Boxer from getting killed!'*

Suddenly the boat grated on sand and at once the mass shook itself into dozens of independent shadows. The light from the star-shells waned as boots pounded on shifting pebbles and men ran crouching into the blackness ahead.

Bernard sensed rather than saw that Boxer was only a yard or so in front of him and his feet lunged at the pebbles, thrusting his body upward towards the low cliff, where the initial impetus soon spent itself and men seemed to mill here and there without purpose or direction.

Boxer's big face appeared out of the murk, and Bernard heard him shout:

"Number One Gully's wired up! We're going to blast out Number Three—come on," and he shot off to the right, fumbling with equipment as he ran.

Bernard sprinted in pursuit, overtaking an officer just as a series of ear-splitting explosions crashed out from the direction of the lighthouse.

"Cannon-fire. . . ! Thank God for the Spits! It'll cover the noise of our torps," gasped the officer. Then, without remembering at all how he came to be there, Bernard was kneeling at the foot of a wide cleft in the cliff-side, struggling with fuses as the first Bangalore torpedo blew a gap in the criss-cross of wire that was stretched tightly across the mouth of the gully.

With the first detonation Bernard's confusion disappeared and with it went all his fears. The habit of military discipline, and month after month of specialised training, reasserted themselves and he became a fiendishly active automaton, linked to Boxer not because Boxer was his twin, but simply because he was his partner in this particular enterprise.

Together they unslung their rifles and struggled up the gulley on the heels of the officer and side by side they swept into the village beyond the cliff-edge and set about winkling the bewildered enemy from the houses and shepherding a flock of sleep dazed civilians into chattering groups as the sub-section established its line of communication to the beach.

The vicious crab slept as the troop took up its position in the scrub, close by the outer section of the battery's wire. There was a murderous rhythm about each move of every man in the section. The two-inch and three-inch mortars were yanked into position and the anti-tank gun dragged stealthily forward to a point where the gunner could hear German voices muttering inside the wire.

Snipers, Bernard and Boxer among them, took up their positions on the very edge of the cover, marking down a light machine-gun position on the roof and the heavy machine-gun posts inside the compound. The sparse shrub twitched with the movement of invisible figures but, miraculously it seemed, they were undetected by the garrison.

Presently a heavy silence descended on the extended group and Bernard, lying prone, could hear Boxer's breathing as he shifted his position slightly, throwing out his elbow in order to get a better purchase on his rifle butt. Inch by inch Bernard turned his head to the right and waited while the mist shredded away. Soon, as the minutes to zero hour ticked by, he could make out his twin's freckled face, streaked green and brown, with its lavish coating of camouflage paint, so that Boxer looked more like a clown than he had ever looked.

Casual voices drifted across the scrub from the interior of the compound. It seemed to Bernard incredible that they could lie here, armed to the teeth and within grenade-throwing distance of the German wire, yet still remain undiscovered in growing daylight. Never before had they achieved this measure of success. Never had the real thing followed so closely the detailed planning of their briefing.

At ten minutes to six, when the last of the mist had

disappeared and a faint roar of battle was beginning to be heard from the east, the order was given to fire and the calm of the morning was shattered by an inferno of sound that seemed to sweep over the ground like a raging tide, swallowing them in vast waves and stunning their senses so that they watched their fingers perform tasks that had no origin in their brains.

Tiny, inconsequent facets of that action, imprinted themselves on Bernard's memory; a German gunner, performing an almost graceful somersault over the light gun on the roof; a figure brought up short in a fast run across the compound and then lifted bodily by a second burst of the anti-tank gun, firing from the trees on his right; a direct hit by a mortar shell on one of the flak towers that seemed under the impact, to shred away like a stack of newspapers in a gale.

Of the main action, and of his own part in it, Bernard remembered nothing, up to the moment that one of the mortar teams dropped a shell into a stack of cordite in the compound and the entire enclosure rose up in a wide sheet of yellow flame, the blast wave striking the line of commandos and pitching them askew like a row of skittles.

Then more facets, each a horror in miniature; burned men appearing and disappearing in front of the wall of smoke; Boxer's jubilant face an inch from his own, screaming something, he knew not what, and pointing wildly to a brace of Verey lights that were soaring into the grey sky beyond the battery.

Bernard recognised this as the signal and once again his training reasserted itself, telling him that it was time to writhe back from the blazing mass and seek what shelter he could find in the heavier undergrowth through which they had advanced.

He began to move at once, fixing his eyes on Boxer's upturned soles and watching them recede as Boxer struggled to his feet to stand waist high in the coarse grass, firing and firing into the belt of flame beyond the remnants of wire.

Then the crab in Bernard's stomach awoke and nipped, so fiercely that he cried out, rising to his knees and madly whirling his left arm.

"Come back, Boxer! Come on back, you bloody fool!"

But Boxer was in no hurry. Men were now doubling back towards the woods on each side of him and as they passed Bernard they shouted and pointed towards the trees but Boxer remained upright against the tatters of the wire, deliberately firing into the smoke wreaths in front of him.

Bernard shouted again and again, forcing the warnings through fumes of cordite that had him by the throat. Behind him and beyond the village he could hear the roar of battle rising from White, Red and Blue beaches, and the scream of aircraft overhead, high-pitched above the sough of naval shells that came rushing over five miles of water to crash on to the Dieppe defences, told Bernard that the planned withdrawal of the mortar troop had been timed to seconds.

Still Boxer remained, twenty yards nearer the compound, obscured every now and again by wreaths of drifting, yellow smoke.

This then was what Pippa must have meant, this was the stark reality of his double burden. "You can't *do* this any longer Bernard, nobody could. . . . !" It was as though she was calling to him across the quivering belt of woodland and urging him, at long last, to look out for himself, to leave Boxer to take his chance.

The film of cordite broke in his throat but cold and impotent rage took its place and he cursed, turning his back on the battery and stumbling off through the low brush in the wake of the anti-tank gunners.

Then the mortar shell burst about midway between himself and Boxer and it was as though a violent gust of wind had struck edgeways at his calves, crumpling him into a compact ball and hurling him forwards and upwards towards the trees.

He felt no pain, no real pain, just a heavy, numbing thump above the elbow of his left arm, but when he tried to scramble up his feet made no contact with the ground and he fell forward on his face again, just as a naval shell struck a clump of pines on the broken skyline and he saw, as in a film, the slim trunks lift and soar away in a wide arc.

Then the world about him dissolved under the continuous impact of high-explosive.

* * * *

Boxer found him lying on his side, with his knees drawn up to his chin and the shattered remains of his rifle still hanging by its sling from his left shoulder.

He saw the gaping wound in his leg first, a wound as big as an orange, with shredded khaki at its edges and blood pumping steadily on to the grass beside him.

Then he saw the obscene angle of his twin's left arm, with bones projecting through tatters of bluish flesh and this was pumping too and staining the grass.

He fell on his knees, calling: "Berni! Berni-boy!" but Berni, when he turned him over, was unconscious, the waxen pallor of his face high-lighting the streaks of green camouflage paint, his eyes closed, his lips and nostrils twitching.

Boxer knew what immediate action he must take. His training had seen to that. He tore out his field-dressing and used it partly as a bandage and partly as a tourniquet on the calf-wound. Then he made a second tourniquet, this time with his lanyard, and checked the flow of blood from the wreck of Bernard's elbow but after that he was bewildered. He could obey orders, both official orders and Bernard's orders, but he had never developed the habit of independent thought, not even under tranquil conditions; now all hell was loose around him, from the town and beaches to the east and north, from the south, where B. and F. troops were assaulting the strong-point, and from above, where dog-fights between Spitfires and enemy fighters were filling the air with the drone of power-dives and the harsh rattle of machine-gun fire.

He could see what had to be done but there seemed to be no way of doing it. Bernard would have to be carried, either to the beach below Vesterival where they had landed an hour ago, or to a casualty clearing-station, if such a thing existed.

Theoretically it was possible to get to the village, where a detachment had been left to keep open the track to the beach but it was one thing to get there alone, taking advantage of every bush and every fold in the ground but quite another to walk there, carrying a wounded man who weighed over twelve stone.

There must, Boxer reasoned, have been some orders issued

to cover such a contingency. Someone, at sometime during briefing, must have explained exactly what to do with casualties but if such orders had indeed been issued he was incapable of remembering them and it was clear that nobody else would return to help him carry Berni.

Berni would have known what to do had it been he, Boxer, who was lying there, with two patched-up wounds. Berni would have cocked his head, screwed his eyes into narrow slits, and then snapped out a few words that would have accomplished the miracle. Berni would have employed his twin's giant strength in some way and Berni would have known just how to cross a mile of ground under the concentration of fire that made entire woods bounce and dance like the scenery in a Disney film.

In the end, Boxer did what first came into his mind. He gathered Berni into his arms and strode off across the quivering landscape in a general northerly direction.

He didn't get very far, however, for even Boxer realised that it was now impossible to penetrate the curtain of fire that the German mortars were laying across the scrub. In addition, enemy aircraft were now swooping low over the clearings and raking the ground with short-range cannon fire. Boxer was accustomed to taking chances but this was no chance at all, just certain death for both of them. Realising this he hesitated on the fringe of woodland, staring about him on all sides in search of temporary shelter, just a place where he could rest, think and work out some kind of plan, the kind of plan that Berni would have hit upon in a second.

Over to his left was a white scar in the heath, a half-completed tank trap, with a lip of concrete overhanging a shallow trench. Boxer ran to it and jumped into the excavation, scrambling forward on his knees until he could lay Berni on a kind of shelf made of unevenly-placed stones.

He was safe here from anything but a direct hit, or point-blank cannon fire and he wiped the sweat and paint from his face with huge, mud-caked hands and peeped over the top of the ditch just in time to see a column of *Stosstruppe* double out from behind a farmhouse building and deploy along the path through the wood.

He knew what they would do the moment they found

sufficient cover. They would fan out, advance on Vesterival and the beach and then snipe at the evacuating commandos until a heavier force arrived to launch a counter-attack.

Their presence meant that retreat to the beach was now impossible, notwithstanding the slackening off of the enemy mortar fire. Then if not north what about south, to join up with B. and F. troops behind the battery? He considered this for a moment and then rejected it as an equally impossible course. Assuming that B. and F. troops had now stormed and demolished the strong-point, which seemed likely enough in view of the presence of the *Stosstruppe*, they would certainly have retreated by the route they had advanced, round the western approach beside the river and then down to the beach at Quiberville for re-embarkation. It was too late to go this way. Even if there were no living Germans between himself and the southern limits of the battery, he could never overtake B. and F. troops whilst carrying a dead weight.

Then there were Berni's wounds to consider. The tourniquets had slowed the bleeding but they did not seem to have checked it altogether. From where he crouched in the ditch Boxer could see blood welling through the leg bandage, slowly but steadily, like the drip of a washerless tap.

The sight galvanised him into action and he bent and picked up Bernard, scrambling out of the tank-trap and heading due west along the fringe of the wood. It was as good a direction as any and it was just possible that he could cross the line of march of the last of the stragglers from B. or F. troops, on their way back to Quiverville beach.

The roar behind him now increased to monstrous proportions. The ground rocked and quivered under the impact of shells and bombs, whole salvos merging into one another, so that a wall of sound rushed down upon him, making thought impossible. He plodded on and as he strode over grass tussocks and low brush he began to plead with Bernard to regain consciousness and restore to him the power of thought.

"Berni! Berni-boy! What about Lovat's mob? What about them, Berni? How about packing it in, Berni? How about getting a Jerry surgeon. Whadysay Berni, whadysay?"

Berni said nothing. His injured arm and leg swung free,

his body nestled close against Boxer's bloodied battledress and his mop of fair hair, freed from the confines of the steel helmet that had been left behind in the tank-trap, stirred slightly in the blast of successive explosions.

Boxer never recalled how or where he encountered the Frenchmen. One moment he seemed to be stumbling across a wilderness of gorse and sparse copse, and the next he was standing in a kind of cellar, lit by two candles and a single lantern that shone down from a nail in the wall.

Three men, all civilians but wearing revolvers and Sten guns, were bending over Berni at a table made of packing cases and another man, with blue-black whiskers, and a beret that was too small for him, was giving Boxer a drink from a bottle.

Perhaps he had been there for hours or perhaps only a few minutes. He did not know because he was dazed with the detonations, with the heat and the maddening indecisions of the last hours or moments. Then men at the table were jabbering French and Boxer remembered but a word or two of the French that he had picked up at Lille in the first winter of the war.

He half-emptied the bottle that the whiskered man was holding and then his brain began to clear a little. He was about to ask where he was when the tallest man among the table group approached him and said, in clipped, precise English:

"The leg and arm will have to go but we cannot amputate here, we have no facilities."

Boxer stared at him. Only the word 'amputate' registered but that was enough.

"You mean, take his leg off? Take Berni's leg off?"

"And the arm! The arm is worse! It is his only chance, my friend."

Boxer reeled and the whiskered man obligingly pushed a backless chair under him, so that he sat down sharply, striking the rim of his helmet against the wall.

"You can't do *that* to Berni. . . ! Berni's my brother! We're twins, me and Berni! You can't take his bloody leg off, you clot!"

The tall man shrugged and turned away. For a moment he

remained quite still, slowly rubbing his chin as though turning over a problem in his mind. Finally he said:

"Is this your Invasion? You must tell me. It is important that we should know."

"Invasion?" thought Boxer. What was the silly sod talking about? Invasion? What the hell had invasion to do with Berni having his leg and arm chopped off?

Boxer then noticed that all four Frenchmen were looking at him and it struck him that some kind of reply to the question was obligatory.

"They told us it was a reccy," he said, "a reccy in force ..." and then, behind all his distress and bewilderment, his confused memory produced a fleeting glimpse of the briefing hall and he heard the briefing officer saying: 'Tell them not to join in! Tell them the real show is later!'

He said, slowly: "No, this is just a big raid! They told us to tell all the civvies it wasn't the Second Front," then, almost savagely, "What you say about Berni? You *sure* you got to amputate? You *quite* sure?"

The four Frenchmen exchanged serious looks. Then the tall one, the doctor apparently, said something that Boxer could not understand and the two men at the table unslung their Sten guns and the small man, the one with the bluish whiskers, crossed over to the corner of the cellar and dropped on hands and knees.

Boxer began to sweat with anxiety and impatience. What were they up to now? Why didn't they buckle to and dress old Berni's wounds? Why were they treating old Berni as a kind of side-show?

Suddenly the doctor seemed to sense his irritation and turned to him, laying a gentle hand on his shoulder.

"We were about to join you, my friend," he said, "but what you have told us is important, not only to us, but to you and to your brother here! You will understand—there is no point in us attacking the Boche, not if you are returning across the Channel! We should be killed, all of us but when you come in force we shall be ready! Perhaps you will tell your officers what I have said?"

Boxer looked from one to the other. Out of the corner of his eye he saw the whiskered man gathering up the firearms and placing them lovingly into a cavity beneath an up-ended flagstone. He looked across at Bernard, still prone on the packing cases.

"You can do *something* for him, can't you?" he pleaded. "You can patch him up, just so as I can carry him back?"

"You would have to wait until tonight," the doctor said. "You would be certainly killed or captured if you showed yourself on the beach in daylight now!"

He paused a moment, adding, "By now they would shoot you down on any beach within miles of Dieppe!"

For a moment but a moment only Boxer forgot Bernard and gave a thought to his own situation.

"What you reckon I'd better do?" he asked.

"That depends upon yourself, my friend," replied the doctor. "If you remain near here we may find some place to conceal you until you can be passed inland to a collecting point. We have an organisation for this but it is something that must not be done in a hurry. You may have to remain hidden for many weeks and after today there will be strict searches throughout this area."

"What about him?" demanded Boxer, "could you look after him too?"

"That is quite impossible, my friend," said the man shaking his head. "Your comrade is seriously wounded, very seriously wounded and we could not hope to conceal a man in that condition!"

Boxer's face flamed and he lost his temper. "Listen you clot, he's my brother, he's my twin brother," he shouted.

The doctor remained impassive but the other men, sensing Boxer's tension, looked up from their task of replacing a flagstone over the arms cache.

"If you wish to stay free you must leave him behind," said the doctor, firmly. "There is no other course and even so your chances are not good."

"*Leave him? Leave him here?*"

"He will get attention. Someone will notify the Germans that he is here. That can be arranged. Henri will say that he found him here in the barn and they would come for him."

"Ar, but when, *when?*" insisted Boxer, "how long would he have to stay here, lying like that?"

The doctor shrugged and the familiar Gallic gesture irritated Boxer so much that he could have struck the man in the face.

"Until tonight perhaps ... they would send an ambulance if they are not too busy with their own wounded."

"Jesus!" Boxer exploded, "you want me to go underground and leave Berni here ŏn the off chance of being picked up by Jerry?"

"You asked for my advice, my friend," said the Frenchman, "we are risking our lives talking to you, do you realise that?"

Boxer had not realised it and the gentle rebuff sobered him. He was slow-witted but he was not an unreasonable man and he remembered now something else they had told him at the briefing, something about civvies who helped the British being shot within minutes of their capture by Germans.

The hopelessness of the situation overwhelmed him. His head felt numb, as though he had just been awakened from a heavy sleep after a terrific bender at the local. He shook himself like a mastiff and sat down on the backless chair from which he had jumped up when he began arguing with the doctor.

"I'm not going to leave him," he faltered, at length, "I ... I just couldn't, not like that! We been together so long you see ... we've *always* been together... ! I got to get him *seen* to by someone. What do you reckon I should do for the best? Where could I *get* him seen to?"

The man with whiskers said something in rapid French, and the doctor heard him out before nodding.

"If you wish to save his life and sacrifice your own chances of escape there is only one. course open to you, my friend. You must take him yourself to the Boche first-aid post beyond the crossroads but you must go there alone. It would be death for us to accompany you."

"You mean, dressed like this?"

"I would advise you to wear some other clothing until you have delivered him. The Boche is very busy and it is probable that they will not stop a civilian carrying a wounded man. If you walk out on to the road as you are they will shoot both of you and investigate afterwards!"

One of the men in the corner began to forage among some racks and eventually produced some filthy overalls. Then the man with whiskers took off his beret and proffered it, grinning.

The doctor said: "It is not much but it may probably get you as far as the post. Wait ... I have a better idea ..." and he rummaged in a crate and produced a small white flag, printed with a red cross.

"Display this as well," he said. "They will be too busy to challenge you before you reach the road block."

Bernard stirred and Boxer approached the table. It crossed his mind that even now Bernard might be able to speak and devise some alternative plan whereby they could be spirited out of this fantastic situation and back to their unit. But Bernard's eyes remained closed and although his lips moved it was only to utter gibberish, not to give Boxer advice or counsel.

Boxer wondered, as he struggled into the overalls, whether to surrender in this fashion was a military crime but the reflection did not make him waver any more than did the thought that he might be shot as a spy if captured on enemy territory in civilian attire. The important thing now was to get Bernard's wounds dressed and to counter that shocking threat of double amputation expressed by this cold fish of a Frenchman. It did not matter very much what happened after that.

As he put aside his rifle and webbing equipment he began to feel more confident. These Frogs seemed to know what they were doing and he had always heard that Jerry behaved well towards British wounded. It might, he reflected, be worse. Bernard was not yet dead, not by any means, and the Frenchmen might be quite wrong about the seriousness of his wounds. Now that he had specific orders again his confusion of mind began to disappear and his natural optimism began to reassert itself. He looked down at himself and a ghost of his habitual grin creased his mouth.

"Christ," he said to his impassive audience, "what a carry-on it is, eh?—What a laugh me and Berni'll have about this lark when we get back to barracks!"

The doctor motioned him to lift Bernard from the packing cases and as he did so Boxer noticed that the two tourniquets had been expertly retied and a fresh bandage added to the dressing on the shattered elbow. Bernard was now breathing steadily and a little colour had returned into his cheeks.

"I gave him an injection," the doctor said, "he will not give you any trouble. If you are stopped do not pretend, my friend. These clothes are simply a ruse to get you as far as the road block and to stop casual shooting! Stick the flag in your brother's belt, so that it can be seen. If they ask you about his dressings tell them it was your own people who attended to him but they left him behind on the beach."

They passed out into the sunshine and for the first time Boxer noticed the strange silence that had descended over the hazy landscape. He did not connect it with the battle, or link the absence of gunfire with the cessation of fighting, and the probable withdrawal of all British troops but he was grateful for it nonetheless and marched firmly down the track indicated by the Frenchmen.

Bernard seemed no heavier to carry than a section of Bangalore torpedo tubing. He strode on into the sun, emerging soon on to a metalled road at a 'T' section and then turning left, as the Frenchman had instructed.

Without warning a convoy of lorries bore down on him, driven at furious speed, and Boxer had to suppress an instinct to flatten himself in the ditch beside the road but the lorries rushed by in a whirl of dust and the helmeted troops standing in the back did not so much as glance at him.

Boxer counted the lorries, six, seven, eight, nine of them, each crammed to capacity with armed men. In their wake came two armoured cars and then, from the opposite direction, a huge touring car, containing officers in steel helmets, decorated with colourful insignia.

It was the staff car that stopped. Bernard heard the screech of brakes on the pavé and a hoarse shout from one of the officers. A man jumped out of the car and came pounding back towards him, shouting questions in a language that Boxer assumed to be German. He remained quite still, his tiny beret perched on the crown of his head, his lumbering frame straining at the clips of the overalls.

Suddenly the German threw back his head and laughed, calling back to the car, which reversed, rapidly. A plump, elderly officer climbed out and approached Boxer, looking him up and down with great interest.

"You are an English soldier?" he said, finally.

It is doubtful if, even had he possessed a fluent command of the French tongue, Boxer would have tried to bluff. He was aware of the utter inadequacy of his disguise and the events of the day had exhausted his powers of thought. He felt terribly tired, tired of thinking and discussing things that he did not begin to understand, tired of weighing possibilities that made no kind of sense to him. The German at least did not beat about the bush, but like the Frenchmen, seemed to be asking a simple question that merited an equally simple answer.

Boxer grinned, then nodded, pleasantly.

"That's right," he said, "I'm taking my brother to see your M.O.!"

After this bland statement several things happened at once. The elderly officer confronting him whistled slowly through his teeth and the man who had first accosted Boxer began to dance and shout, as though he had suddenly been stung by a wasp. Other men climbed out of the car and began to scream at Boxer and then at one another, until at last the elderly man waved his hand and barked something at a corporal who was the driver of the car.

The corporal leaped into the driving seat as though he had been standing on coiled springs and in the midst of all this bustle Boxer found himself jostled into the car, with the officers crowding him from behind. They all seemed terribly excited and in a crazy hurry to get somewhere. When he found that entry into the rear section of the car was difficult without jarring Bernard's legs on the folding spare seat, someone prodded the small of his back with a Mauser pistol. Then, as though by magic, they were all tearing along the road towards a group of buildings in the distance and still he was holding Bernard close against his breast.

When the car screamed to a halt beside the buildings the officer with the pistol motioned him to get out, but Boxer had not been infected by their terrible urgency and said:

"Okay, okay, but take it easy chum! I don't want to knock old Berni, do I?"

For some reason, a reason that Boxer quite failed to grasp, this remark threw the young officer into a frenzy of rage. He waved his pistol right under Bernard's nose and kept bobbing up and down, gurgling and gasping as though in the throes of an epileptic fit.

Then the corporal jumped out and doubled round the car to Boxer's side, where he flung open the door and began to pull frantically at Bernard's webbing belt. This only increased Boxer's obstinacy and he braced himself against the front seats, remaining immovable until the elderly officer suddenly began to rave at the corporal and at the man with the Mauser. At length both officer and corporal skipped smartly away from the car and began to salute, like characters in a musical comedy.

Boxer was aware of this pantomime but without seeming to play an important part in it. He saw the corporal and the man with the pistol turn and run up a concrete path towards a two-storey building that seethed with uniformed men. Then the elderly officer was addressing him in English, kindly it seemed, for the old fellow spoke quite softly, and kept pointing to a pair of stretcher bearers who had bobbed out of the building and were now standing stiffly to attention beside the offside door of the car.

"They will dress your comrade's wounds," said the officer. "Then he will be sent to hospital, before going into honourable captivity, as yourself!" When Boxer still hesitated, he added: "We are not barbarians!"

Boxer found himself liking the plump officer and whenever Boxer took a liking to anyone he was ready to trust them implicitly. He climbed carefully out of the car and laid Bernard on the stretcher. The bearers moved away immediately and he stood watching them as they marched up the path and through the open door into the building.

Bernard's uninjured arm swung down as they negotiated the entrance and Boxer noticed that the Red Cross flag still trailed from its short stick, wedged under Berni's belt. The elderly officer stood silently beside Boxer until the stretcher party had disappeared and while they were still watching a huge private, wearing a camouflaged smock, and holding a sub-machine gun at the ready position, placed himself on the other side of Boxer and stared fixedly into the middle distance.

"Kom!" said the officer at length, "you will now tell me about yourself and why your comrades left you and your comrade behind when they ran away!"

He pointed casually to a shed built under the right-hand wall of the main building and the escort suddenly prodded Boxer with the barrel of his weapon.

They moved off in procession, the officer first, then Boxer, then the soldier with the sub-machine gun. A group of men, paraded at ease under the loggia of the building, watched them with curious eyes.

As he passed them Boxer yawned, prodigiously. "I'd like a kip," he told himself. "Suffering cats, how I'd like a good, long kip!"

CHAPTER XX

Change Of Plan

ODD and unpredictable events kept getting between Esme and Judith all that spring, and late summer found them widely separated and unmarried.

Once they had rediscovered one another it had seemed to them a very simple thing to get married. There existed, of course, the oft-quoted 'exigencies of service' but these could usually be overcome by a little discreet planning or wangling. All that had seemed necessary was to coincide a week's leave, or even a 'forty-eight' and rendezvous within walking distance of a register office. Then they could be married easily enough and speedily enough, even if they had to enlist a couple of strangers as witnesses and forgo the honeymoon until Esme's operational tour had been completed, and he was grounded for the customary six months.

They had no luck, however, no luck at all and were still frantically exchanging telegrams and long, pip-studded 'phone calls, months after Esme's decree had been made absolute.

First Esme's operational tour was cut short less than half-way through and he was packed off on a conversion course to Lancasters, in the far West of Scotland. He was detained here until late spring, thoroughly exasperated with the delay, and unable to get a pass allowing him sufficient time to meet Judy in Northampton and return to camp in time for Monday's training schedule.

Then, when he had at last been posted to a Lancaster squadron, he went suddenly sick with shingles in the head, and was detained in sick quarters for a fortnight. He was given a week's leave on recovery and they could have married then, but by this time Judy had been posted down to St. Eval, and was on a plotter's course that prohibited leave for a further six weeks.

Esme went down to Cornwall and spent an afternoon and an evening with her, but it was impossible, in that short time, to arrange anything very definite, so they agreed to leave it over until September, when he expected to be re-crewed and complete his interrupted tour.

Apart from the frustrating circumstances of their extended separation Esme was at peace with himself these days, having discovered, somewhat to his surprise, that an operational flight was not quite the ordeal he had imagined, and possessed, indeed, certain unlooked for compensations.

Isolated in his turret, as the huge machine lumbered across the empty skies, he found that he was able to divide his powers of concentration into two equal halves. One half was devoted exclusively to keeping a sharp lookout for night-fighters, and the other was free to range, contemplating the various aspects of the journey, the huge and exhilarating emptiness of the sky, the fantastic cloud formations floodlit by slivers of moonshine, the soaring passage of distant tracer, reminding him of Thursday night Crystal Palace fireworks displays that he had witnessed from the bunkers of the links at the end of The Lane. Then there were the occasional jocular exchanges over the intercom and above all the sense of 'belonging' that they brought with them, the sense of adventuring, in matchless company, into infinite space.

Bomber Command losses were high, and were still mounting, but they had not yet attained the terrifying peaks of the winter offensive. In the main Esme's squadron was lucky and the targets assigned to it so far had not been excessively hazardous.

Once they flew all the way down to Turin, and twice to French industrial centres in the Rhône area. The only time that anything really frightening occurred was during their sole trip to the Ruhr, when their starboard outer engine was hit by coastal flak, and they had turned for home after dutifully ditching their bombs in the North Sea.

Mac', the skipper, said that this 'slice of cake' was far too good to last, and that soon they would be assigned targets that invited 'the chop'. Esme thought that he was right, but nonetheless he continued to experience a comforting tranquillity in the long flights and ultimately made the discovery that an actual 'op' was a good deal less nerve-wracking than the constant, last-minute scrubbings, due to sudden changes of weather.

A tour of operations at this time consisted of thirty flights, and Esme chalked up eight without even seeing an enemy fighter, or encountering more than a spattering of flak. He thus acquired the ability to live from day to day, sealing off the future as unknown and unpredictable. He spent most of his free time reading or talking to Snowball, the West Indian wireless-operator. Occasionally he went out on a routine pub-crawl with the crew, but he was never much of a toper and it usually fell to him and the coloured boy to convey the remainder of the crew home to billets.

He wrote Judy long and affectionate letters, the kind of letters that he had always wanted to write to Elaine, but had left unwritten because of the depressing inadequacy of her letters to him. Judy's letters were far more rewarding than the best of Elaine's had been but they were not, somehow, the letters of an engaged girl, but more like those of a woman who had been happily and tranquilly married for years.

Far from disappointing him this strain of hers exactly matched his prevailing mood. He was able to think of her far more objectively than he had ever been able to think of Elaine, and there grew within him, throughout this period of anxiety and suspension, a warm and cosy acceptance of their association, and a conviction that their coming together, after all these years, had been fated. It was as if all their games of make-believe as children had been a planned prelude for a shared existence as adults, and that now nothing was strong enough to deny them one another's company in the years ahead.

He sometimes told himself that it was quite absurd to think of their love in these terms, for he was barely thirty, and she was a year younger, but he would not willingly have exchanged the repose she brought him for the emotional switchback of his life with Elaine. It was good, these days, to have someone like Judy to think about, and it was satisfying to reflect that, when the world eventually sorted itself out, as he believed it must if it was to endure, then he would at least have someone left who shared his memories of sunlit days in the plough-land beyond the Manor Wood, where the scent of wood-smoke drifted across from builders' fires, and thrushes sang in the thickets of the border spinney.

For Esme, as the war entered its fourth year, had become sharply aware of the great contrast between the world of his childhood and boyhood, and the world of today, with its curious mixture of the trivial and the far from trivial, its brutal slang, its blackout, its careless-talk posters, and its books of clothing coupons, all clouding the emotional de- mands of war and the infinite pathos of eager young men gathering together night after night for the lunatic purpose of flying hundreds of miles in order to drop high explosive on people they had neither seen nor expected to see.

He was aware of this contrast but without being over- involved in it. Sometimes it seemed to him that he was watching it without playing any part in it, and without it stirring in him more than the casual interest of a spectator.

He remembered how, when a child, he had conjured with the ridiculous notion that he was the only person alive, and that everyone about him was imagined, and this thought returned to him sometimes when he sat hunched in his turret, remote from everything but the moon, the stars, and the comforting, crowding, unrelated memories of growing up in the Avenue.

Half-way through September Judy wired saying that they could be married almost at once from Miss Somerton's home, in Devon.

It seemed that her plotting course had petered out, and Judy had now been attached to a Transport Unit, and was sent, as sergeant i/c convoy, to various parts of the country. She had a convoy, she told him, going to Southampton mid-week, and she could scramble in a long week-end on her way back to base in Cornwall.

Miss Somerton, her former employer, who still maintained a small riding-school on the moors, south of Exeter, had therefore come forward with an offer of hospitality from Friday to Monday, and Judy hoped that he could take advantage of this unique opportunity.

He wired back immediately, promising to do his utmost to wangle a week-end, even if it meant travelling to and from Lincolnshire by overnight trains.

Jubilantly Judy shepherded her lorries into Southampton, and then caught the first train back to Exeter.

She was glad to be back on familiar, pre-war ground and the hook-nosed Miss Somerton was equally delighted to greet her, and drive her back to the decrepit Georgian manor-farm that she had used as headquarters ever since she had moved her riding-school into the west.

The relation between Judy and Miss Somerton was openly cordial, and covertly sentimental. Maud Somerton had taken her in as a shy and depressed little shop-assistant of sixteen, and had then proceeded to teach her everything that she herself knew of horses, and horsemastership.

Judy had proved a patient and rewarding pupil, and all through the 'thirties' Maud Somerton had regarded her as a mainstay, particularly in respect of the coaching of children. Judy had that essential combination of firmness and gentleness so necessary to the professional equestrienne, and she could control (Maud never discovered just how) a long cavalcade of bowler-hatted little extroverts, all at varying stages of proficiency, and all trying to make themselves heard above the rattle of hooves, as the bored ponies jogged along high-banked, Devon lanes.

Not once in the years that Judy had worked for her, had there been an accident, or even a spill that led to tears and temper. Maud studied her pupil's technique closely but was never able to imitate it. She would follow her out of the courtyard, and watch Judy marshall her little charges and shoo them down the gravelled drive. Sometimes she smiled grimly to herself as she listened to Judy's string of commands and admonitions, recalling, perhaps, the tear-stained little girl she had met by the Roman Well on Shirley Hills so long ago. She would often stand listening until the voices and clatter were lost in the trees. "Keep your hands *down*, Angela dear ... Sarah darling, toes up and out! Monica, love, you look

like a small sack of barley . . . ! Don't *bunch* your reins,
Barbara . . . here, let me show you, now . . . *relax* darling! Hi
there, don't let him nibble! He'll try it on, just as he does
with all of you . . . !" and so on, until the cavalcade was out
of hearing.

Maud would then lounge back to the loose boxes and
begin mucking out, reflecting that 'The Gel', as she invariably
thought of her, must be a born teacher, with the additional
advantages of a natural seat and the softest pair of hands in
the business! Sometimes, as she pondered this, she would
smile with satisfaction and remember how it was she who had
spotted these talents at a glance, before 'The Gel' had so
much as sat upon a horse!

She was by no means as sanguine about 'The Gel's' love
life. She had liked Tim Ascham, the boy whom Judy had
married when war broke out and who had been drowned a
few weeks later, but she was not nearly so sure that she
would like Esme, the boy, she understood, who had caused
the tears visible on Judy's face the first day they had met by
the Roman Well.

Judy had told her that there had never been anyone
else but Esme, and that she had made up her mind to marry
him at the age of six, but Maud Somerton knew rather more
about hard-pad, greasy-heel, and colic, than she knew about
first-love and she had her doubts about 'The Gel' getting hurt
again, as she had been so badly hurt over Tim.

It was a great pity, she thought, that this new man was a
flier, for fliers did not seem to live very long nowadays, and
she did not care to think what she would do with 'The Gel' if
the little soul was unlucky enough to be widowed a second
time. However, if she wanted to get married she should.
After all, young people of her own generation had had their
lives spoiled by one war and here it was, starting all over
again. Perhaps it was best to do what these two intended
doing, to grab what life had to offer day by day, and ignore
the future, if indeed, there was any future in a world where
crushed oats were the price they were asking, and good hay
was unobtainable!

Almost as soon as she met Judy at the station Maud
realised that 'The poor Gel' was finding it difficult to be

philosophical about this wedding. She had always thought of Judy as a tranquil soul untroubled by jitters, even County-ring jitters, but clearly Judy had changed after more than two years out of the saddle, and was now morbidly preoccupied with hazards that had nothing whatever to do with spirited young geldings and traffic-shy mares.

"It's like this, Miss Somerton," Judy confessed to her, during the cross-country journey to the stables; "I've developed a kind of 'thing' about Esme and me lately. It's silly, and it's superstitious, but we're all more or less superstitious in the R.A.F. We go in for signs, and mascots, and crossed fingers, and all that sort of thing! You see, I've been dreaming about marrying Esme ever since I was a child . . . twenty-three years in all, and that's a hell of a long dream! Oh, I know there was Tim, and I loved Tim very dearly, but not in the same way, not in a well . . . not in a kind of 'meant-to-be' way, as I love Esme, and as I think Esme loves me!"

"He was a long time getting round to it," grunted Maud Somerton. "Why didn't he marry you in the first place?"

"Oh, that's a long story," laughed Judy, "and I don't propose to tell it to you now or ever! The fact is, we do love each other, and we've always belonged to each other, but I wish . . . oh, how I wish, that we'd been able to run off and get married the day we realised it last Christmas leave! I'm sure then that everything would have been all right, I'm sure we'd have had some luck, but so many things have happened since and now it all seems . . . well . . . as if a kind of witch's curse was on us, preventing us coming together, no matter how hard we try! First there was Elaine, the girl he married from over the road, and then there was my Tim, and then Esme went air-crew, because he didn't care what happened to him, and then we met up again, just like a miracle when he brought his little girl to my camp, and now . . . well . . . every time we make plans something silly seems to happen, something always pops up and says: 'Oh no you don't, my beauties! Just wait until I've put a spoke in it!' "

"I've never heard such rubbish in my life," exclaimed Maud, her matter-of-fact soul outraged by this kind of talk. "What you need my gel is a thundering good gallop, and fortunately you're just in time to get one! We're cubbing at six o'clock tomorrow, over at Woodbury Castle, and you can give Jason an airing. He's about as stale as you seem to be!"

"Jason! You've still got my Jason!" exclaimed Judy delightedly, "but you wrote and told me you sold him!"

"So I did," said Maud, "to a farmer over at Silverton, but I borrowed him back for a week the moment I heard you were coming, and he's in the blue box right now, eating his head off at about two pounds a mouthful!"

"Oh, you're a darling, an absolute old darling," cried Judy, leaning over the steering wheel, and planting a kiss on Miss Somerton's weatherbeaten cheek. "You planned it all, didn't you? Just like you fixed up the wedding, and I might have known because you've always been nicer to me than anyone in the world!"

"Oh, don't hand me out any of that slop," muttered Maud, but she reminded herself once again that her original encounter with this warm little creature was certainly the most pleasant thing that had ever happened to her.

* * * *

They rode out while it was still dark and picked their way over the common tracks, past the bustling Marine camp and up to the Castle that crowned the ridge above the valley of the Exe.

There were only three or four other riders, the Master, Whip, and a couple of red-faced farmer's lads, riding unclipped cobs.

Judy was exhilarated by the occasion and by the sharp morning air that carried the first nip of autumn, and whipped the colour into her cheeks as she settled herself on Jason and drew his steamy warmth into her calves.

"Let's make it a cracking day, Jason," she whispered, patting the sleek neck, "because Esme's coming today, and tomorrow's my wedding day."

The big horse threw his head about.

"He'll prove a handful, mark my words," said Maud Somerton, watching her. "That fellow, Cotley never took him above a hand-gallop, and he's been lazing about on grass ever since April!"

"Jason and I are on top of the world," Judy told her gaily, "Come on up, old boy," as the little group of horses filed down from the knoll towards Woodbury Wood, "let's find straight away, and then show 'em what the W.A.A.F. can do!"

They found on the edge of the covert, and away they went, over springy grass and dry, stony tracks, with the Whip in the lead, and Judy a length or so behind, shouting for joy as they crashed through flat brakes of yellow gorse, and then galloped across the main road towards the camp.

Half-dressed marines tumbled out of their tents to watch them thunder by, as they followed their line towards Crook's Wood, and a pair of farm-workers, harrowing a long-rested ground beyond Yettington, paused in their work and shouted directions as the pack scrambled through hedges, overran scent, found a new line, and finally poured across the stubble towards the sea.

It was a fast point, as fast as she remembered, and Jason skimmed the banks without seeming to touch them. In the glorious excitement of the moment Judy forgot Esme, the war, the convoys, and the bombing offensive, leaning far over Jason's mane, and nursing him through the gaps with a sure, steady touch and never a thought to the kind of ground she was likely to jump down upon beyond.

Thus she never saw or suspected the taut strand of pig-wire stretched a yard from the hedge, on the far side of the fifth bank.

The Whip, riding a fleet grey, cat-jumped the obstacle, clearing it by inches, but his wild cry of, " 'Ware wire!" startled Jason, less than two yards behind, and the horse faltered, slithering from the crest of the bank and getting his hind legs between wire and hedge. The wire held and he jammed his forelegs into the turf. Judy went over his head and down, face foremost, on to a harrow that was lying at the edge of the field.

She missed the metal, but her shoulder struck the shaft with a sickening jar, breaking her collar-bone, and ripping her hacking jacket from sleeve to collar as she somersaulted across the grass.

Maud Somerton shouted from the far side of the hedge and the Whip reined in and circled back to her.

"You hurt, Miss? Did you hit that blasted harrow?"

Judy struggled to her feet, hugging her right shoulder. Jason was struggling madly against the hedge.

"I don't know . . . damned wire . . . see to the horse, he's caught by the hind legs!"

They freed Jason with clippers and bent to examine his trembling legs. The strand of wire had scored two deep weals above the hocks and for a moment they forgot Judy, busying themselves, as hunting people will, with the distressed animal.

When Maud Somerton crossed over she found that Judy had fainted. Despatching the Whip to stop a car on the main road, she lifted her up and carefully examined the shoulder, remembering as she did so, Judy's half-serious talk of a witch's curse.

"Poor gel," she moaned, "poor, poor gel! She was getting married tomorrow!"

. . . . .

They drove her to the hospital, where the bone was set and then Maud hired a taxi and took her home, sitting holding her in the back, and thanking God over and over again that 'the poor gel' had escaped with a comparatively minor injury.

Judy was very quiet during the short journey, leaning heavily on Maud's shoulder and looking, Maud thought, to be badly shaken by the toss. Her face was still smeared with mud where she had glissaded across the field, and as the taxi pulled up in courtyard Maud noticed that she was weeping.

"Poor Esme," was all she said however, when they put her to bed.

"Never mind about Esme," Maud told her shortly, "get some sleep until he gets here! Then I'll bring you some tea and broth, after I've dealt with the horses and that idiot, Coombes!"

'That idiot, Coombes' was the farmer who owned the field surrounded by pig-wire, and from her room above the hall, where the telephone was installed, Judy heard Maud Somerton railing at him for daring to fence his own property.

In spite of the ceaseless throb of her shoulder, and the wretchedness in her heart, she could not help smiling at the note of protest in Maud's harsh voice. Then she drifted off into an uncomfortable doze that lasted, at intervals, until noon, when her door opened and Esme was standing beside her, holding a tray of tea.

"Well," he said, "if this doesn't beat all! For crying out loud, Judy, this takes the entire, bloody biscuit!"

"Yes," she said, abjectly, "it does rather, doesn't it?" and then, fearfully: "How long have you got, Esme darling? I daresay I could be up and about by Monday."

He looked away, out of the window and across the beech-ringed orchard to the moor.

"Twenty-four hours, Judy! We could have made it, if everything had gone according to plan, but we can't make it now—not a hope—I'm bound to start back in the small hours!"

She understood very well what he was trying to say.

"You mean there's something special on?"

"A flap, and a pretty big one I should say. I had the Devil's own job to get down here at all!"

She was silent for a moment while he poured the tea.

Presently she said: "I'm a Jonah, Esme, just a plain, honest-to-goodness Jonah!"

"We're a couple of Jonahs, Judy and it's beginning to look as if we've always been!"

"I ought to have known that something like this would happen. Now we'll never be married."

He set down the teapot and took both her hands in his.

"Don't talk like that, Judy! Of course we'll be married! You know how long a flap lasts! Damn it, it isn't as if I'd been posted abroad, or was likely to be! As long as I'm flying Lancs I'm here for the duration and you know that as well as I do!"

Suddenly she began to cry again and he forgot the tea tray, kneeling beside her, stroking her hair, and struggling to find words of comfort and reassurance.

"What's so damned important about getting married, Judy? The thing is that we've got one another! That's all that's important to me!"

But it was not, as she was now fully aware, all that was damned important to her; Judy's dream was older than Esme's, reaching back into the long, dry summers of the 'twenties', when they had fished for tadpoles in Keston Ponds, but she knew it was not yet possible to make him understand this, not until they were man and wife, and she could *live* her devotion instead of dreaming it. She stopped crying and asked him for her handbag, complaining that 'she must look a mess', and apologising again for the accident that had shattered their arrangements.

"It's the first time I've ever been hurt in the hunting field," she told him. "I must have been crazy to chance it today, but it was just that I felt ... well ... so terribly excited, and so wildly happy this morning!"

"You and that dear, old fossil downstairs might as well be married to horses!" he teased her. "Here, get some of this soup down you; I'll feed it to you with a spoon, and show you how domesticated I am!"

She was unable to move her right arm, so he balanced the tray on her knees and she steadied it while he fed her a bowl of Maud's vegetable soup. She smiled wanly as she swallowed, and when the bowl was empty he fetched a flannel and washed her face and hands, gaily but tenderly, so that her despondency lifted and they were calm enough to discuss the future.

"I'll desert and come up to the airfield the minute I can struggle into some civvies'," she told him.

"The redcaps would pick you up before you got word to me that you were outside the wire!"

"They don't do anything to deserters in my outfit! They just sack us, as 'non-amenable to discipline'!"

"We can do a lot better than that the minute you're operational," he joked, "I'll oblige you with a 'Clause Eleven' pregnancy discharge!"

"Now that really *is* an idea," she said, "quite the best yet!" and they both laughed, and talked on for a few moments in the ironic idiom which they had used in the camps over the last two years.

Presently they grew serious again, and he got up and looked out into the gathering dusk.

"All this means much more to you than the Avenue now, doesn't it, Judy?"

"Yes," she admitted, "I suppose it does, but I don't think I should have learned to love it so much if it hadn't been for the Avenue. That never seemed to belong to a suburb to me, it was like a piece of Devon that had strayed, and lost itself while playing near London."

"It won't stay like that, Judy, not after the war. It's changing, even now. They've got thousands of Yanks sculling about in our woods, and the old Manor is a Transport H.Q., thick with jeeps and lorries, and crawling with G.I.s all playing baseball! Sometimes I think even the Jerries wouldn't have made such a mess of it!"

"Esme," she said suddenly, as though his words had started a new train of thought, "after the war do you *want* to go back there? Wouldn't you like to live somewhere else, somewere in real country, like this?"

"That would depend on my job, wouldn't it?"

"I suppose so, but couldn't you write anywhere, in a country cottage for instance?"

He was silent for a moment, then he said:

"I shan't write at all after the war, Judy, I've quite made up my mind about that! You see, I'm not really a writer, and I've never convinced myself that I am! I've been kidding myself, right from the start. I told myself I wanted to be a writer, and because I had enough money to keep me from needing a real job I went right on kidding myself until after I joined up! That way wasted the time I might have 'been learning something. I'm through with all that now. After it's over I'm going to farm and that isn't just another dream, because I've got the capital to buy a farm and I've even talked it over with old Harold. He says it can easily be managed if I go the right way about it."

He turned away from the window and came back to the bed.

"Does that scare you, Judy? Do you feel like marrying an amateur farmer, and watching him lose every penny he's got?"

She felt at peace again. His admission had somehow advanced her another step towards fulfilment. It did not seem strange to her that he, who had never turned a spadeful of earth, or learned to milk a cow, should suddenly become obsessed with the idea of becoming a farmer, and earning a living from the soil and the care of animals. She imagined that he must have been drifting in this direction for a long time now, perhaps ever since the days when they had shared the excitement of the first hawthorn blossoms growing along the hedge in Shirley Rise. She remembered now that he had always possessed this deep and unconscious love of things growing. He had always been moved by the sight of the first foxgloves in Manor Wood, and the raw smell of turned soil in the plough-land beyond the wood. She had always admired his determination to become a writer, and had even been slightly awed by his limited successes with B.B.C. features, but she realised now that she could never have taken this work very seriously, and had always half-hoped that he would discover something to replace it.

She was happy too because his plan coincided exactly with her own desires, and with a deep, hidden wish to make a permanent home here in Devon. She wanted to have his children, and she wanted those children to grow up in an unspoiled countryside, where nobody carried umbrellas or caught regular trains, and the steep lanes possessed neither lamposts nor red pillar-boxes.

"I think that's a lovely idea, Esme," she said, "and I can't think of anything I'd like better! I could be a real help to you on a farm, much more of a help than I could ever be as a housewife in the Avenue. I know about chickens, and I know about pigs, and Maud says there'll be money in chickens and pigs after the war. We'll have to learn about cows somewhere, but that ought to be easy for you; after all, you learned how to be an air-gunner, and it can't be nearly as difficult as that!"

When it began to grow dusk Maud tapped on the door with supper for both of them.

"I've looked up your trains and ordered your taxi for eight," she told Esme. "You can get the 8.45 from Exeter, and there's a train from Euston to Grantham at 3.15 in the morning. I've cut you some sandwiches to eat in the train.

They're door-steps, I'm afraid but I'm not much good at sandwiches, am I, Gel?"

"It's very good of you to bother, Miss Somerton," he said. "How long have we got now?"

"About half an hour," she told him, picking up the tea-tray and going out to the landing. "I'll give you a call in plenty of time."

. . . .

The 'flap' Esme had mentioned was apparent as soon as he booked into camp.

He had travelled twelve hours through the night in crowded main-line trains, and most of the journey had been spent in corridors, huddled against kitbags and suitcases. He arrived back in his billet with an aching head, and the sour taste of too many cigarettes in his mouth, to find Snowball waiting with a message from Mac', the skipper.

Briefing, Esme learned, was at midday, and so far the met. reports were encouraging. It looked, said Snowball, like the start of the Big Show, and according to the gen-boys it would begin with a twin-force blitz on two widely-separated areas of the Ruhr.

After breakfast Esme felt more wide-awake and the crew gathered in Mac's billet to await the announcement of briefing over the Tannoy. Esme had to face a barrage of good-natured raillery in respect of his postponed wedding and Judy's hunting accident.

"Well, if you *will* consort with these Tatler types!" said Hawley, the mid-upper gunner: but Mac', Esme's new skipper, told Hawley to 'get stuffed', and expressed genuine sympathy with Esme. Mac' approved of marrying into the W.A.A.F., having himself married an A.C.W. meteorologist less than a year ago.

They sat about round the empty stove, discussing the forth-coming operation in deliberately casual terms. Esme knew that each of them was experiencing the exact duplicate of his own qualms and that each man was using his individual method to conceal them from the other members of the crew.

Snowball, the radio-operator, was steadily dismantling his

portable radio once again. Hawley, when he wasn't recounting ribald and mostly stale stories, was trying to pretend to an interest in an American periodical. 'Greg', the bomb-aimer, was writing a letter home, and finding its composition distressing to judge by his grunts and frequent shifts of posture. Gilbert, the flight-engineer, was methodically cleaning his shoes—why, Esme wondered, when he invariably slopped around camp, town and billets in his heavy flying boots? Time hung very heavily for them until the warning click of the Tannoy gave them the cue to throw aside makeshift occupations, and scramble for the briefing hall.

"This is it," muttered Mac'. "Fingers out, and press on regardless, chaps!"

They learned that they were to attack Hanover and Bremen in two streams, each composed of over four hundred aircraft. A 'spoof' raid was scheduled for the Ruhr, with the object of diverting enemy night-fighter forces and Esme, listening attentively to the string of experts dispensing their detailed information on weather, course, and the kind of opposition they were likely to encounter, was conscious of a thrill that had been absent from previous briefings.

It was soon clear that the gen. merchants had been nearly right for once, and that this was indeed the opening of the offensive Mac' had prophesied for autumn.

Somehow the knowledge drew each of them more closely into the inner vortex of the air war, so that their personal lives, their homes, womenfolk, grumbles and even their small talk were patterns of long ago and had no significance in this smoke-wreathed hall, jammed tight with earnest young men straining every nerve to appear jovial, carefree, and hardboiled.

After briefing the day seemed to pass very quickly, for there was much to do and a long letter to be written to Judy. Esme considered for a moment, writing the kind of letter that some of the married men wrote and left behind, with instructions to post in the event of their failure to get home, but he quickly put the idea aside as phoney-dramatic, and compromised with an affectionate three-page summary of their conversation about the farm. He ended his letter with a

Rabelaisian admonition to prepare for their next rendezvous, planned for a fortnight hence.

He smiled as he sealed the letter, reflecting that its very tone was a signpost into a new era. A few years ago a man could never have expressed himself thus to a young woman he intended to marry, and it was even doubtful if he would have used phrases like this in a letter to a barmaid who was his mistress . . . 'get weaving', 'get your finger out', 'get up them stairs'. . . . Today these exchanges were normal currency between sexes, particularly between men and women serving in the same arm of the forces. He knew, too, that Judy would read into them the same need to conceal his true feelings as he detected in the brittle gaiety of the men around him.

Greg, the bomb-aimer, found words for this thought, as he sealed his own letter, written to his father, a clerk, in Willesden: "What the hell *can* you say to the folks anyway? If you gave 'em pukka gen you'd be on the fizzer for blabbing official secrets, and if you talked a lot of cock about home and beauty they'd read it as a last will and testament, written by a bloke who knew dam' well he was going for a Burton!"

"I wonder," said Mac', seriously for once, "I wonder if men talked as we talk before battles in the past, before Waterloo for instance? I wonder if they wrote home trying to give the impression that it was all a bit of a lark, instead of the bloody shambles they knew it was going to be?"

"It *was* a bit of a lark, then," said Gilbert, the New Zealand Flight Engineer. "It wouldn't scare *me* any to charge a bloody great horse right up to a mob of poor baskets firing bows and arrows! Hell, you had armour all over you didn't you?"

"Not at Waterloo, you clot!" said Esme, grinning, "and I imagine that grapeshot was as bad as flak any day of the week!"

"What exactly *was* grapeshot?" asked Snowball, and they drifted into a technical discussion on the relative armaments of Wellington and Bomber Harris. Esme was the crew's authority on all historical matters and they were still discussing the range of cannon, and the lethal power of horse pistols, when the Waaf arrived in her jeep to take them out to dispersal.

Then, as they bumped over the tarmac towards 'R-for-Ronnie', the familiar flippancy returned, but with it a deliberate putting aside of everything outside the purely technical sphere relating to a seven-hour flight to and from the Continent. Although no one said as much each of them drew fresh confidence from the presence of so many aircraft, and so much deliberate activity, as crews hoisted their parachute packs out of jeeps and climbed, chattering and yelling, into the bellies of the Lancasters, Stirlings and Halifaxes dotted about the flat, Lincolnshire landscape.

Esme settled himself in the tail and swallowed his wakey-wakey pill as the flight commander's car appeared from under the wing to give him the last-minute target information to pass to Mac'.

"Hullo, Skip? The target is Hanover! Hanover!"

"That's a bloody sight healthier than Bremen!" said Mac', kicking off his microphone.

Esme felt no trace of anxiety now, simply a mild, pleasurable excitement, as the four Merlin engines roared into life and they began to taxi into the queue. Then, with the familiar bumping lift, they were away, and looking right down on the queue as they soared off towards the sea, with other aircraft appearing below them, looking like cut-out toys against an orange sky.

. . . .

The Ju. 88 came at them on the port bow about twenty minutes after they had made their bomb run and turned for home.

Up to that moment it had been a placid, uneventful flight, with no coastal flak and no night-fighters in the coastal belt or over the target, just a long, monotonous haul into the south-east, with a glimpse of the diversionary attack on the Ruhr, and one dummy run over the winking city, already lit with fires and pathfinder flares.

"So far, so good," Mac' had said into the intercom, and then the Ju. 88's navigational lights had cut past their tail and Esme was firing a long burst at it and shouting to Mac' to corkscrew before the enemy banked and came in for the kill.

After that scare they bucketed about all over the sky and it was ten minutes before Mac' called up again; Esme noted the urgency in his voice.

"Bloody outer port's cut! Any damage down your way?"

"No," Esme told him, "and we were damned lucky to get away with it! He jumped me out of nowhere!"

"Okay, keep looking!" said Mac', switching off.

Esme stared up and down, to port, to starboard, until his eyes felt as if they were straining at taut strings attached to the back of his skull. He noticed an interruption in the throb of the engines but a general check-up showed that the aircraft was more than capable of getting back to base.

"Thank God for that!" said Gilbert from his panel. "To hell with landing at a strange base where they've run out of beer!"

Another ten minutes passed and they picked up their old course, hoping to lose themselves in the returning stream, but their serenity was gone and Esme was wretchedly aware of his thumping heart, and tried to calm himself by picturing Judy's brown, elfin face as he had bent to kiss it when Maud Somerton had called up to say that his taxi had arrived.

He succeeded, although it required all his powers of concentration. His brain continued to claw him back to the realities of the night, and the terrors they held for a crippled bomber limping home across hundreds of miles of enemy-patrolled sky.

Then, after a long silence, he heard Hawley's thin voice, piping into the intercom from mid-upper turret:

"*Fighter, fighter! Corkscrew!*"

And again came the wild, senseless bucketing, as Mac' took instant evasive action. Then another spasm of fear but before it could overwhelm him, the sudden chatter of Browning guns, a series of dull thumps, and a confused shouting out of which Mac's voice emerged, terribly urgent this time, calling: "*Jump ... jump!*" as Esme found himself ducking under the mid-upper turret and groping his way across the main spar towards the hatch.

He remembered no more than that of the last, mad moments in the shattered aircraft. He supposed that he must

have carried out the routine actions automatically, his brain
relying on the distilled wisdom of months of lectures and
demonstrations, rather than upon any instinctive moves he
made to save his life. The aircraft seemed to be disintegrating
around him and the reek of petrol caught at his throat.
Someone shot out in front of him and he saw Snowball
prancing about near Gilbert's instrument panel. He remembered a knife-thrust of fear as he tumbled headlong into
space; then he was floating, and his chest felt wet and cold,
and the silence around him was so intense that he felt he
could have reached out and gathered it by the armful.

He did not think about landing, or of the men still in the
aircraft, but only of the vast silence of the sky, and his
strange, almost lunatic suspension in it.

CHAPTER XXI

Esme Describes The Avenue

HIS full consciousness returned only when his boots brushed against something that crackled, and in the split-second between this contact and his impact on solid ground, he once more fell back on the instinctive lessons of his training, flexing his knees and rolling over and over in what he later recognised as an almost expert landing.

He detached himself from the parachute and crawled on all fours from under the folds of silk that the light wind was wrapping about him. He reached forward blindly with his hands, and the contact they made with moist earth told him he had lost a glove on the way down and was sifting tilled soil through his numbed fingers.

His right hand was very cold, but the rest of his body felt warm, almost cosily warm. He sat back on his haunches, a yard or so from the billowing canopy, and prodded himself all over, flexing his arms, and slowly and carefully putting weight on each of his knees in turn.

Then he said aloud: "I'm alive! Christ, I'm alive! I made it! Christ, I made it!"

The sound of his voice, uttering these words, made him want to laugh and leap about, like a small boy suddenly presented with an unexpected treat, but he resisted the impulse and thought instead of Judy and all this would mean to her, propped up where he had last seen her in her bare little room in Maud Somerton's Spartan home.

Then, with the memory of Judy, his mind engaged his immediate problems—to stay alive, and to stay free, free to make his way home again somehow, and get to a telephone where he could hear her voice and to tell her that they would be married after all, even if they both had to be wheeled to a register office in bath chairs by her Commando brothers, Berni and Boxer.

He must have been slightly hysterical, for he had even begun to chuckle at the image such a wedding conjured up, when suddenly he remembered that Berni and Boxer were missing, and had not been heard of since the Dieppe raid, more than a month ago.

The thought cheered rather than depressed him, however, for it now seemed to him that he was not alone in the gusty darkness, but that Berni and Boxer might be somewhere around, eager to renew the partnership he had shared with them in the Lower School, before they were split up by Old Longjohn, the Head, and he was set to work in the forcing-house of the Certificate Fifth.

Gradually, he steadied himself until he could think rationally. Gradually, as he sat in the furrow chafing his numbed hand and stretching his legs, he was able to make some kind of shift at assessing his position and chances.

He was almost certainly in France, which was much better than being in Germany. In France there was an active Underground Movement that concerned itself, gallantly and ingeniously so he had heard, with the business of getting stranded air-crew back to Britain.

Meanwhile he had his escape kit, the small folder of silk maps, compass, and French money. He had malted milk tablets in his battledress pocket, and a small rubber bag for water if he could find any.

Little by little he collected himself, even to the point of reckoning up how many hours of darkness were left, but as he gathered up his parachute, and sucked a malted milk tablet, his dominating thought was still one of immense gratitude and surprise at being alive, and this thought was far too absorbing to enable him to spare one as yet for Mac', Snowball, and the others who had shared that last crazy moment in the kite.

He did not even want to think about the actual cause of the disaster, or how and why they had been 'jumped' and shot down, or whether or no Greg had got in a burst at their attacker before the cannon-shells had ripped into the fuselage, and sent them spinning to earth.

He was content, for the time being, to hole up somewhere, and bury his 'chute, and he stumbled off across the soggy ground until he ran headlong into a wooden building, constructed of rough-hewn planks.

Then he remembered his matches and decided to risk striking one. The tiny flame, extinguished after a couple of seconds, showed him that he was standing in the doorless entrance of some kind of barn, piled high with root-crops.

Carefully he felt his way inside and then struck another match. This time he protected the flame from the wind and it flared up, revealing the inside of a gimcrack structure, built on low piles at the extreme edge of the field.

He let the match burn out and then set about burrowing a hole in the roots, stuffing in his parachute and scrambling over the crown of the stack to a hollow against the far wall.

From here, lying on his stomach, he could make out the faint outline of the entrance and beyond it a faint greyness in the sky. He settled himself among the tufted mangolds and it occurred to him that here already was a source of food to supplement his malted milk tablets. He rubbed one of the roots with the palm of his ungloved hand and set his teeth into the rough, gritty surface.

Almost at once he began to retch and between spasms of dry retching he fell asleep, his face pressed to the cold surface of the roots.

＊　＊　＊　＊

It was broad daylight when he awoke and saw, beyond the ridge of mangolds, a slim, middle-aged man enter the shelter, carrying a pitchfork over his shoulder.

He lay quite still and studied the man closely, noting his clothes, his narrow, expressionless face, and his casual demeanour as he fidgeted about near the entrance.

Esme felt stiff and cold, and by no means as elated as when he had entered the barn, for the realities of his situation were much clearer to him by daylight and it was plain to him now that it could only be a matter of time before he was obliged to choose between surrender or making his presence known to the French, if indeed, he was on French soil.

He decided, at length, to stake everything on a straightforward appeal to the Frenchman and was phrasing an introductory speech when another, older man walked quickly into the shed, carrying what appeared to be a canvas shopping bag which he handed to the labourer.

The newcomer was more impressive. He had serious eyes, and a long, waxed moustache that reminded Esme of a paternal figure in an old-fashioned photograph album. He wore a black pork-pie hat, a check coat of stout cloth, baggy breeches, and short, yellow leggings. Mentally Esme named him 'The Agent'.

Neither glanced towards the stack of mangolds where Esme lay but presently, after conversing in low tones to the labourer, the Agent said aloud, and in excellent English:

"Remain where you are! We will come back for you when the first search is finished! Two of your friends are dead and three are already captured. In this bag is wine and bread!"

Esme said nothing, being far too surprised to reply, and in any case it was clear that the Frenchmen did not expect him to speak, for they instantly left the barn, the labourer remaining close to the entrance and busying himself with his pitchfork.

Esme fought a craving to light a cigarette, and fixed his eyes on the bag that the labourer had set down on the lower bank of roots. It was very quiet in the hollow against the planks, and presently he discovered that, by shifting his position somewhat, he could peer through a chink at the hedge that bordered the field.

He was about to wriggle across the roots and secure the bag when he saw through the chink the upper part of what looked like a military vehicle, cruising slowly along the lane. It stopped just beyond the barn and someone got out, calling sharply to the labourer.

Esme burrowed deeper into the roots, finally succeeding in covering himself. He heard brisk steps nearing the barn and then someone entered, approaching so closely to him that he could hear their breathing. He lay quite still, thankful indeed that he had taken the precaution to cover himself for the visitor, whoever it was, actually scrambled up on to the lower bank of roots and kicked his way towards the back of the barn. Then he retreated, climbed down again, and went off. A moment later Esme heard the engine of the vehicle start up in the lane. He remained covered for another ten minutes, then eased himself free, and slid down the shifting roots to fetch the bag. As he did so the labourer slouched in, his face drawn with anxiety.

"*Parti!*" he grunted and waved his hand towards the bag. Esme took out a long-necked bottle of wine, and two broken halves of a French loaf. He was not hungry, but the man obviously wished him to eat, for he waved his arms and nodded his head encouragingly.

The wine helped to restore Esme's confidence, badly shaken by the visit.

"Les Allemands?" he asked.

The stolid man nodded and spat. Then, without another word or sign, he walked out of the barn and across the sloping field in the opposite direction to the lane.

Esme watched him out of sight and carried the bag back to his hollow. His elation was returning and he decided to risk a cigarette, blowing the smoke into the deep hollow where he had hidden himself. He wondered vaguely which of the crew were captured, which of them were dead, and who was still free, but the fate of five of the crew did not depress him overmuch, for he was riding a tide of personal triumph.

Time passed very slowly here among the mangolds and he had leisure to reflect on the immediate past and the long-distant past. It seemed to him, lying in half-light at the back of a French barn, that so far he had achieved very little in life, but that this was unimportant now, for his achievements were on the point of commencing. Perhaps this was his big chance to achieve something. Perhaps this was something he might do well, escape across hundreds of miles of enemy territory, and get home to Judy and the Avenue. Perhaps, indeed, this was the big adventure that he had been seeking ever since he played in Manor Wood, and cast himself in an endless succession of heroic roles, many of them akin to the role he was now playing! He freely admitted to himself that all he had set out to do had not amounted to anything very much. He had dreamed his boyhood away, and then spent the next ten years in haphazard attempts to justify himself to himself, first as a lover, then as a writer, then as a romantic tramp, then as a husband, and finally as an airman, but so far he had made little impression on anyone. Of all the people he had met during thirty years of opportunity he had succeeded only in impressing one—Judy Carver. His romantic idealisation of Elaine was dead but he still smarted at his failure to have aroused in her anything more definite than lazy, good-natured contempt. As a writer his failure was less spectacular, but he did not shrink from admitting that his contributions to literature meant less than a row of pins, or that the urge to write had now burned itself out.

As a working journalist he was also a failure, for he was aware, by this time, that he had lacked the brashness and self-confidence demanded of the professional newspapermen and had, indeed, never considered himself as anything more than a glorified clerk in Fleet Street.

As an air-gunner, he decided, he had come slightly nearer to success, but even here he had ultimately failed the men who had trusted him, and had allowed that first Ju. 88 to rake the port engine before he fired a defensive burst. That, of course, might have happened to anyone, as old Mac' would have to admit, but Mac' was dead or a prisoner, and his tail-gunner's failure to spot the first enemy fighter was surely a powerful factor in the loss of 'R-for-Ronnie'.

Here, at last, however, was a chance to achieve something spectacular, for here, if ever, he was on his own, and facing the heaviest kind of odds!

If he could get home in one piece, instead of going tamely behind barbed wire for the remainder of the war, then at least he would have something to present to Judy to prove to her that he really was something of the man she had believed him to be all those years they had lived side by side in the Avenue. At all events he resolved to try. Dear God, he told himself, how desperately he would try!

It was almost dusk when the Agent returned and summoned him briefly from his nest in the roots. Apart from issuing a curt order to follow him the Frenchman said nothing, and Esme limped stiffly round the barn and into the lane, where the labourer sat perched on the high seat of a two-wheeled farm cart. The cart, thought Esme, looked like an ancient British chariot of the kind Boadicea drove on Westminster Bridge.

The back of the vehicle was piled with kale, but Esme climbed in and was immediately covered. Then the cart moved off down the lane, its axle creaking abominably, and for the better part of an hour Esme lay uncomfortably across its ribbed floor, half smothered under a hundredweight of wet leaves. When at last the cart stopped somebody thrust a hand through the kale and prodded him, so that he sat up, gratefully enough and discovered that it was now dark and pattering with rain.

The Agent appeared at the tailboard and crooked an imperious finger, motioning Esme to get down and move into an adjacent farmyard that was almost knee deep in slush and manure. Esme waded after him and into a low-roofed farm kitchen, lit by a single oil lamp, and furnished with a single table, two chairs and a narrow strip of coconut matting.

A young, oval-faced man sat at the table, writing. He could not have been much more than twenty-five years of age but he was almost bald and his pink skull gleamed nakedly in the soft light of the lamp.

The Agent nudged Esme and waved his hand towards the bald man, who did not, however, look up from his papers, but continued to write steadily.

"This," he said briefly, "is Claude! Claude will talk with you!"

Having said this he left with his customary abruptness, closing the door behind him. Esme was thus left alone with Claude, who showed a disconcerting reluctance to break off his work and greet his visitor.

Esme sat down on the one vacant chair and waited, feeling rather embarrassed. There was a flatness, a businesslike precision about these people, that did not seem to fit his conception of the traditional conspirator. Esme would not have been much surprised to find himself among scowling, bearded men, wearing billowing cloaks, and a murderous array of weapons in their belts. Or, if this note was out of key in modern warfare, then they might at least, he felt, have been

suave, mysterious characters, and have treated him with
elaborate politeness, like the secret agents in Oppenheim
novels.

As it was he already felt half a prisoner, pushed here and
there by poker-faced gaolers, and as the minutes ticked by,
and Claude continued to be absorbed in pen-pushing, Esme
felt inclined to protest, mildly perhaps, but enough to make
this bald-headed Frenchman show some interest in him.

Then, as the man went on writing, he remembered that
each of these men was staking his life on this encounter. The
worst that could happen to him, if a squad of Germans
suddenly descended on the farm, was to be bundled off to a
prison camp, whereas these people, the labourer, the Agent,
and this enigmatic bald fellow, would certainly be marched
into the courtyard and shot out of hand. The recollection
sobered him and he folded his arms and waited, watching the
man's pen fly over the paper until at last he blotted his page
and looked up, straight into Esme's eye.

"You are a member of the crew of the Lancaster, shot
down near here last night?"

The question, spoken in precise English, and with the
suspicion of a lisp, was thrown at him like a challenge, and
Esme recoiled from its icy directness. He recovered, however, and tried to sound casual in his reply.

"That's so! I was the tail-gunner."

"Name?"

Again the sharp note of directness, amounting almost to
rudeness.

"Fraser, Sergeant, Number 926565."

"Your base?"

Esme hesitated. Over and over again, during the security
lectures at F.T.S. and O.T.U. they had stressed the importance of giving no information whatsoever to interrogators,
nothing at all beyond number, rank and name. The bald man
noticed his hesitation and made an impatient gesture.

"Please! I must insist."

Esme quailed under the Frenchman's eye and manner.

"Scratton Wold, in Lincolnshire," he growled.

The man wrote something in a notebook and then leaned

back against the wall, shooting his long, thin legs beneath the table.

"When you are at home, where do you live?"

Esme shrugged. In for a penny, in for a pound, he thought, and this fellow's eye was almost hypnotic.

"Near Croydon, in Surrey."

The man nodded: "*How* near?"

"An outer suburb of Croydon, actually, but you wouldn't know it!"

The man's thin mouth twitched but it was more of a grimace than a smile.

"You would be very surprised what I know my friend," he said, unpleasantly. "Describe to me where you live, describe it exactly or I cannot help you!"

Esme gave it up. He was dominated by the man and his irritation gave place to dismay.

"It's an Avenue, called 'Manor Park Avenue'. I live at Number Twenty-Two. It's a turning off Shirley Rise, that branches off the Millbank Lower Road."

"And where does this 'Lower Road' lead?"

"To London."

"Via?"

"I beg your pardon?"

"To London, through what suburbs?"

The man now sounded like a testy schoolmaster, engaged in establishing the inadequacy of a small boy's excuses.

"Elmers End, Clockhouse, Beckenham, Catford and Ladywell." Mumbled Esme, transported by the litany to the 'up' platform of Woodside, where the porters sang out these names to travellers as the 8.40 drew in from Croydon. 'That ought to satisfy the surly clot', he thought, but it did not, not quite, for the man said:

"This Avenue, 'Manor Park Avenue', what is at the other end of it, going towards Croydon?"

"The Rec'," said Esme, astounded.

"Please?"

Esme's irritation returned. "The recreation ground, but we call it 'The Rec'. It's got tennis courts and a children's giant stride in it. One gate leads into Delhi Road, and Delhi Road runs parallel to the Avenue. The houses of Cawnpore Road back on to it, all down one side. Is there anything else you'd like to know while I'm at it?"

Suddenly the man thawed and smiled, a sweet, winning smile, that transformed his smooth, rubbery face, giving him the ingenuous look of a boy but somehow emphasising the nakedness of his skull.

"Yes, my friend," he lisped gently, "I would like to know if the old Mill is still there, or whether our friends the Boche, have singled it out during a Baedeker raid?"

Esme warmed towards the man. It was as though he had shed his malignant personality like a shirt, and suddenly revealed himself as friend, confidant and neighbour, all in one.

"*You know it? You've been there?*"

"I *lived* there, until 1939! I was in lodgings, in Outram Crescent, whilst I studied at the London School of Chiropody! Perhaps your feet need attention? But no, you did not walk very far, did you? You were wise and found a good place to hide, down among the mangolds?"

They shook hands over the table and Esme produced his cigarettes.

"This is fantastic," he bubbled, "absolutely fantastic."

"No," said Claude, "it is interesting, but it is not fantastic." Many of us spent periods in London, and all of us had to lodge in one suburb or another so why not Croydon? Why not your Avenue, near Shirley Mill?"

"But why don't you check up on papers?" asked Esme, "what about our identity cards?"

"Papers mean nothing, my Shirley friend," said Claude, "for we make them ourselves by the thousand. We take no one on trust however, not even when they drop straight out of the skies, not even when they travel on the old South Eastern and Chatham Railway each morning!"

Esme laughed. "I think my luck is going to turn," he said. "Outram Crescent? Why damn it, that's less than five minutes from the Avenue."

"It is six," said Claude, getting up, loosening the straps of a leather valise that lay on the floor near the table. "I know because I used to walk along the Avenue from the Recreation Ground on my way to visit a certain young lady each Sunday. But perhaps you know her ... 'Edna' she was called, Edna Stanton, and she lived at Number Six, Shirley Rise. Her father was a policeman!"

Esme felt that he would have given a month's pay to have been able to say that he was acquainted with Edna, the policeman's daughter, but he had to shake his head and suggest another possible mutual acquaintance in the person of old Arthur Setter, who sold sweets and tobacco at the corner of Outram Crescent. They drew another blank, for during his sojourn in London Claude had been a non-smoker, and had only become addicted to the habit since taking up the uncertain occupation of a full-time Resistance worker.

In the meantime, however, Claude had unstrapped the valise and was gently prodding its interior. Suddenly a faint hum emerged from the case, and Esme heard the impeccable accents of the B.B.C. announcer, reading the nine o'clock news bulletin. There was a list of familiar items, then:

... "Last night heavy forces of Bomber Command raided Hanover and Bremen, inflicting considerable damage on tractor works and chemical installations in one city, while other heavy forces destroyed port installations at the coastal target. There was strong opposition from enemy flak and night fighter formations; fourteen of our aircraft failed to return. ..."

Claude left him to hear the rest of the bulletin and when he returned he brought with him a flask of cognac and two small wine glasses. Carefully he poured out two measures.

"To the Avenue, to your home, and your friends, Sergeant!"

Esme swallowed the drink and felt its warmth spreading through him. He said, sombrely:

"I've got a girl in the Avenue, my fiancée, actually. She's called Judy ... *Judith,* and I've just remembered, she'll have heard that bulletin, and she'll ring the squadron, poor kid."

"She will face some weeks of wretchedness, my friend," said Claude, "but in the end we shall return you intact to her! Let us drink to that, before we conduct you to safer quarters."

They drank solemnly and as they put down their glasses

the Agent came back and stood just inside the door. The
geniality drained from Claude's face and the keen, searching
look returned to his blue eyes.

"Come," he said briskly.

CHAPTER XXII

Black Week

JIM had lived through other Black Weeks but none so black as this.

He remembered the original Black Week, back in 1900, when the Continent capered with glee to see the arrogant British trounced by a handful of mounted farmers, but that was more than forty years ago, when he had been a footloose young man with no stake in Britain except his national pride. He had felt shamed by the South African defeats but not overwhelmed by them, and his patriotism had not impelled him to join the Volunteers, as many of his contemporaries had done.

There was another Black Week, in July, 1916, and this time the appalling losses on the Somme had touched him personally, for men had died in his arms, and many of these men were his friends.

It was the same some fifteen months later, when the men who replaced the Somme comrades disappeared by the score in the slime of Third Ypres. Jim felt all these losses very keenly, the more because they had appeared pointless to him then and indeed, appeared so still, but he got over them, and in time he almost forgot them.

When the next Black Week came along he was deep in the class struggle, and the failure of the General Strike did more to sour him than had the massacres on the Western Front. Then, twelve years after that, he rode out another Black Week, the week of Munich.

This week had almost driven him to despair, but even the

305

Munich debacle was not a personal tragedy, and once Britain had begun to fight back he soon climbed out of his gloom and became aggressively cheerful about the war, particularly after Russia had joined in and he formed the opinion that Hitler's defeat was a certainty.

This fierce and belligerent optimism had carried him right through the first eight months of 1942. He kept telling Harold that the collapse of German Fascism was now just a matter of time, that Hitler had a war on two fronts, and that America was now free to maintain an ever-increasing flow of war material to Europe. He said that there would be a Second Front at any time now, probably in the early spring of 1943, and that once a bridgehead was established the whole of enslaved Europe would fly to arms and butcher the Nazis wherever they showed their coal-scuttle helmets.

Harold considered that his friend's military judgment (which he had respected in the past) was being warped by enthusiasm, but he did not say so, not until the first rumours of the Dieppe Raid began to circulate. Harold, the cautious solicitor's clerk, was an equally cautious war-prophet, and he could not believe that Churchill would launch a Second Front at this stalemate stage of the war, before more than a trickle of Americans had arrived in Europe. He told Jim so, that fine August morning. He said that, in his opinion, this Dieppe affair was only a large-scale commando raid, and he was understandably smug when the B.B.C. announcer practically quoted him that same evening, and news went round about the high proportion of losses incurred by the attackers.

Jim grunted his disappointment as they sat facing one another at their war council, over the kitchen table of Number Twenty-Two, but he qualified his admission that he had been wrong about Dieppe by saying: "Ah, but they were probing, just probing! They wouldn't do that on this scale if they didn't intend blasting their way in before autumn! Just hang on Harold ... (as though Harold had applied to him for reassurance) ... just hang on, until next week, and you'll see, by God, you'll see!"

Harold had shaken his head and doubted whether we should be ready to invade until late summer of next year. Jim pooh-poohed this outrageously pessimistic forecast, and advised Harold to wait until the twins showed up and gave them some inside wrinkles on the situation. He was extremely anxious to discuss the military situation with the twins, particularly with Bernard, but neither of them did show up that week, and a day or two later the telegram arrived, saying that the boys had failed to return from Dieppe.

Jim was stunned by the news. He sat staring at the telegram for nearly half an hour, before snatching down his cap and striding out across the meadow into Manor Wood, hoping to absorb the shock before reporting the facts to Louise or Judy, or even the pale girl, Pippa, who lodged with Louise, and seemed to have formed such an attachment for young Bernard.

Jim's old seat on the coping beside the lake, where he had done so much of his thinking in years gone by, was no place for meditation now. It was sited within yards of the U.S. Transport Park, and the area around it echoed with the shouts and laughter of at least two hundred G.I.s.

Accordingly, he skirted the lake and pushed on through the wood into the ploughed fields, beyond the last of the trees. Here he sat down on the stile that marked the Kent-Surrey border, and tried to think of his lost boys as part of the inevitable price one paid for the right to live out one's life as a democrat.

He failed of course, failed wretchedly, and that despite his years and years of stern, political schooling, of so much tract reading, of so many fiery speeches about Fascism as the tool of Capitalism and Teuton megalomania that was a menace to free men everywhere.

The death of his boys, he discovered, now seemed to have nothing whatever to do with the things one preached about international events and just as little to do with democratic responsibilities. One was a tragedy, and the others were jumbles of words and pompous attitudes. A month or so ago his two boys had been clumping about the house, shouting and laughing, thumping him between the shoulders, and calling him 'Pop'; now they were bags of bone and corruption, lying in shallow graves on the French Coast, or washing about in the shallows among other flotsam of the attack.

The telegram, indeed, made him feel very differently about

Dieppe as a military event. 'Probing' was all very well, but why probe a hornet's nest with a bunch of twigs? What was the sense of sending men ashore against fixed guns and then, when their heroism had gained a foothold, taking them off again and abandoning the ground to gloating Nazis? This surely, was no better than the Somme, and Passchendaele. This was Old Haig's notion of war, war by attrition!

He tried to extract a crumb of comfort from the word 'missing' in the telegram but he had never been much good at deceiving himself and he had enough battle experience to know the true meaning of the word. 'Missing', to his mind, meant blown to smithereens, or drowned in a shell-crater. He tried to recall a single case of a man being reported missing, who had turned up after the wounded had been gathered in and the attack called off, but he could recall no such a case. He decided that he might as well resign himself here and now to the fact that the twins were dead, and tell Louise so when he broke the news to her. What sense was there in giving her grounds for hope when there were none?

He got up and walked back through the wood, where he suddenly ran into Orrie, the American friend of his twin daughter, Carry.

Orrie hailed him, cheerfully:

"Hiya, Pop! What's noo?"

Jim stopped, remembering that Fetch and Carry would also have to be told, and welcoming this opportunity to be done with the job as speedily as possible.

"My boys ... Bernard and Boxer ... they're missing after Dieppe," he said, and was ashamed at the wobble in his voice.

Orrie's good-natured face clouded.

"Gee, that's bad! That's tough, Pop! Missing? You don't figure they might be prisoners?"

"In *that* shambles? Not a hope, son, but I'd be obliged if you'd break it to the girls. Would you do that for me? I'll tell their other sisters right away."

"Sure, sure Pop, you leave it to me. Hell, I'm sorry, Pop, reel sorry!"

Jim patted his shoulder, and for the first time he welcomed the American alliance into his heart. He went back to the

Avenue, his steps dragging as he crossed the meadow to Number Twenty, and walked down the alley to the back door.

Louise was hanging out washing, her husband's and her lodger's, a comic mixture of coarse woollen underpants and flimsy pink slips. Jim said:

'I've got some bad news, Lou, old girl. You'd better come into the kitchen!"

She took the pegs out of her mouth and followed him inside.

"Is it about the boys, Dad?"

He nodded.

"Dead?"

"I reckon so ... 'missing' it said. It was Dieppe, damned shambles!"

Louise sat down and stared hard at the pattern of the American cloth on the kitchen table. Jim waited for a moment and then reached out and squeezed her shoulder.

"I don't think I was much of a father to them, Lou. I always wrote them off in my mind as gadabouts, with nothing really solid about them. I was wrong ... Christ Almighty, how wrong I was! They had more guts than anyone I knew, and proved it!"

Louise caught up his hand and pressed it against her cheek. Jim noticed how rough was the texture of her skin, so different from that of her younger sisters, and it crossed his mind what a strange mixture his children were. Louise, the patient, sweet-tempered drudge; Judy, the open-air dreamer; the younger twins, Fetch and Carry, a pair of feather-brained extroverts; the boys, Boxer and Bernard, a pair of good, solid, friendly, unimaginative fighting men; and finally Archie ... he had almost forgotten Archie.

Louise withdrew her hand, dabbed her eyes and then jumped up.

"I must tell poor Pippa," she said, "she's upstairs now, I think! Bernard and she love one another, but I told you, didn't I?"

"I knew they were very thick," said Jim, "but it wasn't all that serious, was it?"

"Yes, it was, Dad," Louise told him. "Bernard wrote and wrote, and he never wrote to any of us! She's got his photo in her room, and only yesterday she asked me for any snaps I had of him when he was little. It's funny, I couldn't find any of Bernard by himself, he was always taken with Boxer."

"I can imagine," said Jim, bitterly.

She left him and trudged upstairs. He heard her open the door of the porch room and go in and close it after her, but a moment later they both came out and Pippa, white-faced, burst into the kitchen.

"Have you got the telegram? Could I see the actual telegram?" she demanded.

Jim gave her the telegram and she read it, carefully.

"But they aren't dead, Mr. Carver," she said, quietly. "Neither of them are dead. You'll see."

Jim marvelled at the steadiness of her voice. He had been aware of her about the house for some time now but had never taken much note of her. She was a strange little thing, he decided, mousy but somehow intense, in spite of a natural reserve. He made up his mind that he ought to tell her the truth and spare her endless misery in the future.

"If they're 'missing' from Dieppe it means they're killed, Pippa. They don't take prisoners in that sort of show, it's always kill or be killed. We shall get confirmation sooner or later, when the full casualties reports come in from one source or another, and I don't think it's going to help if we fool ourselves about a thing like this. It's only far worse in the end, you know."

"I can't prove to you they aren't dead, Mr. Carver," she said, "It's just that I'm sure I should know if they were, at least, I'd know if *Bernard* was, and he isn't, Mr. Carver, I'm quite, quite sure he isn't."

"Well," said Jim, slowly, "if that's how you feel I'll go over to the depot at Acton, and see if I can find out anything more definite. Sometimes you don't get official confirmation for months, but you can often get a pretty good idea by talking to their mates."

He paused, regarding her gravely. "Would you like me to do that?"

It was strange, he thought, that he should be asking her a

question like this when she was not even a member of the family.

"Yes, you could do that, Mr. Carver, but I don't care what anyone says at the depot, I'm quite sure they aren't dead!"

He left it at that. Women were funny about this sort of thing. He remembered how, in the last war, there had always been a lot of silly talk of 'women's intuition' and that it had often led to seances, table-rappings, and God knew what other kind of nonsense. He excused himself and went back to Number Twenty-Two, where he wrote a brief note for Harold and strode off down Shirley Rise to catch a 'bus for Acton.

They were very considerate to him at the Depot. He saw a young lieutenant first and was then shown into the major's office. His chat with the officer only confirmed his opinions. They had not heard that any commandos from the twins' section had been taken prisoner and it seemed very unlikely that they would hear so now. The twins' troop had escaped very lightly, one dead, several lightly wounded and Bernard and Boxer missing. He would, if Jim wished it, send for the Sergeant in charge of the withdrawal from the Hess battery, and find out if any more scraps of information were available. Sometimes, he said, the men pieced together what happened by talking among themselves.

Jim saw the Sergeant privately and learned that Boxer had been last seen close against the compound wire, immediately prior to the withdrawal. The sergeant's information regarding Bernard was a little more definite. One of the anti-tank gunners, he said, had seen him fall after a mortar burst, but the man had an idea that he also remembered him getting up again. Bernard's chances, the sergeant added, should be slightly better than Boxer's, for when last seen he had been on the fringe of heavy cover and at least three hundred yards from the enemy wire.

That was all Jim was able to glean and he carried the information back to the Avenue and passed it on to Louise. Then he sat down to write to Judy and when Harold came home he found his friend weeping over a half-completed letter.

Harold was the ideal man in this kind of crisis. Gently he removed the letter, made Jim some strong tea, and then coaxed him up to bed.

Afterwards he sat down himself and wrote the letter to Judy.

* * * *

Judy received the news of 'R.-for-Ronnie's' failure to return to base on the morning after she received Harold's letter.

One of the orderly-room corporals of the squadron put through a call to her, after sorting through Esme's kit at the billet.

It chanced that he was acquainted with both Judy and Esme, having served with them on the Northampton station, prior to Esme's remustering to aircrew. He notified Judy twenty-four hours before sending the official telegram to Esme's next of kin, given on Esme's Form 1580 as '*H. Godbeer, Stepfather*'. The orderly-room staff sometimes strayed outside the limit of official procedure in this manner, and the more intelligent officers encouraged them. It was often kinder, they felt, to notify someone outside the family with the facts, so that the arrival of the casualty report was buffered.

Judy did not answer the 'phone but the corporal insisted on speaking to her personally, so she hoisted herself out of bed and came downstairs without waiting to find her slippers and dressing-gown. She thought that it must be Esme at the end of the line and that Maud had got the name wrong.

The corporal said: "Is that Judy Ascham, the Waaf sergeant who used to be at Queen's Norton, the one who's engaged to Sergeant Fraser?"

Judy said that it was, and asked who was speaking.

"You probably won't remember me," said the voice, "but I was with you at the Northampton dump and I'm an old oppo of Fraser's, in the orderly-room. I'm in Fraser's squadron now, at Scratton Wold."

Judy's heart gave a violent leap, but she said, quite quietly.

"Are you ringing *for* Sergeant Fraser? Is he there?"

The corporal at the other end of the telephone, hesitated before saying:

"It's like this kid, his kite hasn't shown up! We've got no confirmation so far, so I wouldn't take too dim a view yet awhile. They might be anywhere . . . on the run, in the drink, or paddling home. You know how it is, all kinds of crazy things happen on ops!"

"When was it? When did it happen?" she demanded.

"What was that? I can't hear you!"

"When was it and when did it happen?" she shouted.

"Oh, night before last . . . we waited a bit, in case they force-landed at another airfield. One of our kites did in this case. Point is, can you get in touch with his next of kin? They'll be notified as usual, of course, but finding a letter addressed to you in his billet we thought you might like to help by softening up the folks a bit! I rang because I remembered you from Queen's Norton, and because, well, because you're one of us I guess."

Judy said hoarsely: "I'll do that . . . thanks for ringing. . . . I'll tell his stepfather. Just ring me if there's anything fresh!"

"You bet," said the voice and rang off, with an audible sigh of relief.

Judy went slowly upstairs and sat on the bed. She was not overwhelmed with the shock because, strictly speaking, it wasn't a shock at all, but confirmation of weeks and weeks of anxiety about Esme, leading up to a virtual certainty in her mind that she would receive news of this kind at some time or other.

She had certain advantages over her father. She was familiar with this war and did not confuse it with the last. She knew that a percentage of bombers failed to return after each raid, and had never pretended to herself that Esme's might not be one of them. Perhaps this was the reason that the shock of hearing that such a thing had, in fact, taken place, was not as painful as the news that Tim had been drowned en route for Egypt nearly three years before. That had been so early in the war, and had seemed more like an unlucky accident, whereas Esme's loss was now part of the pattern of life, like a deepening of the conspiracy to cheat her out of the future and deprive her, not only of the fulfilment of her dream, but of its background, its Avenue background where the dream had been born.

The war had now rained many blows on the Avenue and many of them had been mortal. It had claimed Eunice, Esme's mother, for whom Judy had had a strong affection. It had taken Boxer and Bernard, Esme's schoolboy companions and her brothers. It had altered the very shape of the Avenue, and destroyed its symmetry by blasting away the three houses opposite and it had, almost in passing, swept away a string of familiars, like Albert Dodge, of Number Ninety-One, and young Hooper, of Number Six. If it went on long enough what would be left for the survivors like herself?

Maud Somerton found her struggling breathlessly into her clothes and at once protested.

"If you leave here you can't do anything, Judy! You can only set yourself back! Why don't you send off the doctor's certificate and ask for an extension of sick leave?"

"I'm not going back to camp, yet," Judy told her, "I'm going home to London! I've got to, Maud, I've got to be where it all happened, because I might be able to get hold of myself there! I know I won't anywhere else, I'll give up and be a damned misery to myself and everyone around me!"

Maud did not argue with her. She felt tired and helpless in the face of this fresh disaster. She was discovering something new about The Gel every day now, a new facet of character, or temperament, that had been quite unsuspected all the years they had worked side by side. She kissed her, roughly, and went downstairs and out into the yard to the stables. She understood horses and she was understanding people less and less as the days went by.

* * * *

During the tedious train journey back to the Avenue Judy took stock of Esme's chances.

She went about it rather like a castaway, turning out his pockets after struggling ashore from the wreck. She examined and weighed each item that might or might not contribute to his survival. She was, of course, working in the dark as far as Esme and Esme's aircraft was concerned, but she had been closely involved in the air war for two and a half years now, and if her assessments were guesses they were at least realistic guesswork.

A good deal, she knew, would depend on where the incident had happened. If 'R-for Ronnie' had been shot down over the target, for instance, she knew that its crew's chances of survival were slight. In that case it had probably gone down in flames, before anyone had a chance to jump, and there were also some disturbing rumours lately about the lynching of air-crew who succeeded in getting down alive.

On the other hand, if the aircraft had been winged by flak, and had limped part-way home, or had been jumped by a night-fighter over France, Holland or Belgium, then it was not impossible that some of the crew might turn up as prisoners of war, or even get home by making the Long Walk.

Such a thing was rare but it had been known to happen. There was a flying officer, at Tangmere, who went out on a fighter sweep in August, 1940 and came breezily into the mess, haggard but jubilant, in April of 1941! She wondered if Esme had the nerve and the physical stamina to imitate such a feat, even if he was presented with the opportunity. She doubted it, for although she had detected a definite stiffening in his character during the last few months, she had no confidence in his luck or her own. Such a thing might happen to another member of the crew, but not to him. Esme was much more likely to have died at twenty thousand feet or, at best, to have descended safely and been scooped into the bag to be packed off into Germany for the duration.

The journey home was a tiring one. She had a corner seat but her shoulder ached every time the train stopped and started, and it seemed always to be stopping or starting with a series of violent jolts. It was so difficult to forget the war during a railway journey these days. The carriages were always jammed with servicemen and service girls, and their bulky assortment of kit. All the newspapers they held in front of them carried screaming headlines about the war in the Far East. Posters on the hoardings outside, that had once advertised Bovril and Guinness, now pleaded with passengers to fly with the R.A.F., to save money, to dig for victory, or to guard very jealously any information they might have that would be useful to the enemy.

Judy closed her eyes and began yet another inventory.

Death? Capture? Escape? Afloat in a dinghy? She decided to play for safety, and settle for capture, although even that meant that they could not be married now until it was all over and who could tell when that was likely to happen? The Japanese were running amok in the East, and the German armies were still surging into Russia. People said that the arrival of the Americans would make a great difference, and that soon the Allies would assault the Fortress of Europe and defeat Germany in France, but suppose such a miracle did happen? Were there not vast areas out East still to be recovered, before men and women who wanted to get married were proof against the threat of being torn apart and sent off in different directions again?

Shifting her position slightly, in order to ease her aching shoulder, Judy silently cursed the war. It was, she reflected, no longer a crusade but simply a dull, dreary habit. People no longer talked of Hitler and Himmler as sadistic monsters but simply as bores, responsible for bull, blackouts, cheerless journeys in uncomfortable trains like this, shortages, sweet rationing, the price of cigarettes and the cost of trunk calls that were poor substitutes for lovers' meetings!

Even inside the R.A.F. and the W.A.A.F. the old Battle of Britain spirit had disappeared. In 1940, everyone had been a volunteer, and the time-honoured rejoinder to a moan about service life had been: 'Shouldn't have joined!' There was no sense in that remark now, not with the steady intakes of thousands of sullen National Service recruits, yet all the time the months were passing, and everyone was getting older. If Esme was a prisoner for any length of time it might even be too late for them to have children!

She thought, objectively, of the child they might have had, for her child, Esme's child, had always played a prominent part in the dream, and now it seemed more important than anything else. She wondered why this should be so. Was it because the dream itself had never been anything more than an urge to renew her childhood and his, and to repeat, through a child, the sweet, sunlit patterns of those summer days in the 'twenties', when they had been growing up in the Avenue? As this fancy struck her she wished with all her heart that Esme's quip about a "Clause Eleven" discharge

had not been a joke. She wished that she really could qualify
for a pregnancy discharge, and get away from kitbags, railway warrants, and heavy, shapeless uniforms. She wished
that she could exchange the whole of it for a red kitchen-fire,
looking over the old Nursery, where the time would have
passed quickly, caring for Esme's baby.

The longing made her eyes prick and she groped for a
handkerchief and blew her nose, for in that instant she
remembered that her decision to settle for Esme being alive,
and a prisoner, was also a fantasy, that it was more than
probable that he was already dead.

When she had elbowed free of the Waterloo platform
crowds, and queued for an unoccupied telephone booth, she
put in a call to Harold's office, in St. Paul's Churchyard.

She knew the number, having passed messages from Esme
to him on several occasions. She was fond of Harold in the
way that she had been fond of Eunice. He had always
seemed to her such a very gentle person, whose very
stuffiness and professional caution were endearing.

She was aware now that Esme meant much to him, and
that he meant as much to Esme. Their mutual regard for one
another reached back to that day on Shirley Hills, when he
had championed them in the matter of Judy's half-crown,
stolen by the hucksters at a confetti booth. Since Eunice had
been killed they had all three grown closer to one another,
and she did not relish the task of breaking the news about
Esme, remembering how shaken Harold had been by his
wife's death at Torquay. She nerved herself to speak casually, however, and decided to make an appointment for his
lunch hour.

"Mr. Godbeer? It's Judy! I'm in town and I'd like to see
you right away. No, Mr. Godbeer, Esme isn't with me, I'm
on my own. It's . . . it's really *about* Esme . . . I'd like to have
a . . . well, a sort of chat about things. Will that be all right?"

Of course it would be all right, and she knew that she
ought not to have stalled, for Harold, who was so used to
having 'little chats' with people, would be certain to jump to
the conclusion that she needed advice or sympathy. Her
nerve had failed her at the final moment, however, and she
could not bring herself to blurt the truth over the telephone.

He had sounded so pleased to hear her voice, and his own voice had been so warm and welcoming. She said:

"No, not at your office . . . let's meet out somewhere . . . let's have a coffee and a sandwich."

They met some twenty minutes later, in a Ludgate Hill snack bar. He came in carrying his rolled up umbrella, and his brown eyes twinkled at her from behind his thick-lensed spectacles.

"My . . . my! But this *is* a pleasant surprise, Judy! I thought you were *hors-de-combat*, for at least another week, and were then due back in Cornwall! Does this mean you're better? What a nuisance it all was, getting crocked like that, and after all the trouble you've been having getting together!"

"We shouldn't have had long together in any case, hardly time enough to get married by special licence." She told him. "Esme only had a few hours, there was a flap on."

"When did he go back?"

"Saturday night."

"He's heard about Bernard and Boxer?"

"Yes, of course, Mr. Godbeer."

She had almost forgotten poor old Bernie and Boxer in her new grief, but she remembered his kindness now and added:

"It was very nice of you to write for Dad. How is he? Has he taken it fairly well?

"No, I'm afraid he hasn't," admitted Harold, helping the waitress to unload her tray on to the marble-topped table. Then, quietly: "Here you are, my dear, I expect you're hungry. I'm glad you've come home though. I daresay you'll find some way to cheer him up. Your sister Louise took it very well, and so did Pippa, Bernard's young lady. She's an odd little thing, she simply won't believe the worst, and keeps saying that we'll hear better news shortly."

Judy realised that she couldn't keep staving it off like this and his remark about Pippa gave her a lead. She took it recklessly.

"I think Pippa's right," she said. "After all, to have someone missing is bad enough, but it's a jolly sight better than hearing they're dead. and it's right to go on hoping as long as you can, don't you think?"

"Well, I don't know," said Harold, stirring his coffee with a pencil because the snack-bar no longer issued spoons. "Your father doesn't think so, he thinks it's better to face the facts and get them over and done with. I don't think the twins could be alive, or we should have heard by now. After all, it's nearly a month. . . ."

He broke off, suddenly and what little colour he possessed left his cheeks. Perhaps he had noticed something hesitant in her manner, or perhaps he suddenly remembered the quaver in her voice when she had telephoned from the station.

"What is it, Judy dear? Is it . . . is it Esme?"

She nodded, unable to speak and watched his eyes mist behind the heavy spectacles. "He's not . . . dead, is he?"

"His aircraft is missing," she managed to say, "it didn't come back from a raid on Hanover the night before last. We lost fourteen that night, remember? I got an inside tip from Esme's station . . . you'll probably be getting the usual gen. from his squadron today, or at latest, tomorrow. I . . . I just thought I'd try and break it to you first!"

He stopped stirring and bent his head low over the table. They were silent for a moment, then, without looking up, he said:

"Tell me, Judy dear, tell me everything you know."

She braced herself and recited the various alternatives, stressing the number of operational crews who had been saved by parachute, and whose names had eventually filtered through to casualties via the Swiss Red Cross.

"Sometimes we hear that more than half of them dodged the chop that way," she said. "It's about a fifty-fifty chance, I suppose, much better than old Bernard's or Boxer's. You see, Esme as a prisoner would be a Luftwaffe pigeon, and they don't get badly treated, not even when they're captured over the target. There's still a bit of chivalry left about the air war!"

Harold raised his head and she could not help noticing how terribly old and lined his face looked. The hair above his small, flattish ears was quite white now, and she remembered that before the war it had been sleek blue-black.

"You must be feeling terrible, Judy, with this coming right

on top of the news about the twins! Can't I take you home? I don't have to go back to the office unless I want to."

She reached across the table and gripped his long, thin fingers. His unselfishness helped her to get things back into a firmer and saner perspective. He must, she was aware, be utterly devastated by the prospect of losing Esme, who was all he had now that Eunice had gone, yet he could still spare a thought for her misery, push his own into the background and grope for the crumb of comfort on her behalf.

"I'm all right, Mr. Godbeer, really I am! It can't be as bad as it seems. They can't all be dead . . . it's just that, well, I got to thinking in the train, I only wish we'd been able to get married after all and that I was having Esme's child. If anything had happened to him. . . ."

An infantryman, loaded with kit, squeezed past the back of her chair and jarred her shoulder. She winced and Harold jumped up.

"You oughtn't to be moving about among people with that bad shoulder," he said, "you ought to be home and resting it."

"It'll heal much quicker this way, the doctor said so! Shall we go now?"

He paid the bill and they went out into the street, looking up at the jagged unfamiliar silhouette of Ludgate Hill. The vast bulk of St. Paul's towered above them, magnified enormously by the desolate acres that surrounded it.

"Just look at that," said Harold, pointing. "I was thinking only yesterday, this ground hasn't been open to the sky since Wren began rebuilding, after the Great Fire! Are you sure you wouldn't like me to take you back to the Avenue?"

"Of course," said Judy, "I got this far on my own, didn't I?" and then, moved by an impulse born of his gentleness, she leaned forward and kissed him softly on the cheek. Before he could speak again she had turned away, leaving him standing on the kerbside.

She caught a train at London Bridge and was back at Woodside inside the hour. She had meant to go straight home, and tell Louise, but when she reached the corner of the Avenue she changed her mind and pushed on up Shirley Rise into open country.

She wanted to make contact with Esme on familiar ground and she knew that the Manor Wood would be full of Americans, who would probably whistle and make friendly approaches, backed by offers of gum and candy. They usually behaved that way towards unaccompanied Waafs and she had never resented it, for their cheerfulness and generosity seemed very welcome in the Britain of 1942, but she knew that today it would get between her and Esme. So she avoided the wood and sought a tiny island of trees that still stood in the ploughed field, beyond the church and could be reached by a beaten track that branched off the main road.

This spinney had been a favourite spot of Esme's who had used it as a headquarters for their varied activities. It had been, among other places, Crusoe's island, the buccaneers' lair at Tortuga, a besieged castle, and the Isle of Avalon. Beyond it, and within two hundred yards of the field in which it stood, they had commenced a new building site, but the outbreak of war checked its development. As soon as war ended, field and spinney would be swallowed up in a vast, housing estate. The war, that had taken so much from the Avenue children, had given the spinney a temporary reprieve and she was grateful.

The beeches, and the larch trees in the little wood were still wearing green. The foxgloves had gone, but there was convolvulus in the hedge and campion growing beside the bank. She sat down and leaned her back against the tallest beech, looking westward, where the afternoon sun lit the suburb beyond the wood.

Her instinct had not been false. Here she felt closer to Esme than she had felt for a long time, closer perhaps than during some of their fleeting meetings of the past few months, for here it was very easy to picture the Esme she had known and loved since the beginning. Here she could see him once more as the earnest, excitable little boy, in grey flannel shorts, who rushed here and there among the trees, calling her, urging her to hurry and take cover, before the cavalry pickets detected them. Here he had taken her by the hand and dragged her down in the brambles, while his eyes swept the line of Manor Wood for troopers, excisemen, Bow Street Runners and 'pitiless dragoons'!

As the afternoon wore on, and the first chill of an autumn evening stole across the stubble, she came to terms with her grief, much as she had been able to do at the corner of Hayes Wood after Tim had been lost and she had at last found refuge in tears.

She did not weep now or feel like weeping. Instead she prayed, as she had so often prayed for Esme in the front bedroom of Number Twenty-Two, after recording the day's progress with him in the diary that she had kept hidden under her clean vests and knickers in the chest of drawers.

It was several years now since she had offered up a prayer of any sort. She remembered that she had not even seen the inside of a church since marrying Tim, and she had never had a thought about religion in the interval. For all that, her prayer came easily, as she sat with her back against the smooth, grey bole of the beech, her hands limp on her lap.

"Give me something to hope for, give old Harold something to hope for! If Bernie and Boxer are gone, then save Esme! Let me have Esme when it's over! Oh God, give me a chance to be a good wife to him, after all this time! Amen!"

White clouds came drifting, the sun dipped, and a stiff breeze whipped the stubble, dislodging a leaf or two from the branches above her. She shivered and got to her feet, retracing her steps to the road and going on down the hill to the Avenue. She had no key, so she knocked at Number Twenty and was admitted by Jack Strawbridge, her big, red-faced brother-in-law.

"Gordamme, it's Judy!" he called back to the kitchen and Louise, her hands dripping, hurried from the sink into the hall and embraced her, delightedly.

"Oh, I'm glad you've come, love!" said Louise, a little breathlessly. "We been having a rare time with Dad, haven't we, Jack? Such a pity it is, *such* a pity!"

"I met Harold Godbeer in town," Judy told her, "and he told me that Dad was taking it pretty badly. There's more news about them, I suppose?"

Jack Strawbridge spoke from the foot of the stairs, and Judy was struck by the foreign note of bitterness in his easy, countryman's voice.

"Ar, but it's not only the twins as've got 'im down, it's that other bliddy brother o' yours, Archie! We got word of 'im today, leastways, your father did! His case comes up Monday and they want your Dad to go down. Derned if *I* would! *Jiggered* if I would, not fer that scow!"

"Shhh, Jack," said Louise, "Judy doesn't even know about it yet! Dad didn't tell her, you great fool!"

Jack looked stupidly at her, clenched his mottled fists and flushed.

"Is that so? Well, I didn't know did I? I thought everyone hereabouts knew!"

Judy looked at Louise, who turned and went back into the kitchen.

"What's happened to Archie?"

"Nothing ain't yet, Judy," mumbled Jack, "but I reckon it will! He was tight, terrible tight must ha' been, and drove into a flock o' people, knockin' 'em all ways, an' now he's up for manslaughter!"

"Where? Where did this happen?"

"I dunno, 'Win' something or other, down your way somewheres! On 'is way to see 'is missis he was, 'er that's left 'im, so they say!"

For a moment Judy felt she wanted to scream and stride about smashing things. The entire world was going relentlessly and malignantly mad! Berni and Boxer dead! Esme shot down! And now Archie up on a manslaughter charge! What else could happen to make a mockery out of the quiet, humdrum lives they had once enjoyed in this little house?

She checked herself and asked, stiffly: "Where is Dad, now?"

"He's in next door," Louise called from the kitchen, "but I wouldn't go in, not yet! I've sent for Miss Clegg, at Number Four, and she's in there, talking to him. Let me get you some tea, love! You must be real starved, coming all that way and you not well!"

Judy handed her attaché case and great-coat to Jack and went into the kitchen. She decided to say nothing for the moment about Esme. God knows, she thought, 'there's enough trouble for everyone, without adding to it!

She sat down near the glowing range and watched Louise

busy herself at the gas-stove. She was not in the least hungry but she knew that Louise would insist that she ate a cooked meal. Louise, she thought, is so lucky that way, she can always put her miseries into a saucepan, a frying-pan, or stir them in with the weekly wash at the copper.

CHAPTER XXII

Edith As Rod And Staff

EDITH CLEGG, of Number Four, was a deeply religious woman. The daughter of a country parson she had been brought up not so much in the fear of the Lord as in fear of the Lord's elect.

As the elder of the rector's two daughters, reared in a remote Devon parish, she had been aware from earliest childhood of the necessity of setting a good example to her father's rustic parishioners, and her behaviour, up to the hour of her sister, Becky's return home after her elopement with a wandering landscape painter, had been exemplary.

She had, until then, taken a leading part in all parochial activities. She had led an utterly blameless private life, and had sat through her father's long, rambling sermons, nodding her head whenever he made a point and doing so, it appeared, in order to demonstrate to the less attentive that her father's interpretation of the Word found favour in her sight.

She was thus, in every respect, a model daughter, and continued so until the sad end to Becky's elopement had presented her with a choice of loyalties. In the furore that had followed Becky's reappearance she discovered, to her great dismay, that the battalions of the elect were in one camp, and that poor Becky was alone in the other.

Up to that moment Edith had taken her New Testament lessons very literally. In so doing she had assumed that her father, his bishop, his churchwardens, the sidesmen, and all the parochial workers, took an equally uncomplicated view of the teachings of Jesus—that is, they would have been ready to vie with one another and the Good Samaritan, in ministering to a traveller who had fallen among thieves. This, for Edith, had been the beauty of the Christian Faith, its stark simplicity, its insistence on hastening at once, and to the exclusion of all personal demands, to the succour of the fallen and distraught. It seemed to Edith a perfectly natural thing to clothe the naked, to bind up the wounds of the afflicted, and to visit the sick, as natural, in fact, as going to bed at night, and getting up in the morning. She was therefore both hurt and astonished when she made the discovery that no one in the parish, not even her father, a professional dispenser of Christianity, appeared to take these injunctions very seriously; as far as poor Becky was concerned not one of them experienced the slightest joy over the reclamation of a sheep that was lost and found again!

This discovery came as a very considerable shock to Edith. It was as though, all her life, she had lived in what she imagined to be a devotedly Christian community and then, one day, it was revealed to her that everyone, from archdeacon to gardener's boy, subscribed to a faith that had but the outward trappings of her own and nothing at all of its spiritual essence.

One moment she was surrounded by people who raised their voices in ecstatic support of Christ's ministrations to the oppressed; the next she was standing alone, watching these same people shoulder Christ out of the way and hurl stone after stone at the crouching adulteress. In fact, it was a good deal worse than this, for poor, confused Becky was not even an adulteress, just a lovesick, young girl who had been maltreated by a young scoundrel and persuaded to run away on a promise of marriage!

When she had brought Becky home and the entire parish, headed by her father, had crossed to the other side just like the passers-by in the parable, Edith's conception of Christianity underwent an immediate transformation. All the outward manifestations of her faith fell away, like so many discarded garments, but, at the same time, her inner core of loving-kindness greatly enlarged itself, broadening her understanding and deepening her convictions, so that soon her entire being glowed with a desire to serve those who stood in need of service.

The nearest of these, both at that time and subsequently, was poor, witless Becky, but after they had left the parish and settled in the Avenue, there was always enough of the glow left over to warm somebody else. That was how she came to mother Ted Hartnell, the jazz drummer, and after Ted, Jean McInroy, the commercial artist, but even her lodgers did not monopolise Edith's radiations, for some of them crossed the road to Number One, where little Miss Baker, the indestructible sufferer from rheumatoid arthritis, could benefit from them and did, for a period of over twenty years.

Edith had one more characteristic seldom found in those reared in the fear of the Lord; an abiding humility. She never once thought of herself as a ministering angel but rather as a clumsy old spinster, anxious (though by no means equipped) to tread the by-paths of righteousness.

That was why she had conceived such a deep-rooted respect for Jim Carver, and invariably followed the advice he gave her on domestic matters. Jim was big, solemn, decisive and reliable; he was, moreover, the father of a large family, and was therefore qualified to give advice on almost anything.

From the day he had conducted her to Westminster to pay homage at the tomb of the Unknown Warrior, Edith had worshipped Jim's spare, solid strength, and the sense of permanence he conveyed to her. She delighted to see him go striding past her window in his A.R.P. outfit or, later on, in his Home Guard uniform. For her he typified the superior wisdom of the male and his quiet, persuasive voice was her favourite music, his rare, but singularly boyish smile a shaft of winter sunshine.

She had rushed to him, of course. the moment she had heard about the fate of the dear twins, Bernard and Boxer, but she was conscious of the inadequacy of any comfort she could bring to him in this field. He was already strong and resolute, and himself a soldier, who understood these things so much better than she did. When he told her that it was folly to hope that they might still be alive and prisoners in

German hands, she believed him. If he didn't know, then who did? He had fought battles long ago, and was still fighting them today!

It was a very different matter, however, when he stood in need of solace a week or two later, after they had told her that his eldest son, Archie, the big grocer whom everyone seemed to think was a bad lot, but who had always been kind and courteous to her personally, was now in serious trouble with the police. Dear Louise, Mr. Carver's eldest girl, had actually asked her to go along and talk her father out of his dumps, for he was said to be taking his fresh trouble very much to heart.

She had been intending to go in any case, but with Louise's blessing she went blithely. Here, she felt, was a situation that demanded something more than a military approach, a situation, indeed, that she felt well qualified to handle. She tripped along the Avenue to Number Twenty-Two and slipped down the alley to the back door, tapping gently on the glass panel and twittering a little at the low growl that greeted her from within.

She found him standing over the gas-stove stirring porridge, and scowling down into a porringer.

On the table, beside him, was a typewritten letter, with a heavily embossed letter-heading, and she recognised it at once as the letter from the solicitors that Louise had spoken about, the one asking him to go down and see his eldest boy at the town where Archie was in such dreadful trouble.

"Let me do that for you, Mr. Carver," she began, putting out her hand to relieve him of the spoon.

"Let me alone!" he growled, in a tone that he had never employed to her in the twenty-odd years she had known him. "This is none of your business and none of anyone's business!"

Once bent upon comforting somebody Edith was not easily repulsed. She hovered a moment and then suddenly snatched the big spoon from his hand and began to stir the porridge.

"If you're miserable it *is* my business!" she said. "I've brought my troubles to you times enough and I wouldn't like to bring any more if you won't let *me* help, when *you* need a friend! Now sit down, eat your porridge, and tell me all about it, and it's not the slightest use trying to keep it to yourself because I won't go away until you have told me, so there!"

He looked at her in astonishment. He had only heard her talk like this on one other occasion, that day in December, 1936, when she had assaulted Mrs. Rolfe, of Number Eight, after Mrs. Rolfe had gloated over Edward VIII's abdication. That had been quite a business and he had been called in as peacemaker. Edith had been terrified at the prospect of being hauled up on a charge of common assault but, not withstanding her fears, she had been unrepentant about striking a blow for the King, to whom she ever afterwards referred as "Poor David".

He sat down at the table, humouring her because he realised that she meant well, and because he had always felt rather protective about the dear old thing, tied to a half-witted sister, and so grateful for his show of friendship. His tolerance, however, did not extend to permitting her to interfere in this matter. Archie was his problem, and nobody else's. It was bad enough possessing a son like Archie, without having to share him with the neighbours. On the subject of Archie, in fact, Jim was very touchy indeed, as Harold Godbeer had discovered when he had prevented Jim from going along to the corner shop and giving Archie a belting for his share in breaking up Esme's marriage.

Glowering at Edith's broad rump, as she bobbed about over the gas stove, Jim asked himself again what he had done to deserve such a son. He could only tell himself, for perhaps the thousandth time during the past twenty-five years, that it all came of his being away at the war during Archie's formative years; that being so, it was surely not his fault that the boy had grown into a shifty, seedy racketeer, entirely without principle and now, it seemed, headed directly for gaol.

Not one of the younger children had given him trouble on this scale. There had been times when the exuberance of the boy twins had made him slightly anxious about their future, and the girl twins, Fetch and Carry, were not much to write home about, but the anxieties Berni, Boxer, Fetch and Carry had caused him, he now accepted as the small change of parenthood, whereas Archie had long represented all that Jim most hated in society as a whole, the small-time capitalist, whose energies were divided between accumulating money by any means presenting itself, and then using it to racket about with other men's wives, harlots, and whisky-drinking cronies.

Damn it, Jim told himself, it would have been better to have a son who was a good, honest safe-cracker! A man would at least know where he stood with a chap like that, someone who came out in the open, and declared an unblushing war on society! As it was, Archie posed as a respectable tradesman, and his off-the-beat activities had not even been suspected in the Avenue until he had been charged with receiving stolen goods! Even then the young scoundrel had talked his way out of the mess as glibly, it would appear, as he had talked his way into the bed of another man's wife! Now, if you please, it was not receiving, but manslaughter! Killing some poor devil who was unlucky enough to get in the way of his big, swanky car, when its driver was stupid with liquor! This was something no father could forgive, for it was an act of selfish brutality that amounted almost to murder. As he considered the contents of the lawyer's letter that lay before him he shook with humiliation, and his brain clouded with a rage that could find no outlet but seethed behind his temples, a volcano of misery and shame.

Edith set down his porridge and put milk and brown sugar on the table.

"Well? Are you going to let me read that letter?" she asked.

Sullenly he pushed the letter towards her and at once began to spoon hot porridge into his mouth, forgetting, in his anger and wretchedness, to cool it with milk.

Edith ignored his splutter, placed her reading spectacles low on her rather pudgy nose, and read:

"Dear Sir,
The above firm is representing your son, Mr. Archibald Edward Carver, at the Quarter Sessions in Wintlebury, commencing Monday, the 29th inst. Our client, whom we understand to be your eldest son, is charged with the man-slaughter of a pedestrian, to wit, Rachel Nixon, who was

*unfortunately killed in a collision at Bishop's Cross, Long
Hayborough, on August 1st, ult., and in which your son was
involved as driver of the car.*

*The present proceedings follow a coroner's verdict adverse
to your son. Mr. Carver has since been charged but released
on bail in his own recognisances, to appear before the Court
on the date specified above.*

*You will pardon us for communicating with you but we do
so in the hope that you will get in touch with us at once and,
we hope, attend the case in court. Mr. Carver has given us
the relevant facts relating to the accident, but seems reluctant to assist us in gathering material that might well prove
helpful. He gave us the address of his wife and we did, of
course, communicate with her, but have so far received no
reply. We then suggested to him that he should communicate
with you, as you might well wish to attend court, but he
preferred not to do so and it was only with the utmost
reluctance that we could persuade him we should get in
touch with you.*

*If you would be good enough to write or communicate
with us by telephone, we would be glad to point out how you
could assist both us and your son. You will not, I imagine,
have to testify in court, for what we are seeking is background material, to assist us in presenting the case to the best
advantage. It is, I regret to say, a difficult case to defend,
and at the moment there would appear to be very little that
can be argued in our client's favour. It is in the hope of
improving this situation that we are communicating with you
as his father.*

> *I remain,*
> *Yours faithfully,*
> *Gilbert Sills*
> *(On behalf of Messrs. Clark, Sills & Son,*
> *Solicitors, Wintlebury, Wilts.)."*

"Well," said Edith, removing her spectacles, and folding
the letter into its original creases, "you'll have to go won't
you, Mr. Carver?"

"Look," said Jim, pushing his porridge plate away, "I said

this was none of your business, Miss Clegg and I meant it! He's made his bed and he can damn well lie on it!"

"Nonsense," said Edith, mildly, "we all make beds badly now and again!"

He rubbed his chin, hardly knowing whether to be angry or amused by her stubbornness. At length he appealed to her humanity.

"See here, Miss Clegg, he's killed someone! Get that into your head—*killed* someone! He's never been any good, and he's never troubled two raps about any of us, so why should I go down there and acknowledge him now? Can you give me one good reason why I should?"

"Why of course I can. I can give you two! He's in trouble and he's your boy," said Edith. "Shall I make you some fresh tea?"

Jim made a gesture of impatience. "No, no tea . . . and he's not in as much trouble as the poor devil he killed, Miss Clegg!"

She said nothing for a moment but regarded the top of his head as he sat slumped over the table with his long chin cupped in his hands. Her heart bled for him. He looked so despondent and there was a tired hopelessness in his posture.

She moved round and sat down, facing him.

"I don't want you to think me impertinent, Mr. Carver," she began, "but I wouldn't be a friend to you if I didn't say exactly what is in my mind about this dreadful business. You won't be angry with me if I do say it, will you?"

He looked at her then and was struck by the troubled earnestness in her prominent, blue eyes.

He saw her as he had never seen her before, not as a plump and rather plain woman of sixty, or thereabouts, who was desperately anxious to please, and nervous of giving offence, but as someone much more like himself, who had been battered and badgered by successive decades of worry, of making ends meet, of facing up to everything that life demanded without sacrificing dignity and without sitting down and letting the current of everyday problems defeat her.

She was, he thought, typical of all the women of her generation, women who had successively challenged the casualty lists of the Somme, unemployment, the slump, and now German Fascism, and all it was trying to do to them. Many had lost husbands, brothers, and sons, and others had seen their homes smashed to pieces under high-explosive. All of them were oppressed by the dozens of petty irritations that the war had swept into their homes, the blackout, the rationing, the constant strain of hunting the shops for something to bring a little sparkle to the table, the constant nag, nag, nag of restrictions that made even a springclean a major operation. Yet, for all this, they had retained both their dignity and courage, and often a sense of humour for good measure.

The reflection softened the sullen outlines of his face and he smiled, acknowledging her right to advise him.

"Go ahead, Miss Clegg," he said wearily, "say anything you feel you must say!"

"Well," she said, "what I did want to say was just this! You're angry and disappointed with Archie, I know, and you've every right to be, but it isn't what he's done that makes you so set against seeing him, or wanting to do anything to help him, you're really angry because he's your son, and you feel responsible for what he's done wrong! Now I'm a fine one to talk I know, because I've never had any children, but if I had, if I'd had seven like you, and six of them were a credit to me but one wasn't, then I hope I should feel that it was right to go out of my way to help the odd one, if only because . . . well . . . because he's the only one who really needs help, don't you think?"

"Supposing I went down," protested Jim, weakening, "supposing I trailed down there and listened to the case? What good would it do? I don't know anything about him. I've hardly spoken to the boy in years."

"I can't tell you that," said Edith, "but I'm sure that when you got there you'd *think* of something, and that just *being* there would help, somehow! Why don't we both go? It wouldn't seem so bad if you had someone to talk to all the way there and all the way back?"

He got up, leaned his hands on the table and regarded her affectionately.

"You mean you'd come ... you'd actually come into court?"

"I'd like to, really I would, Mr. Carver. I'd feel I was ... was *doing* something to pay back."

"You don't owe me anything, Miss Clegg. What can you possibly owe me? Just a few bits of advice, over the years ... damn it, what's that, between neighbours?"

"Oh, it's not just advice," said Edith, emphatically, "it's much more than that! It's you being *here* all the time, someone I could go to whenever I wanted, and your daughter, Louise, she's always helped me with Becky, whenever I needed help. It's more than that too! Where would people like Becky and I be if people like you hadn't fought in the last war, and your boys hadn't gone out to fight in this?"

The irony of it touched him. How many speeches had he made about the folly of sacrificing young lives at the behest of the well-nourished, the profiteers, and the stockholders? How many times had he hectored apathetic audiences about the rich people that poor people were always being asked to die for whenever there was a war? It had never once occurred to him during his pacifist and disarmament campaigns of the 'twenties' and 'thirties', that the sacrifices of Flanders were made also for people like Edith Clegg, and that it was people like her, with so much less to lose, who were readiest to acknowledge the debt! It was queer that she should say a thing like that! It altered a man's entire conception of the background against which wars were fought.

He opened the letter and glanced through it again.

"The Sessions begin on Monday," he said, finally, "and it's Friday today! If we're going there, we'd better start right away. I don't suppose those lawyer fellows work on Sunday!"

. . . . .

They travelled down to Wintlebury that same evening, and put up at 'The Coach and Horses', in the Market Square.

Jim found the private address of Mr. Sills in the telephone directory, and made an appointment to meet him at his office the following morning.

He asked the solicitor how he might locate Archie, but Mr. Sills was unable to help him. Archie, he said was not due to surrender to bail until Monday morning, and he had no idea where he was lodging, if indeed, he was still in the district. "Perhaps my clerk will know," he said, lightly, "we'll ferret it out in the morning."

The clerk did not have Archie's address, which seemed to Jim a very careless way of doing business. He was, in fact, still further depressed by the apathetic approach to the case by Mr. Sills and his staff. They all seemed to think that Archie's case was hopeless.

Archie, Jim learned, was to be represented in Court by a young barrister called Malcolm Betts, and soon Mr. Betts himself put in an appearance. He was a thickset, ruddy-faced man, with an excessively hearty handclasp. He reminded Jim of a county rugby forward, and although he was by no means as depressing about the case as was the solicitor, his breezy comments did not add much to what Jim already knew of the facts.

Edith, who had accompanied Jim to the office, said nothing, and after a lengthy preamble Jim asked Betts, bluntly what chance there was of an acquittal.

"Oh, none, none at all," said the barrister, cheerily. "As a matter of fact we're putting in a plea of 'guilty'. It wouldn't pay us to fight it, we haven't a leg to stand on!"

"But hang it, you did send for me," grumbled Jim.

Mr. Sills did not appear to hear this, but added:

"He was drinking neat brandy all the way down here. When they got him out of the car he could hardly stand, and kept rambling on and on about the money."

"What money?" Jim wanted to know.

"Why the money that his wife stole from him," replied the lawyer.

All this was new to Jim and he said so. The lawyer sifted through some papers and finally unearthed a page of notes, compiled, presumably, at his original interview with Archie.

It contained a reference to the object of Archie's precipitate journey into the West, and the fact that he had considered himself robbed of all his remaining capital.

"Well, surely you'll bring this out in court, won't you?" demanded Jim.

Mr. Sills rubbed his long nose and fixed his eye on the filing cabinet beside the window.

"I don't know about that," chipped in Malcolm Betts.

"From the information your son gave me it seems that it wouldn't do to mention the money! I rather gathered it was ... er ...well—shall we say a little nest-egg, that no one knew about."

"His wife knew about it, didn't she?" said Jim.

"That's so, that's so," agreed the lawyer, unhelpfully, "but where does that get us?"

Suddenly Edith spoke up. Until then she had been sitting some way back from Mr. Sills' table, and they had forgotten her presence.

"It seems to me," she said, with a note of decision in her voice that Jim did not recall as being in any way characteristic of the spinster of Number Four, "it seems to me that you ought to imply that he had a kind of *brainstorm!*"

They all looked at her, Jim in astonishment, Mr. Sills with alarm, and Mr. Malcolm Betts with a lively interest.

"Can you elaborate that a little, madam," he said, politely.

"Certainly," said Edith, pulling her chair a little nearer the table. "Here's a young man who suddenly finds he had been deprived of a large sum of money. Surely you won't need to say *how* he got that money, or even where it was stolen from, will you?"

"Well," said Mr. Betts grinning, "that shouldn't be necessary, unless of course he insists on going into the box."

"Well," continued Edith, "he discovers this loss and it puts everything else out of his head! He rushes off, down to his wife in order to try and get it back, and all the time the thought of that money is going over and over in his head, so much so that he's not even looking where he's going!"

"What about the brandy?" prompted Mr. Sills.

"You can't get around that," mumbled Jim.

"Well, no, you can't, not exactly," said Edith, "but anyone might take a drink under these circumstances. I've known this young man for twenty years, and I've been in and out of his shop almost every day during this time. I've never once seen him the worse for drink, and you could just say he took it to steady himself and wasn't used to it, couldn't you?"

Jim gasped, and Mr. Sills coughed, but Mr. Malcolm Betts gave Edith an unmistakable look of approval.

"That's a line that hadn't occurred to me, I must say," he

exclaimed. "Why, bless my soul, Miss Clegg, you ought to devil for us, you've got a naturally tortuous mind!"

He turned back to Mr. Sills and Jim: "That's not a bad line at all," he said, "at all events, it's a good deal better than nothing! I'll tell you what, we won't question a single witness but simply put in a strong plea of mitigation on the lines she suggests! Colourful too, might even interest the jury! Never know! There's one thing, however, we ought to establish that he's always been known for strict sobriety."

He turned back to Edith. "Look here, madam, would you go into the box as a friend and neighbour of twenty years' standing, and tell the court what you've just told me about never seeing him the worse for drink?"

"Why, of course I would," said Edith, promptly. "I was rather hoping that you might ask me to give evidence of character!"

"Wouldn't it be better if I went in the box," protested Jim, who was beginning to feel out of his depth.

"Not on your life!" rejoined the barrister, "Relatives' testimonies don't amount to a row of pins! Besides, she *looks* so right!"

"Well, it isn't a great deal, Mr. Carver, but it's about the best we can do," Mr. Sills told Jim. "It might influence the sentence, don't you think Mr. Betts?"

"It might, indeed," agreed Betts, glancing across at Edith, with respect. It was not often, he reflected, that old souls who looked as drab and dowdy as this one came forward with any intelligent suggestions. Almost always they fell back on tears and juries were so indifferent to tears.

* * * *

Jim did not see Archie before his name was called in Court. Up to that moment he was on tenterhooks as to whether the defendant would show up, although, during the luncheon recess, when Jim and Edith were eating in a café across the market from the Town Hall, the considerate Mr. Betts sent a note across, saying that Archie had presented himself in Mr. Sills' office and had been informed of the line they were taking, and of Miss Clegg's willingness to testify on his behalf. Jim preferred not to see Archie before the hearing. "There'll be time enough after. They're bound to let us have a word with him, whatever happens," he told Edith.

Archie's case began about 2:30 p.m. and occupied the court until nearly six o'clock. Mr. Sills' forecast had been fairly accurate. By the time the prosecution had presented the facts, and half a dozen witnesses had testified as to Archie's madcap approach round the bend, Jim had made up his mind to expect the worst. He studied Archie closely, and was struck by the immobility of his expression throughout the case. He sat very upright in the dock, his eyes following the movement of witnesses in and out of the witness-box, but never once did he fidget, or turn and look down into the body of the court.

As the repetitive evidence was presented, and the police were called to give details of skid-marks, and general measurements, Jim's attention began to wander in spite of himself, and his mind ranged back to the previous occasion when he had sat in court and heard a case built up against his sons. That was the time when Bernard and Boxer had been charged with driving their motor-cycles through flood-water, and causing the wash to flow into shopkeepers' doorways, but that, he reflected, had been a very different kettle of fish, entirely lacking the solemnity of this hearing. When Bernard and Boxer had been in the dock everyone in the court had openly sympathised with them, and had, indeed, regarded the proceedings as being richly comic. Well, thought Jim, those two turned out all right in the end, bless their jolly hearts. He only wished that Archie had turned out half as well and he wondered, dismally, what he could possibly say to the boy when they did meet.

His thoughts were interrupted by Mr. Betts, opening his speech for the defence, and Jim noted that the barrister was sticking very closely indeed to Edith's suggested approach, a fact that surprised him, for he could not help finding it odd that an elderly, unsophisticated woman like Edith, should be able to point a path to a professional like Betts, or that Betts should be so ready to take advantage of her observations.

Betts did what he could, leading up to the fact that his client was totally unused to spirit-drinking, a claim, thought Jim, that was belied by Archie's mottled complexion as he sat staring blankly at the empty witness box facing him. 'I only hope the young fool isn't exhaling the smell of liquor at this moment,' thought Jim. 'He certainly looks as if he had had a few on the way in!'

A moment later Mr. Betts called Edith, who rose briskly from her seat beside Jim and almost tripped up the short stairway to the witness-box.

"I am calling Miss Edith Clegg as a character witness," explained Mr. Betts. "I do not propose to call any other witnesses, for further than that we are content to throw ourselves on the mercy of the court.

"There remains little to be said, save that my client wishes to express his deepest regret that he was instrumental in bringing about the death of this young woman!"

He turned to Edith, who had now taken the oath.

"Your name is Edith Clegg, and you live at number Four, Manor Park Avenue, a house next door to the defendant's place of business?"

"That's quite true," said Edith, in a strong, clear voice.

"You have known the defendant for how long?"

"For twenty-three years," said Edith, "and that's long before he took over the corner shop."

"During all that time you have seen him and talked with him frequently, I imagine?"

"Almost every day," said Edith, "his shop was so handy for popping in."

"Can you tell us what estimate you formed of Mr. Carver's character?"

"A very good estimate," said Edith, promptly, and Jim, watching closely, saw Archie's expression change slightly, the blankness giving place to a faint look of bewilderment, as though Edith's statement caused him surprise.

"Can you say more than that, Miss Clegg?"

"Only that never once, during that time, did I see him worse for drink, sir," said Edith. "He didn't ever smell of drink, and he was never anything but nice and polite, not only to me, but to everyone along the Avenue. I think. . . ."

But the court was not to hear what Edith thought at that stage, for Mr. Betts lifted his hand and murmured: "Ah-ah!"

in a slightly reproving tone. He beamed at Edith, however as he moved slightly closer to the witness box.

"In fact, you are very surprised to see him here on this grave charge, Miss Clegg?"

"Yes, I am, indeed," said Edith, and then, like a person judging her distance, preparatory to throwing something at a fixed object, she added, "and he simply *couldn't* have been used to drink and that's the top and bottom of the matter!"

The prosecutor rose, smiling indulgently at the witness.

"I take it you were a regular customer of the defendant's, Miss Clegg?"

"Yes, I was," said Edith, tartly, "but what's that got to do with it?"

"No further questions," said the prosecutor, and sat down, exchanging a knowing look with his opposite number.

. . . .

It might, said Mr. Betts, as they stood waiting in the corridor, have been very much worse and the barrister went on to say that things might have gone very badly for Archie, had it not been for the impression created in court by Miss Clegg.

Jim hunched his shoulders. A sentence of eighteen calendar months seemed to him bad enough, and for the first time since he had heard of the accident he found that he could spare a little sympathy for Archie. In 1931 Jim had once spent a day in gaol himself, after he had been involved in Hunger March demonstrations at Marble Arch, but just one day could not be compared to eighteen months, neither could the circumstances accompanying Jim's imprisonment bear comparison with Archie's. Jim had been locked up in the company of a score of Welsh miners, and all of them had been conscious of martyrdom. No such uplift could now sustain Archie, shut behind grey walls for a year and a half, in order to expiate an act of criminal folly that had resulted in the death of a total stranger.

Jim found himself resenting the ebullience of the young barrister, who was behaving, he felt, as though he and Edith had scored a notable victory over the prosecution. Perhaps he was right, perhaps his own frank handling of the case, plus

Edith's statement, had indeed induced the judge to reduce his conception of Archie from a homicidal drunkard to that of a reckless simpleton, but the fact remained that the boy's business life was now in ruins, and he would surely find it very difficult to pick up the threads again, when his sentence had expired.

Thinking this, Jim asked himself whether he would have felt any better if Archie had been acquitted, and he at once decided that he would not. There was the unwritten, as well as the statutory law; a girl's life had been sacrificed and someone, somewhere, had to pay the bill. Who better than the man who had taken that life, accidentally it was true, but in circumstances far more blameworthy than those surrounding an ordinary road fatality?

The usher came to them at last and said that they could see the defendant for a few minutes before he was taken away. The barrister and Mr. Sills at once excused themselves, and Edith looked hesitantly at Jim.

"Would you sooner see him alone, Mr. Carver?"

"No," said Jim, decisively, "I'd much sooner you came with me. That is, if you don't mind coming?"

They followed the usher along a narrow passage, and then down a short flight of steps leading to a barred and sparsely furnished little room, located somewhere in the bowels of the building.

Archie was sitting at a deal table under a fanlight, with the same expression of vacancy on his face, his arms loosely folded, and one plump thigh crossed over the other.

He looked, thought Jim, tired and resigned, and as soon as the usher had been replaced by a uniformed policeman, who remained standing stiffly by the open door, Archie rose with a flicker of a smile and addressed Edith.

"I'm very glad to have a chance of saying 'thank you' Miss Clegg," he told her, and Jim sensed at once that his embarrassment was the less because Edith was there. "You can sit down," he added, pointing to chairs, "they said we'd got a few minutes."

Jim cleared his throat. He was at a loss to know what to say. It seemed almost indecent to refer to the present or future, and he and Archie had drifted apart so long ago that

they shared very few topics connected with the past. Finally
he said:

"You heard about poor old Berni and Boxer?"

"Yes," said Archie, "Williams, at the shop told me, when I
went back there last week. I'm sorry, they were good kids.
You've heard no more since, I suppose?"

"No," said Jim, "nothing more so far."

"What will you do about the shop, Mr. Carver?" asked
Edith, anxiously.

"A man called Saunders is going to buy it," Archie told
them, "and he's agreed to do so over a period and raise a
mortgage, if he can. It'll all be settled one way or the other
by the time I come out."

"You won't have to . . . to *serve* eighteen months, not if
. . ." began Jim, but tailed off, unable to complete the sentence.

"Not if I keep my nose clean? No, about a year," said
Archie, with a flash of his old insolence. Then, turning
frankly to Jim: "It was damned decent of you to come
down, Dad, and I appreciate it much more than you think! It
was more than Maria could bring herself to do!"

Jim detected the bitterness in his son's voice when he spoke
his wife's name.

"What's happening about Maria?" he asked. "Is she still
down in Somerset?"

"I wouldn't know," said Archie, "she and the two younger
kids were there until recently, but it wouldn't surprise me if
she hadn't cleared out by now. She will if she knows what's
good for her!"

"Are you absolutely sure that she ran off with your money?" asked Jim.

"She was the only one who knew it was there, and the only
one who had a key to the place. That's good enough for me,
Dad."

"Well, there's no sense in making more trouble if you do run
across her, son," said Jim, gently. "If you intend to recover it,
do it through the law."

"Ah, but look where the law's landed me," said Archie,
and this time Jim was relieved to see a genuine grin cross his
face. The sudden widening of Archie's mouth reminded him

poignantly of Boxer, and the reminder completed the thaw, so that he said, slowly:

"Is there anything Miss Clegg and I can do for you? Anything about the shop? Or could we send you anything ... cigarettes, or something?"

"No cigarettes," said Archie, "it's a real democracy, once you're inside."

He turned to Edith and smiled. Jim had never realised what a charming smile he had when he cared to use it. "There's one little thing you could do, Miss Clegg . . . you could tell Elaine Fraser what's happened, and send on her address to me."

"She's still in the Avenue," said Jim, shortly, "she lives at Number Forty-Three and I catch a glimpse of her every now and again."

"Oh, well, that's okay, then," said Archie, "tell her I'll write to her there. It'll give her no end of a kick to get a letter with my new address on the top!"

The constable at the door shifted his stand and glanced significantly at the clock in the corridor. A note of strain entered the group. It seemed to Jim that Archie was making up his mind to say something more but was finding it difficult.

"There's one thing you ought to know, Dad ... I haven't told anyone else ... there's really no one to tell, but I think *you* ought to know!"

"Well?"

"My boy ... Tony ... he's dead. He was killed at Tobruk, about a month ago. He got the M.C. you know, he did damn well out there! In a way I'm glad he finished up like that ... I wouldn't have liked him to hear about this lark. It would have upset him pretty much, I imagine!"

Jim could think of no comment to make. Tony was his eldest grandchild and secretly he had been very proud of him, although his long estrangement from Archie had meant that he had never had more than an occasional glimpse of the boy. He knew that Tony had been commissioned, and was serving abroad, but he had never seen him in uniform. Now he would never get to know him and for a moment the

bitterness of this realisation checked his natural sympathy for
Archie.

He saw Edith reach out and touch Archie's sleeve. The movement did not go unnoticed by the policeman at the door, who
half turned into the room.

"I'm afraid time's up," said the officer.

"I'm so sorry, so terribly sorry, Mr. Carver," said Edith,
ignoring the policeman's interruption, and Archie turned
away quickly but not quickly enough, for Jim saw the muscles
of his throat contract and then realised why his son had
looked so vague and uninterested throughout his trial. He
understood that well enough. Even a charge of manslaughter
must seem insignificant beside the certainty of never again
setting eyes on one's eldest child, of knowing that young
Tony, whom Archie had been at such pains to convert into
an English gentleman, was now dead and buried under sand,
thousands of miles away!

The constable touched Jim's elbow. "I'm afraid I'll have to
ask you to leave now," he said.

"Have you notified the boy's school?" asked Jim, suddenly.

"No, but I should have done, they'll be very proud of him
up there. Will you write a line for me?"

"Of course," said Jim, and suddenly shot out his hand in
Archie's direction.

"After this we'll . . . we'll try and manage to see a bit more
of one another, son?"

He hardly had time to notice the pressure of Archie's hand
before he found himself walking along the corridor, with
Edith close beside him. Edith was saying:

"You see, it was all for the best Mr. Carver. It's dreadful I
know but it was all meant to happen. You're friends now,
you're much closer than you've ever been, so in a way it's
been worth it, don't you think?"

Jim said nothing. He felt desperately ashamed of the
choking sensation in his throat and the blur of tears that
prevented him from negotiating the stone staircase without
stumbling. Edith took his arm and they found their way out
into the street.

She led the way across to the café, where they had lunch.

"What you need is a nice strong cup of tea, Mr. Carver.

Our train home isn't until 8.15. I remembered to check it on a timetable this morning."

He looked at her as she was giving the order, and marvelled at her composure, at the steadiness and confidence that seemed to radiate from her stocky little body, and broad, pink face.

"I'll never forget how you've been over this, Edith," he said, hoarsely and was surprised by the blush that followed his first use of her Christian name.

CHAPTER XXIV

Elaine Versus The Deep South

ELAINE was finding the conquest of the Deep South a more difficult task than she had imagined.

It had been very simple to improve upon her chance acquaintance with Lieutenant Woolston Ericssohn, adjutant of the U.S. Transport Depot, stationed so conveniently close to the Avenue. He was easy to get to know, but not nearly so easy to bring to the boil. Indeed, in some respects he was proving the most difficult prospect that Elaine had ever tackled, and there were times when he seemed outside the range of her experience.

The trouble with Woolston was his background. To see him cross the meadow, and enter the gate of Number Four, where he shared a billet with his superior officer, Major Sparkewell, one would have had difficulty in identifying him for what he was, a Southern gentleman, who would have ridden north with Lee, and west with Fighting Joe Johnston and Beau Beauregard. He did not look like a Southern gentleman. It was difficult to picture him in a linen suit and Panama hat, drinking mint julep under his magnolias, as he discussed with other southern gentlemen the theory that Negro slavery was authorised by Holy Writ. Indeed, in appearance he had more in common with, say, a studious middle-aged clerk, content, perhaps, to rub along on a modest sixty dollars a week, earned in a Chicago insurance office, or even a mid-western store. He was thin, pale, slightly below average height, inclined to stoop, and had scrubby fair hair that did not seem to answer to any lotion on sale at the PX counter.

346

He was also near-sighted, and wore rimless spectacles, so that altogether he was a long way removed from the traditional picture of a Confederate officer, inspired by the cinema and popular fiction.

Elaine knew all about these officers. Not only had she seen *'Gone with the Wind'* twice (she felt a strong kinship with Scarlett O'Hara, although she was unable to share her passion for Ashley Wilkes) but she had also read a large number of current American novels, in which heroes called Buck or Red, or Abner, pursued heroines called Kitten, Ellie, or Charmaine. These heroes were always rangey, and ravenhaired, with insolent eyes but chivalrous manners. Not one of them looked like Lieutenant Ericssohn although, as she got to know him better, she had to admit that if one could overlook his physical shortcomings he had the role fairly pat, and had obviously put a great deal of work into its study.

This aspect of Ericssohn had at first occasioned doubts in her mind regarding his bank balance and his ability, if called upon, to fulfil another role that awaited him, the role of Great Provider, but Elaine was not the kind of person to leave a thing like this to chance and lost no time in making enquiries among Ericssohn's associates, with the object of establishing whether his reputed wealth was as substantial as his drawl.

The result of these enquiries reassured her. All the officers and N.C.O.s whom she met at the 'Welcome America' socials and dances in the suburb that summer, confirmed the fact that Ericssohn was indeed 'loaded', and that his late father, of Hintonville, North Carolina, had been.reckoned a wealthy man, even by U.S. standards.

Having satisfied herself in this respect Elaine dismissed from her mind unworthy doubts regarding Lieutenant Ericssohn's intention to deceive, and at once set about modelling herself into the kind of belle that a Southern gentleman would flirt with before leading home to porticoed mansion.

Up to a point she made rapid progress, for she was half-convinced that here, at long last, was a Provider whose provision promised to be limitless, someone who, besides being able to fix her up with terrace, hammock, yacht, sports car, mink, and martinis, was also of a sufficiently manageable disposition to suffer the presence of any number of more exciting courtiers, without making tiresome scenes, or imposing impossible conditions upon his wfe.

The thing to do, she told herself, was to marry him quickly, before some other suburban huntress had assessed his possibilities, and cooled off the more engaging of his associates, younger men with broad shoulders and Clark Gable profiles, but who were not quite so 'loaded' as Lieutenant Ericssohn.

The point to which Elaine did progress during those first few weeks was that step in Southern courtship where the belle is kissed lightly upon the cheek, an inch or so below the nearest eye.

It took Elaine a certain amount of time to adjust herself to the tempo of Southern wooing. She was not accustomed to being kissed below either eye, or to having the tips of her fingers pressed and then decorously released when men said good night to her at the front gate of Number Forty-Three.

Even Esme's Arthurian wooing had been more venturesome than this, for while Esme too had placed her on a pedestal it had remained a mere pedestal, and had never become the dome of the Capitol.

She was tempted, on several occasions during the early stages of their friendship, to take the initiative, and drag the Lieutenant across the threshold of love. Once there she was confident of producing acceleration on his part, but there was something about him that made her hesitate and play for safety.

Meantime, night after night, she cast about for a plan, one that would shift the onus of pace-making to him, and subject his Southern chivalry to a real test. That she did eventually hit upon such a plan and managed, despite all, to bring it to a successful conclusion, was a far greater tribute to her patience than to her ingenuity.

The real difficulty lay in the fact that Ericssohn's masquerade as a gentleman of the Deep South was not really a masquerade at all. It was not and never had been, a deliberate attempt on his part to pretend to anything other than what he believed of himself. Ever since the day, at the age of thirteen, that he had first gazed upon a magnolia, he had been the slave of a dream as demanding as the one Elaine had been serving since she was fifteen. Ericssohn dreamed of a lost civilisation, the civilisation of the Old and Martyred South, and because he had money at his disposal he had already provided himself with a setting for the dream. He was on the point of converting this dream into reality when the first shots descended on Fort Sumpter (in his case, Pearl Harbour) and he hurried away in response to a bugle call, just as any Southern gentleman would have done, without so much as pausing to swat a blue-tailed fly!

To understand Woolston Ericssohn, and the difficulty poor Elaine had with him, it is necessary to know a little of the Lieutenant's actual background, apart from the one he had created for himself.

His grandfather was a Swedish carpenter, who had come to the States in the early 'seventies', and had prospered, if modestly, as a cabinet maker's foreman, in Chicago.

His younger son, Axel Ericssohn, abandoned cabinet-making for real estate, and in the expansion years prior to the First World War he made a limited amount of money, later drifting south-east, a latter-day carpet-bagger some might have said, in order to share in the first of the post-war real estate booms.

Ericssohn senior was a shrewd man, shrewd enough to sell out and move further south into Carolina, long before the market crashed. It was here, in a town called Hintonville, that he finally settled, investing his capital in high-grade timber, which was something he understood better than most people, certainly most people in Hintonville.

Woolston, his eldest son, was a shy young man, much given to study, and to dreaming. It is not known where he first acquired his white-hot passion for the Confederacy, but it was probably as a teeenager in local libraries rich in the legends of the South. Woolston was not in the least interested in his father's business ventures, he left that to his younger brothers, Gustave and Frederick. He himself had other plans, mainly concerned with the resurrection of a civilisation, blotted out by Sherman and his blue-bellies, nearly forty years before Woolston was born.

He would be, he told himself, a perfect Southern gentleman, and he set about making himself one with a single-mindedness that astonished his family and fascinated the entire community in and around Hintonville.

He first spent a term at a Southern military academy, where he learned to ride, shoot and develop a Southern drawl almost indistinguishable from the speech of people who had been born in the South.

His father died in the late nineteen-twenties and left him some money, but when his mother died a few years later Woolston inherited a very considerable sum and was able to return home and purchase a small plantation, at once commencing to build upon it the kind of house that Jefferson Davis would have recognised as the ideal home of a hero of Bull Run.

It was a long time building, and was only two-thirds erected when the bugles shrilled and Woolston forgot all about his splendid new house in his eagerness to rush into battle. It was a pity, he felt, that Sherman was dead, and that he was now called upon to fight side by side with Yankees against such unfamiliar adversaries as Hitler and Hirohito, but there was obviously glory to be won, and perhaps a beautiful belle into the bargain, so he lied about his age and pulled strings to be included in an early draft, thus arriving in England with the American vanguard.

Since then the prospects of glory had faded. He had been bogged down in a dull, London suburb, filling out endless forms, and signing thousands of grubby chits, and doing so, Godammit, at the beck and call of a coarse-mouthed, regular officer who came from Maine.

They told him that things would improve in time, but he was feeling very depressed and homesick on the morning that he met Elaine humping her suitcase from Woodside Station.

Elaine attracted him from the first, winning smile. Not only was she dark and winsome, just like the girls who had sewn sashes and embroidered banners for the heroes of Shiloh, but she was also the first British woman to pay him the compliment of a second glance.

When he began to encounter her regularly, as he passed to and fro along the Avenue, he noticed that she always smiled before lowering her eyes to the pavement, and the time soon came when he nerved himself to speak to her.

He found her shy and demure, but nonetheless extraordinarily patient with him. After their third conversation he began to feel less homesick, for there was much about her that reminded him of the South, her carriage, her low-pitched voice, her shyness and, above all, her obvious deferment to the male. She was the kind of woman, he told himself, who would always remain dependent upon him, and was so different from most of the girls whom he had seen skylarking with the troops in the Recreation Ground and the Manor Wood. He made up his mind to pursue his advantage with her but cautiously, and in a manner befitting a Southern gentleman. He would behave, in fact, just as was prescribed for him in the booklets they were now issuing to the enlisted men, manuals entitled: *How to Behave in Britain.*

It was fortunate for Elaine that Woolston's experience with women were limited to one High School flirtation, and a somewhat anaemic romance with the sister of a cadet at the military college he had attended. Had he been as experienced as most of his comrades at the Depot he must have smelled powder within a week.

There was a quiet desperation about Elaine's stalking of Lieutenant Ericssohn the 'loaded' Southern gentleman.

She was now over thirty, and the Great Provider still eluded her. This, she told herself, might well be her last chance, but it also looked like being her best chance, and she was nervous of making a mistake.

It took her a long time to appreciate the fact that here at last was a man whom one could not play too slowly. The merest hint that she was the kind of woman who welcomed familiarity would, she felt certain, scare him back into a shell, from which he might not emerge until he was posted overseas. On the other hand, no man alive, she felt, could remain satisfied for very long with the pace of their wooing to date, and the deep shadow that hung over her during this stage was the possibility of his hearing Avenue gossip about her divorce. After all, he lived with the Clegg sisters, at Number Four, and although Becky was half-witted, and Edith was anything but a gossip, Edith was friendly with Jim

Carver, who was actually sharing a house with Esme's stepfather, besides being the father of the co-respondent in her case. The risks were therefore considerable.

After due thought she decided that it would be better to tell him about her divorce, and get her story comfortably planted before someone else whispered in his ear.

She told him one night when they were walking back from a social at the Institute Hall in the Lower Road, and at first she was shaken badly by his reception of the news.

"You been married? You actually *been* married? Heck, that's kind of a shock, honey! Tell me about it! How-come you didn't *stay* married?"

She mastered her panic and decided to appeal to his Southern chivalry.

Even Elaine was surprised by the success of this approach. Her impromptu account of her marriage put quite a strain on her powers of invention. She was not a practised liar, never having found it necessary to lie to men once she had let them kiss her, and it was difficult to present poor, lovesick Esme as a vicious wife-beater, or Archie Carver as an honest John Bull, maliciously manoeuvred into the role of co-respondent.

She was a better liar than she had realised. He believed her more readily because the story heightened his own role as protector. Just as Elaine had exhibited those qualities that had once convinced Esme that she was awaiting rescue from her tower at Number Seventeen, so Woolston had no difficulty in seeing her as the long-suffering victim of a sadistic husband.

"He had the most jealous temper imaginable, and whenever he saw me show conventional interest in another man he seemed to go quite mad," she told him. "He would often," she added, almost casually, "pick this kind of quarrel with me and then beat me!"

"You don't say, honey," gasped Woolston. "What did he lam you with, honey?"

"A dog-whip," said Elaine, without hesitation.

"You got a dog?" he asked, irrelevantly.

"Not now," said Elaine, promptly, "he had mine destroyed!"

"He sure sounds a sonofabitch," said Woolston.

At first Elaine told these stories half in jest, for at that stage in their association she had not become fully acclimatised to his almost limitless credulity, but later on, when she realised that she was furthering her cause, she embroidered her tale with graphic details of the kind of scenes that were commonplace in Number Forty-Three when Esme came home on leave, and had worked himself up into one of his jealous frenzies. She also told him more about Archie, who became 'a kindly grocer across the road', and a man who had incurred her husband's enmity by helping her eke out her miserable rations whilst she was living alone through the horrors of the blitz.

"Poor Archie," she sighed, "he had to sell up, and go away on account of the scandal, but his wife didn't divorce him, and I always felt that this was proof that she at least didn't believe any of the things that Esme and his folks spread around about us. Still, the judge did and they took my little girl away from me. I've never set eyes on her since. I could, of course, for they couldn't stop me seeing her every now and again, but I wouldn't want to confuse the poor kid, and I'll just have to wait for her to grow up before she hears the truth about me."

Woolston contributed little to all this, apart from an occasional whistle, a 'Say, honey!', or 'Gee, honey!' Mainly he confined himself to murmurs of sympathy until Elaine described the final scene, the one that occurred after Esme had come home on leave and found that she had gone away in the friendly grocer's car, in order to make preliminary arrangements to abandon him.

"Ah, he was cruel all right, that night," she sighed, "the night I came back into a house that I thought was empty!"

"What did he do?" demanded Woolston, "just what did that sonofabitch do then, honey?"

Elaine had to draw on a never-to-be-forgotten experience in a hotel bedroom, where Audrey the Amazon, wife of her lover, had discovered her in bed with Mr. Tappertitt, the circus-owner.

"He threw me on the bed, knelt on me, and . . . and thrashed me until he was tired, Woolston!"

"Say! With that dog-whip," cried Woolston, in agony.

"No," said Elaine, honestly, "it wasn't a dog-whip that time, it was a hair-brush and he smashed it to pieces on me!"

"He did *that*?"

"That's what he did, and that's what I never told anybody before because I was always so ashamed of marrying a man who could treat a woman like that!"

"Gee, I'd sure like to run across that guy! I'd sure like to meet him," said Woolston, fervently.

Elaine reflected, with some relief, that this was unlikely, for Esme had been swallowed up by the war.

"Oh, it's all over and forgotten now, Woolston," she said, "don't let's talk about it any more, let's talk about us!"

It might be imagined from this kind of exchange, that Elaine was beginning to feel more sure of Woolston, and that she had some kind of confidence in an eventual proposal, in her shy acceptance and in his submission to the military authorities for permission to marry, but as the summer went by, and his autumn kisses continued to fall upon the cheeks rather than the lips, as night followed night, and Woolston never once suggested coming in for a nightcap, she began to grow desperate again. It was then that she conceived the master plan and hurried to put it into execution. She needed an accomplice and luckily one was available in the person of Muriel Payne, who might be described as Elaine's sole woman friend.

Muriel owned a small but expensively equipped gown shop in West Croydon, and had known Elaine for many years. It was Muriel, who, as sales-girl, had sold the original red velvet dance frock that had bewitched Esme at the Stafford-Ffoulkes dance as long ago as 1929, but since then Muriel had risen in her profession, and was now a partner in a prosperous little business.

Elaine liked her. She was hard-fisted, forthright and broad-minded, but Elaine's trust in Muriel did not extend to confiding wholly in her as regards Woolston. She told her enough, however, to secure her light-hearted co-operation in the matter of a telephone call, to be put through to Number Forty-Three at about 3 a.m. At Elaine's urgent request she also gave her a couple of sleeping pills, without enquiring into the use to which they might be put. She knew that Elaine never used sleeping tablets, and was not likely to possess any, for Elaine was a sound sleeper and had not been attended by a doctor since her child was born on the first day of war.

It was an essential factor of Elaine's plan that Lieutenant Ericssohn should at last be prevailed upon to overcome his reluctance to cross her threshold at night. To achieve this, Elaine invented a birthday, which was celebrated, gravely and decorously, by a trip up West, and a supper in Soho, following a visit to the theatre. For the supper, Elaine steered Woolston to the little French café in Dean Street, where Esme had taken her on the day of their reunion and where, in fact, he had proposed to her.

The location meant nothing to her. She was not a sentimentalist and it was simply a convenient place to get the abstemious Woolston to swallow a half-bottle of Burgundy and a few sips of brandy. She managed to slip one of the sleeping tablets into his second cup of coffee.

That evening she worked especially hard to beguile him, encouraging him to talk about his beloved South and regarding him with parted lips while he held forth on the Negro problem, a subject upon which he held bellicose opinions. She struck a mellow chord when she said:

"Woolston, dear . . . you make it all so *alive* . . . over here we've only read about those things, and they never seemed real. I think you Americans are so *good* for us, and so stimulating! I suppose because we're an island we've got so stuffy and self-righteous about everything, and this has resulted in us being . . . well . . . left behind."

"Don't you say that, honey, don't you say that," said Woolston, emphatically. "Why, honey, the thing I most admire 'bout you folk is that you got reel respect for the past, and that's something you just don't find north o' the Mason-Dixon line. Say honey, this place is kinda cosy, how come you know 'bout this caffy?"

She stopped herself saying that Esme had introduced her to it, deciding that it was an evening to forget Esme, with and without dog-whip and hair-brush.

"Oh, my father used to bring me here when I was a little girl," she said. "Daddy's always had good taste. That's why he does so well in the antique business."

"I'd sure like to meet him," said Woolston and Elaine could not help feeling that this admission signified some kind of progress.

"Oh, but you shall, Woolston, you shall! He's a dear, really, and I know he'd go for you because you've got so much in common. . . . You both have . . . well, I like to call it 'male gentleness'. You'd like my Auntie Dolly, too, Daddy's sister, but she's a bit severe, like someone out of a Victorian novel. She's so disgusted with the way people behave nowadays that she doesn't want to meet anyone. That's why she took a little cottage up in the Lake District, but she's always very nice to me and I'm in her will. She's a bit eccentric, of course. Sometimes she stays up all night and goes to bed in the daytime! That's why she often calls me in the middle of the night."

"Calls you? What for, honey?"

"Oh, I don't know," said Elaine, giggling in what she hoped was a fair imitation of Georgian belles at a barbecue, "I think she likes to check up on me now and again—you know what old people are!"

Considering that Aunt Dolly had no existence outside Elaine's imagination and the demands of the master plan this was a creditable effort. It was not, however, entirely impromptu, for the creation of Aunty Dolly, and Aunty Dolly's moral outlook, had been occupying Elaine's thoughts for several days.

"I think you'd better take me home now, Woolston, dear," she said, rising. "It's already after eleven o'clock."

They returned to the Avenue by train and he was mildly gallant in the compartment that they had to themselves. When they reached the short, tiled path up to Number Forty-Three Elaine took a deep breath.

"Look, Woolston, dear, I've just remembered something. I know it's my birthday but I always feel we ought to give things to the people we like on birthdays, so I went out this morning and bought *you* a little present!"

"You did? Say, honey that was mighty foolish of you, but I'll treasure it, I'll treasure it whatever it is! What is it, honey?"

"Only a record . . . a medley of the Deep South, you

know, bits of all the songs that the darkies sing, like 'Dixie'. 'Dixie' is the main theme and I think you'll like it, it's so lovely and banjoey!"

He was touched. "That's mighty nice of you, honey, mighty nice! You sure go out o' yo' way to keep me from bein' homesick, but heck, I don't have a radiogram right here! How'm I gonna hear it played?"

"Oh, that's easy," said Elaine, eagerly. "I've got a portable gramophone, so why not come in for a moment and hear it right now? I'll make you some tea, I always have a pot of tea before I go to bed."

He hesitated and she held her breath.

"It's kinda late, honey! I don't want to compromise you 'mong the neighbours hereabouts!"

"Oh, but you couldn't do that, Woolston, not if you didn't stay! After all, we're only going to play a record, and that's a kind of alibi isn't it? It won't take a minute, really it won't!"

He badly wanted to hear that record, and the Burgundy he had drunk had uplifted him. The wine, the brandy, and her demure companionship, had created within him a mood very conducive to sitting still and listening to banjo melodies of the Deep South.

"Okay, we'll risk it, honey! But you better draw the curtains good! I'd sure hate to hurt your reputation 'round here!"

He followed her inside and through into what had once been the dining-room but was now her bed-sitting-room.

He looked around with interest while she was drawing the heavy blackout curtains but he averted his eyes from the bed. The gramophone and the new record were on a small circular table, close to the gas-fire which she bent down and lit.

"You sure fixed it real pretty in here, honey," he told her and she smiled and told him to make himself comfortable while she put the kettle on for tea.

She made plenty of noise filling the kettle and then kicked off her shoes and tiptoed back into the hall, peering through the crack in the half-open door.'He was sitting on the bed, his back against the padded headboard, and she noticed with satisfaction that he was yawning, prodigiously.

She left him alone while the kettle boiled and then bustled

in with the tray, setting it down and starting up the gramophone. At once his head began to nod to the twang of banjos and he was far too relaxed to notice that a second sleeping pill, powdered this time, went into his cup with the sugar. She poured tea as the record played itself out.

"That was swell, real swell, honey!" he said, with another yawn. "Say, I'm tuckered! You know something? I could go to sleep right here!"

"You mustn't do that, Woolston," she said, with another barbecue giggle, "that really *would* compromise me! Listen to the other side and drink up your tea!"

She turned the record and he sipped his tea. Then, without protest from him, she played the first side over again and refilled his cup. When she turned back to hand it to him he was sound asleep, chin up and mouth open.

She remained very still for a few minutes and then gently lifted the arm of the gramophone and waited again. He did not stir but began to snore, gently and regularly. She turned down the gas, switched off all but the bedside light, and carried the tea tray into the kitchen to wash up.

When she returned he had slithered several inches, and she was able to lift his feet on to the bed and remove his shoes. Her action caused him to slide into an almost recumbent position and she softly adjusted the pillow and loosened his tie. Once he stirred and groaned, but she remained quite still and he did not wake. Finally she threw the eiderdown over his legs, undressed, put on her dressing-gown, and crept from the room, leaving the door ajar.

She was lightly asleep on the front room sofa when she heard the first tinkle of the telephone. She jumped, switched on the light and looked at her watch. It was ten minutes past three. She found her slippers and crept into the hall, peeping through the open door.

He was in the same position, high up on the bed and still sound asleep, but the persistent ringing of the 'phone on the bedside table must have disturbed him for he turned over and uttered a series of short grunts.

She had dreaded this moment. Everything depended on his automatic response to the telephone bell. After all, he was an adjutant and a ringing telephone must be second nature to him. All he had to do was to roll over, grab the receiver, say one word and then Muriel would do the rest.

She waited, biting her lips as the 'phone rang and rang. She found herself praying: "Answer it, Woolston! Answer it, you clot! Everything *depends* on you answering it! My entire future depends on you waking up and grabbing that 'phone!"

She was glad now that she had warned Muriel that he might not answer at once. The damned 'phone must have been ringing five minutes and it was within a foot of his ear! Suddenly and quite unexpectedly he sat up, rolled to the left, and snatched at the receiver.

"Yeah? Yeah? Who is it?"

She almost squealed with relief and then laughter as she studied his bemused expression, so bemused indeed that she was sure he had not yet remembered where he was. Muriel's brittle voice crackled from the 'phone and Elaine heard the words: "Who's that? Who is it? Is that a man? Do you hear me? *Is that a man?*"

She had to bite her hand to check the bubble of laughter, for suddenly he held the 'phone at arm's length, as though it was a scorpion, and his eyes, still blank with bewilderment, roved the room. Muriel's voice continued to crackle but her words were now indistinguishable.

This was Elaine's cue. Deliberately she loosened the girdle of her dressing-gown and hurried into the room throwing herself across the bed and snatching the 'phone from his hand.

"Is that you, Aunt Dolly? Is it you, Auntie? It's Elaine, here, darling! *Who? A man?* Nonsense, darling! There's nobody here but me!"

She heard Woolston hiss and felt him plucking at her dressing-gown.

"I said something," he hissed, "Dogonnit, I opened my big mouth . . . !"

Elaine pretended not to hear him. She was engaged in acting harder than she had ever acted for anyone in the past.

"But of *course* not, darling . . . how *could* there be . . . ? Listen Auntie . . . listen. . . ."

This was Muriel's cue. There was a sharp click as the receiver was replaced. Elaine stared at it for a moment, still sprawled across his knees and then, slamming down the 'phone she sat up and uttered a long, low wail of dismay.

"You . . . you *spoke* to her, Woolston! Oh, but you shouldn't have—you shouldn't have! What *will* she think? Whatever *can* she think? Oh Woolston . . . !" and she climbed off the bed, slumped into the armchair and buried her face in her hands.

He was beside her in an instant, a wincing, quivering figure of shame and contrition.

"I guess it come natural, honey . . . I was dead to the world, and I just grabbed it . . . I wouldn't have done it for the world, honey, you gotter believe that! I'd rather've cut my hand off, so help me, I would!"

"What . . . what did you *say?*" she whimpered.

"I dunno, I don't remember . . . I asked who was calling, I guess. It come natural, honey, startin' up like that!"

"But she'll never forgive me, Woolston, *never!* She'll never even *speak* to me again! And I was the only one in the will! It's even worse than that, she'll write to Daddy, and Daddy'll be down here right away! He'll never believe it was innocent, *nobody* will! Don't you see what a dreadful mess you've made of everything?"

He did, indeed, and groaned aloud.

"How come I'm here? What happened to me? What's the time?" he wanted to know.

"It's after three, and you . . . you just *wouldn't* wake up! It was all that wine, I suppose, and you seemed so terribly tired that I thought I'd leave you to sleep for a bit, and lay down in the other room. It was silly I suppose but how was I to know she'd ring? And how could I dream you'd be silly enough to answer if she did?"

He looked so wretched now that she thought he was going to burst into tears.

She seemed suddenly to realise that her dressing-gown was uncorded and whipped its folds about her. He turned his eyes away.

"Look, honey . . . I feel kinda responsible for this . . . I wouldn't want you to quarrel with your family on my account. You been swell, and me . . . I figure I'd have gone loco here if it hadn't been for you! What say we . . . we *get* married, huh? Then I figure it wouldn't matter how much the old fuddy-duddies talked!"

It was like the final moment of a long and uncertain voyage across stormy waters; it was like the first, friendly twinkle of light, after hours and hours of stumbling along in the dark, but it was also more than that, it was a moment of supreme personal triumph, the climax of a campaign that reached back to the first day she had come to terms with her destiny, the day that she had decided that there was only one worthwhile goal for her, security in the embrace of a man who was 'loaded'!

Yet she was not free to savour the moment, not yet, not until he was safely out of the house and across the road in his billet at Number Four. Until then she must keep the stars from her eyes.

She said, so softly that he had to incline his head to hear her:

"I wouldn't want you to marry me on that account, Woolston. That's the most gallant thing any man ever said to me and I'll always remember it, but what happened just now wasn't your fault, it was an accident." She paused a moment, watching him, then: "Of, course, if you really *want* to ... if it had ever crossed your mind before this dreadful thing happened ... ?"

She must have underestimated herself, for there was really no need to take any more chances. He gave a little yelp and fell forward on his knees, lowering his head to her lap and covering her hands with kisses.

"I guess I'll write to your father right away, honey! I guess I'll tell him what a swell daughter he's got and that I'm crazy to marry her, crazy, d'you hear me?"

She sighed and stroked his stiff, stubby hair.

"I'll try and make a good wife, Woolston darling," she said, and at the moment of saying she meant it.

CHAPTER XXV

Sunshine In November

AS Edgar Frith turned into the Avenue from Shirley Rise, and passed beside the shapeless mound that had once been his home, a shaft of November sunshine lunged at the even numbers opposite like a long, bronze spear, lighting for a moment the russet-coloured brickwork of Number Twenty and Twenty-Two where the rough-cast had fallen away from the space above the porches.

Edgar noted the sunshine and it seemed to him a good omen. It was not often that he returned to the Avenue. His memories of the years he had spent at Number Seventeen were not pleasant memories, nor was he successful in blotting them out when he was separated from Frances.

She was aware of this and had suggested accompanying him to London, but he had a very personal reason for wanting to make this trip alone. He was jealous of her high opinion of his professional judgment, and if Chaffery was going to laugh at him, and tell him to hump his prize back to Wales, mark it forty shillings, and sell it as a garden ornament, he did not want Frances to witness his humiliation.

If this happened, as well it might, then he wanted time to compose himself and rehearse light-hearted acceptance of the disappointment. On the other hand, if Chaffery endorsed his opinion, then he wanted to nurse his triumph in secret all the way home to Llandudno, and burst in upon Frances like a boy running home with news that the world was at his feet. He wanted to run up the stairs into their cosy living room over the shop and shout: "I've done it, Frances! I've done it at last! It's *'right'*, just as I said it was! It's *'right'*, Francie, and you're looking at the man who bought a masterpiece for shillings!"

For nearly forty years he had been dreaming of such a moment. Long before he and Frances had eloped, when he was a shy young salesman in his first job, he had pictured himself coming back from an auction sale with a masterpiece acquired for a few shillings. He had no clear idea what kind of a masterpiece it would be, perhaps a picture, or perhaps just a piece of exquisitely modelled china from one of the early factories. Whatever it was it would be something that would attract the attention and interest of specialists all over the antique world, and drive the other dealers half-mad with jealousy and frustration when they remembered how they too had had an opportunity to buy it, but had overlooked it because they lacked his knowledge.

Every now and again Edgar had come near to fulfilling such a dream. There had been the lost and badly damaged Giovanni Bellini, painted over by a Victorian amateur, the picture that he carefully cleaned and then sold again for a few pounds, only to read in *The Times* a month later that the picture had been resold at Sotheby's for fourteen thousand guineas.

There had been the Bow tea service, almost perfect, that he had purchased privately during the first year that they opened in Llandudno and been obliged to resell for a quick profit, because of the mortgage debt on their premises, and of the urgent necessity to invest in stock and keep the business turning.

Then there had been the 16th century French tapestries, at Gorsehill Hall, which he would have bought had not his courage failed him at the final bid. 'Skipper' Williams had bought those tapestries, and resold them at a huge profit within an hour of the trade knock-out. All these and other opportunities had slipped by, usually because his nerve proved unequal to gambling with Frances' capital, and with two women dependent upon him.

Now the mortgage was paid off and he was holding a fair-sized stock. Now Pippa was earning and living away from them, in London, and he was much more free to speculate and back his judgment to the limit of his means. But then something else had stepped between Edgar and fulfilment, 'Skipper' Williams' wartime reorganisation of 'The Ring', a ring that Edgar had steadfastly refused to enter, because, after a lifetime in the trade, he still possessed a squeamish conscience.

As the war continued and the Ring tightened a notch at every sale, Edgar's conscience began to cost him money. By the autumn of 1942 Williams and his associates, if not exactly ruining him, were at least making his life very difficult, and forcing him out of the sale-rooms.

Edgar had known what to expect, for Williams had warned him that they were determined to do this after Edgar had turned down his final ultimatum at the Gorsehill three-day auction.

"Look-you, Manny," he had said, in his music-hall Welsh accent, "You'll have to come in see, or get out altogether, Manny! Everyone else is in and we won't stand for outsiders keeping the prices up! Now be a sport, Manny, and don't make us freeze you out! It's good friends we can be, if only you'll step down off that high horse of yours, and be reasonable, isn't it?"

But Edgar, although he knew that the threat was not idle, had remained obstinate. He had always operated outside the ring, and he would continue to do so for as long as he was in business. It went against his conscience to see a set of chairs worth at least two hundred pounds bought in by the ring for a tenth of this sum, and then knocked out, immediately after the auction, for its true value, the difference being split between the dealers instead of going into the pocket of the vendor.

There had always been a ring, of course, but in the old days it had been an optional arrangement. A man could join it or stay free of it, and if he stayed out no pressure was put upon him to join. It was very different nowadays! Stock was hard to find, and Edgar did not like the kind of dealer that the ring had attracted since the war, seedy little opportunists for the most part, who attended every auction sale without the slightest intention of acquiring stock, men who were content to hang around, do the bidding for Williams and his associates, and then slink off with their share of the knock-out money.

Williams himself was typical of the kind of man dominating the trade. He had no real business premises but operated from a ramshackle barn on the Fossdyke by-pass. It was getting more and more difficult to combat this kind of competition, for a legitimate antique dealer was faced with the inevitable overheads of a shop, and was obliged to keep a proper set of books, instead of dealing exclusively in cash, thus evading a high proportion of tax.

Edgar had fought back. He had tried, half-heartedly, to organise three or four of the better-class dealers into an opposition, but he had failed, finding that they were afraid of 'Skipper' and his following, and preferred to fall back upon private purchases, rather than compete with the Ring under the auctioneer's rostrum.

He himself went on attending sales, his false teeth clenched in grim determination to go down fighting, but after delivery of Williams' ultimatum it became impossible to hold out any longer. The crisis came at the Tandovery Manor sale, where he was unable to buy a single lot and retired, humiliated, into the garden before noon.

It was then that he had first seen the Cupid. He had been sitting on the low wall of the lily-pond, munching his sandwiches, and the Cupid had seemed to wink at him from its plinth, at the junction of two rose-walk paths.

He got up and walked over for a closer inspection. The little statue was about thirty inches high, with a smooth, pouting, cherubic face and undamaged wings. A person possessing no special interest in statuary could have been excused for passing it without a second glance. It had been there so long that it had merged into the landscape. The muscle crease between the shoulder blades was worn smooth by centuries of Welsh rain, and the toes were hardly distinguishable as separate extremities. The entire body was slumped sullenly on the bow stave, as the eyes surveyed the cloud-masked mountains in the west. Edgar at once christened it 'The Sullen Cupid' and made up his mind to buy it on the spot.

He knew that Williams and the Ring would not dispute it

with him. They hardly ever bothered with outside lots, leaving the contents of sheds and garages to the locals, who often bought in gardening tools and greenhouse equipment for shillings. He went down on his knees in the mud and carefully examined every inch of the Cupid, applying his pocket glass to an indecipherable inscription on the plinth. He could make out four letters, '*ARDI*', which was obviously part of a longer word, so he put his glass away, finished his lunch, and waited until the auctioneer headed the crowd into the sunken garden and began selling the outside lots.

He had to wait a long time and before they reached Lot 1003 which was the Cupid, it was raining hard and almost everyone had drifted away.

"Garden ornament, Lot 1003! What am I bid?" demanded the auctioneer, hunching his shoulders, and glaring round at the dwindling crowd.

"Ten shillings," said Edgar, firmly.

"Any advance on ten? Any advance? Once, twice, three times . . . sold to Mr. Frith," said the auctioneer, with a token tap of his hammer.

A gust of wind almost lifted his hat and he made a wild grab at it. "This is murder!" he said, "we'll finish off in the greenhouse." Then everyone shuffled away, leaving Edgar alone with his Cupid.

He got it to the car with the assistance of one of the auctioneer's men. It was surprisingly heavy and the effort distressed him, bringing on a sharp bout of indigestion. Notwithstanding this, he drove home with a soaring heart, left the Cupid in the car, and hurried upstairs to the kitchen, where Frances was preparing supper.

She looked up and smiled as he bustled in.

"Did you get anything? Were they as horrid as ever, dear?"

"I got The Cupid," he said, breathlessly, unable to keep the jubilation from his voice, "I got The Sullen Cupid and I'll stake my wig that it's 'right'! It's 'right', Francie, it's a wonderful, wonderful buy!"

Frances left the stove and relived him of his dripping raincoat. That was what was wonderful about Frances, she was so expert at catching a man's mood, and never irritated by tut-tutting about chills, wet clothes, and warmed-up meals.

"Tell me, Edgar, tell me all about it!"

He told her as they ate their supper. He said that the Sullen Cupid was no ordinary Cupid, but the work of a master, almost certainly an Italian master. He did not know which master, and would not attempt to guess until he had looked up the books, and scraped the moss and grime from the inscription, but he was quite sure that the Cupid was 'right', as sure as he had been about the tapestries. This time he would take his time over identification and resale. This time he would make quite sure that he and no one else got the credit for the discovery.

He worked on the statue all the following day but succeeded only in deciphering one more letter, a 'B' immediately preceeding the 'ARDI'. It was enough, however, to enlarge his opinion. The Sullen Cupid, he decided, was the work of the same master as the famous Pensive Cupid, now in the Mond collection. It was a creation of Antonio Lombardi, the Venetian responsible for the Doge's tomb, in Venice. It was worth, at a guess, at least four figures, probably much more, and he had bought it for ten shillings!

It did not seem strange to Edgar that he should discover the work of a 15th century Venetian in the garden of a Welsh manor house. He had been in the antique trade far too long to remark upon such things. All these beautiful objects had a wandering destiny, owing allegiance to no one but the man who created them, and who had died, long since, leaving them to drift here and there like ageing wantons, attaching themselves to this owner and that owner, until these custodians died, or needed money and parted from them.

Edgar had seen ancient Chinese porcelain sold from the bedroom mantelshelf of a Shropshire cottage, and the paintings that Dutch masters had painted before the Armada set sail sold in the terrace houses of industrial towns. The vagaries of the trade did not surprise him, but its element of chance occupied his thoughts day and night. As he packed the Cupid into a specially-constructed box and watched the carrier lift it into his lorry en route for the station, he felt like a gambler who, after a lifetime of routine punting, had at last secured a huge bet on a virtual certainty. He drove behind the carrier all the way to the station, and when they arrived he stood close by while they hoisted the box into the luggage van. He could hardly drag himself away to buy his ticket, and when he did he was back again within minutes, taking up a position in the corridor where he could glance into the van at every stop, and make sure that the porter did not toss any baggage on top of his freight.

He was glad now that he had kept in touch with Chaffery, his former employer, who still did business in Croydon and Purley. Chaffery might be a hard-drinking cynic, and one of 'The Boys', and he might boast that he was in the game for profit and nothing else, but Edgar knew him rather better than that, and had not been surprised by his immediate response to the letter telling him of the Sullen Cupid. The dealer had wired: *"Nice going. Stop. Bring it down. Stop. Will get Dixon to confirm."*

Dixon, Edgar recalled, was a West-End dealer, and an acknowledged specialist in Renaissance art. Ordinarily, Edgar would have hesitated to trust him, but he knew that Chaffery was one of his best agents and that Dixon would be certain to give him an unprejudiced opinion. On arrival in Croydon he left the box in Chaffery's back room to await Dixon's visit, and Chaffery promised to telephone the verdict by eight o'clock that same evening.

"It's better that you shouldn't be here when Dixon comes, old man," Chaffery said, and Edgar agreed with him but he did not embarrass his former employer by enquiring what story he had told Dixon. He trusted Chaffery more than he trusted anyone in the trade, having learned his business from the man, and he believed him when Chaffery said: "You've earned a real find, Frith, old boy! You've really earned one! I'll get the truth from Dixon! He won't spoof me. You can rely on it!"

Thus, having settled the major part of his business, Edgar turned to domestic matters, and made his way back to the Avenue.

Elaine had written and told him that she had recently become engaged to an American, and invited him to meet her fiancé. He also wanted to see Pippa again, and enquire about Mr. Carver's boys and poor, old Esme, whose child he and Frances still cared for in Wales.

The thought of the child, Barbara, hardened his heart towards his daughter, Elaine. He found it difficult to understand why she had never wanted to see the baby since the divorce, and had never mentioned her in her letter about the American. He supposed that Elaine must have inherited his first wife's flinty streak, and nothing whatever of his own sentimentality. It was curious, he thought, that Frances' child, Pippa, now meant so much more to him than his own daughter, and seemed to possess far more of his own characteristics than Elaine possessed. He wondered what Elaine would make of her life in the end. Would she find happiness with a second husband, or would she tire of him as quickly as she had tired of Esme and seek excitement in some new relationship? She was not much like her mother in that respect. Esther had found it almost impossible to give herself to one man, much less a string of men, and he wondered if his daughter inherited his own sensuality or if it was sensuality, and not the cold-blooded exploitation of physical attractions in order to get what she wanted from men. He decided that he could not begin to answer this question, for he knew even less of Elaine than he had known of her mother, or brother.

He was still thinking about this when he knocked at her door and she popped her head out of the bathroom window, over the alley, calling down to him.

"Come right in, Daddy! The door's open, and I'm in the bath!"

He went into the hall and was startled when a slim, uniformed man emerged from the front room. Somewhere close by a gramophone was playing and the soldier had to shout above the music to introduce himself.

"Mr. Frith—*sir*—I'm Ericssohn, Lootenen' Ericssohn! I guess you've heard about me! Elaine'll be right down! Would you care for a martini, sir?"

"No," Edgar told him, rather flustered at this unconventional reception, "but you go ahead and have one."

He put his hat and umbrella on the hall-stand and followed

the American into the front room, studying him closely as he bent over the gramophone and stopped the music.

He was surprised at the man's insignificant physique. He always had the notion that Elaine preferred big men, like that young scoundrel, Carver over whom she had made such a fool of herself, and who was now, so he had heard from Pippa, serving a prison sentence for manslaughter.

The Lieutenant mixed himself a drink and tossed it off to cover his obvious embarrassment. Edgar was finding the interview equally painful and wished heartily that Elaine would put in an appearance and get it over.

"Have you two known one another very long?" he ventured, at length.

"All summer," Woolston told him, "I'm billeted just across the road. Lady by the name o' Clegg. Funny little body!"

"Is that so?" Edgar said, but could think of no comment to make on Edith, whom he knew only by sight. "When do you and Elaine propose getting married?"

"Hard to say," the American told him, "we hev to get all the formalities fixed up. There's a heap o' rules and regulations 'bout this kinda thing, sir, and it looks as if our outfit might be moving out pretty soon, to North Africa I guess, or mebbe the Second Front! We'll get around to it, I guess, soon as we can."

It was all so muddled and casual, like the rest of Elaine's life, and like almost everybody's life these days. People decided to get married, divorced and married again, just as though they were making arrangements to go to a ball or on a picnic. Was this haphazardness the result of the war, and had young people behaved like this during the first war? He couldn't recall that they had, but of course there had been Frances and her young officer, the father of Pippa, and that had been haphazard enough. Perhaps he was the only person left alive who yearned for a smooth, settled existence, rooted in one particular spot, and pursuing one particular job?

Elaine floated in on an aroma of lavender bath salts. Her mass of dark hair was tied up in a turban and she wore only a closely-wrapped bath robe and yellow silk bedroom slippers. She kissed him, smelling sweet and fresh, and he marvelled again that he and Esther had been able to produce such a vital, strapping, shapely, uninhibited young woman.

"I hope you two have got the talkie-talkie over by now," she said, and Edgar, noticing a note of coyness in her voice, thought that it went ill with her breezy informality.

He decided that the best thing to do in the circumstances was to match her informality, and said:

"I can't imagine what there is to 'get over' as you say. You wouldn't be likely to take much notice of anything I had to say about getting married!"

He saw at once that he had said the wrong thing, for Elaine's expression hardened, though she still smiled brightly and said, quietly:

"Woolston and I didn't want to make it public without you first having met him, Daddy! Surely you realise that?"

He was out of his depth and must have shown it, for Elaine jumped up from the arm of the chair and gave Woolston a playful push.

"You go and freshen up, darling, while *I* have the little talk with Daddy! Woolston was so keen to meet you, Daddy that he came in straight off duty. Now run along, Sugar, and come back in about twenty minutes. After all, I haven't even seen Daddy myself for a year!"

Woolston let himself be jostled into the hall and Edgar heard them whispering out there. He did not know what to make of all this, and again wished himself safely out of it. Why should she have to do so much pretending in front of this weedy little man? Surely the fellow must realise that her father's permission counted for nothing? Elaine had gone her own way since she was sixteen, and it was too late to stage a dutiful-daughter act now that she was over thirty.

He heard the door close and she came back to him, her expression severe.

"You didn't handle that very well, Daddy. I shall have to put it down to your nervousness!"

"Well *are* you going to get married or aren't you?" demanded Edgar. "If so, what have I got to do with it? You never asked my permission when you married Esme."

"Ah, Esme was quite a different kettle of fish," said Elaine, mixing herself a drink, "this specimen is a Yank, and the Yanks go a bundle on slop, particularly family slop."

"Are you really going to marry him?"

"Well, of course I am, he's rolling in it!"

"Do you love him?"

Elaine regarded him with what might have passed for respectful wonder.

"Are you kidding? *Woolston?* I should say not! When it comes to loving give me a man, not half a pansy turned forty!"

"Well, I don't know," mumbled Edgar, embarrassed, "you really are a queer case and no mistake! Doesn't he know that you don't love him?"

"Not him," said Elaine, sipping her drink, "he's not come to, yet!"

"But it . . . it can't last, a marriage like that, Elaine?"

"Can't it? What about yours and mother's? That lasted long enough, and neither of you were the least bit in love, were you?"

She had scored there and he had to admit it. Who was he to prattle about love and duty, when he had shared the same house with Esther for nearly twenty years but had not shared a bed with her during three parts of that period? Who was he, in fact, to preach about marriage at all, when he had abandoned his family and gone off with Frances to find happiness before it was too late?

"I wouldn't like you to suffer what I suffered, Elaine," he told her, seriously, but she laughed.

"Don't you lose any sleep over that, Dad, I won't! Even if it doesn't work out, divorce is as easy as falling off a wall in the States, and there's always the alimony! It's a woman's country over there!"

He gave it up, as he had always given it up with Elaine. Her grasp of life, or the kind of life that she seemed determined to live, was much surer than his had ever been, but before he began to talk about generalities he was curious to learn why she had set out to become this kind of person in the first place.

"Tell me, Elaine, and without hard feelings either side . . .

is it me and what I did that encouraged you to look at life the way you do?"

"No," she said, "not you, Daddy. Mother perhaps, but certainly not you!"

He was relieved but remained curious.

"Then tell me, Elaine, for I've often wondered, really I have, and sometimes I haven't felt at all happy about it, tell me what makes you so terribly cynical about everything?"

She swung her legs on to the sofa and leaned back, lighting a cigarette and blowing out a long, thin stream of smoke.

"Do you ever think about the time we had together at Number Seventeen? Do you ever remember how dismal and flat it was, never mixing with anyone, never going anywhere, never even talking to one another if we could help it?"

"Yes," he said, quietly, "I remember all that very well, and I'm prepared to admit that you had a rotten time as a kid, about as rotten as any kid ever had."

"That's only part of it," she said, "the thing is, it took me years to realise that *everybody* didn't live like that, that all parents weren't gaolers put there to prevent children from having fun. I suppose I dreamed about escaping for years, not escaping *to* anything but simply escaping from the house, from mother, and from that cane that she used to keep behind the sloppy picture, 'The Tempting Bait', remember?"

He nodded, and she went on.

"I couldn't just run out. First I had to make some kind of plan, and it wasn't until I found the book in the attic that I discovered any sort of plan was ready to hand!"

"What book was that?" he asked, wondering.

She flung an arm over the back of the sofa, lifted a thin, paper-backed book from the end of the top shelf, and tossed it across to him.

He caught it and turned it over in his hands. It was entitled *The Art of Marriage,* and he suddenly remembered the circumstances in which he had bought it, the morning after the miserable failure of his wedding night with Esther. He did not remember having seen it since then, and that must be more than thirty years ago. Esther, he recalled, had done no more than glance at it and its advice had not had the slightest effect in assisting their mutual adjustment.

"When did you first read this?" he asked her.

"Oh, when I was about fifteen, I suppose. I found it in your trunk in the loft. It's pretty corny of course, and the man who wrote it obviously hasn't a clue, but for all that it taught me something I never forgot, and something that I'll always be grateful for."

"What was that?"

"Why, the thing that makes men tick," she said, "at least, from a woman's viewpoint, providing of course she's got common-sense, and the minimum sex-appeal. In the first place I think it taught me *why* people get married, why men voluntarily take on the endless responsibilities of marriage and even rush gaily into it, with their tongues hanging out, simply falling over themselves to shoulder the burden of wife, family, rates, taxes, gas-bills and God knows what else! It's all for that, all for having a woman whenever they want one, and I remember it absolutely astonished me at the time. In a way it still does, but it's just the way they're made, I guess, and most of them couldn't do anything about it even if they wanted to!"

He was silent for a minute, more astonished than shocked. Finally he said:

"I suppose there's a good deal in what you say, Elaine, but it's still only half the answer. I soon found that out with Frances, but I don't suppose I should have ever found the true meaning of marriage if it hadn't been for all those years I spent with your mother! There's a good deal more to marriage than what you say, and I'm surprised that you haven't found that out by this time. The comradeship of marriage is just as important as the physical side, not *more* important, as some people would argue, but *just* as important! It's about fifty-fifty, I'd say, and the odd thing is that one part seems to be quite useless without the other!"

"I daresay you're right," she said, suddenly bored with the conversation, "but how often do you have the luck to find both in a single person?"

"Not very often," he admitted, "not at all often! I suppose that's why Frances and I were so lucky, and so good for each other!"

He got up, stiffly. "Do you really want me to give this chap my official blessing?"

"That's the general idea," she said.

"Then I'll come back about seven-thirty," he told her, "I'm expecting an important 'phone call at eight, and I gave them your number. Meantime, I'd like to pop over and see that chap, Godbeer, and Pippa too, while I'm here. Has anyone heard anything more about Esme?"

"No," she said, "but you'll hear all about him if you go to Number Twenty. That poor Carver kid was all set to move in and marry him when he pranged!"

"Yes, I know," said Edgar, sorrowfully, "I met her in Wales, and I liked her a lot. Is she still in the W.A.A.F.?"

"I imagine so," said Elaine, "but she certainly has a hoodoo on her! That's the second White Knight she's lost in the war!"

Suddenly he found her toughness very irritating and quickly excused himself, letting himself out, and crossing the road to walk along the Avenue to knock at Number Twenty. Louise let him in and at once invited him to take tea and await Pippa's return at five-thirty.

He accepted gratefully, and was there when Jim Carver flung open the kitchen door, shouting and waving a letter in front of Louise. Jim could hardly speak for excitement:

"It's the boys ... they're all right! ... I had this by the afternoon post! Hullo, Mr. Frith! What are you doing here? Where's Jack? Where's Pippa? She'll want to know, she was the one who always said they were safe! It's wonderful isn't it, Frith, old man? Like someone coming back from the dead ... just a prisoner of war letter from young Bernard ... he's in hospital, and Boxer's safe too. Boxer wasn't even wounded! By George, I feel I could go out and get drunk! I can't wait to ring old Harold! Excuse me, Mr. Frith. I've just got to put through a call to Harold, from the call-box at the end of the road! Here's the letter! Read it yourself!"

And he was gone, throwing the letter on the table and as he unfolded it Edgar heard Louise give a long sniff, and then the kitchen door opened again to reveal Pippa, tall, pale Pippa, with her huge, tranquil eyes, so kind and still, yet as reassuring as her mother's.

He started up, holding out the letter, but she only smiled, and said:

"It's all right, Edgar, I met Mr. Carver in the alley. He nearly knocked me over and then he told me! I'm so glad for everyone but it isn't really a surprise to me, you know."

She kissed him and turned to help Louise at the stove. Watching them Edgar thought what a pleasant, friendly house Number Twenty had always been, and what a fool he had been not to come over and get friendly when he had lived across the road all those years. There followed for Edgar one of the liveliest evenings of his life, and one that he was to look back upon with pleasure for years to come.

Jim Carver was back soon after Pippa had arrived, and must have trumpeted his news all the way to and from the kiosk, for soon everyone in the Avenue who had known the twins began to drift along to Number Twenty, and share the Carvers' joy.

Edgar himself took little part in the jollifications. He was content to observe them from a seat beside the stove, but it seemed to him that all the exciting rough and tumble of family life, and all that he had once expected of community life in a suburb, could be found in the tide of gaiety and neighbourliness that foamed into the front and back doors of the Carvers' home that evening. It intrigued him, revealing as it did the spectacular rewards of raising a large family, and it pleased him that Pippa, who had had such a lonely upbringing, was there to share it.

Edith Clegg, and her sister, Becky, from Number Four, were the first two to arrive, and Edith wept when they showed her Bernard's letter and she read that his left arm had been amputated but that his injured leg had been saved. She expressed herself very relieved that the Germans were treating him well and that he had already received his first Red Cross parcel.

Jim said that in view of Bernard's wounds it was possible that he might be repatriated in due course, and at this prophecy Edgar saw Pippa's eyes sparkle. He tried to remember what kind of young man this Bernard was, but could only recall him as a tow-headed urchin, leaping along a chalked-out hopscotch pitch, opposite Number Seventeen, and shouting over his shoulder at his lumbering twin brother.

Philip and Jean Hargreaves looked in after tea, and both wrung Jim's hand. Edgar remembered then that Mrs. Hargreaves, once Miss McInroy, had lodged with Miss Clegg at Number Four, that she had a grave impediment in her speech, and that there had been something about her in the papers not long ago—what was it?—something about her saving the life of the man she afterwards married! Suddenly recalling the story he looked at her with renewed interest, noting that she was pretty, pregnant, and obviously, proud of it. The baby, he heard Hargreaves tell Louise, was expected in the New Year and he was quite certain that it was going to be a boy, so they had already fixed upon the name of 'Winston'.

Edgar smiled at this, and remembered how nearly all the male babies in his own youth had been named after the successful Boer War Generals. Mrs. Hargreaves said very little, speaking only to Edith in the corner of the crowded room, but he noticed that even when she conversed she hardly took her eyes from her big, handsome husband, and when he was speaking she listened carefully to each word he uttered. It was like a fairy-tale romance in reverse, he thought, the princess who rescued and married the prince!

Harold Godbeer, having been notified by 'phone, came hotfoot from Woodside Station, arriving about six o'clock, and when he had finished congratulating Jim, Louise, and Pippa, Edgar coaxed him into his corner, and whispered a word or two in his ear about the Sullen Cupid.

He was flattered by Harold's obvious interest and promised to come across to Number Twenty as soon as he received the expert's verdict from Chaffery. Edgar had always liked Harold, ever since that night that Harold had shown him so much kindness after he had made up his mind to leave Esther, and run away with Frances. He remembered how discreetly and cleverly Godbeer's firm had handled the distasteful business, and he now found an opportunity of telling Harold how grieved he had been to hear of Eunice's tragic death in the hit-and-run raid on Torquay.

Harold looked glum for a moment, but finally smiled and said that it was pleasant to discover that some war stories,

like this one, had happier endings, and then everyone in the
kitchen was silenced by the boisterous Mr. Baskerville, from
Number Eighty-Four and Mr. Baskerville took advantage of
the lull to declare that the treatment of British prisoners of
war was becoming progressively more humane now that the
majority of Germans had become reconciled to the certainty
of defeat!

Mr. Baskerville then treated them all to an optimistic
survey of the war as a whole. He must have received yet
another personal bulletin from Uncle Joe, for he made it
clear that the Germans were in very grave difficulties at
Stalingrad, and that soon the Russian reserve armies would
close their pincers round the dangerously isolated units of the
Southern Spearhead in the Caucasus. Meanwhile, he assured
them, the valiant garrison of Leningrad was already sallying
out to liquidate the half-frozen invaders in the North.

The Arctic convoys, he said, were now pouring into Arch-
angel at the rate of one per week, and the recent victory
of Montgomery, at El Alamein, meant that the Desert Army
could now sweep westward along the entire African sea-
board, and roll up the Afrika Korps like a sheet of wall-
paper!

One way and another it was a very stimulating evening,
and there was so much talk, and so many cups of tea and
cocoa passing around, that Edgar almost forgot the time and
only remembered it when Edith Clegg exclaimed: "Goodness! It's almost eight and I *still* haven't popped across to
Miss Baker and given her our wonderful news!"

Then Edgar withdrew, almost unnoticed, and crossed the
road to his daughter's house, arriving just as the 'phone began
to ring and practically throwing himself across the threshold
at the receiver.

"Hullo, hullo? Is that you, Mr. Chaffery?" he gasped, when
Elaine had left him, closing the door behind her.

"This is me, and we're on a good wicket, old man!"
Chaffery told him. "The expert is here still and he'd like a
word with you, so hold on and I'll fetch him!"

Edgar waited, wiping the perspiration from his forehead,
and trying to recover the breath he had lost in his mad
scramble from Number Twenty.

"Is that you, Frith? Well, I've had a good look, and I'm sure you've got something good! The point is, what do you want to do with it, put it up at Christie's, or take a good profit now? I'm willing to buy, of course, and I'd give you a fair price, allowing for Chaffery's commission, but frankly, if I was in your position, I'd rather have a gamble at Christie's, and that's advising you against my own interests!"

Edgar began to tremble so violently that he could hardly retain his grip upon the receiver. At last he said:

"Is it *really* a Lombardi? Haven't you any doubts at all about it?"

"None," said Dixon, shortly, "it's a Lombardi all right, and I'd stake my reputation on it!"

"Then . . . I . . . I'd like to pay you a valuation fee and . . . and sell it at Christie's," babbled Edgar. "You see, it's . . . it's like this, I've never had a real success before, nothing like this that is, and I think it would do my business so much good if it gets publicity, don't you agree?"

As he said this Edgar could sense the man's disappointment but he answered, "I told you it's against my own interests, Frith, but Chaffery here has more or less explained the set-up and I repeat, I'd honestly advise you to sell it, providing of course, that you hold out for a good reserve."

"Would you . . . would you advise me as regards the amount of the reserve, Mr. Dixon?"

"Naturally, I'll go into it tomorrow. You'd better pop over and see me before you go back to Wales. Good night then, and congratulations!"

"Good night . . . and thank you, thank you so much, Mr. Dixon."

He put down the 'phone and clasped his hands together. All the tea and cocoa he had swallowed at Number Twenty began to gurgle inside him, and a sudden spasm of wind doubled him up, so that he fumbled desperately for his tablets and hurried into the kitchen to pour a glass of hot water from the kettle.

"How was it?" Elaine called from her bedroom. "Are you going to clean up on that statue?"

"It's splendid, just splendid!" he told her, swallowing his crushed tablets, and getting almost instantaneous relief. "It won't make a fortune of course but I ought to see something very substantial, very substantial indeed!"

"Well, bully for you!" said Elaine, and floated into the hall in panties and brassiere. It was odd, thought Edgar, how Elaine always seemed to prefer to walk about half-naked, no matter who was in the house or what time of the day it was.

"Woolston and I are going off to a hop arranged by the U.S. Catering Corps," she told him. "You'll make yourself comfortable here, won't you? There's ham, tomatoes and pickles in the larder, and the spare bed has been made up in the back room. Don't wait up, we shan't be back until around about two!"

He was mildly disappointed. This was his big night and distance prevented him from spending it with Frances. It was, however, not the night to spend alone in a house, eating ham, pickles and tomatoes, before drifting off to bed in an unheated back room.

Suddenly he remembered his promise to Harold and the junketings that were still going on across the road.

"I think I'll 'phone Frances, and then pop over and spend an hour or so with Mr. Godbeer," he told her. "He was very interested in the Cupid, and by the way, they've all had very good news over there today!"

"About Esme?" She showed only the mildest flicker of interest.

"No, about the Carver twins. It seems that they're prisoners of war after all! The little one, Bernard isn't it, he's had his arm amputated by the German doctors."

"Well, I'm glad they're okay," said Elaine, offhandedly. "They were a caution, those two! Hey up," (as the bell rang) "that'll be my beau!" and she opened the door, dressed just as she was, but if Woolston felt any embarrassment he did not show it.

He gave her a spray of orchids and she accepted them as offhandedly as she did most things.

"Thanks, Sugar. Now fix yourself a drink and have your little talk with Daddy while I finish dressing."

Edgar accepted a drink, although he knew that he would suffer for it, and the two of them chatted for a spell in the front room. They did not touch upon the engagement, but discoursed generally about the war, and Edgar was relieved when Elaine swept in, looking, he thought, as beautiful and as exciting as an Anthony Hope heroine. Woolston, who had shown no special interest in Elaine in her lingerie, now jumped up so suddenly that he almost knocked Edgar's glass from his hand.

"Gee, honey! You look swell, real swell! Don't she look good enough to eat, Mr. Frith, don't she now?"

Edgar smiled. The news, the party at Number Twenty, and the American's stiff martini had mellowed him.

"I've always thought her very beautiful," he said, "but of course, I'm prejudiced!"

She kissed him lightly on his forehead and swept up her gloves and bag.

"Come on, Sugar, let's go places," she said, and they went out, leaving him to dial 'trunks' and, as Chaffery might have said, "put the missis in the picture."

*   *   *   *

The neighbours had stopped calling by the time he returned to the Carvers, so Harold suggested that he should share their supper at Number Twenty, for Louise had already had 'a rare day of it' and Jack, her husband, could never stay awake after ten o'clock.

Pippa was in bed and asleep, having already written and posted a letter to Bernard. Jim had slipped off to the local to buy beer, and when he returned all three of them climbed through the fence to Number Twenty and sat down to a hash of spam, powdered egg and fried bread in the kitchen, where Harold explained his newspaper maps of the various fronts that were pinned to the larder door, and staked out with a complex assortment of flag-day emblems.

"This is our G.H.Q., Mr. Frith," he told Edgar, adjusting a cluster of markers around Stalingrad. "We like to keep up with things and see how we stand from day to day, don't we, Jim?"

Edgar was staggered by their detailed knowledge of the fighting on all fronts. Up in Wales he and Frances had not regarded the war in this light, but merely as a kind of backcloth to their everyday lives, and the business of buying and selling stock, or combating the Ring. Now he half-wished that he was living in the Avenue again and in day-to-day touch with people like Harold and Jim, or the boisterous Mr. Baskerville. He would have given much to have dropped in of an evening and talked over the prospects of recapturing Tobruk, or beating the submarine menace. He understood now why Pippa preferred to live in London and merge herself into the war, rather than dream it away in the Welsh hills, or read about it in newspapers and periodicals. He felt, for the first time in his life, a close kinship with the Carvers, the Cleggs, and the Baskervilles, for it struck him that there was infinitely more neighbourliness in the Avenue now than had existed when he and Esther had lived over the road. He even remarked on this and was interested by Harold's frank reply.

"Yes, that's so, isn't it, Jim? If the war's done nothing else its certainly brought us all closer together! We were all inclined to be a bit too stuffy in the old days, don't you think?"

Jim removed his pipe from his mouth and smiled.

"Harold and I lived next door to one another for more than twenty years," he said, "and I don't think we said more than 'Good evening' to one another until the week of Dunkirk, did we, Harold?"

"To tell the truth, I always thought Carver a bit of a Bolshie," added Harold, grinning.

"And I used to quote him as that famous fire-proof character, a Tory working-man, too bloody green to burn!" chuckled Jim.

"Well, I'm still a Conservative in spite of it all," said Harold.

"And I'm still a Socialist, so you see that ours is strictly a wartime coalition, Frith," added Jim.

They sipped their beer and smoked their pipes in an air of rich contentment, until presently Harold said:

"You don't want to go back across the road and play gooseberry to that daughter of yours, when she comes home with her American! Why don't you stay here with us? You can have the porch room, and there's a very comfortable divan in there."

Edgar did not need much persuasion. He was enjoying himself so much that it seemed a pity to put a term to it. It would be great fun, he thought, to have Sunday breakfast in such pleasant company.

He made a formal protest about being a nuisance to people, but they pooh-poohed his objections and soon persuaded him to run across for his bag.

When he returned they had a final beer and·trooped up to bed, and after Harold had brought him a hot-water bottle, Edgar settled himself on the divan, locked his hands behind his head, and reflected what a delightful day it had been. His final thought, as he drifted off to sleep, was how well his digestion had stood up to the terrible buffeting it had received since he had set foot in the Avenue that afternoon. Tea, cocoa, cheese-spread, martini, spam, powdered egg, fried bread, and bottled beer, all in the space of a few hours! Such reckless gluttony would have all but killed him a few days ago, but tonight he knew that he would sleep like a child and he did too, for almost eight hours, until he heard a door bang downstairs and then Jim's rumbling voice and Harold's high-pitched monosyllables answering it.

Presently there was a rattle of tea-cups and the sound of feet on the stairs and Harold came in, beaming, and behind him, Jim, with a Sunday newspaper in his hand.

Both men were in high spirits and he soon discovered why, for Jim threw the *Sunday Express* on the bed and exclaimed:

"Read it! We're ashore in North Africa! Damn it, it's marvelous! Don't you see that Rommel's caught between two fires, and the whole of the French Colonial Empire will come in with us? Look here, Harold, I'm going to have another go at that blasted radio downstairs, and if I can't get anything by the time we've had breakfast I'll step down to Baskerville! He's sure to have the latest, with that damned great set of his!"

Harold smiled, indulgently, like a parent pretending interest in a twelve-year-old's latest enthusiasm, thought Edgar.

"That's Jim, Mr. Frith," he said, as he poured Edgar's tea, "it's just like living with a great schoolboy! But he's not a boy when it comes to action, old man, he's an absolute lion! I don't know what I'd have done without him during the blitz!"

Edgar read the newspaper as he sipped his tea. He felt no ill effects from his outrageous diet of the previous day, only a lazy content to be here among men of his own age, and his own social status, men who seemed eager to give him something that he had never enjoyed before, friendship on equal terms.

The morning sun rose high over the line of Manor Wood and a broad beam stole through the chink in the curtains. An odd fancy struck him that if he and Esther had bought a house on this side of the Avenue, where the morning sun poured in the front instead of the back, then their whole lives might have been as mellow as Jim's and Harold's. Then the thought seemed disloyal to Frances, alone with the baby in Wales, and he dismissed it, jumping out of bed and peeping across at the mound that had been his home.

Harold called from the hall: "Breakfast in ten minutes, Mr. Frith!"

"Thank you," he called, "thank you . . . I'll have a quick wash and shave if I may!"

He pulled the curtains aside and the winter sunshine flooded the little room. The smell of frying drifted up from the kitchen and as he scraped away at his chin he tried to whistle.

It was many years since Edgar Frith had whistled in the act of shaving.

CHAPTER XXVI

New Year Roundabout

TWENTY minutes to midnight, on the last day of December, 1942, and the Avenue nearly half-way through its fourth year of war.

The great hump of rubble, that had been Numbers Thirteen, Fifteen and Seventeen, now possessed a familiar outline, and had become as much a feature of the crescent as the corner shop, or the leaning laburnum in the front-garden of Number Ninety-Seven. Even the presence of G.I.s in the Avenue had lost its novelty and the Avenue rump, at the small-number end, had come to regard them as permanent residents, just like Mr. Baskerville, or Mr. Westerman. Some of the younger residents had even begun to absorb their idioms of speech.

Margy Hartnell, sometime co-director of the Hartnell Eight, saw in the New Year from her former home, at number Forty-Five.

She had left behind a roomful of belongings when she let the house to the Hargreaves, shortly before Philip and Jean were married, and had since written from the North, where she was touring with E.N.S.A., to ask if she could collect them when she returned to London.

She came to the Avenue as dusk fell, on the last day of the old year and Jean, hearing that she had made no arrangements to book a room, insisted that she remained for the night, and packed up her things in the morning.

Margy was much changed these days. Before the war she had been a high-spirited and energetic little woman, driving her husband and his dance orchestra as if they had been an eight-horse team in a rodeo event, herding them from engagement to engagement, popping up beside the drums to sing a number, then descending among the dancers to fish for future dates among committee-men and social secretaries.

She still appeared on public platforms, indeed, she was in great demand as an artist with E.N.S.A. bands touring the camps. Not only was her organising ability much appreciated by E.N.S.A., but her contralto voice had improved and she sang numbers like 'White Cliffs of Dover' and 'Lovely Weekend' in a way that was obviously acceptable to audiences of men uprooted from home and family. This was strange when one thought about it, for Margy Hartnell had never possessed good looks, or the kind of figure that earned the wolf-whistle.

She was small-boned and slightly sallow. Her dark hair was greying a little at the sides, and she never used any of the tricks in the armoury of the popular pin-up vocalists, the slight catch in the voice, or the sudden tearful biting of the lower lip used to regulate the 'drip' of a lyric. She sang her numbers simply, and unpretentiously, and her male audiences accepted the songs for what they were worth. Margy's singing put no strain on their emotions.

She had to make the effort to come home and sort out her things in Number Forty-Five because she was on the point of going abroad on an extended tour.

When she first joined E.N.S.A. she had steadfastly refused to accept engagements that were likely to involve her in an overseas tour, for Ted, her sea-going husband, arrived and departed at irregular and unpredictable intervals.

Sometimes she had no word from him for months at a stretch and then, without warning, she would receive a wire or 'phone call, telling her to jump on a train and make her way to Liverpool, or Barry, or Harwich, and spend a few days with him before he sailed away again.

She lived for these abrupt summonses. Often they were the only proof she had that Ted was still living and not washing about at the bottom of the Atlantic or the Mediterranean, but once the first ecstasy of their reunion had spent itself they almost invariably began to bicker, until Ted grew sullen, and Margy was in tears. Then they would make it up again, and tell each other that it was madness to waste their few precious hours in a quarrel, and they would take a drink or two, and play old records on a portable gramophone, and dance solemnly around a hotel bedroom to the old-fashioned beat of tunes like '*Always*', and '*Missouri City Waltz*', before going to bed and lying awake hour after hour in one another's arms.

They always quarrelled over the same thing, Ted's obstinate refusal to leave the Merchant Navy and organise another dance band ashore.

Ted had changed too. He had never been the same man since a German violinist had told him about what went on in Dachau and Sachsenhausen. After his own terrible experiences adrift in the South Atlantic, Margy thought he would have had enough of adventure and been glad to come ashore, as he might have done with honour, having won himself a medal and passed beyond the age limit of compulsory service. But the medal only seemed to stimulate his martial ardour and after three weeks at home he found himself another berth and sailed off to Quebec.

On the way back his convoy was attacked by aircraft in the Bay of Biscay, and Ted actually operated a gun but he did not tell her about this until much later, after he had taken a short gunnery course, sailed on a Malta convoy, and been shipwrecked for the second time.

He told her very little about his travels and adventures, knowing how bitterly she opposed his participation in the war. He could never persuade her to share his disgust with Hitler and Hitler's methods of waging war. She continued to regard the war as a dreadful bore, a mere nuisance that had been the means of breaking up the orchestra, and sending more than half its members to the Isle of Man. By this time, however, he had learned to accept her attitude, and to write it off as a woman's inability to concern herself with anything outside her purely personal sphere, but it did make things very difficult when it came to saying good-bye again, and it often saddened him to think, as he could not help thinking, that their unique comradeship as business partners and man and wife had been ruined, and could never recover its pre-war harmony.

He was away now, on an Arctic convoy to Murmansk, and she was forced to put him out of mind for days at a time, for the awful risks that he must be running up there in the northern mists simply did not bear thinking about! She therefore absorbed herself in her tours, trailing about from camp to camp in the company of middle-aged musicians, ageing comedians, and bottom-pinching baritones, until the succession of Sunday trains and dismal one-night billets, began to depress her so much that she almost wished she was dead and done with it, and that Ted was dead too, for she told herself that she was not generous enough to think of him married to anyone else after the war.

It was in this wretched frame of mind that she volunteered to join a company about to embark on a North African tour, even though this meant that when Ted came home again she would not be there to join him, wherever he might land. She wondered whether this would annoy him, or whether it would provide fresh fuel for his raging fires of patriotism and give him the chance to boast to his messmates that he now had a wife engaged in overseas combat with Hitler.

Jean Hargreaves felt very sorry for her, particularly as she herself was so settled and happy, in spite of the war and all the upset it had involved. Her baby (already known in advance as 'Winston Hargreaves' along this end of the Avenue) was a few days overdue, and still kicking inside her, instead of in the glossy new pram that awaited it under the stairs, but he could not be long in arriving now, and although she found difficulty in going up and down stairs she felt far better in health than she had ever felt, and Philip, sweet thing, was so wonderfully gentle with her, just like the husbands she had sketched for the magazine illustrations during her ten-year search for the Ideal British Male.

Sometimes, when she answered his quiet smile from the other side of the fireplace, she found it difficult to believe that her quest had ended so spectacularly and that she had actually found the pot of gold under the rainbow.

During the first few weeks of their marriage she had retained a nervous fingertip on the handbrake of happiness, half-certain that, sooner or later, this delicious coast along the levels of content would end at the switchback of disillusion. She would soon, she thought, be brought face to face with some dreadful defect in Philip's character. He would suddenly reveal himself as a secret drinker, or a drug addict, or, if not that, at least display some unpleasant and hitherto unexpected characteristic that destroyed his flawlessness as a mate, a mulish obstinacy perhaps, or clumsiness as a lover, or perhaps just an irritating habit, like the scattering of cigarette ash on her polished floors.

Nothing like this happened, however, and now, to crown her happiness, she was going to have Philip's Winston, and there would probably be a young Philip, or a young Jeannie to follow, so that whole vistas of delight stretched endlessly ahead of them, particularly now that Philip had been invalided from the A.F.S., and held a responsible post with the London Bridge Insurance Company, with a salary and commission of eight hundred a year!

She stayed up with Margy to hear the New Year in on the radio and Philip made tea and brought it in to them on a little tray, spread with a doily!

As the stokes of Big Ben boomed out and 1943 began, he came and sat on the arm of her chair and gently stroked her hair, whilst poor Mrs. Harthell whose own husband was so far away and in so much danger studiously avoided looking at them but sipped her tea in silence as the strains of '*Auld Lang Syne*' issued from the portable.

At a quarter-past twelve when Philip was helping her up the stairs, Jean experienced her first pain and in an instant the serenity of Number Forty-Five was shattered. Margy was called in to assist in getting Jean ready for transfer to the Nursing Home by ambulance and Philip, his firm male poise reduced to a vague dithering that sent him running all over the house with his hands full of "Things-Jean-might-need-at-the-home", was eventually despatched next door to telephone for the doctor, while Margy took firm charge of operations. She was glad to have something practical to think about.

Even the birth of little Winston, however, did not do so very much to disturb the drift of Jean Hargreaves' flower-decked gondola, for the baby was born in less than three hours and by 3 a.m. a pale and distraught Philip was told by a testy doctor that his wife was now sound asleep, that the baby boy weighed seven pounds, that the midwife was extremely capable, and that he would oblige everyone by piping down and going to bed himself!

Philip took the doctor's advice and soon afterwards Margy yawned her way to bed, trying not to remember the occasion when her own child had been still-born in this house, or that the prospect of her and Ted having children in the future was now a remote improbability.

Not that she regretted this very much, nowadays, when all that children seemed to do was to whimper, grow up and suddenly sail away on Arctic convoys, to be bombed, shelled and torpedoed to death!

• • •

Harold Godbeer, of Number Twenty-Two, had a very different kind of adventure that New Year's Eve and it overtook him a mile or so from the Avenue, in the sitting-room of his secretary's home at Elmer's End, an adjoining suburb.

The adventure took him completely by surprise for he never thought of himself as a widower and certainly not as an eligible widower, a man whom a young person could contemplate marrying.

Poor Harold must have been very short-sighted in more ways than one, for the attentions of Miss Redvers, who had been first a typist, and, as he rose in the firm, his personal secretary, seemed to have escaped him altogether. If he had noticed them at all he must have put them down to commercial zeal on Miss Redvers' part; the discovery that she regarded him in any other light than that of an office superior must have been concealed from him by the rampart of his modesty.

It all began innocently enough. About four o'clock in the afternoon, when the city murk was closing in on the office, Blane, the articled junior, tripped into Harold's office with a bottle tucked under either arm.

"Mr. Stillman's compliments and here's a couple of the old and best from the Admiral's cellar," he chirruped, depositing the grimy bottles on Harold's spotless blotter.

Harold inspected the bottles with interest. They had come,

as he knew, from the famous cellar of the late Admiral Hilton, whose estate they were dealing with at the moment. Harold had had a good deal to do with the old gentleman and the port, he presumed, was a kind of legacy, presented via Mr. Stillman in acknowledgement of his services during the Admiral's illness.

"I say, but that's very handsome of Mr. Stillman!" he exclaimed, and then, remembering that it was Old Year's Night and that his girls and Blane, had served him dutifully throughout the year; "What about cracking one now, and drinking to victory in 1943."

Young Blane thought this was an excellent idea and rummaged about for sherry glasses. He found four, and a corkscrew, while Harold carefully removed the cork and sniffed the bottle appreciatively.

"I don't suppose we shall ever have a chance of drinking anything better than this," he told Miss Redvers, and Miss Caughlin, the typist, when they had been summoned from the outer office. "I believe the Admiral was regarded as the best judge of port in London! Well, Blane, you do the honours," and he motioned to the girls to lift their glasses.

"Er . . . here's to next New Year's Day on the top of the Brandenburg Gate," proposed Blane, and emptied his glass at a draught.

"I say, you should *sip* port, young fellow," advised Harold, "this is superb . . . quite superb, don't *you* think so, Miss Redvers?"

"I'm afraid I'm not very used to good port," admitted Miss Redvers, flushing slightly, "a mild sherry, or gin and orange, is about all we ever run to at home. Still, it does give you a kind of . . . of glow right through, doesn't it?"

"That's putting it mildly" giggled Miss Caughlin. "Two of these and I should float all the way to the tube!"

The wine did seem to introduce a 'glow right through' as she put it and Harold's eyes twinkled mischievously behind his spectacles. "Let's have one more," he suggested and immediately refilled their glasses.

Blane left the office smacking his lips and Miss Caughlin giggled again, said she had "simply thousands of letters to finish", and soon followed him.

Harold had intended dictating a letter before five, but he discovered that he did not feel at all disposed to scrutinise the documents on his desk, in pursuance of Messrs. Heslop and Garratt's search queries regarding the Fisher conveyance.

The flavour of Admiral Hilton's old port had lifted him above such things and he preferred, instead, to lean back on his swivel chair and contemplate Miss Redvers as she rattled away on her big typewriter beside the window.

How long had he known her? Ten years? Twenty? Where did she live and what were her ambitions, if she had any? How was it that she was still unmarried? She wasn't a bad-looking girl, a little heavy perhaps, and with a bit of a stoop, but not really bad-looking, with her sleek brown hair and big brown eyes. They could be very kind eyes too, he reflected, remembering how gentle she had been with him on that awful day they had phoned through from Torquay about Eunice. Eunice's eyes had been china blue and she had been much more finely made than Miss Redvers. Odd that he should be sitting here comparing them, as dusk closed in over St. Paul's Churchyard. What was her Christian name? Was it something modern, like Diana, or Shirley, or was it an old-fashioned name, like Jane, or Mary? Surely he ought to know what her name was? He had had her insurance card in the file for years and only had to glance at it!

Before he quite realised what he was saying he had asked her.

"By the way, what *is* your Christian name, Miss Redvers?"

She stopped typing instantly and he saw her brace her plump shoulders. Good heavens, he thought, now I've offended the girl. It must be the port. Who could imagine that two glasses of port would make a man my age start playing the fool with the female staff?

She wasn't offended, however, simply surprised, and mildly amused. She swung round on her typist's stool and smiled across at him and the smile reassured him. He was quite right, he decided, she wasn't at all plain, with her short, straight nose, firmly rounded chin and kind brown eyes. Only her mouth was wrong, it was too small somehow and too puckered, like a sulky baby's, and anyway it looked all wrong on her, as if it had been added after the other features and really belonged to someone younger and slimmer than Miss Redvers!

"Do you really mean to say that you don't *know*, Mr. Godbeer," she said, still smiling, and looking, he thought, very pleased with herself all of a sudden.

"I admit that I should, but I'm afraid I don't," he told her defiantly, and made a mental note that he would think twice before distributing old port to the office staff in future.

"It's 'Kathleen'," she said, "but everyone calls me 'Kay' and I like 'Kay' much better."

"Really," said Harold, politely, "that's quite a nice name— Kay—yes, that's really quite nice," and he tried to end the conversation by bending anew over the Fisher conveyance.

She would not, however, take the cue from him, but continued to sit facing his way, her hands loose on her lap.

Presently, she said:

"Are you doing anything special tonight, Mr. Godbeer?"

He answered without thinking completely forgetting that it was Old Year's Night, and wondering vaguely what made her ask such a question.

"No . . . no, I don't think so! Should I be?"

"It's Old Year's Night . . . most people do something or go somewhere, don't they?"

"Yes, I suppose they do," he answered, "but my friend, Mr. Carver, the man I told you about, is on a long-distance job and he won't be back until after midnight. It's a pity really, as we should have seen the New Year in together and listened to the radio, but he's working part-time now for the transport firm that employed him a long time ago and as I said, he won't be back from Leicester until very late."

He could not imagine why he should be telling her all this rigmarole but it was safer than discussing her name and she seemed interested. He noticed that the port, or his sudden interest in her name had animated her and that her eyes sparkled and her cheeks were pinker than usual.

"Would you like to . . . to come to a little party?"

She spoke diffidently and with what seemed to him a considerable effort.

"A party? Where?"

"At my home . . . just the family you know, we'd love to

have you and it seems so silly to see the new year in all by yourself. Do come, Mr. Godbeer!"

"Where do you live?"

She laughed at that and hoisted herself off the stool to cross over to sit in the chair that she used when he was dictating.

"Oh dear! You aren't very flattering, are you?"

"Isn't it Streatham?" he said, feeling vaguely apologetic.

"No, and it hasn't been Streatham since the blitz," she laughed. "It's Elmers End, right on your doorstep. You could easily get a bus home afterwards, they run until twelve-thirty."

His reserve was fighting a losing battle with the port. He said to himself: "And why not? Why ever not? She's a nice girl, a sensible girl, and it would be interesting to see how she lived and what her parents were like. What should I do with myself if I went home? Cook some supper, read the evening paper and sit over the fire until the small hours waiting for Jim."

"Are you quite sure that your people would like me to come?" he asked.

"Why of course I am! Daddy would be thrilled. He's heard about you for years, and Mother too."

"Well, I must say it's very kind of you," said Harold, "and I . . . I'd like to come, if you're absolutely sure they won't mind."

He got up, feeling elated and she jumped up too, looking prettier than he had ever thought her capable of looking.

"You oughtn't to waste time taking me to a party," he said jocularly, "you should concentrate on the younger bloods!"

Instantly he was sorry he had made the remark, for her eager look faded and was replaced by an almost sullen expression.

"I'm not the slightest bit interested in 'young bloods'!" she said. "They're all show-offs!" Suddenly she became very business-like. "Shall we do that letter to Heslop and Garratt before we close down?"

"No," he told her, "that port doesn't seem to go along with Heslop and Garratt! We'll leave it until tomorrow."

He got his hat and coat and she covered the typewriter, afterwards disappearing into the cloakroom where she remained a long time. When she emerged he noticed that she had reddened her lips, powdered her nose, and done something to her hair. They went out into the drizzle and along to the station but without saying anything more to one another before reaching the 'bus stop.

The London Bridge train was packed and they were unable to exchange another word until they had struggled out on to the platform at Elmers End, to find that it was now raining heavily. He put up his umbrella and held it over her.

"You lead the way," he said and was a little alarmed at the readiness she showed in taking his arm.

She lived, he discovered, in one of the larger bungalows on a new estate that reached out towards the northern fringe of the golf links, bordering Shirley Rise. The bungalow was squat and red-tiled, with a rough-cast finish and a well-kept garden. Inside, the furniture was new and the colours bright, a little too bright for his taste. The family seemed disposed towards dramatic mural decorations and he noticed particularly a flight of plaster geese, moulded in diminishing sizes, and disappearing across the hall towards the dining-room.

Her father, he found, was employed at the gasworks, in Lewisham. He was an elderly, brisk little man, obviously delighted to see him. He at once whisked away Harold's coat and umbrella and conducted him into the lounge, where several other people were finishing their tea.

"It's my boss, Mr. Godbeer," announced Miss Redvers, generally, "but don't let's bother with formal introductions because he isn't very good at remembering names, are you Mr. Godbeer?"

He said no, he was afraid he wasn't, and it struck him that she seemed to possess two quite distinct personalities, one for the office and another for home. The office personality, the one he had always thought of as being exclusively Miss Redvers, was a stranger to this after-office hours girl, who was relaxed and altogether less mousey. The Miss Redvers who sat typing at the window overlooking St. Paul's Churchyard, would never have said a thing like that, not even after an entire bottle of the Admiral's port!

He shook hands with her mother, brother, and sister, and her sister's young man, who was wearing the uniform of the gunners, and a bombardier's chevrons. They seemed to be a jolly, normal family, much devoted to one another and extremely welcoming towards him. After tea (a very extravagant tea for wartime, he thought!) they all helped mother to clear away and wash up. Then Kay took out some Bach records and put them on the radiogram, telling him to make himself comfortable and talk to Daddy whilst she popped up and changed.

He sat there for more than half an hour, listening to Bach and attempting also to listen to Mr. Redvers. The little man talked conventionally about the war and shortages and the garden that he was making out at the back.

"It's clay," he said, "heavy clay, and I find it terribly tough going. It's always the same, of course, when you move into new property. I've dug out at least five tons of half-bricks and old iron, in the two years I've been here. You've no idea what they dumped there—bicycle frames, bedsteads, even enamel chamber-pots!"

Harold said he could well imagine, contenting himself with monosyllabic replies. He felt relaxed and comfortable. The glow of the port had not died away when Mrs. Redvers came in with sherry. Then Kay reappeared, and Harold only just prevented himself from exclaiming aloud, for he had expected her to appear in something quiet and comfortable, but she now looked as if she was dressed for a ball. She wore a bright, yellow frock, with a spray of artificial flowers fastened to the shoulder, and her hair had been groomed until it looked as soft and sleek as a film star's. As he stared at her the brown eyes smiled into his in a way that they had never smiled in the past.

After supper (they did seem to consume huge quantities of food, thought Harold) they pulled back the furniture and the bombardier and Kay's sister, Peggy, began to dance. Kay tried to persuade Harold to dance with her but he was firm in his protests and said that he had never learned to dance, not even in his youth, and would much prefer not to start now, notwithstanding the Admiral's port and her father's sherry.

She did not seem to mind one way or the other but perched herself happily on the arm of his chair, tapping away

with her right foot, and when Peggy and the Bombardier
were tired of dancing they tuned in to the Home Service and
heard the news, and the first part of the New Year programmes. At ten o'clock the Bombardier said that he would have
to catch his 'bus and Peggy went off with him, telling them
that she wouldn't be long. Mr. Redvers then said that he
didn't think he would wait up for midnight as he had welcomed too many new years already, but when Harold protested that he too should be going, both Mr. and Mrs.
Redvers exclaimed that he must do no such thing but must sit
right here until 1943, and then catch the twelve-twenty 'bus
that passed the door and dropped him within two hundred
yards of his home.

Harold would have much preferred to leave but they were
all so insistent that it seemed rude to make an issue of it, so
Kay fetched him another plate of trifle and while he was
eating it, her brother, Sam and Mr. and Mrs. Redvers melted
away and he was alone with Kay.

The sudden cessation of the family's chatter made him feel
rather nervous and when Kay switched the radio off and put
on a Strauss record, he said:

"Has your mother gone to bed too, Miss Redvers?"

She pretended not to hear the question and busied herself
with the radiogram, remaining beside it until the record was
well started and the familiar melody of *'Tales from Vienna
Woods'* filled the room.

Then she looked up and smiled.

"Are you always going to stick to 'Miss Redvers'?" she
asked. Apparently noticing the expression of alarm that followed this question she added: "I wouldn't expect you to call
me 'Kay' at the office, of course, but it does sound terribly
stuffy here, don't you think?"

"I think your family are very charming ... Kay," he
conceded, "it was most kind indeed of you all to bother with
me tonight."

"Have you really enjoyed yourself?" she asked gravely.
"You needn't mind telling me ... I did rather rush you into
it!"

"Nonsense," he said, relieved by her admission, which
seemed to him to herald the return of the familiar Miss

Redvers, "I've enjoyed myself immensely and I'm very glad
indeed that you thought of asking me." He paused a moment
before adding, banteringly; "I half expected to meet your
young man, Kay."

"I haven't got a young man," said Miss Redvers, remaining
coiled beside the radiogram and looking away from him.

"Oh, come now," he chaffed, "you aren't going to tell me
that you dressed up like that for me?"

"As a matter of fact, I did," she said, and this time looked
at him with disconcerting directness, so that it was his turn to
look away.

"Does that surprise you so much, Mr. Godbeer?"

"Yes," he said, wriggling, "it certainly does!" With an
effort he rallied a little, "Bless you, Miss Red . . . *Kay*, what's
the point in impressing *me*? I'm old enough to be your
father."

"Do you know how old *I* am?" she asked, in the same
steady voice. "After all, you didn't know my Christian name,
did you?"

He had no answer to this, so after a slight pause, she
added: "Well? *Do* you?"

"No," he said, frostily, "I'm afraid I don't! Your age is on
your insurance card no doubt, but I don't remember looking
at it."

At the mention of the insurance card she laughed outright
and he decided that he did not like the key of her laughter. It
was hollow, almost harsh, and he began to feel more nervous
than ever.

Even yet, however, he did not feel personally involved.
Away at the back of his mind he began to form the opinion
that she was in some kind of trouble, and was anxious to
discuss it with him, but was finding the subject very difficult
to broach.

He decided to make a start. "What's the matter, Miss
Redvers? Are you unhappy about something? Can I help? I
would, of course, surely you know that?"

The effect of his question was startling. She jumped up and
crossed to the window, moving very swiftly. He caught the
gleam of tears in her eyes. It embarrassed him to think that
her sister, Peggy might return at any moment, and find them

alone together and her in tears, but it seemed callous to ignore her distress altogether.

"Well, Kay," he said, kindly, "you can confide in me if you like, I'm a good deal older than you and I might. . . ."

Suddenly she whipped round on him and he was horrified to see that her face was now twisted with misery. She no longer looked the least bit attractive and her pursy little mouth was screwed into a tight, red knot.

"What *is* it, Kay?"

"It's *you!*" she snapped, "it's your continual harping on age! You talk as if there was thirty years between us! You don't know how old I am but I know how old you are! I've always known, you're fifty-seven next March and that makes you just nineteen when I was born! Well, I suppose you *could* have been my father, but it wouldn't be very likely, would it?"

He sat quite still, his hands grasping his knees, his mouth slightly open. "Good gracious!" he thought, "now I am in a fix! It's me that she's after! *Me!*"

He was the more surprised because he had never thought of himself as even eligible. Eunice was dead, of course, but that only made him technically available to someone like Miss Redvers, for he had never once contemplated remarriage, not to her, or to anyone else!

Even in the pain and bewilderment of the moment it crossed his mind that this was a strange attitude on his part, that a second marriage should have occupied his thoughts at least occasionally, but the truth was it had not, and he supposed that she could hardly be blamed for imagining that it must have done.

He thought back, quickly but systematically, over his relationship with this girl in all the years that had led up to this extraordinary situation. Had he ever, by word, deed or glance, encouraged her to think one day he might marry her? He had been kind and considerate, he hoped, ever since she had been sent into him as a copy-typist, long before the war, but beyond that he could recall paying her no special attentions, certainly not to the degree of encouraging her to believe that he would ever propose marriage to her!

Reassured on this point his bewilderment suddenly gave way to indignation.

"I say, look here . . . Miss Redvers," he spluttered, 'just what's in your mind? Just what are you trying to imply?"

She began to weep in earnest then, the tears streaming down her plump cheeks and her shoulders quivering with an emotion that she made no attempt to restrain, while he, on his part, began to panic, thinking of her parents just across the passage, and of her sister, Peggy, whose key might grate in the lock at any moment.

He jumped up and took her by the hand, leading her over to the arm-chair beside the fire.

"Now . . . now take a hold of yourself, Miss Redvers . . . please . . . I beg of you . . . you've really no right to . . . to carry on like this . . . it makes me feel dreadful! Here, use this!" and he whipped his handkerchief from his breast pocket and pushed it into her hands, afterwards retreating to the far side of the fireplace.

To his immense relief she made the effort, dabbing her eyes and indulging in a series of prolonged gulps.

"There now," he encouraged, "there's no need to get hysterical, is there? If you . . . you want to say anything, then perhaps you'd better say it, before your sister comes back."

"She . . . won't come in here when she comes back," said Kay, "they've all gone out of their way to leave us alone!"

He glanced about him like a trapped animal, too frightened to feel anger at the perfidy of womankind. He realised now that he must get out of the house somehow, and with dignity, but at the moment he could think of no way of achieving this, for his legal mind was still obsessed with the frightful possibilities of doing the wrong thing in the wrong way.

He sat quite still and fought for calmness; presently he was able to address her in a fairly reasoned tone.

"Do you mean to say that . . . that your inviting me here was part of a . . . a *plan*, Miss Redvers?"

Her tears ceased to flow and now it was she who looked frightened.

"Oh, *no* . . . ! Not like that, Mr. Godbeer! Really it wasn't, it's all *much* more complicated! You see, it all goes back to before . . . well, before you lost your wife!"

"Indeed," said Harold, with an edge to his voice that made her heart leap. "And just how, may I ask? Just how, and why?"

"I'm afraid I . . . I've always given them the wrong impression," said Miss Redvers, so wretchedly that he at once began to feel renewed compassion for her. "I . . . well, I suppose I pretended you . . . you liked me when I first became your secretary and then, when your wife was killed, I suppose they got the impression that we might. . . ."

His eyes began to glitter again as her voice tailed away. "Well?"

"Oh, Mr. Godbeer, you must think I'm a terrible person but it didn't seem bad at the time, really it didn't! It seemed a kind of . . . well, a kind of *game* I was playing with them, with myself even!"

She had not expressed herself very clearly but because he was a gentle, sensitive person, her rambling explanation was almost adequate. The anger and indignation went out of him and he felt only pity, mingled with embarrassment. Beyond these feelings, hidden shamefully away at the bottom of his large heart, was something else, a tiny spark of pride that refused to be extinguished by the douches of guilt he applied to it. After all, she was only thirty-seven, and earlier in the evening, when she had swept into the room in that pretty yellow dress and high-heeled shoes, she had looked quite desirable, the kind of woman indeed that men a good deal younger and more flighty than he would have liked to have kissed. Yet, for all that and for years on end if she was to be believed, she had had eyes only for him, a fifty-six-year-old managing clerk, earning eight-pounds-ten a week, less National Insurance! It was incredible but, no matter how one looked at it, it was also very flattering!

He switched his mind back to her and wished that he could think of some way to help her over the next few days. He could imagine what those days would mean for her, with the family waiting, hopefully, at first, then with deepening disappointment, for the announcement that she was to marry Mr. Godbeer at last. She could never return to the office after this, of course, it would be too embarrassing for both of them, and the memory of this evening would cloud their minds all the time he was dictating and whenever their heads came together over a lease, or a brief. This, he told himself, was a great pity, for she was very good at her work and he would miss her; nevertheless she would have to go and he felt sure that she herself would be the first to admit as much.

"I'm sorry if you've been hurt, Kay," he said at length and for the first time his use of her Christian name came naturally to him. "Is there anything at all I can do? Anything that might ... er ... smooth things over, I mean? I've always thought of you as a nice girl and I always will, so don't let that part of it worry you. It's just that. ..."

She handed him his handkerchief and made a brave attempt to smile.

"You don't have to make excuses, Mr. Godbeer," she said quietly. "I'm the one who has to do that."

She got up and switched on the radio. There was a click and a faint hum. "We've missed the New Year, I'm afraid, but you've still time for your 'bus, if you hurry."

She went out and returned with his hat, coat and umbrella.

"Won't you walk to the stop with me?"

"No, not if you don't mind," she said, "I must look like hell."

"Will you ... would you like to take a few days off and then ring me at the office?"

She reflected. "Yes, I'll do that if I may, I'll go off on a bit of a holiday and ring you on Monday."

She held out her hand and he squeezed it. "I can only say that I ... I'm as sorry as it's possible to be."

"Don't mope about it, Kay ... but you didn't let me finish what I was going to say."

"I said you didn't have to say anything, Mr. Godbeer!"

"But I'd like to because it ... well because it may help to explain things. I was very much in love with my wife, and I suppose I still am, and always will be! People like me never do get married again, not after a certain age anyway, but you ... well, it's ridiculous to think that thirty-seven is old and you've got to stop thinking it is, really you have! That's all I wanted to say. Good night, Kay."

"Good night, Mr. Godbeer."

She opened the front door and he went out. The rain had stopped and the pavements gleamed in the swift glow of the hall light and then went black again as she shut the door. He stood blinking for a moment, trying to accustom his eyes to the darkness. Then, feeling for his pocket torch and switching it on he made his way carefully along to the 'bus stop.

The air was not cold but fresh and sweet after so many hours in an overheated room. He felt glad to be in the open again and glad that this astonishing incident was now behind him. There would be loose ends, of course, but they could be tied now that she had come to her senses, poor girl.

He looked anxiously down the road and was relieved to see the masked headlights of the 'bus approaching.

"I'd better tell someone," he said to himself, "I'd better confide in someone, just to be on the safe side, and that someone will have to be old Jim. Thank God, there's Jim! Thank God, we're such good friends!"

* * * *

New Year celebrations inside the county gaol, where Archie Carver was serving his sentence, were limited to a film show and an extra half-hour's free association on Old Year's Night.

The film was a Laurel and Hardy, and Archie enjoyed it much more than he had imagined he would, for he had never liked this comedy team in the days when he could visit any cinema that he cared to visit.

That was one of the remarkable things about losing one's freedom and living a strictly regimented life, where every moment of one's time was accounted for in advance, and one knew, with certainty, that the unexpected could not happen. Under these conditions one's sense of values changed, changed so much, and so quickly, that one's entire outlook became warped. Trivialities developed into enormously important issues and what had once been an important issue became less than a triviality, and was brought to mind only after concentrated effort.

Income-tax, for instance.

There had been a time, not so long ago if one reckoned by the calendar, when income-tax was a very important matter indeed, often occupying a man's thoughts from morning to night. In here, however, nobody gave a damn about income-tax, no one so much as mentioned it. The possession of a cigarette stub was far more important than all the money in the coffers of the Inland Revenue.

Women, too!

Women had always engaged Archie's attention if but lightly, for no woman had ever dominated it, or claimed any of the time that he devoted to business matters. Yet in here his mind was obsessed with women, and with one woman particularly, so that he found himself remembering the smallest particular of his association with Elaine Fraser and the capaciousness of his memory regarding her astonished him.

He could recall, for example, exactly how she had stood when she was regarding herself in the mirror before getting into bed with him. Without him knowing it his mind must have formed a minutely accurate picture of her pose, with both hands resting lightly on the glass-topped dressing-table, her body and one foot thrust forward, inclining one buttock towards him in what now seemed a provocative posture.

He remembered her clear, white skin, and the spread of her thick curls on the pillow! He remembered her frank, laughing sensuality, and the sense of repose that she brought to him after a day spent wrestling with travellers, coupons, and stock returns.

He yearned for her as he had never yearned for any human being; beside her the contents of all the tills in London seemed less than a heap of packing-case shavings.

He always began to think of Elaine and to examine his memories of her the moment they had dispersed to their cells and the clanging of steel doors had receded along the gallery.

This was usually his time for a systematic probe into the facts and coincidences that had cost him his freedom. The nightly marshalling of this chain of events had helped him over those first, hideous weeks, until he landed the soft job in the store, and had something else to occupy his mind.

He would ask himself just where he began to go wrong and would fix the starting-point at the purchase of those two crates of spirits from the egregious Mr. Swift. From here he would slowly trace his run of bad luck to his row with the accountant, his settlement with the Inland Revenue, his failure to change the lock on the store-room in the yard, his mad rush into the West to recover his reserve capital, up to the very moment of the impact with the cyclists on the main road.

After that he found it difficult to remember the order of events and his memories of the inquest and trial were confused. He knew that at some time between these events they

had given him a wire or a letter, informing him that Tony had been killed in action in North Africa, and that it had seemed to him at the time that the people who brought him this news were sadists who enjoyed pounding and pummelling a prostrate man.

The news of Tony, however, and the abrupt change in his life that immediately followed it, had done a good deal to help him, for it had lifted the burden of guilt from his shoulders and enabled him to wipe away the memory of death that had burdened his conscience.

Archie was coarse-grained, greedy and almost completely selfish, but he was not inhuman and the knowledge that he had snuffed out somebody's life had troubled him for many weeks.

As the year wore on, however and he slipped into the routine of prison life, it began to trouble him much less, for it seemed to him that Tony's death, and the time he was spending in this half-world, more than atoned for the girl's death. As the weeks passed this idea strengthened in his mind and he began to regain his self-confidence.

His strongest characteristics had always been self-reliance and the habit of thinking along constructive lines, and these came to his rescue during the long hours that he remained shut away from distractions. In the long silences that followed lock-up he was able to go back over his life phase by phase, and re-examine all his decisions, not only those decisions regarding the management of his businesses, but those affecting his relationships with all kinds of people. He learned a great deal from these inquests and one of the first things he learned was the value of privacy, the kind of privacy that only a sentence of imprisonment can provide.

This was an aspect of prison life that surprised him. He remembered, years ago, hearing someone express satisfaction at the news of a notoriously work-shy man being sent to prison. "That'll teach him to work," the person exclaimed, and for some reason Archie had never forgotten the remark.

He now had an opportunity of testing the statement and found that it was wholly false. Nobody, he soon decided, had ever learned how to work in a prison, for a prison was surely the laziest place in the world, and its routine the most leisurely ever contrived by human beings.

Inside a prison only the privileged would work a normal span of hours. The others filled in their time as best they could and the constant struggle to find tasks that would occupy mind and hand was, to Archie at any rate, the most punishing feature of his sentence. He had been lucky, inasmuch as the prison staff soon came to recognise his organising ability, and made him a storekeeper, where his detailed knowledge of everyday commodities proved invaluable and he was able to set about reorganising the antiquated issue and withdrawal system of stores. This not only helped him to occupy his mind but it also recommended him to the elderly officer in charge of the department. Soon he was recognised as a model prisoner, bent on giving no trouble and gaining the maximum remission of sentence.

It was after supper, when he was back in his cell, that he had to make a conscious effort to think constructively and to discipline his thoughts to follow a set pattern. He had never been in the habit of spending much time in bed and was therefore seldom able to get to sleep until after midnight. This left him four hours in which to meditate and it was at this time, when he had temporarily exhausted all other sources, that his thoughts began to centre on Elaine.

On the final night of the old year he found it impossible to think of anyone else, for he remembered that they had spent Old Year's Night together two years before, and had seen 1941 launched at a dance, organised by a Polish relief organisation, at Lewisham.

It had been, he recalled, an entirely satisfactory evening.

They had danced until midnight and then driven off in his car to Shirley Hills, parking on a high, windy ridge, where they could look down on blacked-out London, silent under a brilliant moon and a sitting target for the Luftwaffe.

There had been plenty of night flares and distant explosions, an occasional flicker of tracer and here and there, a small fire, but it had all seemed to have little to do with them, for they had had plenty to drink and were in high spirits.

They had watched the show for a while and then climbed into the back of the car and made love. Elaine, he remembered, had been particularly demanding that night and he had put this down to the excitement of the raid and the amount of gin and Pims Number One she had consumed at the dance. Afterwards, as was their custom, they talked, quietly and amiably and he had sensed very strongly the kinship that made her company so rewarding. She had said to him on that occasion:

"Have you ever been in love with anyone, Archie? Have you ever *wanted* to love anyone?"

He had never found it necessary to lie to her and he was truthful now.

"Ever since the world began people have talked an awful lot of drivel about love, Elaine. Why the hell have they always had to wrap it up in cellophane? I've never minded admitting to myself that it's an appetite and neither have you, so don't ever try and sell me anything different will you?"

She had laughed at that and asked for a cigarette but presently she had said:

"About love, Archie! An awful lot of people have believed in it for a long time. We couldn't be wrong I suppose?"

"Not a chance, Elaine, not a chance!"

She had nodded, and pulled hard at the cigarette. Suddenly she had tossed it away and laughed again.

"Okay, it's an appetite! How often are you hungry, Archie?"

"You ought to be able to work that one out!" he said.

"Now you're trying to sell *me* something," she chuckled. "I'm the only larder you visit!"

"I sometimes think that you could be," he told her serious-ly and his reply must have stopped her from pursuing the subject, for she was silent all the way home, as though contemplating the implications of his remark.

They had never discussed love again, although their associ-ation had continued right up to the time that he began floundering with the Inland Revenue claims. Later she had drifted away with her Dutch merchant captain. He had not seen her after that and it was not until he went to prison that he began to think of her again.

Up to then she had been the last of a long line of larders, no more or less to him than Rita Ramage, his first mistress, or Gloria, the saucy shop-girl who had lifted nearly a hun-dred pounds from his wallet, or any other of the casual associations he had formed during his limited spare time over the years.

It was prison and the privacy of his cell that had changed this, for in here he never once thought of Rita or Gloria, but only of her and of all the good times they had spent togeth-er. Ultimately she came to mean much more than an attrac-tive and obliging woman. As time went by she began to represent freedom in the abstract, and everything one as-sociated with what went on outside the walls.

Lying on his cot, the rough blankets drawn up to his chin, he became reconciled to his conception of Elaine, and having at last made up his mind decided that he would write to her and ask her to come and visit him. He had a visit due to him and there was no one else whom he wanted to see in here. He thought it unlikely that she would respond to the first invitation, but at least it was worth trying, for either way it would help him. If she ignored his letter, then his resent-ment might enable him to put her out of mind along with all the others, but if she replied, if she actually came, then it must mean that he was as firmly rooted in her consciousness as she was in his and that surely gave him something to hope for?

Decision had always been Archie's sedative and having made this decision he was able to dismiss her and all she stood for until the letter was written. He turned over on his side and reached over to tuck the trailing blanket under his shoulder; by the time 1943 was fifteen minutes' old he was asleep and snoring gently.

CHAPTER XXVII

Boxer Diverts The Third Reich

SEVERAL hundred miles from the spot where Archie lay musing about Elaine, another man who had worn out shoe leather on the Avenue pavements was also in captivity, but he was enclosed by barbed wire instead of brick walls, and was watched, not by warders, but by harassed German reservists.

Like his brother, Archie, Boxer soon came to terms with his gaolers. Some of them were quick to respond to the wide, innocent smile that had once disarmed suburban grocers, and set them poking into their bins for broken biscuits, but there the parallel ended, for Boxer, unlike Archie, might almost be said to have been enjoying his captivity.

Boxer had always been receptive to new scenes and new sources of fun, and his travels up and down the Third Reich during the last few months had presented him with plenty of both. For various reasons, most of them traceable to Boxer's eccentric sense of humour, his was far from being a static captivity, and his captors seemed determined to ensure that he should not stagnate behind one particular network of barbed wire.

A succession of schoolmasters had, as it were, broken their teeth upon Boxer's intellect, and his original German captor, the portly and well-meaning Major General von Haussman, was neither more patient nor more ingenious than the men who had superintended Boxer's education. Judged by standards then existing among high-ranking German officers, von Haussman was a very patient soul indeed and his forbearance, throughout the period immediately following Boxer's amiable surrender, had a good deal to do with his prisoner's subsequent migrations.

It was because Major General von Haussman had had so much faith in his own powers of persuasion that Boxer did not go straight into the bag with all the other Dieppe prisoners. The Major General had been struck by Boxer's ingenuousness the very first moment he set eyes on him, as he trudged along carrying his wounded brother to the enemy medical centre.

Von Haussman reasoned that a man who would march thus into the midst of an army, assembled for the sole purpose of exterminating him, and lay claim to that army's resources as trustingly as this soldier had done, must necessarily be lacking in intelligence, and was therefore likely to prove a promising subject for interrogation.

The Major General had had experience of questioning British prisoners during the dog days of 1940. He had found them, almost without exception, to be stubborn, security-conscious, and singularly unhelpful. They told him their number, rank and name and then, when asked for further information, yawned in his face. They were impervious to threats and indifferent to blandishments. They even refused to fill out Red Cross forms, which thoughtful Intelligence officers had prepared for them, with the object of alleviating the anxiety of loved ones at home. In short, the information of military value that Major General von Haussman extracted from captured British soldiers could have been scratched on an identity disc, and would have discouraged most examiners to the point of despair.

Major General von Haussman, however, was a patient optimist, always confident that something rewarding was just around the corner. By the time he had completed his preliminary examination of Boxer he was convinced that he had at last stumbled upon a very promising source of information, one that, wisely and carefully handled, might prove more fruitful than any number of dossiers compiled inside the established prison camps.

His aide, the slim, superior, buck-toothed Captain Engelstein, did not share his faith in Boxer, but he too made an error in his estimate of the prisoner, for both officers took one look at the big commando and decided that he was very stupid. The Major General persuaded himself that Boxer's stupidity could be coaxed into showing a profit. Agreed on this they then formed diverse opinions of their prisoner's worth, for the Captain concluded that the big head behind the amiable grin held nothing whatever of military value.

Both men were in error. Boxer was not stupid. All his life he had been lazy, easily led, unimaginative, and slow-thinking, but he was not stupid. What the German officers did not know, and what they could be forgiven for not knowing, was that up to the moment of capture Boxer's brains had never been exercised, his brother, Bernard, having done Boxer's thinking for the better part of twenty-five years.

Boxer's dominant characteristic had always been his sense of humour and once his nagging anxiety regarding Bernard's hurts had been allayed, and the Germans had persuaded him that his twin would be given instant medical aid, in the best traditions of warfare between two civilised nations, it was his sense of humour that crept out to sun itself. The field of opportunity it was offered was immense and, quick to appreciate this, it at once went to work on the nearest subject. This happened to be poor Major General von Haussman, a mere fortifications expert, but a man with earnest ambitions to adventure into the realms of military intelligence.

The initial interview between General and Private took place in a small hut, close to the Field Dressing Station, where Bernard was having his wounds dressed.

The Major General, having dismissed his aide, settled himself comfortably and went merrily to work to win Boxer's confidence.

First he praised him for his care of his wounded brother and said that Boxer's fraternal solicitude had touched his heart. He then went on to assure Boxer, in an accent that reminded his prisoner of all the music-hall and barrack-room jokes he had ever heard about Germans, that from this point on Boxer need have no fears but that his brother would receive humane and skilful treatment at the hands of his late enemies. Von Haussman stressed the word 'late', pointing out that Boxer must now cease to regard the Germans as opponents, but rather as his hosts.

"For you, my brave man, the vor it iss over," he announced. "For you it iss the honourable captivity!"

He then went on to talk of other matters, of the gallant failure of the Dieppe Raid, of the excellence of the German coastal defences and the impossibility of penetrating them no matter what weight of armament was brought to bear upon them from the sea or air. He gave Boxer a black cheroot to smoke and talked to him as he might have conversed with a keen young junior, placed under his care.

Boxer was fascinated by the General's expansiveness and listened very attentively, despite the fact that he was now feeling extremely sleeply, and was obliged to stifle a series of long, yammering yawns.

Major General von Haussman noticed these yawns but he took no offence and despatched his orderly for a pint of black coffee, urging Boxer to refresh himself after his Herculean exertions. Boxer accepted the coffee gratefully and swallowed the jugful while his host went on to talk of military matters, presently sliding smoothly from this topic to that of Anglo-German relations, and the tragedy of the present conflict between cousins.

"I haf the goot friends in England," he confided. "It iss wrong that we should quarrel so bad when we are cousins, iss it not?"

Boxer had never thought of himself as in any way related to the Germans but he was ready to try, providing this particular cousin would encourage him with something to eat, and a chance to get a good, long kip on the floor. Seeing no point in beating about the bush with a man so obviously obliging as the Major General, he said, simply and straight forwardly:

"I'm very hungry, sir! They pinched my iron rations on the way in here."

If von Haussman was a little surprised by this ingenuous remark he did not show it, but sent instantly for some vegetable soup and a long, French loaf, of the kind that Boxer had learned to appreciate in 1940. Whilst Boxer ate, the officer went on talking, gently and persistently, until suddenly he stopped and asked a direct question.

"You set out from vere, last night?"

Boxer had been expecting something like this and had an answer ready, but he thought it best to pretend to ponder awhile. The Major General watched him, his eyes bright with hope.

At length Boxer said, slowly and clearly:

"From a little place we call 'Bolloxhaven', sir!"

The Major General knitted his brows. He was very familiar with the Channel and East Coast ports and had been expecting to hear the word 'Folkestone', 'Dover' or 'Broadstairs'. He had studied many up-to-date maps but he could not recall ever having seen or heard of 'Bolloxhaven'. He said so, quite politely.

Boxer shrugged. "It's a long way up the creek," he said, helpfully, and was slightly relieved to see the Major General smile.

"Ah—yes! A code name standing for . . . ?"

"I dunno what it stands for," said Boxer quickly, "you see, I'd never been there before last night!"

The Major General murmured something and then wrote on his pad. When he looked up Boxer was asleep, his head and shoulders on the trestle table. After regarding him paternally for a moment or two Major General Haussman summoned the orderly and told him that the prisoner would remain under guard in the hut, and was not on any account to be disturbed until the following morning.

They locked the hut and posted a sentry at the door. The sentry was changed every three hours throughout the night, but Boxer did not hear them stamping and shouting outside. It was dusk when he half-awoke and saw that they had placed a straw mattress and two grey blankets on the floor beside him. He rolled off the chair on to the mattress, pulled the blankets over him, and went to sleep again at once, remembering nothing more until a helmeted infantryman stamped in with his breakfast, placed it on the table and went out again without a word.

For a moment or two Boxer had difficulty in remembering where he was and by the time he had remembered, the

Major General had entered the hut and was informing him
that his brother had now been removed to a military hospital
and that the doctor attending him had hopes of saving both
leg and arm.

"When he iss recovered you vill together be vonce more,"
he added. "Then, perhaps, the vor vill von be!"

The news cheered Boxer, who now felt refreshed, relaxed
and eager to pass a pleasant hour or so with the German
brass, particularly as he had acquired a taste for the General's cheroots. If, in exchange for this unexpectedly lavish
hospitality, the old boy wanted to talk about the war then
Boxer was willing to humour him, and give him something to
write down on his little old pad! It would be wrong, of
course, to tell a Jerry anything that might be useful to
him—they had been very insistent about that at the assault
training centre—but surely there could be no harm at all in
pulling the old chap's leg a little? After all, it was a long time,
since he had had such an opportunity, and it would be
something to tell old Berni when they patched him up and
brought him along.

He wondered, a little vaguely, what this silly old basket
would most like to hear—something about the bombing
maybe, or perhaps something a bit more spectacular, like
'Exercise Spy-hunt' the training scheme the Commandos had
enjoyed so much in North Wales, earlier that summer.

Boxer finally decided that a highly-coloured version of this
story offered the best possibilities, and at once launched into
an account of an exercise in which two Commandos, playing
the roles of two German agents landed by U-boat had been
instructed to make their way to an air-field twenty miles
inland, while the rest of the troop set out to hunt them down.

He told the story well, with many a reminiscent chuckle
but he forgot to mention that the two spies, finally located
under a road bridge and 'shot out of hand', had been Ginger
and Dusty, two men from 'A' troop, and that Ginger, an
excellent Cockney mimic, had amused them all by *'ad lib-
bing'* his part in broken English and squealing for mercy as
he crawled about round the feet of the hysterical 'firing-
squad.'

The Major General was obviously very interested in this

story and wrote a number of things down on his pad, after which he beamed at Boxer, ordered up luncheon and five more cheroots, and promised to visit him again before he was sent along to the prisoners' collecting point.

He never paid his third visit, and Boxer never saw him again. Late that afternoon the door of the hut crashed open and two German privates, armed to the teeth, came in at the double, with Captain Engelstein, the Major General's aide at their heels.

Before Boxer understood what was happening to him he was handcuffed, bundled to his feet, and almost thrown out of the hut and into a canvas-covered van that was standing in the yard outside. The two soldiers leaped in after him, but the Captain remained prancing about outside, howling, gibbering, and waving his arms like a man in a fit.

Boxer knew no word of German, so that everything the Captain said was incomprehensible but the tirade seemed to be having a curious effect on the escort, who kept glaring at Boxer as though he was a wild beast, and slapping their rifle butts, as though to remind themselves that they were not defenceless against him.

Once he had recovered from his surprise Boxed settled down in the van to enjoy the pantomime. It was the first time that he had ever witnessed a traditional German 'flap', and he found it fascinating. It was minutes before he realised that the Captain's outburst was directed at him, and not at the guards, for the engine of the van refused to start and suddenly everybody was bundled out into the yard again and rushed into an open lorry, where the pantomime began all over again and the Captain, viewed from the tailboard, seemed to be having a second seizure.

He looked so diverting as he hopped about in his highly-polished boots, his narrow face purpling, and his long, aristocratic hands fluttering, that Boxer was unable to prevent himself from chortling openly and asking, of the nearest guard, "what all the panic was about?" His chuckle, and the question that followed it, had a distressing effect on everyone. The officer screamed something at the guard, who at once jabbed his rifle butt into Boxer's stomach, completely winding him and converting his amusement into speechless indignation.

He managed to gasp, "What the bloody hell . . ." as the lorry started, but the sudden jerk deposited all three of them on the floor. Dragged to his feet, and hounded into the corner against the driver's screen, Boxer began to reflect upon the incomprehensible nature of an enemy who one moment plied him with coffee, soup, cheroots and amiable conversation, and the next treated him as though he alone stood between the Wehrmacht and world conquest.

He never did discover the true cause of his rapid transition from privileged prisoner to prisoner extraordinary. Nobody explained to him, at least not in English, that a few moments before he was bustled from the hut Major General Haussman had received a terse telephone message from Military Intelligence, and had gathered therefrom that if 'Bolloxhaven' was indeed the British Army's code name for Newhaven, Deal, Tilbury or Folkestone, it was not in general use above the rank of Corporal.

He also learned, to his surprise, that if enemy agents had been landed on the Welsh coast by U-boat, in June of this year, then they had arrived there without the authority or assistance of the Bureau of Espionage.

Boxer might have guessed all this, of course and might even have occupied the bumpy journey inland by putting two and two together, but he remained mystified, for he had already forgotten the details of his little chat with Major General Haussman, and in any case he had plenty of other things to think about, for the lorry was being driven at breakneck speed and it was all he could do, manacled as he was, to remain in an upright position.

It would be interesting to follow Boxer through his tour of Occupied France, Occupied Belgium, Occupied Holland, and, ultimately Germany itself, but it would be a long and tedious journey, and would not teach us anything new about Boxer.

In the two or three months that followed his capture he was treated as a special prisoner, inasmuch as he was subjected to more interrogations than was usual in the case of captured private soldiers; he was also distinguished from

other prisoners of war by manacles and comparative isolation.

The manacles did not worry him overmuch. He was of a
mechanical turn of mind and soon learned how to slip them
off whenever he was alone. Moreover, once out of range of
the explosive Captain Engelstein, nobody took the handcuffs
very seriously. Neither, in fact, did his interrogators seem to
take him seriously, despite the special report that accompanied him wherever he went, and although he did not recall
much of his conversation with the General, or link it in any
way with the special treatment accorded him, he made no
further attempts to amuse himself at the expense of subsequent interrogators. Variations of his original narrative would
have put too severe a strain upon his imagination.

It was not until he was drafted to a working-camp, and
treated as an ordinary prisoner, that his originality began to
flower again, for here he found several kindred spirits who
had persuaded themselves that the shortest route back to
their favourite pubs and girl-friends was a route signposted
with acts of sabotage.

This, indeed, was the favourite pastime of British prisoners
in the camp near Augsburg, to which Boxer was sent in the
spring of 1943, and Boxer, everybody soon decided, was
eminently suited for the role of Jolly Saboteur. His wide,
vacant grin seemed to hypnotise the elderly guards and the
civilians about the place for it seemed that Major General
Haussman was not alone in mistaking his mildness and joviality for clownish stupidity of a high order. That was why
everyone gave Boxer so much rope, and when his natural
amiability was supplemented by the hoarded contents of Red
Cross parcels, which included packets of Virginian cigarettes
and chocolate, there was simply no holding him back.

At the Augsburg camp the prisoners were employed on a
busy railway siding, sited at the foot of a long gradient that
connected a sawmill with its goods depot.

The engines used in transporting the timber were operated
by German civilians, but the coupling and uncoupling of the
wagons was left to prisoners.

Nobody connected Boxer with the mysterious uncoupling
of a long train of empty wagons shortly before dusk one

evening, and nobody blamed him when fifty-seven trucks slid away from the stationary engine and rumbled at gathering speed down the long incline, to pile into an ungainly pyramid at the Augsburg siding.

The driver and fireman of the train had last seen Boxer and all the other prisoners at the main siding, when they had set off on the final trip of the day, and there were no prisoners up at the sawmill, since it was after dark when the engine arrived and all the prisoners were then being paraded for lock-up.

The act of sabotage was therefore credited to parachutists and the fireman and driver were sent to haul trucks across the white plains of the Ostfront. Boxer obligingly helped to clear away the wreckage, and tidy up the siding, and was later included in a batch of men sent to live in wired billets adjoining the mill itself. Here they worked at felling timber and hauling it back to the mill, pending the repair of the depot.

It was very pleasant down here in the springtime. The work was hard but the life was healthy and agreeable. Sometimes the smell of sawn pines would remind Boxer of the building sites in and around the suburb at home, and he would experience a pang or two of homesickness, not so much for the Avenue, but for his lost boyhood, and for Berni.

He had, however, received some reassuring news of Bernard, via his father. It was sad to reflect that henceforth Berni would have to face life with one arm but that, Boxer reasoned, was better than losing an arm and a leg, and in any case Pop had written to say that there was hope of Berni being repatriated in the next exchange of severely wounded prisoners. This would mean, of course, that old Berni would never be able to join him here in Germany, but there were compensations, amusing compensations some of them, such as the elimination of Little Willie, the short-tempered overseer.

Little Willie had arrived from Munich to keep a fatherly eye on the prisoners in case those fiendish parachutists began fresh mischief, and Boxer had no trouble at all with him, for the overseer reserved his spite for smaller men, men like

'Tich' Hoskins. Hoskins, who was a friendly little man, was sent to the cooler for twenty-one days, after something had gone wrong with one of the circular saws.

Boxer was fond of Tich, who reminded him a little of old Berni, and when Tich had been cuffed, harangued and marched off, Boxer made up his mind that it was time somebody did something about Little Willie. There was a Polish medical orderly on the camp who was known to be bitterly hostile to the Jerries, and Boxer sought him out and had a little talk with him. He came from the Medical hut with a small packet of powder, concealed in the toe of his sock.

That night Little Willie was found outside his quarters on hands and knees, vomiting at irregular intervals, and groaning piteously between spasms. Everyone thought he was drunk and two of the guards carried him off to bed, but in the morning Little Willie was much worse, and the next day he was hurried off to Augsburg military hospital.

Nobody connected Boxer with the overseer's sudden illness, for no one recalled that Boxer had been in the habit of giving Little Willie bars of chocolate in return for an extra long mid-morning break in the clearings. Someone might have remembered, had it not been for the serious outbreak of fire at the mills before Little Willie's replacement arrived, but all else was forgotten in the closing-down of the manufactory and the transfer of prisoners to the Earberg area, where they were set to work on road-making in summer-heat, and sometimes referred nostalgically to Little Willie and the Augsburg pine forests.

Boxer did not remain in the road-gang very long. After a month or so he changed identities with a lieutenant in the Gunners, who suggested the switch when the British officer prisoners passed the road-makers on the way to baths each Monday.

The switch was easily arranged and Boxer found himself with a brand new identity, henceforth being known as Lieutenant A. S. C. Burne-Cookham, R.A., or 'Algy', who shared a hut with fifty-one other officers.

Every one of these men seemed to regard Boxer as a fine sportsman, who had done Algy, their comrade, a great service by consenting to change places with him, but Boxer found it difficult to regard the change in this light. Outside the wire he had been operating a concrete-mixer in blistering summer heat, whereas inside it there was nothing to do but lounge, play rounders, read magazines, or indulge in what the officers called 'stooging' for their escapes.

Boxer was astonished at the amount of time these keen types devoted to the planning of escapes, particularly as hardly any of these escapes resulted in more than a few days' freedom for the escapers, some of whom were eager to face terrible risks to get outside the wire.

Almost invariably the venturesome were back in the cooler, turning over the problems of yet another bid to get out, and some of their endeavours involved an immense amount of physical toil. There were, for instance, no fewer than five tunnels under construction, and for a spell Boxer worked in one of them, but the Escape Committee soon recognised the fact that, muscular and willing though he was, he was of far more use to them as a diversionist, particularly when what they called 'a wire job' was coming up, and the alert sentries in the elevated look-out towers had to have their attention engaged for a few moments.

Boxer, it was discovered, had a whole repertoire of diversional tactics, some of them picked up during his pre-war tours in the company of stunt men and professional acrobats, and others acquired during his captivity.

One of his popular turns was a fifty-yard stroll past the look-out towers walking on his hands, a feat which never failed to attract the astonished gaze of the sentries. Another, and somewhat similar trick, was his comic 'crab-walk,' a style of progression that fascinated all who witnessed it. For this diversion he would point his toes inward and form a curious diamond-shaped aperture with his long legs, walking thus along the extreme inside edge of the trip wire, balanced on the sides of his feet.

No matter how many times the guards saw this performance they never ceased to be intrigued and amused by it. They looked down into the compound and shook with laughter while, higher up the wire, enterprising young men went to work with homemade cutters and sawed their way out to a brief spell of freedom.

Boxer's summer season in Oflag vaudeville came to an end
with the sudden reappearance of an emaciated Lieutenant
Burne-Cookham, R.A., who had been recaptured in the
Schaffhausen Bulge after more than five weeks on the run.

Side by side in front of the glum Commandant, the two
men were seen not to be very much alike after all and Boxer
was marched out of the camp to the accompaniment of
cheers and good wishes. He spent a month in cells, before
being transferred to a 'Naughty Boys' ' camp, near Cassel.

He welcomed the change, for he had not altogether approved of the officers' preoccupation with tunnels and wire-
jobs.

They tried to persuade him that it was a soldiers' patriotic
duty to escape, and get home in order to continue the war,
but Boxer's rapidly developing powers of reasoning told him
that it was surely folly to go all the way home in order to
fight one's way all the way back to Germany again! If one
was already here, then surely it was more logical to stay and
look around for some way in which Hitler might be
harassed? Even if opportunities were limited now they might
not always be so, and in any case it was refreshing to stick
around and bait poor old Jerry. He rose to a bait more
spectacularly than even Boxer's schoolmasters had risen in
the old days, and it was a pity that old Berni wasn't here to
share in the fun. Life in Germany, Boxer decided, was really
one long, rewarding game of knocking-down-ginger!

The new camp to which he was sent was a lively one, for
here were assembled, in a single, mediaeval building, all the
other ranks who would have qualified for Colditz, the famous
Bad Boys' Camp, had they been officers.

The inmates welcomed Boxer with open arms and it was
here that he earned the nom-de-guerre of 'The Gaffer',
awarded in recognition of his leadership, enterprise and,
above all, his remarkable ability to acquire contraband articles. Whether it was his light touch, or whether he still relied
on that ingenuous, split-melon smile, his fellow prisoners
were never able to determine, but almost every day Boxer
would deliver some useful article to the Guards' Sergeant
Major in nominal authority over the prisoners.

One day it was a civilian's Homburg hat, the next a coil of

wire, the day after a pickaxe, and the day after that a wad of German marks, or a railway time-table.

One morning he turned up with half a ladder, that had to be returned because there was no room to stow it in the contraband cache under the washhouse floor. The Sergeant Major was impressed by the yield, and promised to recommend Boxer for a medal after the war. This promise must have inspired Boxer to even greater efforts, for the following day he turned up with an Iron Cross, whereupon the Sergeant Major, wiping the perspiration from his brow, exclaimed:

"All I can say is, thank Christ you weren't in my unit when we quartered in the Tower! God Almighty, you'd have walked off with the perishing Crown Jewels, and flogged 'em in Houndsditch!"

And here, for a year or more, we must leave Boxer, in no way oppressed by captivity, but finding in it the means to keep everyone around him happy and amused. He missed Bernard, of course, so much so that he tried hard not to think about him, but it was rather pleasant sometimes to be able to act on one's own initiative, and discover exactly how one could get along without prefacing every proposal with a "Whatdysay, Berni? Whatdysay?"

CHAPTER XXVIII

'La Gloire'

"ONE of the first things one has to learn about the pursuit of La Gloire, is that it can be a tiring and tedious business," said Claude, rolling a cigarette to and fro between thin lips, and slamming home the magazine of the Sten gun.

Esme agreed, quoting Jim Carver, veteran of World War One.

"I had a chap next door to me in the Avenue, the father of the girl I'm engaged to as a matter of fact. He served right through the Quatorze...." (Esme had dropped into the French habit of distinguishing the two conflicts as 'Le Quatorze' and simply 'La Guerre') "and I once asked him what war was really like. I never forgot his reply. He said: 'If you could reduce the time I spent as a soldier to an hour, I was scared stiff one minute, frozen stiff nine minutes, and bored stiff the other fifty'!"

The Frenchman laughed and laid the Sten gun on Esme's bed. "Your prospective father-in-law is a realist," he said. "Now you must get some sleep. I will call you when Maurice arrives and when we are ready to move."

He shook hands and as he left the attic, and descended the uncarpeted stairs to the room above the watchmender's workshop, Esme reflected that Claude was right about La Gloire. It had indeed been a tedious business, in spite of constant movement, and constant alarms.

Most of the time he had spent in Northern France Esme had been cooped up in attic bedrooms like this, attempting, by one means or another, to pass lonely hours until his journey into the south-west could be arranged.

He realised, of course, that enormous care had to be exercised by these people, each of whom was risking his or her life by contact with him. He had learned, from Claude and his deputies, something about the expanding network of the French underground movement, of its passwords, daggers, forged passes, secret conclaves and all the trappings one had associated in pre-war days with light fiction. By now he was aware from personal experience how difficult and dangerous was a simple movement from district to district in France, where German troops were stationed in every small town, and Vichy agents, informers and collaborators were established inside every Government department. He knew all this, but it did not check his impatience to begin his journey home, to be able to walk the streets by day or night, free of the nagging fear of sudden arrest, and the betrayal of friends that might follow his arrest.

Sometimes he almost wished that he had been captured that first day in the mangold shed near the scene of the crash. He reasoned that, if this had happened, then at least he would have been among his own kind, able to come to terms with life and await the end of the war. He would also have been in a position to acquaint Judy and old Harold that he was alive. Situated as he was now this was out of the question and he did not care to reflect on Judy's wretchedness, or Harold's silent grief, for surely they must suppose him dead now that news of the surviving members of his Lancaster had had time to filter back to Air Ministry Casualties.

His admiration for the Resistance people was extreme, but sometimes, in the loneliness of his hide-outs, he could not help feeling that their heroism was wasted, for all their efforts over the past two years had resulted in nothing more than the smuggling home of a hundred or so evaders, trained men like himself, capable of re-entering the struggle, and what was a hundred men in a war of these proportions? How could their sacrifices and ingenuity affect the outcome of the war by a single day? Was it really worth risking their lives to prevent the capture of a few stray airmen, or to damage a section of railway track? Did it really matter to the war effort if he got home again, or if a small local factory continued to manufacture haversacks and respirators for the Germans?

During one of these pessimistic moods he discussed the subject with Claude, the Group Leader. They always talked English, for Esme found it cheering to converse in his own tongue with someone who had actually known the Avenue, and had waited at the 'bus stop, at the foot of Shirley Rise, on sunny mornings when the hawthorn was in blossom along the golf links hedge.

"You are regarding it too closely, or perhaps not closely enough, my friend," Claude had told him. "We do not do this so much for you as for ourselves! It is not as important to us that you should get home but that we should risk our lives trying to outwit the Boche! You see, my friend, we Frenchmen helped to murder Western civilisation, 1940. Yes, my friend, we did it by sloth and by cynicism. You have read Oscar Wilde, of course?"

"His plays?" queried Esme.

"No, no, his plays are gilded trifles," said Claude, impatiently, "for he wrote them before he had learned truth through suffering. I refer to his great work, 'The Ballad of Reading Gaol'."

He pronounced it 'Reeding' and Esme grinned.

"It's 'Redding', like 'bedding'," he said, for Claude was always anxious to have his pronunciation corrected, "but what's the connection, Claude?"

"It is what happened to us in 1940," said Claude. "You remember?—

'Yet each man kills the thing he loves
By each let this be heard,
Some do it with a bitter look,
Some with a flattering word,
The coward does it with a kiss,
The brave man with a sword!' "

Esme protested, for it seemed to him monstrous that this gallant young man should continue to feel so humiliated by his country's collapse.

"You take too much on yourselves," he said, "You couldn't control your crooked politicians, any more than we could galvanise our wishful-thinking bunch into positive action, in 1938! The fact is, the whole damned lot of us had a horror of starting up another war, and we kept telling ourselves that it wouldn't happen! I was as bad as anyone else and I don't mind admitting it now! There was only one chap in our Avenue who saw what was happening, that chap I told you about, Jim Carver. The rest of us backed Chamberlain and his piece of paper, and don't let any Britisher tell you differently!"

"That may be so," replied Claude, "but when it did happen you preferred to die rather than give up. Each of you, the highest and the lowest! That is something of which you should always be proud, my friend!"

Esme wondered whether this was an exaggeration on the part of the Frenchman and decided that perhaps, after all, it was not. He had seen the suburb under non-stop bombardment and had sensed the spirit of defiance in people like Edith Clegg, and little Miss Baker across the road. Supposing England, or any other country, had been isolated and pounded in this ruthless manner? Suppose its fighting men had been thrown back on a defenceless base, and its food supplies menaced by U-boat blockade. Would that country have continued to resist or would it, like France, have glumly sued for peace and accepted German domination?

He decided at once that this was one of those silly 'if' questions that had no real answer. . . . 'If there had been tanks at the Battle of Hastings'. 'If Napoleon had actually landed the Grande Armée on the shores of Kent. . . .' Who could tell? One could only judge these matters by what did occur, not by what might have occurred.

He made up his mind, however, to spare the Frenchman's pride and said: "We were saved by the Ditch, Claude and without it we'd have been no tougher than you people! Apart from that, I can't see a cagey old Devonshire farmer risking his neck to get a French aviator back into the fight, as you're doing right now!"

"You are kind but not quite honest," smiled Claude, and the topic was dropped.

About two months after his first interview with Claude in the farmhouse, Esme had a very pleasant surprise.

One afternoon, Claude came to his hide-out over a butcher's shop in a little village, near Lille, and told him that he was about to meet an old friend. A few minutes later Snowball, the West Indian wireless operator, was shown into the room, displaying perfect teeth in a delighted grin but no surprise at all at their reunion, having heard some time ago that Esme was still free, and in hiding.

They spent an animated hour in one another's company before Claude said they must part, for Snowball's journey to Paris had been arranged, and he was leaving that night, disguised as a French Colonial N.C.O.

"For him it was easy," Claude said, when Esme protested bitterly at Snowball's priority. "For you, perhaps, there is something important that has to be done first!"

"What do you mean by that?" asked Esme, noticing that Claude avoided his eye.

"There is some information that your people would like to have, and it is possible that you might be the right man to convey it to them!" said Claude, quietly.

He went on to discuss a mysterious activity of the Germans in parts of the Pas de Calais coast. Nobody he said, knew the precise purpose of these activities, for as yet they were limited to large-scale diggings, tunnellings, and the laying down of wide-gauge railway tracks.

"Maybe it's a new series of radar stations," said Esme.

"It is more than that my friend," said Claude, "it is some kind of long-range weapon ... rockets perhaps, or something like rockets. We have reports from at least a dozen centres. At Siracourt and Mimoyecques, for instance, thousands of Russian slave labourers are employed. At Nieppe, near Armentières, a small forest has been closed in with camouflage netting."

"You mean that you want me to memorise details and report back to A.M.?" asked Esme, anxiously.

"That must depend upon you," Claude told him, "for you are an airman, and it is not for me to ask you to become a spy! As I have told you before, if you are caught now you have an identity disc and would go, after some questioning no doubt, into a prisoner of war camp. If we were caught it would be the firing squad or, at best, deportation to Germany, and slow death when we got there!"

"What exactly do you want me to do?" asked Esme, his stomach sinking.

For answer Claude rose and went across to his valise, which he unstrapped, taking out a small, leather-bound volume. Esme saw that it was an anthology of French verse but when Claude opened it he saw a hollowed-out section in the leaves. From the hollow the Frenchman extracted a small sheaf of tissue papers, each sheet being covered with drawings.

"It is of great importance that these sketches should reach your Intelligence without delay," he said, bluntly.

"May I look at them?"

"Of course."

Esme smoothed the sheets and examined them carefully. Each was covered with fine tracing in indelible ink, and the spaces beneath the drawings were filled with rows of tiny figures that looked like a text illustrating the sketches.

"Are these drawings of the places you mentioned?" he asked.

"There are three more to come," said Claude. "Our people are getting them for you now."

"So that's why I've been kept hanging about for so long?" said Esme.

Claude shrugged. "You are at liberty to refuse to have anything to do with them," said Claude. "If you were caught with them you would of course, be treated as a spy!"

"Don't you have special couriers to transmit this kind of information?"

"We do have couriers," said Claude, "but two have been caught this month, and a third is in hospital with pneumonia. Well, my Avenue friend, what is it to be? A simple evader or a special agent?"

"You don't leave me much choice do you?" said Esme, unhappily.

The Frenchman patted his shoulder. "I will arrange a rendezvous with Martin, in order that he should explain them to you. What little we know your people shall know," he said.

"I'm not much good at anything as involved as this," mumbled Esme.

"We shall see," promised Claude and left him to his thoughts.

The meeting with Martin took place about a fortnight later. Martin, in the role of a French policeman, had reconnoitred two of the sites, and had detailed information on those at Siracourt, Watten, and Wizernes, all in the Channel coast area.

As far as Esme could gather the diggings were of two distinct types, the one a huge, sunken mushroom, made of reinforced concrete, and the other a more open site, usually situated on the edge of a wood, with a large timber platform fed by a railway track. The greater part of the track was concealed in a tunnel.

Martin was convinced that they were designed for some kind of long-range gun, but he told Esme that one of his party, an engineer by profession, was of the opinion that they were connected with long-range secret weapons, possibly pilotless missiles. Whatever they were, the sites were all near the coast, and it therefore followed that any projectile leaving them would be aimed at south-east England.

A few days after Martin's visit Esme was moved again, this time to a watchmaker's house in a village a few miles outside Paris.

The watchmaker, an elderly man, was a collector of antique clocks, and his house was full of clocks, some of them dating back to the early eighteenth century.

All day long his clocks were chiming and the old man would sometimes conduct Esme on a tour of the collection, here touching a clock lovingly on its base of decorated porcelain, or there making a minute adjustment to a timepiece representing a tournament, in which tiny armoured knights charged one another each time the hour struck.

At a certain time each evening the watchmender would put a finger on his lips and take Esme into the workroom, where he would lift a loose floorboard behind his counter. He would emerge holding a tiny radio set, so small and gimcrack that it reminded Esme of the crystal sets that had been so popular in the Avenue when he was a child.

On this tiny instrument they would listen to the B.B.C. news and when the bulletin was over the old man would wink and say: "It is a useful contrivance, but not as beautiful as the least of my clocks, Sergeant!"

Esme was here when Claude arrived one night with the last of the drawings and news that he was to be ready to leave France the following night.

"You will not be going overland, my friend," he said. "We have decided to send you home by Anson aircraft."

"By Anson . . . ? You mean, I'll fly out from a secret landing field?"

"Of a kind, yes," smiled Claude, "but the runway is not so perfect! With luck, you will survive to be in London this time tomorrow. After that they will give you leave, perhaps, and you will be able to surprise your fiancée, Judith. You will kiss her twice, tenderly, once for yourself, and once in memory of the Shirley policeman's daughter, who was so cold, and so frightened of falling in love with a foreigner!"

Esme was so excited by the prospect of being in England again in less than twenty-four hours that he was obliged to leave his preparations to Claude. Under the Frenchman's instructions he used adhesive tape to fasten the drawings to the inside of his thigh, and then covered the bulge with a circle of adhesive paster.

"It would not fool the most stupid of the Gestapo but at least you could shed your clothes and still retain them!" he said. "If we are challenged at any stage of our journey I advise you to rely more upon this and upon your powers of flight," and he gave Esme the loaded Sten gun.

Esme was too nervous and excited to take Claude's advice and go to sleep, pending Martin's arrival with the lorry. He lay on his mattress in the watchmender's attic listening to the sleet slashing against the small window pane, and wondering if this weather would mean a postponement of the flight. They still had to cover several hundred kilometres to the pick-up point, which was located south-west of Paris, and Claude had told him that they would be making the middle step of the journey by rail and using a slow train as the safest means of early morning travel. He was to make this journey as a Belgian gas-fitter, and his identity card had been made out in the name of Adolphe Picart, with his own photograph attached.

Carefully he went over the story that he was to use if challenged. He was a native of Dakar and had spent most of his life in the colony, which accounted for his accent. He was employed by the firm of Lamartine et fils, heat-engineers, of Brussels, and was going to Bordeaux to help in the installation of a new gasometer.

It all sounded so pat and Esme, who had always spoken reasonably good French, was confident that he could pass for a Frenchman with the majority of Germans. At all events, Claude said that this was so, and Claude knew his business. If they encountered collaborators, however, it would probably mean using the gun, which was to be carried in Esme's tool-bag.

At first light, Claude said, a lorry would call for them and convey them both to a small railway station about five kilometres away. From here, they would travel second-class to Orleans, where a car would pick them up and take them south-west across the old Vichy demarcation line to the air strip.

Esme had been awaiting the day of departure with extreme impatience but now that it had arrived he felt far more nervous than at any time during his period on the run. So many things could go wrong at the last moment and if something did go wrong, and he was caught and searched, the probable results did not bear thinking about.

He tried, as he lay on his rustling mattress staring up at the vague outline of the high window, to comfort himself with the thought that here, at last, was a situation that he had been rehearsing since childhood. Here was high adventure and romance, the chance he had always longed for in order to prove to himself that he was capable of transforming day-dreams into reality. 'Down, Judy, down! The cavalry patrols are searching for us!' 'Quiet, Judy, quiet! The snap of a twig will betray us!'

Well, here were Gestapo squads, more to be dreaded than any cavalry patrol, and all keeping a sharp look-out for him;

and here was a situation where the snap of a twig might well lead straight to Fresnes Gaol, or Vincennes, where an account of his activities over the past few months would be gouged or beaten from him, involving not only his own death, but the betrayal of every Frenchman who had housed and fed him since the previous September!

The reflection brought no glow of pride and certainly no surge of excitement, only a dry, parched feeling in the throat, and a persistent waiting-to-see-the-headmaster sensation in the pit of his stomach. He decided, without shame, that he was not, after all, an adventurer, and that in future the exploits of fictitious heroes would provide him with all the excitement he demanded of life. No longer did he see himself as Jim Hawkins, or Brigadier Gerard. The mantle of the elect had fallen from him and he envied only people like Mr. Baskerville, or old Harold, both, no doubt, tucked up in their warm beds in the Avenue, awaiting the dawn of another day that would begin with the arrival of the 8.40 at the Woodside 'up' platform.

* * * *

He leaped from his mattress at the sound of a car braking in the street below.

His instincts, sharpened by the weeks he had spent in hiding, were as keen as an animal's, and he slipped noiselessly across the room and opened the door an inch, standing quite still, and listening intently for the sound of Claude's movements below.

It was still dark, but his luminous watch showed him that it was not yet the hour that the lorry was expected. He was about to cross to the window again, and look down into the street, when he heard the terrifying crash of splintering woodwork, then a confused uproar from the landing below.

He had no time to experience terror, or even to tell himself that this was the evader's nightmare, a raid in the middle of the night! Everything, from the first crack of the street door, seemed to happen with the speed of light, and everything he did from then on was dictated by blind instinct.

He heard someone shout: "No, m'sieur, no! Go, see for

yourself!" and then the crash of boots on the lower flight of stairs.

Almost at once there was a volley of shots and a sudden glow of subdued light spreading up from the narrow staircase well, and faintly illuminating the small landing outside his attic.

Into this rectangle of light ran a uniformed man, brandishing a revolver, and as Esme flung open the door something whipped sharply at his right arm.

From below Claude shouted a warning and without being able to distinguish the actual words Esme interpreted his yell as a command to fight his way downstairs.

He did not even remember having picked up the Sten gun but it was here, held in his left hand, with the metal butt pressed hard against his hip.

At the moment the man on the stair fired Esme's finger closed on the trigger, and he fired a full burst without the least attempt to aim. Then, still holding the gun, he ran across the landing and down the stairs into the pool of light, where Claude was standing astride the bodies of two men in black uniforms.

Two yards away, close to the living-room door, was the watchmender. He was sitting with his back to the door frame, his bare feet thrust out at a wide angle.

At the moment of reaching Claude, and before he had fully absorbed the scene on the landing, Esme heard a strange, bumping sound immediately behind him, and he turned to see the body of the man he had killed roll down the short flight of stairs and come to rest at his feet.

He stared at it in amazement, noting its slow, almost graceful progress and he was still staring when Claude caught him by the arm and dragged him down the remaining stairs, into the hall and through the swing doors to the old man's workshop.

The moment they entered the room there was more shouting from the street, and somebody fired a volley through the shop window. The bullets must have smashed into the row of clocks on the shelves behind the counter, for Esme heard a confused metallic clang, but Claude made no comment, maintaining his grip on Esme's sleeve and dragging him on through the door leading to the kitchen, and down a narrow passage into the yard. As they crossed the enclosure he spoke for the first time.

"Reload under the wall and follow me out!"

Esme did as he was told, holding the gun between his knees while he fumbled for the ammunition that was loose in his jacket pocket. He heard Claude unbolt the back gate that led, he remembered, into a covered archway and from thence to a network of alleys, serving the huddle of houses at the back.

"Give me the Sten! Give it to me!" snapped Claude, and tore the gun from Esme, dropping his own automatic to the stones.

Side by side they ran out of the archway and down the first alley to the right, but as they emerged someone came pounding over the cobbles from the direction of the shop-front and Claude suddenly stopped, faced about, and called over his shoulder to Esme.

"The lorry is at the end of the lane ... Martin ... get to him!"

Then followed another burst of firing, the flash of the gun lighting up the dripping walls of the alley, and Esme saw nothing more than that of the fight but dashed on into the darkness ahead, emerging, in less than thirty seconds, on the main road, where he ran full tilt into a vehicle parked right across the mouth of the lane.

The force of the collision winded him and he felt an agonising pain in his shins where they had met the running board. He recoiled from the stationary vehicle but somebody reached out and pulled him into the driving cabin. Instantly, with the door swinging loose, the lorry shot away, twisting this way and that as it took corners at breakneck speed, and headed for the open country.

Slowly, as he recovered from the shock of the impact, Esme was conscious of two other things apart from the painful smart of his bashed shins. One was the ceaseless thresh-thresh of the windscreen wipers, fighting the steady slash of rain, the other a strange, spreading numbness in the upper part of his right arm. Then followed a heavy drowsiness, that seemed to pluck at his senses, preventing him from thinking of anything but sleep.

Everything, he felt, as the lorry rushed forward, was driving him towards sleep, the airlessness of the cabin, the almost hypnotic swish-swish of the windscreen wipers, and the numbness of his arm, that now seemed to be spreading upwards to his brain. He found that he could not even count how many other men were with him in the front of the lorry, and which of them was actually at the wheel.

Presently the turning and twisting of the lorry ceased and it settled down into a steady rush through the rain. Esme was about to ask where they were going, and whether or not Claude was safe in the back, but his drowsiness overcame him and he let his head fall on the shoulder of the man on his left, remembering nothing more until he opened his eyes and looked into the face of a pretty girl about eighteen who was stooping over him and shaking him gently.

"M'sieur . . . Sergeant . . . ! Can you walk . . . ? Must we carry you to the aircraft?"

He sat up quickly, and winced with pain. His left hand shot to the source of pain, the upper part of his right arm, and he discovered that it was heavily bandaged and that he had scarcely any feeling in his right hand. He felt dizzy as he struggled to his feet and the girl put her arm round his waist to steady him.

"We must hurry, m'sieur . . . ! The Anson can only remain a very few minutes!"

It was still dark as they limped together into the open, and it occurred to Esme what a desperately long night it had been. The wind, however, helped to clear his head a little and he said:

"What happened to Claude? Did Claude come with us, in that lorry?"

"No, M'sieur," the girl said very soberly, "Claude was killed last night, and you were lucky to escape yourself! You must take things very quietly, Sergeant. You have lost a great deal of blood from your wound. Lean on me, Sergeant, but hurry. . . . Please hurry!"

Two other figures materialised out of the darkness and the girl called to them. Esme felt himself lifted and carried sedan-fashion across uneven ground. Then, directly ahead, he saw the aircraft, with a few bobbing lights about it and the rain glistening on its fuselage. The girl, now at his elbow, said: "Lift him inside ... no, no, wait ... ! Martin said I must find out about the papers ... !"

Suddenly Esme's brain cleared and he remembered, for a moment or two, all that had happened since he had jumped up from his mattress on hearing the car brake in the street below.

"I've still got the bloody papers," he grumbled, sleepily, "I've got them safe, just where Claude stuck them, and you can tell Claude I'll give his regards to that bloody policeman's daughter, the one that wouldn't play ball the way he wanted to!"

He had forgotten that Claude was dead, and perhaps this was the reason why the girl would not accept his statement about the papers, but tore open his trousers and thrust her hand against his thigh. Her action embarrassed him and he shouted: "Hi, what the hell?" but the girl only made the kind of soothing noise that a busy nurse makes at a bedside, and after running her hand across both thighs, and locating the bulge of plaster, she turned to the men who were lifting him into the aircraft.

"It is in order, he has them safe!"

Then she bent swiftly forward as the men stepped away and planted a kiss on his cheek.

"Bon Voyage, Sergeant!" she whispered, breathlessly.

He noticed then how young and how pretty she was, and he wanted to ask her how she had become mixed in this crazy cloak-and-dagger nonsense, and why she wasn't home and in bed, instead of sloping about the open country, and lifting men into aircraft in the middle of the night.

The roar of the unthrottled engine blotted out further thoughts of her and he said to a man in a windcheater who was sitting close beside him: "I'm bloody cold! Hasn't anyone got flying-kit in this kite?"

"Relax, cobber," said the man, in a strong Australian accent. "You're on your way home, kiddo, so what the hell are you bellyaching about?"

CHAPTER XXIX

Open House

THERE was a brief period, in the summer of 1943, when the war that had already lasted nearly as long as its predecessor was almost forgotten by the people of the Avenue.

This was in the week when the majority of them became, for a few days, at least, a closer-knit community than they had ever been in the past, even during the worst nights of the blitz.

Then, for the first time since the Avenue houses had been built, the people of the big-number end mixed freely with the rump of the Golf links' end, and there was a coming and going between houses, and a glib exchange of Christian names, that belonged more properly to a country village than to a suburb twelve miles from London Stone.

The occasion was the double wedding of two of the Avenue's fighting men, Private Bernard Carver, repatriated after more than eight months in German hospitals, and Flight Sergeant Esme Fraser, recently back from the dead, and due to be decorated for exceptional devotion to duty.

The idea of a double wedding was Pippa's, but the idea of converting the weddings into an Avenue occasion was Harold's and that of his friend, Jim Carver. In the event there was no double wedding in the real sense, for Esme was a divorcee, and he and Judy could not be married in Shirley Church, like Pippa and Bernard, but this circumstance made little or no difference to the main event, for the plan to invite at least half the Avenue to a combined wedding breakfast in the gardens of numbers Twenty and Twenty-Two, had taken

438

firm root in Harold's heart, and fired the imagination of both Pippa and Jim. Thus, the marriage of one couple in church, and the other almost simultaneously in a register office, at Croydon, did not even complicate the arrangements.

The Avenue gathered for the Church wedding but toasts were held back until the smaller family party, who had been attending Esme's and Judy's wedding, returned to the Avenue soon after midday. Then the neighbours began to crowd into Numbers Twenty and Twenty-Two, where the first thing they witnessed was a lively little ceremony sponsored by Harold and Jim.

This was the symbolic demolition of the highboard fence that had separated the two verandahs and gardens for more then thirty years.

There were, of course, identical fences between all the houses in the crescent. They were constructed of thin, overlapping boards, seven feet high at the verandah ends, and shortening to four foot where they had passed the tiny tool-sheds, and outside W.C.s, to join the paling fence separating back gardens from alley and Nursery.

For some time now the fence between Numbers Twenty and Twenty-Two had been no more than a token boundary. As long ago as the 'twenties', when Judy had been the playmate of Esme, and living on very friendly terms with Eunice Godbeer, his mother, there had been a swinging plank, held in place by a single nail. Later, when Jim moved into Number Twenty-Two to share quarters with Harold, this plank had been removed altogether and chopped up for firewood, but the fence as a whole remained and up to the outbreak of war it had been given an annual coat of creosote on each side by Harold and Jack Strawbridge respectively.

The notion of pulling it down did not occur to Harold or Jim until the week of the weddings.

He and Harold were sitting in the kitchen of Number Twenty-Two, working out the seating arrangements for the event while Louise, Edith Clegg, Jean Hargreaves, and Mrs. Hooper, of Number Six, were hard at work in the adjoining kitchen, sorting the combined resources of the Avenue in preparation for the wedding breakfast.

Almost everybody had contributed something to the feast.

Tins of spam were much in evidence, and there were even three or four hoarded tins of sliced peaches and apricots. There were the ingredients of scores of pasties, sausage rolls, and cakes, two dozen eggs (the product of Mrs. Hooper's visit to her sister on a farm, near Penshurst) and a limited supply of gin, rum, and minerals, procured, somehow or other, by the obliging Mr. Saunders, who had succeeded Archie as proprietor of the corner shop.

The four women had formed themselves into a kind of committee under the chairmanship of Louise Strawbridge, and the men were content to leave them to organise the food and to concentrate upon the problem of accommodating nearly one hundred people in a garden strip measuring about twenty-five yards by ten yards.

Chairs were to be had in plenty, for these, plus two long trestle tables, had been borrowed from the Delhi Road Church Institute, but Jim said that when the tables were erected, and the chairs arranged around them, there wouldn't be room to pass the bottle, much less to jive, as his daughters, Fetch and Carry obviously intended to jive with their American friends from the Manor Wood depot.

Harold said: "It's a pity we can't have it in two gardens, old man!"

"Well, and why can't we?" asked Jim, suddenly.

"There's the fence!"

"Then to hell with the fence!" retorted Jim.

They sat smiling at one another for a few seconds, both instantly appreciating the enormous significance of the proposal.

For years now, it seemed, they had been ducking to and fro through the narrow gap between the two main supports of the fence, but the idea of removing the barrier altogether had never occurred to either of them. It did now and it appealed to them immensely, for each felt that in some way the removal of the fence would cement a friendship forged in the fires of war and ensure that this friendship survived the war. Never again, now that Esme and Judy were marrying, would Numbers Twenty and Twenty-Two be two houses, indeed, if one thought about it they had ceased to be two dwellings on the day that Harold had made his first tentative suggestion that Jim should move in and keep him company until Eunice returned from Torquay.

Now Eunice would never return, and Harold supposed, rather glumly, that once Hitler had crossed into the shades in pursuit of Kaiser Wilhelm and everyone had made a victory bonfire of their blackouts, Jim would return to his own home, Esme would make a home of his own somewhere, and he, Harold, would be left in lonely isolation at Number Twenty-Two. No wonder that the idea of pulling down the fence struck him as a very happy one indeed.

Jim, for his part, no longer regarded himself as a lodger in Harold's house. Ever since Bernard's return the accommodation in Number Twenty had been almost as cramped as it had been when all the children were growing up and all his family had lived at home. Louise and Jack occupied the front bedroom, Pippa had the back bedroom, the twin girls slept on camp beds in the parlour, and Bernard was temporarily accommodated among Jim's yellowing pamphlets in the little room over the porch. There was no place for him any more, for even if the twins married Louise would need an extra room when Boxer came home, and would doubtless like to keep a spare room for any other members of the family who visited her after they had married and moved away, so he too thought the idea of destroying the fence a very sensible one, and they at once got down to practicalities.

"We could do it right away," he told Harold, "it's rotten right through at the far end and only needs a pushover!"

"No," said Harold, his brown eyes sparkling behind his thick-lensed spectacles, "let's make a kind of ceremony of it! Let's do it tomorrow, in front of everyone!"

Jim at once saw what he was getting at and approved. It matched his own feelings about the Avenue since Churchill had taken charge of the war. The levelling of the fence would be symbolic of the unity of the British, of the sinking of party differences and social distinctions, and of the Avenue's implacable determination to scorch German fascism from the face of the earth!

"Very well," he agreed, "we'll do it before the toasts, and we'll make a proper old issue of it!"

And so they did, watched by a large and enthusiastic

audience, for by the time they had returned home with the second bridal couple, the house and garden of number Twenty was teeming with guests, and Pippa, with Bernard standing shyly beside her, had as much as she could do to keep the party from beginning prematurely, and was glad to step aside in favour of Judy, who, as a sergeant-instructor in the W.A.A.F and an ex-marshal of Pony Clubs, was much more at home with exuberance en masse.

The symbolic levelling of the fence, with Jim swinging a 14-lb. sledge hammer at the verandah end, and Harold (assisted by an uplifted Mr. Baskerville) at the nursery end, was a spectacular opening to a party that, from its outset, proved the most joyful and uninhibited in the Avenue's history.

Not even on Armistice Day, 1918, or subsequently, when almost every thoroughfare in the suburb celebrated its VE Day by a communal meal in the open street, did the Avenue let its hair so far down as it did upon this occasion.

This may, of course, have been partly due to the presence of Mitch and Orrie, the American boy friends of the younger Carver twins, for it was they who provided the music, and the howl of their amplified records could be heard as far away as Cawnpore Road, but Jim and Harold preferred to think that the success of the party lay in the genuine goodwill of neighbouring families, people who shared their own joy in the miraculous return of not one, but two prospective bridegrooms!

'The Unlikes', of course, had always been popular along the crescent, ever since the days when they had enlivened the district, with their games of string-and-parcel and knocking-down-ginger, but the sudden popularity of Esme was more difficult to understand, for he had always been regarded as an aloof young man, and had never made many friends in the Avenue. Perhaps, Harold reflected, people like the Cleggs, the Baskervilles, and the Westermans, recognised in the story of Esme and Judy a real-life fairy-tale to which, as yet, there was no happy ending, or perhaps they simply identified him with the R.A.F., that had performed such wonders in 1940, and was now engaged in giving the Germans regular draughts of their own medicine.

Jim watched the neighbours congratulating the couples, as Esme, Judy, Pippa and Bernard stood close together on the verandah of Number Twenty-Two, and it seemed to him that here, at long last, was the first real evidence he had ever had that his old dream of a social millennium might be achieved during his lifetime! These people, and their sons and daughters overseas, were surely demonstrating the ascendancy of the common man over power groups and despots everywhere, and when at last final victory was won they would enter upon their reward—a sane, just, class-free world!

The sun shone brilliantly but Jim saw that there was a far more subtle radiance at work in the two gardens. Baskerville, for instance, was actually listening to someone, and Westerman, for once, was not obsessed with the necessity of turning every remark into a feeble joke. Instead they were both listening attentively to Hargreaves, the ex-fire chief, who was commenting on a sheaf of snapshots that featured his six months' old son, Winston.

Jim marvelled at his audience's patience and its ability to assume interest, for not only were Baskerville and Westerman notorious talkers, but both had already reared families of their own!

Down against the loganberry bush that straggled along the fence dividing Number Twenty and Number Eighteen, dear old Edith Clegg was persuading Mrs. Hooper, and Mrs. Dodge, of Number Six and Ninety-One, to try yet another of Louise's sausage rolls. One would not have imagined, Jim thought, as he studied their animated faces, that each of these women had lost an only child in this war, and that for them there could be no hope of weddings, or a tribe of grandchildren in the future. They could have been forgiven, he thought, for looking glum and envious, but instead they looked gay and eager. As he watched, he saw them bite into rolls and smile at Edith, and he realised that Edith too was remembering young Hooper of the *Royal Oak*, and young Albert Dodge, the paratrooper, and was making a special effort to draw these two women into the community of the living.

Jim saw that old Mrs. Coombes was there, recounting her interminable story of the night that the bomb had disposed of all but her in Numbers Thirteen, Fifteen and Seventeen. Everyone along the Avenue must have heard that story by now, but Mr. Burridge, of Number Ten was listening attentively to it, and plying the leathery old girl with gin as she told it, illustrating her life-preserving dive in to the stair-cupboard by broad sweeps of her hands.

Mrs. Barnmeade was there, whose father-in-law, the punctilious A.R.P. warden, had been the Avenue's first casualty as long ago as the phoney war period. Everyone seemed to be there, everyone except Elaine Frith, Esme's first wife, who could hardly be expected to put in an appearance, any more than could his son, Archie, for Archie, Jim recalled with a pang, was still doing time in a West Country county gaol, just as Boxer (who would have enjoyed an occasion like this so much!) was doing a different kind of time, somewhere in Germany.

Jim's thoughts were interrupted by the tentative approach of Edgar Frith, who had travelled all the way from Wales, accompanied by his wife, Frances, and Esme's little daughter, Barbara, in order to give Pippa away.

Edgar was delighted to find himself related to big Jim Carver. He had never forgotten the genial hospitality Jim and Harold had shown him at Number Twenty-Two, on the occasion of his trip to town with the Sullen Cupid.

Cupid had now been sold, and Edgar was the richer by two thousand guineas, as well as the reputation for 'spotting a right buy' that he had always craved, but he had already set aside a substantial part of the money to install Pippa, and her disabled husband, in a little garage on the Caernarvon Road.

The project, which he regarded as a kind of dowry, was still very much in the air, but Edgar thought that Pippa would soon be able to convince Bernard that it was an excellent chance to overcome his handicap before the war ended, and men came swarming out of the forces to compete with him in civilian life. After all, Bernard, so he understood, was an experienced motor mechanic, and there should be money to be made in garages once this tiresome petrol-rationing was abolished.

Edgar, however, had not approached Jim with the idea of

enlisting his support in the garage plan, but simply to ask him whether he thought it would be bad taste to convey a message to Esme Fraser from his ex-wife, Elaine, of Number Forty-Three.

"It's put me in rather a spot, Carver," he complained. "You see, Frances and I had to call on the girl to show her little Barbara, and she'll be remarrying herself very soon, or so I understand. It was all rather awkward, but well . . . I did promise that I'd try and buttonhole Esme, and give him her message!"

"What was the message?" growled Jim, for he still disliked and distrusted Elaine.

"Oh, just that she wishes him the best, you know," said Edgar, more cheerfully. "She's an odd girl . . . always has been . . . but I think she really means this, in fact, I'm quite sure she does!"

"Well, I suppose there's no harm in passing that kind of message," said Jim, doubtfully. "What do you think, Mrs. Frith?"

He addressed Frances, whom he had met for the first time that day. He liked her, recognising at once the enormous influence she exercised over this pleasant but rather dithery little chap, and comparing her very favourably to her predecessor, Esther, whose body he had helped to dig out of Number Seventeen more than two years ago.

"I'm afraid Edgar hasn't told you everything," said Frances, with a smile. "The fact is, Elaine is here now, and she'd rather like to wish both Esme and Judy good luck!"

"I don't see her," said Jim, looking round and frowning. He had never forgiven Elaine for associating with Archie, a civilian, while her husband was serving in the Forces, and he now found himself irritated by her brashness in gate-crashing the wedding breakfast of her former husband.

"Well, not *here*, exactly, but over there, at the bend in the alley," said Frances. "Would you like *me* to ask Esme?"

"Yes, I would," said Jim, gratefully, and watched her cross the lawn and whisper something into Esme's ear. He saw Esme's look of surprise and saw him turn to Judy, who smiled and nodded. "She *would*, of course", thought Jim, watching very closely. "There's not a spark of malice in

Judy!" He remembered now his favourite daughter's apathetic face and manner during the period that followed her sudden switch from a job at Boots', in the Lower Road, to the new and, to him, improbable job at a riding stable, near Keston. That must have been about the time that Esme had jilted her for Elaine, and had almost broken the kid's heart, but he had been years discovering this and had not even heard about it until shortly after Esme had been reported missing, and Judy had told him everything about her childhood love for the boy.

It was strange, he thought, how long it took a man to find out important things about people, even when they were one's own flesh and blood.

He saw both Esme and Judy detach themselves from the knot of people round the lawn and follow Frances down to the back gate and out of sight along the narrow alley that ran between the blocks of houses.

Then Carry's G.I., Orrie, switched the music off, and Harold called upon everyone to fill their glasses and asked if someone would propose a toast to the happy couples before they set out on their honeymoon.

"Lord bless us, are they going on their honeymoon as a foursome?" shouted Mr. Westerman, unable to resist such an opportunity.

There was a burst of laughter, and renewed laughter when Harold replied, quite seriously, "No, no! Of course not! They're going off in different directions!"

Then, to his relief, Jim saw Esme and Judy return, and at once stepped down on to the lawn and told Harold that he would propose the joint toast if that was what Harold wanted.

It was just what Harold did want, for he knew himself to be a hopeless public speaker, so Jim plodded back to the verandah of Twenty-Two, climbed on a chair, clapped his hands, and shouted for silence in his best open-air-rally voice.

Ten years ago, Jim Carver would have improved the occasion by airing his views on the state of the world. Two years ago he might have introduced into the toast a few comments on the activities of Government contract profiteers, and the danger of bad faith with our ally, Soviet

Russia, but since the day that he had mourned his twins, and had seen one of them miraculously restored to him, he had gone a long way towards acquiring a political tolerance that his committee would have labelled 'typically bourgeois' in pre-war campaigning days.

It was enough for him, for the moment at all events, to rejoice that Bernard had found a girl who would love and care for him, in spite of his grave disablement, that Judy had also found and claimed the man she loved, and that poor old Boxer was out of the war, and safe behind German wire, where he would have to stay whether he liked it or not until the Third Reich was hammered to pieces and he could return home again.

In view of all this he contented himself with a conventional little speech, wishing the two couples great happiness, and a safe passage to victory. Just before he stepped down, however, he caught the eye of Mrs. Hooper of Number Six, and on the spur of the moment he added. "There's just one other thing I would like to say, ladies and gentlemen! In proposing a toast to my son, Bernard, my daughter, Judith, and to their respective bride and groom, I think it only right to couple with it the name of Bernard's brother, known to most of you as 'Boxer' and with the people of this Avenue who have already given their lives in the struggle to sit upon that unmitigated little scoundrel! I won't mention all their names, for this isn't a day for sadness, but I would like all the people here who have lost anyone to know that we do sometimes think of them, and remember them with gratitude!"

There was a moment's silence when he stepped off the chair and Mrs. Hooper's eyes met those of Mrs. Dodge. Harold, listening intently from the far end of the garden, began to think of Eunice, and how she would have revelled in all this sociability on her doorstep, but he recollected himself in time and raised his glass, calling loudly on brides and grooms, and looking encouragingly at Esme for a response. Esme realised that something was expected of him as Judy squeezed his hand, so he cleared his throat and said:

"Thank you, Jim, thank you on behalf of my wife, myself and Bernard and Pippa here. When I was in France not long ago I met a lot of people who reminded me very much of the kind of people here today. One of them actually knew this Avenue, he'd lodged just round the corner, in Cawnpore Road. He was killed, helping to get me back, and I mention him only because it seems to me that he was typical of all the people over there who haven't given up, any more than we gave up at the time of Dunkirk. In saying 'thank you' for all the good wishes we've had showered on us today, I'd like to propose a toast to the people I've learned to believe in since all this uproar and muddle started. I'd like you to drink to ordinary people in roads like this all over the world!"

He looked at Judy and smiled as Jim, delighted by the unexpected context of Esme's speech, shouted: 'Hear, hear!' at the top of his voice, and came striding across the lawn to shake his son-in-law's hand.

He did so joyfully, as though, for the first time, he was welcoming a fellow-crusader into the family, someone whom the war had managed to convert from a moody, dreamy, youth into a man with whom he had affinity. He did not arrive at this conclusion at once, for he was a slow, deliberate thinker, who needed time to digest impressions, but as he slapped Esme on the shoulder, and smiled into Judy's radiant face, it did cross his mind that his daughter must have been far more discerning than he to have recognised Esme for the kind of person he was all those years ago, when they had played together as children.

The thought was like a dash of sugar on a flame, the flame of faith that was already burning so brightly today and the flame shot up, warming him through and through.

"By God!" he said to himself, as they began to sort themselves out for the usual Avenue send-off, "By God, but things are beginning to work out after all! In spite of all that drag between the wars, in spite of Chamberlain and his umbrella, and all the sickening inertia these people showed up to the moment of Dunkirk, things are really beginning to work out and give a chap something to hope for in the future!"

* * * *

Esme had not really cared for the idea of a reception and

Avenue garden party but on leaving hospital, with his wound healed, he had realised that a get-together was important to Jim and Harold and had therefore raised no objections when Judy sounded him on the matter.

Nothing mattered now that the weight of fear had been lifted from him, and he had the additional satisfaction of knowing that he had, almost against his will, at last achieved something useful. Whatever happened now he would always be able to recall the terse congratulations of the grey-haired Air Commodore in M.I., who had interviewed him in Whitehall on the day he was discharged from hospital.

"I've been asked to tell you from a somewhat higher level that those drawings, and the information about them that you dictated in hospital, were worth the risks you took to get them out, Sergeant," the old boy had said. "We knew a good deal of what was going on over there, of course, but this is the first real confirmation we've had, and you seem to have put up a good show—in my opinion, a damned good show! I daresay you'll hear more of it, but in the meantime we'd like to regrade you, and have you join us here after your leave. Would you care for that?"

On learning that he was being asked to join a Branch of Military Intelligence for special duties, and work from London in liaison with the Free French forces, Esme said that he would like it very much indeed. For one thing it would mean the end of operational flying, and for another it was certain to prove interesting. He filled out a number of forms, passed through a couple of interviews, and went out to 'phone the news to Judy, who had by that time returned to Cornwall.

She had come up to London on a forty-eight-hour pass the moment that she learned he was home and when he saw her walk shyly into the ward his heart had nearly burst with tenderness.

She had bent over the bed and kissed him, not in the way that she had kissed him when they had rediscovered one another on Manor Island, or later during their unsatisfactory courtship when they were stationed hundreds of miles apart but gently and firmly, as though she was sure that this time there were to be no more delays and separations, and no more frantic rendezvous arranged by 'phone or wire, but the permanence for which she had yearned all her life and a certainty of at last being able to prove herself capable of translating her dream into warm, substantial reality.

Esme had never thought of Judy as being a pretty girl, 'elfish' was the word he had sometimes used to sum up her small, regular features, light brown hair, and mild, brown eyes, but she looked very pretty now, with high colour under the tan of her cheeks, and eyes alight with joy.

He took stock of her anew. Ever since the day, now eighteen months behind them, when they had made their mutual discovery opposite the old Manor he had valued her warm companionship and the sense of repose that she brought him, but not until this moment had he felt drawn to her physically as compellingly as he had once been drawn to Elaine. She was, he decided, not only sweet, loyal and utterly reliable, but exciting in a way that she had never seemed exciting in the past. All his adult life he had been searching for the lady in the tower, a woman whose image he had conjured from the pages of *Idylls of the King*, in his grandmother's library at Kensington. Elaine's dark good looks, her white skin, and possibly her elusiveness throughout his adolescence, must have blinded him to the presence of the real princess whose tower was next door.

Judy had always played a part in his dreams, but it had been a walking-on part, the role of shield-bearer. Now, without trumpets or drums, she had moved into the centre of the stage, and had suddenly become the woman he would continue to weave his dreams around, a woman, who, so unlike Elaine, would regard such inclusion as the highest compliment he could pay her.

Lying back on his pillows after she had left, and studying the butter-coloured distemper of the ward ceiling he felt happier, and more confident than he had ever felt in his life. The little probationer, who had returned from showing Judy out, came over and collected his tea-tray and looked down on him with a sly smile.

"Well?" she said, "when's the happy day, Sergeant?"

"As soon as I can get to hell out of here," he told her with a grin.

*   *   *   *   *

They drove on into the sunset, nursing the noisy engine of the old Ford Eight that he had bought from the warrant officer in the next bed at hospital. They were heading, ultimately, for Maud Somerton's place, in Devon, but as it was late afternoon when they left the Avenue after the reception they did not expect to get more than half-way that night.

They said little for there was not much need to talk. They had known one another for so long and they had no new confidences to exchange and certainly no necessity to release the pressure of excitement with small talk. They had done with small talk a long time ago, and they could say all they wanted to say, for the moment at least, by an exchange of glances, or a slight movement on the part of Judy on the worn, leather seat beside him.

Towards twilight they came to the fringe of the New Forest and turned off the main road, near Romsey. Presently they came to a small, half-timbered hotel, called *The Hart* and Esme got out and went into the lobby.

He came out a moment later and nodded and Judy took her bag and followed him inside. They were shown up to a large, low-ceilinged room, with a large bay window, looking over the forest.

"Just for one night?" asked the old man, who had followed them in.

"That's right," Esme told him and then, as a spot of confetti flung by Edith detached itself from Judy's collar. "You might as well know! We're on our honeymoon!"

"You don't have to tell me that," said the old man, solemnly. "I bin a Boots best part of me life, sir!"

They all laughed but without embarrassment, and Esme gave him half a crown.

"Thank you, sir, I'll bring the rest of the stuff up right away," he said, and left, gently closing the door.

Judy sat down to comb the confetti from her hair and for a moment he watched her from the bed. When she saw in the mirror's reflection that he was watching, she suddenly stopped combing.

"Come and see if you can get it out," she said.

He got up, crossed the room and stood closely behind her,

letting his hands rest on her shoulders and then slip down and meet across her breasts.

He felt her tremble slightly as she said:

"We've been lucky, Esme darling, so terribly lucky, all the way through!"

"Does that make you anxious?" he asked, remembering her forebodings on the occasion that should have been their wedding night nearly a year ago.

"No . . . no, it doesn't, Esme, not any more, not now we're actually married! I feel as if we'll always be lucky after this about children, jobs, each other—everything! I suppose that's because today somehow rounds everything off and gives a kind of *shape* to my life, as far as you're concerned in it anyway! Can you understand that, Esme darling? *Can* you?"

He nodded into the mirror and lowered his head so that his cheek touched her hair. They remained thus until the old man, returning with the baggage, came bumping along the corridor and paused outside the door, announcing his presence with an exaggerated cough.

. . . .

Two hundred miles away to the north-west the other Avenue honeymooners were sitting side by side in the dining-car of the Holyhead train. On the same express, but several coaches away, were Edgar, Frances, and little Barbara, now fast asleep on Frances' shoulder.

The steward had just served the second course, pale, grisly meat, swimming in thin gravy. Pippa, pulling a wry face, leaned over Bernard to cut it for him.

"I wouldn't bother," said Bernard, grinning, "it doesn't look worth it! What did we come in here for? I'm not hungry, not after all that stuff Louise dished up at the reception."

"That was hours ago," said Pippa, and then, cheerfully, "I expect the dessert will be better."

"I can cope with the dessert," said Bernard. "From now on Pip concentrate on the spoon vittles! They stop me feeling so bloody helpless!"

She was sorry then that they had come into the diner. She hated him to be reminded of the difficulties of his everyday existence, of his inability to tie knots, to do up buttons, to cut up his food.

They had not been so fortunate as Esme and Judy in arriving at a readjustment, for the roots of their association were nearer the surface and their future was more uncertain.

He had needed very patient handling during the first weeks of his return. She found that she could cope with his disability if she avoided making an issue of it. She encouraged him to take the army physiotherapists seriously during his bi-weekly visits to the hospital. She had even managed to escape from the camouflage-netting shed, in order to travel to and fro with him, but she had much more difficulty with a hurt inside him that had little to do with his empty sleeve, or the limp that had resulted from the severed muscles of his leg.

He spoke very little during those first days of his return and everybody at Number Twenty went out of their way to avoid mentioning Boxer, although it seemed strange to them to have Bernard about the house without hearing Boxer's laugh, or the thump of his boots on the stairs.

Pippa took Bernard for one or two walks across Shirley Hills and sometimes they went to the cinema in the evening. They discovered, however, that they were slightly embarrassed when they were alone together and it was not until he had been back in the Avenue for nearly a month that Pippa made any progress with him.

She was lying awake in the porch room one night, when she heard him come out of his room and go downstairs.

She slipped a raincoat over her nightdress and went after him, with the idea of brewing some tea, but when she looked into the kitchen and dining-room he was not there. She thought at first that he must have gone for a walk, then she saw the glow of his cigarette at the bottom of the garden.

She called: "Shall I make some tea, Bernard?"

He came up to the verandah and flicked the cigarette-end over the fence into Number Eighteen.

"No, Pip, I'm okay! I just couldn't sleep. Go back to bed, kid."

She hesitated, standing just inside the french windows but he turned his back on her and deliberately lit another cigarette. In the flare of the match she saw that his face was drawn and blank. She made up her mind, stepped out on to the verandah and stood close to him.

"It's Boxer, isn't it, Bernard?"

"Oh, for Christ's sake . . . !" he began explosively but checked himself, reached out and patted her shoulder. "I'm sorry, Pip! There's damn all anyone can do about it! I'll be okay, only give me time, for God's sake give me time to get used to it!"

The shoulder pat and the manner it was administered made her feel desperate. She realised that if she was to achieve anything at all with him she must take the lead now—this instant. No amount of time would make any difference to him, not so long as he was left floundering about on his own with his thoughts pounding the treadmill of memory.

"You'll have to talk about it some time, Berni," she said, firmly. "You might as well start now and tell me! If you only knew it I'm the person who can help, because I'm the only one who has ever thought of you and Boxer as two persons and not one!"

He looked closely at her then, holding her in his glance for nearly a minute. Finally, he said:

"That was the one time that I left him to cope on his own, the *one* time, Pip! He wouldn't come away when we began pulling back but just stood there, firing into the battery! It was so bloody silly when you think of it. He couldn't have been firing *at* anything, there was so much smoke! Then, when I copped it, it was him who found *me* and carried me about for hours. I don't know how the hell he did it under those conditions but he did, somehow, and he got tourniquets and dressings on me somewhere or other. I wouldn't be here now but for that, they told me so in the Jerry hospital. Then, I began thinking what it meant. It meant that he could have got clean away, without any trouble . . . almost everyone in our troop did, you know, but old Boxer couldn't have tried to get back to the beach. He just picked me up and walked slap through it all, right into the Jerry lines and gave himself up! It's so damned funny that he should have done that, after me turning my back on him the way I did!"

"Why do you feel so bad about it," she asked quietly. "Why aren't you proud of him? You ought to be!"

He shook his head impatiently.

"I'm telling you, it was only a minute or so after I'd turned my back on him! Don't you see, Pip? I was fed up to the back teeth with him! I remembered everything you'd said to me, that I couldn't go on and on looking out for him the way I'd always done! Then he went and did a thing like that for me! I can't get that out of my head!"

She was silent a moment, considering. "You're looking at it all wrong, Bernard," she said at length. "Sit down and listen to me. You've got to start looking at it the way it really is, and you've got to begin right here and now!"

She pushed him towards the deck chair that stood against the boundary fence and took a seat facing him on the low railing separating the tiny verandah from the garden.

"You being hit like that was the luckiest thing that ever happened to Boxer," she said. "It gave him the one chance he's ever had of being someone, of doing something on his own and out of his own head, instead of just something you told him to do! Now then—listen Berni—how do you know that it hasn't done him a tremendous amount of good? How can you tell whether he's the same person any more, now that he hasn't got you to do all his thinking for him? You just turn that over for a minute or two while I go in and make some tea!"

She left him sitting there looking out over the moonlit Nursery. When she returned with the tea he was still there and she noticed that his cigarette was carrying an inch and a half of ash.

"Well?"

Suddenly he threw away the butt and sat forward.

"It adds up!" he said. "It adds up, Pip!" He got up. "Turn on the dining-room light a minute!"

She put down the tea and went back into the room to switch on the light. He took a much creased letter from his battledress pocket and spread it out on his knees.

"There's a bit here from one of his letters that Dad showed me. It puzzled me Pip but now it doesn't. Listen: *'. . . it isn't as bad as you think being here, I've got a new*

name. I'm "The Gaffer." . . . ' What exactly is a *'gaffer'*, Pip,
I always thought it was some kind of boss?"

"It is," she told him, "it's a name they sometimes give the
head of a gang of workmen, up north."

"The *head*, you say?"

"Yes. A kind of foreman, who gives the orders!"

He began to show excitement. "That's what I thought it
meant, but it seemed so funny old Boxer being a gaffer and
giving orders. D'you really think. . . ."

"I've always thought that you never gave him a chance,
Bernard," she said, "so what's the point of torturing yourself
for the one you couldn't help giving him? Here, drink your
tea, and then go back to bed and to sleep, silly!"

He was silent for a while, slowly stirring his cup, then
laying down the spoon and lifting it to his lips. When he had
emptied it he said:

"Do you really want us to get married, Pip? Are you quite
sure you aren't doing it because I'm like this now?"

"That's right," she said with a smile, "now begin worrying
about that side of it! At least I can do something about
that!"

She did too, for afterwards he was much easier to manage
and she soon discovered that by far the best way of handling
him was to bully him.

Louise would sometimes hear her teaching him to reload
his safety razor with one hand and would smile and nod to
herself, as Pippa's voice came from the bathroom—"Now
then, you'll only drop it if you scoop it towards you, stupid!
Press your thumb against the handle and wedge the razor
against the back of the basin. . . . Here, let me show you . . .
like *that!*"

Or when she was in his bedroom, teaching him to knot his
tie—"Hold the thin end against your chest with your elbow,
silly, then flick the broad end over and through . . . *that's*
better, you'll get the hang of it in no time, so long as you
think and aren't in such a dreadful hurry all the time!"

"She's quite wonderful," Louise said to herself. "How
lucky we are to have her here and so much in love with
him!"

It wasn't always as easy as this, of course. Sometimes his

helplessness would infuriate him and he would fling things about in a rage, weeping with frustration at his seeming inability to perform the kind of task that people with two hands perform unconsciously. Then she would suddenly stop bullying him and adopt different tactics, talking to him as a patient mother soothes a highly-strung child; "Steady, Berni; all right, let's have a bit of a breather and then tackle it again. There's absolutely *no hurry*, dearest! Just relax, and let's find out exactly where we went wrong!"

Slowly but appreciably she made progress, better and more spectacular progress than the professional physiotherapists were making at the hospital. Jim watched her sometimes out of the corner of his eye, marvelling at her skill and limitless patience and Louise watched too, her heart swelling with love for this tall, sallow, ungainly girl, whose devotion was like something out of a romantic book or film, and not at all the kind of thing one stumbled across in everyday life along the Avenue.

The crisis, for both of them, was delayed until the third week of their honeymoon when they were alone in the chalet that Edgar had rented for them among the sandhills, near Rhosneigr.

Edgar had pushed on in secret with his plans for 'the little garage' but he decided that there was no necessity to hurry the young couple, for Bernard had been granted a month's demobilisation leave and was already in receipt of his disability pension and back pay.

The Army medical people had recommended plenty of sea-bathing as likely to be beneficial to the muscles of his injured leg and Bernard, much to his surprise, found that he could swim almost as well with one arm as he had been able to do with two.

Every morning, rain or shine, he and Pippa ran down to the beach and plunged into the bay, shouting and laughing in the shallow water, and splashing one another like two town children on holiday. Then they would swim out into deeper water and Bernard would roll over and do a series of porpoise dives, exhulting in an element where his handicap no longer existed.

One morning, when they had been enjoying themselves like

this for half an hour, a sudden shower of rain drove them inshore to retrieve their single bathing towel, and Pippa, leaping from the water, shouted: "Race you to the towel, Berni!"

She was long-legged and very fleet, and in the exhilaration of the moment she completely forgot about his stiff leg, and raced up to the chalet, where she had dried herself and peeled off her costume by the time he had joined her.

"Here, Slowcoach," she said, laughing, and threw him the towel as he climbed the three steps into the chalet. He grabbed at it but missed, and as he bent to retrieve it he misjudged his distance striking his forehead a sharp blow against the corner of the awning rail.

It might have been the familiar ache in his leg, awakened by the sprint, the sharp pain of the blow, or the realisation that even a simple act like reaching down for a towel was now distorted into a problem. It might have been any one of these things coming after months of pain and anxiety, but whatever it was he screamed and rushed into the chalet, slamming the door. A few minutes later Pippa found him on his knees, sobbing into a cushion, his body twisted with a distress that could find no other relief but in the helpless sobbing of a child.

She took the towel and gently dried his shoulders, saying nothing until his body ceased to shake and he remained there, kneeling, his face buried in the cushion.

It was some time before she could trust herself to speak. When her own tears ceased to flow she whispered: "Better now, Berni darling?"

He kept his face turned away from her but he could not conceal his scars and she saw, with infinite compassion, the ugly, puckered knot three inches below his left shoulder. She looked at it intently and her glance travelled down to the wasted calf, pitted wih craters of grafted flesh.

She touched him lightly. "You don't need to worry, Berni, there's only me here. Don't be ashamed, Berni darling! I wonder it hasn't happened long before, it was bound to, you know and it can only do you good!"

He still kept his face averted from her so she laid aside the towel and dropped on her knees, throwing her arms round his shoulders and straining him to her. They remained thus for more than a minute. Then, still not looking at her, he said:

"It makes everything so bloody lopsided, Pip. It's something you just can't explain to anyone, not even to a doctor!"

"You don't have to explain it to anyone," she told him and laying her cheek against his shoulders she kissed the stump of his arm again and again.

At the touch of her lips he turned suddenly and took her face in his hand, staring down at it and reading in her eyes a reflection of his own misery and deprivation.

"It's worse when you forget, Pip! You wouldn't think you could forget but you do, and when something makes you remember again it's like facing it all over again!"

"It'll get better, Berni dear. You'll stop forgetting and stop remembering. It'll be like a scar that you got when you were a baby, something that's there but is now simply a part of you!"

He wanted more than he had ever wanted anything to be reassured and convinced.

"How can you know that, Pip? How can you be sure of it, without having been carved about, like me?"

"I was sure that you weren't dead, Berni."

He nodded. "That's so! Pop and Louise told me about that! What made you so sure? How is it that you've always known about me and about Boxer?"

She smiled and shook her head: "I can't tell you that, Bernard. There just aren't the right words to explain a thing like that, but I always *have* known, haven't I? So why can't you take everything I tell you about yourself and about 'us' on trust? Why don't you trust me, for instance, if I can tell you what's the best thing for us to do right now?"

"What is the best thing, Pip?"

"To start working, Berni! To start working now, today!"

"You mean that garage your father's always hinting about?"

"Why not. Why ever not? That's something you *can* do, Berni and if it isn't wrong to borrow from banks why should it be wrong to borrow from people like Mummy and Edgar, people who haven't actually fought in the war, but want to feel that they're helping the people who have?"

He got to his feet, picked up the towel and stood near the window looking out over the sea. Watching him she saw his hand open and shut. Then, when he turned back to her, she saw that he was smiling, with the tears still wet on his cheeks.

His voice, so tremulous a moment before, was now level and assured. He said:

"Okay, Pip! If you say it's right then it *is* right! Make some coffee and we'll hop the next 'bus to the mainland and see about it!"

It was as though the magic of her faith had swept like a beam into the darkest corners of his mind and she saw with joy that the battle was almost won, that from now on there would be fewer and fewer moody silences, that ultimately he must come to regard the past as the past, without the power to sour present and future. He threw her the towel and went into the bedroom, whistling.

She stood up rubbing her neck and called to him.

"We're out of milk, we haven't fetched it from the kiosk! I'll go and get it now!"

She went out under the awning and began to descend the steps to the beach. Then she stopped, throwing back her head and laughing.

"What's the joke?" he called through the open shutter.

She came back into the chalet and stood in the doorway, still laughing.

"I was going to the kiosk for the milk! Like this . . . in just a bathing cap!"

CHAPTER XXX

Wolf Hunt

THE taxi set down Elaine at the foot of the steep ramp that led up to the gates of the County Gaol.

She looked up at the red-brick walls that seemed immensely high from where she stood and then at the iron-studded gates, with the little wicket gate cut in the main door. She wondered if one simply rang the bell, as though seeking admission to an ordinary house, or whether somebody now watching from a window would come out and check on credentials, before permitting her to cross the threshold.

Now that she was actually here, and standing outside the gaol she was a little scared by the occasion. She had never been so near to a prison before, indeed, she did not recall ever having seen a prison, except on the cinema screen. Her knowledge of prisons, and of prison customs, was therefore confined to what she had learned from American films. Hundreds of men, she remembered, milled about the big yards in loose jackets and caps with big peaks. From time to time they were chivvied by men carrying guns, and in every film that she had seen about prisons the inmates spent their time hatching plots to escape and eventually did escape, against a background of wild confusion, the crackle of fire-arms and the blare of sirens.

Standing at the foot of the ramp, and warmed by the afternoon sun, Elaine would not have been much surprised to see something like this happen before her eyes; instead, a deep silence brooded over the building, so deep that it was difficult to imagine that hundreds of men were living on the

461

far side of the wall, and that somewhere among them was Archie Carver, now in the eleventh month of his sentence and about to receive his first visitor.

She shook off the feeling of awe and walked firmly up the ramp to the wicket gate, where a printed notice said: 'Please Ring'.

She pulled hard at a metal rod that looked like the flush lever of an old-fashioned lavatory and heard the bell jangle far beyond the gates.

Presently, and after a certain amount of shuffling and jangling, the wicket gate opened and a red-faced young man in a drab, navy blue uniform put out his head and smiled at her.

"This way, Miss," he said, without any preliminaries.

Elaine smiled back at him, and was relieved to see the look of interest that invariably showed in men's faces whenever her smile was directed upon them. With more confidence she tucked her handbag under her arm and stepped briskly through the wicket gate into a narrow yard hemmed in by sheds.

The gate clinked behind her and the smiling, beefy young man pointed to the nearest shed.

"In there, Miss," he said very politely.

"Thank you," said Elaine, rewarding him with another dazzling smile.

The feeling of awe and bewilderment left her, exorcised by the flattering attention of the young officer.

. . . .

Elaine's presence in the County Gaol was due to a curious incident that had taken place in the meadow behind Number Forty-Three, about a week before.

Archie's letter inviting her to visit him had now been tucked away in her handbag for six months or more. She had received and read it with surprise, for she had almost forgotten Archie and, more particularly, where Archie was situated.

Time slipped away so quickly for Elaine these days and she had been amazed to discover on reckoning up that it was now more than two years since she and Archie had spent that lively week in Blackpool; it was therefore, almost eighteen months since she had last seen him at her solicitor's, when they met to discuss the divorce.

Since then things had been shaping rather well for Elaine. She wore a sapphire and diamond engagement ring that must have cost her fiancé at least two hundred pounds. The centre stone was so large that she sometimes found it difficult to believe that it was real, and only slipped it on when she accompanied Woolston on their tri-weekly jaunts to town. She had left it behind today, deciding that it wasn't the kind of thing one took inside a county gaol.

She had acquired, in addition, a mink stole. Woolston was very clever at thinking up just the kind of gifts she liked, and the stole had arrived at Number Forty-Three by special delivery on Christmas Eve.

On New Year's Eve, only a day or so before she had received Archie's letter, Woolston turned up with a large amethyst brooch, and a month later, on the occasion of her birthday, in early February, he had presented her with a huge vanity box, made of soft leather and containing at least three dozen accessories, each mounted in silver!

He showered gifts on her, all kinds of gifts, and on every kind of occasion. He seemed to be able to lay his hands on everything that a girl was likely to need, but could never hope to buy on the miserable allocation of clothing coupons they issued nowadays. Her last book of coupons was still intact (it was the only complete book of coupons in the Avenue) for on Woolston's weekly day off from the depot they usually spent the whole day in town and made a systematic round of the shops.

Woolston told her to buy whatever she wanted to buy and sat close at hand whilst she made her choices. He was unlike any other man she had met. Not only did he encourage her to spend but also showed an intelligent interest in her purchases. In addition his taste was excellent.

"Not that, Honey! That's not you, Sugar! You want something a shade lighter. Try the ice blue, Lover!"

At first Elaine found this sort of thing exciting, but it astonished her to discover how quickly she learned to take it for granted. As the summer wore on, and they passed the

first anniversary of their engagement, she began to wish that
he would show her attentions of another kind, attentions that
had nothing to do with the outward trappings of courtship,
but could be regarded as evidence that she produced an
effect upon him as a woman, and not simply as a well-
groomed and expensively-dressed companion in a theatre or a
restaurant.

She told herself that it was ridiculous to quibble with
Fortune when she was basking in Fortune's smiles, when any
woman in the whole of wartime London would have rushed
to change places with her, and enjoy his prodigal generosity,
but despite his attentiveness, and the steady flow of expensive
gifts, Elaine had begun to feel more and more uneasy about
Lieutenant Ericssohn's qualifications as a lover. She found it
impossible to get used to his curious offhandedness when they
were alone, and enjoying the privacy of Number Forty-
Three.

Every man with whom she had been alone in the past had
set out to make the most of it, but here was Woolston. to
whom she was officially engaged and to whom, presumably,
she was soon to be married, not seeming to mind whether he
was alone with her or not.

She gave him plenty of opportunities. When he called for
her to go out she usually greeted him in her underclothes,
exuding, moreover, the expensive perfumes that he was always bringing her. She played soft, dreamy numbers on the
gramophone until some of her records began to fault. When
they returned, late at night, she mixed him drinks that would
have encouraged most of the Englishmen she had known to
pounce before she had time to turn on the gas-fire and warm
the room! On two occasions she had called to him to bring
her things she needed while she was in the bath, but he had
only drifted in with a magazine in his hand and put the
articles she had demanded on the chair, going out again
without so much as a glance at her.

At first she put it all down to his Southern chivalry, to a
code that strictly forbade him to take advantage of her until
they were actually man and wife. Even so, it was disturbing
to have to admit that he seemed in no hurry at all to get
married, and that whenever she raised the subject he began

to talk vaguely of prospects of being sent overseas at any moment, or stress the difficulties of coaxing the requisite permits and sanctions out of Uncle Sam.

All things considered he was the most baffling man she had ever encountered. With any other man, with anyone less generous, or less obviously pleased to be seen in her company, she might have resolved her doubts by openly inviting seduction, and thus bringing matters to a head but all her instincts warned her against taking this irrevocable step, for Great Providers, as she had already discovered to her cost, did not grow on the Avenue laburnums, and unless she could be absolutely certain of so arranging matters that they resulted in immediate marriage then perhaps it was better to be satisfied with a good night kiss in the hall, the kind of kiss that no man, not even Esme as a callow youth, had offered as a pledge of desire.

Matters stood like this on the night of the wolf hunt, the night that she was confronted with an aspect of the Deep South that had so far been confined to the cinema and the popular novel.

They had returned late to Number Forty-Three after a visit to the West End, to see the long-running farce *Arsenic and Old Lace* and she had gone into the kitchen to make coffee.

It was an airless night, so she opened the kitchen door and as she was getting milk from the pantry she heard a disturbance in the meadow behind the house. At first she took little note of it, the G.I.s were always skylarking out there with girls, but suddenly the vague sounds became sharper and a girl screamed above the growl of men's voices. Because there was urgency in the scream she ran to Woolston, whom she surprised, peeping out through the curtains.

"You'd better go out there," she said, "it sounds as if someone's in trouble!"

At that moment the girl screamed again, and they heard the slam of their back gate and running feet on the path. Elaine hurried back into the kitchen just as a tousled girl in her late 'teens rushed in, slamming and locking the door, and putting her back to it.

Elaine recognised the girl at once. She was one of the

Rawlinsons, from Number Seventy or thereabouts, a teeming, ing, slightly rackety family, who had moved in to the Avenue from a bombed area nearer the city. The girl was badly scared and almost incoherent.

"What's happening out there?" Elaine asked her. "What's going on?"

The girl began to sob and Elaine led her away from the door and pushed her into a chair. Woolston came in from the sitting-room but even before the girl began to speak Elaine noticed that his expression was curiously bleak.

In a few minutes the girl calmed down sufficiently to pour out a story. She and a coloured American had been crossing the meadow from the wood when they had been set upon by a party of white Americans, half a dozen or so, and all apparently drunk. They had attacked Buck, the Negro, and two of them had held her and finally dragged her away from the group, and shouted at her to go home. She had run into Number Forty-Three because she saw a chink of light.

As she finished her story renewed uproar broke out from the meadow. There was the sound of scuffling, general shouting, and then one loud cry and the thud of running feet.

"Go out and stop it, Woolston," said Elaine, "I'll look after the girl."

She stopped, for he did not move, and his expression hardened as he said:

"You get that broad outer here, honey! It's just a wolf hunt, and that nigger had it coming to him, I guess!"

She stared at him, uncomprehendingly, and then, as she realised what was in his mind, she jumped back from the girl and faced him, angrily.

"You can't just stand there and do nothing," she shouted, "you're an officer and you've got to stop them!"

"Honey, you wouldn't understand! You just get that broad outa here, like I said!"

"If you won't go, I will," snapped Elaine and unlocked the door. He was beside her instantly, his hand on hers.

"Okay, okay!" he said, savagely, "but I don't want to get mixed up in this business. I tell you that nigger was uppity and had it comin' to him!"

He tore open the door and went into the garden. They

heard his unhurried steps on the path as the last shouts subsided. Elaine turned to the Rawlinson girl.

"Are you all right? You sure you're all right?"

"Yes," said the girl, beginning to snivel again. "I ... I don't know why they set upon him like that, he wasn't doing anything ... he was nice ... !"

"You get on home as quick as you can. ... Here, go this way through the front, and don't say anything about this, d'you understand? If you like you can come and see me tomorrow, but don't go near that camp again!"

She half-pushed the girl into the hall and opened the front door.

"Remember, don't go near that camp again!"

The girl seemed dazed but Elaine pushed her out and shut the door, returning to the kitchen as Woolston came in. She was surprised to see that he was smiling.

"Well?"

"It was like I said, they just beat him up a little."

"Did you catch any of them?"

His eyes opened wide. "Catch them? No, honey, I didn't aim to let 'em see *me* around!"

"But what's happened to the Negro?" Elaine demanded.

"He's still out there, I guess. I don't figger he'll neck any more white girls for the duration."

"You mean ... he's injured?"

Woolston locked the door and remained with his back to it.

"Listen, honey, don't you worry yourself over that nigger! He's had it comin' to him a long time and I guess the boys just got around to fixing him! Hi, where you goin' now?"

"I'm going to 'phone the police," said Elaine, flatly.

He jumped forward. "Police! Goddam it, you can't bring civilians into a thing like this! Don't you go near that 'phone, honey!"

She looked him up and down and there was contempt in the glance.

"Listen to me, Woolston. A man's lying out there injured, and I don't give a damn whether he's black, white or khaki, he's going to get attention so long as I know about it! Now then, do you notify the police and ambulance or do I?"

He met her eyes and realised there was no evading the issue. He sighed and hitched his belt.

"Okay, okay, but you're playin' with fire, honey! I'll get on to the dee-pot since you insist, but right after that you an' me got talking to do!"

He 'phoned the depot and within minutes they heard a car move along the cart track between Number Nineteen and the bombed site. He went out to the gate again but was back in a few moments. He found her in the sitting-room, swallowing a large gin.

"You got to get one thing straight, honey," he told her, helping himself to a drink. "Where I come from you don't stick your neck out when folks are taking it out on an uppity nigger! If you don't want to take part yourself you don't see nothing, and you don't hear nothing, get me?"

She realised then that she was seeing a different Woolston, a stranger with eyes that somehow reminded her of the fanatical eyes of old Holy Joe, the suburb's sandwich man, who throughout her childhood, had patrolled the streets with a sandwich-board bearing the crimson-lettered warning: *'Beware of the Wrath to Come!'* She was aware, of course, of his attitude towards coloured people, and his laconic comments on the subject had been supplemented by odd references to the problem in books and newspapers, but until now she had never been aware that his approach was anything more than an idiosyncrasy on his part, and on the part of Southerners generally. It had never seemed a prejudice strong enough to sanction a brutal assault on another human being, or a callousness permitting an officer to leave one of his men lying injured and unattended in a field.

She was so shocked that she felt slightly sick and wanted to be rid of him as quickly as possible. She put down her glass and went into the hall.

"You'd better go now, Woolston. We'll talk about it to-morrow!"

He nodded, slowly, as though he was relieved that she showed no further disposition to discuss the matter.

"Okay," he said, shortly, "Good night, honey!" and he kissed her cheek with his customary detachment.

She went back to the kitchen and made some coffee,

taking it into the bedroom and sitting in front of the gas-fire, brooding on the incident.

How could people be so inhuman as that? How could a person as mature as Woolston justify such an act in this day and age? What was it to him, or to those other men, that the girl Rawlinson liked to walk out with a coloured soldier? What would it be like in America, where this kind of thing was presumably commonplace? *Wolf hunt! He had it coming to him! He was uppity, so beat him, kill him!*

Suddenly, and with an odd sense of relief, she began to think of Archie, and Archie's letter.

She wondered why he should suddenly come into her mind, at a moment like this, when she was feeling upset, confused and frightened. Could it be because, of all the men in whose arms she had lain, Archie alone seemed strong, sane, and predictable?

She found his letter, reading it again in the light of the bedside lamp. She knew then that she would go and see him, soon, as soon as it could be arranged, for there was no one else who could advise her about Woolston, the man whom she was supposed to be marrying, for somehow, from someone, she had to have advice, even if it meant going inside a prison to get it. She had never needed advice before, but she needed it now, and Archie was the only person qualified to give the kind of advice she sought.

She made up her mind instantly and, as always once she had made a decision, she felt better at once. She undressed quickly, finished her coffee, and turned out the light, listening. Presently, the sound she was waiting for came from the cart track, the slow crunch of tyres on loose gravel, as a vehicle pulled out of the track and turned right towards Shirley Rise.

By the time the beat of its engine had died away she was asleep.

The two radiant smiles that Elaine had bestowed upon the young prison officer showed an immediate profit. She was directed to the centre seat in the visitor's room, where couples faced one another over the wire grill that topped a long counter, and the chair she was given was thus the chair furthest from the warders, who seated themselves one at each end of the long room.

Archie was already there awaiting her and she was agreeably surprised by his appearance. He had lost a good deal of his flabbiness and he looked, she thought, surprisingly fit and alert. The excitement of her visit had brought a heavy flush to his cheeks, and when she smiled at him through the wire mesh, his eyes lit up with pleasure and he braced his broad shoulders in a way she remembered him doing in the past whenever he was on the point of cracking a joke.

He cracked one now, a small and ironic one, but a joke that lacked wryness.

"Well, Elaine, and how's this for a nice, country seat? Big place! Takes a lot of your money to keep it up!"

"You look wonderfully fit, Archie," she told him. "How are you doing?"

"Time," he said cheerfully, "but not much more of it!"

"You mean you'll be out soon?"

The eagerness in her voice did not escape him, and his grin broadened.

"In less than two months but what's that to you? You're tied up with a rich Yank, I hear!"

"Who told you that?"

"Oh, I heard it from the Old Man. He and I have more or less made it up, you know!"

"He's been here to visit you?"

"No, he wanted to but I wouldn't let him. He writes tho', and so does that dear little body at Number Four, Edith Clegg."

"Well, I never!" exclaimed Elaine, surprised without knowing why.

"Tell me about this Yank, Elaine. Is he really in the dough, I mean, apart from what those boys pick up in the forces over here?"

"He's got plenty of money," said Elaine, slowly. "He owns a lot of property in the South."

"And I must say you look as if he was throwing it about!" said Archie, with a wink.

She was a little disconcerted by his manner. Without knowing exactly what to expect she had taken it for granted that he would be subdued by his circumstances, or, if he showed spirit (which she thought more than likely) then he would also show bitterness. As it was, his attitude indicated neither meekness or defiance. He was certainly not cowed, and he obviously did not resent her enjoying good luck, so much better luck than he had enjoyed of late.

She wondered if he had come to terms with his sentence and whether the experience had done anything to blunt the cutting edge of his aggressive egotism. Almost immediately he indicated that this was so. Looking straight into her eyes he said:

"Well, jolly good luck to you, Elaine! I'm glad one of us backed a winner!"

"I'm not at all sure that Woolston *is* what you'd call a winner," she heard herself saying.

She had not meant to give so much away but somehow she had lost the initiative. "He's got money, Archie, stacks and stacks of it I imagine, but well . . . I don't know. . . . !"

She stopped, biting her lower lip, uncertain how she could explain the impulse that had driven her to visit him. She realised that she could hardly discuss the wolf hunt or express the doubts about Woolston within hearing of prison officers, and all these other people conducting their low conversations on each side of her, but she nevertheless felt the need to give him some sort of hint, something to think about, and hope for, during the interval that must elapse before she visited him again, or their paths crossed again after his release.

"Well, Elaine?"

He was waiting, his face alight with interest.

"I don't know . . . he's . . . he's so *slow*, . . . Sometimes I think he's . . . well . . . almost . . . you know. . . ."

"A queer?"

"Well, a bit of one."

He threw back his head and laughed, and at the sound of his laughter the red-faced officer looked up sharply, and the tiny woman sitting beside Elaine glanced at Archie reproachfully, as though he was mocking the solemnity of place and occasion.

"I'm sorry, Elaine," he apologised, "but it strikes me as so funny, you getting mixed up with that kind of monkey!

Still. . . ." Suddenly he was quite serious again "I wouldn't let *that* worry you, not if you can actually land him, of course! I've heard about marriages like that and they can be made to work, although that may seem a bit of a tall story! Maybe you could come to some kind of arrangement later on and that's been known too, believe me!"

She was irritated now, and annoyed with herself for giving him such a splendid opening. She looked sideways at the warder, hoping that he would stand up and say it was time to go, but Archie was very quick to notice the change and at once set out to mend matters.

"Let's forget the Yank, Elaine. Tell me about the Avenue. We've only got another minute or so!"

"There's nothing you don't know about the dreary old Avenue, if you've been hearing from your father and Miss Clegg," she told him. "You'll have heard all about the double wedding, of course. I saw Esme and your sister, Judy that day, and I wished them both luck. They're going to be all right now. Esme's over me completely and she's madly in love with him. She always had been, you know."

Suddenly he wasn't listening to her and she noticed that he glanced urgently at the big clock behind her.

"I'd just like to say thanks a million for coming right down here, Elaine," he said, breathlessly. "It was good of you and I'm damned if I'll ever forget it! Not many people would have come in the circumstances, hardly anyone, in fact! Believe me, Elaine, I do wish you all the luck in the world with the Yank and no hard feelings!"

She too sensed the urgency of the moment and suddenly her mood changed again and she felt glad, very glad, that she had come. She realised now that her instinct had been right, and that the visit had done a good deal to steady her.

"If I can return the compliment I'd like to say that I think you've stood up to everything wonderfully, Archie," she told him sincerely.

"Oh, *that!*" he shrugged, and she noticed how wide and splendidly muscled were his shoulders, compared with Woolston's.

"I had it coming to me, Elaine," he said, "and I'm not sore, not really sore! I sat up and begged for it, and I don't hold it against anyone for dishing it out! There's one thing about this place—it does give you a chance to think. I always imagined that I planned things when I was outside, but I didn't you know. In the main I always acted on impulse and chanced my luck! Well, this business has taught me one thing. It doesn't do to rely on luck, Elaine. I'll know better next time!"

"What are you going to do when you get out, Archie?"

"Depends on capital," he told her, "I've got two thousand from the corner shop. That's not much I know, and the place would have fetched six after the war, when there'll be a terrific rush for small businesses with living accommodation, but it's two thousand better than nothing, and I'll start up again, somehow, some place! I'm not worried!"

"No, you're not are you?" she said, wonderingly. "You're not nearly so worried as the people. . . ." She had been on the point of saying 'the people outside', but she checked herself, and said "as most people."

The beefy young officer stood up and coughed, and the women on each side of Elaine scraped their chairs. Then the other officer barked an order. "It's like talking to a pack of dogs," Elaine thought, as, with a final wink, Archie stood, turned smartly right, and joined the file of men that was already shuffling past her on the far side of the wire.

Elaine followed the other warder out into the yard and retrieved her belongings at the brick shed. A few minutes later she was walking briskly down the concrete ramp towards the town. She had a very thoughtful look as she stood with a group of other visitors waiting for the lights to turn green before crossing the road.

"He's got so much guts," she said to herself. "I never dreamed that he had that much guts!" And as she said it her mind drifted away from Archie to contemplate the word 'guts' in the abstract.

There were so many variations of the term—guts to charge a machine-gun, the kind of guts that people said Esme had shown, by avoiding capture and working his way home to Judith after already screwing up his courage to breaking-point to fly on operations. Then there were the day-by-day guts, the kind that had revealed itself so readily in the

Avenue during the bombing, and finally her own kind of guts, the guts to make a plan, and stick to it, no matter what people said, or how it affected those one lived among!

Could Woolston lay claim to any one of these? Would he, for instance, on finding his world in ruins, brace up and grin, as Archie had grinned when she faced him across that awful wire netting?

She doubted it. She doubted it very much but was there any way of finding out for certain?

Still musing she passed into the main hall of the station and lost herself in the bustle attending an incoming train.

CHAPTER XXXI

Sicilian Encounter

MARGY HARTNELL and her ENSA concert party had followed
the armies across the Mediterranean to Sicily.

They crossed in September of 1943, when Mussolini's Italy
was on the point of collapse and fighting had all but ceased
on the island.

They were based for a time on Taomina, the honeymoon
town under the slopes of Etna, and here, in a huge marquee,
or in an open amphitheatre, they gave a concert each night
and played to capacity houses.

Privately Margy did not think much of their programmes.
There was no real talent in the party and under different
conditions it would have had difficulty in attracting a paying
audience in a garrison town on a Saturday night. Out here,
however, there was no competition and almost any kind of
song, mime or dance was well received by the troops, who
laughed uproariously at jokes that had been cracked in the
musical-halls of their grandfathers.

Margy acted as relief pianist and instrumentalist, but on
certain evenings she had her own vocal spot and sometimes
led the community singing. She also played the trumpet but
she was at her best with the piano accordion, the 'squeezebox' as it was called by the audiences.

All kinds of men crowded into the marquee to hear her
play numbers like *'Lili Marlene'*, and often someone would
send up a special request. She liked special requests, for they
enabled her to establish a closer contact with her audience,
and when a request was handed up she always asked the

applicant to identify himself and shout out the branch of the service he represented.

"Here's someone who wants *'Lovely Week-end'*," she would announce. "Who is it? Come on now, where are you hiding, Charlie? I'm not going to play it unless you stand up like a man and show yourself! Come on, you can't be so shy, or you wouldn't have a lovely week-end to remember!"

Then a young man in khaki, or in navy blue, would bob up from the back and call out something facetious, such as: "It's not me, it's my mate Bert, Gorgeous! He wants *'Lovely Week-end'* because his last one is still costing him seven-and-a-tanner a week," and the joker would subside, in a scuffle and a gale of laughter.

When she was not on stage Margy would sometimes go round and stand at the back of the tent, looking across the serried rows of heads to the stage, and speculating on the men who so obviously enjoyed these corny programmes.

Such a variety of men she encountered; kilted Jocks, Red Devils, Desert Rats, with complexions walnut brown after two years 'in the Blue', grounded fighter-pilots, with their ridiculous moustaches, noisy Free French, broad-shouldered Poles and stolid Dutch, light-hearted British tars, in their flopping bell-bottoms, Royal Engineers, Gunners, and aloof Task Force officers, with the strain of past missions in their eyes.

There were men in their greying fifties, and boys still in their 'teens; there were saucy men, who slipped an arm around her waist, and shy men who blushed when she asked to see a photograph of their girl friend. There were Americans, who looked at her in a certain way, and excessively polite Americans, who called her 'ma'am', and came to attention when she spoke to them. There were all kinds of men, every kind of man, but never a merchant sailor, never Ted, with his slow, self-effacing smile, and rhythm-tapping foot, the man who (how many centuries ago?) had drifted into her Woolworth's Store on the Old Orchard Road, where she was once employed as song-plugger, and asked her to play *'Wonderful Amy'*, the hit of the hour, on the Store gramophone.

Sometimes, she told herself, she was a fool to spend so

much time thinking about Ted. She was only thirty-one and still mildly attractive in a *petite,* 'gypsyish' way. Scores of men would have been glad to invite her out to a meal, to flatter her and pet her perhaps, in the back of a car, and some might have made her feel that, even though time was racing by, and the war went on and on, it was still pleasant to lie in a man's arms, and hear him make an issue of the Mediterranean moon.

She never did give any particular man individual encouragement but continued to mother them *en masse,* to ask after their girl friends, and sing their request numbers, numbers that had, for almost every one of them, some special significance in prewar years.

One stuffy night the atmosphere was so close and heavy that Oscar, the manager, ordered the stage to be reversed and the concert performed in the open air, with the audience crowding into a vast circle under a full moon.

During Margy's second turn with the piano-accordion a man at the back stood up after she had finished playing *'Johnny Zero',* for an American, and called, loudly and clearly:

" *'Stormy Weather'!* Give us *'Stormy Weather'!"*

His request was followed by a volley of others, demands for *'Waltzing Matilda', 'Sally',* and the eternal favourite, *'Lili Marlene',* but the soldier who wanted *'Stormy Weather'* had been the first, so she moved down-stage, smiled into the sea of upturned faces and said:

"You're lucky, soldier! That's an old favourite of mine, chum, so with your permission I'll get rid of the squeezebox and *sing* it! Are you with me, Ernie?" as the pianist sidled in from the wings, and Eddy Marks, the tenor, relieved her of the accordion.

'Stormy Weather' had considerable significance for her. Years ago, during their honeymoon at Blackpool, she and Ted had sat in a box at the Tower Theatre, and heard Gracie Fields sing it when it was a new and popular number.

She moved across to the piano and began to sing, her mind re-creating the surroundings in which she had first heard the song, and her voice easily adapting itself to the strident sadness of the dirge.

'Can't go *on* . . .
Everything I had is gone,
Stormy Weather!
Since my man and I ain't together,
Keeps raining all the ti-ime . . .
Keeps raining all—the—time!'

She must have excelled herself, for the applause was thunderous and interspersed with a chorus of appreciative whistles that continued for almost a minute.

She patted the pianist on the shoulder and then saw Oscar signalling an encore from the wings. She was tired, and needed a drink, but she could not help being encouraged by the reception. She looked out across the crowded amphitheatre, peering through almost motionless clouds of tobacco smoke that hung above the bowl like an awning.

She lifted her hand for silence and the applause died away. "Okay, boys! Just one more! What'll you have? Make it snappy!"

At least a dozen men stood up but one, well away at the back, was a split second in advance of his competitors. He leapt to his feet and shouted:

" *'Margy'*! Sing *'Margy'*!"

His voice was at once lost in scattered shouts from all points of the circle, but Margy had heard him and she waved, frantically, for silence.

"Okay! *'Margy'* it is! Are you ready, Ernie?"

They sailed into the number and as she sang it she reflected that it must be all of fifteen years' old, that she had sung it in her Woolworth's days, and that Ted had always regarded it as 'her' tune. It was a good, nostalgic number, with plenty of swing and all the zest of the late 'twenties', when everybody seemed to have such a good time on so little money, and nobody had ever heard of Hitler or concentration camps.

When she was about half-way through she noticed, but without paying special attention to it, a small stir away at the edge of the circle. Then she saw a man threading his way carefully between the rows of seated figures, and making his way towards the narrow gangway between the converging lines of backless benches.

There was something vaguely familiar about the man's movements, something that disconcerted her, so that she turned her head away from the audience and fixed her eyes on the spur of rock, marking the right-hand boundary of the valley.

Then, when she was half-way through the second chorus, she saw the man more clearly. He was now ascending the short flight of steps that led to the stage and for another second or so she went on singing, wondering what the man could be doing there, and why he should have chosen this particular moment to climb from the auditorium.

Ernie, at the piano, must have been wondering the same thing, for he faltered, and the accompaniment petered out as the man moved into the direct light of the footlights. She saw then, and with a cry that ended the number on a kind of squeak, that the man was Ted and that he was holding out his arms and speaking to her.

Below her the audience seemed to go mad. Men sprang to their feet in hundreds and began shouting at the top of their voices. Ernie had left the piano stool and Oscar, the manager, had jumped out from the wings. She felt faint and dizzy with the uproar.

Then Ted's arms were around her and his mouth was pressed to hers and nothing else mattered, not the audience, the concert, or the war! She felt herself lifted and carried across to the piano, where she was dumped and temporarily abandoned, while Ted turned to the audience and waved his hands semaphore fashion, the way he had always asked for silence when about to announce one of her special numbers at a dance at home.

"*Okay*, fellers! *Okay!* You can shout your heads off but I can explain everything! Listen, fellers, *listen*, everyone! Margy here's my wife, and I haven't seen her in over a year, so what would you do, fellers? What would you do if you found yourself put ashore in Valetta, heard that your own missus was handy, and then had the chance of a hop over here in a Dakota?"

His speech produced a roar that eclipsed its forerunner.

The men nearest the stage began to bunch forward, and those further back climbed up on the benches and began to caper about, waving their caps and behaving, Margy thought, like supporters at a Cup Final when their team had scored a winning goal during extra time.

It was Oscar, the manager-comedian, who at last managed to quieten them.

He waddled down to the footlights and stood beside Ted. He was still wearing baggy, checked trousers, and the billy-cock hat he had used in the preceding act.

"*Quiet!*" he shouted, in his harsh, costermonger's voice. "*Quiet!* you bell-toothed bush-monkeys! This is an occasion! This is really something, fellers! *Quiet! Listen!* Quiet, can't you?"

Slowly the uproar subsided but a continuous murmur persisted as Oscar put his arm on Ted's shoulder and began to speak again.

"This isn't a gag, fellers! Take it from me, chaps, it's no gag! Honest-to-God, I didn't know a thing about it, and neither did Margy! Damn it, you've only got to look at the gal! This is on the level, fellers! This chap really is her old pot-an'-pan. Ain't that so, Margy? Tell 'em, kid. Ain't that so?"

Margy nodded, happily, but she was unable to speak.

"What you chaps *don't* know," went on Oscar confidentially, warming to his work as impresario, and rubbing his hands with professional glee, "is that this chap *here*, Margy's old man, is *Ted Hartnell*, a famous, pro' band-leader and a jazz-drummer, and an artist who 'as appeared many times on the B.B.C.! Now ain't that so, Teddy-boy? Ain't that so?"

Ted had no chance to confirm or deny, for Oscar's announcement created a renewed storm of cheers. When he had won another respite he went on to say that 'maybe— *maybe* mindyew, Ted and Margy would do a special number right here, after which he was sure the audience would excuse 'em further participation in the concert, because I reckon they got a ruddy sight more urgent things to do!"

A roar of laughter, and a storm of hand-clapping greeted this announcement and Ted grinned as he returned to the piano and held a short consultation with Ernie and Margy.

Finally he came back to Oscar and whispered something to him, whereupon Oscar nodded eagerly, and then addressed himself to the audience yet again.

"They're going to give you something *real* appropriate, fellers ... something *local* you might say, or as-near-as-dammit local!"

He raised his voice to an agonised howl: "Margy's gonner sing, with Ted Hartnell accompanying on the drums, that old-time popular number known to all an' everyone of you, 'The Isle of Capri'."

He bowed himself back into the wings as the grinning drummer bustled on with a set of drums. The drummer arranged his frame and placed a chair for Ted in front of it, then skipped off-stage and left the field free to Ted, Margy and Ernie at the piano.

Margy dabbed her eyes, slipped off the piano and moved down-stage with her hands clasped, waiting through the introductory bars with a demureness more reminiscent of a Victorian ballad-singer than an ENSA camp canary.

She sang the lyric quietly and sweetly, without the 'give' that Ted had always associated with her delivery of vocal numbers and then, after a verse and chorus, she stepped back and nodded to Ernie, and Ted addressed himself wholeheartedly to the drums and swept into a hotted-up version in his best dance-hall manner.

The troops loved it and applause broke out before he had worked his way through the chorus. He hurled himself at kettle-drum, side-drum, triangle and cymbals, while Ernie's fingers flew faster and faster over the keys, until at last Ernie gave up and sat back, while Ted entered upon one of his prolonged flourishes submerged in the full tide of applause that swept over the stage.

Watching him from her stand near the piano, Margy's heart nearly burst with pride, for it was clear to her that three years at sea, and all his dreadful experiences, had done nothing to destroy his touch. Here he was, the same old Ted, beating it up and beating it up as if his life depended on sustaining the merciless tattoo of flailing drumsticks.

The very sight of him, sweating and beaming over the skins, renewed all her hope in the future. Hero he might be,

George Medal winner, and merchant-seaman for the duration, but nonetheless he was still her Ted, ace-drummer of the suburbs, and pivot of the Hartnell Eight!

"Ted," she breathed, "Ted, you're wonderful ... wonderful!"

He finished with a final lunge at the cymbals and abruptly turned his back on the audience, crossing up-stage to her, taking her hand, and leading her down-stage to make a bow to the boys.

They remained standing there a moment and then, with the roar of applause ringing in their ears, they ran into the wings, past Oscar and others, who thumped their shoulders, and jumped down into the empty marquee that had been the auditorium.

As they crossed it and slowed down a sudden pang assailed her and she asked, breathlessly:

"How long have you got, Ted? How *long*, darling?"

He dragged her from the tent and pushed her into a jeep that was standing parked against the wall of a shattered villa.

"Just tonight, Margy! Just the one night, so let's make the most of it, honey!"

He jumped in and started the engine as a dozen questions rose to her mind. How did he get here, how did he find out about her being here? Why did he have to return so soon? Who owned the jeep he was driving? She put none of the questions to him, for there was no time to waste on questions.

"A mile or so out of town, Ted ... there's a kind of garden, overlooking the sea. Lots of flowers grow there, thousands and thousands of flowers, and they smell heavenly! Oh, Ted darling! This is a miracle, a lovely, lovely miracle!"

"Yes, and you have to make 'em happen these days," he said grimly, groping impatiently for her hand as the jeep roared down the white ribbon of road.

CHAPTER XXXII

Elaine Goes Back On Dreams

ARCHIE was discharged from prison at 7.50 a.m. on October 1st, 1943.

The prison staff, from Governor downwards, were genuinely sorry to see the last of him, for he left behind him not only a superbly well-ordered store but any number of interesting ideas related to store-keeping and the art of indenting for stores generally. In a quiet and tactful manner he had put several harassed officers in the way of improving themselves, and the Governor wrote on his report! *'Seldom in my experience has a man in my charge shown more keenness to make use of such opportunities as present themselves during a sentence of imprisonment.'*

Archie left prison without a trace of bitterness but in spite of this his original attitude to society had undergone no fundamental change during the past twelve months. He had freely acknowledged his debt to society as regards the girl he had killed. Having settled that debt with a whole year of his life, he now went out into the world again without the slightest disposition to apologise to anyone.

In some ways he had reaped material benefit from his experience, for not only had he found plenty of spare time in which to think, but time in which to read. He had wasted no time on fiction but concentrated on a close study of various technical volumes, beginning with *Everyman His Own Lawyer*, and ending, during the final month of his sentence, with the patient digestion of a massive work, entitled *Gutteridge's Ownership of Property*.

483

The Governor had shaken hands with him very cordially and in wishing him the best of luck had asked him if he had any ideas regarding his own future.

"First, I intend to make some money, sir," said Archie, so promptly and confidently that the Governor, a solemn man, had laughed outright.

That was indeed Archie's main intention as the gates closed behind him and he stepped out into the crispness of an autumn morning.

It ought not, he reflected, to be so very difficult for he was far from destitute, and had a credit balance of just over two thousand, the proceeds of the sale of the corner shop. In addition, he was fighting fit and told himself that he had never felt better. This, very possibly, had something to do with his enforced abstemiousness, and his very modest consumption of tobacco during the past year. He realised as much and had accordingly made at least one good resolution whilst in gaol. He would keep off spirits! His long hours of soul-searching during the period between lights-out and sleep, had convinced him that here was the root cause of all his troubles. During the year preceding the climax his brain had never been sufficiently clear to cope with sudden emergencies. He reasoned that had it been then he would never have bought those NAAFI goods, not at any rate, without covering the trail more efficiently than that idiot, Swift had covered his!

Neither would a sober man have quarrelled with his accountant in wartime, whereas the final blackout, after the discovery that his Floating Reserve had been stolen, must certainly be traced to excessive spirit-drinking over a long period.

Well, decided Archie, hitching his belt and sniffing the heady air of freedom, here's an end to all that! From now on it's a glass of bitter or nothing at all!

He had also made up his mind not to return to the grocery trade. There was plenty of money in it, would always be money in it, particularly during wartime, but the retention of a worthwhile margin of profits was becoming a job for a trained accountant, and Archie had never enjoyed wrestling with columns of figures. In his view it occupied far too much time, time that a businessman ought to employ more profitably. Cheap property might be a better bet, providing one had the capital, but his recent study of the property market had convinced him that two thousand pounds was insufficient capital to begin business on the scale that he contemplated. He decided, therefore, that there would have to be an intermediate effort, something to do with cars, perhaps, or something where a maximum stock could be procured with the minimum outlay.

He occupied his mind on these matters as he walked down the long, concrete ramp, that led away from the prison, consciously disciplining his thoughts because he did not want to start thinking about Elaine.

He had been immensely braced by her visit but subsequently cast down by her failure to repeat it, or to answer either of the letters he had written to her during the last two months.

His common sense told him that he could hardly expect her to welcome a renewal of their association. She had been a good deal cleverer than he and had apparently secured her future with this wealthy American. He might have competed with the Yank in the past, when he had plenty of money, but such capital as he now possessed he needed, every single penny of it, and Archie had never expected a girl to associate with him for the sake of his company alone, certainly not a girl like Elaine, who had even fewer illusions than himself.

All the same, he had rather hoped that she would have written at least once and wished him good luck on coming out. He would not have interpreted such a message as anything but a gesture of comradeship, made for old times' sake. There was after all, a limit to a man's self-sufficiency, and Archie had now reached the age when he needed at least one confidant to combat his increasing fear of loneliness. Maria had never been a confidante, not even in the earliest days of their marriage, and the only human beings in whom Archie had confided during the last twenty years had been his father-in-law, old Toni Piretta, and his own son, Anthony, and now both were dead. His two younger children, James and Juanita, he would have had difficulty in recognising in the street, and anyway, since the theft of the money, and his arrival in gaol, he had neither seen nor communicated with his wife or children. There was his father, now disposed to be friendly, but the gulf between them was far too wide to be bridged, save by occasional handshakes and family gossip. The best they could hope for was to be civil to one another on the few occasions that they were likely to meet and Archie, on his part, had every intention of prolonging the truce with his father into the future.

Turning these matters over in his mind he reached the road that wound past the foot of the prison approach and stood indecisively at the pedestrian crossing, leading to a footpath that divided the two blocks of buildings between the main road and the railway station.

It was still only a few minutes past eight o'clock and his train was not due to leave for town until nine-forty. He wondered what to do with his first ninety minutes of freedom and had almost made up his mind to go to the station buffet and buy himself some tea and a newspaper, when a persistent hooting attracted his attention.

He looked towards the town and saw a solitary, saloon car, parked just beyond the studs.

He shaded his eyes against the strong morning sun and suddenly his heart glowed with pleasure, for he recognised the woman sitting in the driver's seat as Elaine.

In a moment he was beside her and was surprised to find that she was alone.

"Since when did you own a car?" he demanded.

"Since this morning," she told him, smiling. "I got myself driven down here and then hired this one locally, giving your name as a reference!"

"Good God," he exclaimed, "I'm a gaolbird! How did you manage to talk them into that?"

"Oh, I can talk men into anything," she replied, jocularly. "Besides, the car's hired out in my name, and I'm legally responsible. You were banned from driving, weren't you?"

"For three years," he said, getting in and watching her make a few practice gear-changes, "but the ban ought to be lifted long before that. We're working on it now—they went to no end of trouble to prepare the ground when I told them that I was wanting to buy a van and start up again. You've no idea ... me and the Gov, we're just like that in there!" and he crossed his fingers and slapped her on the knee.

"I knew you'd like to be driven back," she said, "so I came down here yesterday and fixed it. We can return the car at the London depot."

He regarded her with affection and admiration. She looked, he thought, more attractive than ever, in her neat olive-green two-piece, absurdly small hat with eye-veil, and long French gloves. She was thinner too, particularly about the face and her appearance had the stamp of the West End salons, from freshly-permed hair, down to expensive-looking Italian shoes.

"You look like the answer to a young lag's prayer!" he told her. "Why didn't you tell me you were coming down?"

"Let's go!" she said, "we don't want to hold an inquest under the wall, do we?"

He laughed, and pinched her thigh, as she clumsily let out the clutch. The big car lumbered off, lazily, and with a persistent squeak issuing from somewhere near the rear of the chassis.

"Could we stop somewhere for breakfast?" he asked her. "I'm supposed to have had mine but I was so keyed up that I couldn't swallow a mouthful!"

"Neither could I," said Elaine, "but in my case it wasn't excitement, it was getting up so damned early! Why do they have to turn you chaps loose in the small hours? There's cigarettes in my handbag, help yourself!"

"You always were a lazy little bitch," he said, "but by God, am I pleased to see you!"

"Thank you, Archie," she said, so demurely that he laughed again and the sound of his own laughter lifted his spirits to such a peak that he had to resist an impulse to sing. She settled down to drive, snuggling down in the seat like a Persian cat, he thought, glancing sideways at her—and he proceeded to light two cigarettes, one of which he stuck between her lips. He drew the smoke down into his lungs and blew it out slowly through his nose.

"This is the life, Elaine," he told her, as the old car coasted down the hill into open country.

. . . .

It was understandable that Elaine felt no urge to discuss her last minute decision to meet him at the gaol gates. Her appearance there was, in a sense, a surprise to herself, for it was not until the early afternoon of the previous day that she had finally made up her mind to come.

The decision had been the result of a fresh wave of doubt in respect of the wisdom of marriage to Lieutenant Ericssohn. Elaine was always having doubts nowadays, and was in fact, far less sure of herself than she had ever been, but it would be difficult to attribute her uncertainties and strange loss of direction to any one particular factor of her life.

For some time now she had settled for the fact that Woolston, viewed solely as a lover, was a pitiful substitute for any of the men in her past. He claimed to be thirty-nine, but she estimated his correct age to be somewhere around forty-five and sometimes he behaved towards her as if he was already a grandfather.

Sometimes it seemed as if her doubts stemmed from her sheer inability to rouse in him any physical desire, for this made her conscious of her own age in a way that she had never been aware of it prior to her engagement.

She told herself over and over again that it had never been an intention on her part to seek a lover in this latest association, that Woolston was billed in her mind as The Great Provider, not The Great Lover. She went on to tell herself that, once she was safely settled in the States, admittedly a woman's country, she could afford to overlook his undistinguished appearance, his absurdly old-fashioned air of patronage towards her as a woman, his undeniable fuddy-duddiness, and his distressing lack of virility. All these drawbacks were trivial in a man who was able to buy a mink stole as though he was purchasing a box of chocolates.

How often had she convinced herself that this was the kind of man for whom she had been looking all these years? What did it matter if he was middle-aged, a foreigner, and tiresome fusspot? He was rich, and he liked to be seen moving with her among younger and envious officers. He flaunted her like a captured banner at unit dances, and other social occasions, and as long as he felt like that about her he would continue to pay for the privilege. If he was disinclined to exact the customary payment then so much the better! What woman in her senses would want to be pawed by Woolston?

This line of reasoning made good sense to Elaine, but it brought her no permanent reassurance. She could not even explain to herself why it did not, for over the years she had lost the habit of self-scrutiny. She had made a plan and satisfied herself that it was a good plan. When Woolston Ericssohn had crossed her path her instincts, or what she had mistaken for her instincts had told her that here was the means of attaining her object, here was the provider of house, terrace, yacht, car, hammock, courtiers, and all the clothes and adornments that she was ever likely to need! The real trouble lay in the fact that plan and instincts were now sadly at variance. For the time being the plan had lulled her instincts, and, as time went on, she came to understand that her mounting uncertainty was merely the manifestation of their reawakening.

The plan had been all very well in its way, but it had originated in her head and Elaine, who did not know herself nearly as well as she imagined she did, was a sensual woman, to whom the attentions of a virile man, a healthy, normal man like Archie Carver, were a physical necessity. It was on this very issue, indeed, that she had first quarrelled with Esme, resenting her elevation to the role of a beautiful but remote lady-in-the-tower. Furthermore, it was this characteristic that had drawn her, but without her being fully aware of the fact, to Eugene, to Tappertitt, the little circus owner, to Archie himself, and to the Dutch sea-captain.

Woolston Ericssohn, notwithstanding his enormous financial lead over every predecessor, simply did not measure up to her requirements. It might have been different had he been a tolerant, easy-going man, the kind of middle-aged husband content to look the other way if she sought consolation among younger men, but she was aware that this was not the case, that in addition to being pompous and pettifogging, he was also jealous and dictatorial, the kind of man who was certain to make endless scenes about other men and, if provoked, to meet infidelity with spite.

There was something else about the American that caused her uneasiness. She had been more shocked than she had realised over the attack upon the Negro in the Manor meadow. Basically a very tolerant person she had found it impossible to regard this incident as the inevitable outcome of a coloured man's association with a white girl, and the assault had revealed to her the wide gulf existing between the people of the suburbs, of which she would always be one, and these high-spirited, open-handed extroverts now living in their midst.

One thought of them as being the same people but they were not, for beside them the people of the Avenue were like a group of tired old aunts and uncles, trying to smile at the horseplay of children at a party, simply because they felt it was expected of them. In so many ways the Americans resembled children. They had the same impulsive generosity, the same sudden streaks of cruelty, and the same brutal intolerance for those who did not conform; Woolston, for all that he was an officer, and a mature man of substance, was no different from the G.I.'s who had actually engaged in the wolf hunt. What would it be like to have to share his prejudices day in, day out? What would it be like never to see Piccadilly Circus again, or the shops in Bond Street, or even the wide curve of the Avenue?

She took her misgivings to her sole woman friend, Muriel Payne, the gown-shop ally of the night of her engagement, but she received scant sympathy in this quarter. Muriel, at thirty-five, had been twice divorced and was now living with a third man, who was reported to have made a small fortune out of the manufacture of army huts.

"What do you care how old he is?" Muriel had exclaimed. "Why should you care if he doesn't burst a blood vessel when he sees you in your scanties? You're going to marry him, aren't you? And he's loaded, isn't he? What's come over you lately, Elaine? What on earth are you bitching about? I always thought you fancied yourself queening it under the magnolias?"

"But Muriel, he's so . . . so self-righteous in some ways, and so hopelessly adolescent . . . !"

"What do you expect of a man who coughs up for this as

though he was buying you a choc-ice in a cinema?" demanded Muriel, holding up the mink stole, that Elaine had thrown across a display stand when she entered the salon. "Look here, Elaine, I'm your friend, and because I was, I did all I could to help land him, didn't I? Well, be your age, and for God's sake stop looking a Derby winner in the mouth! You play along with Woolston, right up to the minute he says 'I Will', because if you ditch him, or even think of ditching him, so help me I'll move in myself!"

Elaine took her advice, and did not answer Archie's letters, but two days before his release-date something happened that was to resolve her doubts once and for all.

Woolston invited her to meet his colonel and in her presence the two of them at once began to discuss plans for a wedding in the locality of the depot.

It seemed that the colonel, who was the most naïve American Elaine had yet encountered, had some fantastic idea of using the wedding to further Anglo-American relations in the area. He planned a bumper reception in the forecourt of the Old Manor, inviting, as guests of the U.S. Army, a hundred or more of the local residents on whom the American technicians had been billeted during the past twelve months.

Elaine was alarmed by this suggestion but the colonel was so obviously good-intentioned that she did not like to hurt his feelings by a flat rejection of the idea and simply told him that she had been contemplating a very quiet wedding, and would require time to consider his generous offer and all it implied.

At this Woolston dropped a second bombshell. There was unfortunately, not very much time to think about it, for he had been posted back home, pending promotion and a command at a new training depot, in Virginia.

For a moment Elaine's clouded expression cleared as she recognised certain possibilities in this turn of events. If Woolston departed for the States, and paid her a generous allowance, then there might be something in favour of getting married almost at once. It was unlikely that arrangements could be made for her to join him whilst the war continued, and the end of it was not yet in sight. Anything could happen between now and then, and Elaine had never been a person to take the distant future into consideration.

The Colonel, however, poured a cold douche on this hopeful shoot before it had showed an inch above ground.

"Ordin-ar-ily," he said, with the indulgent smile of a film uncle, "ordin-ar-ily that would mean you kids would be separated by three thousand miles of ocean for the dooration, but it so happens we can get around that one! Yes, ma'am, we been right here figuring a way o' flying you back within a month of *Captain* Ericssohn taking up his appointment. Now I wouldn't say that is according to the book of rules, but I figure it *can* be done, Mrs. Fraser, unofficially that is!"

Elaine could only murmur a polite reply and excuse herself as rapidly as possible. She wanted time to think. She wanted to go somewhere alone, where she could fight this idiotic wave of panic that was now threatening to submerge her altogether.

She told Woolston that she "simply had to consult Daddy", and as 'Daddy' lived right up in Llandudno, this meant that she would be away for at least two days! She promised to 'phone him on arrival in North Wales, and call again the moment she had discussed, 'with Daddy the Colonel's wonderful offer about the wedding.'

Even as she said this she knew that she would not go to Wales but to a drab town in the West, where there was a high red-brick wall and a steep, concrete ramp leading up to a gate in it.

She hurried back to the Avenue and at once began to pack. All the time she was throwing things into her small suitcase she was telling herself that she was stark, staring mad, but she continued to pack, nevertheless, thrusting reason into the innermost recesses of her mind, and conversing aloud with herself as she opened and closed drawers. "I don't care! I must get away! I don't care! Maybe I *will* go through with it in the end, but right now I must get away! I must see Archie, just once more perhaps, but I must see him! I must!"

When she had finished packing, and was crossing the hall to open the front door, she saw Woolston's silhouette against the coloured glass panel. She guessed that he must be calling on her with an offer to run her over to Euston and she did not want to go to Euston but to Waterloo. She felt incapable of pretending any longer, so she tiptoed through the kitchen, out of the back door, and along the garden alley to a point where she could slip through the shattered palings into the meadow and thence into Shirley Rise. This was the route that Archie had used early in the war, when paying her his Saturday night calls but she did not remember this, she was far too preoccupied in getting past the end of the Avenue without being spotted by Woolston.

. . . . .

They had breakfast in the 'Coach and Horses', a village hostelry a few miles short of Salisbury.

It was a good breakfast by wartime standards, porridge, sausage and tomatoes, toast and marmalade, and reasonably strong coffee.

When they were drinking their second cup Elaine noticed that he had hardly spoken during the meal. She said, banteringly.

"You've hardly looked at me, Archie! Is it because you were so hungry?"

"Yes, but not for grub," he told her, quietly.

"You haven't even kissed me, either!"

She said this lightly but he did not receive it so.

"If I did I wouldn't be answerable for the immediate consequences!" he said, seriously, "I've never seen you looking so wonderful, and I didn't ought to have to remind you that I haven't had a woman in more than twelve months!"

She laughed, partly at his solemn tone, but more for sheer joy at being once more in the company of someone so stimulated by her. She had almost forgotten what it was like to be coveted.

"Poor Archie! Self-denial was never your strong suit, was it?"

He looked up and she was amazed to see that his face was troubled and that her banter was actually hurting him.

"It's not that, Elaine, and it's not just that you happen to be a woman, or that you look so exciting!"

She had never heard him speak like this before and her curiosity was aroused.

"Well, tell me, Archie?"

"Oh, to hell with it! You tell me about your Yank!"

"No, because Woolston isn't important today and you are, Archie!"

He considered this for a moment. Finally he said, but without looking at her:

"No one's ever done a thing like this for me! Come to think of it, no one's ever shown me much decency or consideration. People have been all kinds of things to me, Elaine, nasty, patronising, servile . . . you know . . . but always with their eye on the ball! No one's ever made the kind of effort you've made by coming down today, by getting this car and going to the trouble to look like you do! I won't ever forget that, Elaine, not even if we never saw one another again after today! That's something I'll always remember and I suppose it makes a man feel that there must be some better way of showing his appreciation than by the usual way!"

She was touched by his words, more moved by them than she had been moved by anything anyone had ever said to her in the past. She was also amazed with herself for feeling so drawn towards him, so strongly that she dare not let him see it. She stood up, turning her back on him, and pretending to search for something in her bag.

"Get the bill and let's go, Archie! Wait, you'll want some money!"

She began to fumble in the handbag but he stopped her.

"Okay, I'll see to this! They never turn a lag loose without money!"

He took out a small roll of notes, money that he had had in his wallet when he began his sentence, and the two or three pounds that had been issued to him with his civilian clothes and railway warrant.

She went out first and when he rejoined her in the car he noticed that her expression was strained and that her bantering mood of the first stage of their journey had gone.

"Don't let's go straight home, Archie!"

He paused, his hand on the door handle.

"Where then?"

"I don't know! Anywhere! Do you know anywhere round here?"

"Bournemouth isn't far."

"All right then, let it be Bournemouth!"

He climbed in and sat silently beside her. She moved off with another clash, driving in second gear until reaching a junction with a painted out signpost. She took the right-hand fork and headed for the coast, and for several miles neither of them spoke. Then Elaine said:

"Do you know of a decent hotel in Bournemouth?"

He glanced at her and noticed that her expression was the same. Suddenly she steered into a lay-by and stopped the car.

At once he began to protest. "You'd better get back to town, Elaine! This is crazy and you know it's crazy! The last thing I want to do right now is put a spoke in your wheel. You'll be getting married to that Yank and. . . ."

"I'm not going to marry the Yank! It's all over now, Archie!"

"You mean you've broken it off . . . to come here, like this?"

"No, but I mean to break it off. . . . I don't want to go through with it, so for God's sake don't try and talk me back into it!"

He was quiet for a moment. When he spoke it seemed to her that he was choosing words as carefully as a man chooses his steps down a steep, dangerous path.

"Listen, Elaine! I've got about two thousand saved from the wreck, and I've almost decided how to use it in order to get up again! I'm over forty, forty-two to be exact, and it's not going to be all that easy! I've never proposed marriage to anyone . . . Old Toni fixed my marriage with Maria, and neither of us had much say in the matter. It was purely a business arrangement anyway, and now I can't marry you because Maria's a Catholic, and she'd never divorce me! Well, that's how it is, so there's not much in it for you, is there? I will say this though. If you meant what you said just now, if you've really thought about it and that's why you're here, then I'll do everything I can to make a go of it. If I didn't succeed, and we came a mucker, then you'd be absolutely free to pack it in, and I'd never hold it against you, never in this world! Is that sort of proposition any good to you, Elaine?"

She closed her eyes and threw back her head, so that her neck was pressed hard against the threadbare cretonne of the seat-cover. He noticed then that her hands were trembling so violently that she lost her grip on her handbag and it slid from her lap on to the floor.

He required a powerful effort to prevent himself from twisting round and taking her in his arms, but he made the effort, knowing that, at this moment of time, a frenzied embrace would only exacerbate their problem.

"You've got to have time to think about it, Elaine?"

She twisted round and faced him. "I don't *need* any more time," she shouted. "It's the only kind of proposition that interests me!"

She seized his hand and pressed it hard against her breasts and with a wonder too deep and bewildering for words he saw that she was crying. The sight of her tears calmed him more than anything else could have done.

He freed his hand and ran the palm gently round the smooth contours of her chin. Then he kissed her very lightly on the forehead.

"Okay, then! We'll make it, Elaine, and even if we don't, we'll have a hell of a good time trying! Here. . . ." He bent and retrieved her handbag, and tilted the driving mirror in her direction. "Get busy on your face before we hit Bournemouth! We can make it in twenty minutes if this vintage model holds out!"

He started the engine as, methodically and expertly, she began to repair her make-up.

"I don't know why I should waste time doing this," she said at length.

"Neither do I," he replied, "but do it! Bournemouth is almost sophisticated these days!"

CHAPTER XXXIII

D-Day Roundabout

ON the evening of the 5th of June, 1944, Jim Carver was despatched by his firm to make a delivery at a large Ordnance depot, near Basingstoke.

All day he had been helping to load tool-kits into the lorries and completing the papers that would pass him in and out of the camp. He wondered, as he set off at sunset, whether the crates he was now transporting were designed for the long-awaited invasion but decided not, for by now, he had almost lost faith in the great project.

His optimism of June and December, 1941, had ebbed throughout the subsequent year, to flow back for a spell on the tide of the North African invasion, and reach its high-water mark in the early autumn of 1943, when Italy surrendered and began 'to work her passage home.'

That was the moment, Jim decided, for the all-out assault on the northern shores of the Continent, for what could be more promising than to hammer Hitler on three fronts?

It was all very well for old Winnie to talk about 'probing the soft underbelly of Europe', and 'the matchless valour of our allies, the Russians', now slogging away at German eastern frontiers, but what were we and the Yanks doing, apart from footling about Southern Italy, and hammering the Nazis from the skies?

What was needed now was an irresistible drive from the north-west, an invasion mounted on a scale so formidable (and 'formidable' was one of Winnie's favourite words these days, wasn't it) that the whole structure of Occupied Europe collapsed, and Resistance movements everywhere surged into the open and began to hound the invaders over the Rhine.

Such a course, felt Jim, was so obvious that he was astonished that Eisenhower and Monty did not insist upon it taking place at once ... this very moment, before the Germans in Italy consolidated, and they and their snivelling satellites in the East had a chance to dig in behind the Carpathians.

Nothing happened, and the delay from September, 1943 onwards had soured him and awakened his pre-war suspicions of Churchill. What, he asked himself, was the old chap waiting for? Was it, as some were saying, for the Russians to bleed themselves white, so that post-war Europe would lie at the feet of the British and Americans?

Harold, of course, pooh-poohed this idea. Sitting over their maps in the kitchen of Number Twenty-Two, the Avenue strategists argued more acrimoniously than they had argued since Dunkirk.

"I must say that view's a bit thick, old man!" Harold protested. "After all, as I've told you again and again, we daren't risk a repulse when we do start. If we break our teeth on *Festung Europa*, as we did, I'm now persuaded, at Dieppe, then the war will last another three years, and the Russians will get so discouraged that they'll probably dig in around Warsaw!"

"Damn it," roared Jim, "would you blame 'em? What sort of encouragement are they getting? Here's Stalin, screaming for a Second Front and has been, for months! All he gets is a shush-shush-now-now from our play-it-safe boys, and a few tramp-steamers full of aircraft spares!"

"Come now," countered Harold, "you're not going to tell me that the Reds could have got this far without our material, are you?"

"I ruddy well am!" said Jim. "Do you think their offensive depends on the trickle that gets through on the Arctic convoys? That wouldn't equip a division, take it from me!"

"I certainly won't take it from you, old man," said Harold, stiffly, "or from that idiot, Baskerville, either! To hear *him* talk, on the way to the station sometimes, you'd imagine that he was in hourly telephonic communication with Moscow!

Westerman's as bad, too! He nearly fell out of the carriage with laughter when we passed an outrageous notice, painted on the side of a bombed building, in the Lower Road yesterday!"

"What sort of notice?" asked Jim, his curiosity getting the better of his impatience.

"One of those *'Second Front Now'* notices, scrawled up by somebody as reckless as yourself," growled Harold, "only this one was different for underneath it had got, *'We Bull, While Russia Bleeds!'* Oh, so you find it funny, do you?"

Jim did and chuckled, the story restoring his humour somewhat.

"It only goes to show that public opinion as a whole, is in favour of invasion, Harold," he said.

"Then public opinion doesn't know what it's blathering about," snapped Harold, "and anyway, I'm late for my train, so you'll have to wash up the breakfast things!"

He grabbed his coat, attaché case and umbrella and swept out, leaving Jim grinning. 'Dear old Harold,' he thought, as the front door banged, 'I daresay he'd carry a torch for Goering, provided someone tied a blue ribbon round his fat neck!'

The unloading of the convoy occupied most of the night, and Jim, as the last driver in line, was the last to leave the camp.

He drove out on to the Great West Road just as the sky in the east began to brighten and promise a fine day. The road was unusually empty. All the way to the Staines bottleneck he did not meet, or overtake more than half a dozen vehicles.

"It might be a peace-time Sunday before the after breakfast exodus begins," he told himself, as he slipped into neutral at the first set of traffic lights beyond the Hounslow junction.

A tanker drew up beside him, awaiting the lights, and a white-faced Cockney popped his head out of the cabin and whistled:

"Oi, mate! 'Eard the noos?"

"No," said Jim, "what news?"

"We've done it," said the Cockney, "we gorn an' invaded! Someone gimme the tip, back in Staines!"

"You sure . . . you absolutely sure?" shouted Jim.

"You betcher life, cock! It's the real thing! Hey up, she's green! So long, cock, see you in Gay Paree, eh?" and the petrol-lorry slid away, leaving Jim fumbling madly with his gears, urged on by the insistent hooting of the cars behind.

He drove on until he drew level with a roadside pull-up that he sometimes used when travelling this route. A group of men were standing at the counter flap, all engaged in animated conversation. Jim braked and almost flung himself out of the cabin.

"Is it true?" he demanded, of the nearest truck driver and when the man said that it was he thumped him on the shoulders and pranced about like a child, exclaiming, "I can't believe it! Damn it, I can't believe it!"

He seemed to have selected the surliest man in the group.

"I dunno why," said the man, whose tea had been slopped by Jim's excited caperings, "you bin expecting it 'aven't you, 'cos if you 'aven't you muster bin holed up somewhere since the Christmas before last!"

"How are we doing? How's it going?" demanded Jim.

"Christ knows!" said the man, "I wasn't there, was I?" and he flicked the dribbles of tea from his leather jerkin, and growled "Another cup, Lil" to the girl behind the counter.

An American Negro, eyes rolling under a huge forage cap, tugged at Jim's sleeve.

"Dey's asho', Mister! Dere was sumphin on de radio, so I heard!"

"Thank you, son," said Jim, "I expect it was just the bare announcement, I'll get home and tune in!"

He hesitated a moment, anxious to mark the occasion with some kind of gesture. The Negro was in the act of fumbling in his breeches for money to pay for his tea and sandwich.

"Have this on us, chum!" said Jim, and slapped down half a crown. Without waiting for tea or change, he strode back to his lorry, jumped in and pulled out on to the main road. If he chose his route carefully, he decided, he might be able to get back to the Avenue before Harold left for his train. He must discuss this with somebody and who better than Harold?

Harold had been gone some time when Jim came slamming into Number Twenty-Two. He had an appointment in chambers at Lincoln's Inn and caught an earlier train, for old Mr. Stillman, his employer, was down with bronchitis, and there was so much to do at the office. Because of this break in his routine he arrived at Lincoln's Inn without knowing of the landings and from then on, until past ten o'clock, he was closely occupied with the brief on which they were seeking counsel's opinion.

It was a complicated brief and Harold was a conscientious man, otherwise he might have noticed the atmosphere of suppressed excitement in the comings and goings of Sir Henry Chipping's staff. As it was he finished his work, noticed nothing unusual, handed the papers to an elderly clerk in the outer office, and went out into the Strand. He decided to treat himself to a cup of coffee and a roll, before returning to his own premises in St. Paul's Churchyard.

At the entrance to the little café that he used whenever he was in the Law Courts area, he had to step smartly back on to the pavement, in order to avoid a recklessly driven taxi, and in so doing he cannoned into a young woman, immediately behind him.

"I say, I'm most frightfully sorry!" apologised Harold sweeping off his hat. Then he gasped and his eyes sparkled with pleasure. "Well bless my soul! If it isn't Miss Redvers . . . Kay! It is, isn't it?"

It was indeed, but a very different Miss Redvers from the plump and rather dowdy girl who had worked alongside him for so long and had embarrassed him so dreadfully on Old Year's Night, eighteen months ago. She looked younger, livelier and altogether more sophisticated. She had lost weight, her figure had noticeably improved, and the clothes she was wearing looked far more expensive than the drab business costumes she had worn when she worked at Stillman and Vickers.

"This is remarkable, Miss Redvers! Fancy meeting you, like this!"

"Bumping into me would be a more accurate way of putting it, Mr. Godbeer," she laughed, and he noticed at once that she seemed far more assured and at ease with him than she had been at any time in the past.

"You look splendid, absolutely splendid, Kay! What are you doing? Where are you working? I say, I was just about to have a coffee, why don't you join me?"

"I'd love to," said Kay, leading the way into the café.

He went to the counter and returned to their table with two coffees, two rolls, and a pat of butter the size of a marble.

"No sugar, thanks, I don't want to put it all on again," she told him, "and I can only stop a few minutes anyway, we're terribly busy today as you can well imagine!"

"Where do you work? Didn't you go to Heslopp's, after you left us?"

"No," she confessed, with a fleeting smile, "I didn't even apply to Heslopp's. I work for the Ministry of Information, in Bloomsbury." She paused, then added, impressively, "I'm a private secretary to Marcus Wilmott!"

Harold gathered from her tone that he ought to know all about Marcus Wilmott but he did not and compromised with a polite nod. The new Miss Redvers, however, was far more observant than the old one and laughed outright.

"Why, you old fraud! You haven't a clue who he is, now have you?"

"No," he admitted ruefully, "I'm afraid I haven't! Who is he?"

"He's the big noise in Neutral Press Hand-outs," she told him. "He was a well-known journalist before the war and wrote a lot of popular travel books, the 'I-Spy' series ... remember? *I Spy Bulgaria, I Spy Chile.* He's really quite famous!"

"Is he nice?" asked Harold, reproving a small imp of jealousy, for he found to his dismay that he was slightly intimidated by her poise and whiff of patronage.

"He certainly *is*," said Kay, enthusiastically, and then, coyly, "as a matter of fact we're engaged, look!"

She pulled off her glove, thrust her hand in his direction, and spread the fingers. He saw a large engagement ring, an opal set in diamonds.

"My word!" he exclaimed, biting back an impulse to remind her that opals were reputed to be unlucky. "That's a corker! I say, I do congratulate you! The girls at the office will be terribly excited to hear about this! Do you mind if I tell them?"

"Not in the least," said Kay, "but I expect they'll have plenty else to gossip about today, won't they?"

"Why should they?" he demanded, "what's special today?"

She looked at him with surprise. "You mean you haven't heard about the invasion? I thought you were always up-to-the-minute with war news!"

"*Invasion?*" His jaw dropped and he whipped off his spectacles. "You mean *THE* invasion? *Today?*"

"Oh, Harold, you're priceless!" she giggled. "You must be the only person in Europe who doesn't know about it by now! We landed in France about six o'clock this morning!"

"God bless my soul!" said Harold, faintly. "Is *that* what everybody was so fidgety about in Sir Henry's office? But this is magnificent! . . . You say we got ashore . . . ? Was it very terrible? . . . Was it like Dieppe?"

"No," she said, soothingly, "not a bit like Dieppe. It seems to have been a picnic so far, all except at one spot, where some of the Americans ran into trouble. It was brilliantly planned, and I suppose all our bluff came off so much better than we could have hoped. The major landings were at Avranches and it looks as though the idea to cut off the Cherbourg peninsula will work out just as they planned."

"How do you know so much about it, Kay? Is it in the papers already?"

She laughed again and it struck him once more how very sure of herself she was, and what a remarkable transformation her personality had undergone in less than two years.

"Oh, I've been up to my neck in it for weeks," she told him. "It was to have been yesterday but it was postponed, on account of weather. Look here, why don't you come back to the office with me and meet Marcus? He's sure to have all the latest handouts and you'll learn a lot more from him than you'll read in the late editions!"

He was elated by the proposal and he could not help thinking how much Jim would envy him this remarkable opportunity.

"I'd love to come, providing it's not ... well ... not secret or anything," he told her.

"Oh, you're a very discreet person or I wouldn't have asked you," she said, and again he sensed patronage in her manner.

He was however, duly impressed by the bustle at the Ministry of Information, now housed, he discovered, in the London University, a building he had never previously entered.

File-bearing men and girls were running up and down staircases, office doors were opening and shutting, and everywhere along the corridors he could hear the tinkle of telephone bells.

Gravely she presented him to Marcus Wilmott, a thick-set, rather fruity man, about forty. Harold took an instant dislike to him, deciding that the fellow was far too conscious of his own importance, and very much inclined, thought Harold, to talk down to all the underlings who approached his desk, in the hope of impressing his visitor.

To Harold, however, whom Kay introduced as 'her old boss and a real sweetie!' he was cordial, and happy to 'put him in the picture' about the latest news from the Continent.

"It all seems to have gone fairly smoothly so far," he told Harold, "but of course there'll be a counter-attack as soon as Rommel sizes up the situation and regroups his armour! The thing is, will the weather hold? If it breaks up then Mulberry is sure to run into trouble."

Kay must have noted the puzzled frown that crossed Harold's face and at once took pity on him. She looked at Wilmott who smiled, wagged his finger and then appeared to relent.

"Mulberry," he said, "is ... er ... well, something they'll use for the build-up. It's a code name, of course, like 'Pluto'."

"What's 'Pluto'?" asked Harold seeing that it was clearly expected of him.

"I'm afraid 'Pluto', like 'Mulberry' is still top secret, old chap," said Marcus, with an irritating smile, "but you'll hear quite a bit about both, once we've consolidated!"

The 'phone rang and he snatched the receiver, just as

Harold was asking himself why Wilmott spoke the pronoun "we," as if Harold was a chance visitor from Siam, and not a fellow-countryman with a stake in the enterprise.

"Wilmott here! Right away? Yes . . . yes . . . naturally I will!"

He slammed down the receiver and stood up, extending a flabby hand.

"Well, I'm afraid you'll have to excuse us right now, old chap. Top-level hand-out over at A.M.! I shall need you, Kay, and it looks as if we shall have to skip lunch!"

They shook hands and as Kay showed Harold to the lift he noticed that she seemed slightly subdued. It was the effect of a few minutes with Marcus Wilmott, he supposed, for he himself felt somewhat intimidated and was secretly grateful for the 'phone call that had cut short their interview.

"I can't tell you how nice it's been seeing you again, Harold," she said, as they shook hands.

"It's been a wonderful experience for me," said Harold, "not only meeting you like this, but coming here, on a *day* like this! My word, but won't Jim Carver, my neighbour, be envious when I tell him!"

As he said this he felt a yearning to be with Jim and away from all these bustling, knowing people, and their self-conscious superiority. He distrusted their profundity. Each of them wore leeriness like a buttonhole. The people really engaged in this business, he told himself, were a long, long way from this marble rabbit warren, clambering ashore under fire most probably, and not making nearly so much fuss about it either! He was genuinely glad, however, to note the astonishing rehabilitation of Kay Redvers, for he had always had a bit of a conscience about her. He said, as they parted:

"I'm sure you'll be very happy, Kay. When do you intend getting married? I ask because . . . well . . . I'd like to send you a little something!"

"Oh, as soon as Marcus gets his divorce," she said airily and as the lift descended Harold reflected rather sadly that hardly anybody got engaged and married in the old-fashioned way nowadays, for they all seemed to hop on and off the bridal car as if they were changing 'buses. Then, as he walked out into the Square, he forgot Kay, and began to think about the Invasion, and what he was now in a position to tell Baskerville and Westerman if he met them on the 5.15 that night.

"I wonder," he mused, as he walked briskly into Kingsway, "I wonder if Esme's in it, or that jazzy sailor from over the road? It's a pity about Jim's boys, Berni and Boxer. They went through all the worst of it and now, when the great day arrives, one is out of the army altogether, and the other poor devil will hear about it from the Germans!"

* * * * *

Esme did not take part in the invasion but he none the less spent a very busy day at the Headquarters of the Free French, decoding short-wave messages originating from places like Grenoble and Limoges.

He was so absorbed in his work that he did not even think of Judy, or remember that this was the end of her first week in Devon as a civilian once more, or that the invasion would certainly mean that he would not be seeing her for some considerable time, for the C.O. had already warned him that when the bridgehead expanded he would have to fly to France and make personal contact with the Free Forces of the Interior.

Down in Devonshire, in the riotously overgrown garden of 'The Shillets', the tumbledown house and small-holding they had leased the day after she had discovered that she was pregnant, Judy Fraser scarcely gave a thought to D-Day. Her whole mind and body was occupied with the business of making a home out of what had been a wilderness.

They had discovered 'The Shillets' during a spring ramble, while on a week's leave at Maud Somerton's home.

It was a ramshackle, two-storey house, part Elizabethan, part Georgian, part mid-Victorian, and had been, successively, a farm, a manor house, a timber-merchant's depot, and then a farm again. Nobody appeared to have lived in it for several years and the only sound section of its structure was its red-pantiled roof, that seemed to have kept it from falling into hopeless decay.

It stood on a knoll, about fifty yards from the shallow

River Otter, where the stream swept in a wide and final curve to the sea. The seventy acres attached to the house were mostly sterile orchard and coppice, with three or four steep fields that might, if resown, support a small herd.

There was plenty of stabling and a vast assortment of outbuildings at the side, but what had attracted them at the outset was the mellow, lichen-covered façade, with its bulging latticed panes, and high Doric portico, enclosed by a small forecourt that had once been paved, but was now broken up and waist high with dock and cow-parsley.

They explored it eagerly, passing through the low-ceilinged hall and across the vast kitchen into the walled garden behind the stables. Here the afternoon sun beat down on a wild tangle of plants and fruit bushes, all long since run to seed; beyond, in the direction of the birch coppice, where the ground dipped towards the fields, primroses grew in huge, straggling clumps, and the unkempt hedge was already gay with dog-violet, campion and convolvulus.

"It's absolutely enchanting," Judy had exclaimed, "I can't think why it's still empty at a time like this."

"Take a look at the kitchen," said Esme, "and then ask yourself if you'd like to work in it!"

They went back to the kitchen and paced out the forty-seven strides from rusted range to dining-room.

"The meal might conceivably have been hot when it started," said Esme, "but it would be a dam' cold roast by the time you sat down to it!"

"I wouldn't have a kitchen here at all," Judy told him. "I'd make a new kitchen out of the butler's pantry, and use this for a washroom and drying room. I'd have the hall relaid with wooden blocks and use rugs, instead of this awful linoleum that some vandal has laid down! I'd make an inner glass door, so that the beauty of the old one was preserved, but the draughts were excluded. I'd take out that dreadful modern fireplace and expose the old one, the great big one that you could burn half a tree on! I'd have it looking wonderful if I had a thousand or so to spend on doing it!"

He was very quiet after that and left her to wander about upstairs. She heard his footfalls echoing as she sat in the sunny window seat and looked out across the ruined flower garden to the gleaming curve of the little river.

Presently he came down and stood quietly behind her.

"Are you glad about the baby, Judy?"

"Terribly glad, you know I am."

"How long will it take you to get your ticket?"

"Oh, about three weeks. I've got girls out in less!"

"Then supposing we did take this place?"

She turned and caught his hand. "You mean it? You mean that you like it as well?"

"I know that this is what I want to do after the war, to live in a place like this, and try and make something out of it, but I wouldn't want it if you didn't. It would be terribly hard going for a while, Judy, and one way and another we should have to stake pretty well everything we've got!"

"Oh, Esme, let's do it, *let's do it!*" she cried, leaping up and embracing him. "I know I'd like it but I was never quite sure that you would, in spite of all you said about wanting to farm. We could make this place live again! It would be like . . . like . . ."

She broke off, noting that his eyes were smiling.

"Like the old Manor," he completed.

"Yes, and I thought of that the moment I saw it! Did you, Esme?"

He nodded, squeezing her hand.

"Let's go and tell Maud and see what she has to say about it. I'll wager she knows more about it than the local agent."

He was quite right. Maud knew all about 'The Shillets' and its long record of failure. It was owned by the Markover Estate and could be had on a long repairing lease. Everyone, it seemed, had gone broke at 'The Shillets', possibly because it was too big to run as a private house and too small to pay as a farm.

"You can't farm seventy acres," she told them, "it's neither one thing nor the other. You could do chickens and pigs there, I imagine, there's quite enough land for that, and maybe keep a cow for your own use, but you'd have to supplement your income somehow . . . take summer visitors, or run a riding-school."

"I couldn't do that," said Judy, "it wouldn't be fair on you, Maud."

"I don't see why," said Maud, slowly, "seeing that I'm giving up in a year or so. Maybe we could do some sort of deal and I could stay on as a sleeping partner—no, no, wait. . . ." As Judy began to exclaim, "First I'd have to go out there and have a good look at the stabling and lofts. How about tomorrow?"

And so, miraculously, it was settled in a matter of days, and Judy went down to stay with Maud as soon as she was discharged, while Esme set about getting estimates from local builders for the extensive renovations that were necessary.

By D-Day some progress had been made, although the house was still far from habitable. Judy rode out there every day, encouraged by the local doctor's pronouncement that gentle horse-exercise, far from being dangerous to a woman in the early stages of pregnancy, was the best way of keeping her muscles relaxed and 'letting Nature get on with the job in her own way.'

She was here now, using the trowel on the forget-me-not bed, and pouring cans of weed-killer between the cracked paving stones of the forecourt. She was so happy, and so absorbed throughout the day, that when Maud came for her, leading a quiet cob for the ride home, she did not even remember about the invasion until Maud said:

"Trot on, trot on! I want to hear the six o'clock bulletin, gel!"

Then Judy remembered that there was a war on, and that she had promised to be in for Esme's bi-weekly 'phone call.

"That's odd," she said, "I'd completely forgotten it *was* D-Day! That fireplace is coming along nicely but there's so many idiotic restrictions about building. Mr. Perry says we'll have to apply for a supplementary licence if we're going to re-build the sties!"

. . . .

One member of the Avenue rump, who did play an active part in the landings was Ted Hartnell, ship's gunner, but it was by no means as active a part as he would have wished and he was bitterly disappoined when the Luftwaffe failed to show up in great numbers. Night fell off the littered beach without him having been able to train his sights on a single enemy aircraft.

He was so cast down by the scarcity of enemy aircraft that he complained bitterly to the cook, when he went below for his cocoa.

"It's enough to drive a man back to Civvy Street," he grunted, as though the cook had the ordering of Luftwaffe sorties in the west. "Where do you suppose they've got to? There were always plenty of the bastards around on the Malta runs, weren't there? And they came low enough when we were slopping about in life-jackets, didn't they? Here we are, right on their bloody doorstep, and not one of 'em's got the guts to take a crack at us! I tell you chum, it's enough to make a man go to the skipper and ask for his ticket!"

His chagrin at being so cheated was not counterfeit, for Ted Hartnell was an implacable Nazi-hater, and was here off the beaches from choice, having gone to considerable trouble to get himself transferred to a vessel earmarked for D-Day service.

Now he felt badly let down, like a huntsman who has been promised a cracking day with a famous pack, and has gone on to draw coverts from dawn to dusk without a whiff of scent.

The cook, an elderly seaman, with most of his troubles behind him, did not share Ted's disappointment.

"You don't know when you're well off, mate!" he growled. "All I c'n say is, thank Gawd they did stay away! And for why? Because I don't go for the kind o' visiting cards they use and that's straight!"

Ted finished his cocoa and went on deck again, taking up his position in the bows, and searching the expanse of sea between anchorage and shore. He had completed his tour of duty and had only to summon his relief, but he was reluctant to call it a day. He had all manner of scores to settle with the Luftwaffe and there would never be another chance like this, not if he lived to be a hundred.

Ted was well over forty now, and until 1939 he had never harboured a spiteful thought for anyone. His transition, from amiable jazz-drummer to fire-eating ship's gunner, had begun

long before the Nazis had fired a shot in his direction, and his
sea service in the Atlantic and Mediterranean, had confirmed
him in the belief that killing Nazis was the only worthwhile job
for a man who called himself a man.

The Nazis, on their part, had done their best to reciprocate
his animosity. They had torpedoed him in the South Atlantic,
and set him adrift for the better part of a fortnight, on a
spoonful of water a day. They had then machine-gunned him
all the way from Gibraltar to Malta and back, and they had
fired long bursts at him when he was clinging to an over-
turned lifeboat in the Bay of Biscay. Finally, as though despairing of killing him, they had turned their guns on his property
in the Avenue, cracked all his windows, and brought the ceilings
down. Despite all this he was still here, searching the sea and
sky for a target and finding none.

It was, as he said, enough to drive a man back to Civvy
Street.

* * * *

Two honorary members of the Avenue community did find
targets on that day.

Orrie and Mitch, boy-friends of the younger Carver twins,
Fetch and Carry, were ashore on Omaha beach at first light,
and manoeuvred their vehicles through the intricate network
of underwater obstructions that had already accounted for
most of their section.

By eight a.m. Omaha Beach was a shambles. Dead men
had piled up in the shallows, and wrecked vehicles were
almost wheel to wheel along the tide line.

It was not part of the official duty of Orrie and Mitch to
assault German strong-points, but in the kind of mix-up that
ensued on Omaha beach that morning anything could happen, and they soon found themselves being used as infantry.

The two Americans did not share Ted Hartnell's crusading
fervour for Democracy, but they were extremely interested
in personal survival, and at that particular time and place the
elimination of certain strong-points seemed the only way to
ensure such survival.

With Rangers, and other assault troops, they blasted their

way into the sandhills and shot Germans at close range, after which they gave a hand with the wounded and then helped in the buildup of ammunition on the hard-won beach-head.

They did their duty, with something to spare, but they did not pretend to themselves, or to each other, that it had been the kind of day they would look back upon with pleasure.

"I'd sure like to git to hell outa this," admitted Orrie, after darkness had fallen, and they lay in a slit trench trying to sleep above the roar of a naval barrage.

"Me, too," confessed Mitch, "I don't aim to be no hero, Bud, never did and never will! Them dolls back home ain't gonna believe about this, Orrie!"

"No," said Orrie, glumly, "but I sure ain't gonner waste no time convincing 'em, just so I get back in one piece! I'm gonna have other things on my mind right then, I guess!"

Presently the stream of naval shells overhead ceased. An officer looked into the trench and told them that word had come through from other sectors further east that British and Canadian units had made good their landings, and were advancing rapidly inland.

"We don't really belong with this outfit," Mitch told him, hopefully, "we're transport drivers, and we sorter got lost early on."

"Is that so?" said the officer, reflectively. "Well, I'm kinder lost myself, boys, but who the hell isn't?"

He moved on and when it was darker and quieter the two friends fell to discussing the twins again. Their situation increased their intimacy and they spoke more freely than they had ever spoken in the past.

"You aim to marry that doll o' yours, Mitch?" asked Orrie, presently.

"Yeah, I guess so, we have kinder talked it over," admitted Mitch. Then: "How about you and Carry?"

"Aw, we'll get around to it, mebbe," said Orrie, laconically, "and when we do, what-say we make it a double?"

"Could be," said Mitch, adding thoughtfully, "if we get into that trucking business, like we figured, we could set up house together. Then, maybe, we could swop dolls whenever we felt like it, for so help me, Orrie, I can't never tell one from the other, can you?"

Orrie was thoughtful for a spell. Finally, he said: "Mitch, here's sumphin I ain't never told you before! You remember that night at the Searchlight Battery dance, when I climbed in the wrong truck? Well, fact is it was dark, and I got to necking your dame by mistake!"

He expected Mitch to exclaim but instead the other received the confession with a gruff laugh.

"You think that kinda funny, Mitch?" demanded Orrie, indignantly.

"I sure do," said Mitch, "because it so happens that I made the same mistake the same night, and your dame didn't so much as squawk, so I reckon them two was ribbing us, Orrie!"

There was a silence for a moment, then Orrie said:

"How'd you make out with mine, Mitch? Honest, now!"

"How'd you?"

"I'm asking *you*, Mitch!"

"Okay! Pretty fair, I'd say! And you, Orrie?"

"Fair to middlin'," admitted Orrie.

There was another pause, broken by Mitch, who said:

"You figger we'd better let on we know 'bout it, Orrie?"

Orrie considered. "No, I guess not," he said at length. "Dames are funny that way. They don't mind kickin' over the traces now an' again, just so they c'n still let on to 'emselves they ain't. I figger we'll keep this one up our sleeves and make other mistakes, mebbe!"

"I'm easy," said Mitch and then, dismissing the women; "Jeese! I dunno what I'd give for a smoke, Orrie!"

"Me, too," said Orrie, "but I guess that'd be sticking our necks out, Bud!"

Presently the shelling ceased altogether and they slept.

* * * *

Far away to the south-east, some hundreds of miles from Omaha beach, a man who had not been seen in the Avenue for almost two years was celebrating D-Day in his own way. He was sitting in the latrine of a prison camp barrack block, absorbed in putting his final touches to a curious piece of handiwork.

The task was being performed in the uncertain light of a

home-made dip, constructed of a tin of meat fat and a twisted pyjama cord. The light was very bad and the materials inadequate, but he seemed, nonetheless, to be making good progress, for presently he laid his work aside, rose, took a metal skewer from his pocket, and began to address himself to the padlock on the wash-house door.

When he had picked the lock he whistled and looked over his shoulder at another man, who had been standing in the shadows behind him. This man was now examining what appeared to be a large oval picture frame.

"That's first-rate, Boxer," said the other man. "Are we ready to hang it now?"

"Just about, Whitey," said Boxer, and opened the door a crack in order to look across the wide yard towards the garrison wire.

The beam of a searchlight swung slowly across the big compound, paused for a moment on the big canteen building, then passed on, leaving the prisoners' barracks in darkness.

"*Now*," said Boxer, and dived into the open, with Whitey close on his heels.

Their excursion was a direct result of the D-Day landings, news of which had come through on 'Anna', the illicit camp radio, within two hours of the invasion.

The prisoners were jubilant and their guards had been correspondingly nervous all day.

Apart from a good deal of skylarking, however, the day seemed to have passed quietly enough, far too quietly for Boxer, who began to feel restless towards evening and drifted over to see his friend, Corporal White, who lived across the compound.

"Seems tame, not to do *nothing* to show '*em!*" he told Whitey. "Damn it, we've always celebrated good news in some way, haven't we, and this is the biggest news we've ever had, isn't it?"

"Sarnt-Major said to take it easy, Boxer," said Whitey despondently. "He says old Jerry's sure to be trigger-happy for a week or so!"

"Aw, what the hell," grumbled Boxer, "I don't mean nothing like *that!* I mean just a bit of a lark! Listen, Whitey, I got a little pepper-upper, that's a hundred per cent safe, and will only take the two of us! We don't need to say nothing to the others, not till it's in the bag!"

Corporal White had had a wide experience of Boxer's 'pepper-uppers' in the past year or so, and although curious he was nevertheless guarded in his reply.

"What is it?" he asked, "you tell me, and let me judge for myself."

Boxer told him and Whitey chuckled, appreciatively.

"Cor! No harm in that," he admitted, "no harm at all! You say you can get hold of a picture of Adolf?"

"Easy," said Boxer, "and we can take our pick of frames, can't we?"

"I'm on," said Corporal White, "only let it be a surprise, to all the others. We can fix it in the canteen, high up above the service hatch, so don't say nothing 'till it's all fixed!"

They perfected and planted their 'pepper-upper' and were back in their own huts within twenty minutes of leaving the barrack. It was not until after roll-call the following morning that their handiwork was appreciated by the prisoners as a whole.

The duty officer heard howls of laughter issuing from the canteen, as he made his final check of numbers, preparatory to handing in the parade states into the guardroom.

He was curious to discover the cause of the merriment. It did not sound the kind of disturbance that called for disciplinary action, but more like a display of high spirits that needed prompt investigation before it overreached itself and got out of hand.

He called a corporal and two elderly reservists, and marched them in to the canteen, where the prisoners were awaiting their meal.

His arrival was the signal for renewed laughter. Howls of delight greeted the squad's arrival, and the men made way for him, respectfully, as he walked down the long building towards the serving hatches at the far end. It was here that the most of the kriegies were gathered, and the laughter was loudest and most persistent.

Then he stopped, ten yards short of the hatch, as his gaze rose slowly above the level of the aperture, and came to rest on an astonishing addition to canteen furniture.

High above his head, so high that it could only be reached by a ladder, hung a large coloured print of the Fuehrer. It was one of the portraits sent out to the camps in batches by one of the Berlin illustrated papers, and it showed the Fuehrer in pensive mood, staring down into the hall with that look of brooding sadness so typical of his recent portraits. It was framed, neatly enough, in a lavatory seat, and underneath it, in large, paint-scrawled letters, was the legend: *Have this one on me, chaps!*

Boxer heard the duty officer's squeal of rage and at once clutched Whitey for support. Together, and in the midst of a shouting, laughing throng, they reeled against the deal table. Tears filled Boxer's eyes as he stamped his large feet in a paroxysm of mirth. He laughed openly and shamelessly, for Boxer had always enjoyed his own jokes as much as anyone else.

CHAPTER XXXIV

'Crossbow'

IN the early hours of June 14th, 1944, Jim Carver was returning empty from a delivery in the West Midlands, when he passed what appeared to be the scene of a routine bomb-incident.

He stopped because he was curious. The scene had a familiar air, uniformed men standing beside their parked lorries, a vast heap of rubble, a tangle of fire hoses on the pavement, and a fire-tender parked alongside the wide gap in the terrace.

He thought: "My word, but that must have been a big one! I didn't know there had been a raid last night," and he climbed out of his cabin, and touched a tin-hatted warden on the arm.

"What was it? A blockbuster?"

"We're not sure," said the warden, "I think it was jet-tisoned. Somebody didn't want to fly all the way home with it, I suppose, but whatever it was it was a nasty packet, one of the worst we've had!"

"Damn it, I thought we'd finished with this sort of thing," said Jim.

"So did everybody," said the man, shortly and moved away to help a group of men in battledress demolish a tottering chimney-stack.

Jim went back to his lorry and drove slowly into the West End, via the Bayswater Road. The traffic was light and there seemed to be few people about, although it was now approaching the first rush hour. He was tired and longed for bed. "I'm getting too long in the tooth for these all-night jobs," he told himself. "Thank God it all seems to be finishing, and we shall be able to take things a little easier. What a hell of a time it's lasted, already nearly five years!"

He reached home, turned in, and slept until Harold came home at six. Harold called up from the hall:

"You about, Jim?"

"I soon will be! Put the kettle on, Harold!"

He came downstairs in his pyjamas, unshaved and with his grey hair sticking up on end.

"I've slept the clock round! I was all in when I got back, soon after you left this morning. I passed a nasty incident on the way. Did you get anything over this side?"

"I heard them banging away at something," said Harold, "but it didn't sound much like a raid, more like a single aircraft, out of control. As a matter of fact there's a rumour in the City that it was the first of them."

"First of what?" asked Jim, "what rubbish are they talking in your office now?"

"Secret-weapon talk," said Harold, "Hitler's last fling. They say this one was a pilotless 'plane, called the 'V.1'."

He was surprised when Jim failed to pooh-pooh the idea.

"I suppose it's possible," he said, remembering the size of the gap in the row of houses he had passed early in the day. "I wonder if our people are on to it?"

They were, as he had ample opportunity to discover during the latter part of the week, when delivering to Eastbourne and Hythe. By that time the run from Lambeth to the East Sussex coast, had become known as 'Doodlebug Alley', and a succession of strange, speeding missiles, looking like crossbows, and sounding like a two-stroke motor-cycle being driven across the sky, were streaming in from the Pas de Calais coast, each heading in the general direction of the capital.

At first, Jim did not take them very seriously. He fell back on his old method of personal reassurance, the line that he had taken throughout the blitz. London was a big place, and if one's chances of being hit during an attack by two hundred bombers was small, then how much better were they of dodging a single warhead, without a human brain to guide it?

He pulled in on the way through Norwood one morning and watched a V.1. pass directly overhead, honking its way north-east, and suddenly cutting out as it dived silently to earth.

It fell short of the main target, somewhere in the direction of New Cross, but he distinctly felt the vibration, and saw the vast plume of yellowish smoke mushroom into the sky.

He watched the street come to life again, shoppers emerging slowly from doorways into which they had crouched when the V.1's engine had cut, and its dive had begun. Then he looked more closely at a middle-aged woman's face, as she straightened herself beside his lorry. There was fear in her face, fear and infinite strain, but when she saw him looking at her, her mouth twitched into a nervous smile.

"That's another that missed us, anyway," she said but the tremor in her voice belied the flippancy of the remark.

"They don't seem to be having much effect," said Jim. "Of all the things that little maniac has tried so far this is certainly the daftest!"

"I don't know about that," said the woman, grimly, "they kill people, don't they? I passed a place yesterday in Beckenham, where they say one of 'em wiped out about fifty. Hit a chain store, so they said, and made a rare mess of it, I can tell you!"

He missed the note of joviality that he had learned to expect from strangers recounting a bomb story.

"Have the people round here really got the wind up about them?" he wanted to know.

"Yes, they have," said the woman, "and I'll tell you why. It's because you can see 'em coming!"

That, Jim discovered, was the general opinion along 'Doodlebug Alley' during the next few weeks. You could see them coming, and were therefore presented with a choice of where to run. There was a kind of suspended horror about them after their engine had cut, for although one knew full well that they were going to dive one could never be sure whether they would land a mile away, or a few yards away. Sometimes they were as long as ten seconds in descending after their honk had ceased, and in that ten seconds it was possible to die half a dozen times.

There was another aspect about them that worried Jim. They came at the end of nearly five years of war, at a time when Londoners had persuaded themselves that the worst was behind them. People were so tired, and so bored, and many, in spite of everything the papers said about food calories, were badly undernourished.

Suppose, Jim asked himself, the V-1. was to be followed by V.2 and V.3. Suppose the inflow of missiles was stepped up until one was falling on London every few seconds? How long could an exhausted population stand up to that kind of attack?

He was partly reassured, in July, after an unofficial visit to the coastal defence-belt.

Delivering crude oil containers, to a depot near Winchelsea, he passed teams of sunburned R.A.F. men, camping beside their moored barrage balloons and he could see for himself the long line of balloons gleaming across the sky as far as the Kent horizon.

A corporal told him that the barrage had already hooked down quite a number of bombs and would claim more as soon as it thickened.

There was also, he learned, an ack-ack belt nearer the coast, and beyond that a Channel fighter patrol supplementing the one attacking V.1's from inland bases.

Lying on his back, in a field near Rye marshes one morning Jim watched a Tempest assail one of the missiles, speeding up behind it and firing tracer into the tail, until the flying-bomb began to glow and falter, twisting and turning as though to shake off its pursuer, but ultimately blowing up with a roar as the fighter-plane zoomed into a victory roll and bore off towards the coast.

"By God, but that was marvellous, marvellous!" Jim said to himself. "If only old Harold had been here to see it."

The visit to the coast improved his morale. For once, he told himself, the authorities appeared to be tackling an emergency with speed and imagination, and when he read in the papers that the first flying-bomb launching base had been captured in France he felt as elated as he had been by news of the German surrender at Stalingrad the previous year.

His faith in the staying power of the Londoner received an additional boost one sunny afternoon in August, when he happened to be crossing Leicester Square, on his way home after a call at the company's office.

His attention was attracted, as always with Jim, by a crowd of people assembled in Great Newport Street, near the tube station.

Assuming it to be another incident he hurried over to offer assistance, but when he joined the crowd he found that it was not the kind of incident he had imagined but merely a large group of pedestrians engaged in watching a window-cleaner rescue a trapped pigeon.

The pigeon had wedged itself behind the wired-up window of a tall building and was resisting all efforts to be freed. Balanced on an extended ladder the man had already loosened the corner of the netting but the pigeon had flown into the top left-hand corner, where the rescuer was finding it difficult to reach.

The crowd continued to grow, and so did its interest in the rescue. Men and women began to call out advice. "Come down and move the ladder further over!" "Rip that other corner away, chum!" until a man in authority, presumably he who occupied the offices behind the window, emerged from the building and called: "Hold on! I'll nip up and help you from inside!"

At this the crowd cheered and a policeman, smiling broadly, began to ascend the ladder.

"I've got a pair of cutters here," he shouted to the perched window-cleaner.

The street was now jammed with people, but nobody appeared to heed the familiar honk-honk of an approaching V.1. Jim heard it clearly and marvelled, half-expecting the crowd to scatter, and dive for cover, but not one person moved. All remained gazing upwards towards the second-storey window and there was renewed cheering when the window opened and the man who had promised assistance reappeared, waving a rolled-up newspaper in an attempt to frighten the bird into the window-cleaner's grasp.

Overhead the honking suddenly ceased and a few people near Jim glanced up at the patch of open sky between the eaves.

"Hey up!" said a Covent Garden carter, grimacing at Jim, "here comes another bloody doodlebug! Hold on to yer 'at, mate!"

A shattering explosion came from the general direction of the Strand but the crowd hardly flinched, for at that moment the window-cleaner grabbed the pigeon by its legs and frenzied cheering broke out on all sides.

The policeman reached up and took the bird, holding it close against him as he descended. The man in the office window beamed down on the crowd.

"Is it okay?" asked the carter, shouldering his way to the foot of the ladder.

"Looks so," said the policeman and suddenly tossed the bird into the air.

They watched its flight as it soared away towards St. Martin-in-the-Fields and then the policeman, suddenly recollecting his duty, shouted, "Now then everybody! Move along there, move along!"

Jim walked thoughtfully into Charing Cross Road and down the incline towards the station. The incident had impressed him more favourably than anything he had witnessed since Dunkirk. Was this, he wondered, an unconscious demonstration of the spirit of the people who had survived so many desperate situations during the last ten centuries? Was this the secret of their survival, often against impossible odds, and in the face of all intelligent predictions?

That bomb! It could have destroyed every one of them! It could have sent window-cleaner, pigeon, policeman and spectators into Covent Garden, and gouged a hole in Great Newport Street large enough to hold twenty double-decker buses! This, in fact, was what it was meant to do! For this it had been assembled in Germany, transported hundreds of miles to the coast, and launched across the Channel and the length and breadth of Kent.

But no one had taken the slightest notice of it! They were all much too taken up with the rescue of a stray pigeon, trapped behind splinter-wire! Not even the trench-veterans of the First World War had faced a bombardment with this serenity, so what did it matter how many secret weapons were being assembled in the Reich factories, when each of them must take second-place to a trapped pigeon?

He caught his train and read the war news all the way to Woodside. The German counter-attack at Mortain had been thwarted by rocket-firing Typhoons. The Ploesti oil-wells had been plastered by the Ninth U.S. Army Air Force. The Yanks were hammering away at the outer ring of Japanese conquests in the Pacific. The Russians were advancing on Warsaw. The Allies were in command of the whole of Southern Italy and were surging north to the Po. The war, surely, was practically won, and would have been, damn it, if the mutinous Junkers' time-bomb had been more strategically placed in 'that little maniac's' headquarters on the Eastern Front.

The links were bathed in a golden light as he turned into Shirley Rise and strode up the incline towards the Avenue. Somebody called to him as he crossed the road and turning his head he saw that it was Edith Clegg, presumably returning home after the matinée at the Odeon.

He waited for her to catch him up. "Hullo there, Miss Clegg! What a lovely afternoon."

He noticed then that her face was grey and that she was breathless. She looked indeed, as though she had just run the whole length of the Lower Road, and he wondered vaguely why she should be in such a prodigious hurry to get home for tea.

"What's the matter, Miss Clegg? Is your sister missing again?"

Edith reached him, sobbing for breath and clutched his arm.

"They 'phoned ... it's *us* ... one of those awful doodle-bugs ... !"

She was unable to say more but there was no need. Jim seized her by the hand and together they began to run along the pavement to the corner shop.

When they reached it they stopped and stared blankly at one another. Where the shop had been was now a vast array of tumbled bricks and shattered paving stones, and the Avenue was full of people, scrambling here and there over mounds of rubble.

Every house on the even side, from the corner shop to the bend in the crescent, was down, and beyond the wreckage a line of ambulances reached away out of sight towards the Rec' gates.

CHAPTER XXXV

Edith Expands

HAROLD had taken an afternoon off that Friday. It was not his habit to take afternoons off but Mr. Stillman, the senior partner of the firm, had been insisting that Harold looked very peaky these days, and shortly after his own convalescence he took a good look at his clerk, complimented him on the way he had coped during the last few months, and told his partner, Vickars that "something should be done about that chap, Godbeer before he gets wise to himself, and demands a rise in salary on pain of resignation!"

Vickars agreed. For a long time now he had appreciated Harold's worth. It was not often, he reflected that one could buy so much loyalty for under five hundred a year.

"We ought to send him off on a holiday," he told Stillman.

"Not that I think he'd ever leave us, but we don't want him going sick, not with business as good as it is!"

"Then we'll not only make him take a holiday, we'll give him a bonus," said Stillman. "How about twenty-five?"

"Make it fifty," said Vickars, "he'll never get over that!"

So Harold was summoned to the senior partner's office and offered a cheque for fifty pounds, on condition that he took a fortnight's holiday, commencing that very day.

"Have you got somewhere to go?" Stillman wanted to know.

Harold, who was quite stunned by his employers' generosity, mumbled something about Devonshire.

"Nice hotel?"

"My daughter-in-law's got a farm down there, Mr. Stillman, and I daresay she'd have me, if I wrote to her."

"You've no time to write, 'phone!" said Stillman, "and when you get there take things easy, and don't go volunteering for anything! I don't want to see you here until a fortnight on Monday, understand?"

Harold 'phoned Judy, who said that she would be delighted to put him up. She had good daily help now and 'The Shillets' was just about habitable. No, she wouldn't go to a lot of trouble, and she wouldn't put herself out for him. He could please himself what he did during the day and she would be very glad of his company in the evenings! Yes, he was to catch the 9.30 from Waterloo, change at Sidmouth Junction, change at Tipton St. John's, and she would meet him there in the trap! No, she wasn't an invalid simply because she was five months' pregnant, and was perfectly strong enough to drive a trap along a few country by-roads!

After this encouraging conversation Harold began to feel excited about his holiday. He was very fond of Judy and guessed how lonely she must be, since Esme had gone over to France, and was not able to write much on account of his mysterious comings and goings in recently-liberated territory.

He caught the 12.50 from London Bridge and was back in the Avenue in time for a cold lunch. After lunch he changed into tweeds and completed his packing, not forgetting to turn out his fishing-rod, for Judy had told him there was trout in the pool opposite the farm.

He had never done very much fishing, although he had owned the rod for more than twenty years. He had always fancied himself as a fisherman and had promised himself that on his retirement he would take up fishing seriously.

He carried the rod down to the verandah and stood facing the double gardens, practising a few casts. The sun over the old Nursery was bright and warm, and the sounds of the suburb seemed to carry a long way in the stillness of the summer afternoon. He could hear children playing in Delhi Road and the familiar whirr of lawn-mowers higher up the Avenue. It reminded him of Saturday afternoons in peace-time, when the song of the suburb was always heard so clearly at weekends.

Presently one of the Jarvis girls at Number Eight turned on a radio, and Harold recognised the music of one of his old favourites, '*The Student Prince*'.

He put down his rod and eased himself into a deck-chair. He remembered having taken Eunice to see '*The Student Prince*' when it was a hit show in the West End, and the songs always made him feel young but pleasantly sad, as though he too had once raised his tankard to Cathy, in Old Heidelburg.

As he sat there listening Louise popped her head out of the kitchen door of Number Twenty.

"Would you like a cup of tea, Uncle Harold? I'm making some now, for Jack. He's in the nursery, working."

Harold thanked her and said that he would like a cup of tea very much indeed. It was all he needed to make him feel that his holiday had really commenced.

Louise called Jack, who came clumping along the gravelled alley dividing gardens and nursery, and lazily, Harold watched his slow, ponderous movements, as he cleaned his spade, and carefully scraped his boots. How lucky I am, mused Harold, to have such wonderful neighbours, and what fools we all were to be so stiff and formal with one another during all those years between the wars!

At that moment, as Jack was about half-way up the path, they both heard the familiar honking, beyond the wood.

"Hullo! I thought it was time we were due for one of those infernal things," grumbled Harold.

"Aw, giddon! Us don't take no notice o' they," said Jack, shading his eyes and looking carelessly into the sky.

"I'll come and drink my tea in the kitchen," said Harold, struggling up from his deck-chair.

The *bub-bub-bub* of the flying-bomb suddenly ceased and was succeeded by a curious swishing sound, rising in key to a wild, screaming wail.

"Good Lord . . . !" shouted Harold and saw fear in Jack's eyes as, together, they leaped from the verandah towards the open back door of Number Twenty.

. . . .

Becky was also in her back garden when the flying-bomb landed.

She was standing on a box placed against the nursery fence of Number Four and calling to her strays, 'Mittens' and 'Mog.'

In the years before the war, when her own cat, Lickapaw, had been alive, Becky Clegg had had no time at all for the nursery strays, and had actively discouraged Lickapaw from associating with them, but that was because they tempted Lickapaw to stay out all night and sometimes to remain away from home for nearly a week.

Now that her own cat was dead, and his inscribed headboard stood under the loganberries, Becky had forgiven all the cats that lived in Delhi Road and used the nursery as a hunting-ground. 'Mittens' and 'Mog' were her favourites, for she had got it into her head that they had been orphaned by the 1940 bomb that demolished the corner block, and had since lived wild, subsisting on what they could catch, or on the bounty of Avenue housewives.

This was not so, for both cats had good homes of their own, but Edith had never told her this, for she knew that Becky liked going down to the fish shop in the Lower Road each day, and buying them scraps. She liked to make sure that they actually got the fish, and it was part of her ritual to climb on the box at tea-time and call them by name. They were much more punctual to meals than Lickapaw had been and it was rare that they did not come running to her summons, or the smell of fish-heads.

They came now, a black cat, with snow-white paws, and a lean, thickly-barred tabby, and as they ran they mewed with delight and Becky exclaimed.

"Oh, you dears! Oh, you loves! Aren't you good things to come so quickly? You were waiting for me, now weren't you?"

She heard the honk of the V.1 and remembered Edith's instructions. Whenever she heard one of those nasty things she was to stop whatever she was doing and run under the stairs. So many had passed over just lately, however, and it was very tiresome to have to jump down, before she had time to give Mittens and Mog their rations. They would be so disappointed, she thought, if she snatched the fish away just as they were reaching up for it, and they would surely never trust her again! So she decided to ignore the horrid noise and finish what she was doing. She leaned over the fence and called: "Never mind the old Doodlebug dears, never mind, then!"

Suddenly everything around her seemed to rise up and turn different colours, orange, purple and silvery grey. For some reason the box on which she was standing slid away from her feet, leaving her clinging to the tall fence, which her weight must be pulling down, for the air around her was filled with a rending, crackling sound.

She thought, as she fell: "Oh, dear, Edith *will* be angry, she will be terribly angry about breaking the fence . . . !"

. . . .

The bomb came in slantwise from the extreme south-western corner of Manor Wood, striking the Avenue oblique-ly at Number Thirty-Eight, after skimming over the chimneys of the odd numbers, opposite.

It exploded on the upper storeys of the block and its fin was later found as far away as the hawthorn hedge that bordered the links in Shirley Rise.

It had no business to approach from this angle and should have come in from the south-east, or at any rate from due south, but its mechanism had been slightly damaged by an ack-ack splinter, and it had been behaving eccentrically all the way from the coast, widening its line of approach, and losing height far more rapidly than its despatchers had planned.

It demolished every house between Number Thirty-Eight and the corner shop, nineteen in all, besides shattering parts of the even numbers opposite, and sending a solid chunk of Mr. Saunder's yard wall right through the front of Number One. It killed twenty-one of the residents at that end of the crescent and it injured another eighteen.

Jack Strawbridge and his wife, Louise, were killed outright, in the kitchen of Number Twenty, Jack as he crossed the threshold, with Harold at his heels, and Louise as she moved away from the gas-stove, carrying the teapot.

Harold was lifted and flung outwards, towards the nursery,

where he landed amidst debris on the vegetable rows that Jack had quitted but a moment before.

Becky Clegg was killed by blast at the bottom of her garden, and Miss Baker had a miraculous escape when masonry was hurled into her front room, at Number One, killing the local Health Visitor who was making a routine call on her.

Mrs. Westerman and Mrs. Baskerville were killed in the corner shop, along with Mr. Saunders, Archie's successor, and his shopgirl, Letty Jarvis. The two customers had been buying their weekend rations, and enjoying a pleasant little gossip about the Norton girl, Amy, who had just given birth to a coloured baby at her aunt's home in Lucknow Road.

Letty Jarvis's sister, Cora, who had been listening to excerpts of 'The Student Prince' on the radio, was killed at Number Eight, which was bad luck indeed, for the Jarvises were newcomers to this end and their old home, Number Eighty-Six, was untouched by the bomb.

Mrs. Hooper was killed under the stairs at Number Six, and old Mrs. Coombes, who had survived a direct hit on her home in 1941, was killed in the open as she slipped out to post a letter to Bombardier Crispin, in Italy.

When the dust settled the rescue teams found that their way into the Avenue from Shirley Rise was blocked and consequently had to approach the scene from the Rec' end. They found that the far end of the crescent had been virtually wiped out.

Jim Carver, having led the gibbering Edith away and handed her over to some people in Shirley Rise, ploughed his way over the loose debris that now covered the unrecognisable yard of the corner shop. He stood for a moment on the site of Number Four, with tears streaming down his face and the muscles of his throat twitching.

In the last few years he had witnessed a large number of incidents but he had never looked upon such horror as this, not even on the Western Front. Body after body was lifted from the rubble and carried to the line of ambulances that were queueing further down the Avenue. Members of heavy rescue teams were calling to one another to lift beams and clear away what seemed to Jim to be whole acres of shattered bricks. Every now and again they came upon someone whom Jim recognised, and when the still figure of Becky was found, and he saw that she was not disfigured, he sponged her face and tried to take a more active part in the work.

It was useless, however. His brain seemed numbed and his legs and arms weighted down, so that it required an immense effort to move across the uneven ground.

He thought: "Thank God old Harold wasn't here! Thank God he won't be home yet! I'll go down to Woodside and meet the train! I wouldn't like him to see this, it would upset him for months!"

Then young Baskerville called him from the rear of the nearest ambulance. He saw that the boy's face was ashen and wondered vaguely whether he had been on the spot when it happened.

"Mr. Carver! Will you go and tell my Dad about Mum, Mr. Carver? I ought to but I can't, I just can't! Shopping she was, getting the rations. Look at her, Mr. Carver, just look at her!"

Jim glanced at the shapeless bundle under the stained blanket and looked quickly away again.

"All right, son," he said wearily, "I'll tell him. You get yourself some tea from the mobile canteen. I'll tell your Dad about Mum!"

He made a great effort to collect himself and clambered across to the warden who was directing operations.

"How many?" he asked, hoarsely.

"Over twenty so far, Jim," said the warden. "Christ! Did you ever see such a shambles?"

The man who had succeeded Jim as chief of the heavy rescue squad now approached him.

"This is your road, isn't it, Carver?"

"Yes," said Jim, "and I've got to find out about my daughter and son-in-law. They were in Number Twenty, right in the path of the bloody thing!"

"Hopner's making some sort of list," said the man. "Some of the locals are helping him with it! He's over there, on the old bomb site."

He moved over and saw from Hopner's failure to meet his eyes that Jack and Louise were among the dead. He looked

over his shoulder at the list and it seemed at first as though
almost everyone he knew was on it ... Jack, dear old Lou,
Becky Clegg, Mrs. Baskerville, Mrs. Westerman, the two
Jarvis girls, Mrs. Hooper, old Mrs. Coombes ... merciful
God, how many more?

Somebody touched his arm. It was an A.F.S. man that he
knew, from the Upper Road depot.

"There's a chap here asking for you, Carver, one of the
injured. Can you spare a minute?"

Jim left Hopner and followed the man over the rubble that
had been Twenty and Twenty-Two, and into the garden
behind, now knee deep in litter. A small group of ambulance
men were standing round a stretcher placed on a cleared
space. The man on the stretcher was Harold.

"Hullo, Jim!"

The voice was barely a whisper but the eyes smiled. Jim
fell on his knees, unable to say a word, but taking Harold's
hand in both of his and pressing it.

"I came home early, Jim," said Harold, as though to
convince Jim that it really was he who was lying on the
stretcher. "What happened to Louise and Jack? Are they all
right?"

Jim found his voice but hardly recognised it.

"Never mind anyone else, how about you?"

"It's my leg, I think," said Harold and shuddered violently.
"Thing is, I've lost my damned glasses! Do you think you
could find my glasses, Jim? They must be somewhere
around!"

Jim glanced at the confusion around him and then back at
Harold. He saw that his friend's face was drained of colour
and that his hair was white with brick dust. His eyes travelled
lower down the stretcher and he saw that two ambulance
men were applying a tourniquet to the right leg and that
Harold's left leg and left arm were already swathed in bandages.
Was Harold, too, going to die?

"I'll have a look round, Harold," he faltered, "and then
bring 'em along to the hospital." Then, his brain clearing
somewhat: "I tell you what old chap, I'll phone your occulist
and see if he can rustle up a spare pair. You'll need 'em in
dock you know, you'll want to read. Take it easy right now,

Harold. . . ." As the men lifted the stretcher, and one of them shook his head at Jim and frowned. "I'll come along to the hospital as soon as they let me, how's that?"

A look of desperation showed in Harold's grimy face and he half rolled on the stretcher, shooting out his right hand and plucking the seam of Jim's trousers.

"Don't leave me, Jim, *don't!*"

"I'm not leaving you, Harold. I'm taking you to the ambulance and I'll be around all the time!"

They picked their way into the Avenue and moved down to an ambulance that stood outside Number Forty. Gently Jim disengaged Harold's hand as they slid the stretcher inside and closed the doors.

"How badly is he hurt?" Jim asked, of the remaining stretcher-bearer.

"Difficult to say," said the man, "deep cuts and compound fracture of the right leg and other fractures in the left leg and left arm. Ribs caught it too, by the look of things. He was blown about twenty-five yards, clean over the fence!"

Jim turned away and then seemed to lose his sense of direction. He kept telling himself that he should be doing something useful, instead of drifting about and looking on, while others worked at rescue, but the shock had made conscious thought impossible and he remained standing irresolute where the cart track broke the sweep of the odd numbers. It seemed to him the one recognisable spot in the Avenue.

He was still standing there when Edith found him. She came scrambling over the loose bricks from the direction of Shirley Rise and it seemed to him that she showed remarkable agility and resolution. When she reached him she smiled and caught up his hand.

"I had to come the minute I heard, Mr. Carver! Oh, you poor dear. . . . They told me about your daughter and son-in-law, and I had to come, I knew you'd need somebody!"

He looked at her in astonishment. Did she also know about her own sister and all the others?

"It's terrible I know," said Edith, "but it's better than any of them being terribly injured and suffering. They couldn't have known anything about it. . . . Just a terrible bang. I'm sure Becky didn't know anything about it, poor lamb!"

The numbness began to lift from his head. Then she did know and yet, in the midst of her wild grief, her instinctive concern had been not for herself, or even for Becky, but for him! Less than half an hour ago she had been hysterical with shock and now here she was, having learned the worst, scrambling over piles of rubbish to console and comfort him!

"Where are you going to sleep tonight, Edith?" he asked, taking her arm. "Almost everyone we knew is homeless or with too much trouble of their own."

"I've thought of that," she said, "and Mrs. Foxley, that nice little woman you left me with in Shirley Rise, is fixing it up right now. The sister of the manager at my cinema runs a little hotel. . . . You probably know it, it's called 'The Priory', at the corner of Outram Crescent. I've been there to dinner, and it's ever so nice and homely. I thought I'd go there and there's a room for you too, if you'd like it. I asked Mrs. Foxley to ask her to keep you one!"

It was astonishing, he thought, how steady and clear-thinking she was, and how impressively she had risen to the occasion while he, a man, and a professional rescue-worker, had gone to pieces under the impact.

She was leading him gently away from the Avenue and down Shirley Rise to Mrs. Foxley's and as she led, and he followed without protest, she chattered away as if she was organising a Bank Holiday excursion.

"You'd better have some tea now, and then a good hot bath, Mr. Carver. Afterwards we'll come round and see if we can salvage anything. I don't suppose everything will have been smashed or buried. We can borrow a couple of suitcases, I suppose. Mrs. Foxley said she knew where she could lay hands on some, and then we'd better get a taxi and go round to The Priory. I mean, it's no good hanging around here until dark, is it? It'll only make us all the more morbid and miserable!"

He made no reply and she glanced at him sympathetically, imagining that he was still brooding about his losses, but she was wrong; he was trying to find words to express his admiration of her courage, but could find none that he considered adequate.

CHAPTER XXXVI

Christmas Roundabout

NO snow fell in the suburb that Christmas, the last Christmas of the war, but those who were left in the Avenue would have welcomed a flurry, just enough, perhaps, to cover the new scars at the short number end.

As it was the crescent had a dismal, slovenly look, the neat houses tapering off into a row of hovels and, finally, into mere heaps of brick from the point beyond Number Forty, now the last intact home on that side of the road.

The uneven side looked more itself, for there were still curtains in the windows, although every pane of glass was heavily criss-crossed with new adhesive tape. Many of the front-gardens were sadly overgrown and neglected, but at least they were free of half-bricks and stacks of chipped slates. Even here, however, deterioration began about half-way along the crescent, at Number Forty to be exact, where the roofs were covered with tarpaulins stretching as far as the end of the block.

On the Shirley side of the cart-track there was not a great deal of difference between the odd and even sides. The odd houses were still standing, but few of them were occupied and one was almost demolished. It was easy to distinguish between the old and new wounds on this side. Time had done a great deal to heal the 1941 gap, and coarse grass was growing over the mounds that had been Numbers Seventeen, Fifteen and Thirteen. People living higher up the Avenue, however, had almost forgotten this incident and when they talked of The Bomb they now meant the flying-bomb of 1944, not the comparative pin-prick of 1941.

Very little of value had been salvaged from the even number ruins. They curved away from Number Thirty-Eight to the site of the corner shop, looking like a vast tumulus.

In a sense they were a burial mound, for two of the people killed there had not yet been accounted for and were presumed to be lying under the debris.

The autumn rains had softened the outlines of the long cairn, but here and there were pathetic reminders of the families who had lived on this spot, a splintered clothes horse that had belonged to Mrs. Hooper, some sodden clothing that had been hanging on the line in the garden of Number Eight, and a soggy pile of Jim's pamphlets, still held together with picture wire.

The survivors were right to prefer snow to the sleet that drove in from the east that Christmas. Snow would have been a cleaner, softer mantle than the December murk.

• • • •

Jim and Edith spent that Christmas with Bernard and Pippa, in their bungalow on the road to Caernarvon. They had been invited down to Devonshire by Judith, but Edith reminded Jim that Judith, already in charge of Esme's five-year-old Barbara, was expecting her own baby within weeks and would have as much as she could do looking after herself. Esme was still in France and had only been home for a few days in early autumn, when they all thought that Harold was going to die.

Pippa made her father-in-law and Edith very welcome, and Edgar and Frances drove over from Llandudno on Christmas morning. One aspect of the visit did a good deal to cheer Jim, who was recovering but slowly from the shock of losing Louise, Jack, all his personal possessions, and the solid comfort of Harold's matchless companionship in a single afternoon. He was relieved to see that Bernard was now quite himself again and that his marriage to Pippa was obviously a great success.

Old Bernard, Jim decided, had overcome his handicap with courage and resolution, but it was clear that he owed as much to Pippa as to his own determination. He still limped slightly but it was wonderful to see him work the petrol pumps and even change the wheel of a car with his single arm.

He had always been tough and wiry but Jim was struck by the tremendous strength he displayed with his over-worked right hand, and the dexterity he showed in bracing tools against his chest, and even using his teeth when he needed to shift his grip on a wrench or a length of chain.

He looked very well, thought Jim, but what was more important he looked serene and happy. There was a smooth, matter-of-fact comradeship between him and his wife, that had its basis in the girl's casual attitude towards him, as though they were brother and sister rather than man and wife.

They shared the work both in garage and kitchen, and Pippa told Jim that they would continue to do this until they could afford hired help, or at least until her baby arrived in June. The prospect of yet another grandchild pleased Jim and he praised her decision to start a family instead of waiting, as so many young people seemed to do nowadays, until it was too late. Pippa was quite frank about the baby.

"It would have been a jolly sight more sensible to wait, Mr. Carver," she said. "I do all the books, and I work the pumps whenever Berni's at work in the shed. I don't know how I'll cope with it all when there's a baby to see to, but we'll manage somehow. We have so far!"

"I think you've coped marvellously," Jim told her, "and what's more I think you've worked wonders with Berni!"

"It wasn't me, it was the garage," admitted Pippa smiling. "This dump was a godsend—finding something that he could do right away! We even cut our honeymoon short to get it started!"

"How did Berni feel about having the baby?" he wanted to know.

"I'm afraid I didn't consult him," said Pippa, laughing, "it was my idea, just something else I thought might be good for him!"

Jim kissed her impulsively. It was not often that he kissed

anyone uninvited, but he felt moved by her friendliness and by her vast stock of common sense.

"I think he's a damned lucky chap, in spite of all his injuries," he told her.

. . . .

It was probably this talk with Pippa that set Jim thinking about his own future that Christmas afternoon.

After dinner he suggested a walk but everybody except Edith declined. Edgar wanted to listen to the King's speech, and Frances had promised to do some mending for Pippa. Bernard said he had urgent work to do on a customer's car that had been promised for Boxing Day, and Pippa preferred to doze beside the fire, so Jim and Edith went out along the main road and walked into Caernarvon to have a look at the castle.

The castle was shut but they made a circuit of the walls and then sat down to enjoy the pale sunshine on a seat overlooking the little harbour. He told her about his chat with Pippa and how good she was for Bernard.

"I only hope young Boxer's as lucky, when he gets home," he said.

"Oh, I don't think that's a matter of luck," said Edith seriously. "I think it's much more a question of whether one takes a short or a long-term policy in life."

"Just what do you mean by that, Edith?" he asked, amused by her solemnity.

"Well, it's just that I don't think people really *do* fall in love with one another, like everyone imagines they do, and like they do at the pictures," said Edith. "I think most successful marriages don't begin that way at all, but simply arise out of people saying to themselves, 'I'm all right on my own now, but will I still be satisfied with life when I'm over forty?' You see, I've always thought it needed much more courage for a man to get married than it does for a woman! A young man can have a very nice time nowadays if he stays single, and keeps all his money, but if he takes a longer view, and marries somebody who attracts him, he gets the benefits later on, when there's somebody there to take an interest in him, and he's got a stake in life with his children, just as you have!"

"Well, I suppose there's something in that," admitted Jim, "and I should be in a position to judge, but as you've seen for yourself, children grow up and make homes for themselves, and you never mean as much to them as you like to pretend to yourself! It's the people of your own generation that count when you're getting on in years. I'm fond of my bunch, and I'm more interested in them now than I was when they were kids, but if I was completely honest I'd say that you and old Harold Godbeer meant much more to me than any of them!"

He said this casually and conversationally, shooting out his long legs and leaning back against the wall, his hands clasped behind his head. He did not notice that she looked away from him quickly, and stared out over the burnished surface of the water between the quay and the tip of Anglesey.

She said, at length: "I'd never have got through it all if you hadn't been in the Avenue, Mr. Carver!"

He looked at her curiously. She did not seem to be relaxed as he was but rather tense and her pudgy little hands were occupied in twisting and twisting the handle of her handbag.

"That's nonsense," he told her, shortly, "for you pulled yourself together much quicker than I did! It was a case of me relying on you when Lou and Jack were killed, and even before that if you come to think of it! What about the time the twins were missing, and the other time, when we had all that upset about Archie?"

"Oh, I didn't do much," said Edith, "it was just that I was there to talk to. I know you always had Mr. Godbeer to confide in, but sometimes a woman's better, and besides, I've always been able to go to you about Becky and our money troubles, haven't I?"

He thought back over their relationship. He had known her now twenty-four years, and during all that time she did not seem to have changed much. He remembered how she had looked that winter afternoon, when he took her up to the Abbey to see the Unknown Warrior's tomb. Even then she had had iron-grey hair, and had walked as though her shoes were too small for her. She was one of those women who always looked to be in their early fifties, who must have aged very quickly up to that point and then come to terms with life, and refused to grow any older. It was not how she looked, however, that interested him. What he liked about Edith was her unswerving loyalty to everyone she knew, and to the Avenue-dwellers as a community. In all the time he had known her, her placidity had never deserted her, and when it came to a crisis there was nobody quite like her, as she had demonstrated so remarkably during the court proceedings against Archie and when almost everyone had had everything in their lives shattered by the flying-bomb.

He wondered where she found such tranquility. Was it in her religious upbringing in a remote Devon vicarage, or had it been acquired, slowly and painfully, during her lifetime as nurse to an invalid sister? How would such staunchness be rewarded? Would she (as she herself doubtless believed) enter into ultimate peace and glory upon death, or would she struggle on until she was too feeble to trot to and from the cinema, or to look after lodgers, and finally end up in some kind of institution for the aged? The latter alternative seemed to him, who lacked faith in an Afterlife, the more probable, and it filled him with a sense of compassion so strong that he reached out and took hold of the hand that was plucking so nervously at the handbag strap.

"What are we going to do with ourselves now, Edith? The war's almost over but when it is, when everything starts up again, what are *we* going to do?"

"Mr. Baskerville told me the Government would rebuild our houses," said Edith. "There's some sort of resettlement grant for people like us, isn't there?"

"Do you really want to go back there?" asked Jim. "It can never be the same, you know, and almost everyone around will be a stranger."

"Where else could I go?" she asked him.

"We could find another house, or even go and live in the country, near Judy," Jim heard himself saying.

"*We?* You mean ... *together?*"

She was looking at him now and her face was blank with surprise, so blank indeed that he could not help smiling into it. When he did, the surprise faded and there came into her prominent grey eyes a light that he had never seen there before.

"Why not? We've always got on so well, and although I haven't much to offer I can still work! I'm still as fit as I ever was, and we wouldn't be so lonely, either of us! There is one thing, however, you'd have to stop calling me 'Mr. Carver'. I think you'd find it difficult after all these years, but you'd have to try! Perhaps you could begin by calling me 'James' and work up to 'Jim' in time for the Silver Wedding!"

At the word 'wedding' she started, and suddenly withdrew her hand and looked away. He saw that there were tears in her eyes and his protective instinct was aroused. He said:

"Now, now Edith, don't upset yourself about it! We're old friends, and you don't have to agree for fear of offending me. Why don't you think about it? There's no hurry after all these years, surely!"

"I . . . I'm sorry I'm making such a goose of myself," said Edith, gulping, "but . . . well . . . I just can't imagine anyone wanting to . . . to marry me at my age, especially someone like you, somebody I've always so admired!"

The compliment embarrassed him a little, so that he sounded slightly gruff.

"Don't harp on about age, Edith! Great Scott, I could give you a year or two I know! Well, what do you think? Shall we go home and tell everybody, or shall we keep it a secret and suddenly spring it on them?"

She dabbed her eyes, swallowed twice, and smiled. She had never smiled at him in that way before. Her round face seemed to reflect the radiance of the winter sunshine and she looked, for a moment or two, almost young.

"Certainly not, Jim," she said. "I'm so . . . so proud that I want everybody to know about it! Everybody, d'you understand?"

• • • •

On Christmas afternoon Judy went up to the paddock and saddled 'Gramp', the aged pony, for Barbara's after-dinner constitutional.

Strictly speaking Barbara was still on the leading-rein but

today she would have to go as far as the viaduct unaccompanied, for Judy was far too big to climb on a horse, even a pony as stolid and docile as old 'Gramp'.

Her size, which seemed to have increased very suddenly, was a great joke with herself, Maud Somerton, and even little Barbara.

"Had a case like you at Firhill once, long before your time," joked Maud, in her harsh, keep-those-elbows-in, voice. "Mare they sent me was supposed to be in foal but wasn't showing at all! Thought it might be a rabbit, if anything! Then, almost overnight, she blew herself out like a turkey-cock and finally presented us with 'Gilpin.' You remember 'Gilpin', don't you? Stood sixteen hands and made a cracking good hunter once he'd learned his manners!"

"I remember 'Gilpin' very well," laughed Judy, "and he had a nasty habit of lashing out when you least expected it just like mine does!"

"Good sign, good sign," said Maud, as though she had been instrumental in bringing a thousand babies into the world, and had watched their mothers through all stages of pregnancy.

Barbara trotted off down the lane and Judy remained leaning on the paddock gate, thinking how much like Elaine Barbara was, with her coal-black curls bobbing on her neat shoulders, and her plump little calves coaxing the reluctant Gramp into a trot.

It was very still out here, with the trees bare against the wan afternoon sun, so still indeed that she could hear the water swirling over the pebbles in the wide curve of the river. The leaves on the two big chestnuts across the lane seemed reluctant to fall, and their colour was exciting, bronze, wine-red, and the palest green, spotted with rust. Behind her the smoke rose up straight from the oldest of the chimneys, a part of the original building that they had been able to save.

She surveyed the paddock and house with quiet pride, for she had a sense of having created it. They would always stay here now, she told herself, she, Esme, the child, Barbara, and perhaps other children. When she was over forty they would be shouting to one another in the old orchard, catching their ponies and stealing one another's bridles and saddle girths for gymkhanas, quarrelling perhaps, but not seriously, for surely nobody could really quarrel in the midst of all this peace and loveliness. Later, when she and Esme had entered their fifties, the children would be grown up themselves, and probably bringing their fiancées home for inspection.

Perhaps Esme's stepfather, Harold, would come to live with them when he was better. Harold would like it here, pottering about the sheds, and fishing in the pool and the children would like him too, for he was a gentle little man who had suffered much. Esme, she felt sure, would be happy here, and would find himself at last in the excitement of raising pigs, and stepping up on the output of the hens in the deep-litter sheds. Later on they might experiment with a few Guernseys, and Judy could almost see Esme driving them in from the sloping meadow at milking-time and calling, softly, as the farmers round here always called their cows: "Hoo-*ooo*! Hoo-*ooooo*!"

Louise and old Jack, particularly Jack, would have liked it here at holiday times. A shadow crossed her face as she thought of Lou and Jack, and of all the people at the small-number end of the Avenue. How lucky had she been to have Esme away in France when it happened, and how lucky too to have been down here herself, where nobody bothered to drop bombs any more.

The clack-clack of Gramp's hooves, returning up the lane, disturbed a cock pheasant and it flew, panic-stricken, from a clump of golden bracken in the hedge. The harsh '*Kar-Kark*' reminded her of the first pheasants she had ever seen, in the plough-land beyond Manor Wood, and this made her think of Esme again and yearn for him.

She smiled to herself. They said that one didn't think of one's husband in that way during pregnancy but, as usual, they didn't know what they were talking about. She needed Esme most desperately, needed to feel his arms round her and his cheek against hers, needed his presence about the house, and his whistle on the stairs. The smile faded.

"Oh, God," she prayed aloud, "make the damned thing end quickly, *quickly!*"

"What?" called Barbara, as she trotted up.

"Nothing, darling," smiled Judy, "I only said, 'What a lovely pheasant'!"

"Gramp is so lazy," complained Barbara. "Shall we give him a big feed of oats for a Christmas present?"

"No, darling, he's too old for oats," said Judy, "Give him a mangold, and listen to the lovely, greedy way he crunches it!"

She turned her back on the lane and walked behind the pony up to the path to the tack-room. Behind her the short, winter afternoon died, as the red sun dipped behind the ridge.

 . . . .

Elaine came out of the downstairs bedroom of Number Forty-Three about eight o'clock on Christmas morning and padded into the kitchen to make tea.

While she waited for the kettle to boil she opened the back door and stood for a moment looking out over the brick-strewn meadow towards the silent woods.

She glanced left, towards the mound that had been her home throughout childhood and adolescence, but she did not remember it as such, for she was not a woman who derived any pleasure from reminiscence. She was much more at home in present and future.

She had never regretted her decision to turn her back on dreams, and take pot-luck with Archie but as she stood looking out over the meadow she thought that she had had more than enough of the Avenue, and that it was high time they got themselves a flat, instead of scheming and working day and night to provide flats for other people. That was their means of livelihood it was true, but after all, they were doing very well now, and had already made a clear three thousand out of conversion and key-money.

They would do even better, she reflected, when the real rush began, when the young men and girls came surging out of the Forces, clamouring for homes of their own, even if those homes had to consist of an eighth part of the living-space in a two-storey Victorian villa, divided up by sheets of hardboard.

There was no getting away from it, when it came to

making something out of nothing Archie was a dabster, an absolute dabster! Who but he could have made four tolerable flats out of that dreadful semi-detached ruin in Outram Crescent? Who but Archie could have squeezed three hundred a year from a coach-house, converted into a bungalow, and furnished with a few strips of Wilton carpet and some café chairs, bought for five shillings apiece at an auction?

The whistling kettle interrupted her reflections. She made the tea and carried the tray into the bedroom. Archie was still fast asleep and she prodded him with her foot.

"Come on! Get weaving! You've got to see that rascal, Corbett this morning, haven't you? He'll sell to someone else if you don't clinch the deal over a bottle of Christmas cheer!"

He sat up, rubbed his eyes and yawned.

"Damn Corbett," he said, but his mind instantly grappled the problem. "He wants too much for that place and I'd doubt if I'd ever get sanction to convert. The main fabric's unsafe!"

She sat on the bed, sipping her tea. "Offer him a hundred less and see how he reacts!"

"Might be worth a try," agreed Archie, "but hell, it's Christmas Day, don't we ever get a break?"

"Not while the going's so good," said Elaine. "Help yourself, it's sugared!"

He did not reach for the cup, however, but leaned over and groped in the pocket of his jacket that was hanging beside the bed. She heard the faint, pleasing rustle of tissue paper.

"What have you got there?"

"A little gee-gaw for a bad girl," he said.

Her hand shot out and she snatched a little box from him. She slammed down her half-empty cup and stood up, whipping off the lid and plucking the bracelet from its soft bed.

It was an expensive piece of jewellery, far more expensive than she could have hoped for in their present circumstances.

"Archie!" she exclaimed, breathlessly, "this must have set you back far too much!"

"Not nearly as much as you'd think," he said, casually.

"It's not new of course, I'm damned if I'm paying purchase-tax on that kind of bauble! I got it below cost from Freeman. Remember Freeman? He was that chap we let into Number Thirty-Five, Cawnpore Road. He was so grateful that he really did hold the price down. I know that because I went straight and had the damn thing valued by Izzy Marks!"

She shouted with laughter. How like Archie it was to get a substantial reduction on a bracelet in exchange for a flat, and then run round the corner to another dealer in order to make quite sure that he was getting good value! She didn't know which to admire the most, Archie or the Christmas gift. She slipped it on and regarded it at arm's length.

"Archie, it's a honey," she told him, "and it really is a surprise, one hell of a surprise!"

"You like it?" he said, enjoying her delight.

"Do I *like* it! Move over and let me show you how much I like it!"

"No, no!" he protested, laughing. "Damn it woman, I want my tea, and besides, you're quite right about Corbett, we ought to clinch before he calls in anyone else."

"Are you spurning me?" demanded Elaine.

"Not exactly," said Archie, chuckling, "but there's a time and place for everything.... No honestly ... honestly, I really do want my tea, I. . . ."

She kissed him hard on the mouth and he let his tea grow cold. It was usually this way with Elaine, there was always fun and horseplay in their association, and he could find no words to express his gratitude to her. He never thought about any other woman nowadays, hardly so much as looked at one. There was money-making, and there was Elaine and this was more than enough for a man in his forty-fourth year.

* * * *

The sons and daughters of the Avenue were scattered far and wide that Christmas, further and wider indeed than they had ever been in preceding Christmases of the war.

Ted Hartnell bathed that Christmas Day in New Caledonia. The eldest of the Baskerville boys sweated it out on the beach at Port Darwin. Joe Crispin, of Number Fifteen, got helplessly drunk on vino, in Bari. Boxer Carver spent a quiet Christmas day in the cooler, where he was half-way through a twenty-one day sentence for giving a comic and much-appreciated imitation of Reichsmarshal Goering. Boxer was glad of the rest, however, for he had been tunnelling very energetically of late, and the emergency exit was now complete and sealed, an insurance against Jerry's mad-dog reprisals, when the curtain came down on the Reich that was to have lasted a thousand years.

Twenty-one days in the cooler was not the ordeal it once had been. The camp guards were very docile these days, and rare indeed were the frenzied Teuton flaps, that Boxer had so loved to witness. It was difficult to induce a flap among guards, so elderly and so dispirited, had they become, and even some of the officers were half-tamed.

Boxer, in fact, was getting rather bored with prison camp life, and had almost made up his mind to persuade Whitey to join him in a hike to the nearest frontier when they were returned to the compound. Whitey (who had impersonated Doctor Goebbels in the impromptu pantomime) was now in the adjoining cell, and occasionally they shouted messages to one another. This was against regulations of course, but old Sag-Guts, the corporal of the guard, was a tired, tolerant man. At this moment he was snug in the guardroom, listening to a sixteen-year-old-boy playing *'Heilige Nacht'* on a harmonica. Strains of the familiar melody reached Boxer in his cell and made him think of Avenue Christmases of twenty years ago.

"I say, Whitey! You there, Whitey?" he bawled.

" 'Course I'm here! Where the hell else would I be?" Whitey called back.

"Can you hear that Jerry playing a mouth-organ?"

"Sure! Sounds proper seasonable, don't it?"

"You ever go carol singing as a kid, Whitey?"

"Sure I did, every year! Did you?"

"You bet, me an' my brother Berni! We used to make enough for Christmas presents. *'Wence-lass'* we always sang tho', but I could never remember more'n the first verse!"

" *'Hark the Herald Angels'* was my favourite," shouted Whitey. "You know that one?"

" 'Course I do! Let's sing it now! Ready?"

They began to bawl *'Hark! the Herald Angels Sing'* in competition with the mouth-organ, and Boxer's split-melon grin widened and widened as he bellowed:

> 'Hark! the Herald Angels sing-hing
> Beecham's pills are just the thing . . . !'

The parody shocked Whitey, who was a great believer in Christmas. He called:

"Pack it in, Boxer! You aren't singing it right!"

"Oh, I forgot the ruddy thing!" said Boxer. "Sing something else, sing *'Nancy Brown'!* I go for *'Nancy Brown'!"*

"Okay!" called Whitey, mollified by the request, and as the boy in the guard-room finished his carol Whitey's hoarse voice began to echo through the block.

> 'Down in West Virginny
> Lived a girl named Nancy Brown.
> She was sweeter than the sweetest
> Of any girl in town. . . .'

Boxer's grin settled on his face as he lay listening to Nancy's successive rejections of a long string of suitors, until
. . .

> 'Came along the City Slicker
> With his hundred dollar bills!
> He put Nancy in his Packard
> And he drove her to the hills
> She stayed up in the mountain
> She stayed up in that mountain
> She stayed up in that mountain all that night!
> She came down next morning early
> More a woman than a girlie
> And her Pappy drove that hussy out of sight!'

Boxer hugged himself with glee. He had heard Whitey sing *'Nancy Brown'* a hundred times but he never tired of it; he never tired of any old and tried diversion, or of familiar songs like *'Coal Black Mammy'*, or games like the string-and-parcel and knocking-down-ginger. He was a genial, simple soul, and found his pleasures in genial, simple things.

* * * *

Four hundred miles to the west of Boxer's cell Esme was not finding life so simple; that morning he was tired, hungry, and exasperated.

He had promised Smithy, his driver, that they would be in Paris for Christmas, in time to pick up their accumulated mail at the American Express Office, and maybe coax a good Christmas dinner out of S.H.A.E.F., but their van had broken down for the tenth time during their journey up from Toulouse, and now that an obliging village mechanic had at last got it going again they were still hundreds of kilometres short of Paris.

Esme had been feeling very homesick indeed during the last few weeks, far more so in fact than he had felt during his previous wanderings on the Continent, for then he had been on the run, and there had been so much to occupy his mind, whereas now France was practically cleared of Germans, and free movement from department to department was limited only by broken bridges and the extreme scarcity of petrol.

He had covered thousands of miles since the Allied breakout, in August, and now the war seemed to have left him far behind.

Officially he was supposed to be photographing bomb-damage; unofficially he was 'showing the flag' and collecting scraps of information about the resistance groups. It was tiring, unrewarding work, entailing long journeys by road and air, and it did not seem to be serving a useful purpose now that the Germans were fighting on their own frontiers.

Throughout the autumn, when he had driven south-west from Brussels across the plain of France, and into the remote provinces of Anjou and Poitou, his interest in the people of the liberated towns had kept boredom at bay. Now the resistance groups were beginning to squabble among themselves and his interest flagged. He realised also how tired he was, and how worried a man could be, with a wife having her first baby hundreds of miles away.

Exhaustion and worry made him moody, and sometimes the efforts to support himself and his driver, in a country that had been milked dry by four years' enemy occupation, almost overwhelmed him.

Air Ministry had said: 'Live on the country' and the order had seemed almost romantic when issued in a warm office, in King Charles Street, Whitehall. It was far from being romantic down here, where whole communities were existing without heat, light, medical supplies, or transport and sometimes without the barest necessities of life.

The strain of war had converted Esme into a heavy smoker but all his cigarettes had been dissipated as currency in the south. In addition, he was constantly immobilised by lack of petrol, and for food he could only vary the eternity of American 'K' rations with small quantities of goats' milk cheese and wine, cadged from the desperate locals.

Such money he had carried with him had already been spent on food and black market petrol, he had been forced to sell his flying boots in Bordeaux, and his watch in Limoges. At last he gave up the struggle, sent off a signal from Toulouse, and headed back to base on his own responsibility.

Christmas morning found him probing through yellow fog towards Orleans, where he overtook a long and dripping column of German prisoners, and learned from their guards that there was a U.S. Transit camp a kilometre further on.

Travelling at a walking pace he eventually located the camp and drove into the wired enclosure. A prim little lieutenant approached him as he jumped from the van.

"You got authority to drive in here, man?"

Sullenly, Esme produced his pass. He was accustomed by now to the strange contradictions of the U.S.A. Military machine, in which earnest young officers insisted that every 'i' was dotted, and every 't' crossed, but real problems were referred to the nearest 'top sergeant'.

"I guess anyone could have this kind of credential," said the man, removing his pince-nez spectacles.

Esme lost patience.

"Oh, for crying out loud! The bloody thing's got Eisenhower's signature on it! I'm out of grub and out of gas and I've got to get to Paris! Who's in charge around here?"

The officer was a stickler for the book.

"You got an identity card?"

Esme wearily produced his identity card and Smithy, the A.C.2 driver, winked at him from the lorry.

The officer made a great show of examining the blue card.

"What day were you born on, soldier?" he asked, unexpectedly.

Esme opened his mouth to protest but at that moment a tall sergeant loomed out of the fog and at once took charge of the situation.

"This guy's okay," he told the officer and then, addressing Esme directly: "I guess you don't remember me, Bud, but I was a guest at yore weddin'!"

Esme blinked. "My wedding . . . ?"

"Sure thing! Our outfit was located in that ruin, 'cross the way. Here, take a looksee Bud, maybe this rings a bell somewheres?"

He extracted a wallet from his overall pocket and presented Esme with a postcard-size photograph. In the yellow glow of the headlamps Esme at once recognised Judy's twin-sisters, Fetch and Carry, photographed on what was obviously the steps of the old pavilion in the 'Rec'. Enthusiastically he clasped the sergeant's hand.

"By God, but this is a bit of luck! You must be Carry's Yank, Orrie?"

The sergeant grinned. "No, sir! 'Fetch' is my dame, and I'm Mitch! When do we celebrate?"

The lieutenant looked harassed.

"You say you can vouch for this man, sergeant?"

"Sure, sure," said Mitch, so airily that Esme, inwardly chuckling, would not have been the slightest bit surprised if he had added: "Run away an' play someplace else, Bud!"

They went into the canteen, where Mitch ordered beans, bacon, and steaming cans of coffee, too hot to hold. He did not eat himself but sat on a box, beaming at Esme.

Presently Orrie drifted in but on learning that Esme and

his driver were without stocks of food, petrol and cigarettes he went away again, returning later with two cartons of Chesterfields, and a promise that all Esme's other needs were being attended to.

Esme could not help comparing their generosity and easy friendliness with their officer's frigidity, and reminded himself, for the twentieth time during his dealings with Americans, that it was highly dangerous to generalise about them.

They exchanged bits of news and Esme was able to startle the two Americans by informing them that the twins were now employed at an American Service club, in Oxford, whither they had gone in early autumn after the general Avenue exodus following the bomb.

Esme gathered that the twins were not over-conscientious correspondents, for neither Mitch nor Orrie had heard from them in more than two months.

"Are you two really serious about those kids?" he asked, adopting the role of brother-in-law.

"Sure are," Mitch told him, "and we got it all fixed. We're aimin' to set up as a foursome, in Cleveland, Ohio. Brother o' mine's got a used-car business up there and me and Orrie, we figger on taking over soon as this outing's over! Say, I remember Fetch tellin' me your outfit was 'Top Secret!' You ought to be wised up on this Goddam war. How long d'you figger it'll last, Bud?"

"That's anyone's guess," said Esme, smiling, "but when we're through over here don't forget we've still got the Far East to tidy up!"

"Aw, the U.S. Marines'll rub out the Nips, brother," said Orrie. "Don't you worry none about the East!"

"I hope so," said Esme, wondering at their cheerfulness, and comparing it with his own despondency. Perhaps they were younger and that much fresher, or perhaps their slaphappy confidence stemmed from their country's overwhelming superiority in technical equipment. It crossed his mind then that Anglo-Saxon leadership had slipped away from Britain during the last year or so, and had now passed into the hands of these big, gangling men, with their fussy little officers, and their undeniable know-how. He found that the prospect of hanging on to American shirt-tails after the war did not touch his national pride. All he wanted, all he would ask of life in the future, was to be left alone on his seventy-acre plot, and never asked to travel further afield than Exeter on market days.

He stood up and shook hands with Mitch and Orrie.

"So long then, and nice to have run into you! If I get home before you do I'll call up the girls and tell them how we met here, on Christmas day!"

"You do that!" said Orrie, eagerly, as Esme found his driver, climbed into the lorry, and drove out along the Orleans Road.

It was strange, he thought, as he broke open the cigarette carton and pocketed a packet of Chesterfield, how he could never get away from the Avenue, no matter how wide and far he travelled. There had been his encounter with Judy on the night he walked out on Elaine, with Barbara in his arms. There had been poor old Claude, and his unrewarding courtship of the policeman's daughter, in Shirley Rise. And the Avenue, or what little was left of it, had cropped up again in the persons of the two genial Americans, who were going to make G.I. brides of two Avenue girls, and take them home to Cleveland, Ohio, to help run a used car business!

Esme saw the Avenue not as it had been the last time he was home on leave, the compassionate leave they had granted him in order to see poor old Harold in hospital, but the Avenue as it was in his boyhood, the long, sweeping crescent that had always seemed to seal off London's advance into the countryside, and he was surprised to discover that he still thought of it with warmth and affection.

Was there anyone still living in the small-number end now, he wondered, anyone who, despite bombs, doodlebugs and rockets, still garrisoned this advanced sector of London?

. . . .

There was someone still in residence at the short number end, but it was a mere token garrison.

Little Miss Baker, of Number One, was celebraing Christmas alone in her dilapidated front-room, having resisted renewed attempts on the parts of relatives, friends and Council officials to dislodge her.

There she sat, with her cat, Charlotte, and her budgerigar, Alfred, reading at random from her stained and tattered copy of Rupert Brooke's poems, the book that someone had salvaged from the debris that littered the room after the ceiling had fallen on the Health Visitor, the previous August.

Like their mistress both cat and budgerigar had survived the catastrophe. Charlotte had once been Mrs. Crispin's cat, of Number Fifteen, and Alfred had been Mrs. Westerman's bird, and had been presented to Miss Baker by Mr. Westerman after his wife's death in the corner shop. Westerman was away all day at work, and felt that Alfred would die of grief if left in solitude.

Rough and ready repairs had been made to the front room. A stout beam and some wide planks held up what remained of the ceiling, the windows had been fitted with heavy wooden shutters, now thrown back to reveal the crisscrossed pattern of adhesive tape stuck across the new glass, but apart from these repairs the room was much as it had been throughout the war, and the long period preceding the war. A steel engraving of 'The Charge of the Scots Greys, at Waterloo' still hung over the sideboard. A coloured print of Queen Victoria, as she had looked at the time of her first jubilee, was still in place over the radio table, and there was still the same Persian rug, badly discoloured by crushed plaster, in front of the fire.

Despite the makeshift repairs it was very cosy in here. The fire burned brightly, throwing leaping shadows on the wall opposite, and the kettle sang on the hob as the respectful tones of the B.B.C. announcer warned listeners that His Majesty the King was about to deliver his Christmas message. Miss Baker softly closed her Rupert Brooke, took off her spectacles, folded her hands on her lap and addressed the sleeping Charlotte at her feet.

"Lottie," she said, looking round her with an air of satisfaction not far short of smugness, "Lottie my girl, whatever made them think that I wanted to share Christmas with anyone but you and Alfred? They're all very kind, Lottie, and I suppose they mean well enough, but when it comes to asking us to give in to that little Jackanapes at the last moment they're knocking at the wrong number, eh, Alfred?"

Alfred, the budgerigar, cocked his small head on one side and whistled. He was not a talking budgerigar, but his whistle was low and melodious.

"Shush, Alfred!" said Miss Baker, severely. "Didn't you hear? It's the King!"

CHAPTER XXXVII

The Coming Of Arthur

IT is not often that a man attends his own wedding in the morning and is also present at the birth of his own grandson before midnight the same day, but such a rare privilege was Jim Carver's, on January 22nd, 1945.

It was a crowded day for Jim, and one that he was likely to remember with pleasure for the rest of his life. He and Edith had not intended to rush matters in this fashion, although both were in favour of a quiet wedding early in the morning, with possibly the twins, Fetch and Carry, as witnesses, and Edgar Frith as dispenser of the bride.

The Third Reich, however, once more took a hand in Jim's affairs, planting a V.2 within fifty yards of the private hotel where Jim and Edith had gone, after losing their homes in the summer.

The hotel was not destroyed but its structure was badly shaken and it was declared unsafe. All the guests had therefore to move out at short notice, and seek alternative accommodation. In January, 1945 this was more than a mere inconvenience. For people possessed of a small income it came near to being an impossibility.

Jim found a temporary lodging with the Westermans and spent the second week of the new year combing the suburb for a furnished flat, but without success. He was offered one or two third-storey bed-sitting-rooms in the Woodside and Clockhouse areas, but the rental demanded was prohibitive, and the lodgings offered no kind of permanence.

Neither he nor Edith were without means. Both had been

working full-time throughout the greater part of the war, and they could also expect compensation for the destruction of their homes and goods by enemy action, but Jim reasoned that he was now well over sixty, and Edith was not much younger, so that neither could expect to continue in full work for very much longer. They would therefore have to exercise caution in matters of finance.

Jim would have preferred to buy a house and be done with it, for it was clear that the price of property would rise very sharply the moment the war was over. The only houses that were for sale, however, were in a pitiable state of repair, and even had he settled on one it would have been impossible to find a builder to make it habitable.

Tramping the suburbs all that week he was reminded of his long search for work during the early nineteen-twenties. His faith in the British working-class received some unpleasant shocks during the quest, and he was disgusted by the rapacity of some of the owners of small and dingy property. The comradeship that had existed between people during the blitz, and subsequently, seemed to have disappeared in the dust of the V.1s and V.2s. For the most part people were tired, sour, greedy and disinclined to be helpful. They were sorry, they told him, for those of their neighbours who had lost homes, but their sympathy did not extend to letting rooms or selling furniture at reasonable rates. On the seventh day of his quest he came home greatly discouraged, stopping at the corner of Shirley Rise to 'phone Edith, who was temporarily accommodated in a Cawnpore Road bed-sitter. He was surprised by the chirpiness of her voice when he reported failure.

"Never mind, never mind! I've had a visitor, Jim! Yes, you know him, of course you know him! He's your boy, Archie!"

"Archie? How on earth did Archie know where you were living?"

"Oh, he found out, he's good at finding things out! Listen, Jim, he's still living at Number Forty-Three, and he's most anxious to contact you! I think he's heard about a house. No, dear, I didn't have to tell him about us because he knew! I don't know *how* he knew, Jim, but he did, and he was very

sweet about it, very sweet indeed! Where are you speaking
from, Jim? Well, why don't you pop along and see him now?
He was going straight home. Well, you never know do you?
He might know of something to suit us!"

Jim made his way up to the Avenue with mixed feelings.
He had seen and spoken to Archie several times during the
last year, and together they had attended the funeral of Lou
and Jack, in August, but although their relationship was
cordial enough on the surface, Jim still harboured a vague
distrust for his son, and his misgivings had been increased
when he learned that Archie was living openly with a woman
who was not his wife and who possessed an unsavoury
reputation in the suburb. He supposed that he was fair-
minded enough to admit that this was not his business,
particularly as Archie was now over forty, but when this fact
was added to Archie's own reputation it did not encourage
him to be proud of the boy. He had wished more than once
that Archie would either leave the Avenue or pull himself
together and try to achieve some kind of respectability.

He wondered why Archie should have gone to the trouble
of seeking out Edith, instead of making a direct approach to
himself. Perhaps it was because Edith had spoken up for him
in the witness-box and he remembered her as a 'soft touch',
or perhaps he needed help once again, and was reluctant to
ask it of his father?

Frowning over these possibilities Jim knocked at the door
of Number Forty-Three and was promptly admitted by
Elaine, who greeted him cheerfully, and called up the stairs
to Archie before showing him into the front room and asking
him if he would care for a drink.

Jim said that he would like a beer and Elaine disappeared
to get it, while Archie, in vest and trousers, and with lather
drying on his broad, red face, came into the room and shook
hands.

"I hear you're looking for somewhere to live, Dad?" he
said directly.

"That's so and I just got your message from Edith. I didn't
know you knew about me and Miss Clegg, we've told hardly
anyone down here as yet."

"Oh, I get around," said Archie, with a grin, "and I'd like

to say right out that I'm all in favour! That old duck is an absolute sweetie-pie and if I can do anything for her I'll do it, quite apart from helping you out of a jam! How would you like this place?"

"This place? You mean, this house?"

"Sure! Why not? You'd be near everyone you knew, everyone that's alive and kicking that is!"

"Are you and. . . . Are you moving?"

"We're going out to Chislehurst the day after tomorrow. We've got a peach of a place out there, a small country house, standing in its own grounds. Southern aspect, easy garden, and one of the best views for miles around!"

"Didn't it cost you a packet, a place like that?"

"No," said Archie, with a mischievous grin that recalled to Jim how he had looked as a boy. "But we won't go into that right now! The point is, this place is vacant as from Wednesday, and I'd like you and Miss Clegg to have it as a wedding present!"

Jim sat bolt upright, almost knocking over the glass of beer that Elaine was handing to him at that moment.

"*Wedding present!* You mean . . . you want to *give* us the house?"

"Now don't go all high-hat, Dad," growled Archie. "Look at it squarely from her point of view as well as your own! You're not chickens, either of you, and you can't afford to splash everything you've saved on a terrace house at present-day prices! You'll be buying at a peak and you've got your old age to think of! No matter where you go you won't rent a furnished place in or out of London that won't set you back at least a fiver a week; and even then it won't really be furnished, just dolled up with rubbish. I'd *like* to give you something, I never have, so far as I remember, and it's like I said, Edith Clegg was wonderful to me when I was up against it, and I hate being in anyone's debt! That's one characteristic that I did inherit from you!"

Jim slowly recovered from the initial shock of the offer and said, slowly:

"Well, I must say it's . . . it's uncommonly generous of you, Archie, and I appreciate it, upon my soul I do! But I just couldn't accept a wedding present from you that was the equivalent of two thousand pounds! You can't afford to throw money about like that!"

"How do you know what I can afford?" demanded Archie, so sharply that Elaine at once intervened, sitting down opposite Jim and throwing one elegant leg over the other in a way that revealed to him a flurry of silk and lace.

It was curious, Jim reflected, that Elaine Frith always looked and behaved like a high-class tart, yet her parents had been so respectable and she couldn't be half as bad as people made out, for this house must surely belong to her, having been made over to her by Esme at the time of their divorce.

She embarrassed him somewhat by appearing to have read his thoughts.

"It was my house," she told him, "but it isn't now! Archie bought it from me, a year ago and he paid cash for it with the first money he earned when he started up again. We both want you to have it, because you and Miss Clegg have had such a shocking run of luck lately."

She smiled very sweetly, Jim thought and noticed for the first time that she was an exceptionally attractive woman.

"Now why don't you just say 'yes' and let Archie feel that he's done at least one thing in his life without making a clear profit? It'll do him no end of good and it'll solve your problem on the spot!"

"Well," began Jim, already wavering, "I don't know. . . . It's extraordinarily generous of you both, but why not let me buy it at the price he paid you? Or better still, why not sell it for its pre-war price?"

"——!" said Archie, bluntly. "You'll have it for nix, or you won't have it at all! I'll 'phone my solicitors and get the thing fixed up straight away."

He turned to Elaine. "Give Dad another beer while I get on to Kirtlebury. You'll have to go in and see him, of course. How about Monday, ten o'clock?"

"Monday'll do," said Jim, overwhelmed, "but. . . ."

Archie abruptly left the room as Elaine got up to fill his glass.

"Has Judy had her baby yet?" she asked and, when he told her that it was a week overdue she went on to ask if Esme had been home lately and how little Barbara was settling down in Devonshire. She spoke without a trace of embarrassment, referring to her daughter Barbara as though she was a neighbour's child.

Jim heard Archie talking rapidly on the 'phone in the next room and sipped his beer thoughtfully.

"I don't know anything about people," he told himself. "The older I get the less I know, and I suppose I'll end up by knowing nothing at all, no more than the day I was born!"

. . . .

It was all settled to everyone's satisfaction. Jim brought his few personal possessions along the following day, and Archie and Elaine moved out before the end of the week. Edith accepted a pressing offer by Miss Baker to be married from Number One, and accordingly left her lodgings and returned to the Avenue two or three days before the wedding.

It was not such a quiet wedding after all. Archie and Elaine joined Edgar Frith, and his wife, Frances at the church, and a small group of the older residents, from the big-number end of the Avenue, called in to drink their health. Among the droppers-in were Philip and Jean Hargreaves, now Jim's next-door neighbours, and there was quite an old-fashioned send-off when Jim and Edith quitted Number One for the station.

They intended leaving London from Waterloo, on their way down to Exeter. Edith had expressed a desire to show Jim the village on the North Devon coast, where she had grown up and which she had not visited for ten years, but they did not go directly to the station, for they had an important call to make *en route*, and the taxi driver had instructions to convey them to the local station.

Jim shouted: "Hi!" when the hire-car driver took them speeding past Woodside, but the driver grinned and called over his shoulder: "The gentleman told me to take you all the way to Waterloo and paid me in advance, sir!"

"That must have been Archie again," said Edith. "He'll never have a penny to bless himself with if he carries on like that!"

"But we don't want to go to Waterloo yet," Jim told the

driver, "we've got to look in on someone at Westminster Hospital!"

"Oh, dear, I'd quite forgot poor Mr. Godbeer," said Edith. "Drop us at the Westminster Hospital and we'll get a taxi on from there, driver."

Jim had paid Harold a weekly visit ever since he had been fit enough to receive visitors. Harold was making slow but steady progress, and could now hobble about the ward on crutches but Jim was increasingly worried by his friend's occasional fits of depression and had been fighting them for several weeks.

They had managed to save Harold's legs but the chest wound had almost caused his death during the relapse, in October. Harold's chest had always been his weak spot and when he developed pneumonia, after two months in hospital, Jim gave him up for lost and had only just convinced himself that Harold would, despite everything, ultimately recover from the terrible injuries he had received when the blast had flung him across the garden into the Nursery.

Harold shared his surprise and in his more cheerful moments he even joked about it.

"I've been lying here thinking how much it takes to kill a man," he told Jim, one afternoon. "Here's me, still alive after all that, yet I can remember the time when I thought I was committing suicide by going down to Woodside without a scarf on a frosty morning!"

"The Hun certainly had it in for you and yours, Harold," said Jim, doing his best to sound jocular, although the surgeon had told him privately that Harold would be unlikely to recover the full use of his legs. "You must be as tough as hickory, in spite of all that fussing and dosing and gargling you used to do before you caught your train every morning!"

Harold had been pleased about the wedding and had asked Jim to bring Edith to the hospital before they went away. Visiting hours, however, did not officially begin until afternoon, and so he had to cajole special permission from the senior sister.

He was granted the favour and was awaiting them in his wheel-chair when they were shown into a side ward, whither

Harold had propelled himself as soon as morning dressings began in the General ward.

Jim felt a little shy presenting Edith as his wife, but Edith at once took the initiative and planted a big, motherly kiss on Harold's pale forehead.

"You never thought *this* would happen, did you, Mr. Godbeer?" she exclaimed, and Jim reflected that her entire personality had changed since his Christmas proposal at Caernarvon. He had been conditioned, more or less gradually, to full recognition of her worth in a crisis, but from the moment he had suggested that they should get married all her natural hesitancy of speech and manner had evaporated like mist in sunshine. Where she had apologised and sometimes stammered, she now bubbled and beamed; her appearance had changed too, for she already looked younger and much more alert. At all the other Avenue weddings that she had attended she had worn her tight green costume, bought in the 'twenties' and not only sadly out of fashion, but faded and strained at the seams. The old green costume was not having its customary wedding airing today. Instead, she looked smart and trim in a new, tailored two-piece, with hat, gloves, shoes and handbag to match.

Harold was quick to notice the change and teased her, gently.

"My word, Miss Clegg, it looks to me as if you've been buying clothing coupons on the black market!"

"Oh, but I have," replied Edith, unblushingly, "the woman at the place where I was lodging sold me eight of them for two pounds! Was that a fair price do you think?"

"I'm afraid I wouldn't know," said Harold, chuckling, "I always made do on my issue! Will you two be seeing our Judy while you're in the West?"

"It depends," Jim told him. "She's expecting her baby any time now and I've arranged to ring her from Exeter. We shall go up to North Devon first and try and see her on the way back, at the week-end. How are you coming along, Harold? You look mobile enough in that odd contraption."

Harold's invalid testiness returned.

"Oh, I can move around," he said glumly, "but I get so

damned bored! Do you know how long I've been cooped up here now?"

Jim did know, to the very day, but he quickly by-passed the subject and told Harold how Archie had made them a wedding present of Number Forty-Three and that they would therefore continue to live in what was left of the Avenue. Harold whistled but Jim, who knew him very well by this time, noticed a look of sadness steal over his face.

"Oh, well, I suppose I shall have to go back into digs," he said, dismally, "and I can't say I like the idea at all, but there's no sense in buying another house at my time of life."

Edith decided that she did not like this line of talk at all.

"Now just you stop that, Mr. Godbeer," she said, severely. "You've as many years ahead of you as we have and you know very well that if you want a little place to yourself you can always have part of our house. We should all get along very well together, I'm sure!"

The idea appealed to Jim and he said so at once, but Harold shook his head. Despite the happy occasion he seemed very cast down, thought Jim.

"I couldn't do that," he said, "although it's very kind of you both to offer. You see, the surgeon's told me about my legs and I don't want to be a nuisance to anyone. If I did make a fair recovery I'd have to get a place of my own somewhere, and teach myself to stop relying on other people. You understand that, don't you, Jim?"

Jim did. It was exactly how he would feel in Harold's circumstances but he said:

"There's no doubt about you making an almost hundred per cent recovery, Harold, so snap out of it! When they discharge you from here you'd better arrange to spend a few months with us, at least until you find your feet again!" Then, warily: "Exactly *what* did the surgeon tell you?"

"That the best I can hope for is to be able to get up and down stairs but that I should never be able to do without irons and never be able to walk more than a short distance at a time. It seems that my left leg is now over an inch shorter than the right."

"People have got about with worse," said Jim. "Look at Miss Baker, in Number One."

"Yes, I think of her a good deal," said Harold, wistfully, "but look here," he made a determined effort to shake off his gloom, "this isn't a day for my troubles, I've got something for you! One of the probationers went out and bought it for me and if you don't like it, say so, and we'll send her out to get something else!"

He fumbled in the folds of the plaid rug that lay across his knees and his hand emerged, holding a long flattish carton, carefully wrapped in Christmas greetings' paper.

"May we open it here?" asked Jim, after Edith had expressed delight.

"I think you'd better," said Harold, "you may want to change your minds. It's a bit unusual but I wanted to give you something more personal than a toast-rack or a pyrex dish!"

The gift was a set of four exquisitely-painted miniatures in oils, all landscapes, and each framed in spinet keys. Jim gasped with surprise and Edith took refuge in a stammer.

"Why they're bbbbeautiful, Mr. Godbeer! Quite bbbbeautiful! I've never had a present anything like that but, bless you, they must have cost a dreadful lot of money and it's nnnaughty of you, very naughty indeed!"

Harold made little clicking noises with his tongue. "They're by a chap called Kirkwright, a pupil of Isabey so I'm told. I checked up on them with Edgar Frith, he knows all about such things, and he says they weren't all that expensive! They aren't old masters, or anything, but I . . . well . . . liked them, and I thought they'd look nice on each side of your fireplace. Little landscapes like that make a room look furnished, if you know what I mean."

A little probationer with fair hair and china blue eyes peeped into the side ward and addressed Harold with the brittle gaiety that young nurses reserve for male patients who have passed the age of fifty.

"Come along, Mr. Godbeer! It's your turn now! We mustn't keep Mr. Hobson waiting, must we?"

Harold, who had been enjoying his dispensation up to then, glowered at her. "I'll keep him waiting as long as I damn well please," he growled, so sourly that Jim and Edith exchanged puzzled glances.

"Now, now, Mr. Godbeer, we don't want a tantrum do we?" said the girl, hovering at the door.

"That's how they address you in here," grumbled Harold, completely ignoring her. "Just as if you were about nine and having your tonsils out! 'We must brush our teeth, mustn't we?' 'It's time for our supper, isn't it?' You put up with it at first, but in time you revolt, that is if they haven't cut your spirit out on one of their damned operating tables!"

Jim had never heard Harold talk or behave in this way, and thought he would try and sweeten the atmosphere with a little joke.

"Is he a terribly difficult patient, nurse?" he asked, smiling.

"He wasn't, until he was allowed up," said the probationer, unsmilingly. "Now do come along, Mr. Godbeer, or you'll get me into trouble with Sister!"

Harold had now lapsed into a sulk and he looked so much like a thwarted adolescent that Jim had great difficulty in keeping a straight face.

"Pop on down and get a taxi, Edith," he said, "I'll bring him along in one minute, nurse!"

The probationer shrugged and left, Edith giving Harold another kiss and following her, after receiving a sly nudge from Jim.

When they were alone, Jim said:

"You're a good deal lower than you were last week, Harold. Is there any special reason?"

"Yes, there is," said Harold, who now looked a little ashamed of himself.

"Well?"

"I didn't tell you everything just now. The fact is that Hollandby, the top surgeon, was here on Monday. He says he could promise a much better recovery if I submitted to another operation in a few weeks' time."

He avoided looking at Jim and his fingers plucked nervously at the folds of the rug. Jim saw that his hand shook and that the taut skin of his forehead was glistening with perspiration. He put his arm on Harold's shoulder and at his touch Harold shuddered.

"I can't face up to another, Jim, I can't! It may sound

dam' silly to you but it's the truth! I've had as much as I can stand! All I want is to get out of here and make do, even if I have to crawl about on hands and knees!"

Jim kicked the door shut. "Tell me! Tell me exactly what difference this new op is likely to make! Come on, you can tell me, old chap."

With a big effort Harold pulled himself together.

"Hollandby says they'd have to break the right leg again and reset it. It isn't anyone's fault, just my age, I imagine! If I gave them the go-ahead, and it worked out as they hoped, then I'd have to spend a few weeks at their physiotherapy centre, in Sussex. After that they say I'll still limp but not nearly so badly as if they patch me and send me out as I am."

Jim considered; he was trying hard to put himself in Harold's place. A few more weeks of pain and anxiety, weighed against the prospect of an almost complete cure. He knew at once what he would decide but then, he had not lain here for months in pain and fear, as Harold had done. It was easy to make a brave decision when one was fit and active. A man could stand so much pain and uncertainty and then, when the limit was reached, not one more twinge, or one more doubt.

He said, slowly: "It isn't a thing I'd like to advise you about, Harold. If it was me I'd have it done but you know your own breaking strain, and if it's going to drain you of what reserves you've got left, then maybe it's better to settle for half a loaf. That's something only you know about!"

"I keep asking myself if it's worth it," said Harold.

This was a question on which Jim felt that he could advise.

"Damn it, Harold, of course it's worth it! Look at it this way, you've worked hard ever since you were a kid, and after this no doubt you'll retire, and take things easy. You've got through the worst of it, not only all the years of hard grind that led up to retirement, but through the war and this fearful bashing they gave you! Isn't it a pity to chuck away the twenty odd years of peace you've earned for the sake of one more spurt?"

"You're taking it for granted that I'll make old bones and I won't Jim, not after this," said Harold.

"Damn it, you'll live as long as I will!" said Jim emphatically. "It isn't your injuries that makes you think your life has been shortened, but lying here, with so much time on your hands! Listen, Harold old man, do you remember that night we got to know one another, at the time of Dunkirk?"

"Yes, of course I remember it, Jim!"

"Well, I'll tell you something! You did me more good that night than anyone ever did in the whole of my life! I was ready to pack it in there and then, but it was you who gave me something to hope for, and something to fight for, simply by being who you are and what you are, an ordinary chap next door, with enough guts to hang on and hang on, until the muddlers like me got their second wind! I reckon you can scrape the barrel now, and find enough to go through with this job, and if you do, then you'll be out in time to enjoy that little bastard's wake, over in Berlin!"

Harold's thin lips twitched and Jim was relieved to see that he was now smiling again.

"Good old Jim," he said, at length, "you're always on the look-out for someone to canonise aren't you?"

"I've always believed that it's been a battle as to who could hang on the longest," said Jim, "and what goes for all of us goes for you! It's a bit more than that too," he went on, dropping his voice, "as far as I'm concerned winning the war wouldn't mean a damn thing if you didn't come through it!"

"You really mean that, don't you, Jim?" said Harold.

"Yes, I do! It's odd but somehow you ... you kind of symbolise this war for me! You always have!"

Harold was silent a moment and then swivelled his chair. Jim noticed that he had braced himself and was smiling broadly now.

"All right, Jim, I'll go through with it and thanks for everything! You'd better call them and. . . ."

But there was no need to call anybody. The door opened and the Sister appeared, clothed in starch and fury.

"You really must come *at once*, Godbeer!" she snapped. "Is this all the thanks I get, for arranging a special visit?"

"I'm coming, I'm coming," said Harold, wearily, as the Sister whirled him round, and whisked him past Jim into the corridor. And then, as a parting shot: "We've got our own Hitlers, Jim. This dam' place is crawling with 'em!"

* * * *

Judy was alone in the house with Barbara when Jim telephoned from Exeter.

Mrs. Cousins, the daily from the village, had sent a message to say that she was in bed with influenza and Ernie, the poultryman, had gone off to Exeter market to buy a second-hand hover for the spring chicks.

When the 'phone rang Judy had just had her first pain and she was sitting on the broad, bottom stair, still gasping. She called to Barbara, who was crayoning at the kitchen table.

"See who it is, Baba! Answer it for Mummy!"

She had been 'Mummy' to Barbara ever since they had moved into The Shillets, six months ago, and it had not taken the child very long to adjust herself to the relationship. The only other mother Barbara remembered was Frances, in Llandudno, and she retained memories of Pippa, but they were fading. She was a lively, intelligent child and Judy had found her such good company that she had put off starting her at school, although she had been five in September. She decided to wait until her own baby was born and Mrs. Cousin's daughter, Thirza, came to live in.

Barbara came trotting out of the kitchen and reached up for the receiver. She liked answering the telephone.

"This-is-the-Shillets-and-it's-Baba-speaking," she recited gaily. She called across to Judy on the stairs. "It's Grandfather Carver, and he's in Exeter!"

Judy experienced relief. Now that the baby was actually coming some of her confidence had deserted her and the arrival of Jim in Devon was reassuring.

She struggled to her feet and crossed the hall.

"Hullo, Dad? Where are you?"

"At the Station and we can't get a good train to North Devon until four. We thought about staying in Exeter for the night, there's no sense in pushing on, and arriving long after dark. How are you, Judy-girl?"

"I'm fine but. . . ."

The second pain gripped her and she broke off, squeaking

into the 'phone, so that he instantly became anxious and said, quickly: "Are you still there Judy? Is that you, Judy?"

She gritted her teeth and sat down on the chair under the 'phone.

"Listen, Dad, I think it's started . . . yes, just now . . . of all times! . . . I'll have to ring off now and get somebody!"

His voice sounded desperately anxious. "Who's there? Who's with you, Judy?"

"Nobody, except Baba, but don't fuss, Dad, I'll get someone. It's all fixed!"

"I'll come, Judy, I'll come over straight away!"

She nodded and replaced the receiver, clasping the arms of the chair and shooting out her legs as the pains wracked her, and lights exploded into the sun patterns before the open door.

The spasm passed and she realised that she would have to think and act fast. Jim's arrival was a stroke of luck but he could not get here for over an hour, even if he was lucky enough to find a cab at the station. Ernie, the poultryman, would not be back from the market until after three o'clock, and Maud Somerton, whom she had promised to ring, would be in the stable yard and seldom answered the telephone at this time of day. She took advantage of a lull in the pain to pick up the receiver and ask for Doctor Christie's number. She liked and trusted Christie, a brusque, elderly doctor, who rode to hounds. The Doctor's secretary told her he was over at the Cottage Hospital but that she would try and get him at once. She then began to explain that he was due to perform a minor operation there at 3 p.m., but Judy cut her short as the pains began again.

"Get him or his partner. . . . I'll send someone down for Nurse Rawley! My baby's on its way!"

The woman at the other end of the 'phone began to exclaim but Judy dropped the receiver and called loudly to Barbara, who had drifted back into the kitchen.

"Baba! Are you there, Baba?"

Barbara came running, startled by the urgency in Judy's voice. Judy sat down again and beckoned to the child.

"Listen Baba, this is important! I want you to saddle old Gramp and ride down to Mrs. Southcott, at the *Ring o'*

Bells! Tell her Mummy's baby's coming, and she's to get Nurse Rawley, and if she can't get the nurse tell her to come herself, d'you understand, dear?"

The child regarded her with mild wonder. She knew all about the baby and was intrigued by the prospect of a brother who, for some inexplicable reason, was at present living inside Mummy, and taking his time about joining them, but the prospect of actually saddling up the pony, and riding down to the village without an escort, drove everything else from her mind, and she began to hop about the hall in her delight.

"Do you understand what you've got to do, Baba?" asked Judy, impatiently.

"Yes, yes," chanted Barbara, "ride Gramp down to Mrs. Southcott and tell her the baby's here. I'll make him gallop—I'll shake him up!"

"The baby's coming ... and get nurse, try and get nurse!"

The child nodded and clattered away. Judy heard her feet flying across the cobbled yard to the stables. Between the waves of pain she fought panic, for now that she was alone in the house and the prospect of losing the baby, as a result of her own carelessness in not making better arrangements, began to assume terrifying proportions.

Only last night, when Doctor Christie had looked in, it had all seemed a bit of a joke, and he had commended her on her lack of fuss, but now it seemed to her an act of madness to have left everything to chance and relied upon a five-year-old child to bring help when it was needed.

She dragged herself upstairs and was relieved to hear Gramp's hooves clatter over the flagstones of the path, leading to the lane. She leaned heavily on the window-sill and waited to see pony and rider emerge from behind the chestnuts and canter off towards the village.

Then, as the pain receded for a moment, the incongruity of the situation struck her, and she clawed her way to the bed, rolling over on her back and thinking how strange it was that Esme's first child should be called upon to play such a spectacular part in the arrival of Esme's second child, while Esme himself was. . . . God knew where!

The pain became almost continuous then and she drew up her knees and moaned, trying to fix her mind on something pleasant in the past, something offering a refuge from the agony and terror of the present. She shut her eyes tightly and deliberately conjured up a picture of the ploughed ridge beyond Manor Wood, where it swept up to the spinney and the county border, but the figure that emerged from the wood and climbed the slope towards the spinney, was not Esme, but Boxer, her brother. Hands in trouser pockets he kicked at stones as he walked over the furrows and she saw that his lips were pursed in a whistle. She wanted, most desperately, to know what tune he was whistling. For some reason this became terribly important as she struggled to seal herself off from a fresh surge of pain, and concentrate on the slouching figure of Boxer mounting towards the skyline of the field.

Then, just as he reached it, she heard his whistle clearly. He was whistling a tune that she always associated with those days in the Avenue. It was *'Coal-Black Mammy'* and she heard him as clearly as though he was standing at the foot of the bed. Her own lips formed the words.

> 'Not a cent, not a cent
> And my clothes are only lent. . . .'

Then he passed over the skyline, the room went dark and the pain became so intolerable that she screamed.

· · · · ·

The car that Jim had at last managed to find deposited him and Edith at the foot of the lane, and they were obliged to struggle up the muddy path to the farm on foot. He saw at once, however, that his worst fears were unfulfilled, for Judy was obviously no longer alone. A battered Morris, the doctor's, he assumed, was parked under the chestnuts, and as he and Edith hurried into the garden an elderly woman in mud-splashed riding-boots and a hacking jacket green with age hailed them from the porch.

"Mr. Carver? Silliest thing, we've never met! I'm Maud Somerton, and you'll be glad to hear the Gel's fine! It's a boy, a monstrous, hairy, little brute! He was born before the doctor got here, if you please!"

Jim gasped with relief. "God, but I was worried," he admitted, and then, recollecting his manners: "How do you do, Miss Somerton? This is my wife, and we were only married this morning!"

They shook hands and Edith winced under Maud's grip. The anxiety, the rush from the station, and the final sprint up the sloshy lane, had left her breathless and dishevelled. A hank of grey hair had broken loose from under her new straw hat, and her neat, brown shoes and stockings were coated with mud.

"You look all in, the pair of you!" said Miss Somerton briefly. "Come inside, and let me get you something! Doctor's still upstairs! Nurse arrived after it was all over! I told the Gel that woman was no dam' good! Lucky old Nell Southcott came back with the child!"

They went into the big kitchen, where a log fire burned brightly, and Jim sniffed the air appreciatively. Although an inveterate town-dweller he had always loved the smell of a farm-kitchen, and the hiss and splutter of burning wood.

Barbara came prancing out of the buttery and jumped at him.

"The baby's here, the baby's here!" she chanted, "and it was me and Gramp who fetched everybody from the pub!"

"She rode the pony down to the Southcotts," Miss Somerton explained. "Now leave them alone, Baba, and let them get their breath! Have you given old Gramp a good rub down?"

"Yes, and I've put his rug on," said Barbara, smugly.

"Good girl, good girl," said Miss Somerton, absently, and to Edith, "I expect you could do with some tea. Help yourself to sugar!"

Jim and Edith sat drinking tea in the kitchen while Maud Somerton talked inconsequently of Judy, how happy she was down here, and what a flair the Gel had for teaching children to ride. Jim smiled, enjoying his relief, and remembering all the stories that Judy had told him about this terse, leathery, old riding-mistress.

"You changed her life, Miss Somerton," he told her, gratefully. "She worships you, you know!"

Maud snorted. "Rubbish!" she snapped, "she's got no time for anybody but that airman husband of hers! When is he likely to be home?"

"I shouldn't think it'll be long now," said Jim, "we shall soon have the blighters on the run again!"

"By God and about time," said Miss Somerton, explosively. "Do you know what they're asking for hay this winter?"

Jim never learned the current price of hay for at this point the old doctor bustled in, purple-faced and wheezing. Jim shook hands with him and reflected, while doing so, that to live down here was to transport oneself back into George III's reign. People still sent children on horseback for midwives, and doctors looked like hunting squires in 18th-century hunting prints.

"How is she, doctor?" he asked.

"First-rate!" said Doctor Christie, "and that's the way to have them! I don't know what people want with nursing homes and what-not. Damned badly-run places, most of 'em, nothing like your own home! You'd better feed her some broth now, Maud, and I'll ring through before I turn in. Nurse'll be here for a week or so. Will you be staying on, Mr. Carver?"

"I'm afraid we shall have to, just for tonight," said Jim, apologetically. "We were on our way to North Devon when it happened and we were only married this morning!"

"Good God!" exclaimed the doctor. "Well, I daresay Nell Southcott will look after you, and congratulations on both events! I'd better be off now. Old Mark Phillips, over at Coombe Brake, will die tonight. Pity! I made sure he'd make his century."

"I thought he had," said Maud, off-handedly.

"Ninety-eight," said Doctor Christie, "Ah well, we can't all do it, can we Mrs. Carver?"

"Nnno," said Edith, doubtfully, "I suppose not, Doctor!"

Mrs. Southcott, a sharp-nosed, cheerful woman, about Jim's age, came downstairs and introduced herself, apparently accepting this interruption of her life very philosophically. After telephoning her daughter at the *Ring o' Bells* she made up the beds for Jim, Edith and the nurse, and afterwards helped Edith to prepare a meal of eggs and bacon, stewed fruit and another vast pot of tea. Maud finished her meal first and put Baba to bed, afterwards going out to replenish the wood pile. Before she left she went upstairs to see Judy and called down, saying that Jim and Edith could look in and see her before they went to bed.

"You go, Jim," said Edith, shyly. "I'm sure she'd rather see you alone. Tell her I'll see her in the morning."

He climbed the broad, uneven stairs, and Maud pointed out the bedroom. On the landing he met the nurse, who told him that Judy had had one good sleep but was probably ready for another.

"I won't stay a minute," Jim promised.

He went in a little fearfully and found her sitting up, sipping a mug of Ovaltine.

A bright coal fire was burning in the high grate and the new curtains were closely drawn. The panelled room looked cosy and inviting. The baby's cot stood beside the bed, furthermost from the fire, and the room was lit by a single, pink-shaded bedside light. The air of comfort and elegance astonished him, for his acquaintance with the kitchen had prepared him for spartan bedrooms.

"Hullo, there," she called, cheerfully. "Well, I managed it!"

She could not keep the note of triumph from her voice and he was excited at seeing her so strong and confident. He did not remember ever having noticed the lustre of her thick, chestnut hair, or the rich bloom on her cheeks. She not only looked happy but in radiant health, and his mind went back to his first wife, Ada, and the birth of their eldest child, poor old Louise, in the drab, two-roomed flat they had occupied when Queen Victoria was still on the throne. It seemed several centuries ago.

"I'm so glad you were around," she said, kissing him. "Where's Edith?"

"Downstairs," he told her, "and she's tired out! She said she'll come in and see you in the morning. We'll be staying tonight, there's no help for it. That Mrs. Southcott and Miss Somerton have seen to us."

"Did it go off all right, the wedding?" she wanted to know.

"It went fine! Archie and Elaine were there. He gave us the house you know, and Edgar Frith gave Edith away. It was very quiet, of course, but everyone was friendly. They're a friendly bunch in the Avenue."

"Yes," she said, "they always were, weren't they? Don't you want to see the baby?"

He clapped his hand to his head. "Good Lord, I'd actually forgotten! I was so worried when I heard you were all alone but I needn't have been need I? The entire district seems to be on tap!"

"In a way it's just like the Avenue," she said. "The people around are all that really count, Dad!"

She leaned over and reached into the cot, pulling the blue blanket on one side. Jim caught a glimpse of a brick-red, puckered face, crowned with a sparse halo of dark, brown hair.

"Isn't he wonderful?" said Judy. "He weighs eight-and-a-half already!"

"He's fine, Judy. What are you calling him?"

"I don't know, I can't make up my mind. It would have been 'James', but you've already got one James, Archie's second. I would have liked 'Esme' but Esme doesn't like the name much. He says it's a bit girlish. What do you think of 'Harold'?"

"It would be a wonderful tonic for old Harold, but I can't honestly say I'm gone on the name, are you?"

"No," she said, "it's not an open-airey name is it? It's too 'officy', somehow! I say, I've got an idea! Reach me that book, the green one, with gold lettering."

He gave her the book, a small leather-bound volume of Tennyson's poems, and she put down her Ovaltine mug and began to flick through the pages.

"I can't think why I didn't have this brainwave before! Listen."

She began to read and it was clear that she was very familiar with the passage, for she read it rapidly and without trace of hesitancy:

'And that same night the night of the New Year,
　By reason of the bitterness and grief,
　That vext his mother, all before his time,
　Was Arthur born, and all as soon as born,
　Delivered at the postern-gate
　To Merlin, to be holden far apart
　Until his hour should come;'

She closed the book and smiled.

"That'll do," she said, "We'll call him 'Arthur'! That'll give old Esme no end of a kick, you see if it doesn't!"

"He wasn't born before his time, he was a good bit overdue wasn't he?" said Jim, smiling.

"That's poetic licence," said Judy, "Esme's a glutton for poetic licence—always was!"

He knew little or nothing of her childhood games beside the lake in Manor Wood. In those days all his spare time had been taken up with politics and he had hardly noticed the children, unless they got in his way. He saw now that she too had remembered this, for she was not really conscious of him any longer, but sat propped up, her hands folded, her mind exploring a special preserve that was her own and Esme's. He did not like to trespass any longer so kissed her, softly.

"Good night, Judy love."

"Good night, Dad."

He went out and she glanced at the baby before turning off the bedside light. She felt tired, but relaxed and comfortable. The coals rustled in the grate and shadows danced across the ceiling.

Arthur! After all this time! The Coming of Arthur! How would that strike Esme when he heard about today's event and came rushing home to see his child? Would it strike him as rather forced and silly? Would he prefer a name that had no bearing on the old Manor that had been 'many towered Camelot', and the lake that was the mere into which so many Excaliburs had been flung?

What exactly was 'samite' that had clothed the mystic arm? For years now she had been meaning to look it up in a dictionary, but she never had and still thought of it as a kind of fine cotton, like the material of the powder-puff handkerchief that Esme had once bought her at Woolworths, in the Old Orchard Road.

The nurse looked in and said something but she was asleep.

CHAPTER XXXVIII

King Boxer The First

THE Germans had a word for it; they called it *'Fernheh'*, a craving to wander into strange, far-off places.

Boxer had been a victim of *'Fernheh'* ever since new leaves had begun to show on the trees outside the compound, and the smell of spring came to compete with the smell of barrack-room brews.

He had made up his mind to leave camp by one of the tunnels, both of which had been nearing completion, when he began his last spell in the cooler, but when he came out he was told that one tunnel had caved in, and that the other had been discovered by the security patrols, so that he was pondering the possibilities of an independent escape when the Allies crossed the Rhine and the Great Exodus began.

Life became more exciting but infinitely more strenuous for everyone. The prisoners were marched from camp to camp, aimlessly it seemed to Boxer, who had never bothered to study the war situation as a whole, and therefore had scant sympathy with the generally-held opinion that escape, at this stage, was not only a waste of time but a dangerous enterprise.

He argued that, under existing conditions, it was absurdly easy to escape on the march. The reservists who guarded the column hardly bothered to count them at the end of the day's march. In a sense the captives had become gaolers and the tough Coldstreamer, who had been the Senior N.C.O. at the camp for the past two years, was now principal adviser of the harassed Commandant and his despairing staff.

Boxer had rather liked the guardsman in his former role, but he did not understand the Sergeant Major's current antipathy towards a general dispersal of prisoners into the surrounding countryside.

The Coldstreamer, not distinguished for his patience, did his best to explain to Boxer.

"Look, you clot," he announced. "The entire bloody country's in chaos, so the only smart thing to do now is to stick close to the Krauts who know us, and who look upon us as their insurance! The woods are stiff with deserters, Hitler Youth, Werewolves and all kinds of thugs, most of 'em prepared to cut your throat for the scrapings of a Red Cross parcel! So don't get the idea that you can survive out there, or make your own way back to our lines! You'll stay put and you'll like it, until Jerry packs in, get me?"

Boxer could not see it this way. In the early stages of his captivity he had not concerned himself very much with the business of escape. It had seemed to him, at that time, much more practical to remain in Germany and occupy oneself baiting Germans. Today, with the Jerries running here, there and everywhere like a bunch of scalded cats, there was no longer any point in baiting them. They would not rise to a bait, no matter what one did or said. Nothing would induce them to start one of those delightful flaps that Boxer enjoyed so much. Accordingly, he reasoned, one might just as well pack it in, slide off towards home, and call it a day, taking one's chance with the wild men in the woods. Surely that was more sensible than to continue to march up and down slushy roads, sleep in crowded barns and insanitary transit camps, and exist on next to nothing?

He consulted Whitey, his friend, on the subject, but it seemed that even Whitey had been won over to the Sergeant Major's point of view and firmly rejected the idea of dodging the column.

"Aw, lay orf it, Gaffer!" he told Boxer. "Where's the sense in takin' any more bloody chances? We'll all be out of it any'ow inside a week or two."

Boxer was disappointed but by no means discouraged. If Whitey and all the others preferred to wear out their boot leather in marching here and there sooner than chance it in the woods, then he would go off alone and seek out whatever new adventures Fate had in store for him.

He checked his kit, donned every garment he possessed, risked a post-war court-martial by helping himself to two tins of beans from the shrinking communal store, and strolled over to the improvised latrine behind the cattle sheds where they happened to be billeted for the night.

The latrine was guarded by a single German, a small defeated man, recently invalided from the Russian Front. Boxer gave him a cigarette and told him to look the other way, while he climbed out behind the latrine and jumped down into the adjoining pasture land.

Ten minutes later he was inside the woods and walking due west by the setting sun.

He had studied a map a day or so before he had made his final decision, and had made a rough copy of it on the back of a carton. This map, a blanket and his two tins of beans, comprised his entire escape kit, but his lack of equipment did not worry him overmuch. For years now he had been an expert picker-up-of-trifles and he had no doubt but that he would come across all he needed.

He was not disappointed. That inscrutable Providence said to watch over drunkards, children and incurable optimists, smiled down on him from the hour of his departure. Before darkness fell he emerged from the woods to cross a small open patch, where a second-class road had been cut through the forest. Lying on its side in the ditch, where it had been flung by the bombs of attacking aircraft, was a lorry, and under the lorry, overlooked by salvage team and passing marauders, was an unopened crate of pilchards.

Boxer prised off the lid and counted the tins, more than a hundred of them. He found a piece of angle iron from the canopy and employed it as an opener, eating two tins of pilchards on the spot and then going to sleep on the leather cushions inside the driving-cabin.

He awoke at first light upon hearing the sound of dragging footsteps in the dead leaves alongside the road. Squinting through the shattered windscreen of the lorry he saw that it was nothing to get alarmed about, for the glade was empty except for a young woman who was poking about among the debris between the lorry and the trees.

She was an odd, bedraggled creature, wrapped in what appeared to be a few yards of coarse sacking and a yellow gas-cape. Her head was bare and her black hair hung about her face like a tattered mat.

Boxer climbed out of the lorry and called across to her. At the sound of his voice she ran crouching into the wood but when she saw that he was alone, and unarmed, she stopped on the edge of the trees and looked back, poised to continue her flight.

Boxer had not been a prisoner in Germany for more than two and a half years without learning that the major preoccupation of a woman attired as this one must be a search for food, and he knew at once that hunger alone prevented her from diving into the woods like a startled hare.

He guessed that she must be one of the hundreds of thousands of foreign workers who had been uprooted in recent weeks by the turmoil inside Germany, and was now scratching about for the means of existence. He reached back into the driving cabin and held up a tin of pilchards.

"Pilchards!" he shouted. "Very good! Very nice!" and he smacked his lips and rubbed his stomach.

The woman's teeth flashed in a smile but she still hesitated. He turned his back on her and sat down to open the tin. When he glanced over his shoulder three women were regarding him from the bushes. All were dressed in bizarre odds and ends, and one of them, whose grey hair was tied under a long, green scarf, wore German jackboots several sizes too large for her.

He dug the angle-iron into the pilchards and forked a large piece of fish into his mouth.

"Pilchards!" he said again. "Smashing!"

Step by step they advanced out of the woods and Boxer then saw that one of the newcomers was a child, about thirteen. He beckoned to her and she suddenly began to run towards him. He ripped off the remainder of the lid and handed the tin to her, chuckling as she fell upon it and began cramming fragments of the fish into her mouth. He opened the driving-cabin door and pointed to the crate.

"Help yourselves," he said genially, "they didn't cost me nothing!"

His gesture must have removed the last vestiges of suspicion from the two women, for they dived into the cabin, dragged the crate into the open and seizing a tin apiece at once commenced to pound them with stones.

"Here, half a tick, half a tick, don't be so bloody greedy!" he protested, and skillfully opened another tin with his piece of iron. The child smiled up at him between large mouthfuls and her pinched face became smeared with tomato sauce, so that it looked startlingly like blood against the pallor of her cheeks.

"You poor bastards," said Boxer feelingly, "I bet you haven't seen nothing like this in weeks!"

Between them they accounted for seven tins and then they began to address him in high-pitched, gobbling voices.

"Me no savvy! Me Soldat English!" he explained.

They appeared to understand the word 'English' for the child began to caper. The young woman who had been first on the scene evidently mistook him for the advance guard of the British army, for she beamed and pretended to shoot, pointing towards the west.

"No," said Boxer, comprehending, "I'm just a kriegie on the run, a prisoner . . . look!" and he went through an ingenious pantomime intended to establish his status. The two women looked so downcast at this that he decided to cheer them up by switching to a second pantomime, this time aimed at impressing upon them the nearness of British troops.

"*Waldkappel!*" he said, repeating the name of the town from which his column had been evacuated less than a week ago. "The British at Waldkappel! Bom-bom!" and he made noises suggestive of an attack by tanks.

This seemed to confuse them but they did not press the point and presently the young woman beckoned to him and advanced a few steps towards the wood.

At that moment Boxer heard the whine of approaching aircraft and decided that there were healthier places to stand about than an open clearing. He picked up the crate, which he was just able to carry, and followed the trio into the trees, flattening himself as the aircraft zoomed down on the clearing and then skimmed lightly away again. Boxer noticed that it was an American Thunderbolt and its presence cheered him.

"Yanks," he told the women and supplemented the information by champing his jaws in the hope of indicating chewing-gum. The women nodded. They had evidently seen a number of American aircraft in the area and the crone in the jack-boots began a conversation with the younger woman that ended in her laying hands on the crate at Boxer's feet.

Boxer was having none of this. He was prepared to share his find but not to give it away.

"No bloody fear," he said shortly, "where this goes I go, savvy?"

Presumably they did, for the young woman beckoned and went on ahead, pushing along a winding path for the best part of half a mile and then leaving it to break through a thick screen of bushes into a circular clearing about a hundred yards square.

Exerting himself to the utmost Boxer struggled along behind her, gasping and grunting under the weight of the box, and when he had burst through the bushes, and slithered down a slope into the clearing he found himself in an extensive bivouac, consisting of half a dozen roughly-constructed huts, inhabited by at least two dozen refugees, all but one of them women and children.

His first thought was that his pilchards would not survive very long in this kind of company and he was half inclined to retreat but the bank that he had descended was slippery and he was quite exhausted by the walk from the road, so he sat down on his crate as the best means of protecting it and waited for the women to explain his presence to the only man in the group, an aged, yellow-faced derelict, wearing a buttonless tunic and huge, baggy breeches, made from an army blanket.

Boxer took an instant dislike to the old man, who did not seem very welcoming, but he was relieved to discover that the old fellow understood English and could speak it reasonably well between his harsh bouts of coughing.

He was able to explain that the women in the clearing

were a party of Russian slave-labourers, recently employed in
a factory at Mulhausen, and that when the factory had been
destroyed by American aircraft a week or so ago their hut-
ments had been set on fire, and the inmates had scattered in all
directions.

Germany, the old man insisted, was *kaput!* The Russians
were advancing rapidly from the south-east and were not
meeting with much opposition. He seemed to be far better
informed on the situation than was Boxer, for he said that it
was not the British who had attacked Waldkappel recently
but the Americans, who were using 'thousands and thousands
of tanks!' It would not be long, he added, before the Americans and Russians joined hands inside Germany, but in the
meantime they would have to stay hidden and live as best
they could. He was a talkative old man once he got started
and went on to say that he was a Belgian, who had been sent
to Germany early in the war to work in a glass foundry. He
did not explain how he came to be here in the company of
the Russian women and Boxer did not ask him, for the
Belgian's explanations had taken a long time and he had tired
of the strain of attempting to follow him.

While they were conferring the women gathered in an
admiring semi-circle around Boxer and every now and again
one of them reached out and touched him. As they did this
each kept her eyes fixed on him and whenever he met the
gaze of old or young they smiled and made little murmuring
noises. He found their attentions soothing and pleasantly
distracting, and soon his natural geniality urged him to show
some response to their welcome.

He got up and opened the crate and at once the women's
murmurs rose to an excited cooing. Solemnly he placed one
tin in each pair of outstretched hands, ignoring the surly
protests of the Belgian at his elbow, who was evidently
distressed by his generosity.

While the women were resorting to various means of opening the tins the young woman who had guided him to the
camp signalled to him to follow her across the clearing and
into a hut, that stood a little apart from the others.

He went inside and found nothing but a couch of heaped
up dead leaves and an empty mess tin. She pointed to the

heap of leaves and then at Boxer, from which he gathered that this hut was to be his quarters, and that she now regarded him and herself as joint custodians of the crate.

He signified that he understood her and placed the crate as far from the entrance as possible. As he did so he remembered his tins of beans and took them from his haversack. The woman hissed and glanced fearfully over her shoulder, before taking up a position that blocked the small entrance. He opened the tin and poured the beans into the mess tin, placing the half empty tin under the leaves. He possessed a spoon and began to use it, for the pilchards had proved an unsatisfactory breakfast. He had never liked pilchards but he had always loved beans. He ate them steadily and the woman did not take her eyes from him.

After a while he began to feel restless under her unwavering stare. He was prepared to dispense pilchards but two tins of beans, he told himself, would not go very far among this rabble, and he would be wise to conserve his stock against an uncertain future.

The woman's eyes, however, continued to battle with his caution, and at length he groped under the leaves and handed her the half-full tin.

She fell upon it with the same ravening hunger as she had shown earlier in the day, and when the beans were gone she thrust her tongue into the tin and licked it as clean as a cat's plate. When it was empty she sighed and made a series of signs that he could not understand. She was still trying to explain something when the Belgian came into the hut and proposed that he should guard the pilchards, whilst Boxer took two or three of the younger women out on a foraging and reconnaissance expedition.

For some reason that he could not explain Boxer trusted the woman more than he trusted the Belgian. He was getting very good at sign-language by this time and soon made her understand that she was to stay with the crate while he and the old man were away from the clearing.

The Belgian began to argue but Boxer cut him short. "You bloody well do as I say and don't chew the cud, gran'pa!" he said, so firmly that the old man followed him over the bank and through the bushes to the track.

They spent the afternoon skirting along the edge of the woods in search of turnips. Several aircraft passed over but they were too high to be identified.

Once, in the far distance, they saw a German motorised column pass along the skyline, and towards evening they paused to listen to a steady boom of artillery that seemed to come from the east and not the west as he would have expected.

They explored an abandoned farmhouse but found nothing worth carrying away and dusk was falling when they returned to the bivouac, to find the Russian girl sitting cross-legged on the pile of leaves, a heavy cudgel on her lap.

She said something to the old Belgian who merely grunted. When Boxer asked what she had said he hunched his shoulders and pointed at the cudgel.

"They came but she struck them," he said, laconically.

"Good for you, Olga!" said Boxer and patted her shoulder.

Without quite knowing how it came about Boxer now assumed full leadership of the group. The old man hung about uncertainly and the woman looked at Boxer interrogatively, as though awaiting orders. Outside, between the hut and a smokeless fire, the other women and children were gathered expectantly and Boxer, having glanced at the group, and then at the woman with the cudgel, understood that some decision was expected of him.

"Are they waiting about for their rations?" he asked the old man.

The Belgian's eyes narrowed and he glanced contemptuously at the woman on the couch.

"Send her away," he said, "it is time that we made a plan!"

Boxer signalled to the woman to leave them and she rose very reluctantly, moving just outside the entrance and facing inwards, her back to the crowd.

The old man began to grope for words, but there was no mistaking the urgency of the message he wished to convey.

"It is best you and I leave here," he said, "there is not enough to feed these women!"

Boxer was outraged. "Well, you mean old bastard!" he

exclaimed. "Leave these kids to starve and go off with the lot? Not bloody likely, Grandpa! If anyone goes short it's going to be you, chum!"

He did not understand why he should take this attitude. After all, the old chap was talking good sense, and pilchards that would keep two for a fortnight would only last a couple of days shared among the twenty-four starvelings in the clearing.

He certainly had not intended to get himself mixed up with these people, for it was surely neither the time nor the place to add to one's responsibilities, but now that they were looking to him for leadership he found it impossible to abandon them.

"If you think you'd get along better on your own take four tins and clear off now," he told the Belgian. "Me? I'm going to get some organisation into this outfit!"

He walked out of the hut and addressed the girl, whom he now thought of as 'Olga'. Olga was the only Russian name he knew, apart from 'Ivan'.

"Get 'em lined up, Olga," he said and supplemented his order by signs.

The girl understood at once and began to marshal the refugees into a queue. He went back to the hut, where the Belgian was already helping himself from the crate.

"I said *four*, Grandpa, not forty-four!"

He slapped the old man's hand and counted out four tins.

"Now scram, Grandpa!" He pointed to the door and repeated: "Scram! Vamoose! Allez-allez, you thieving old basket!"

The man shrugged and left the hut. Boxer did not reflect much upon the problem of communicating with these people without an interpreter, even such an inadequate interpreter as the Belgian. He told himself that he would manage somehow, and he and Olga dragged the crate into the open where he began issuing tins. This done he returned, opened his last tin of beans and shared it with the girl.

It was dark now and he wondered about the fires but decided that they would have to risk advertising their presence. The huts were little more than shelters and it was cold.

He sat down on the leaves and tried to think. What the hell could you do for these people? To judge by the constant rumble of guns, and the almost continuous drone of aircraft overhead, fighting was now going on all around them. This little glade was as safe as anywhere, he supposed, and certainly safer than trekking east or west along roads or forest tracks. Tanks and motorised infantry would use the tracks, particularly with so many hostile aircraft overhead, and some of the Yanks were not over particular in their choice of targets—his own column had been strafed four times in its movements from camp to camp.

If they remained here, however, they would have to be fed and the pilchards would not last much longer. His frown of concentration turned on the girl, who was cleaning the communal mess-tin and spoon with handfuls of leaves.

Watching her Boxer relaxed, thinking her action typical of her entire sex. Louise, his sister, would have done just that, even under these conditions. Here was artillery grumbling all round them, the sky vibrating with bombers, and twenty-two women and children trying to sleep in home-made huts on a supper of tinned pilchards, yet Olga still practised the trade of housewife! He wondered how old she was and how she came to be here. He yearned to confide in her and ask her advice, but knowing no single word of Russian, he realised that this was not possible. The fire outside had burned up and its glow lit up the hut as she laid down the burnished mess-tin and picked up her cudgel, seating herself on the crate, folding her arms, and leaning her body on the flimsy wall. She was evidently taking her responsibilities as sentry very seriously.

"You can't sit like that all night, Olga," he said. "They won't try anything, so long as I'm here!"

She smiled and threw back her mop of hair. He got up and spread his blanket on the leaves, pointing first to her and then to himself. She understood this readily enough but indicated by signs that he should lie down first and when he did so she lay down beside him and threw the edge of the blanket over his shoulders, jerking it towards her so that they were pressed together in its fold.

He was surprised by her warmth and by the softness of the thick couch of leaves. Nestling there, with her arm across his shoulder in order to hold the blanket in place, he reflected that it had been quite a day. It promised to be quite another, tomorrow, but he would not think about that now. Something would turn up, just as it always did.

It was years since Boxer had held a women in his arms but he experienced no desire for this one and this fact also surprised him. Was it the cold, the years of celibacy behind wire, or the strange, overriding conviction that this girl, now seeking to comfort him, was not a woman at all in that sense but a kind of mother, doing duty for all mothers, everywhere.

He considered this fancy for a moment and then, the moment before sleep overtook him, the humour of the situation struck him and with it the need to make a mental note of it in order to recount the story to Bernard. He had so many stories to tell Berni, but this, surely, was the richest of them! A woman and a bed in exchange for a crate of tinned pilchards!

Even as he fell asleep his face split in his habitual grin.

*   *   *

Boxer remained in the clearing for fourteen days and the period proved to be the final stage in the true discovery of himself as an individual.

Ever since that August day almost three years ago, when he had been faced with the terrible necessity of making a whole series of decisions regarding the disposal of Bernard, Boxer had been moving steadily towards the achievement of independence.

His experiences in the prison camps had given him plenty of opportunity to exercise ingenuity, but inside there had always been expert advice available and, in addition, a certain pattern to which even inveterate practical jokers like Boxer were obliged to conform. Here, in the clearing, there was no single person with whom he could confer, and the only pattern that emerged was that of staying out of sight and staying fed until either the Americans or the Russians showed up, and he could hand over his charges to someone better equipped to look after them.

His luck, however, did not desert him, for on the second

day, while on a reconnaissance along the edge of the forest, he found a hamlet from which the inhabitants appeared to have evacuated themselves in haste.

He made a thorough search of two small farms and located two sacks of oatmeal in an abandoned perambulator. He wheeled them home in triumph and there was joy and thanksgiving in the bivouac that night, for every person in camp had two helpings of porridge, as well as their usual ration of pilchards.

On the fourth day the population of the clearing was augmented by a party of German civilians from a town on the other side of the river that they could see from the fringe of the woods.

The party consisted of three elderly men, five middle-aged women, and seven assorted children. One of the women, a school-teacher, could speak both English and Polish, and was able to understand sufficient of Boxer's orders to transmit them to the Russians.

The two groups displayed no animosity towards one another and neither questioned his authority. Outside on the plain there was war and here, deep in the woods, was a limited measure of security, hot food, and partial shelter from rain and cold. This, for the terrified refugees, was all that mattered for the moment, and as the thunder of guns increased from the west more and more fugitives began to trickle into the clearing, some of them bringing stocks of food that went into a communal larder.

More huts were built, a regular system of reconnaissance was organised, and a permanent patrol set to watch the junction of the forest path and the road where Boxer had first encountered the Russians. Rumours circulated in the camp with the persistence of the aircraft patrols overhead, and Boxer issued orders for the huts to be moved and rebuilt under the trees, leaving the open section of the clearing free in case the settlement should be mistaken for a troop concentration and bombed.

Once or twice, German motorised columns rumbled along the road within half a mile of the camp, but no units penetrated the belt of undergrowth that screened the clearing from the track. Such fires as they used were built under the close-set trees and a watch was maintained on each in order to keep it as smokeless as possible.

Even so, on the fifth day, a grizzled forester wearing a uniform that reminded Boxer of the Sherwood Forest outlaws featured in the two-penny magazines of his youth, came into the camp and handed Boxer his shotgun.

In a conversation conducted through the school-teacher the forester assured Boxer that he' was not, and had never been, a member of the Nazi party, but had been enrolled in a specially-formed unit for the defence of the district against anticipated paratroop attacks, in February. There were many such as he in the district, he said, and they would be happy to surrender to units of the British, or the Americans. Meantime, pending arrival of the main forces of the Allies, he would be glad to act as forest guide to the refugees. He made no secret of the fact that he wished to shed his quasi-military status as rapidly as possible.

Boxer did not know what to make of all this and was by no means sure of the attitude he ought to maintain towards Germans carrying arms. After some thought he decided to abandon his role of P.O.W. and take an altogether more active part in the war. Convinced of the sincerity of the forester he accepted his shotgun and ammunition, and sent him to watch the cross-roads. This was certainly a risk now that the man had found the clearing, but it was one that Boxer was obliged to take, for there were no facilities for holding the man prisoner in the clearing.

Two days later there were even more startling developments. The forester reported to the school-teacher that he had made contact with a group of armed civilians, whom he had persuaded to surrender. He assured Boxer that there would be no trouble with these people, some of whom he knew, and all of whom were men over forty, hastily enlisted for home defence during the last two months.

They marched into the clearing the following morning and stacked their arms outside Boxer's hut. There were twenty-nine of them in all and the leader behaved towards Boxer as though he had been a conquering general.

By this time Boxer was getting used to authority and was even attired for it. They had brought him a British officer's

pack, found abandoned along the route of one of the
P.O.W.'s forced marches, and he had decked himself out in
an infantry captain's cap and battledress, so that he was
ready for the second mass surrender, this time of a party of
regular troops, located by the patrols of the first party and
conducted to the clearing by night.

This latest batch consisted of forty-three men under the
command of a bewildered junior officer. The officer, Boxer
noted, was at the end of his tether, and had been hoping to
surrender for days. He spoke English and told Boxer that he
and his half-company had not slept for four nights and had
marched over two hundred miles since the unit was despatched to the Wanfred sector, a fortnight ago.

The men were too exhausted to eat and lay about round
the fires, the subject of sour complaints on the part of women
trying to prepare meals with improvised utensils.

There was no serious food problem now, however, for the
obliging forester had shown them where they could find meal,
root crops, and maize in abundance. More and more huts and
a few tents sprang up, and when Boxer conducted a census
he found that there were over two hundred prisoners and
refugees in the clearing and more coming in each day.

He formed a kind of staff from the Russian girl, Olga, the
German school-teacher and the forester, and they discussed
their various problems round his fire. It was here that the
forester told him that he could, if he wished, make contact
with American tank units, who were about to cross the river
and by-pass the forest to the south. Boxer decided to take his
advice, for it seemed to him that if he continued to rule the
clearing the entire population of Germany might sooner or
later find its way there and deposit its manifold problems in
his lap.

He set Olga and the Russian women to guard the rifles and
followed the forester along a series of tracks that led south
through a part of the woods that he had not yet explored.

On the way they heard small-arms' fire, coming from the
direction of the river and later a dull, heavy explosion. When
they emerged from the woods on to the river road they saw
the tail-end of a German column, disappearing at speed into

the east. Across the river were puffs of smoke that indicated the presence of American artillery.

They settled themselves on a wooded ridge overlooking the stream and within hailing distance of the damaged bridge. The bridge had evidently been blown up that morning and its demolition must have been the explosion they had heard. Boxer decided that the charges must have been faulty, for only one arch had been severed and even this was still practicable to pedestrian traffic.

About noon the first American infantry began to cross, led by small groups of heavily-laden men, who picked their way carefully across the twisted girders and ultimately formed up on the bank. The nearest of them were about a hundred yards away when Boxer stood up and shouted. The immediate response was a smart volley, that whipped through the branches of the trees under which they were standing. Boxer was indignant.

"Well, stone the bloody crows!" he exclaimed, subsiding quickly.

When he cautiously raised his head again a patrol of four men were fanning out in the undergrowth immediately below them. They moved with elaborate caution and Boxer, watching them closely, could not restrain a chuckle.

"So help me, if I had a Tommy I could pick all four off in one burst!" he told the stolid forester.

He saw what he must do. He was accustomed now to making swift decisions and remembered that his long woollen socks were white, or had once been white. He kicked off his boot, peeled off a sock, and raised it on a length of twig that the forester passed to him.

A moment later a voice below called sharply:

"Stand up, don't stir, and keep your hands above your head, Kraut!"

Boxer stood up, grinning, and saw that the foremost man of the patrol, a broad-faced corporal, was already within thirty yards of the ridge.

"I'm no bloody Kraut, Yank!" said Boxer, genially. "I'm a P.O.W. on the run, and I've got a whole army of Krauts falling over 'emselves to surrender!"

They took both him and the forester before the officer, a

major, who was polite and incredulous, but not inclined to be helpful.

"You say you're a P.O.W. and you've got two hundred Krauts rounded up in the woods, Captain?"

"They're not *all* Krauts," said Boxer, modestly. "Some of 'em are Russians, and lots of 'em are just kids!"

"I don't get it, Captain," said the American, bluntly.

"Well, there's not all that to it," said Boxer, patiently. "They were wandering all over the auction, and they just moved in on me! You give me the word and I'll fetch 'em over. They'll be eating out of your hand, the lot of 'em!"

"I can't take over two hundred prisoners," protested the American, "this is a combat unit!" Then, doubtfully. "Where d'you say these Krauts are located, Captain?"

"I can take you there," said Boxer, "but I'm not really a Captain, I just borrowed this kit! It's like this see; Old Jerry, he always goes for officer's tabs, and I might have had trouble with 'em if they'd known I was just an O.R."

The officer sighed at this additional complication. "Well, I guess I'd better send someone along to collect 'em," he said. "This goddamned war don't go by the books any more! I guess I'd better put through a call to Corps H.Q. 'bout this, Captain!"

"Yes, sir, you do that," said Boxer, "but don't forget to put 'em wise about my real rank. You can collect a packet of trouble for impersonating an officer in my outfit!"

"You can in any outfit," said the Major, grimly.

A sergeant and ten men accompanied Boxer to the clearing and in the early afternoon the exodus began.

Boxer and Olga led the column and the G.I.s watched in astonishment as it emerged from the woods into the April twilight beside the river.

The officer counted them in and ordered up extra rations. He seemed to have shed his initial bewilderment and welcomed Boxer with far more cordiality than he had shown earlier in the day. He had made arrangements, he said, to convey Boxer to the nearest British unit that very night, in accordance with a special drill laid down for freed prisoners of war, but before Boxer parted from him he made a confession over a generous tot of whiskey.

"You know something, feller? I didn't believe you, not until I actually set eyes on this rabble!"

"No," said Boxer philosophically, "and I don't reckon anyone else is going to believe me back home!"

He finished his drink, shook hands with the Major, and climbed into the jeep that was awaiting him at the end of the patched-up bridge.

Olga must have been watching, for she hurriedly detached herself from the group of women standing beside the road and ran towards him, shouting something that he could not understand. He realised then that he would never see Olga again and the thought tempered his pleasure at the prospect of meeting British troops again.

"So long, Olga!" he said gently, "I'm going to miss you, sister!"

She caught and kissed his hand but he hastily withdrew it when he saw the jeep driver's knowing grin.

"Looks like you bin frattin' in them woods, Limey," he said.

"It wasn't like that, chum," insisted Boxer, as the jeep sped across the bridge, "believe it or not, it wasn't that way at all!"

He pondered a moment, then added: "Queer that! Don't ask me *why* it wasn't, but it wasn't!"

CHAPTER XXXIX

The Squib

JIM had expected the end to arrive with an explosion that would echo round the world.

Just as he had begun this war with notions based on the last, and had imagined that the winter of 1939 would find millions of men facing one another from a network of ditches, so he had taken it for granted that VE day (or, as he preferred to think of it, "Armistice Day") would be a repetition of November 11th, 1918, with hysterical mobs thronging the West End, and soldiers riding on the bonnets of taxis.

Up to 10 a.m. on May 8th nothing like this had taken place in or around the Avenue. In some unlooked-for fashion the end seemed to have stolen up on them, and tapped them on the shoulder. Announcements prophesying the total collapse of Germany had been dribbling out of the radio throughout the preceding week, and the most sensational event of this season of victory so far had been the spectacular end of Mussolini, upside down on a Milan lamp-bracket, his mistress beside him, displaying voluminous underpants.

These pictures had caused a mild sensation in the Avenue but after all, nobody had ever taken Mussolini very seriously, and what happened to him was irrelevant now that Italy had been out of the war for almost two years!

There had been news of exciting advances of the Russians on all sectors, and not long ago a statement about "the Battle of Berlin", but there was nothing unexpected about this either. The Russians had been making dramatic advances ever since Stalingrad, and even a Russophile as ardent as Jim thought that it was high time they hoisted the red flag on the Chancellory!

All the capital cities had been liberated, and everywhere the hated Gestapo was being hunted down by blood-thirsty partisans. In spite of all this, however, the war continued, and there had been a good deal of gloomy talk of a last-ditch resistance in the Dolomites, the Hartz Mountains, and even Berchtesgaden! There was also much speculation on the probable flight of Hitler, Himmler, Goering and Goebbels to the Argentine, by U-Boat.

Then came the more heartening reports of Hitler's suicide in the Bunker and of his replacement, as supreme Commander of the armed forces, by Admiral Doenitz, whose name meant very little in the Avenue. Jim found it very muddling and, in many ways, rather disappointing. More than ever he missed old Harold, and the discussions they might have had over the morning and evening news bulletins.

On the night of May 7th, when it was officially announced that the war might be considered as won, he went to bed with a feeling that he had been cheated of something, and when he took a stroll as far as the Rec' after breakfast, and saw no flags displayed in the Avenue, he returned to Edith in a bewildered and slightly tetchy frame of mind.

"I'm hanged if I know what to make of it all!" he told his wife, when she asked him if the jollifications had begun. "It might be an ordinary Sunday in peace-time! There's a kind of Bank Holiday air about the streets, as though everyone was lying in and taking tea up to bed! How would you like to go up West, Edith? After all, we must do something to celebrate!"

But Edith did not want to go up West. She was frightened of crowds and if she trod pavements for any length of time her feet began to give her trouble.

"I'd be a terrible drag on you, Jim dear," she said. "You go by yourself and then come home and tell me all about it tonight! I'd much sooner slip down and do what I've got to do at the Granada. Then I can slip in and watch the second half of '*A Tree Grows in Brooklyn*'. It's such a nice film, and I've only seen the first half, because we were so busy all day yesterday!"

Jim could not help smiling. Here, at least, was total victory! Dictators everywhere were dead, or in hiding. Whole populations had been freed from under the iron heel of Fascism. There would be no more bombs, no more rockets, no more casualties. Yet all Edith wanted to do was to see the second half of 'A Tree Grows in Brooklyn' at a suburban cinema!

He was grateful, nonetheless, for her decision meant that he would see more, and be free to explore further afield. He went upstairs and put on his best navy-blue suit and his strongest and most comfortable pair of boots. As an afterthought he pinned his medal ribbons on his jacket. He did not often wear medal ribbons, and they were usually aired but once a year, at the Legion Armistice Day service, but today seemed a fitting occasion to display them. He selected a favourite walking-stick from the up-ended drainpipe in the hall, kissed Edith and set out along the Avenue, his eye cocked for any sign that today was the greatest day in recorded history.

He found the same Bank Holiday air at the station. Everyone, it seemed, was taking advantage of the public holiday and lazing about the house. It was not until he arrived at Charing Cross that he found indications that others, besides himself, expected something of the occasion. The streets were filling rapidly, and crowds were converging on Whitehall. He followed their drift and accosted a man of about his own age, who was also displaying the 1914 star.

"What's happening? Is it anything special?"

The man was friendly. "They say Winnie's going to announce the victory officially," he said.

"Where from?" said Jim, eagerly.

"From the Air Ministry, so I hear," said the veteran.

"Why not from the Palace balcony I wonder?" said Jim. "That's where all the hoo-hah began last time! Were you lucky enough to be on leave?"

"No," said the man. "I was in France. I'd just gone back after a long spell in hospital. Whiff of gas on the Albert Sector, and it still bothers me a bit. I see you had a good innings out there. Were you at First Wypers?"

"Not exactly," Jim told him, "I was over there in November '14, but I didn't go up the line until Neuve Chappelle!"

"Ah, that was a real bloody shambles!" said the man. "I copped my first packet there. A sniper got me in the backside! I lost a lot of good pals in that show."

"Me, too," said Jim.

They moved along Whitehall and the crowd was denser here. Soon a surge of people forced them apart and Jim made his way through the close ranks that were massed opposite Richmond Terrace, flattening himself against the wall as police began to clear a passage for a car that was moving out of Downing Street.

"Is that Winnie?" he demanded of a sailor, close by.

"No chum, it's Smuts!"

Smuts, thought Jim! The little chap who had given everybody so much trouble at the end of the Boer War, now the war before last! The crowd began to cheer and Jim smiled, grimly. Who would have supposed that a London crowd would one day cheer a Boer irregular in Whitehall? It looked as though, years hence, Field Marshal Rommel would get an ovation as he passed the Cenotaph!

Then he remembered that Rommel was dead, along with Hitler, Mussolini, Goebbels and most of the other villains in the piece! Not only the principals either! Dear old Louise and Jack Strawbridge were dead, so were two of the Friths, most of the Crispins, young Albert Dodge, young Hooper of Number Six, Mrs. Westerman, Mrs. Baskerville, and dozens of others who had been minding their own business in the Avenue when Chamberlain came home from Berchtesgaden with his little piece of paper!

Well, at least *that* bunch hadn't died in vain! At least they had helped to show the world that people who lived in terraced houses in British suburbs would not tolerate gangster diplomacy and mass murder indefinitely, and if the politicians did not bungle this peace, as they had bungled the last, then the survivors might hope to profit from the sacrifices of the last six years. In that case Old Harold's shattered health and Bernard's empty sleeve could be regarded as small investments in democracy!

His thoughts were interrupted by a vast heave of the

crowd that now surrounded two sides of the Air Ministry building. At the same time a rushing sound, like a huge sigh, issued from Parliament Square, and as it swept past Jim it was taken up by the masses thronging Whitehall as far as Nelson's column, where it seemed to burst into a roar the like of which Jim had never before heard.

He stood on his toes and looked up at the first floor windows opposite, seeing a group of people moving out on the balcony and waving at the sea of faces below them. Excitement gripped him as he recognised the thick-set figure of Churchill, standing slightly in advance of the group, one hand raised and fluttering.

The shout that accompanied his recognition sounded like the crash of a tidal wave on a reef. It rocked the buildings and bounced back, reverberating in every direction. Jim saw men and women beside him with their mouths wide open but he was unable to hear any sounds that emerged from their throats; each individual shout was lost in that vast avalanche of sound, directed up at the figure on the balcony.

Suddenly there was silence, almost complete silence, as though someone had slammed a sound-proof door on the ovation. In the two-second pause that followed it was even possible to hear a woman in front of him hiss: "Shush-shush!" as though there had been need for shushing.

Jim remembered only the first four words of the Premier's announcement and he never afterwards forgot them, for to him they emphasised the genius of a man who had shown himself superior to every other politician in history at the art of gauging the temper of British people.

"This is *your* victory ... !" began Churchill and the statement proved too much for the hushed crowds, for once more the wall of sound rushed down Whitehall, and was taken up by thousands too far away to see the balcony, or to know what was happening there.

After that VE Day seemed to change into top gear and Jim was able to sense relief and gladness in the people about him. For an hour or so everybody shed their inhibitions, and it looked, for a while, as if the Armistice Day scenes were about to be repeated. Jim saw a soldier embrace a W.A.A.F. underneath the commemorative plaque to Charles I's execution outside the banqueting hall of Whitehall Palace. He saw half a dozen G.I.'s jiving in the middle of Charing Cross Road. He saw an A.T.C. girl shin up a lamp-post in Westminster Bridge Road, and he saw a smiling, well-dressed Mr. Aneurin Bevan patted on the back, as he walked sedately past the statue of Abraham Lincoln in Parliament Square.

He ate his sandwiches in St. James's Gardens and when he had rested a little made his way to Westminster Hospital, to call on Harold.

Harold was almost well now, as well as he ever would be, but he had stayed on an extra week or so in order to avail himself of a second and more advanced course of physiotherapy.

Jim found him dressed and hobbling up and down the ward with the aid of two, rubber-tipped sticks. His face lit up when Jim called to him from the door and he came bustling over looking more cheerful and considerably more animated than Jim recalled him looking since August.

"I knew you'd come, I knew it!" he exclaimed. "I said to Mr. Crutchley here, as soon as I heard the news last night, I said: 'You see, old Jim Carver'll show up tomorrow, you see if he doesn't!' Didn't I say that, Mr. Crutchley? Didn't I? And here you are, fresh from seeing the sights, I'll be bound! Now sit down, Jim, sit down and tell us old crocks all about it!"

Jim sat on one of the beds and described Churchill's announcement of the victory, and the wonderful ovation he had been given by the crowds in Whitehall. He soon saw, however, that Harold was not really interested in the VE Day celebrations. Hospital life had narrowed his outlook and both he and Mr. Crutchley would have much preferred to have discussed their injuries and courses of treatment.

Despite the occasion, and despite the warmth of his welcome in the ward, Jim was unable to rid himself of a conviction that the gaiety of these men was brittle and had been assumed partly for his benefit and partly because all the healthy people with whom they came into contact expected cheerfulness from them.

Harold, he thought, was spry enough, but perhaps a little too spry, too prone to express himself extravagantly, and altogether too eager to demonstrate how active he had become under his last course of treatment.

"He's changed," Jim told himself, sadly, as Harold joked and laughed with the legless Mr. Crutchley, who lay in the bed opposite. "He's not the same fussy and straitlaced old Harold any more, since they began messing about with his arms and legs and ribs! They've taken some of the starchiness out of him it's true, but damn it, I'd grown to love the starchiness because it was part of Harold, a far more endearing part of him than all this perkiness they've stuffed in its place!"

He made a determined effort to rediscover the old Harold by trying to open a discussion on the probable fate of the surviving Nazi leaders.

"They'll probably put 'em all on trial and hang the whole bunch," he said, though he did not for one moment believe this, having once fallen victim to the "Hang the Kaiser" election slogan.

"Not them," growled Mr. Crutchley, from across the ward. "They'll more likely make 'em Knights of the Bloody Garter!" and at once switched the conversation back to a patient who had gone off his head and been taken away to the asylum the night before last.

Suddenly Jim felt an urge to return to the streets. The air of 1939 cynicism and "littleness" was poisoning the ward, and he wanted to be among people who had ceased to doubt and who believed, as he did, in the splendour of the British victory.

As he shook hands with Harold, however, a flash of their old comradeship showed in Harold's smile.

"Well, Jim," he said, "so it *did* happen after all! We finally beat the bastards, didn't we?"

Jim looked at him, noting his sunken cheeks, his stoop, and the transparency of the veins on the back of his hands, and suddenly Harold seemed to symbolise everything that the Avenue had sold, pawned and sacrificed to prevent the Fascists from moving in, and disposing of their futures and their children's futures.

He put his arms round Harold and held him so tightly that

Harold suddenly went limp and dropped one of his sticks to the floor.

"Yes, Harold old chap, we certainly did beat the bastards, and don't let anyone ever tell you in years to come that we didn't!"

.   .   .   .   .

He bought himself some tea in a Lyons' and then decided to have a last look around the West End, before making his way back to Charing Cross.

All the outward signs of another Mafeking night were manifest but somehow they failed to convince him. It was like some of the English carnivals he had attended as a young man, in towns like Bognor, and Southend. People thronged the streets and smiled as the tableaux trundled by, but none wore paper hats as though they enjoyed wearing them. There was extravagance and forced gaiety in the air, but it was impossible to rid oneself of the feeling that everybody had come out of doors to watch somebody else play the fool, and that each of the impromptu side-shows that offered itself as a diversion, was stage-managed by a few lucky peple who had found something alcoholic to drink.

In Trafalgar Square Jim watched a party of sailors fall in and out of the fountains. They were not nearly so intoxicated as they pretended to be and their movements were deliberately unsteady, like those of a music-hall comedian performing an act.

Not far away, in Cockspur Street, he watched a more original mafficker mount the empty plinth of George III's statue, and proceed to sell the National Gallery by auction. In Haymarket he passed a procession of Servicemen and Servicewomen, marching sheepishly behind a man with a Union Jack fixed to a shutter pole.

Only in Piccadilly Circus was there any real sign of hysteria and here it had little to do with the victory.

The crowd in the Circus was dense and increasing all the time, fed by a steady flow of sightseers from Shaftsbury Avenue and Haymarket. Jim found himself half-carried to the base of the boarded-up statue of Eros, where everyone's eyes were turned towards an unusual spectacle at the corner of Regent Street.

Here an entrance to the Underground was protected by a structure of planks, that formed a kind of hut, and on the platform made by the roof of this structure an exceptionally pretty girl was undressing.

The crowd was obviously delighted and roared encouragement. An obliging spotlight-manipulator, sited on the roof of a building across the circus, swung the light on the act.

The girl was not alone on the elevated platform. On her right was an American G.I., who seemed to be enjoying the role of impresario, and on her left was a diminutive civilian, an earnest young man wearing horn-rimmed spectacles, who appeared determined to prevent the strip-tease from reaching its logical climax.

The ministrations of these two men diverted the thousands of spectators as much as the act itself. When Jim arrived in front of Eros the little civilian seemed to be fighting a losing battle, for the girl's shoes and dress had already been flung to the cheering ranks below, and in spite of his tortured protests she was now in the act of peeling off a white slip.

The G.I., who was solemnly drunk, continued to bow and wave a proprietary hand towards the girl. A moment later off came the slip and a roar of approval greeted the girl's appearance in flimsy underwear.

Jim stared open mouthed at the spectacle. He had lived within a 'bus ride of Piccadilly Circus most of his life, and had seen a variety of spectacles on this very spot, but never anything quite like this. He was so surprised and shocked that he could not even find anything amusing in the curious contest that was being waged between the unhappy civilian and the expansive G.I.

These two had now fallen to pushing one another behind the girl. There was nothing very active about their quarrel and neither was in danger of falling off the platform. They simply stood shoulder to shoulder, as though daring one another to aim the first blow, and they reminded Jim of two characters in an old-fashioned comedy.

Meanwhile, the girl, who seemed to be ignoring them,

stepped out of her knickers and turned her attention to her suspenders.

The G.I. stood aside for a moment, in order to throw the abandoned panties to the crowd. He then returned to continue his dispute with the despairing civilian, who now appeared to be weighed down by shame and dismay.

At this point in the proceedings a squad of grinning policemen managed to force their way through the crowd and reach the foot of the platform. The crowd began to boo, but good naturedly as the spotlight turned upon an officer in the act of scaling the platform, whereupon the G.I. again abandoned the civilian, this time to argue with the policeman. The civilian at once took this opportunity to check the striptease.

As the girl began to unzip her foundation garment he exerted himself to hold it in place. The girl wriggled, the crowd screamed with laughter, and the game little man held on, at length receiving some much needed assistance in the persons of two other constables.

Between them they managed to dislodge the girl and drag her to the edge of the platform, where more policemen awaited her with upraised arms.

A naval officer, standing close to Jim, exclaimed: "Now I've seen everything!"

"I've seen too much," grunted Jim and turning, forced his way through the crowd and along Coventry Street, towards Charing Cross Road.

The crowd outside the station was so dense that he abandoned the idea of returning home by train and went on down Whitehall, toward Lambeth, to look for a 'bus.

He was tired now and felt deflated. He told himself that it was nonsense to be so depressed by the lack of spontaneity in the celebrations, or the unpleasant impression that remained in his mind after watching the Piccadilly strip-tease. For all that, he grew more and more depressed as he waited in a queue for the Croydon 'bus. He tried, during the long journey home, to analyse the true causes of his depression. Had it really much to do with the forlorn carnival air of the streets, of Harold's facetious preoccupation with his hurts, or with the strange, despairing muddle in which the war had ended?

On consideration he thought not and blamed, instead, the reaction that was surely inevitable after such a prolonged period of strain.

In addition, away at the back of his mind, a number of small irritations had been building up during the last few weeks and now he had leisure to examine them one by one.

He did not like the behaviour of some of the liberated peoples, particularly the French, who were said to be parading shaven women round their market-squares, as a reprisal for their alleged association with Germans during the occupation. This was not the kind of war-aim that he had envisaged throughout the heat of the day; it was far too close to the very thing they had been fighting all these years. Neither had he liked the ghoulish murder of Mussolini and his mistress, Clara Petacci, for this he felt, outraged public decency. He was worried by the growing friction between the British and Americans on one side, and the Russians and Americans on the other, and also by some of the recent public statements from Washington about the avowed intentions of Joe Stalin. To Jim, these utterances seemed to aim mortal wounds at a peace yet to be established. On the other hand, he had been equally disturbed by the Red Army's callous abandonment of the Warsaw patriots the previous summer, for this indicated that there might, after all, be some truth in the Right wing's warnings of Russian hegemony of Eastern Europe after the war!

These and other facets of the war disturbed him. Jim was a simple straightforward man and so far the peace held no promise of working out in a simple, straightforward way! Already reaction was setting in among certain groups of the Left, groups to which Jim had once wholeheartedly subscribed. Socialists were beginning to call Churchill the champion of Big Business and the war-profiteers. There would be an election soon and then, he supposed, the old game of mud-slinging would begin all over again, the Right seeking to entrench themselves against the Unions, the Left, demanding big-scale nationalisation and vast multiplication of tiresome Government controls!

Was left-wing reform really any solution to the problems

of a tired and a frustrated electorate? Could nationalisation and social security on the scale of the Beveridge Plan, really be provided out of an empty exchequer?

The war, they said, had cost the country thirteen millions a day, and it had gone on for nearly six years! There was still Japan to be accounted for, and Britain's overseas credits had been mortgaged in the desperate days of 1940! Where then would the money come from for increased pensions, and a huge reconstruction programme? From America, in the form of loans? Surely that would mean that the British were shackled to American capital for good, and thus tied to Washington's coat-tails in matters of foreign policy? Where might that lead? To another thumping great war, he'd be bound!

He got off the 'bus at Cawnpore Road and walked slowly back to the Rec' end of the Avenue, pondering these things.

He had to admit that there remained, in his heart and head, scarcely one good, honest, pre-war conviction! He had been, successively, an ardent trade unionist, a militant striker, a Socialist of the Centre, a fire-eating pacifist, a fanatical anti-Fascist, a jingo, a pro-Churchill vanguardist, a pro-Russian extremist, and was now inclining towards left-wing Liberalism! He was still, thank God, actively anti-Fascist, and as such could still regard the war as justly waged and justly won, but what would emerge from all this rubble and blather? How had his ancient dream of the Brotherhood of Man and the final renunciation of war been furthered by the overthrow of Hitler and all that overthrow had cost the suburb in blood and treasure?

He turned despondently into the big-number end of the crescent, and as he did so it suddenly occurred to him that there was something odd about the Avenue. For a moment he did not realise what it was and then, catching his breath, he noticed that at least half the houses in the terrace were brazenly defying the blackout regulations, regulations that were still in force!

Lights blazed from at least twenty windows and as he passed Number One Hundred and Twelve, where the big lilac still inclined towards the front-garden of Number One Hundred and Ten, the sounds of a party issued from front-room windows and he heard young voices raised in song.

He paused for a moment to listen. Half a dozen people were bawling a number that he had never much liked, *"There'll Always Be An England"*. Popular as it had been during the earlier stages of the war, he had always felt slightly embarrassed when he had heard it sung, for it was the kind of song that he associated with Kipling's verse and the smug, music-hall patriotism of the nineteen-hundreds. It was a silly song just as silly as that other popular tune, the one about hanging washing on the Siegfried Line.

Tonight, however, it was not so much the song that impressed him as the realisation that the party at Number One Hundred and Twelve was the first real sign he had seen of the Avenue's return to normal.

Lights were blazing and people were singing, with all their windows open and uncurtained! He could see, through the sprigs of unkempt privet, the bobbing heads of men and girls in uniform, and he could hear, above the words of the song, the heartening sound of laughter and gay, young voices.

He did not know who was living in Number One Hundred and Twelve these days but that did not seem important. Somebody lived there, and obviously somebody who liked to see young people enjoy themselves. Surely the important thing was that young people were still able to enjoy themselves, no matter what things were said or done in the chancellories of the world! That human right had been won back for them at El Alamein, Cassino and Avranches and a pledge of it had been written in vapour trails over half Europe. These people, the people now singing *"There'll Always Be An England"* were obviously not worried about the drawing of new frontiers, or the balancing of budgets, and after all why the hell should they be? They had been groping about in a blackout and humping their packs all over the world for years on end and many of them, poor devils, had never had a chance to enjoy youth as it should be enjoyed before being slowed down by the doubts and difficulties of middle-age!

To blazes with the bloody politicians, thought Jim! Let them eat their brains out for a change, and let places like the

Avenue work out their own salvation! After all, people had prophesied (and he among them) that Britain was too stale and lazy to fight Hitler, but these prophets had been sadly wrong, and he himself had been just as wrong! When the Avenue had been put to the test in 1940 and subsequently, how superbly it had risen to the challenge! And so it would again and again, in spite of every sign to the contrary!

The people of all the avenues round here had had their lights switched off and after grousing a little, and fumbling about for a spell, they had stretched themselves, got up, and promptly turned them on again, administering as they did so a hefty kick in the pants to the strutting bullies who had challenged their liberty in the first place! That was all that had really happened, and that was all that ever would happen when foreigners tried to push them around in the future!

In a far more cheerful frame of mind Jim walked the remaining distance to Number Forty-Three and put his key in the lock. He had no time however to turn it, for at once the door flew open, and Edith greeted him, her face flushed, her whole manner as eager as a girl's.

"Jim, oh *Jim*! You'll never guess, you. . . ."

But Jim did not have to guess, for even as he put his hands on her shoulders, and kissed her cheek, a once-familiar laugh was heard in the kitchen, a kind of whooping neigh that had once accompanied the rat-tat of countless games of knocking-down-ginger along the terrace.

Jim rushed across the hall as Boxer lumbered from out of the kitchen.

"Wotcher, Pop? How you doin', Pop?"

Pop was now doing very well indeed, although he would have found great difficulty in saying so! He threw his arms around his son and, as he did so, his glance travelled over Boxer's shoulder and through the open kitchen door to the table, beside the gas-stove. It was heaped with tins and cartons, scores of tins and cartons, so many that some had fallen off on to the tiled floor and lay on top of a concertinaed kitbag.

It was as though Boxer had realised that the sands of wartime licence were running out, that soon, inevitably, 'scrounging' would be called 'stealing' again, and that he had best make the most of his opportunities.

"I stopped off at a Yank depot during the flight to Brussels," he explained, modestly. "The lads at the airfield told me you people was still rationed, so I just scouted around a bit! Mum says she can use 'em, but I got fags for you, Pop!"

" '*Mum*'," said Edith, ecstatically. "He said 'Mum'! Did you hear him, Jim?"

"Yes," said Jim, gently releasing Boxer's right hand, "I heard him, Edith! God bless you, boy, you haven't changed a bit, not a bit! I'll ring Bernard. Bernard'll want to know! Bernard'll want to hear straight away!"

As he picked up the 'phone and dialled trunks Jim reflected that VE Day had not been such a damp squib after all.

CHAPTER XL

The Bulldozers

IN the first week of March 1947, the long hard frost broke at last, and the snowbanks that had lain for so long under the Avenue's dwarf walls crinkled into yellow slush and were soon swept into the gutters by gleeful householders.

It had been the longest and coldest winter that most of them could remember, the kind of winter depicted on Christmas cards that showed oxen being roasted whole on the frozen Thames, and mail coaches floundering in snowdrifts.

Ever since the first week of the New Year the rounded hill marking the spot where Numbers Thirteen, Fifteen and Seventeen had stood, and the long, untidy barrow opposite, that was all that remained of the short-number terrace on the even side, had been mantled in snow. The road between the pavements had been treacherous under inches of hard-packed ice, and the few vehicles that used it, Corporation refuse lorries, and tradesmen's vans, wore chains that clanked dolorously as they moved along towards the deserted Rec'.

People had remained indoors as much as possible and housewives like Edith, who were getting on in years, and not sure of themselves on the glacial pavements, had given their Lower Road shopping commissions to the men.

The meadow behind the Avenue still lay under a sheet of untrodden snow, and the Manor Wood, blue and silent under heavy skies, looked sad and sombre, as though each tree had read its death sentence in the marks scored on its trunk by the surveying team, who had spent so much time in the wood during the preceding autumn.

• • •

The bulldozers and grabs moved in on the first Monday in March.

Jim Carver, who had been down to the Lower Road for Edith's shopping, saw them breast the slope of Shirley Rise and grind into the eastern end of the Avenue, grouping about the flatter section of rubble, where his own and Harold's house had stood.

He realised then that the day had arrived, and that soon the whole of this end of the Avenue would be demolished as a new road was driven across the meadow, and through the wood to join the Holly Wood Estate in the south-east. And even this would be but a beginning. Soon a network of smaller roads, terraces, and closes, would branch off the new high-way, and within a year, or maybe less, the wood would be gone to make room for development known as Manor Wood Estate.

No longer would the Avenue be a salient, marking the furthest advance of south-eastern London. Any day now the long, curving line would break, and all that bombs had left of the crescent would become just another road, like Cawnpore Road, or Lucknow Road, hemmed in back and front with houses, shops, 'bus shelters and perhaps even a cinema or two.

The Clerk of Works set up his headquarters in a large hut sited in the Old Nursery, just behind the house that Edith and Becky had inhabited from the year of King George V's coronation until August, 1944.

From this hut a stream of orders went out to the shock brigades in their row of canvas huts dotted about the mead-ow, and within forty-eight hours of the arrival of the first bulldozer an order for a general advance was given. An hour later mechanical grabs had begun to bite into the mound opposite Number Twenty and Twenty-Two, flattening it in conformity with the meadow, and driving a broad furrow down the old cart-track that crossed the meadow to the wood.

At the same time other grabs began to gnaw their way along the Avenue on the even side, stopping short at Number

Thirty-Six, the first of the undamaged houses on that side. Then a bulldozer attacked the recently vacated houses that stretched due west from Number One, the house from which the indestructible Miss Baker had at last been dislodged, afterwards pushing on towards that point on the odd side, where the wounds inflicted by the 1941 bombs made its work look effortless.

The sun shone brightly all that week and after so many dull days indoors most of the people comprising the Avenue rump came out to watch the men and machines at their work.

It was a sadly reduced group, however, who watched the opening up of the cart-track on that crisp March morning, for most of the families who had lived at the Shirley Rise end of the Avenue between the wars were now scattered and broken up.

Jim was there with Edith, for Number Forty-Three was not involved in the operation, and beside them stood Philip and Jean Hargreaves, and their four-year old son, Winston, who regarded the grab with a mixture of delight, fascination and awe.

The widowed Mr. Baskerville, of Number Ninety-Seven, was there, enjoying a retirement that gave him the leisure he craved to grow huge, yellow chrysanthemums in a home-made greenhouse built on the site of his bomb-proof shelter.

The widowed Mr. Westerman was there, from Number Ninety-Eight, not yet retired, but expecting to be within a few months, and already anticipating his old age by taking a day off on account of a touch of lumbago, that should have kept him indoors notwithstanding the sunshine.

Mr. Westerman was moved to make one of the feeblest of his jokes. Watching a bulldozer lunge at the exposed wall of Number Eleven, he said: "The Luftwaffe couldn't shift us but the Socialist Minister of Housing has!"

Nobody laughed and the joke fell flatter than most of Mr. Westerman's jokes. Jim was too unsure of himself politically to defend the Socialists, as Mr. Westerman had rather hoped he would, and the others, having regard to the Avenue's

losses, regarded jokes about the Luftwaffe as being in doubtful taste.

Mrs. Dodge, of Number Ninety-One was there, remembering that her son, Albert had operated a mechanical grab,
before he threw up his job in 1940, and became a paratrooper. Mrs. Jarvis, and one or two others were there, but hardly
any of the younger folk, for most of these had gone away to
make homes for themselves, some as far as Canada and
Australia, others only five minutes' walk south and east of the
Avenue.

Esme and Judy Fraser were nearly two hundred miles west
of their old homes when the first of the tree-felling teams
went to work on their wood with cross-cuts and tackle, but
nevertheless the day was something of an occasion for them,
for the sun that had converted the snow-crust into slush in
the Avenue had thawed West Country lanes almost a week
before, and on the first really sunny day Judy proposed they
should harness old Gramp to the trap and take a picnic to
the Castle, above the estuary.

Esme, who had passed a difficult seven weeks during the
frost, grumbled that he could ill-afford the time but Judy
talked him into taking a day's holiday and they all drove up
the rutted lanes to the plateau.

Here they turned Gramp loose to browse among the gorse
and spread ground sheets in the lee of the larch coppice. On
all sides of them the undulating countryside was rapidly
shedding its quilt of snow, and the lower slopes of the valleys
were already showing wide, unbroken stretches of green and
gold. To the west the river was like a shining blade, thrusting
towards the sea, but the Haldon Hills, on the far bank, still
wore their crowns of snow.

Judy lifted Arthur from the trap and Barbara, gumbooted
and mufflered, at once took charge of him, and led him away
to feed the birds among the trees on the ancient earthwork.
From where she sat, unpacking the lunch, Judy could hear
their voices carry across the brake. For her too, the winter
had been a hard one. For almost a fortnight The Shillets had
been cut off from the village, so that they had been truly
self-supporting, with plenty of eggs, bacon, milk and vegeta-

bles, but no meat, and, for the last five days of the frost, no sugar or flour.

Esme returned with an armful of wood and began to build a fire.

"A hot drink will do the children good," he said. "Make a wind-shield Judy, while I light up!"

She knelt beside him, holding her duffle coat by the hem and when he glanced up he looked into her eyes and noted their sparkle and the pink flush of her cheeks. He thought of her then as she had looked to him on that frosty day on the Manor island and the memory encouraged him to forget the fire for a moment, to take her face in his hands and kiss her lips.

The unexpected kiss heightened the colour of her cheeks, but she said, lightly: "Now then, now then! You were supposed to be lighting a fire!"

"I don't need one when you look like you do this morning," he told her.

She put her head to one side, smiling.

"It's nice to hear you say something like that again," she said. "I was beginning to wonder if it was the work, the cold spell, or me!"

"It was all three," he said, sitting back on his heels as the twigs began to crackle, "but now that spring's here we'll see what we can do about it!"

He rose to his feet and called: "Hi, Babs! Arthur! The fire's going! Get some sticks!"

At that moment, had they known it, a tall beech came crashing down on the very spot where they had first met and because they were sentimentalists they would have been interested. They did not know, however, for they did not think of the Avenue much these days. There is always so much to do on a farm.

* * *

Nearly three hundred miles north-west of Esme's picnic that sparkling morning Pippa left the petrol pumps to cross the road and collect a parcel from the G.P.O. van that had stopped opposite the bungalow gate.

"It's from Boxer!" she called to Bernard, who was lying on his back under a Bedford van in the garage.

He scrambled out, his fair hair streaked with oil from a leak that he had not yet located.

"Open it up, Pip," he shouted and began to wash at the workshop tap.

Pippa cut the string and tugged at the wrappings. The postmark said *"British Forces Overseas"* and the object inside the parcel puzzled her for a moment. She shook away the shavings that cushioned it, and put it down on the bench.

She saw then that it was one of those traditional German jokes, a model of a privvy, with a heavily-moustached man sitting on the seat, a contented look on his face and a large pipe in his mouth. Printed on the door, which could be opened and shut, was a legend in Gothic script but she knew no German and neither did Bernard, who came over and examined the novelty with interest.

"That's about typical of Boxer!" he said. "Wasn't there a letter inside?"

They searched the wrappings and found a single sheet of notepaper, covered with Boxer's huge, childish scrawl.

"Dear Berni and Pip" it ran, *"I thought you might like this for the mantelpiece of the new bungalow. They are all the rage over here and I meant to tell you what it says on the door but I've forgotten. I can still only swear in German and shout 'Raus-raus!' at the civvies who crawl round us like no one's business and say they never wanted to fight Britain. I haven't come across one bloke who was a Nazi yet but I'm on the track of a bint I chummed up with on the way out. She's a Russky and I've always wanted to catch up with her again. I've just heard she's still in the Western Zone, and working as a skivvy so you mite have some news that will shake you soon so long now as ever Boxer."*

"Whatever does he mean by all that?" asked Pippa.

Bernard scratched his head. "I suppose he means he's traced Olga," he said. "Olga was the girl he told us about, the one he met when he was on the run."

"Does 'bint' mean a woman?" asked Pippa.

"Yes, and the only woman I heard of him meeting over there was this Russian!"

He folded the note and placed it carefully in his overall pocket. "Can you beat that? Boxer, married?"

"He isn't married yet, is he?" said Pippa, who was never able to understand Boxer's letters.

"No, but if I know him he soon will be," said Bernard. "He's a case and no mistake! What makes him imagine the Welsh would stand for Jerry's lavatory humour? *On our mantelpiece!* What do you know about that?"

Pippa laughed and began rewrapping the gift.

"It was nice of him to remember your birthday anyway, Berni."

"He dam' well ought to," said Bernard, "it's his too, isn't it?"

A lorry pulled in beside the pumps and Pippa left him to attend to it. Bernard smiled to himself, contemplating the irony of his twin's return to Germany as a regular, after spending nearly three years there as a prisoner of war.

His thoughts were interrupted by a loud wail from the perambulator, wedged against the pillars of the bungalow porch. He crossed the gravelled path between workshop and dwelling and bent to retrieve a woolly elephant that Jimmy, the younger of his two boys, had flung to the ground.

"Eddy!" he called, to a plump three-year-old playing bricks on the floor of the front room. "Keep an eye on Jimmy, son! Mummy and I are busy this morning! Catch!" as he tossed the package through the open window, "It's a present from Uncle Boxer!"

The child scrambled to his feet and ran towards the parcel. Bernard returned to the workshop, picked up his spanner and crawled under the Bedford again. Presently, to an accompaniment of regular taps and bangs, Pippa heard him whistling a melody that she always associated with him and Boxer. She supposed that his twin's letter had put it into his head again, for presently the whistle ceased and he began to sing the words:

"Everybody's doin' it, doin' it, doin' it!"

She began to whistle it herself as she went in to prepare their midday meal.

As she stirred the stew a bulldozer lurched over the rubble that had been her husband's home for twenty-five years, and her own for the greater part of the war, but neither she nor Bernard thought of the Avenue as home any longer. They had paid a ten per cent deposit on a home and were paying off the remainder gallon by gallon, as vehicles passed in and out of Caernarvon.

. . . .

Harold was on his way back to the Avenue when the bulldozers began to demolish the odd side of the crescent.

He was returning from his first holiday since the summer of 1939, when he and Eunice had spent a quiet but enjoyable fortnight at Newquay.

The long frost had immobilised him, for although he was walking very well now he did not care to risk a heavy fall on the iced-over pavements and Mrs. Harvey, his landlady at Number Eighty-Eight, was a very active little woman and had undertaken to do all his errands during the cold spell.

Harold had not accepted Jim's offer to take a flat at Number Forty-Three but in the end he had been unable to tear himself away from the Avenue and had rented the upper half of Mrs. Harvey's house, lower down the crescent.

He did so because he was determined to establish his independence but this he failed to do, for Mrs. Harvey, and her unmarried sister, Norma, made much more fuss of "our gentleman upstairs" than Jim and Edith would have done.

His unexpected and out-of-season holiday had been the result of a flattering invitation on the part of Mr. Stillman, his former employer, who had asked him to spend a week at his Sussex home, in order to assist him in drawing up a will.

Harold had been delighted by the invitation and agreeably surprised by his welcome, for Mr. Stillman loomed very large in Harold's estimation, and was said to be worth six figures.

Harold had been made an executor and treated like a distinguished guest during his stay, but now that everything was signed and sealed he was secretly glad to be returning to his own easy-chair, and to the society of people like Jim,

Edith, and Mrs. Harvey, and even little Miss Baker, who now watched the Avenue parade from a more central window, at Number Sixty-Two.

Harold had found peace in the year that followed his discharge from hospital. He had still not quite recovered from his surprise at being alive and mobile, but he no longer missed the bustle and gossip at the office in St. Paul's Churchyard, preferring to sit and re-read the classics, beginning with George Eliot, and ending with Robert Louis Stevenson; this was something he had always told himself he would do on his retirement.

He did a bit of gardening too, discovering a friend and ally in the person of Mr. Baskerville, the chrysanthemum-grower. Mr. Baskerville, Harold now admitted, was not nearly such a bore once he had a trowel in his hand, and was pottering about between his greenhouse and the rockery that he was rebuilding in the front garden. They became, in fact, firm friends during the first summer of peace, and conferred with one another about the imminent collapse of British economy, now that the Socialists dominated Parliament. He remained close friends with Jim, of course, but Jim had Edith, and Baskerville was a widower, like himself.

Jim saw Harold turn into the Avenue from Shirley Rise and hailed him as he stepped over the litter that strewed the broken pavements.

"Hi, Harold! You're just in time! You've got a new address now! It's to be plain *'Manor Road'* from now on, and the road across to the woods is to be *'Manor Park Drive'* if you've ever heard such nonsense!"

"By George!" exclaimed Harold, surveying the activity, "They are making a bit of a mess of the place, aren't they?"

"Twelve hundred houses are going up so they tell me," said Jim, shouting against the stuttering roar of a pneumatic drill, outside Number Nine. "I'm damned if I can see who's going to live in all of 'em!"

"They'll ruin us before they've finished," screamed Harold, "you see if they don't! You and that precious Attlee of yours!"

Ten years ago Jim would have swallowed this bait and at

once opened a heated discussion in support of Socialist housing policy, but today he was content to laugh and slap Harold on the back.

"The politicians'll ruin us, no matter who's in," he predicted, "It's six of one and half a dozen of the other if you ask me! What we really need is a national revival of the Liberal party, and we'll get it before long, you see if we don't! Did you have a good time with the nobs, down in Sussex?"

"Yes," shouted Harold, "I had a very good time indeed, but I'm glad to be back, Jim, very glad to be back! Will you and Edith come over after supper? I've so much to tell you."

"We'd like to," said Jim, "put the kettle on about eight!"

Harold left him and picked his way along the Avenue to Number Eighty-Eight, and as he turned in at the gate he looked back at the changing outline of the short-number end.

"Manor Road," he said to himself. "It doesn't sound so expensive as 'Manor Park Avenue', but I expect we'll get used to it, like everything else that's happened around here in the last twenty-five years!"

· · · ·

Only a mile or so from the Avenue Archie was turning into the short drive that led to 'Pine Hollow', the white, detached house that he had originally bought with the idea of converting into luxury flats, but had decided to occupy himself when Elaine had told him that he would be a father once again in February, '46.

Elaine was by no means as astonished at the prospect of this child's arrival as she had been by the prediction of Esme's child, in the last winter of the peace. In fact it was a matter of surprise that she had not conceived long ago, and for a time she kept the information to herself, slightly apprehensive as to how Archie would accept it, for there was still little prospect of their being in a position to marry.

Archie's wife, Maria, had never offered him a divorce, although they had recently learned through a lawyer that she was now considering living in Italy. If she did go abroad, then Elaine supposed that it might be possible to get the divorce, but she did not give the matter much thought. She felt far more married to Archie than she had been to Esme, and had no cause to regret her snap decision on the Bourne-mouth Road, back in 1943.

Archie had gone a long way in the last four years. The string of village pop-ins, of which he had been so proud before the war, seemed a trivial little enterprise in retrospect, for he had now a stake in twelve blocks of flats, besides owning half a dozen tall, Victorian houses, accommodating four to five tenants and bringing in some two thousand a year. He also owned 'Pine Hollow', worth at least another eight thousand at today's market price, and all his investments outside the realm of bricks and mortar were sound and rewarding.

One way and another Elaine had lost very little by switching from Woolston to Archie, for Archie was not the kind of man who would stop at twenty thousand, but would go on making money all his life. Elaine was confident of this, and equally confident that the money he made would be shared with her.

His enthusiasm when she finally told him about the child was almost embarrassing.

"What *you*? Us? A kid?" he kept repeating, until she felt obliged to remind him that she was only thirty-six, and could hardly be expected to regard conception as a miracle.

After that he was never seen in an ill-humour, not even when things did not fall out as he planned in business. He insisted that they resold the house they had intended occupy-ing after handing over Number Forty-Three to Jim, and went to live in 'Pine Hollow', which had six bedrooms, and stood in four acres of cultivated garden.

'Pine Hollow' actually possessed a flagged terrace, with a shingled roof over it, and when Elaine referred jokingly to her old daydream of the hammock he startled her one morning by fixing a hammock to the main supports outside the lounge.

By that time, however, she was too advanced in pregnancy to be able to use it, and tried to persuade Archie to climb in but without success. Archie had never been the kind of man to while away his time in a hammock, and was not going to begin now, when property prices were soaring to astronomi-

cal figures, and families were holding out key-money for a
dingy top-floor, furnished with odds and ends from the junk
sheds!

The child, another girl, was born on Elaine's birthday in
February, and Archie insisted that they should name her
Louise, in memory of his favourite sister. He found a nannie
and Elaine retired, promptly and gratefully, from the cares
of motherhood, spending many anxious hours in front of the
mirror, in order to convince herself that her figure had not
been impaired. She need not have worried. Even had her
waist-line disappeared altogether it is doubtful whether Archie would have noticed it, for her power to attract him
seemed to wax rather than wane with the passing years. He
still possessed in generous measure the lustiness she had
sought in him, but since his post-war successes another element had entered their partnership and she had proved a real
asset to him in business, particularly when it entailed the
adroit handling of middle-aged men.

Sometimes he would bring her a difficult client who needed, he said, the kind of pushover that she could provide, and
almost always she succeeded where he had failed. It was never
necessary to go to extreme lengths with these gentlemen. All
they sought, it seemed, was a little flattery and chin-
chuckling, to restore to them some of the confidence that
their wives had neglected to nurse. Elaine was quite superb at
this kind of thing, and after introducing her Archie would retire "to run his eye over a lease or two", leaving the field
open to Elaine.

When he returned the visitors were usually in a more expansive mood than when they had first been introduced to
Elaine, but her part in this little game was a close secret.
Archie invariably introduced her as ". . . the wife, a real sweetie,
but she hasn't a clue, old man!"

The day the bulldozers arrived to give the *coup-de grâce* to
the short-number end of the Avenue, Archie brought home a
balding gentleman named Spright, who managed a small building firm in the area, and with whom Archie was anxious to
come to terms.

He left Mr. Spright in the lounge after giving Elaine a

quick briefing in the cloakroom, and subsequently excused himself, retiring to his office-study for an hour or so.

When he rejoined them, Mr. Spright's original estimate for converting a pair of Archie's semi-detached houses into four two-bedroomed flats was ready to drop by several hundreds of pounds, and Elaine was insisting that he stayed on for dinner and told her a little more of his fascinating hobby of trick-photography.

"Perhaps you'd like to take a tricksy picture of me," she suggested, coyly. "I like having my pictures taken, don't I Archie?"

Archie said that she did indeed and proved it by showing Mr. Spright an enlarged snapshot of Elaine in a bikini that had been taken during a brief holiday at San Marino the previous summer.

Perhaps this was why Archie and Elaine continued to prosper. The Mr. Sprights operated individually, whereas Archie and Elaine now operated as a team.

Archie had passed the end of the Avenue that very afternoon and had noticed what was happening down there, but when they retired to bed that night, with Mr. Spright's contract safely in the strong-box, he did not tell her that the bulldozers were advancing over the meadow behind her old home but instead discussed Mr. Spright's unusual hobby, and what an important part hobbies sometimes played in the world of commerce. He did not think that Elaine would be very interested in what was going on in the Avenue, for the Avenue was now a long way behind them.

· · · · ·

The girl Carver twins, who had been known as 'the Likes', and who had been born and reared in Number Twenty, heard of the demolition in a long letter from Jim, written when the work had entered upon its second stage.

The twins had long since qualified as G.I. brides, and had sailed to the States in a specially-chartered war bride liner, caled *Nevada*. It was not to Nevada that they went, however, but to Cleveland, Ohio, whither Mitch and Orrie, their husbands, had preceded them almost a year ago.

Fetch and Carry had far less trouble adjusting themselves

to their new country than the majority of their fellow brides. They had shed their insularity years ago, as long ago as 1942, when the American vanguard first appeared in the suburb.

Even before then they had already commenced their transformation at the Odeon, in the Lower Road, so that when they actually found themselves in Cleveland they were more American than the Americans, and some of their neighbours had difficulty in remembering they had been British.

They talked like Americans, and they dressed like Americans. They scorned the use of table knives like the Americans, and it took them less than a week to acquire the American woman's attitude towards their husbands' little weaknesses.

Mitch and Orrie, who were already well established in the trucking business, were somewhat dismayed by this final act of acclimatisation. One of the principal characteristics of British girls that had recommended itself to the G.I.s as a whole, had been the lip-service British girls paid to the traditional superiority of the male.

They were therefore disconcerted by the speed with which Fetch and Carry set about proving that America was a woman's country, making inroads into money that their husbands had set aside for business expansions and cheerfully entering into a sheaf of hire-purchase agreements when such money was not readily forthcoming.

"Maybe we was in too much of a hurry to get 'em back here," Orrie confided to Mitch one day, after a lively domestic dispute about the purchase of kitchen equipment. "Maybe these dames wouldn't expect the moon if they was still rationed, like all the rest o' their folks!"

Mitch, the laconic, had nodded. "When we get that next truck Orrie, we'll figger some way to send 'em home on a vacation," he said and left it at that.

Fetch opened Jim's letter and read it aloud to Carry. "They're pulling down our end of the Avenue," she exclaimed. "What you know 'bout that, Carry?"

"They c'n have it, sister!" said Carry, standing sideways in front of a mirror, in order to discover whether the new gown

that had arrived that morning did or did not "do" something
for her.

"Yep," said Fetch, reflectively, "gimme the States any time!
On'y Yanks know how to treat a woman!"

· · · ·

Two other former residents of the Avenue received news
of its demolition through the post.

Jean Hargreaves, née McInroy, who had succeeded Ted
Hartnell as lodger at Number Four, and whose husband had
subsequently purchased Number Forty-Five from Margy,
Ted's wife, when Ted was away at sea, had kept in touch
with the Hartnells after they had settled in the holiday resort
of Sandridge Bay, on the east coast.

Ted had left the sea and picked up the threads of his
pre-war life within a week of Hitler's suicide in the bunker.
There had been no point in remaining separated from Margy
after that. The task he had set himself, when he first learned
of the goings-on in concentration camps, was now accomplished, and he might as well return to civvy street. Hitler,
Himmler and Goebbels were dead, and Goering, God rot his
distended belly, was in close confinement and due, no doubt,
to be hanged, although Ted would have much preferred him
to have been burned at the stake. The gates of all the
concentration camps had been flung open, to reveal to every
Doubting Thomas the actuality of the conditions therein, conditions faithfully described to him by the Bavarian violinist as
long ago as 1939.

Perhaps Ted Hartnell's most satisfying memory of the war
was the moment that he picked up a newspaper and was
confronted with a picture of Kramer, the "Beast of Belsen",
scowling, unshaven and, what was even better, heavily manacled! Ted took particular note of the newsreel shots dealing
with the interior of Belsen after the British troops had
penetrated the compound, and he rubbed his hands with glee
when he learned that German civilians had been compelled
to witness the film, in order to make quite sure that concentration camps had not been hush-hush factories for the manufacture of secret weapons.

If Ted could have had his way he would have preserved at

least one concentration camp, in order to accommodate a selected group of war-criminals, and he would have staffed this camp with Polish, Dutch and Czechoslovakian patriots. This however, was now a matter for the politicians, and Ted had no wish to become a politician. Neither, for that matter, had he any wish to become a dance band leader again, at least, not if it meant that he had to live out of sight of the sea.

Something had brought about a permanent change in Ted Hartnell during his voyages back and forth across the Atlantic, and up and down the Mediterranean. The smell of the sea had performed an act of alchemy on his blood and he discovered to his dismay that he could not face life without it! The stale, dusty atmosphere of a suburban dance hall now made him gasp like a fish, and although, as a drummer and an inspirer of rhythm, he was as good as ever, he derived no real joy in the work, and poor Margy thus found herself faced with a new set of worries, for how else could they earn a living?

She was almost in despair when Ted bounded up with a copy of the trade paper and showed her an advertisement that he had ringed in blue pencil.

It seemed that Sandridge Bay, a thriving resort with a big future on the holiday map, was advertising for an experienced dance orchestra leader, who was to act as an all the year round entertainments' manager! The salary offered was eight hundred a year, plus a bonus when the foreshore income increased above a certain figure.

"It's tailored for us, Margy," he had exclaimed. "We organise all the dances and entertainments and we live practically on the beach! Why hang it, Margy, I don't see why we can't live on a boat!"

"Do you want to live on a boat?" she had demanded, coldly.

"Well, of course I do," he admitted, "there's no rates to pay if you live on a boat!"

Luckily poor Margy had learned patience during the last five years, and she decided there and then that she might as well make the best of a bad job.

As it turned out it was not really a bad job at all, for Ted

was a huge success at Sandridge Bay, and after a few weeks
in lodgings she had been glad to move on to a cabin-cruiser
that he had bought at a give-away price.

The vessel, renamed *Margy*, was moored to the quay in the
harbour, and once she had got used to walking up and down a
sloping gangway, instead of in and out of a front door,
Margy began to take great pride in her namesake, keeping it
trim and spotlessly clean.

It was here, after the postman serving the harbour area
had thrown the mail at her from the quayside, that Margy
read Jean's description of the last days of Manor Park
Avenue. She was interested, and so was Ted in a half-hearted
way, but before she had finished reading the letter she noticed
that a gull had spotted the ship's bell and she laid aside the
sheets to find her duster and a tin of metal polish.

Ted finished the letter as she went to work.

"I wonder how many of the old lot are still there?" he said.

For a moment, but a moment only, his mind held a picture
of the front-room of Number Four as it was twenty years
ago, when he and Edith, and poor old Becky, had played
'*Valencia*', and '*Yes, Sir, that's my Baby*' on the old cottage
piano. Then Margy interrupted his thoughts by saying:

"I got a new record while I was shopping. It's a man
playing a zither and it's got a good beat. Have you ever
played a zither, Ted?"

"I've played everything," boasted Ted, vaguely, and laying
down the letter he got up and leaned on the rail, sniffing the
salt-laden breeze that always seemed so much fresher and
more invigorating down here than it was back in the town.

•   •   •   •

After Jim and Edith had heard Harold's account of his
holiday, and had returned home that March night, Edith said
she was tired and would go straight to bed.

Jim did not feel sleepy, so after he had filled Edith's hot
water bottle he brewed himself another pot of tea in the
kitchen and then took a turn down the back garden in order
to enjoy a final pipe in the open.

He opened the back gate and looked out across the meadow. The moon was on the wane but the sky was bright with

stars, and he could just see the dark line of the woods and the huddle of heavy equipment that the builders' teams had parked in the cart-track.

Only that morning he had viewed the bulldozers with a detached and technical interest but tonight he resented them, for it was as though they had come here to demolish the mile-stones in his memory, milestones that reached back through the war and the days of appeasement, to the slump, the General Strike, and the day in 1919 when he had first made his way here from the Ostend leave-boat to find his first wife lying dead from Spanish 'flu.

He had known none of these people then, indeed, he had possessed no friends outside the army, for throughout his earlier years he had never remained long enough in one street to convert nodding acquaintances into neighbours like Edith, Harold, or even the Hargreaves, next door. He was glad now that Ada, his wife, had found this place, for through the decades behind him he had come to love and cherish it.

Was that possible? Could one love bricks and mortar? Perhaps not, perhaps he would have learned to value the flesh and blood inhabiting any such row of houses, for in their comradeship, if one was patient enough, was truth.

He was sixty-seven now and it was time to take stock of his convictions. His own life did not seem to have amounted to much. He had wasted so much time on politics and it was only now that he was coming to realise that politics were really people, the kind of people who lived in these Avenues.

He let himself out of the back gate and wandered along as far as the cart track and then back once more into the moonlit avenue, crossing the road to stand on the spot where his front gate had been.

He looked west along the silent crescent and his conviction grew that here, and here only, was the real answer to all the questions that he had been asking himself for more than half a century. It was not possible to learn about people from books and pamphlets, and therefore it surely followed that it was not possible to learn how to govern from these sources. To understand, and evaluate democracy, one had to live in a place like this, and live here for a very long time! One had to see all the penny-plain democrats at their weddings and funerals; one had to watch how they behaved under fire, but most of all one had to understand and sympathise with their dreams.

Until one had learned this, words and phrases, like 'democracy', 'public opinion', 'floating vote', and 'electorate' were meaningless, just so many sounds, set down in Hansard, or spouted from platforms, but at least, in his sixty-seventh year, he had learned this lesson, and that it was about all that remained of the mountain of opinions and convictions he had accumulated in the course of his life.

Only a hard core of that mountain now remained, the simple conviction that these people were important, and that their dreams were important, for it was their dreams that fashioned the civilisation they had fought to preserve, not once but twice in his own lifetime!

Their lives, for the most part, were mean and crabbed, and in the mass he had often found them slothful, bigoted and even cowardly. Individually, however, they were none of these things. They were energetic, steadfast, large-hearted and brave as lions.

That was what living in this Avenue had taught him, and by God, it was something worth learning! If the politicians Left, Right and Centre learned as much in the decade ahead then they could all hope to profit by the past, and shape some kind of future for children waiting to be born!

The stillness of the night began to have a soothing effect upon him and gradually he extracted peace and contentment from the silence.

He knocked out his pipe and crossed to the shadows of the uneven side. Over in the woods an owl hooted twice and Jim wondered where the owl would hunt when the trees of Manor Wood had been felled. Then he remembered that there were plenty of other woods in a line from here to the coast, and that soon a new avenue would mark the limit of London's advance into the south-east. The thought comforted him as he let himself into Number Forty-Three and went quietly upstairs to the front bedroom.

Edith was sound asleep and he undressed in the glow of the street lamp, taking as he did so, a final look through the curtains. After the clamour of the day the Avenue was very still and silent under the stars.

R. F. Delderfield

THE DREAMING SUBURB

On the outside the Avenue appeared so peaceful . . .

Jim Carver – A tough, resolute war veteran, he returns from the trenches to build a better life for his family only to find his wife dead.

Archie Carver – Jim's oldest son, smart, ruthless, he has a quick eye for financial profits and beautiful women.

Elaine Frith – Seductive and ambitious, she uses her charms to snare any man she thinks will bring her wealth.

The First World War ends and the soldiers return to the peaceful Avenue. On the surface their homes look just the same but behind the carefully tended front gardens everything has changed, and their families' lives in the next twenty years will be as turbulent as any they have known.

'R.F. Delderfield is a born storyteller' *Sunday Mirror*

HODDER

R. F. Delderfield

DIANA

As a young girl Diana is irrepressible, untameable and, to the orphaned John, endlessly fascinating. Only daughter of a wealthy businessman, she is drawn both to a rigorous outdoor life in the West Country with her horses and the glittering London society that will be her destiny.

They spend a magical unconventional childhood together but Diana's ambition, her passion for life that makes her so desirable, pulls her away from all that makes her happy. The fierce friendship that grew inevitably to love, develops as inevitably to conflict and a betrayal that will mark them both – until the trials of war offers them redemption.

'Highly recommended. Combines tension with a splendid sense of atmosphere and vivid characterisation. An excellent read' *Sunday Express*

HODDER